EARTHLING!

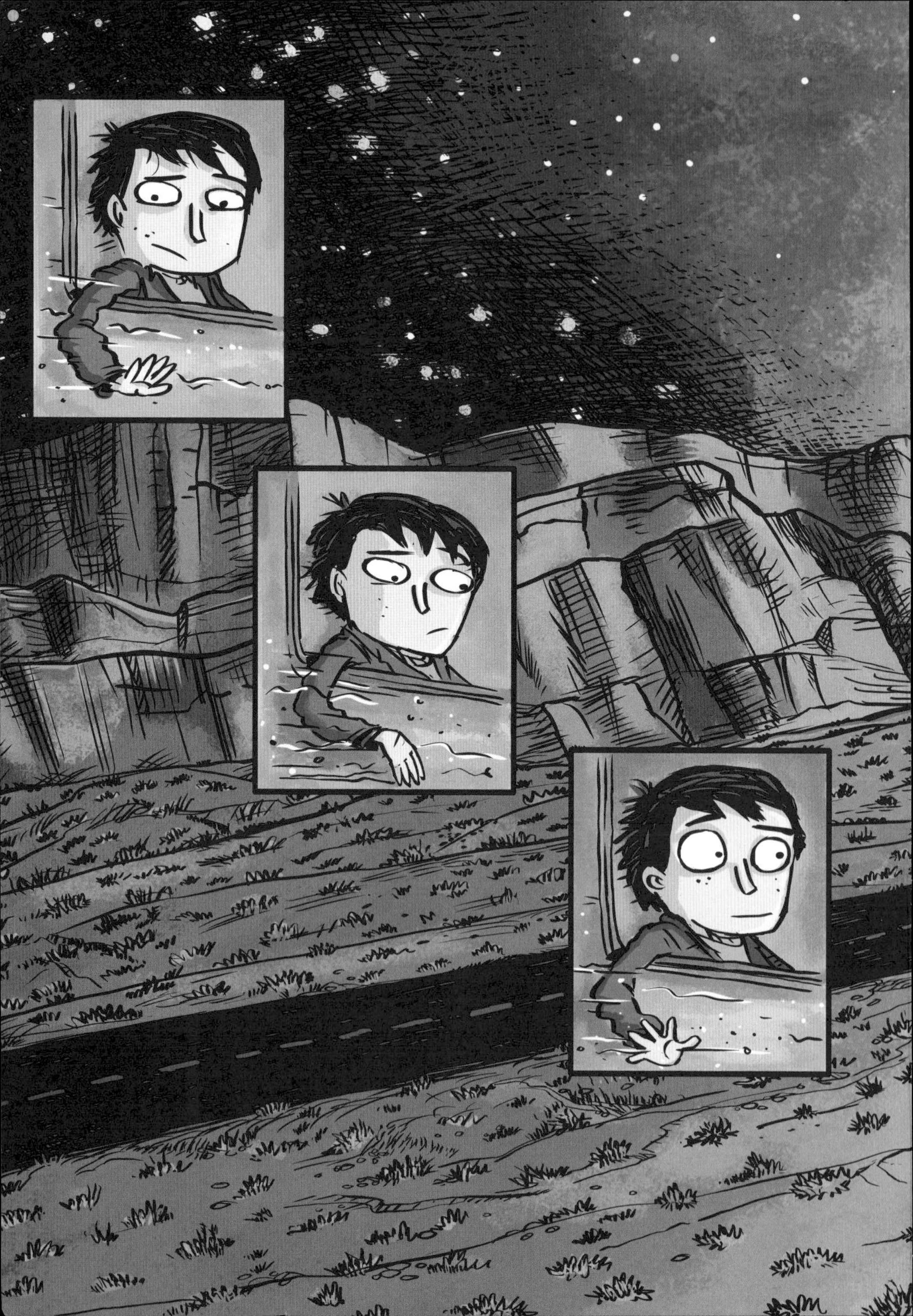

EARTHLING!

WRITTEN AND ILLUSTRATED BY MARK FEARING
CREATED BY MARK FEARING AND TIM RUMMEL

chronicle books · san francisco

CHAPTER 1

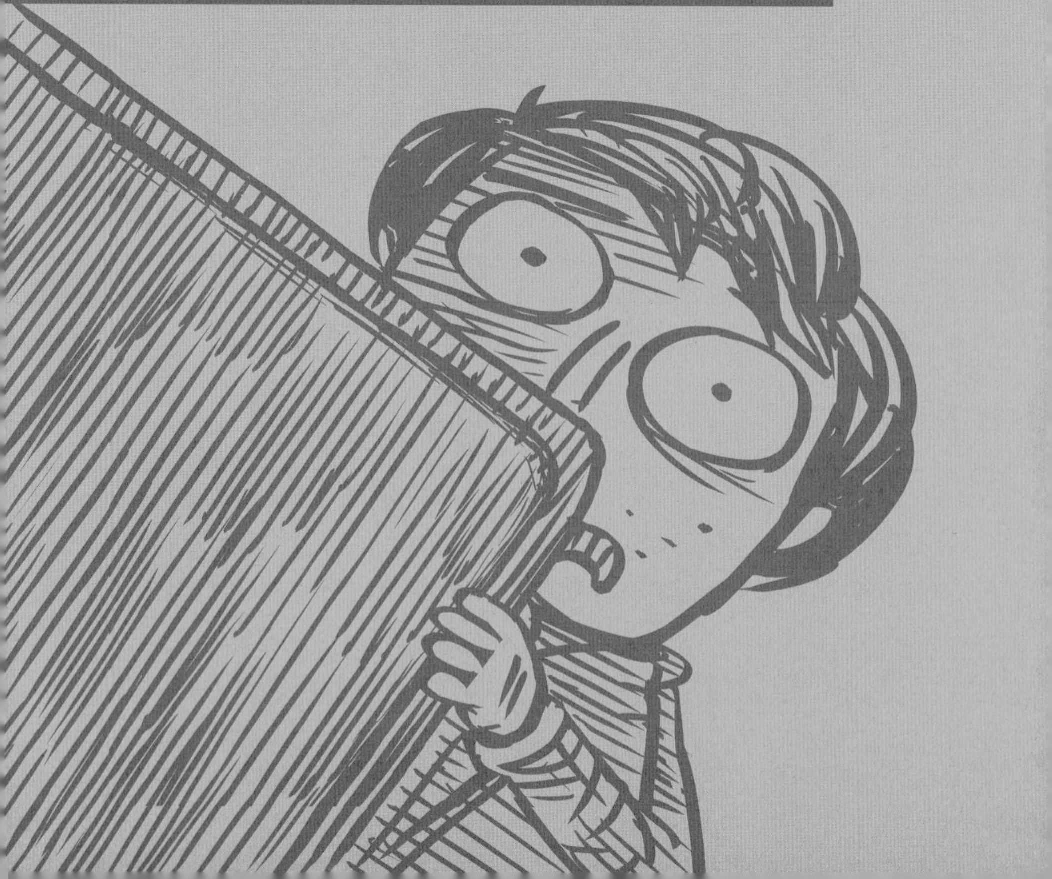

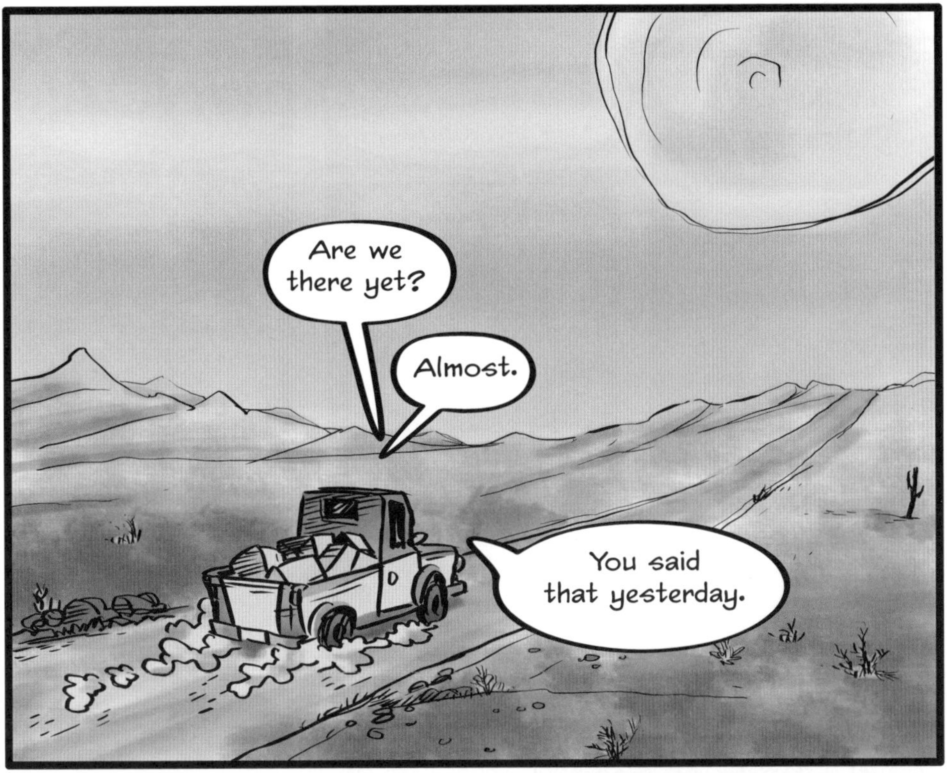
Are we there yet?
Almost.
You said that yesterday.

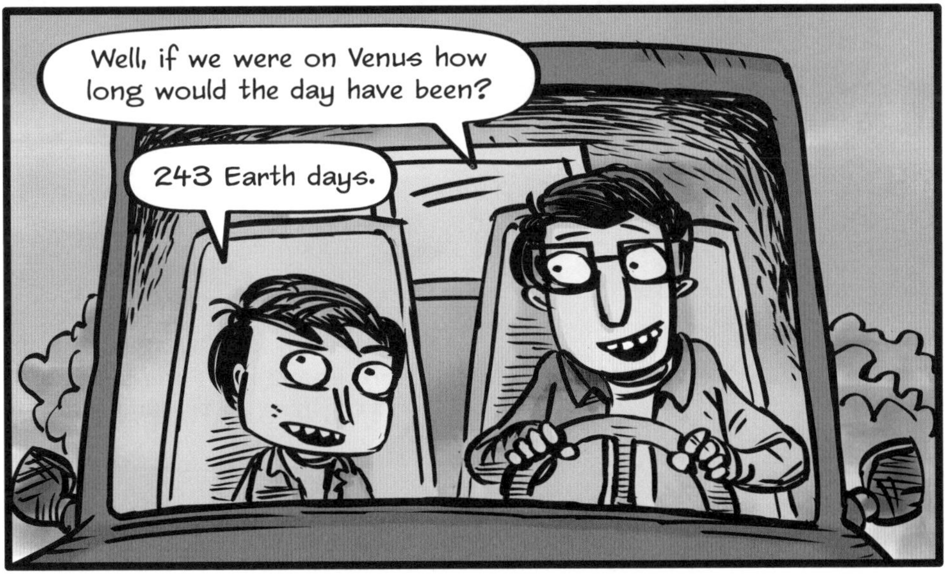
Well, if we were on Venus how long would the day have been?
243 Earth days.

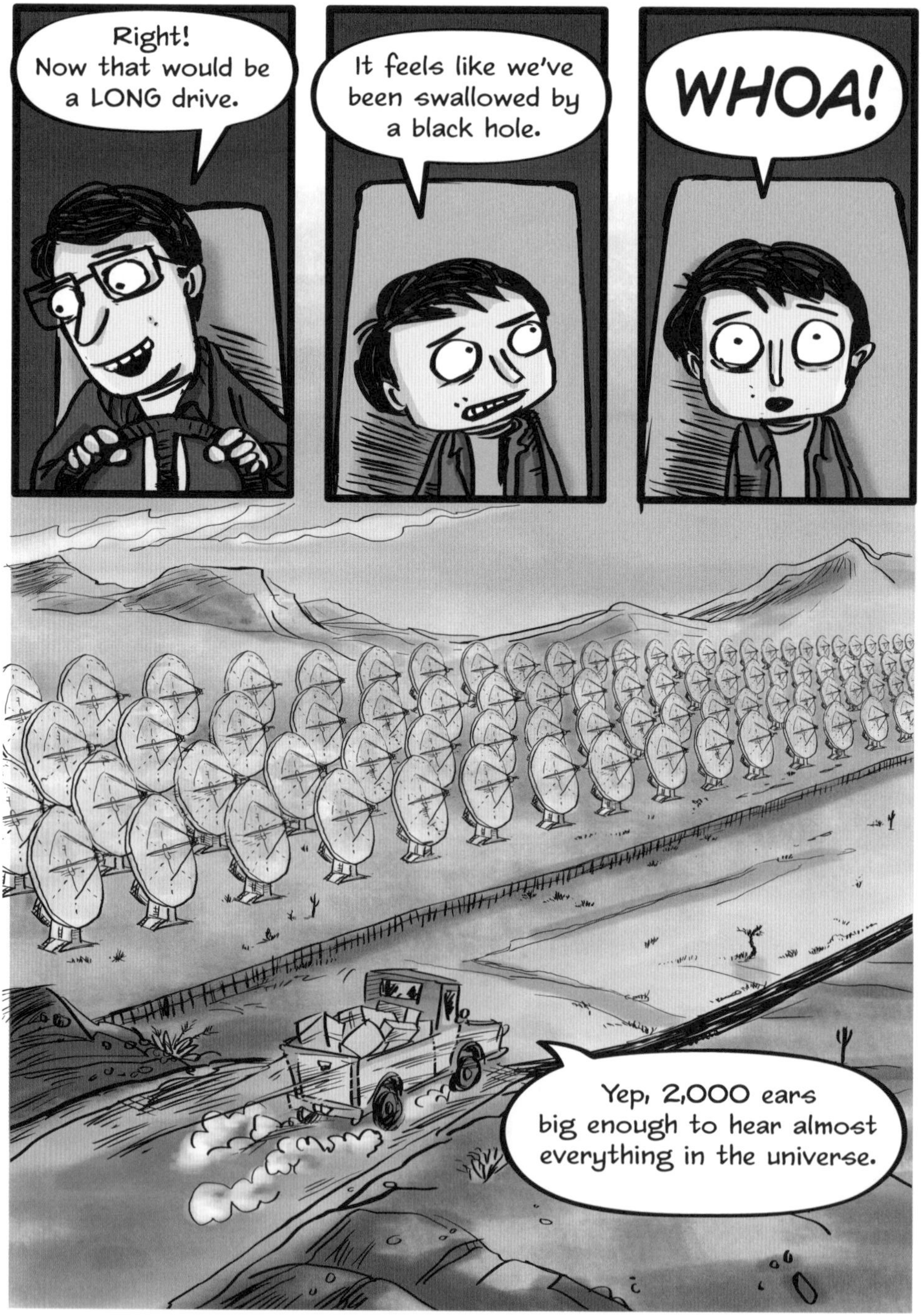
Right! Now that would be a LONG drive.
It feels like we've been swallowed by a black hole.
WHOA!
Yep, 2,000 ears big enough to hear almost everything in the universe.

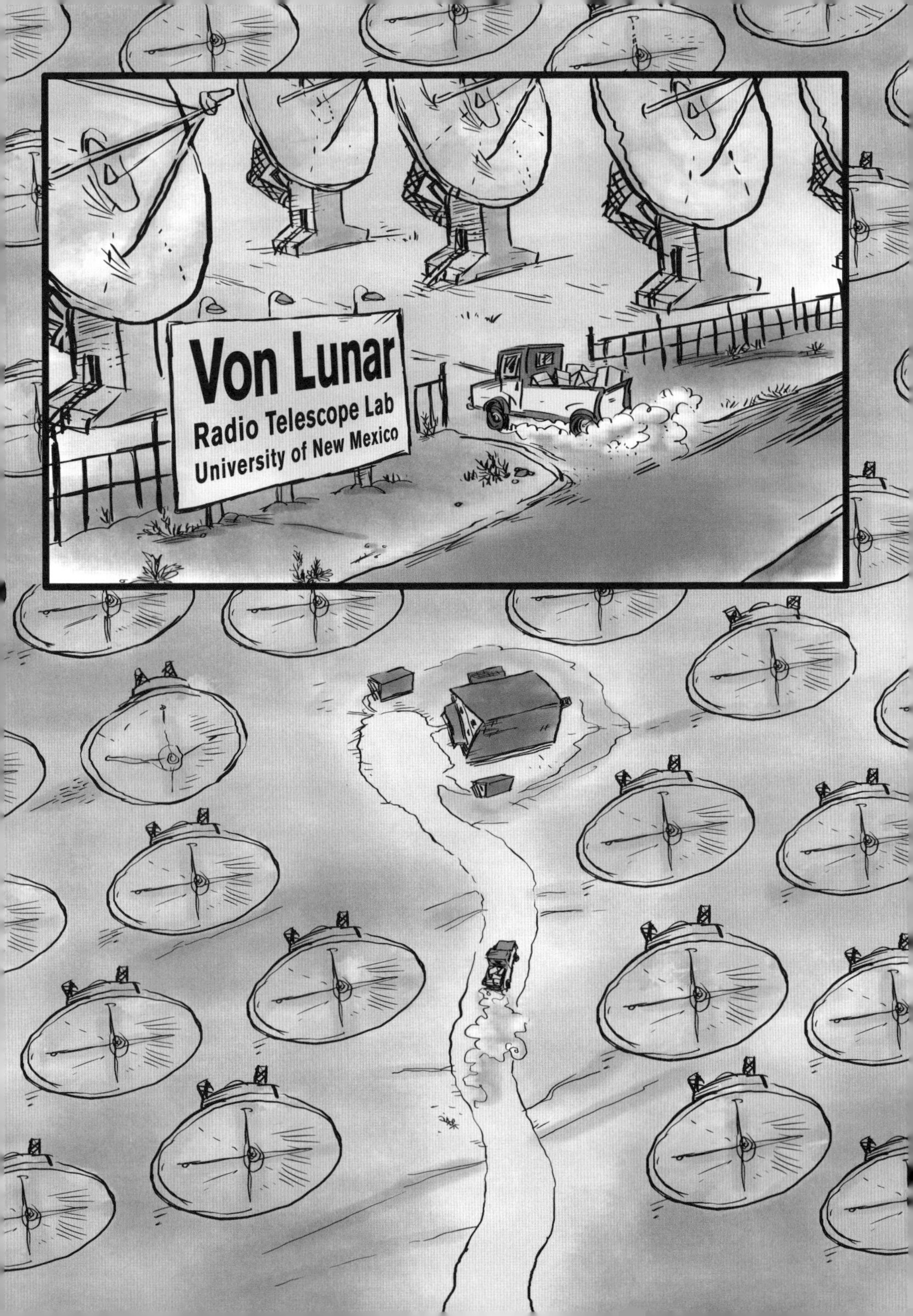
Von Lunar
Radio Telescope Lab
University of New Mexico

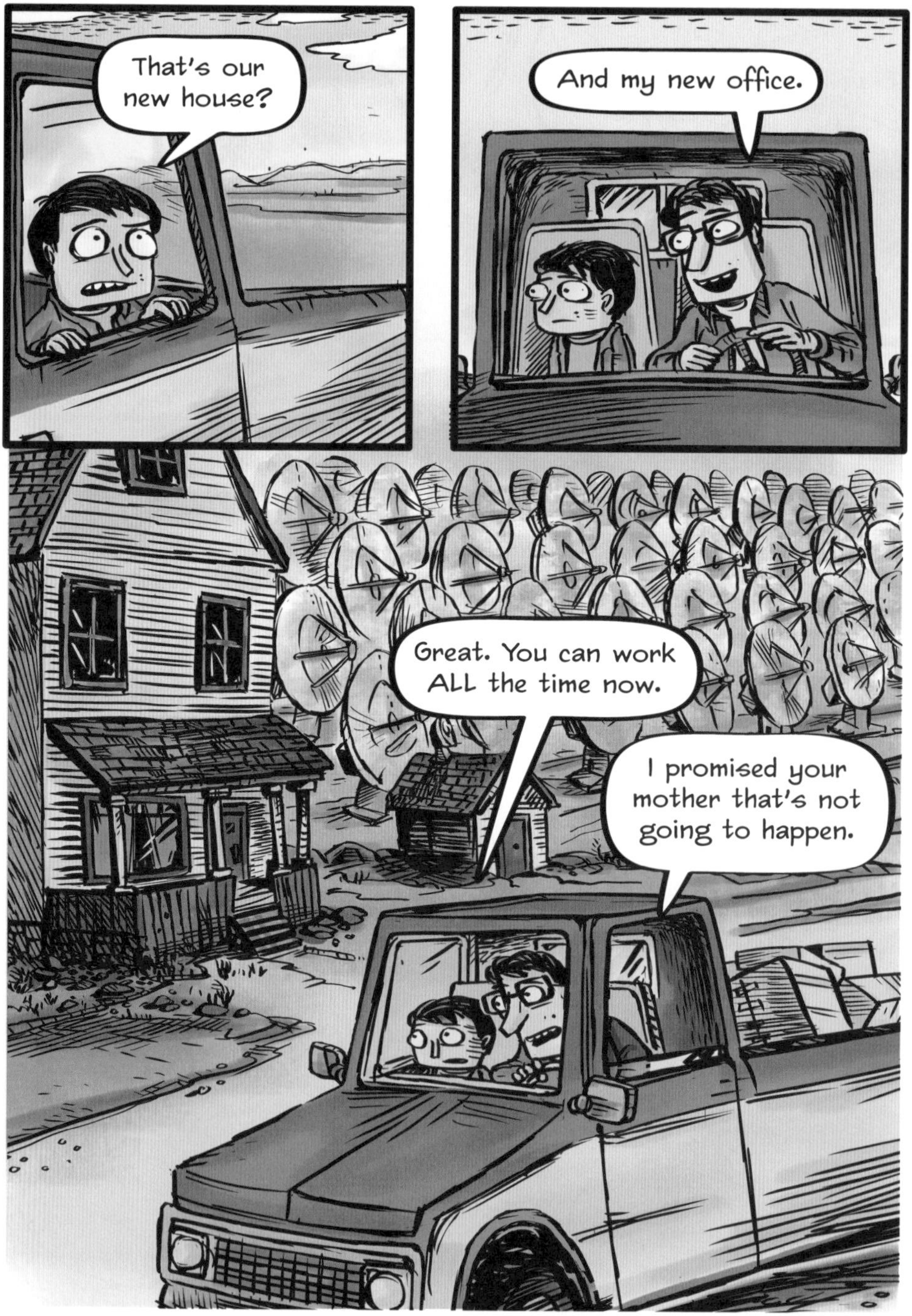
That's our new house?
And my new office.
Great. You can work ALL the time now.
I promised your mother that's not going to happen.

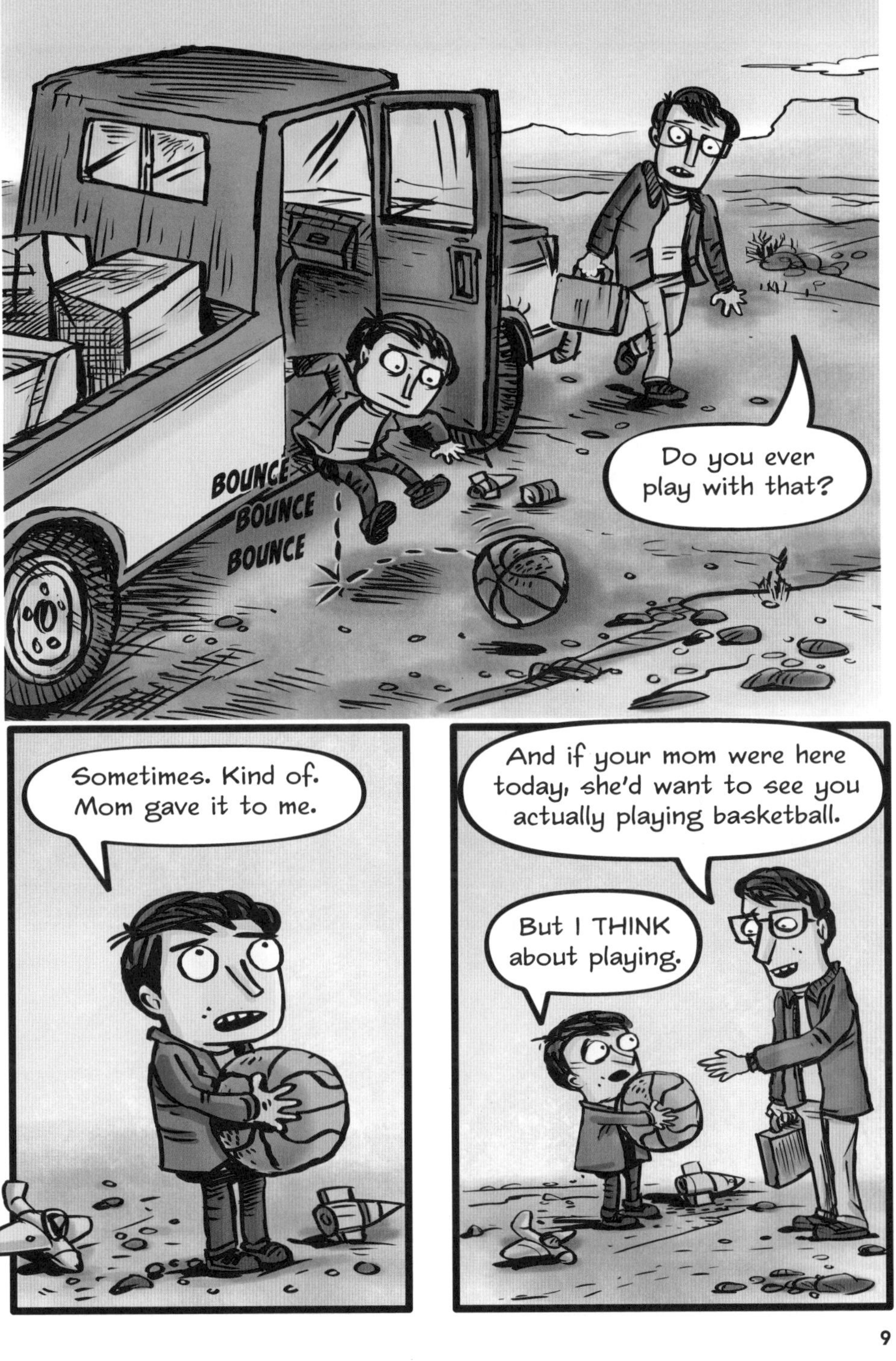
BOUNCE
BOUNCE
BOUNCE
Do you ever play with that?
Sometimes. Kind of. Mom gave it to me.
And if your mom were here today, she'd want to see you actually playing basketball.
But I THINK about playing.

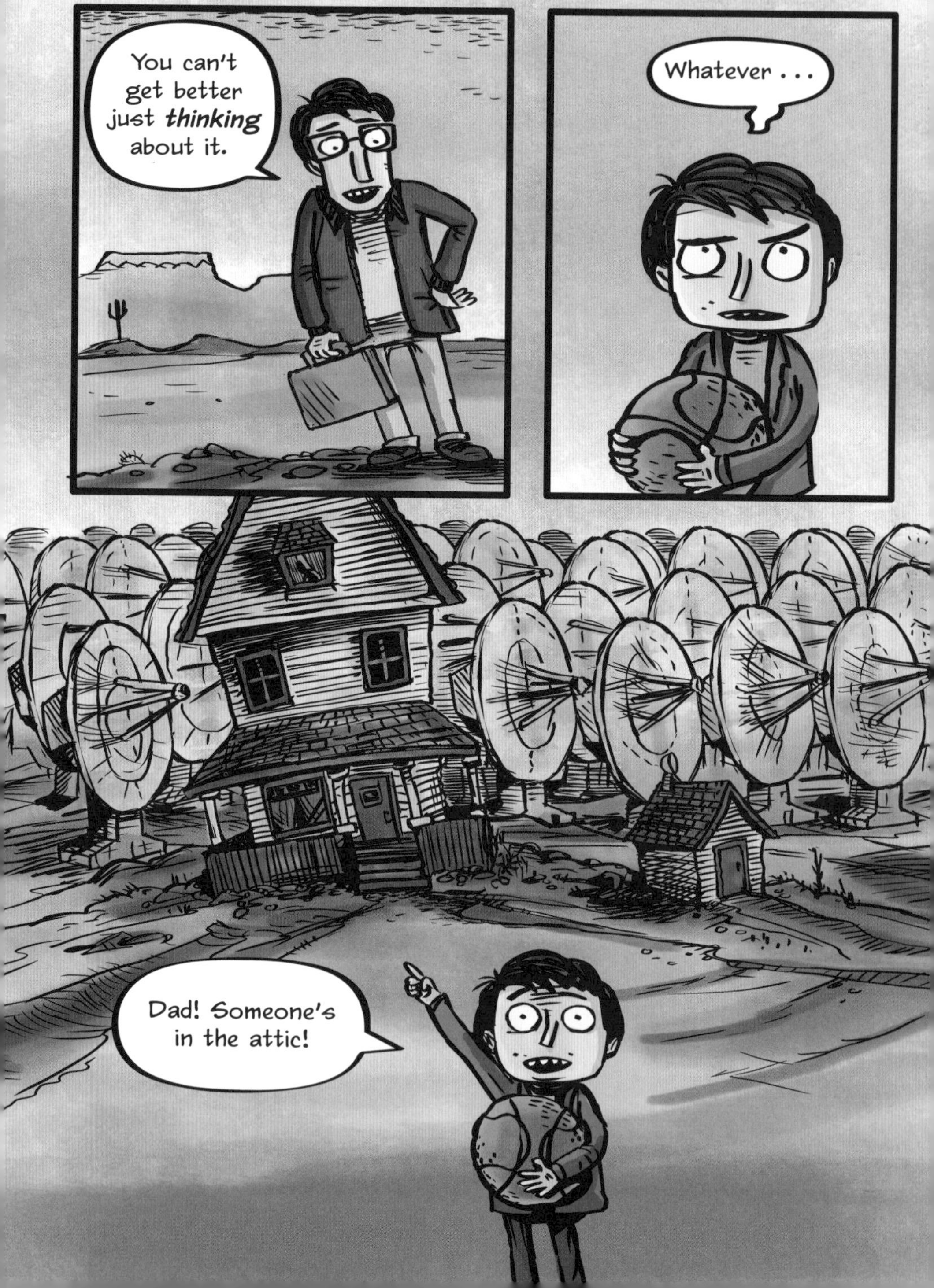
You can't get better just ***thinking*** about it.
Whatever . . .
Dad! Someone's in the attic!

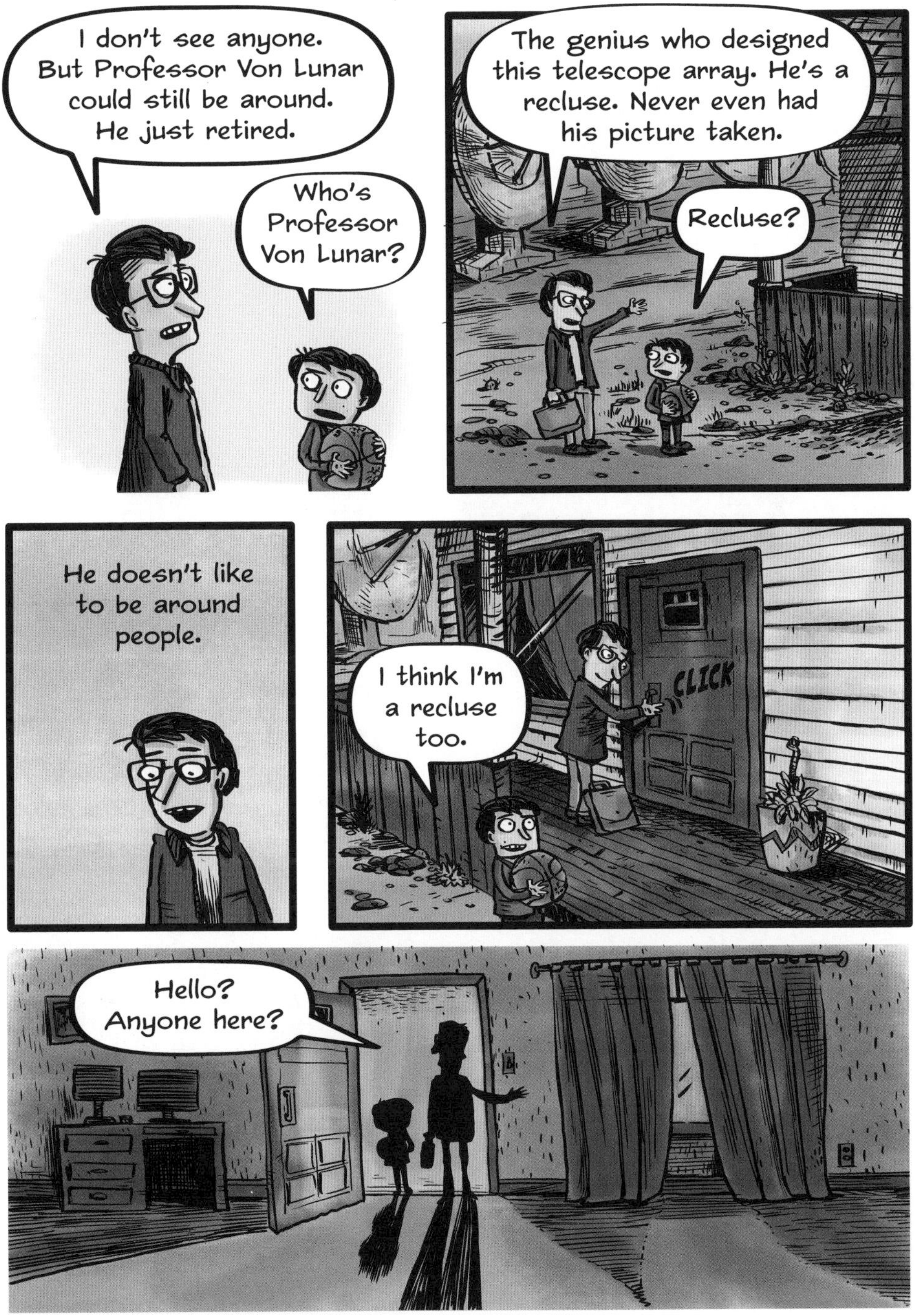
I don't see anyone. But Professor Von Lunar could still be around. He just retired.
Who's Professor Von Lunar?
The genius who designed this telescope array. He's a recluse. Never even had his picture taken.
Recluse?
He doesn't like to be around people.
I think I'm a recluse too.
CLICK
Hello? Anyone here?

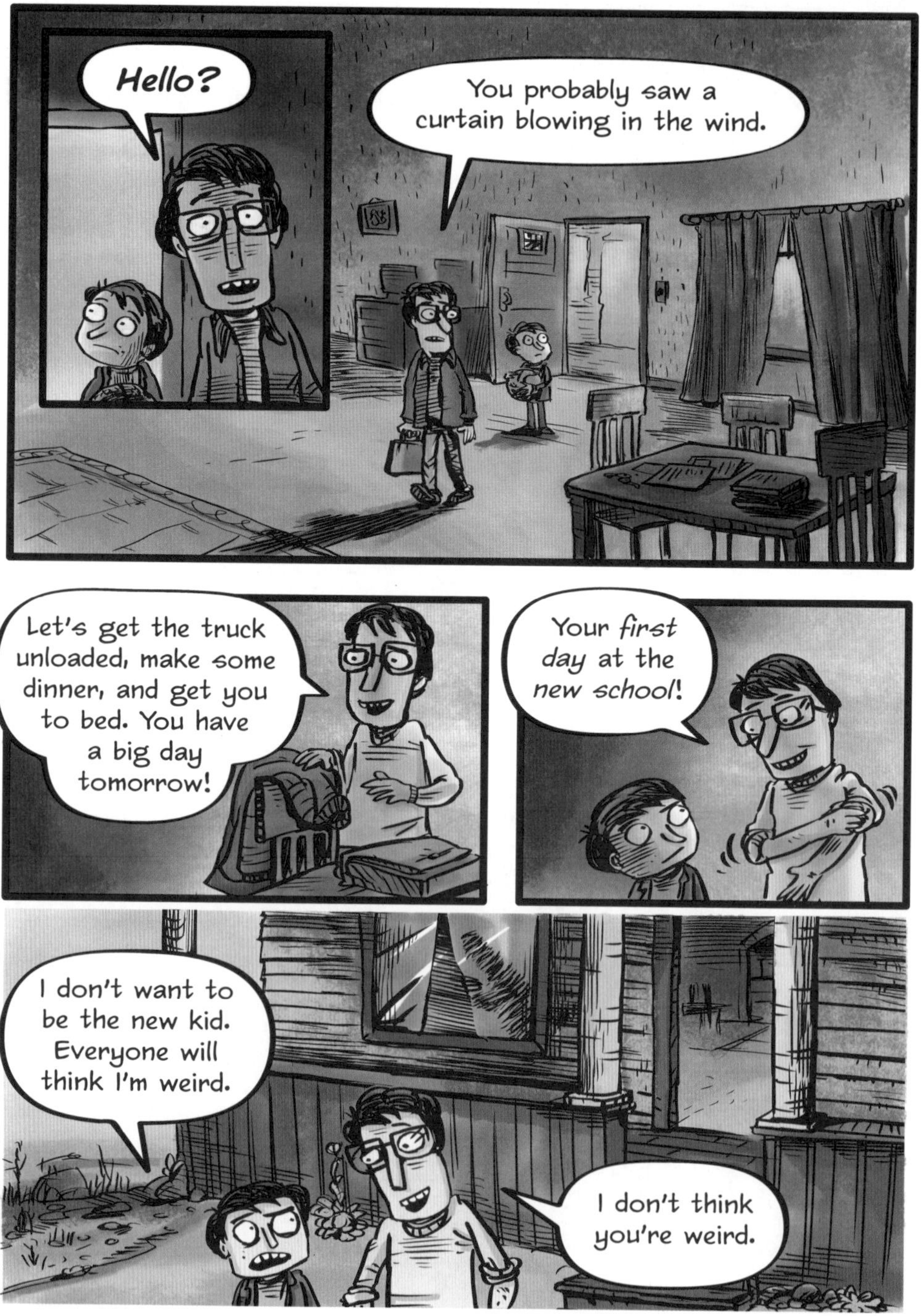
Hello?
You probably saw a curtain blowing in the wind.
Let's get the truck unloaded, make some dinner, and get you to bed. You have a big day tomorrow!
Your *first* day at the *new school*!
I don't want to be the new kid. Everyone will think I'm weird.
I don't think you're weird.

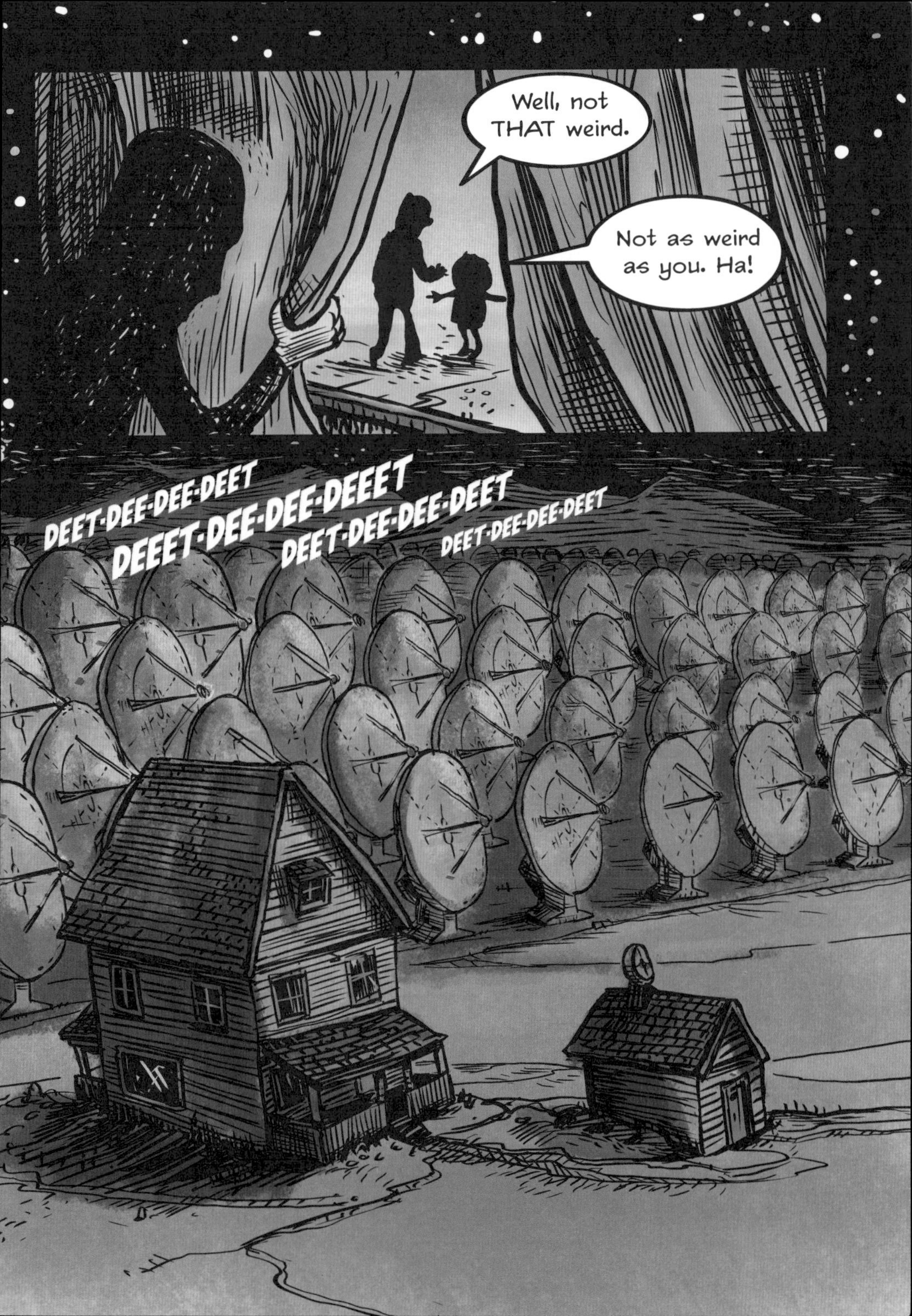
Well, not THAT weird.
Not as weird as you. Ha!
DEET-DEE-DEE-DEET
DEEET-DEE-DEE-DEEET
DEET-DEE-DEE-DEET
DEET-DEE-DEE-DEET

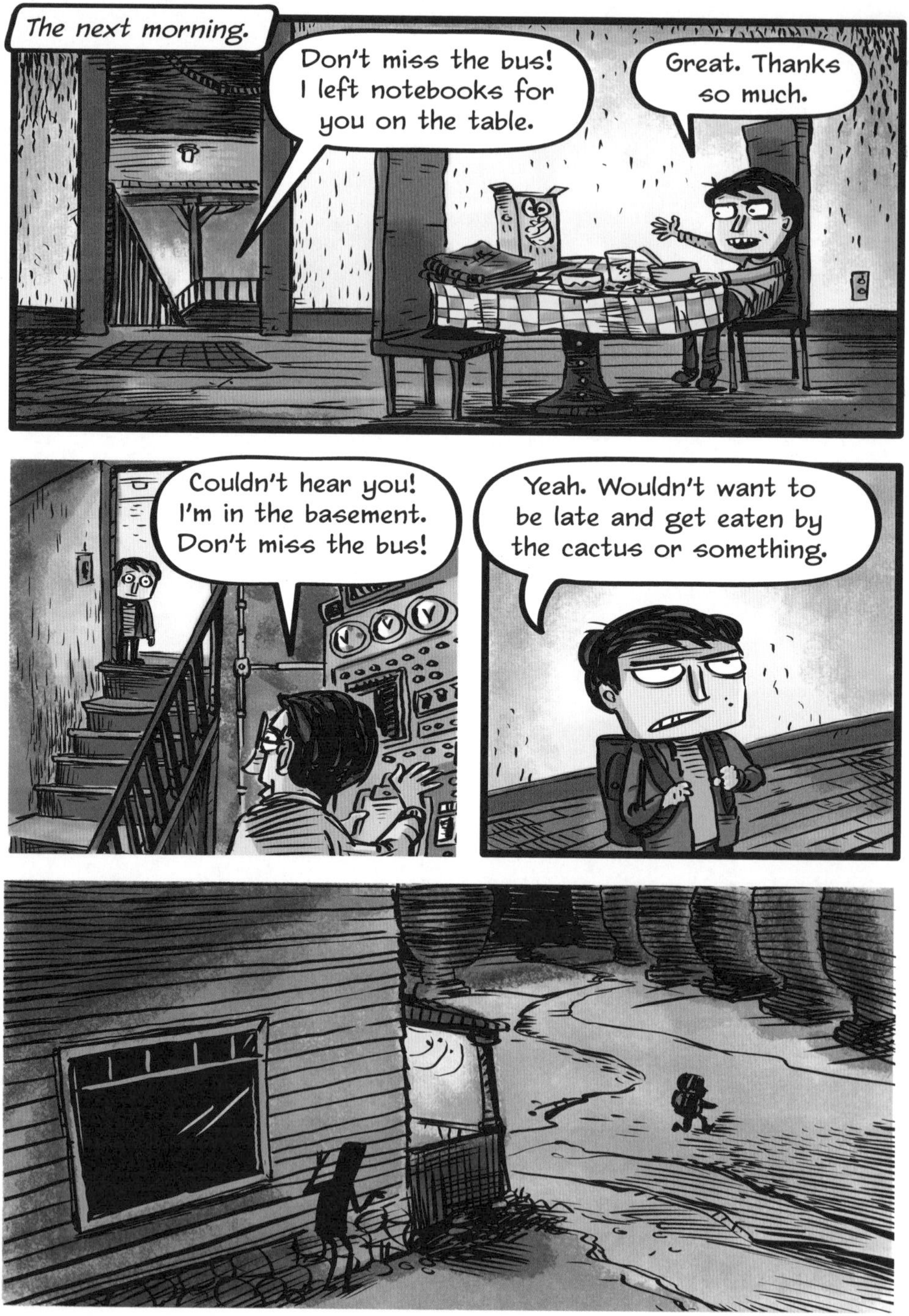
The next morning.
Don't miss the bus! I left notebooks for you on the table.
Great. Thanks so much.
Couldn't hear you! I'm in the basement. Don't miss the bus!
Yeah. Wouldn't want to be late and get eaten by the cactus or something.

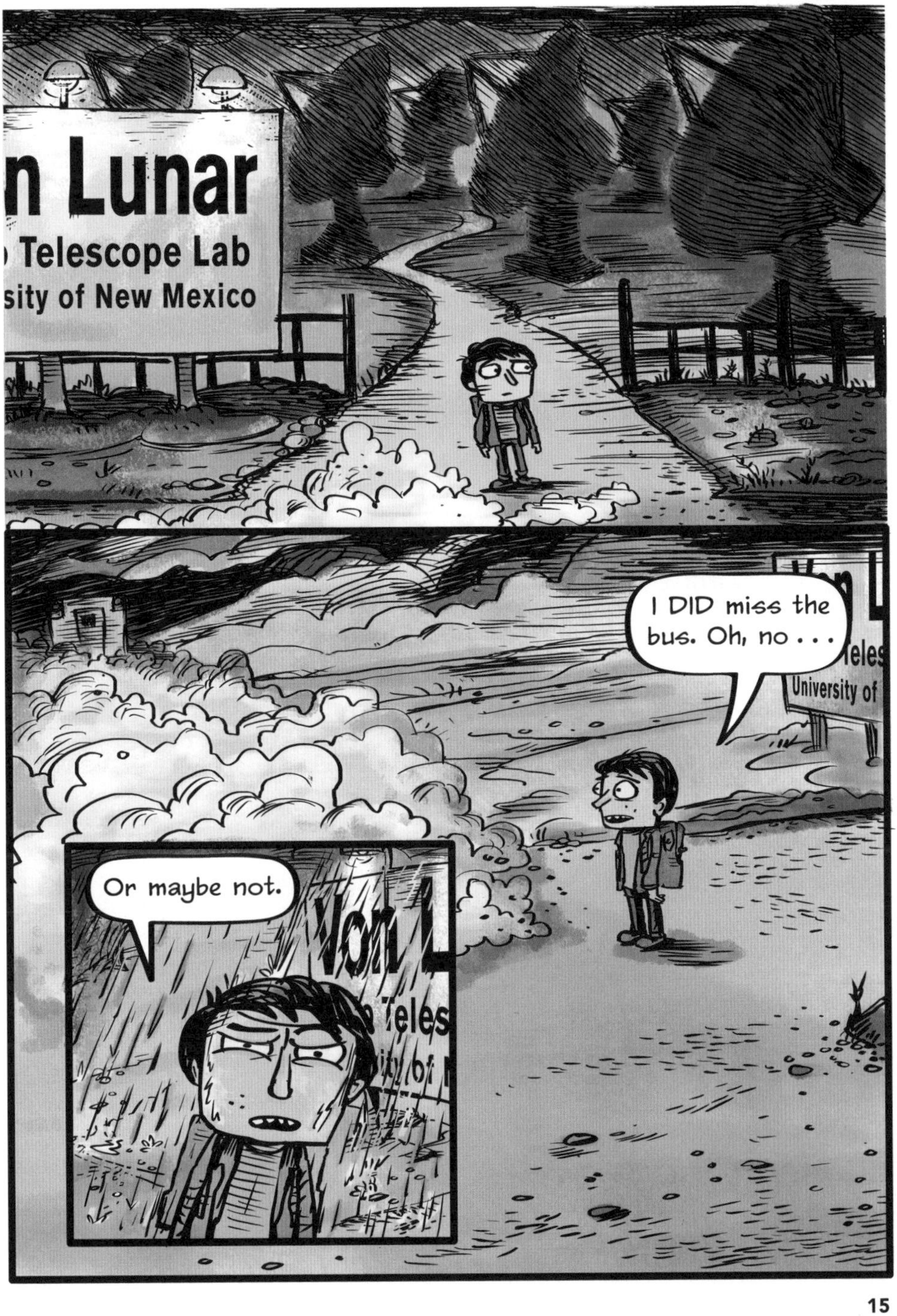
n Lunar
Telescope Lab
sity of New Mexico
I DID miss the bus. Oh, no . . .
Or maybe not.

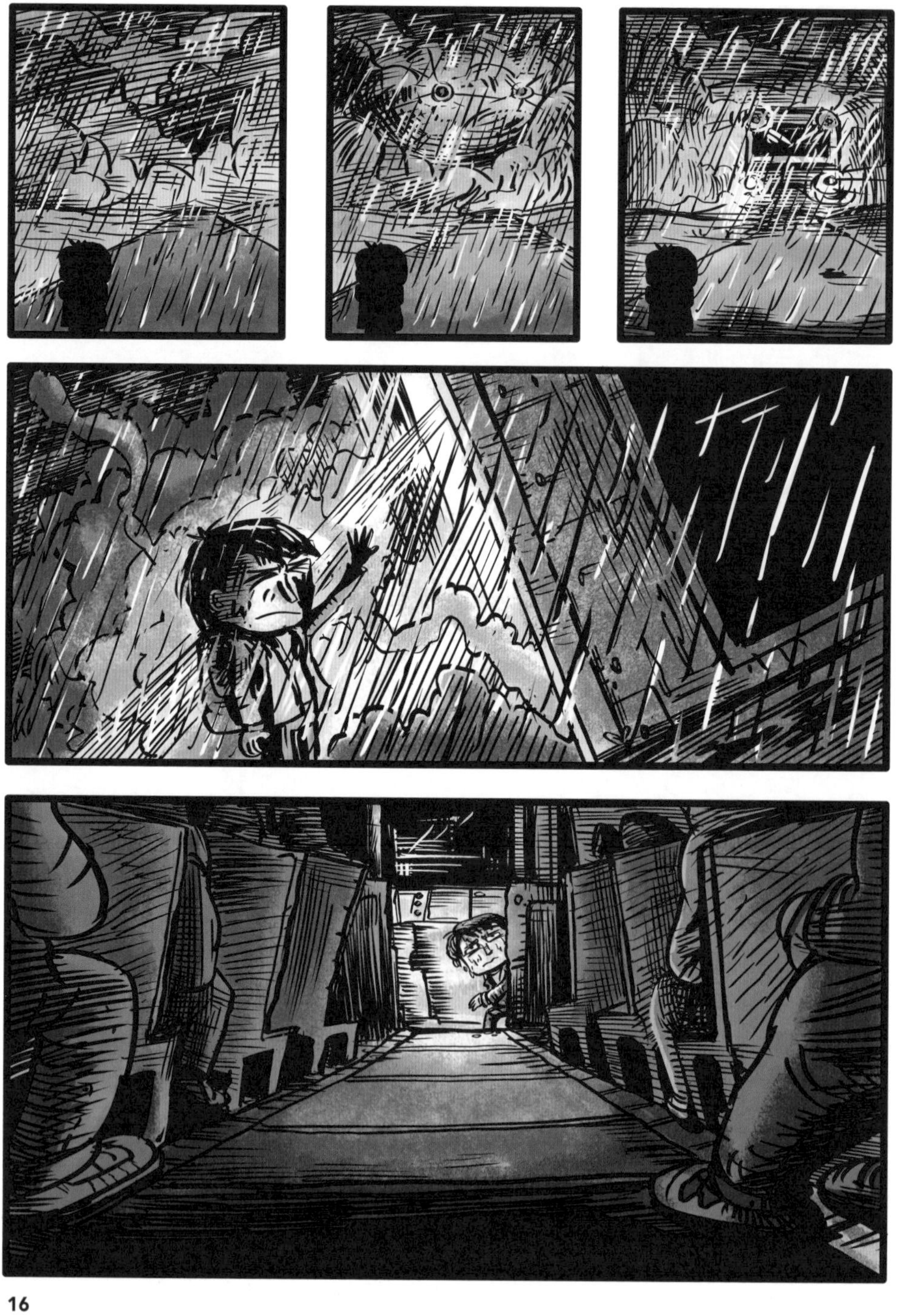

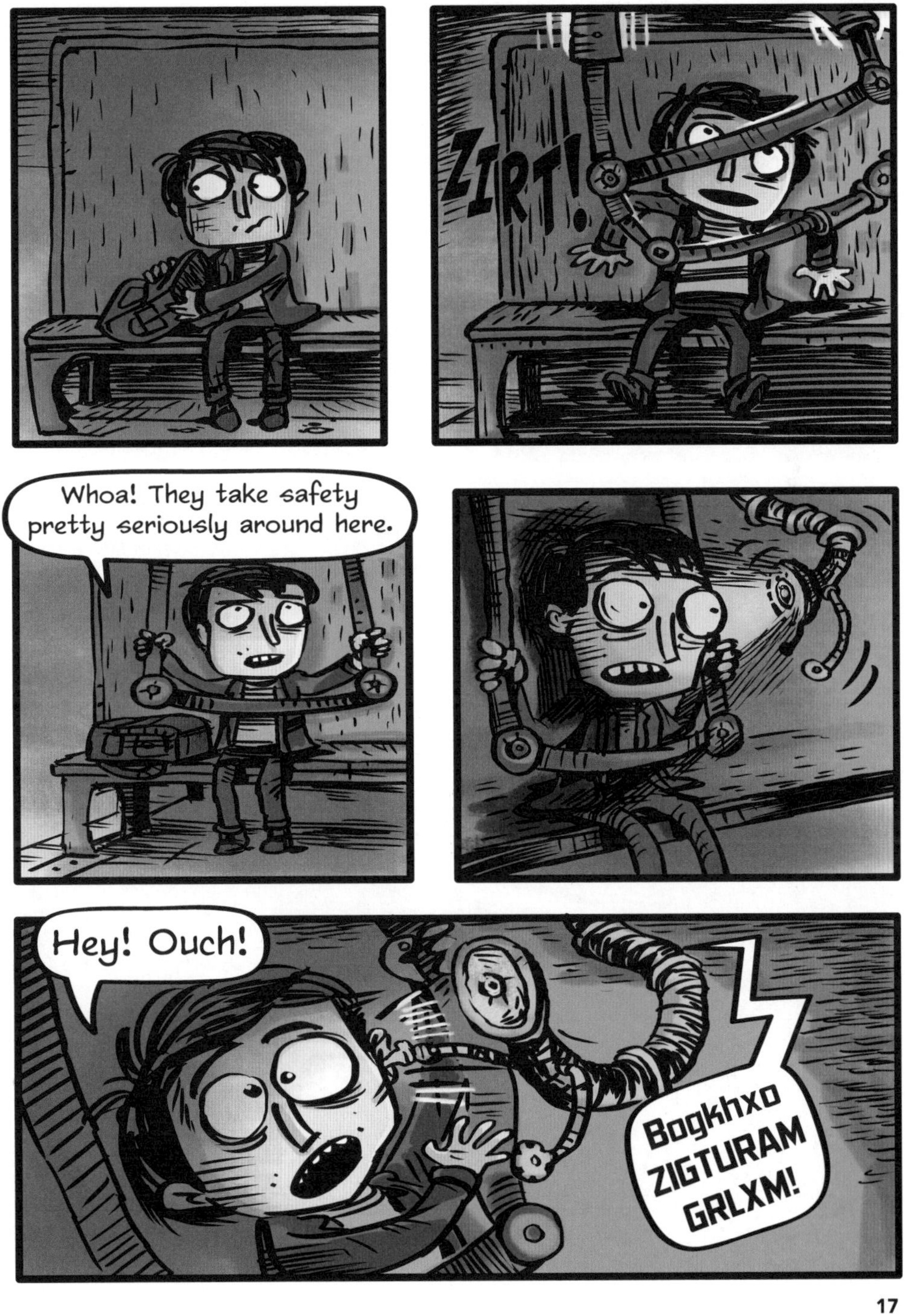
ZIRT!
Whoa! They take safety pretty seriously around here.
Hey! Ouch!
Bogkhxo ZIGTURAM GRLXM!

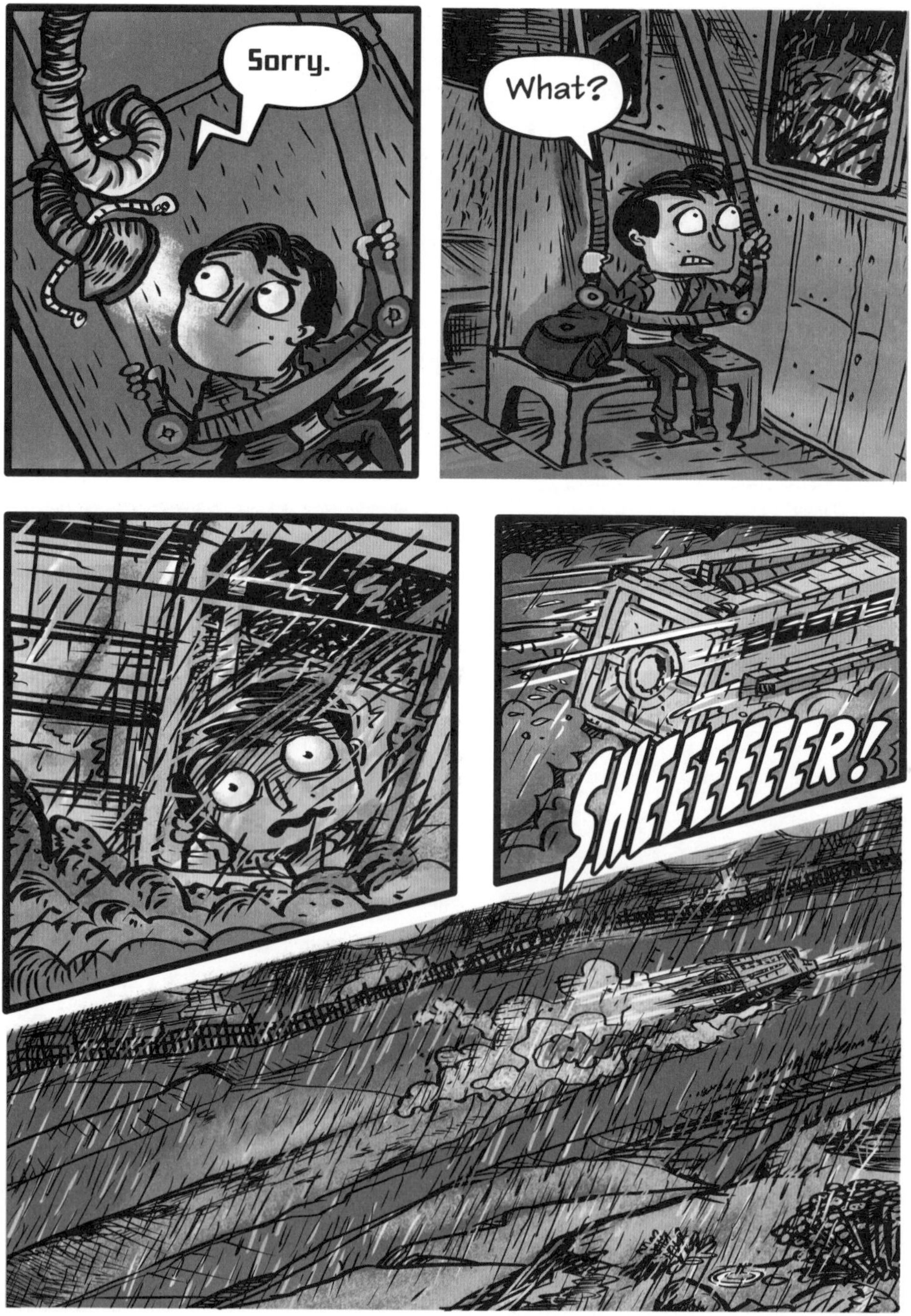
Sorry.
What?
SHEEEEEER!

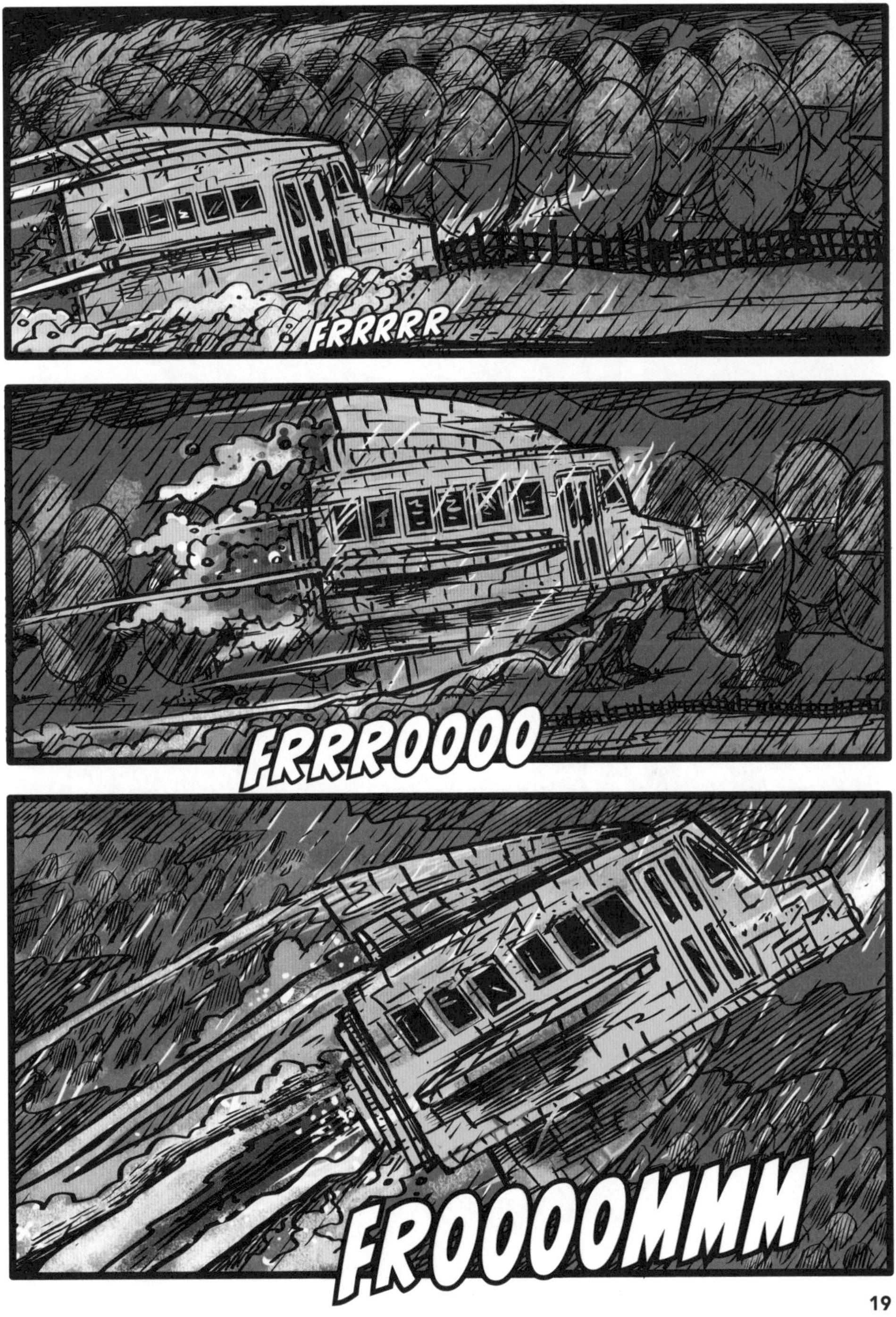
FRRRRR
FRRROOOO
FROOOOMMM

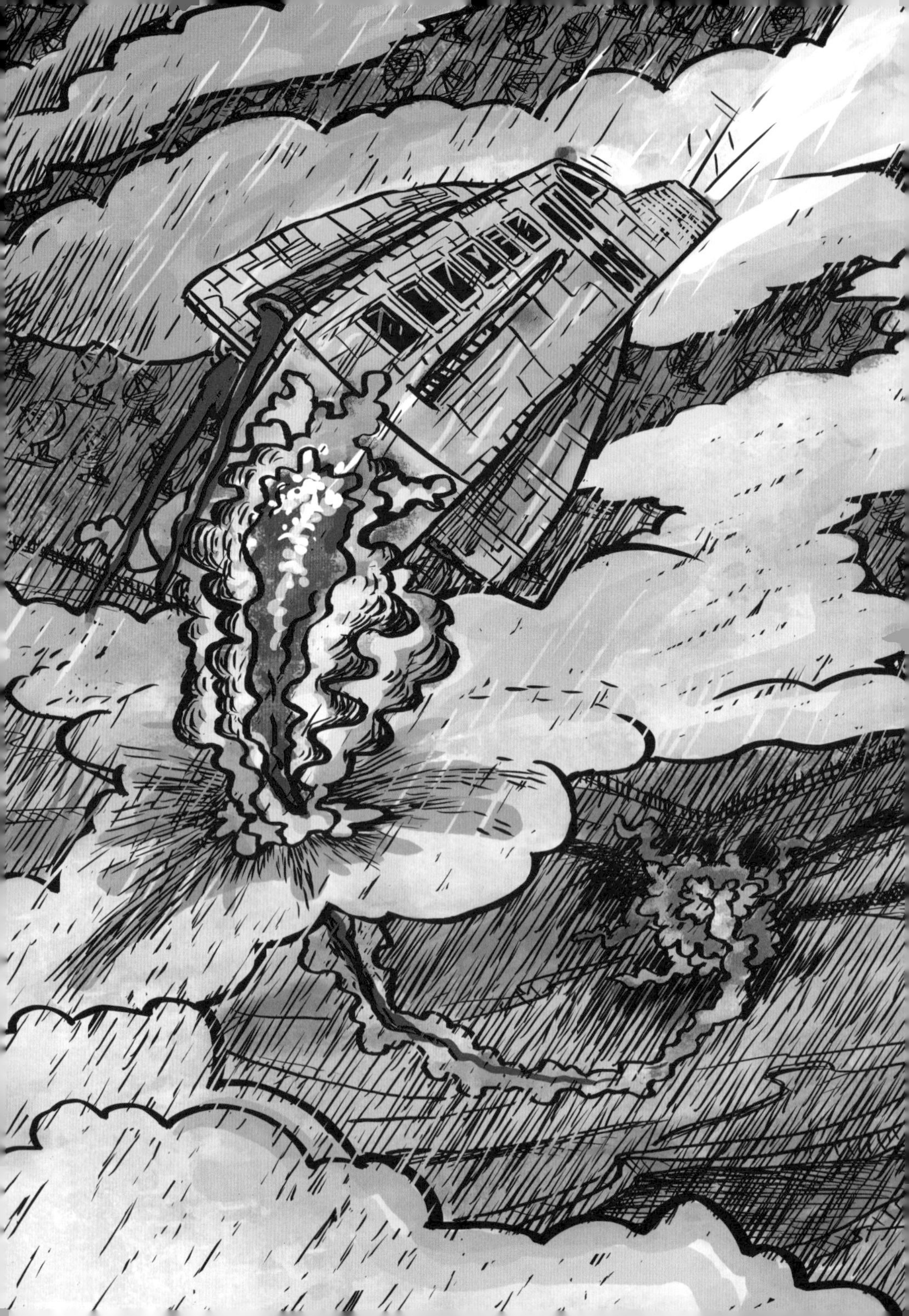

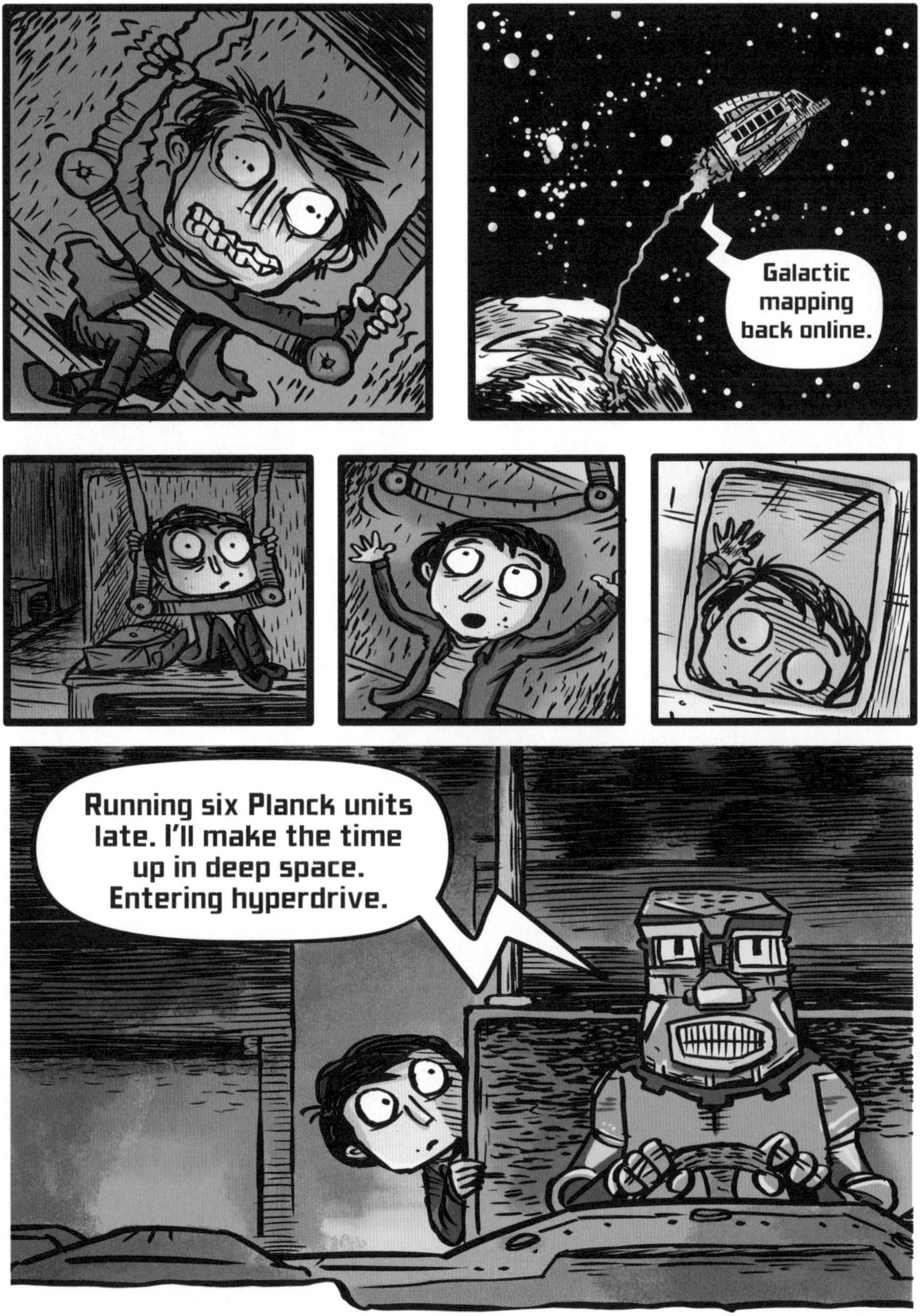
Galactic mapping back online.
Running six Planck units late. I'll make the time up in deep space. Entering hyperdrive.

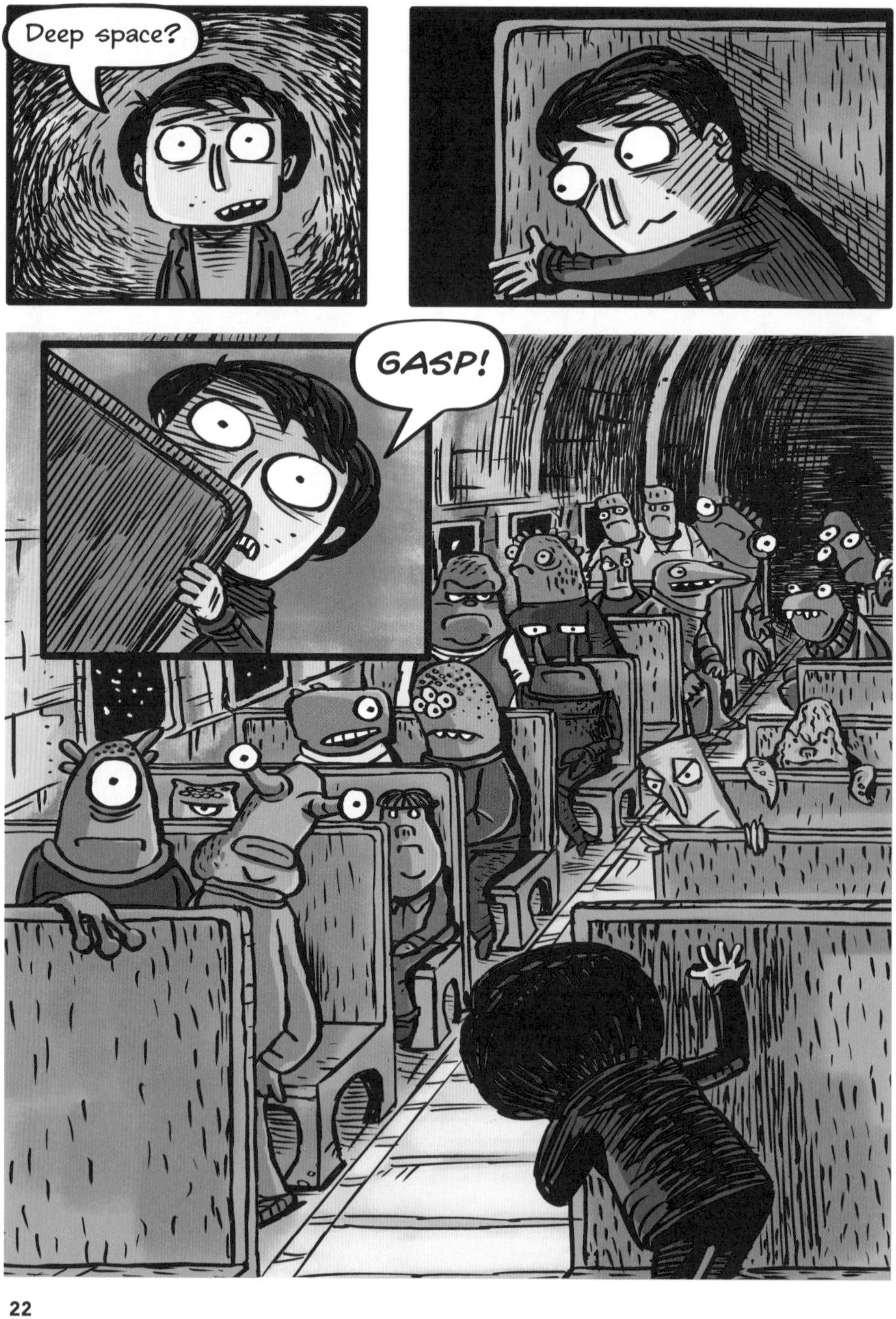
Deep space?
GASP!

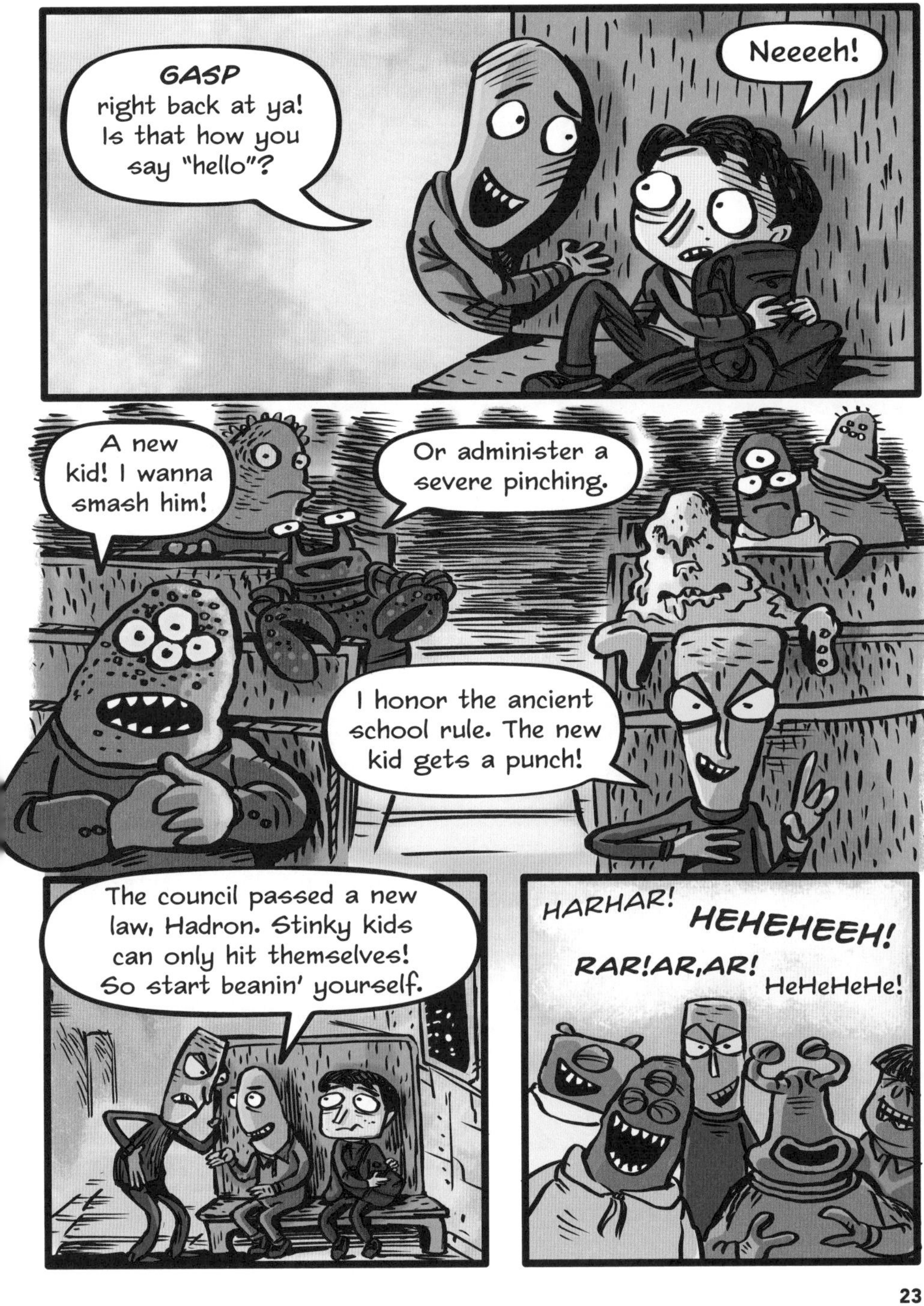
GASP
right back at ya! Is that how you say "hello"?
Neeeeh!
A new kid! I wanna smash him!
Or administer a severe pinching.
I honor the ancient school rule. The new kid gets a punch!
The council passed a new law, Hadron. Stinky kids can only hit themselves! So start beanin' yourself.
HARHAR!
HEHEHEEEH!
RAR!AR,AR!
HeHeHeHe!

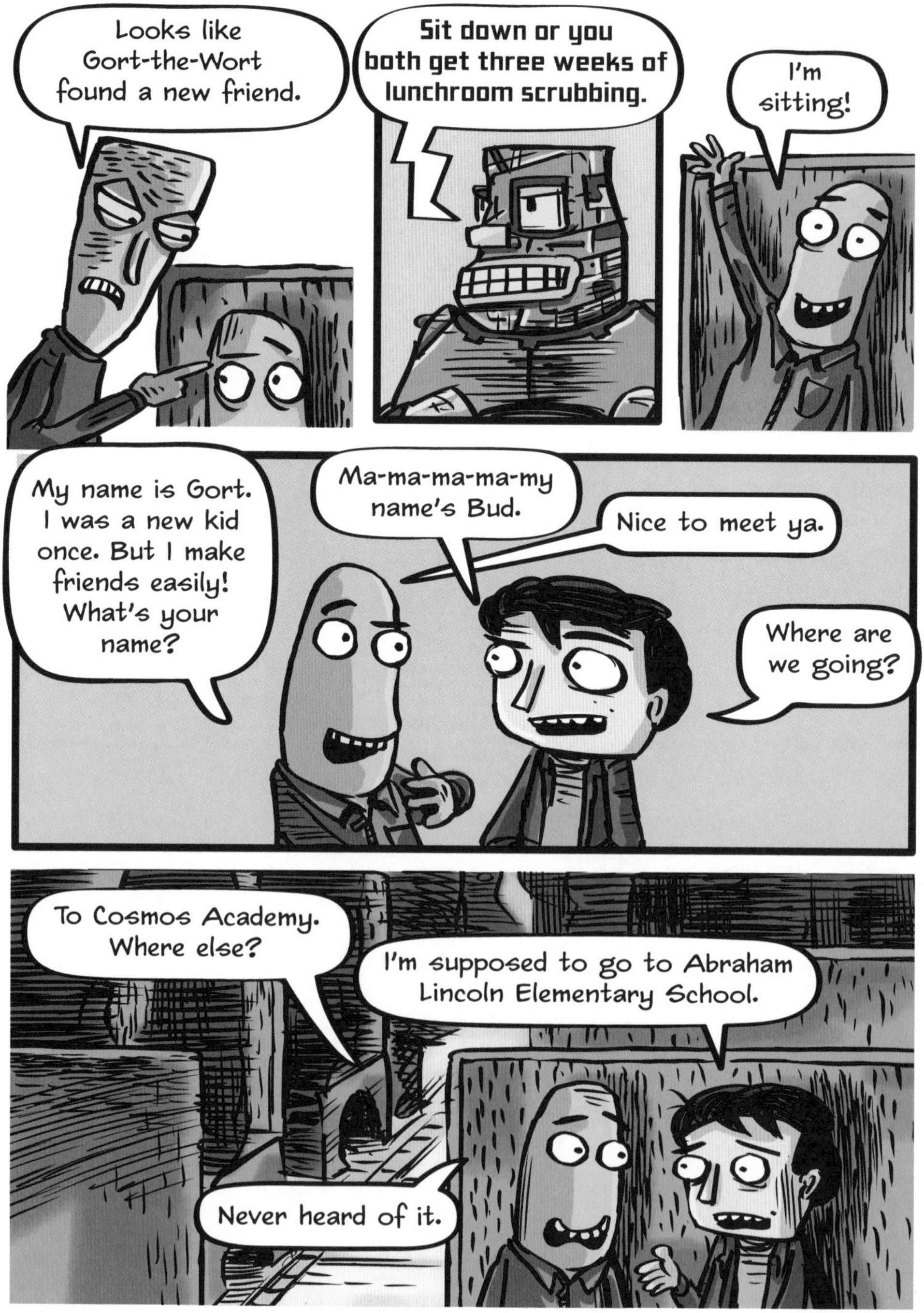
Looks like Gort-the-Wort found a new friend.
Sit down or you both get three weeks of lunchroom scrubbing.
I'm sitting!
My name is Gort. I was a new kid once. But I make friends easily! What's your name?
Ma-ma-ma-ma-my name's Bud.
Nice to meet ya.
Where are we going?
To Cosmos Academy. Where else?
I'm supposed to go to Abraham Lincoln Elementary School.
Never heard of it.

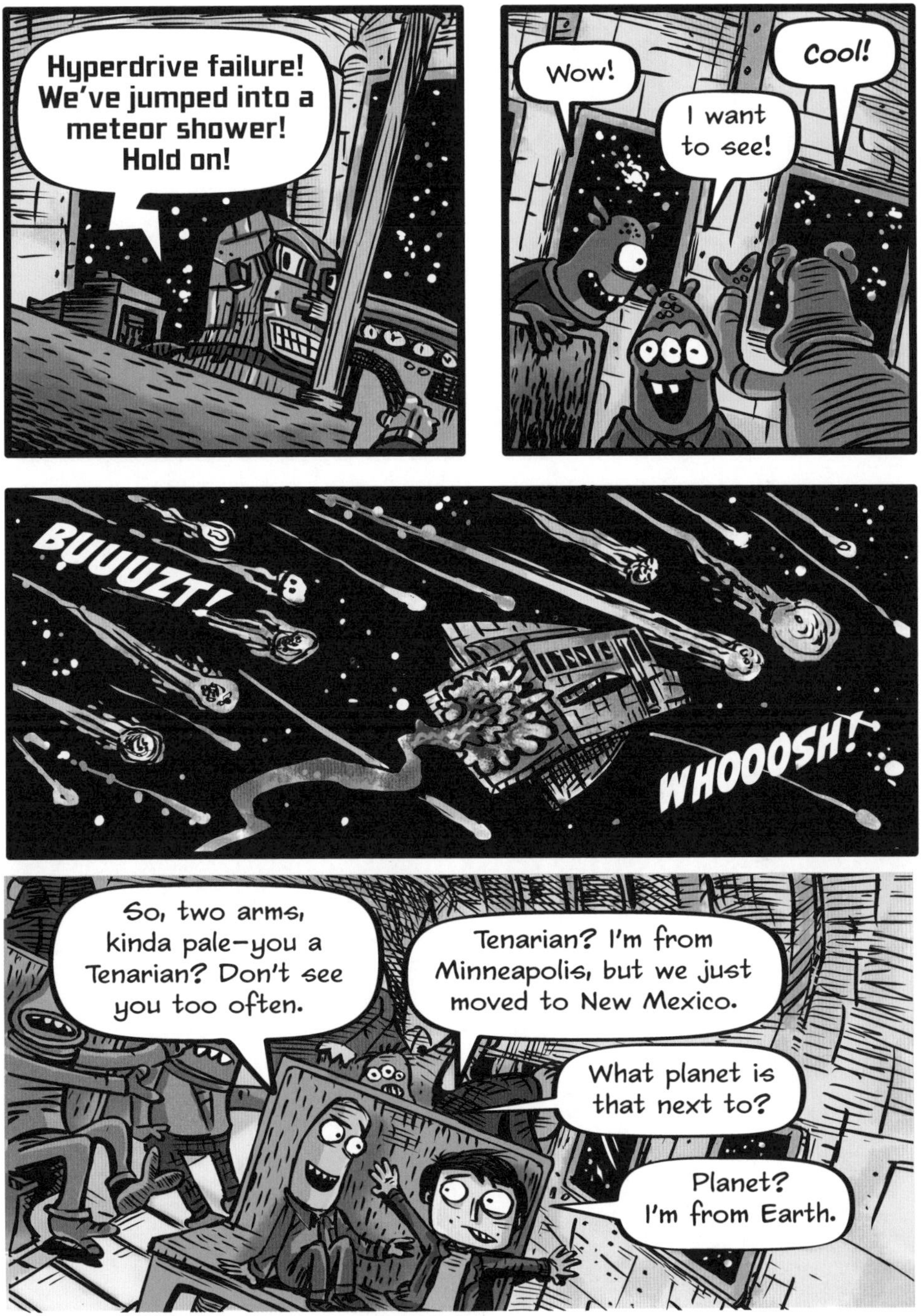
Hyperdrive failure! We've jumped into a meteor shower! Hold on!
Wow!
I want to see!
Cool!
BUUUZT!
WHOOOSH!
So, two arms, kinda pale—you a Tenarian? Don't see you too often.
Tenarian? I'm from Minneapolis, but we just moved to New Mexico.
What planet is that next to?
Planet? I'm from Earth.

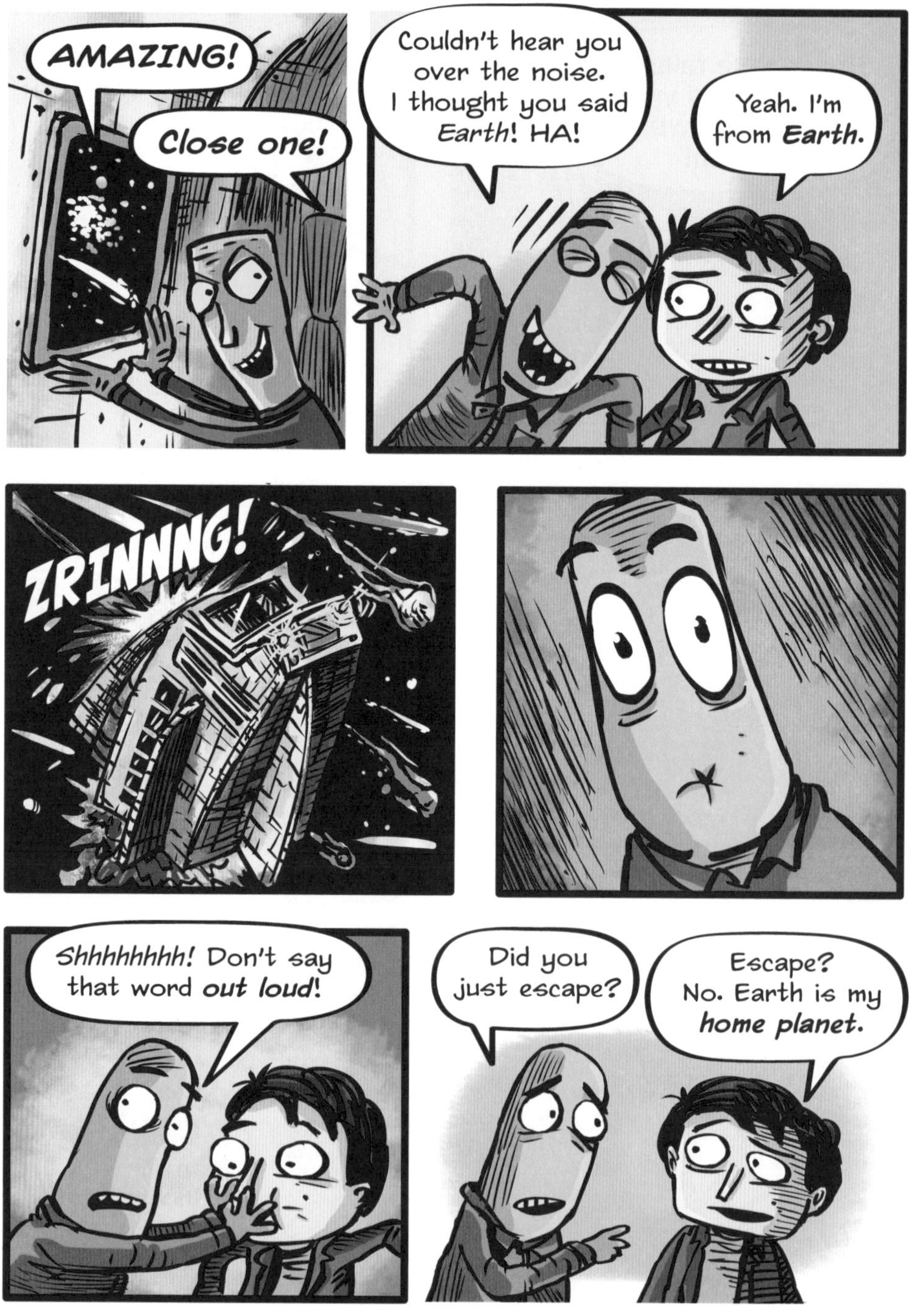
AMAZING!
Close one!
Couldn't hear you over the noise. I thought you said *Earth*! HA!
Yeah. I'm from **Earth.**
ZRINNNG!
Shhhhhhhh! Don't say that word **out loud**!
Did you just escape?
Escape? No. Earth is my **home planet.**

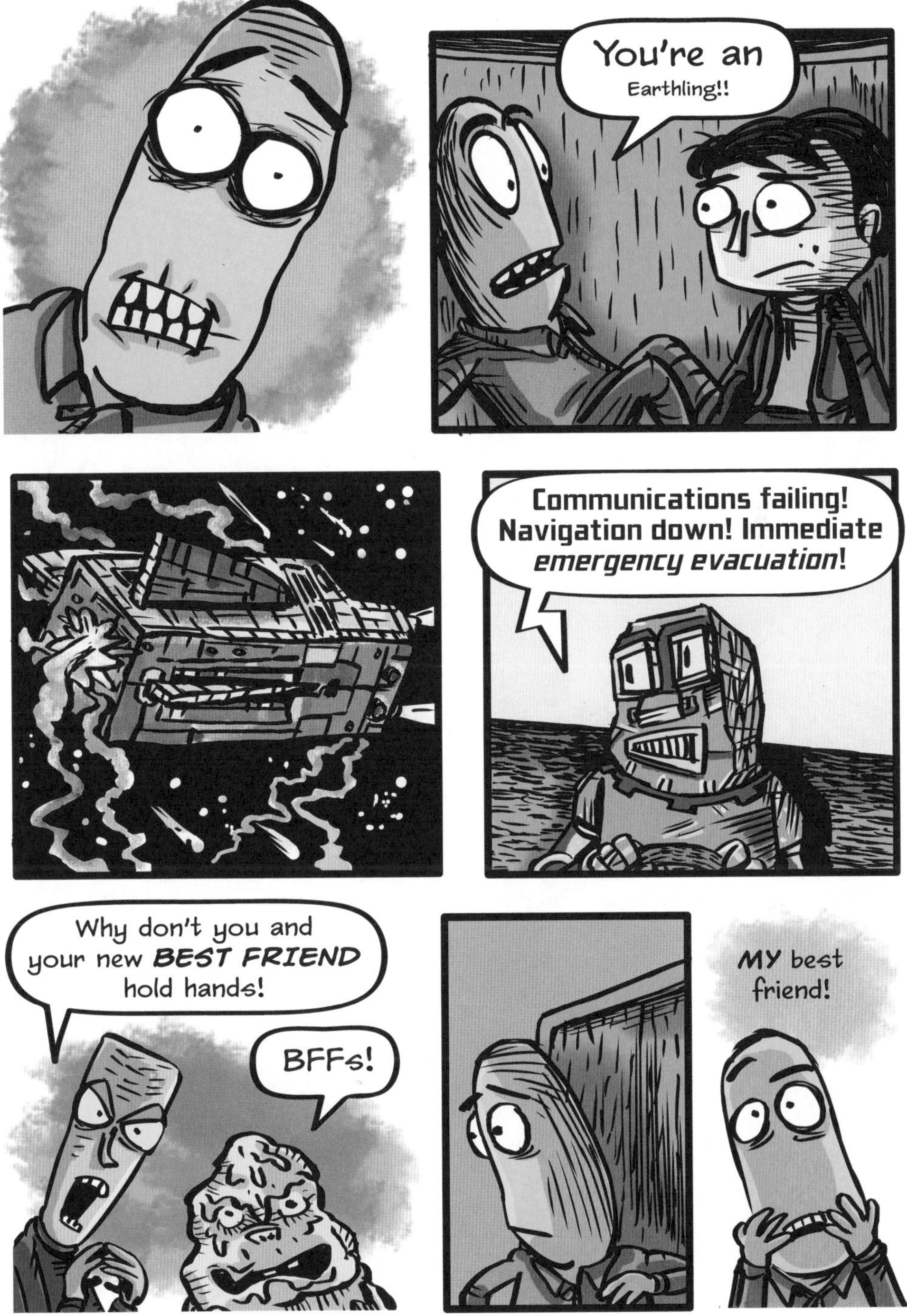
You're an Earthling!!
Communications failing! Navigation down! Immediate *emergency evacuation*!
Why don't you and your new **BEST FRIEND** hold hands!
BFFs!
MY best friend!

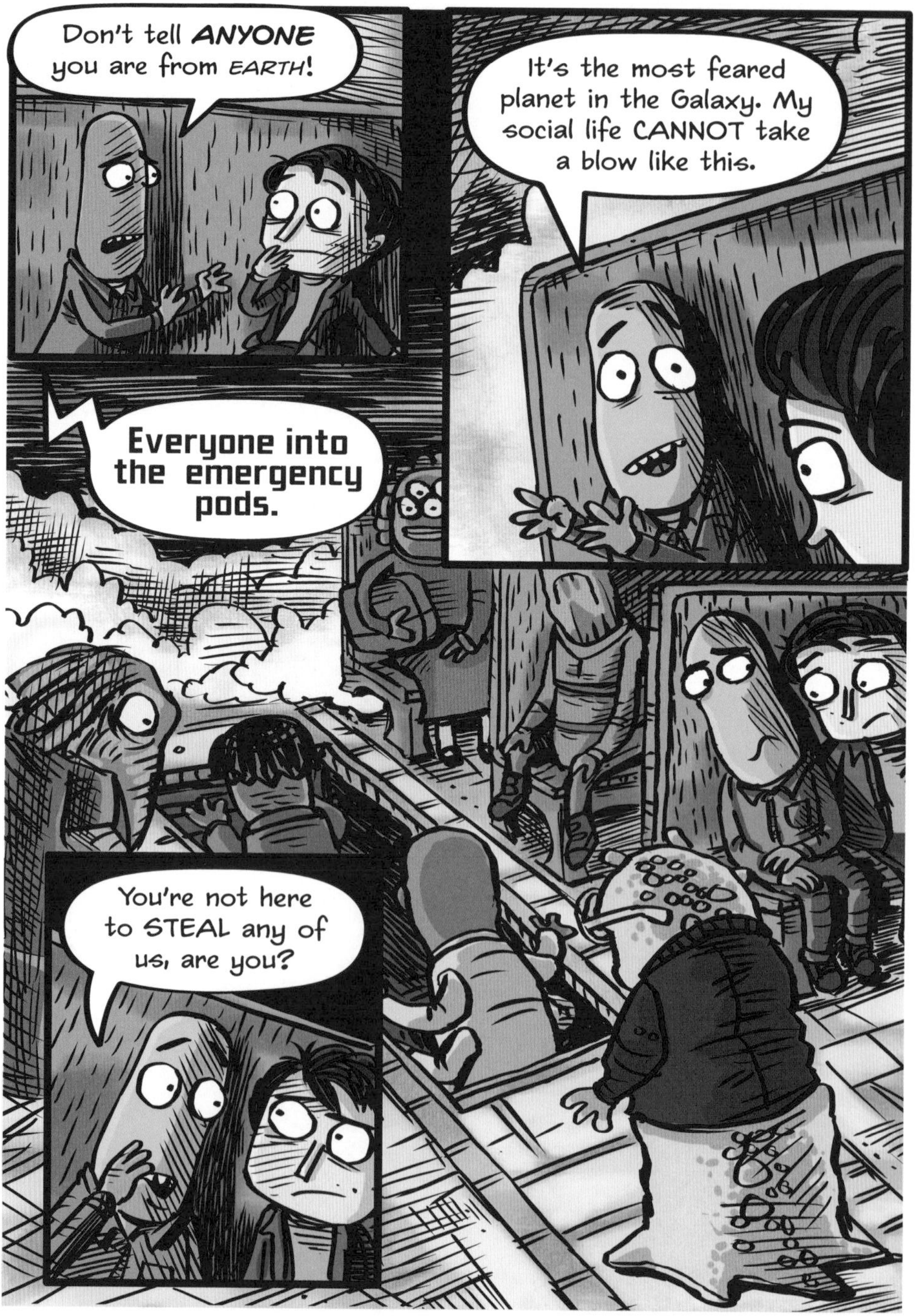
Don't tell ANYONE you are from EARTH!
It's the most feared planet in the Galaxy. My social life CANNOT take a blow like this.
Everyone into the emergency pods.
You're not here to STEAL any of us, are you?

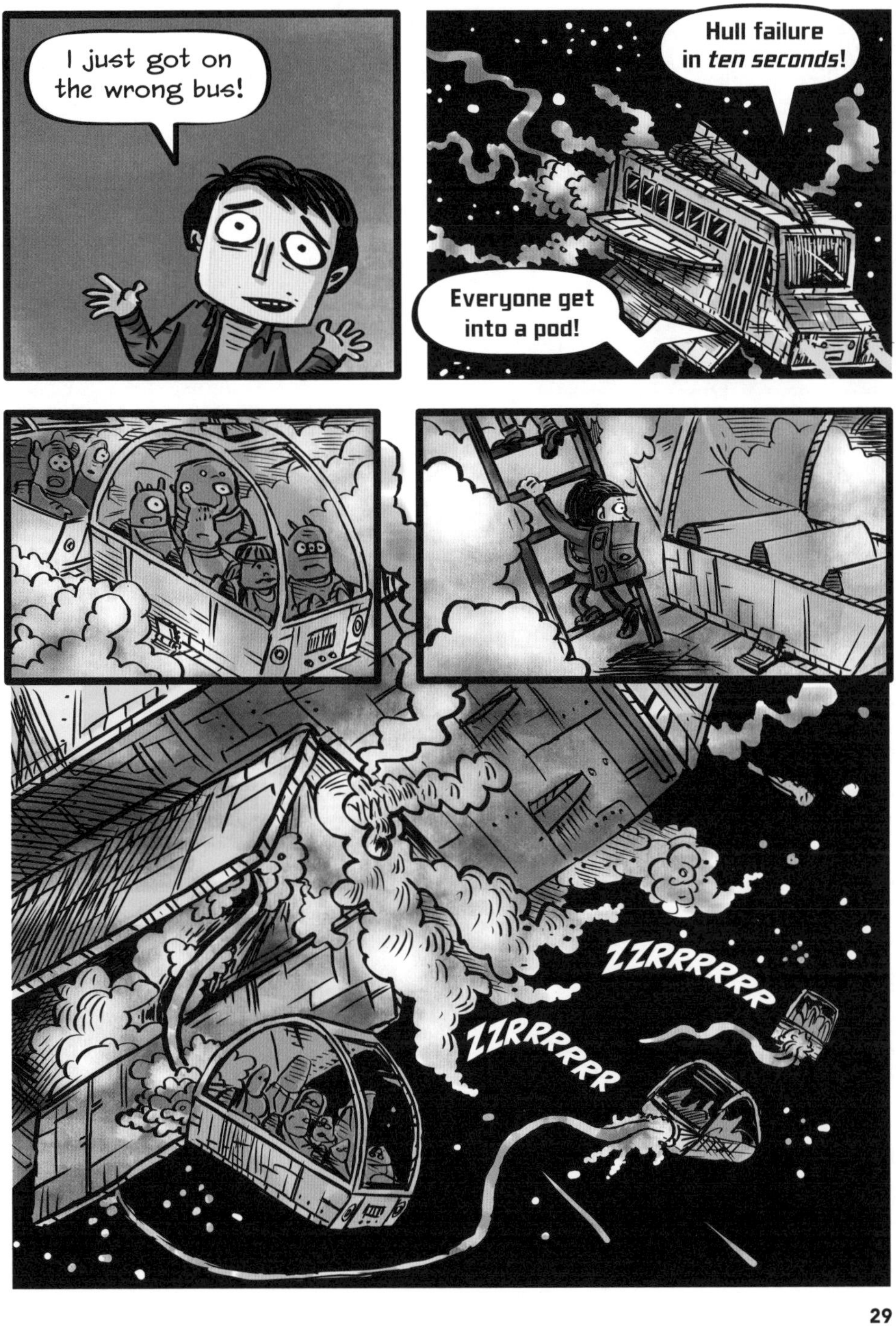
I just got on the wrong bus!
Hull failure in *ten seconds*!
Everyone get into a pod!
ZZRRRRRR
ZZRRRRRR

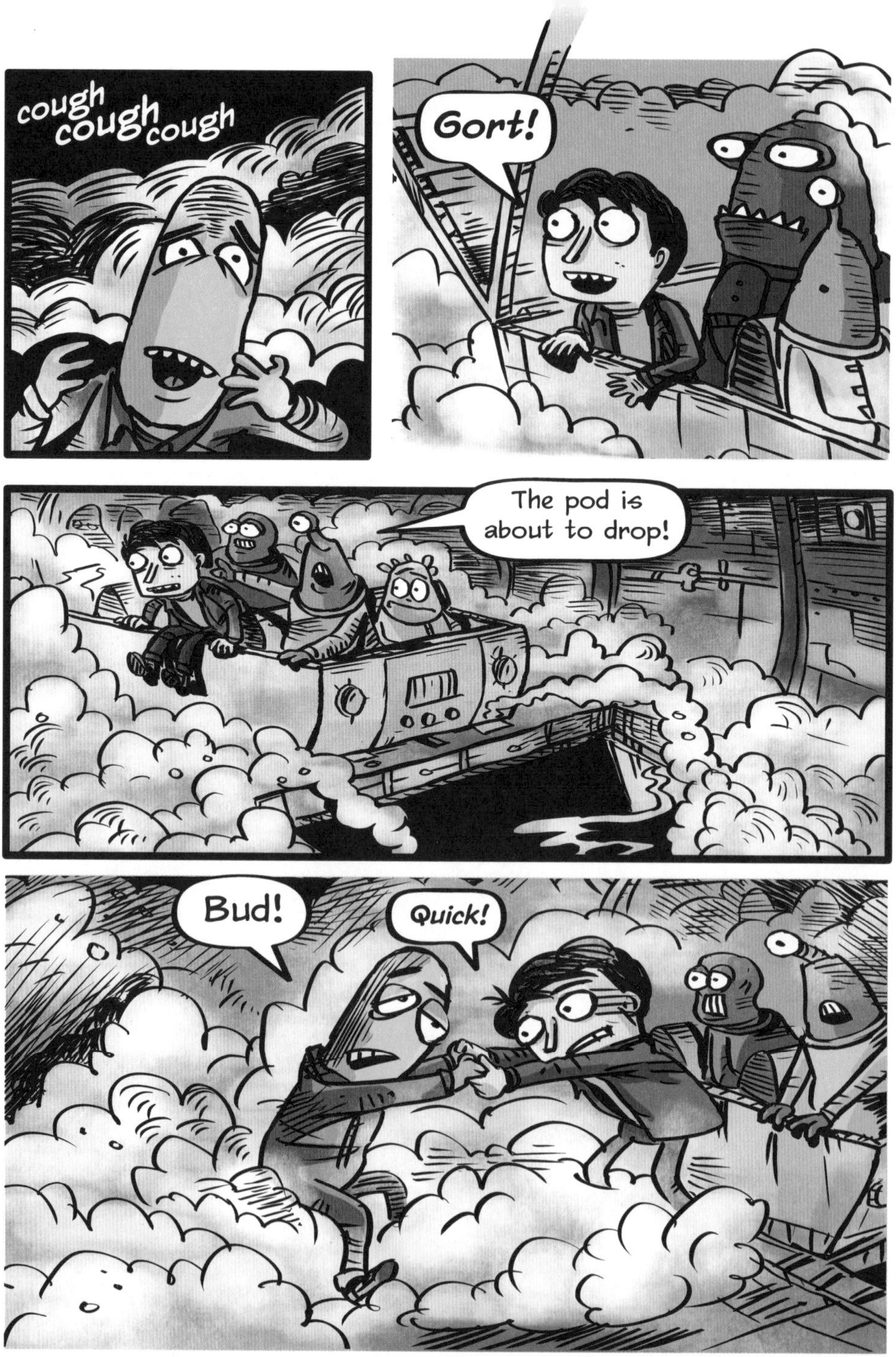
cough cough cough
Gort!
The pod is about to drop!
Bud!
Quick!

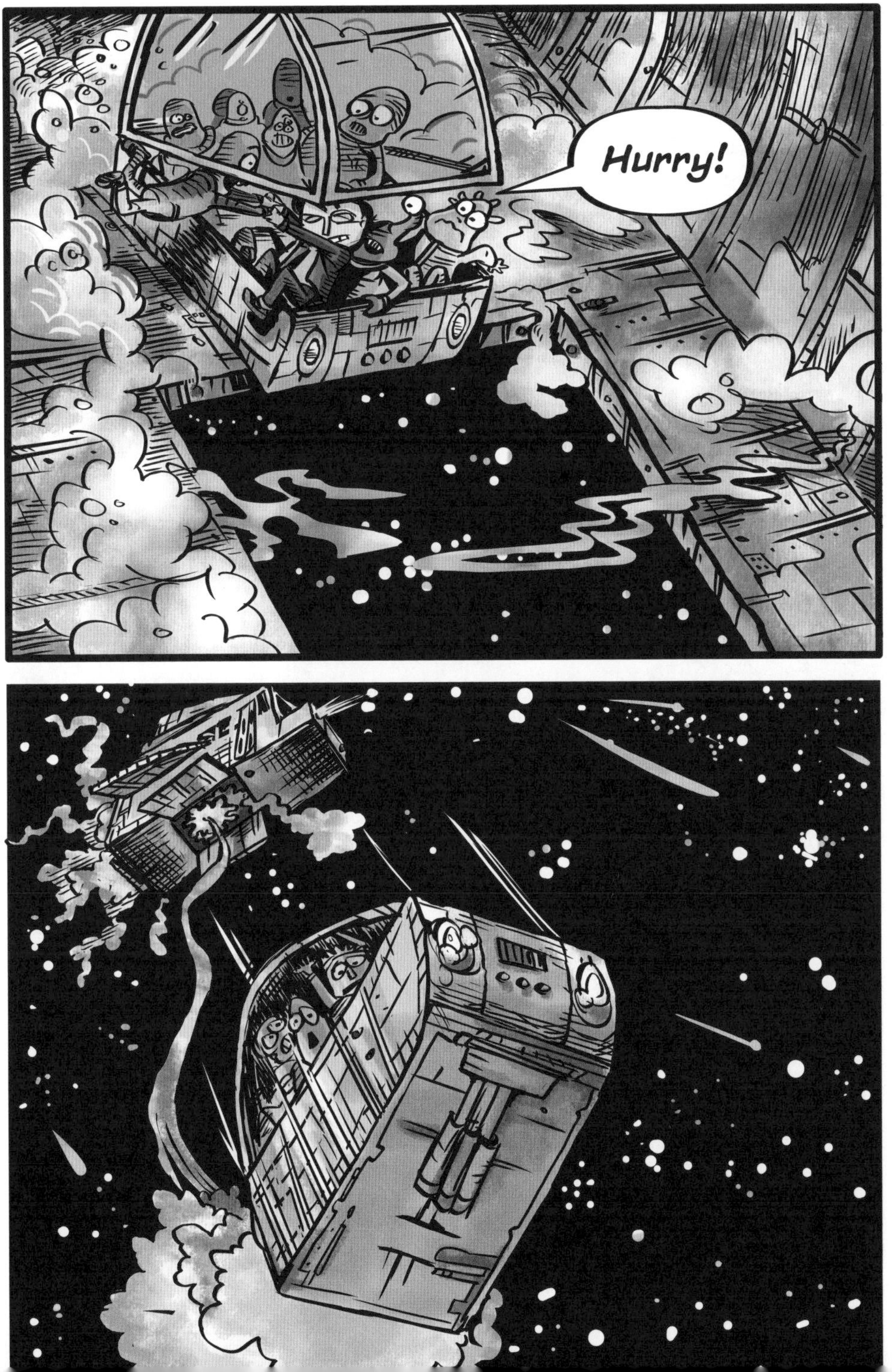
Hurry!

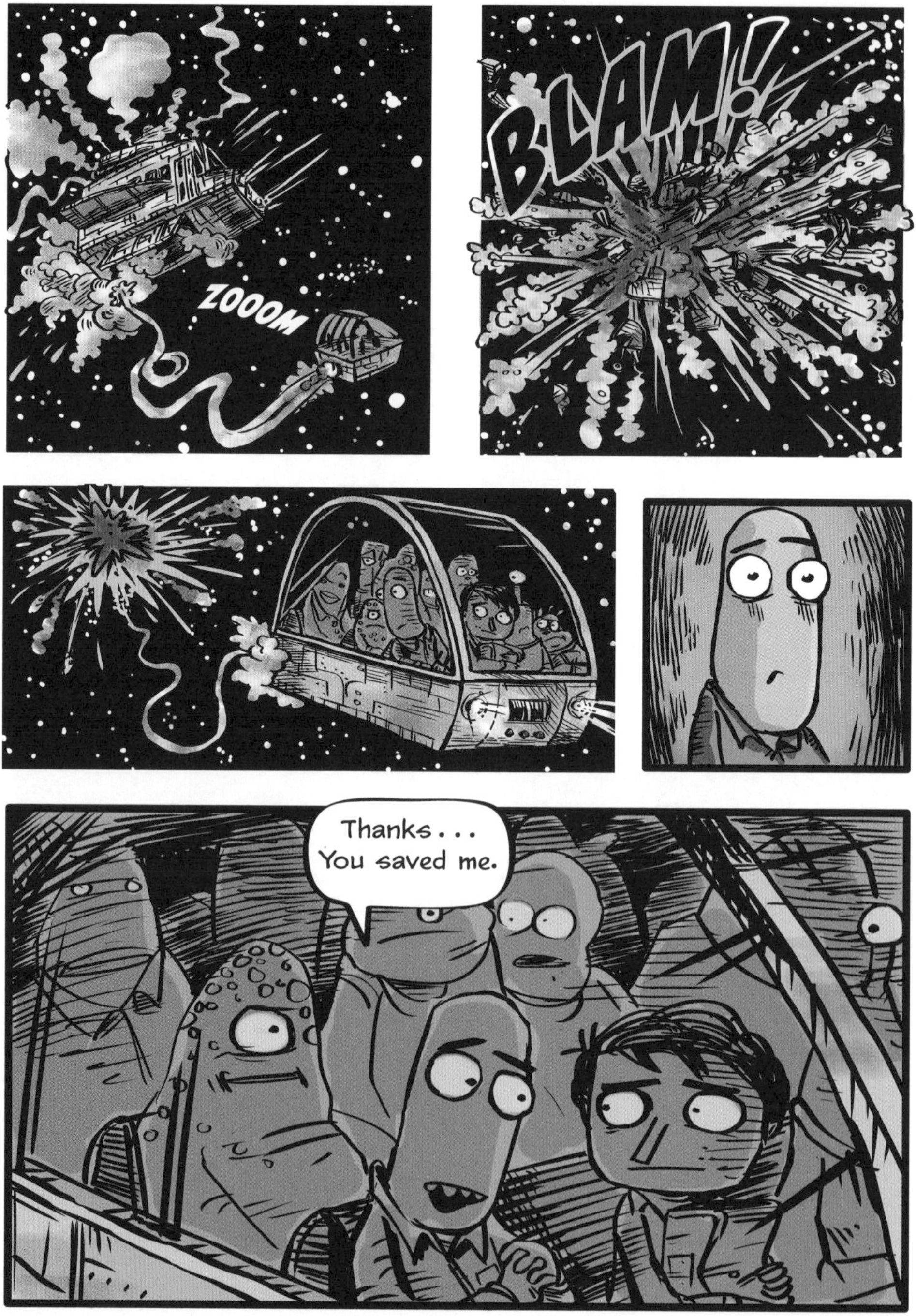
ZOOOM
BLAM!
Thanks . . . You saved me.

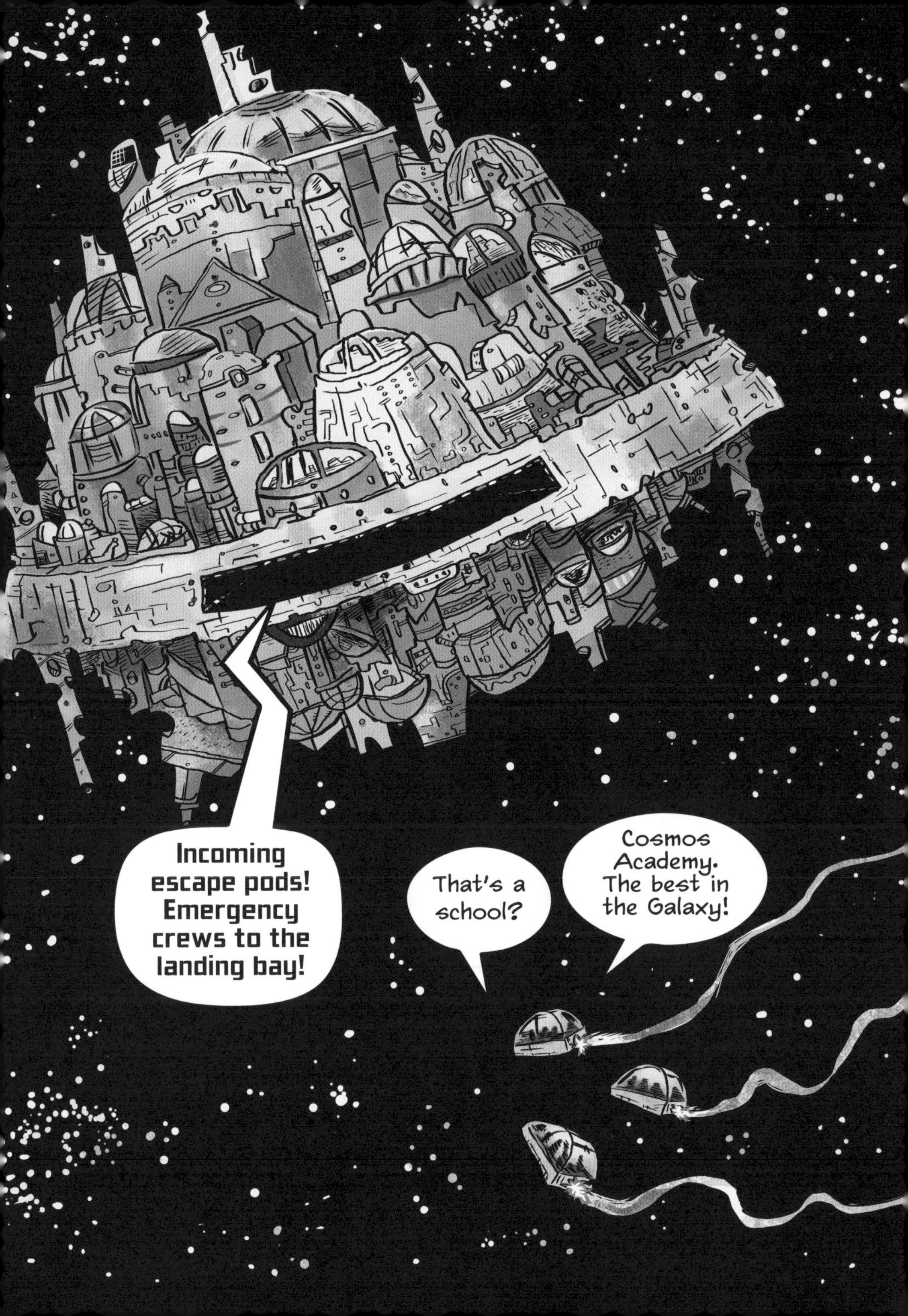
Incoming escape pods! Emergency crews to the landing bay!
That's a school?
Cosmos Academy. The best in the Galaxy!

CHAPTER 2

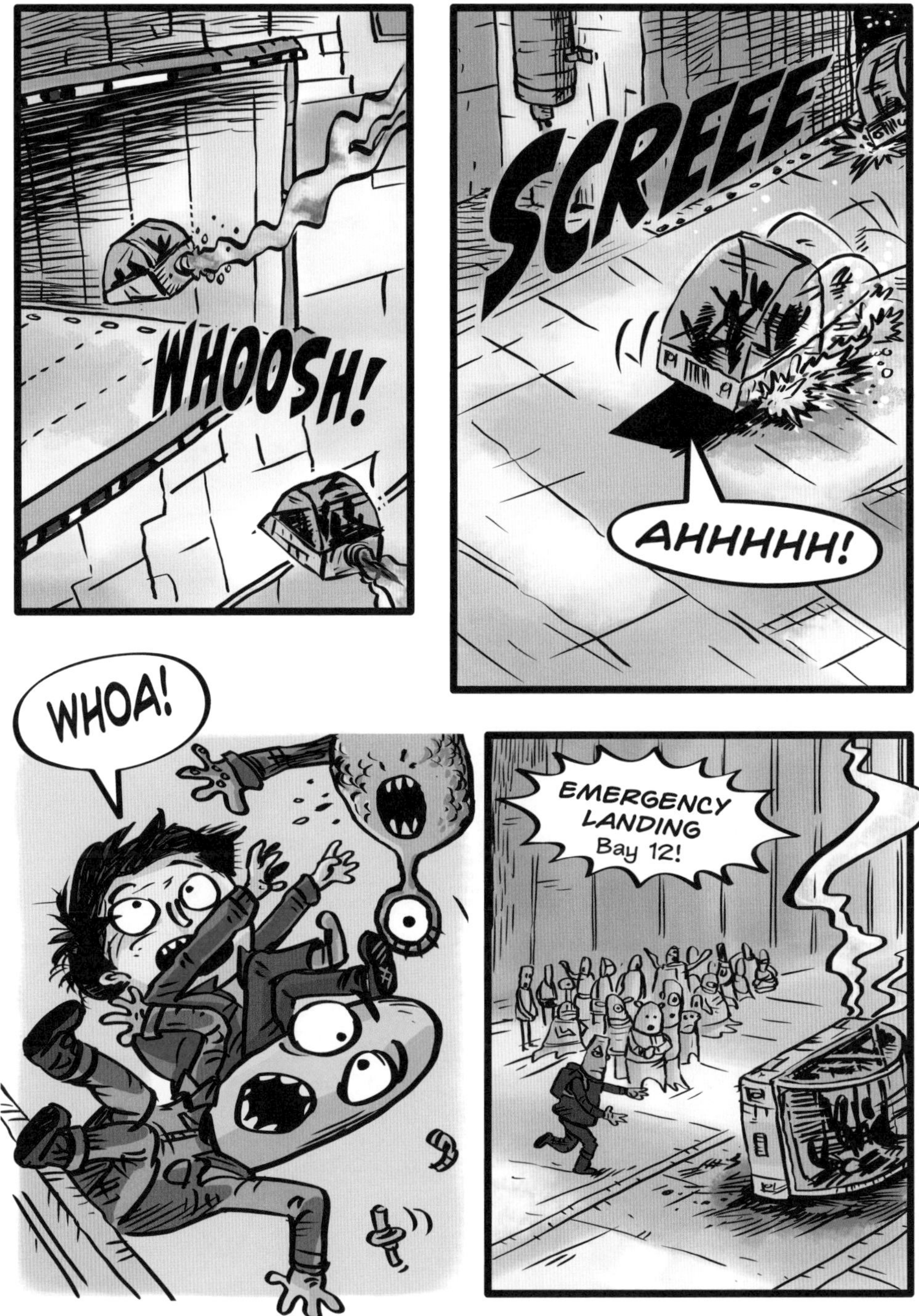
WHOOSH!
SCREEE
AHHHHH!
WHOA!
EMERGENCY LANDING Bay 12!

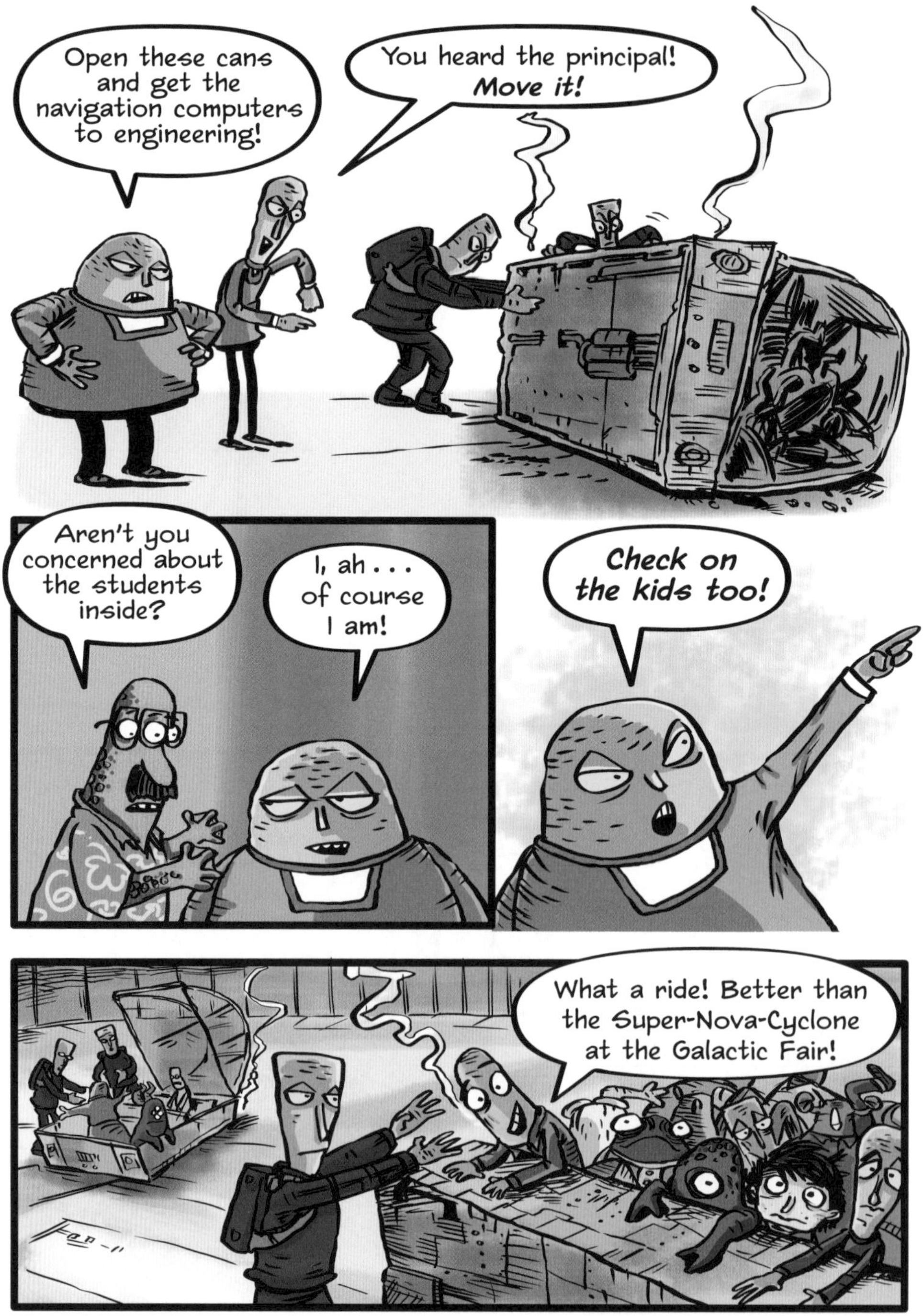
Open these cans and get the navigation computers to engineering!
You heard the principal! *Move it!*
Aren't you concerned about the students inside?
I, ah . . . of course I am!
Check on the kids too!
What a ride! Better than the Super-Nova-Cyclone at the Galactic Fair!

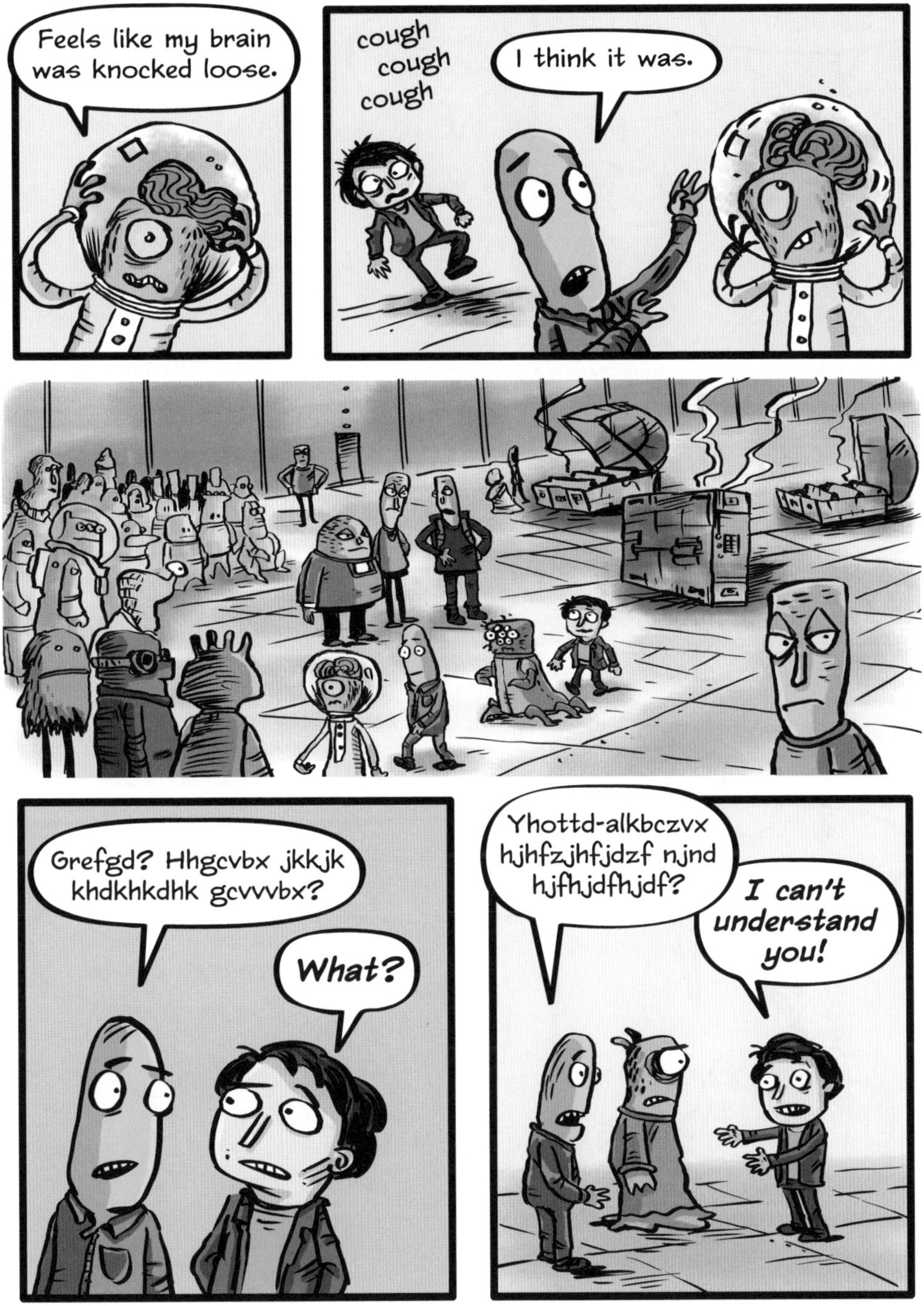

Feels like my brain was knocked loose.
cough cough cough
I think it was.
Grefgd? Hhgcvbx jkkjk khdkhkdhk gcvvvbx?
What?
Yhottd-alkbczvx hjhfzjhfjdzf njnd hjfhjdfhjdf?
I can't understand you!

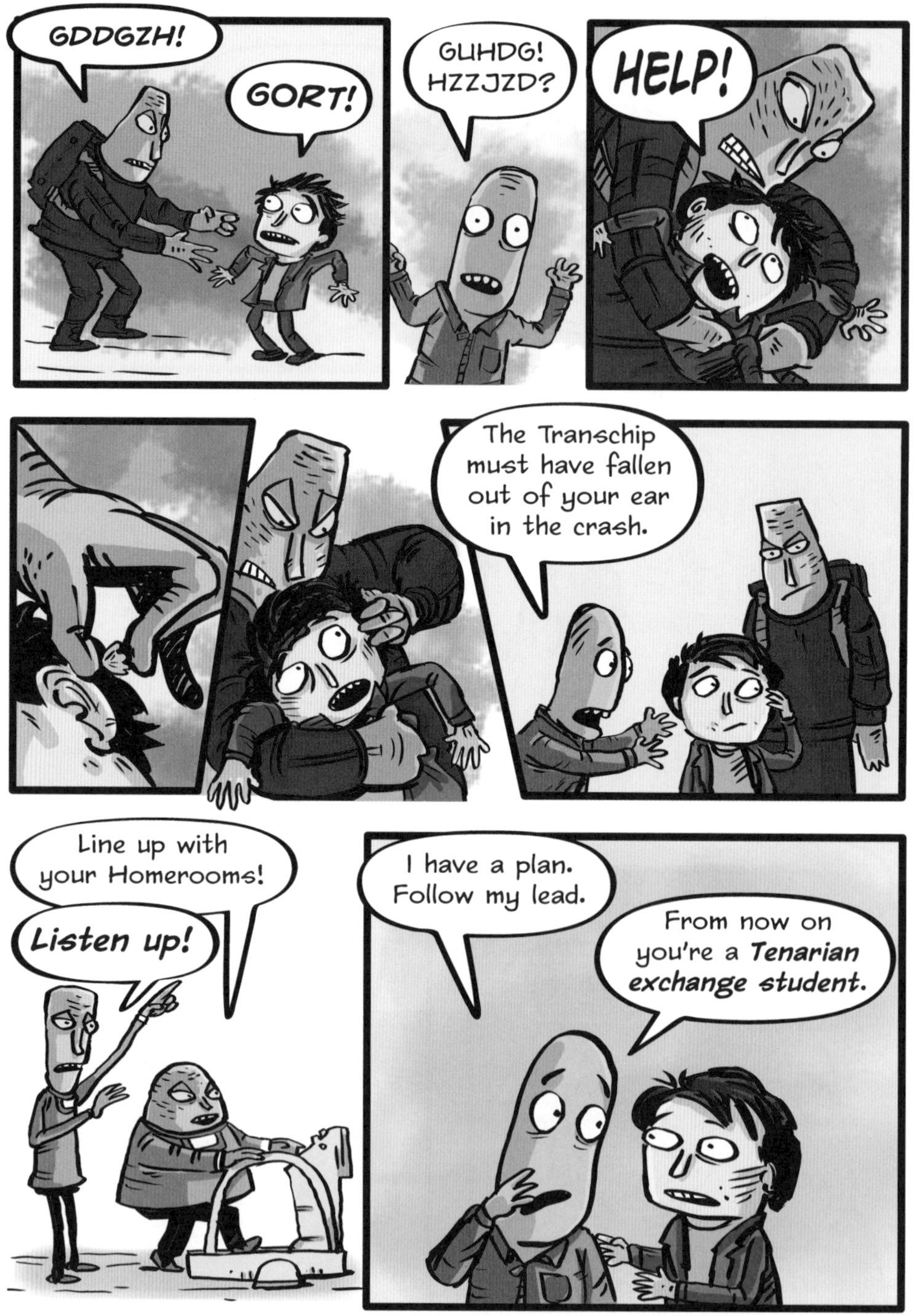
GDDGZH!
GORT!
GUHDG! HZZJZD?
HELP!
The Transchip must have fallen out of your ear in the crash.
Line up with your Homerooms!
Listen up!
I have a plan. Follow my lead.
From now on you're a *Tenarian exchange student*.

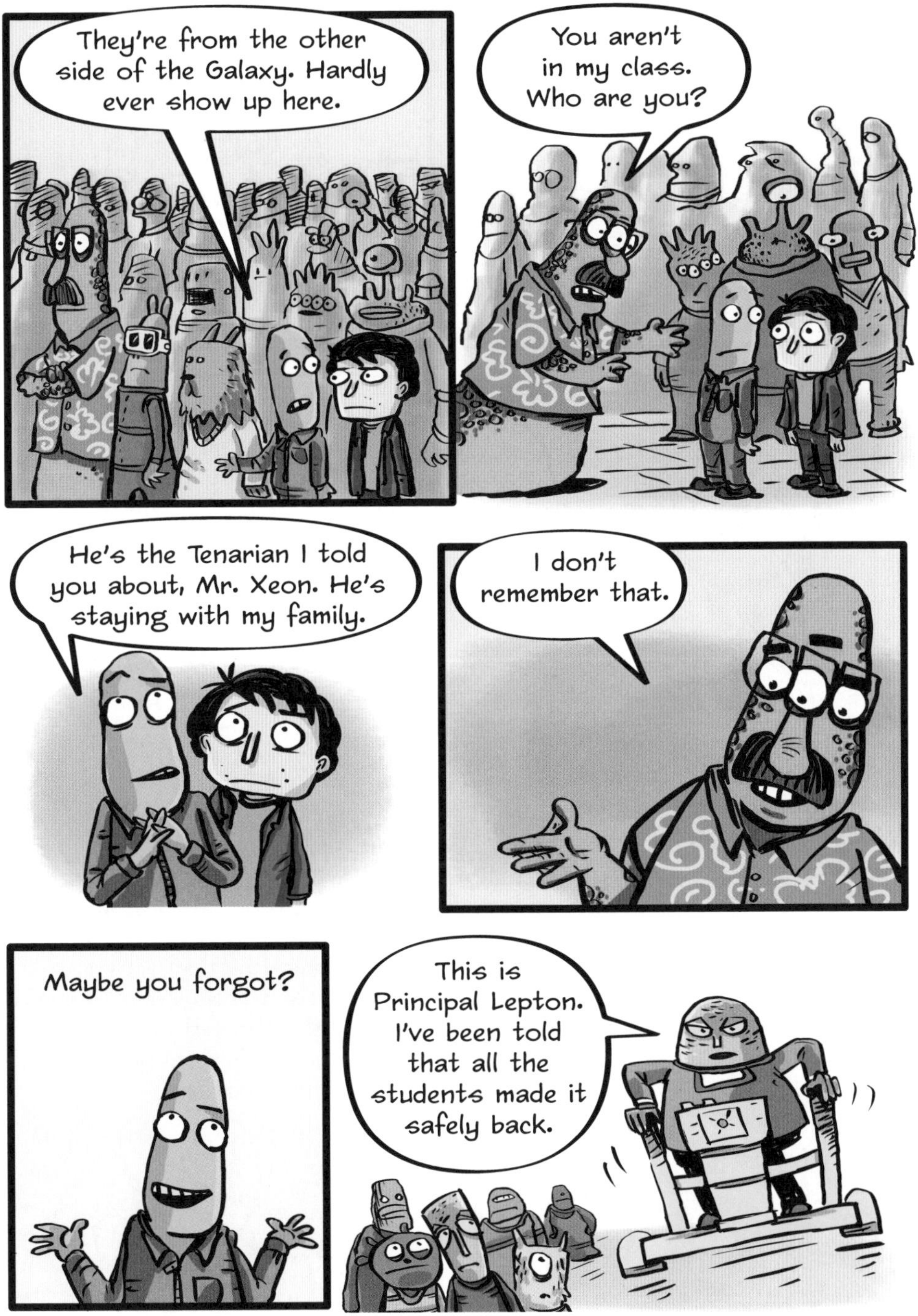
They're from the other side of the Galaxy. Hardly ever show up here.
You aren't in my class. Who are you?
He's the Tenarian I told you about, Mr. Xeon. He's staying with my family.
I don't remember that.
Maybe you forgot?
This is Principal Lepton. I've been told that all the students made it safely back.

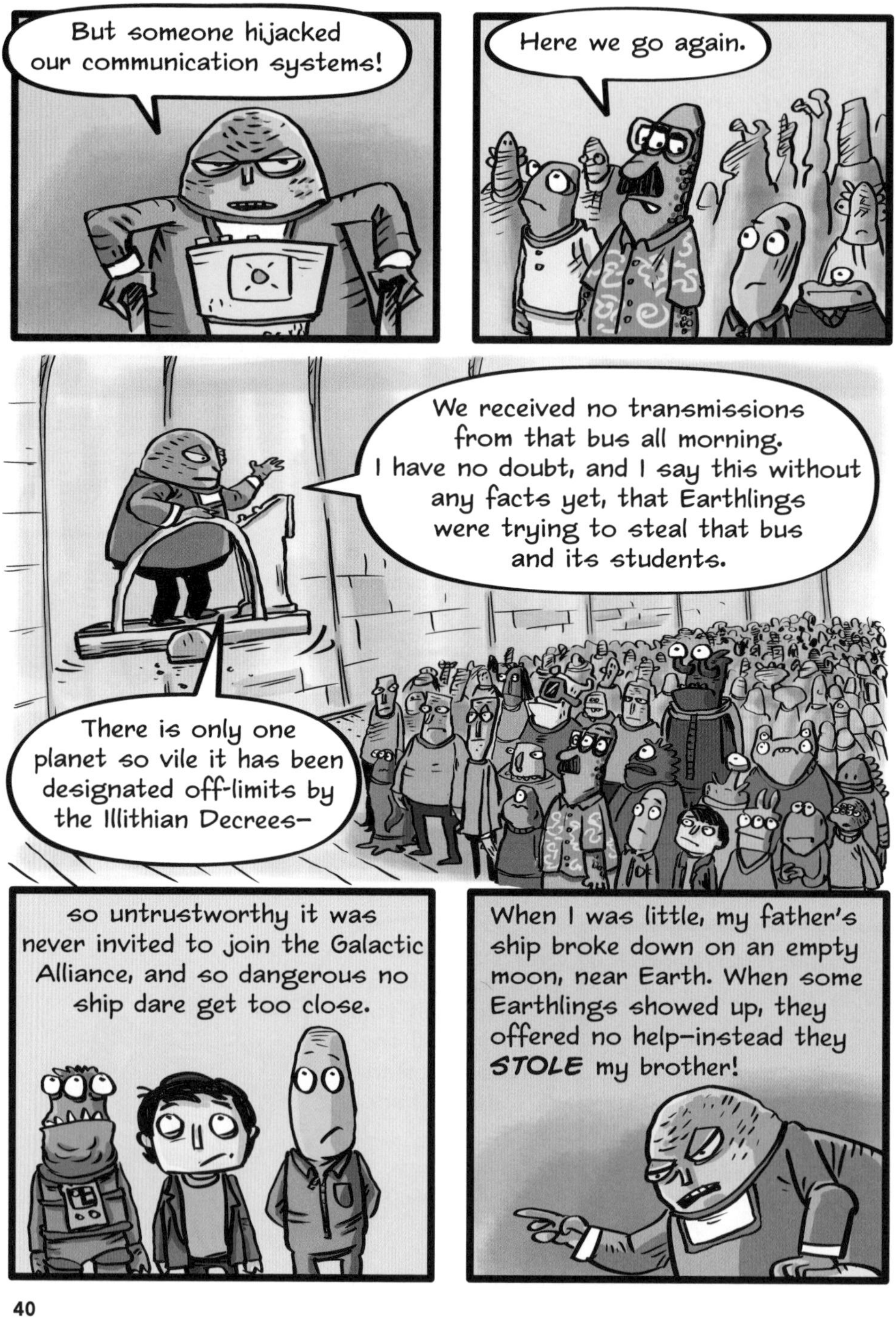

But someone hijacked our communication systems!
Here we go again.
We received no transmissions from that bus all morning. I have no doubt, and I say this without any facts yet, that Earthlings were trying to steal that bus and its students.
There is only one planet so vile it has been designated off-limits by the Illithian Decrees–
so untrustworthy it was never invited to join the Galactic Alliance, and so dangerous no ship dare get too close.
When I was little, my father's ship broke down on an empty moon, near Earth. When some Earthlings showed up, they offered no help–instead they STOLE my brother!

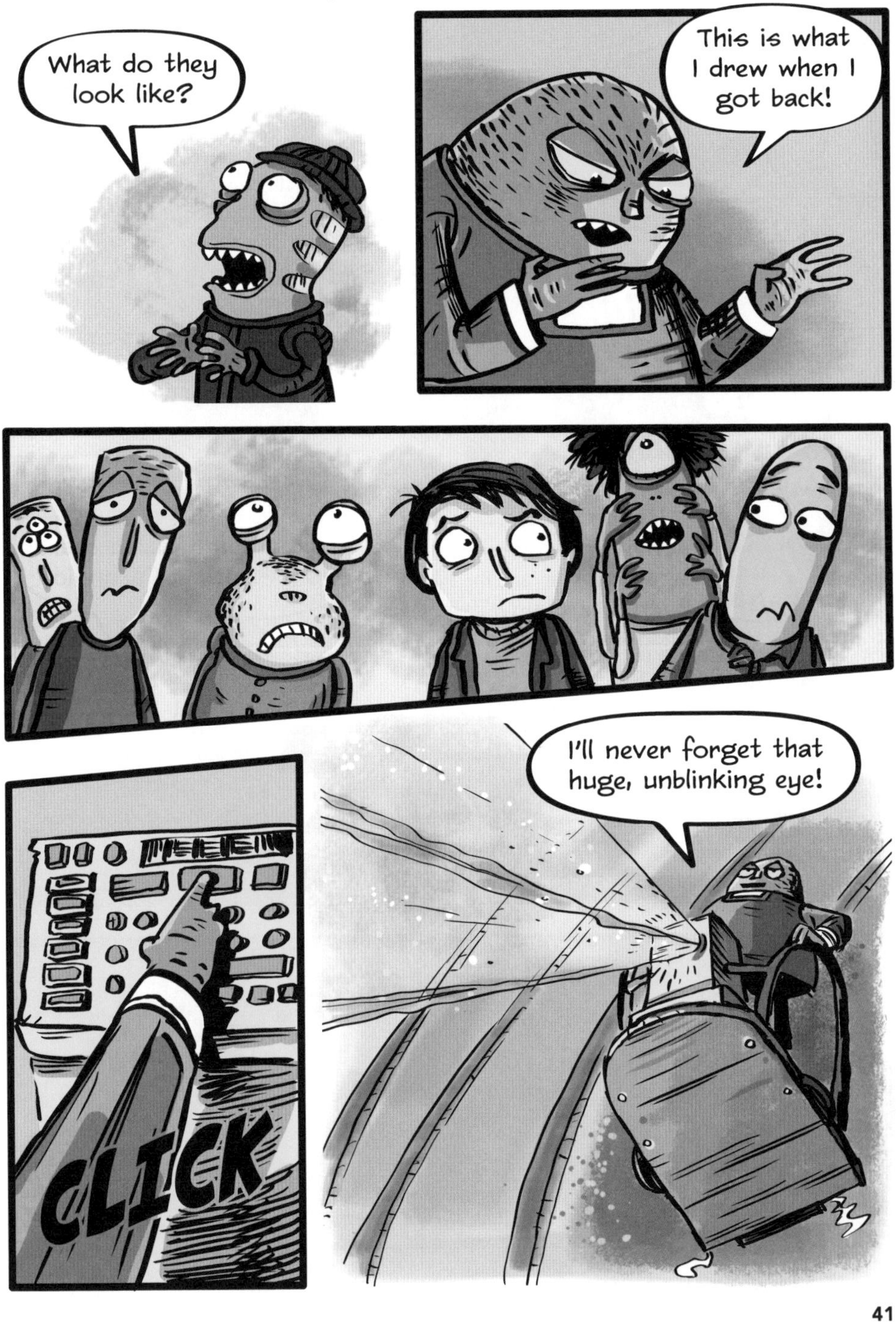
What do they look like?
This is what I drew when I got back!
CLICK
I'll never forget that huge, unblinking eye!

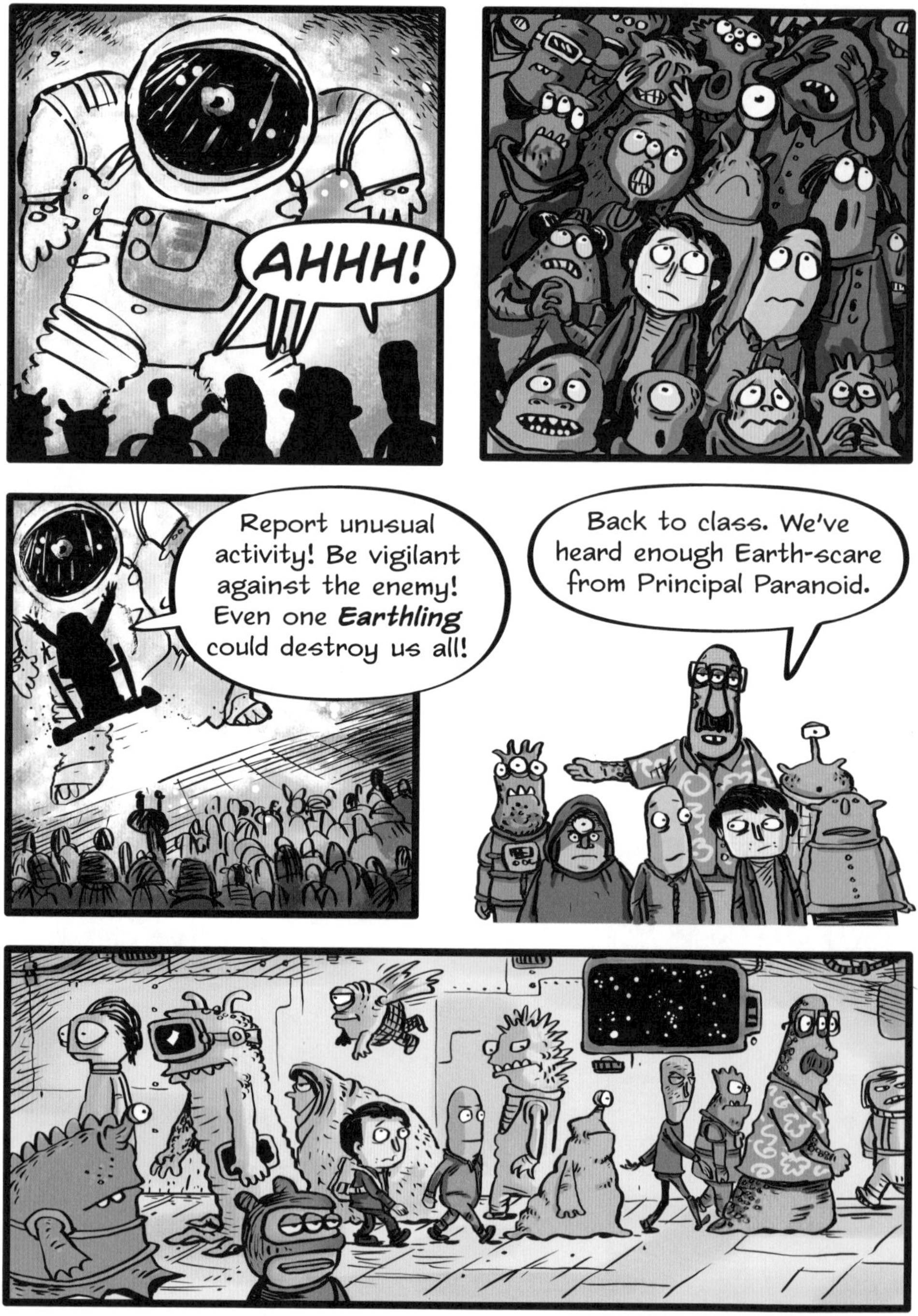
AHHH!
Report unusual activity! Be vigilant against the enemy! Even one *Earthling* could destroy us all!
Back to class. We've heard enough Earth-scare from Principal Paranoid.

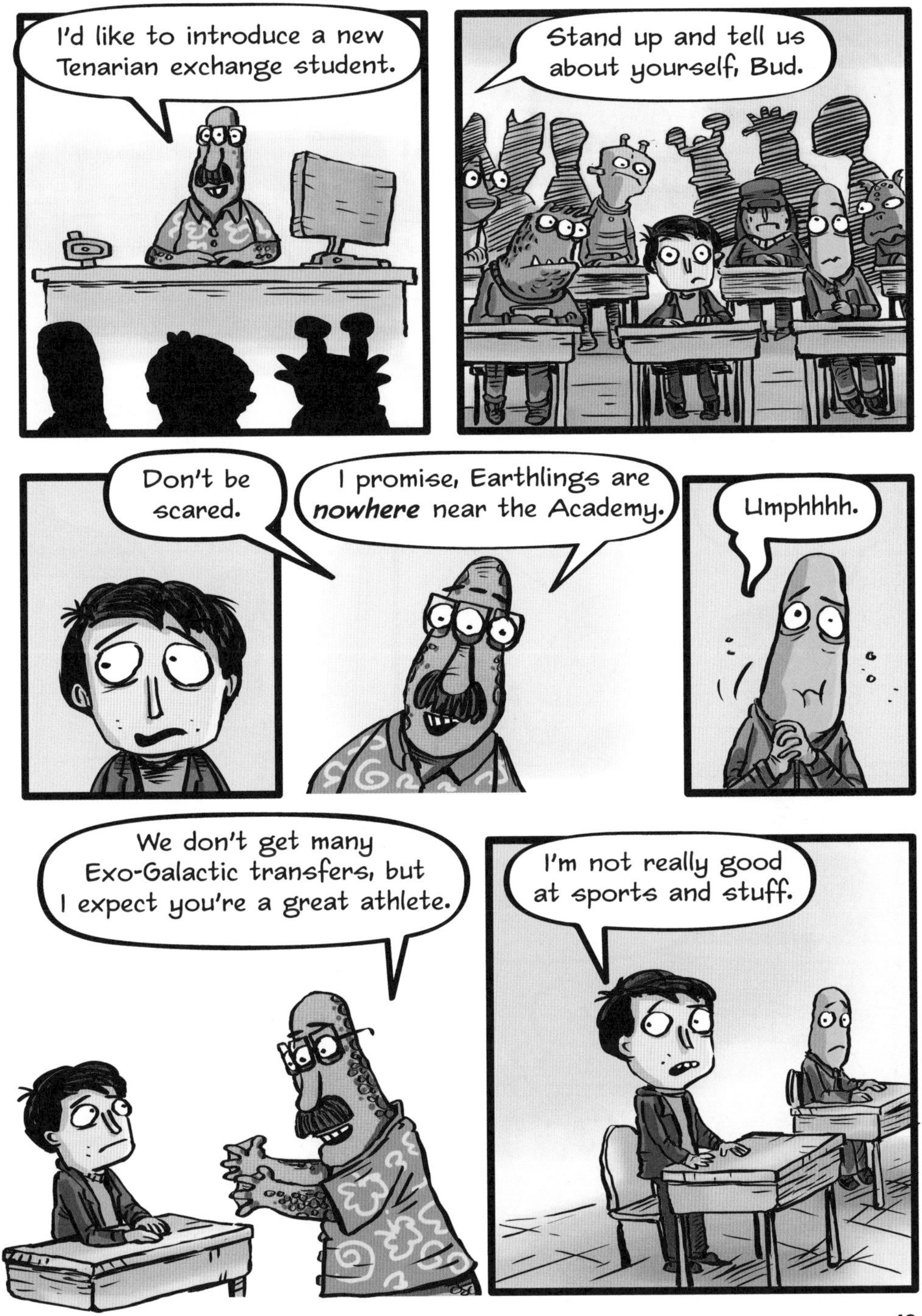
I'd like to introduce a new Tenarian exchange student.
Stand up and tell us about yourself, Bud.
Don't be scared.
I promise, Earthlings are *nowhere* near the Academy.
Umphhhh.
We don't get many Exo-Galactic transfers, but I expect you're a great athlete.
I'm not really good at sports and stuff.

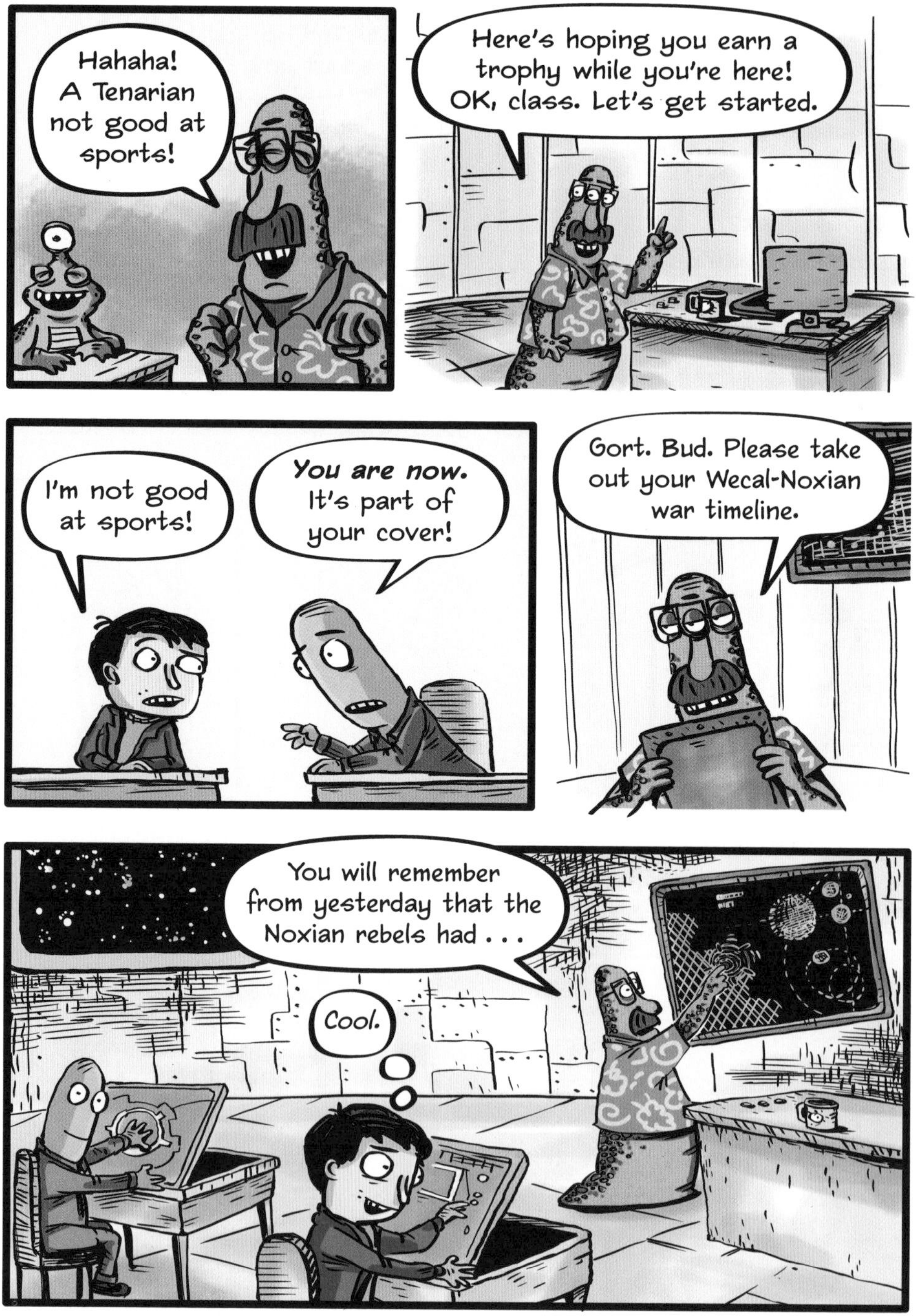
Hahaha! A Tenarian not good at sports!
Here's hoping you earn a trophy while you're here! OK, class. Let's get started.
I'm not good at sports!
You are now. It's part of your cover!
Gort. Bud. Please take out your Wecal-Noxian war timeline.
You will remember from yesterday that the Noxian rebels had . . .
Cool.

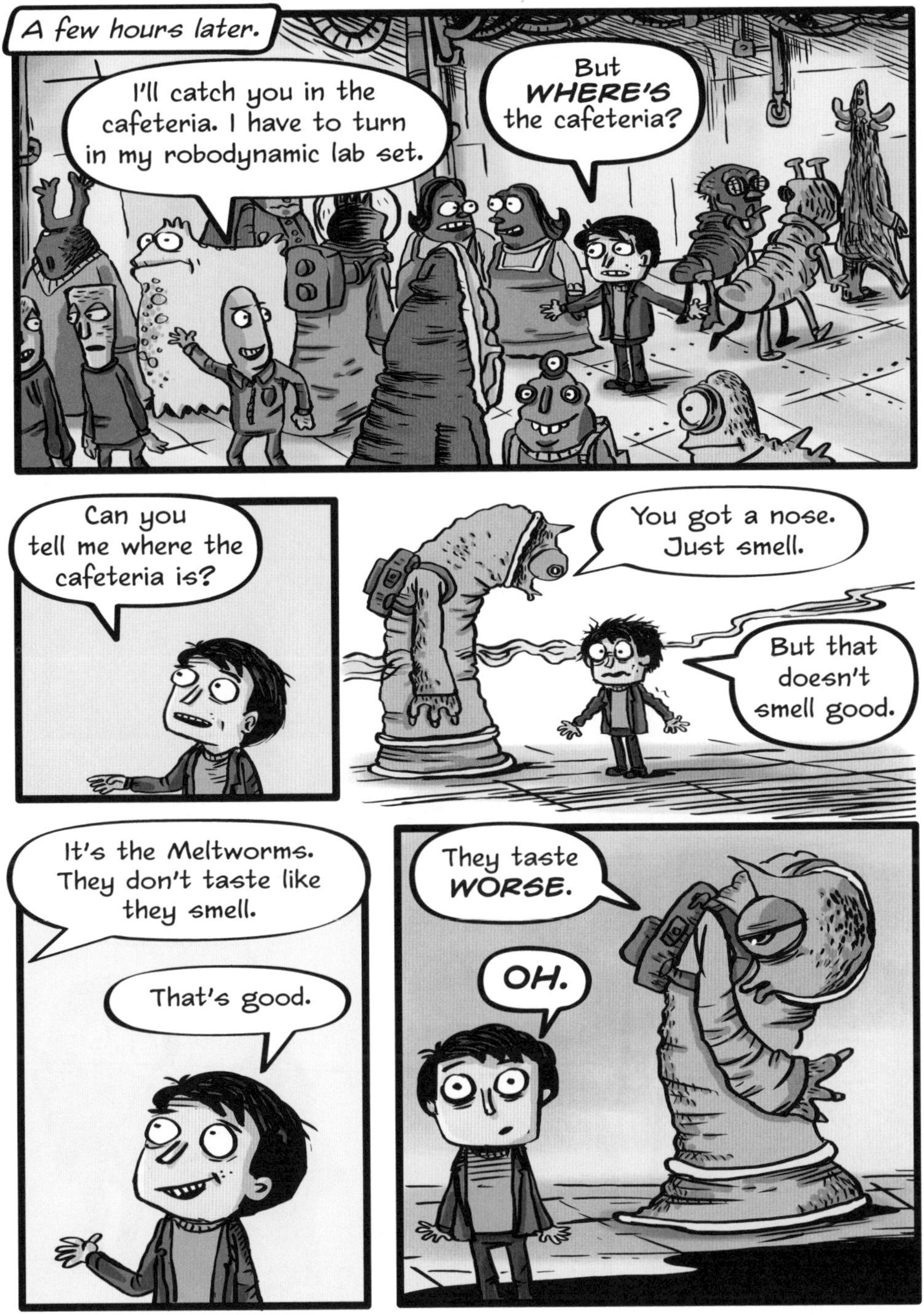
A few hours later.
I'll catch you in the cafeteria. I have to turn in my robodynamic lab set.
But WHERE'S the cafeteria?
Can you tell me where the cafeteria is?
You got a nose. Just smell.
But that doesn't smell good.
It's the Meltworms. They don't taste like they smell.
That's good.
They taste WORSE.
OH.

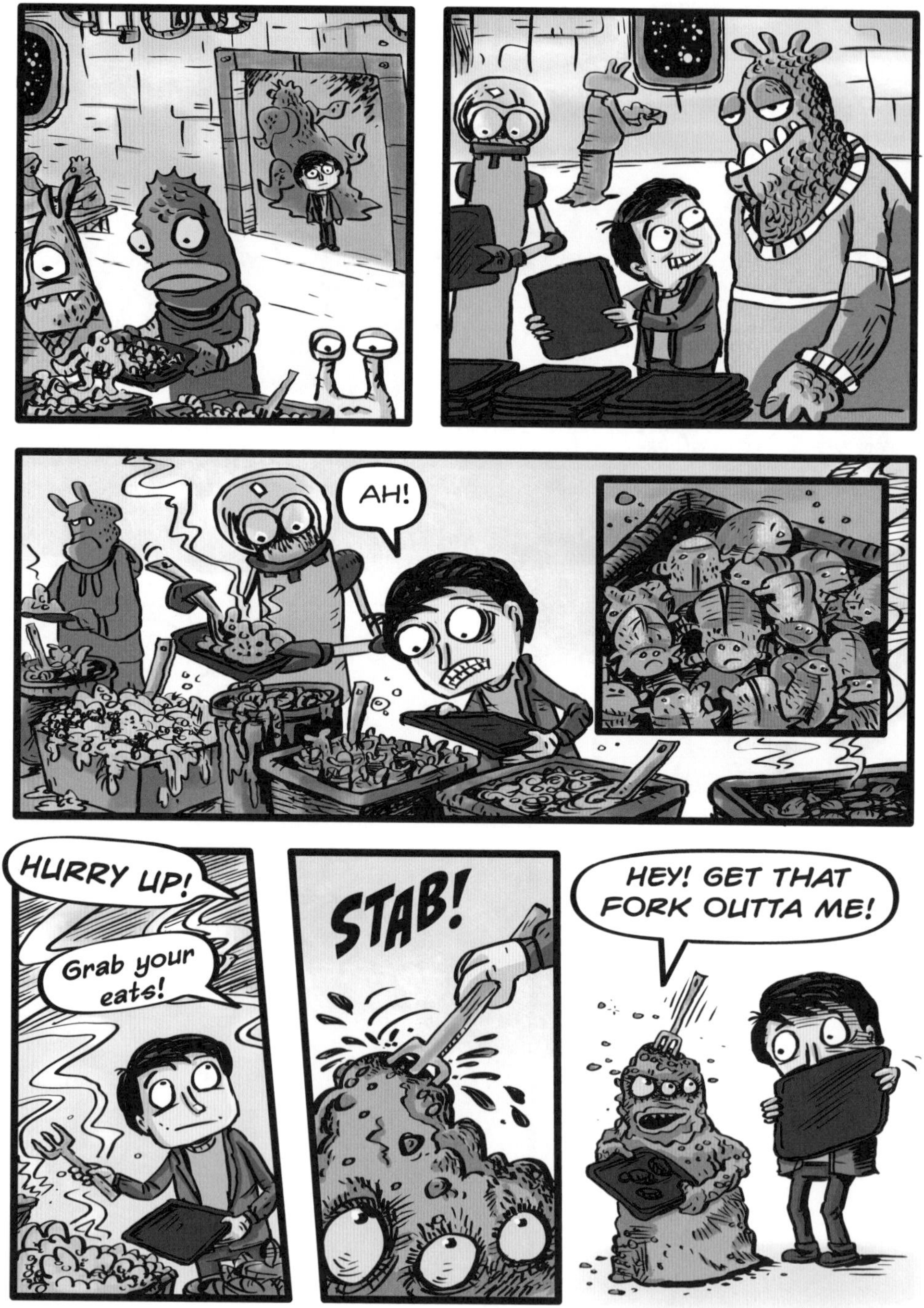
AH!
HURRY UP!
Grab your eats!
STAB!
HEY! GET THAT FORK OUTTA ME!

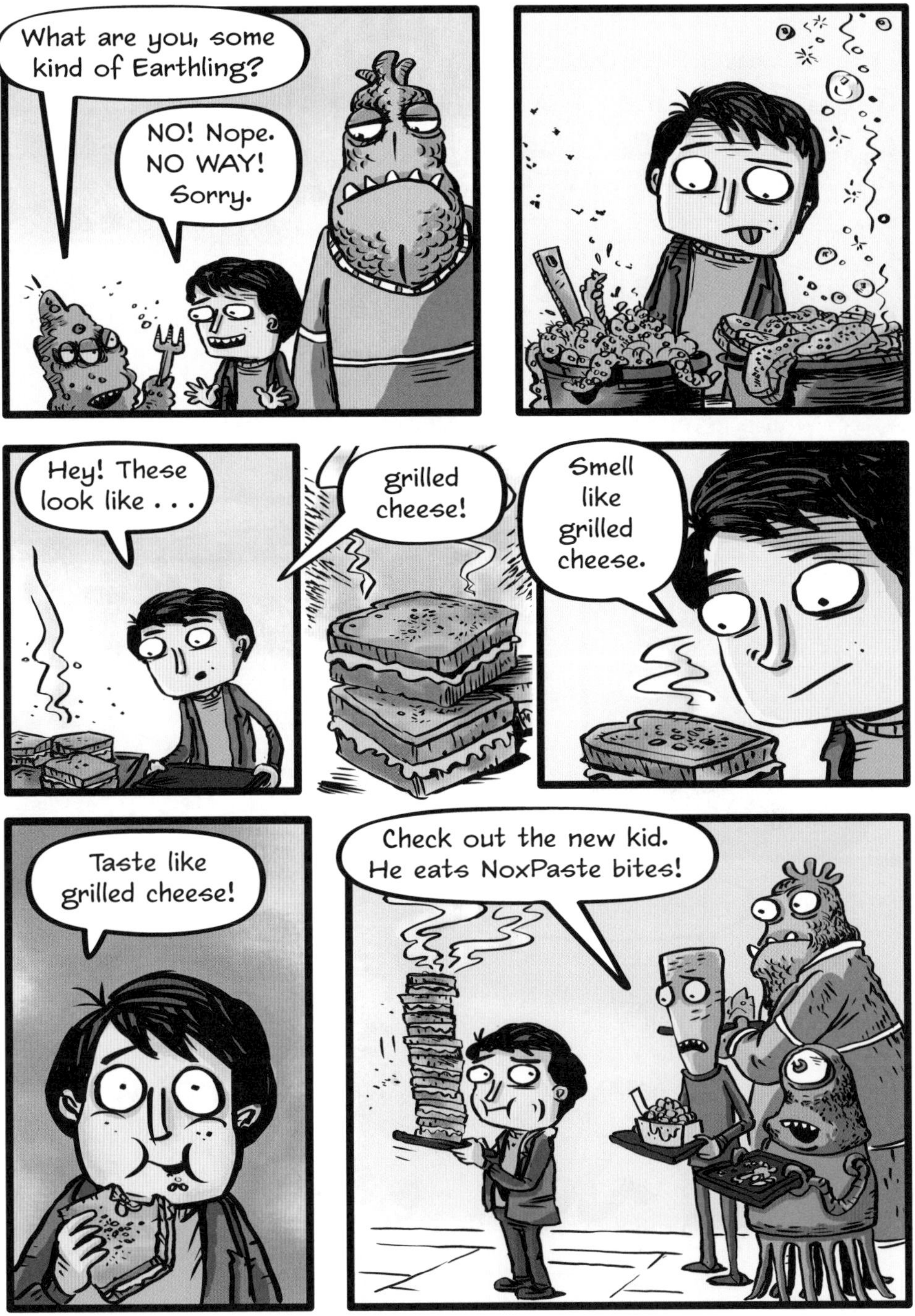
What are you, some kind of Earthling?
NO! Nope. NO WAY! Sorry.
Hey! These look like . . .
grilled cheese!
Smell like grilled cheese.
Taste like grilled cheese!
Check out the new kid. He eats NoxPaste bites!

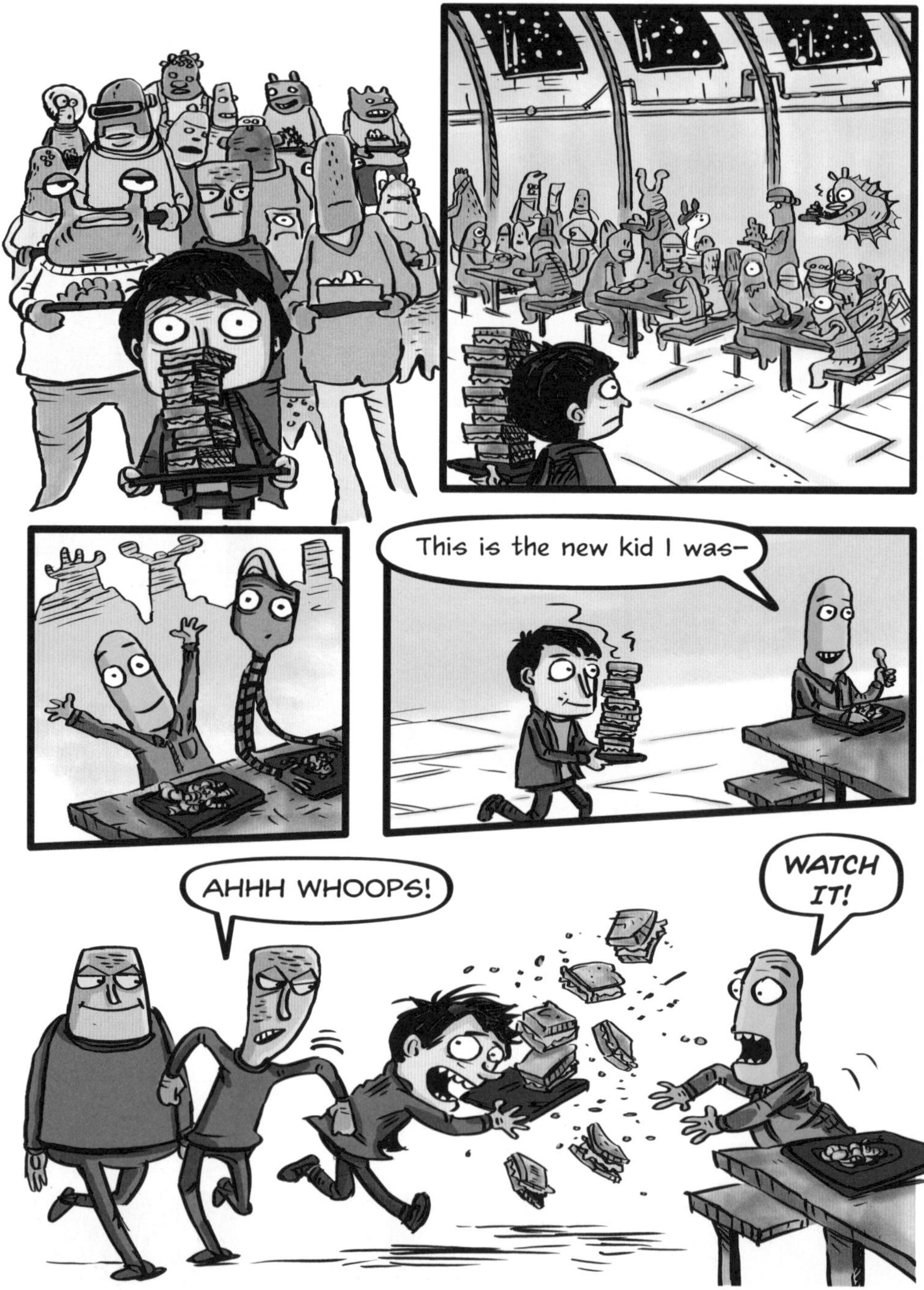
This is the new kid I was-
AHHH WHOOPS!
WATCH IT!

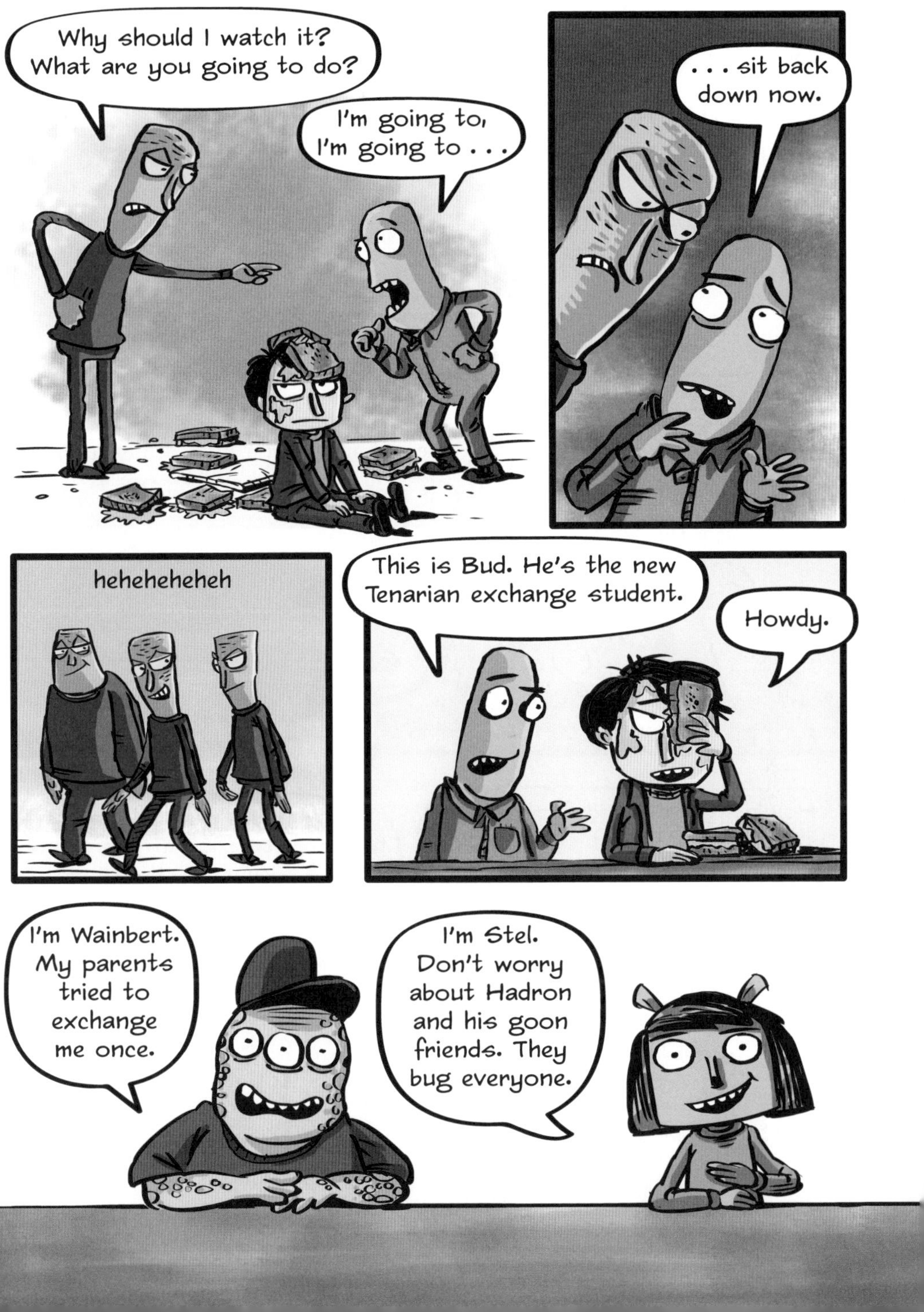
Why should I watch it? What are you going to do?
I'm going to, I'm going to . . .
. . . sit back down now.
heheheheheh
This is Bud. He's the new Tenarian exchange student.
Howdy.
I'm Wainbert. My parents tried to exchange me once.
I'm Stel. Don't worry about Hadron and his goon friends. They bug everyone.

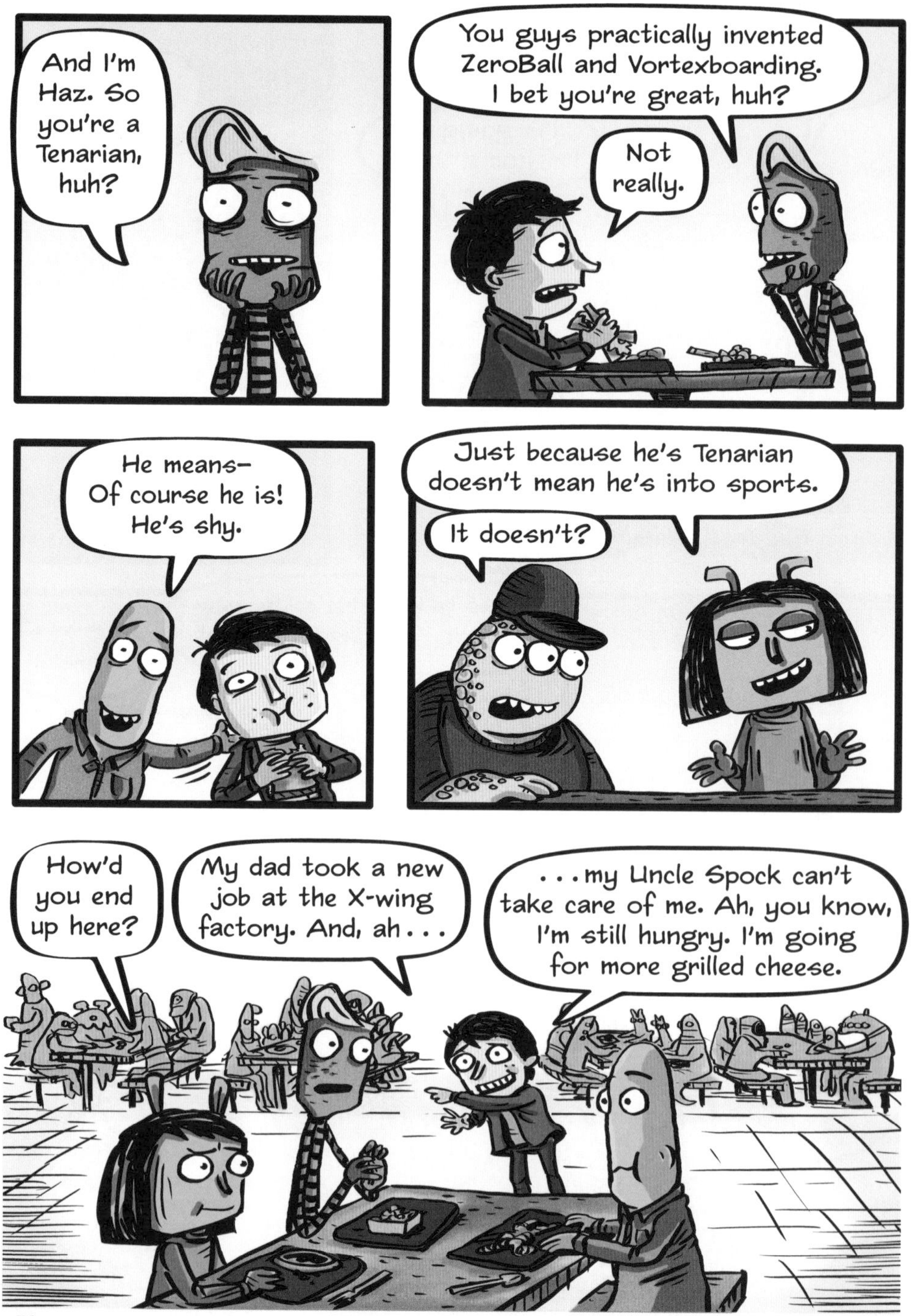
And I'm Haz. So you're a Tenarian, huh?
You guys practically invented ZeroBall and Vortexboarding. I bet you're great, huh?
Not really.
He means— Of course he is! He's shy.
Just because he's Tenarian doesn't mean he's into sports.
It doesn't?
How'd you end up here?
My dad took a new job at the X-wing factory. And, ah . . .
. . . my Uncle Spock can't take care of me. Ah, you know, I'm still hungry. I'm going for more grilled cheese.

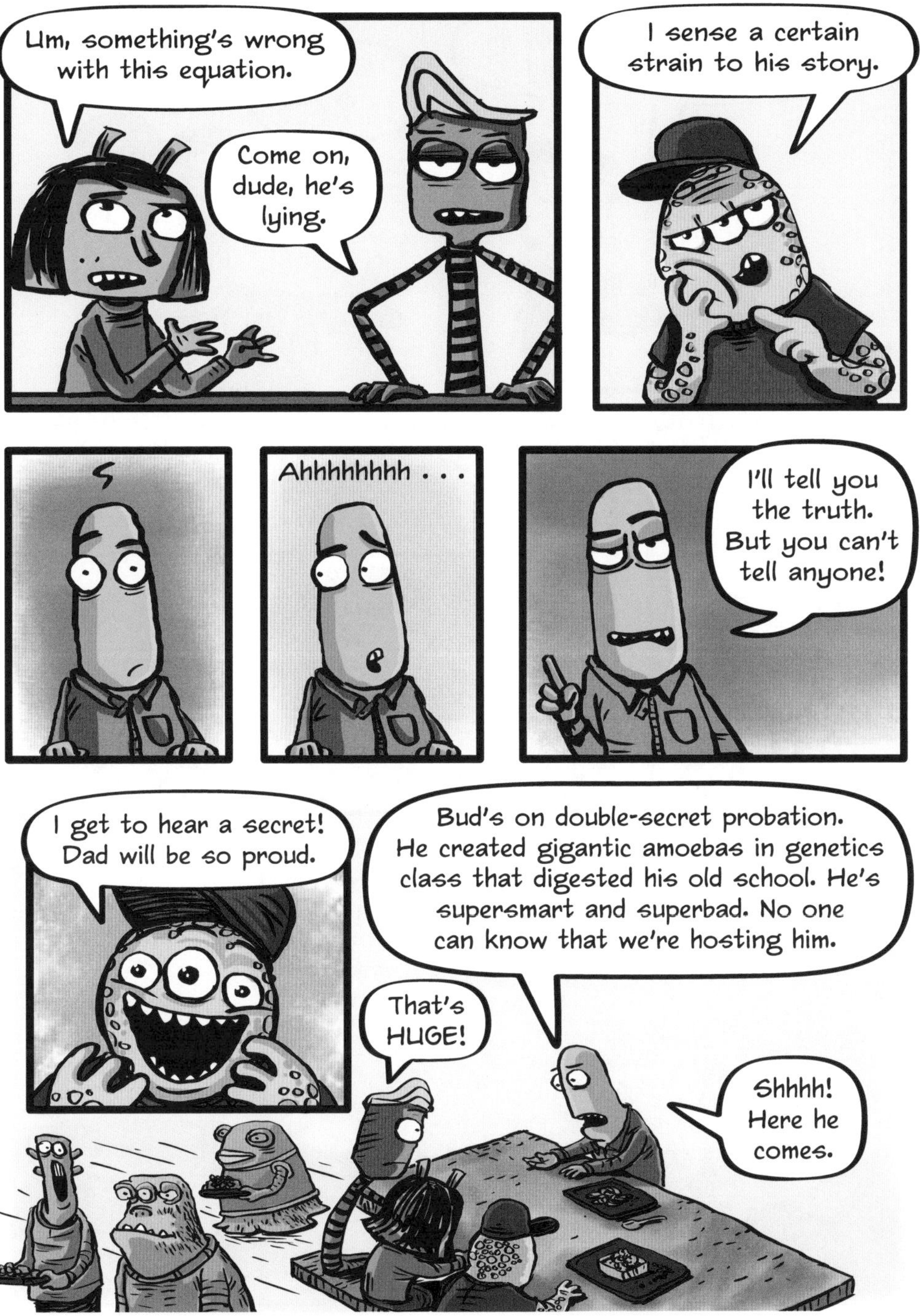

Um, something's wrong with this equation.
Come on, dude, he's lying.
I sense a certain strain to his story.
Ahhhhhhh . . .
I'll tell you the truth. But you can't tell anyone!
I get to hear a secret! Dad will be so proud.
Bud's on double-secret probation. He created gigantic amoebas in genetics class that digested his old school. He's supersmart and superbad. No one can know that we're hosting him.
That's HUGE!
Shhhh! Here he comes.

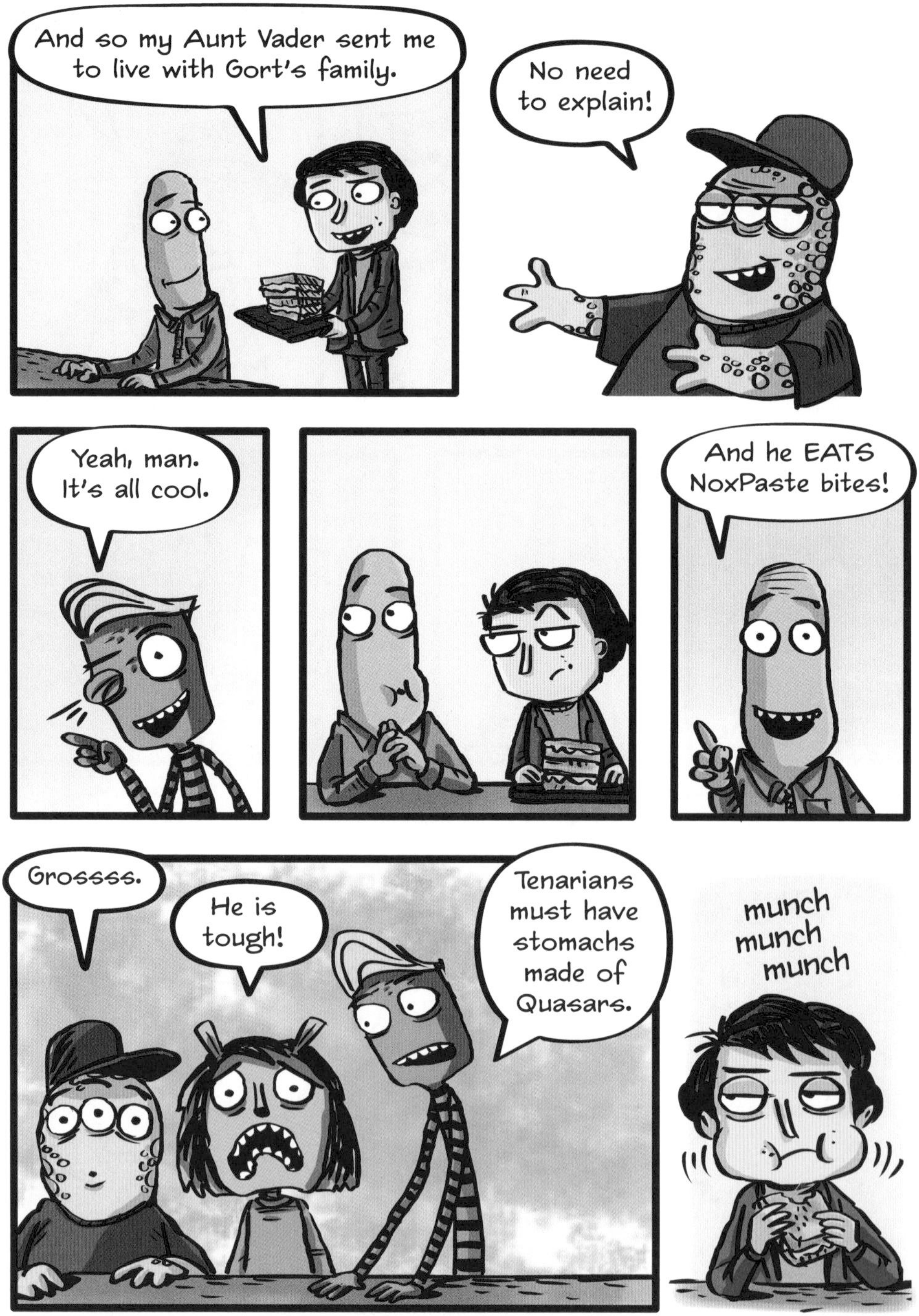
And so my Aunt Vader sent me to live with Gort's family.
No need to explain!
Yeah, man. It's all cool.
And he EATS NoxPaste bites!
Grosssss.
He is tough!
Tenarians must have stomachs made of Quasars.
munch munch munch

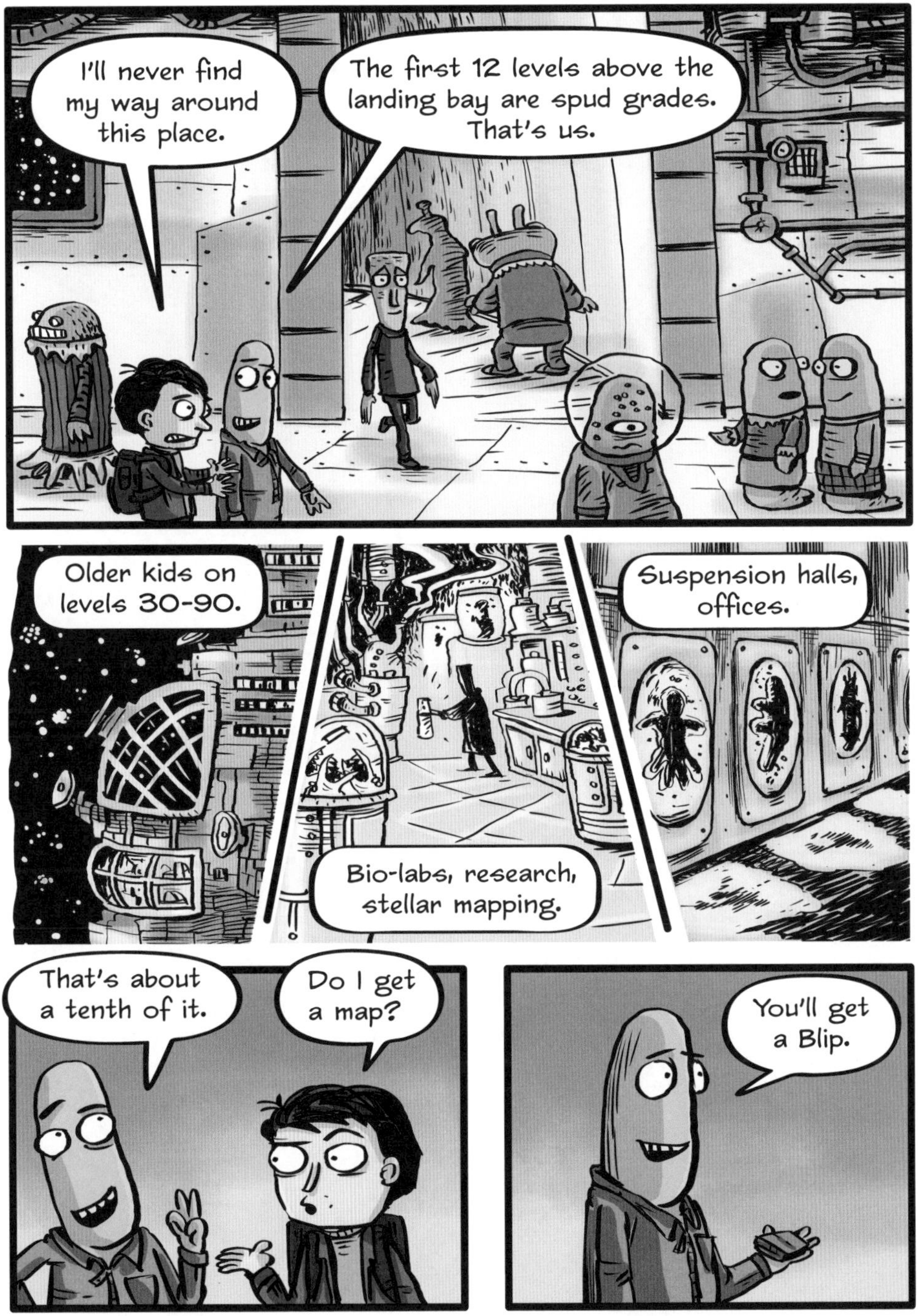
I'll never find my way around this place.
The first 12 levels above the landing bay are spud grades. That's us.
Older kids on levels 30-90.
Bio-labs, research, stellar mapping.
Suspension halls, offices.
That's about a tenth of it.
Do I get a map?
You'll get a Blip.

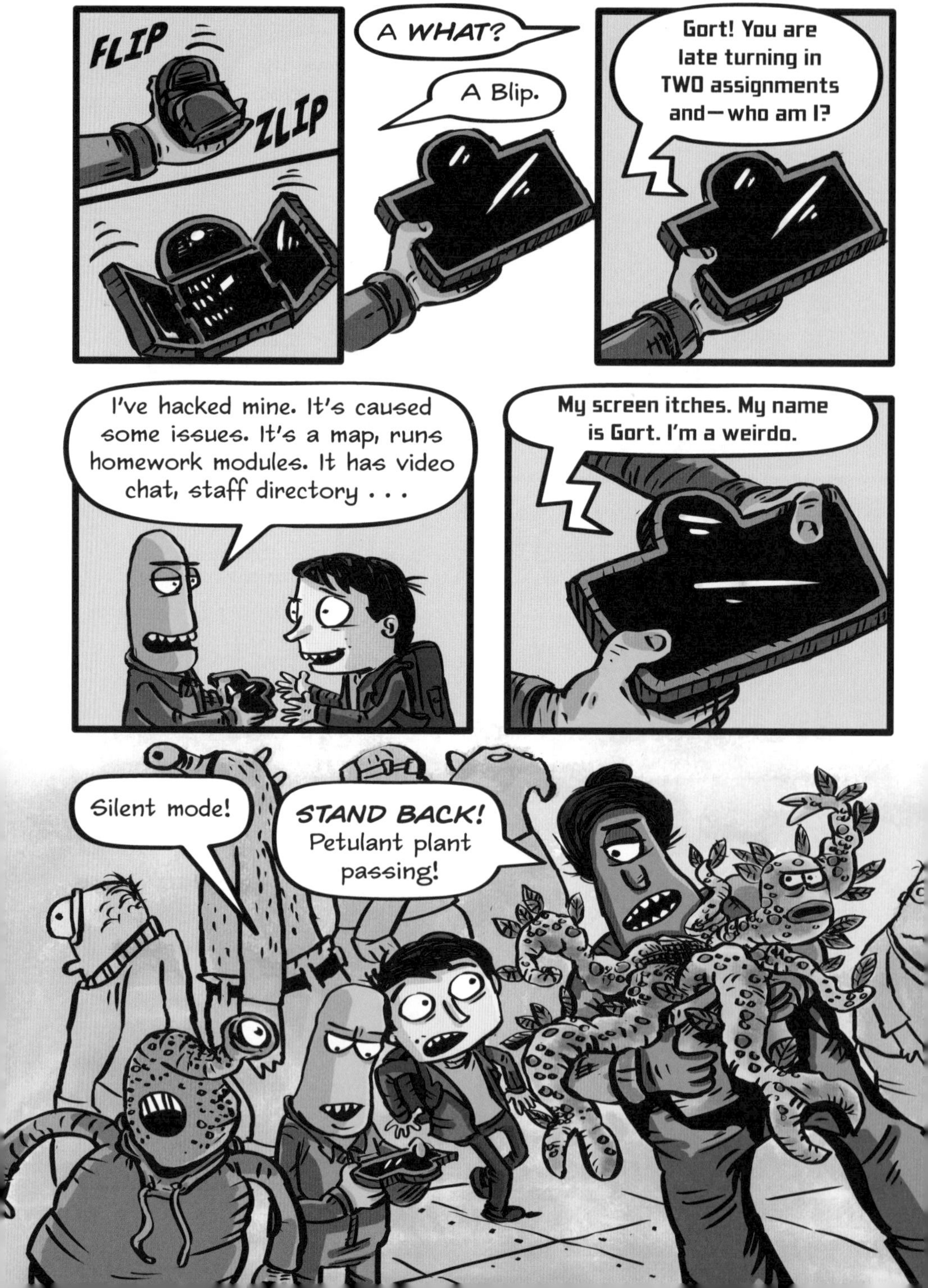
FLIP
ZLIP
A WHAT?
A Blip.
Gort! You are late turning in TWO assignments and—who am I?
I've hacked mine. It's caused some issues. It's a map, runs homework modules. It has video chat, staff directory . . .
My screen itches. My name is Gort. I'm a weirdo.
Silent mode!
STAND BACK! Petulant plant passing!

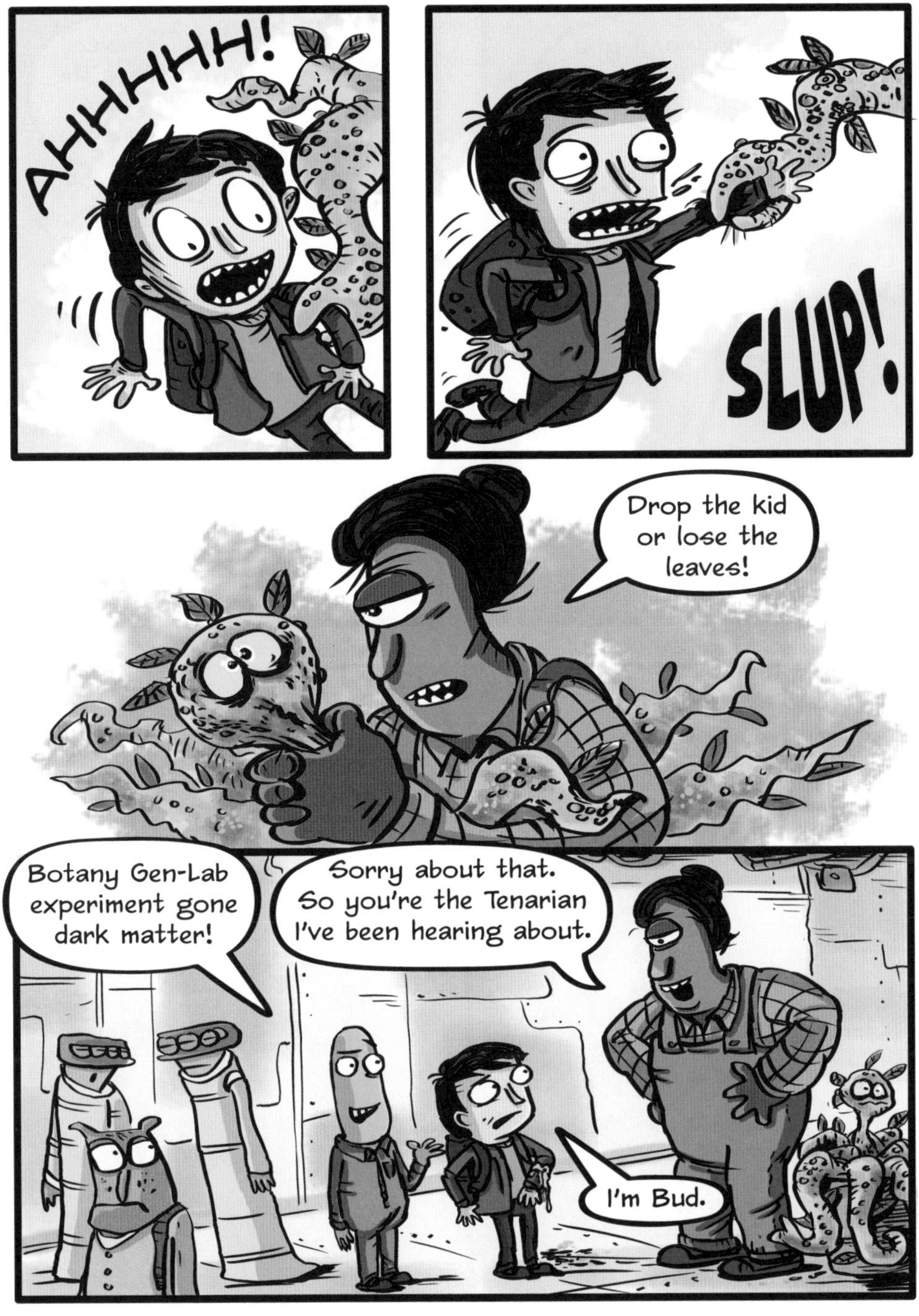
AHHHHH!
SLUP!
Drop the kid or lose the leaves!
Botany Gen-Lab experiment gone dark matter!
Sorry about that. So you're the Tenarian I've been hearing about.
I'm Bud.

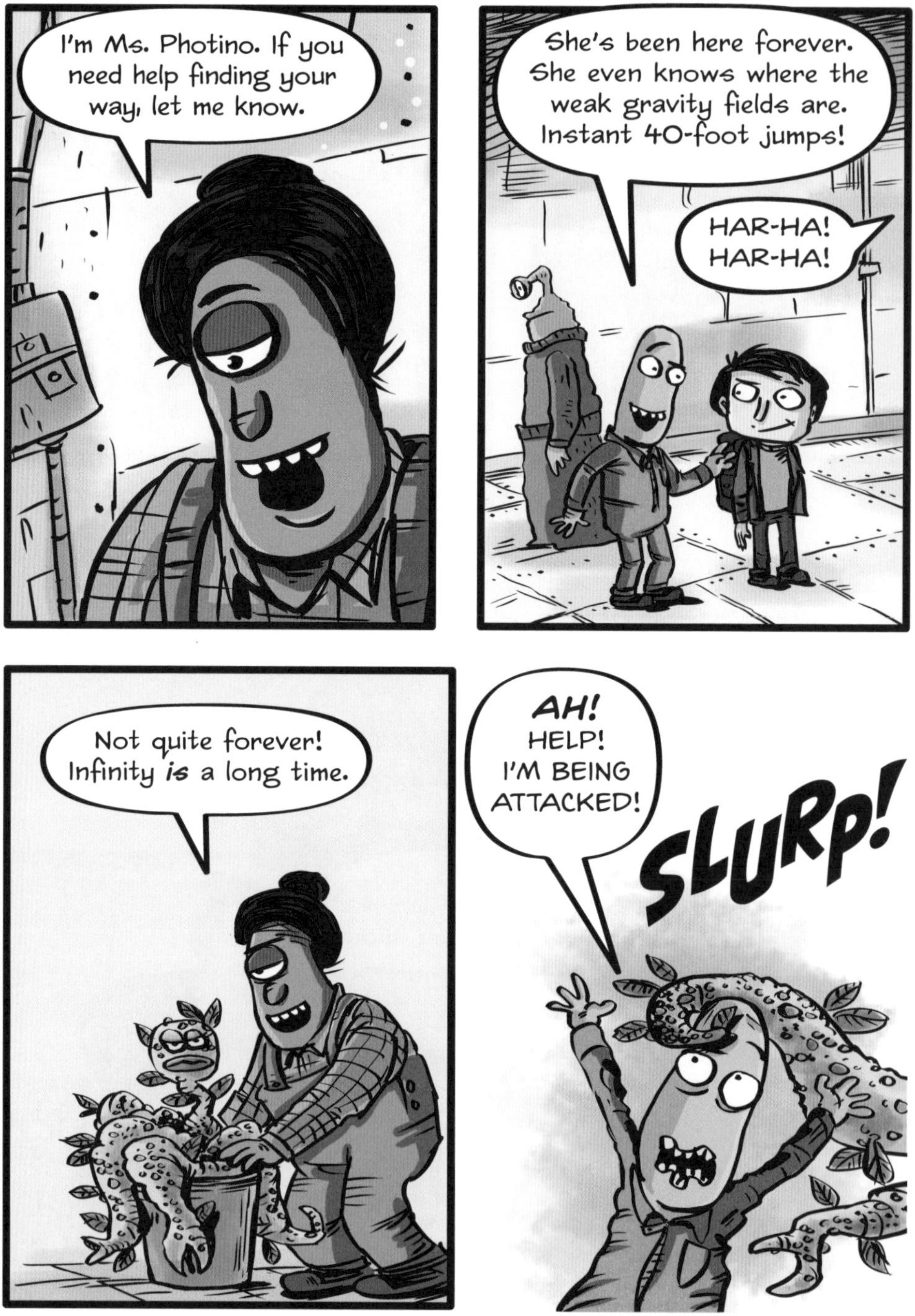
I'm Ms. Photino. If you need help finding your way, let me know.
She's been here forever. She even knows where the weak gravity fields are. Instant 40-foot jumps!
HAR-HA! HAR-HA!
Not quite forever! Infinity *is* a long time.
AH! HELP! I'M BEING ATTACKED!
SLURP!

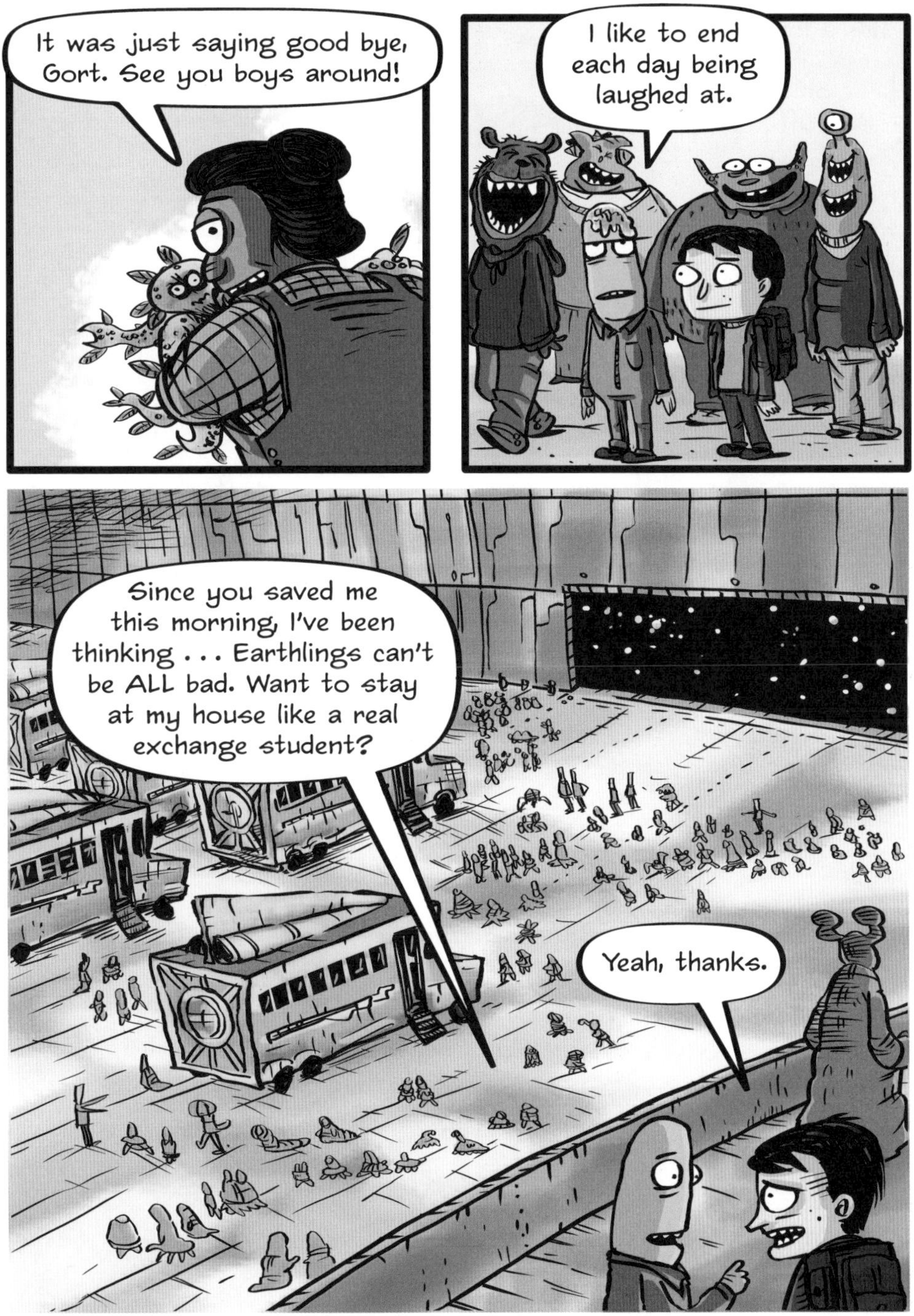
It was just saying good bye, Gort. See you boys around!
I like to end each day being laughed at.
Since you saved me this morning, I've been thinking . . . Earthlings can't be ALL bad. Want to stay at my house like a real exchange student?
Yeah, thanks.

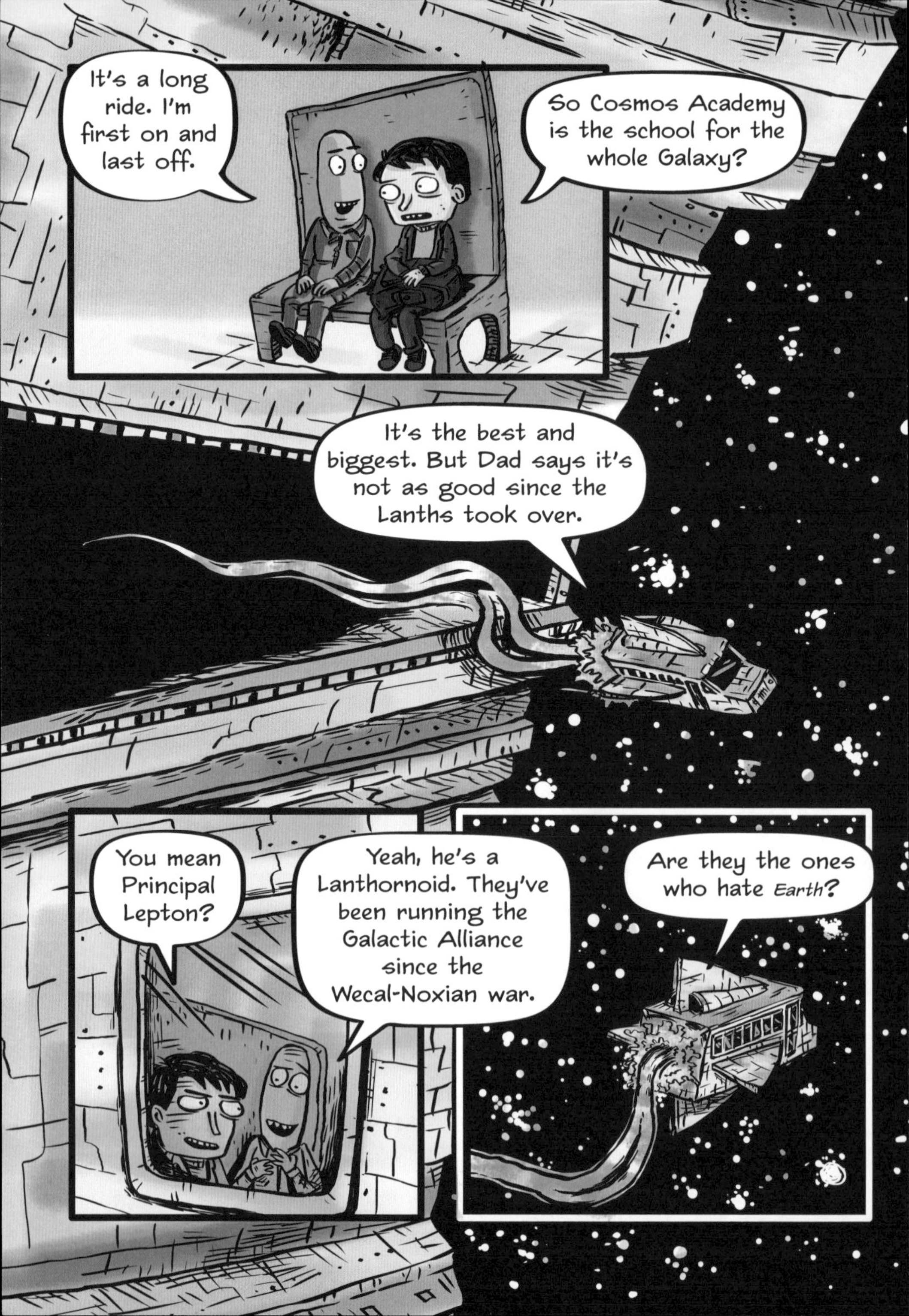
It's a long ride. I'm first on and last off.
So Cosmos Academy is the school for the whole Galaxy?
It's the best and biggest. But Dad says it's not as good since the Lanths took over.
You mean Principal Lepton?
Yeah, he's a Lanthornoid. They've been running the Galactic Alliance since the Wecal-Noxian war.
Are they the ones who hate *Earth*?

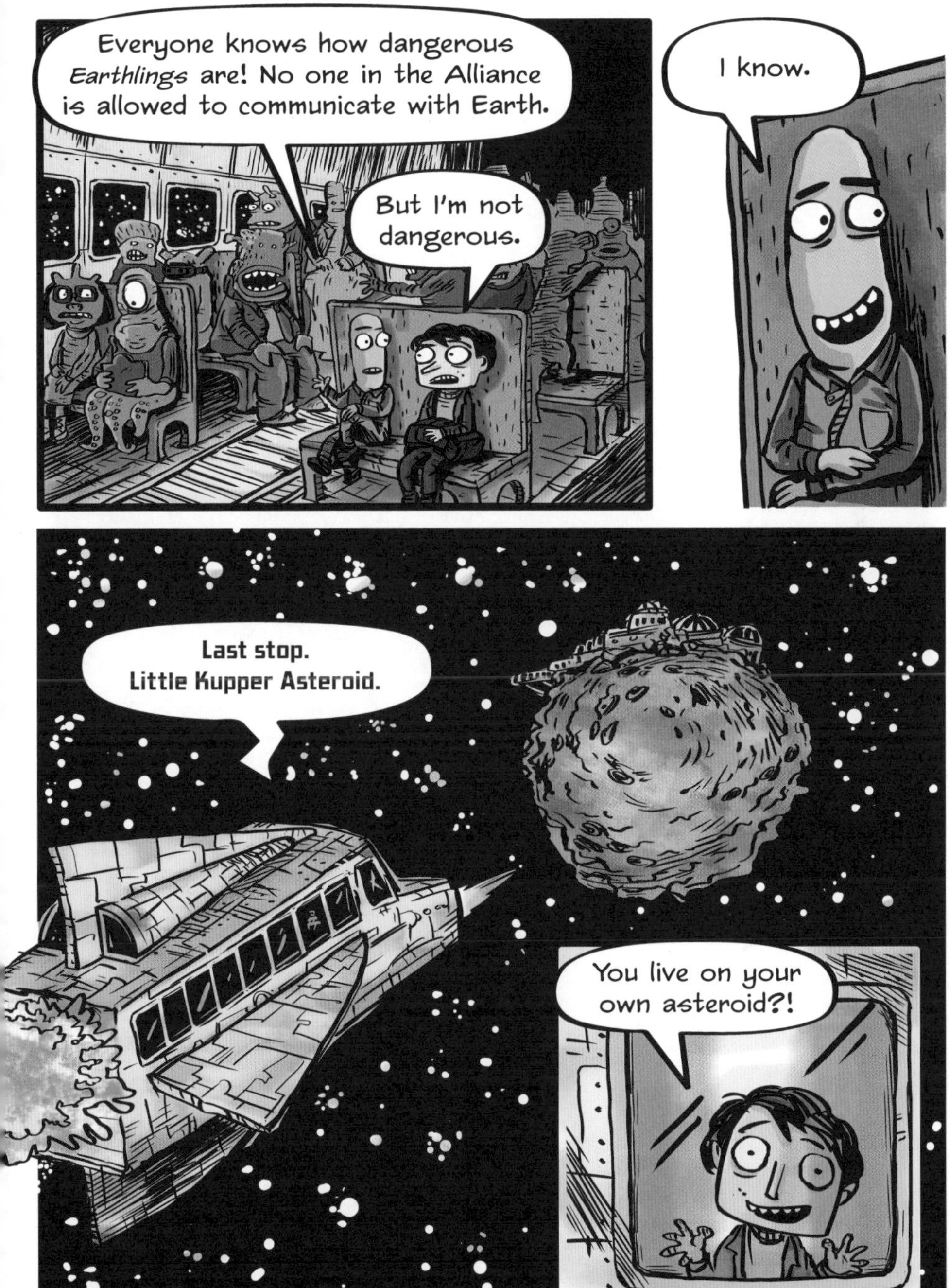
Everyone knows how dangerous *Earthlings* are! No one in the Alliance is allowed to communicate with Earth.
But I'm not dangerous.
I know.
Last stop. Little Kupper Asteroid.
You live on your own asteroid?!

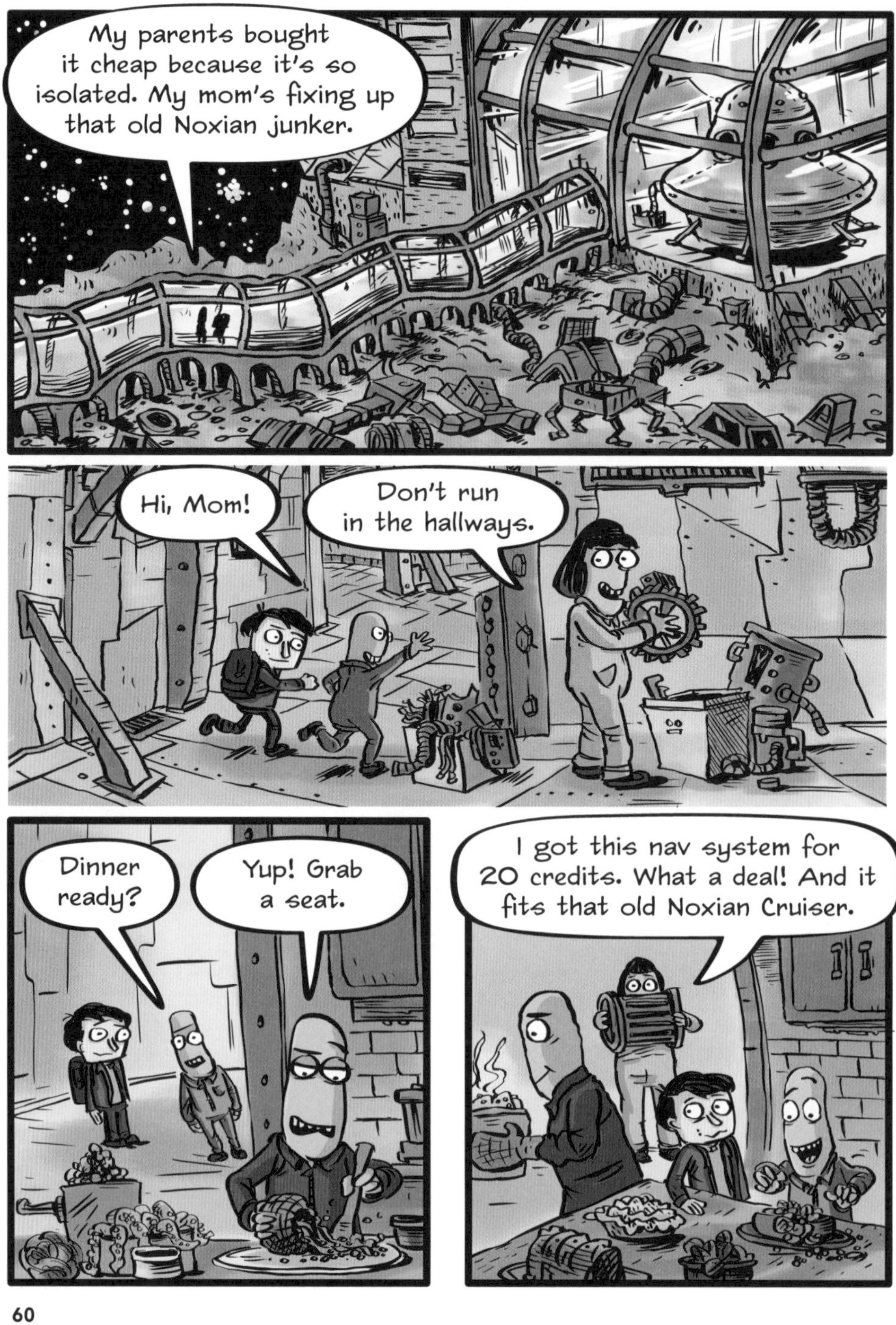
My parents bought it cheap because it's so isolated. My mom's fixing up that old Noxian junker.
Hi, Mom!
Don't run in the hallways.
Dinner ready?
Yup! Grab a seat.
I got this nav system for 20 credits. What a deal! And it fits that old Noxian Cruiser.

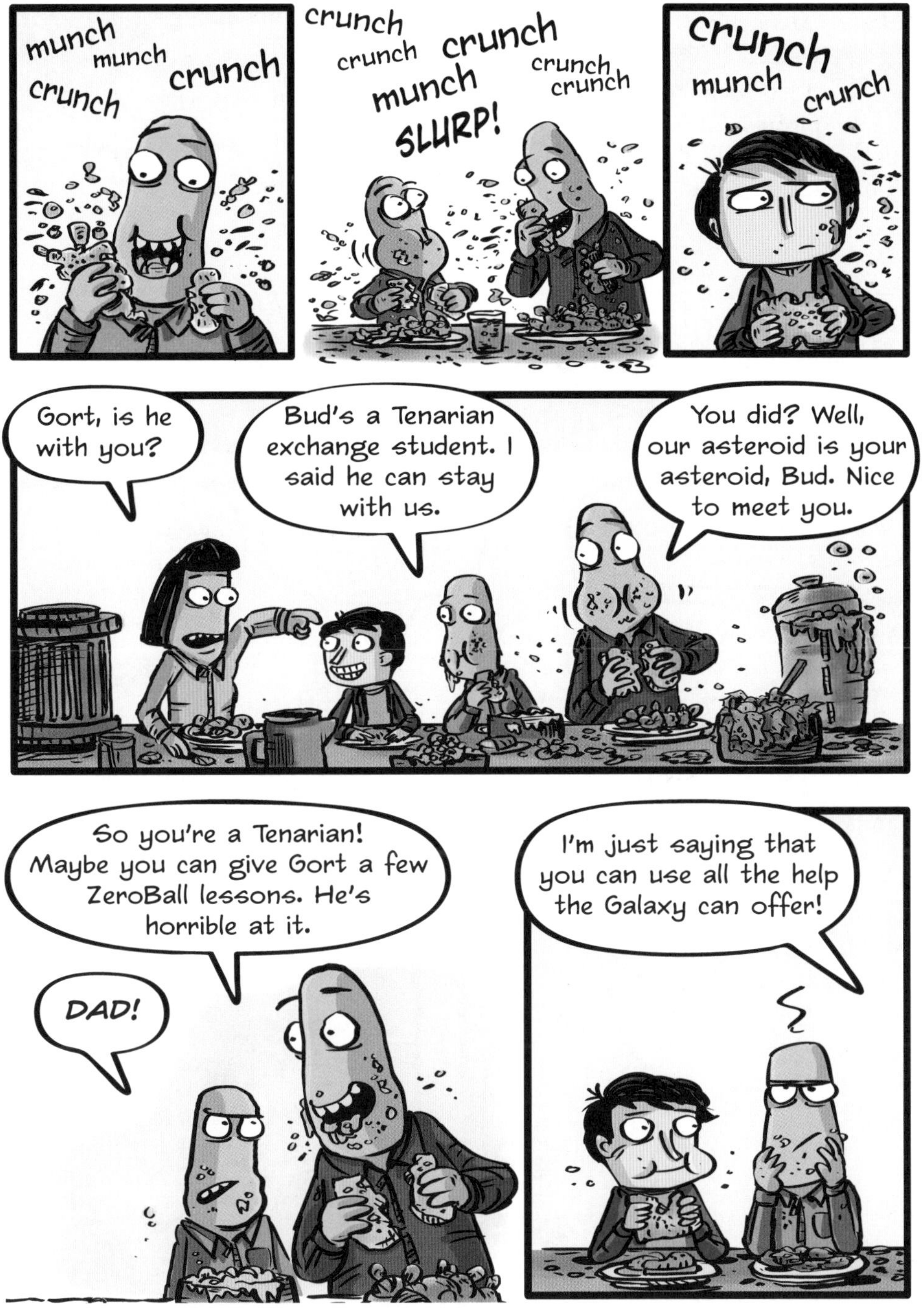
munch
munch
crunch
crunch
crunch
crunch
crunch
munch
SLURP!
crunch
crunch
crunch
munch
crunch
Gort, is he with you?
Bud's a Tenarian exchange student. I said he can stay with us.
You did? Well, our asteroid is your asteroid, Bud. Nice to meet you.
So you're a Tenarian! Maybe you can give Gort a few ZeroBall lessons. He's horrible at it.
DAD!
I'm just saying that you can use all the help the Galaxy can offer!

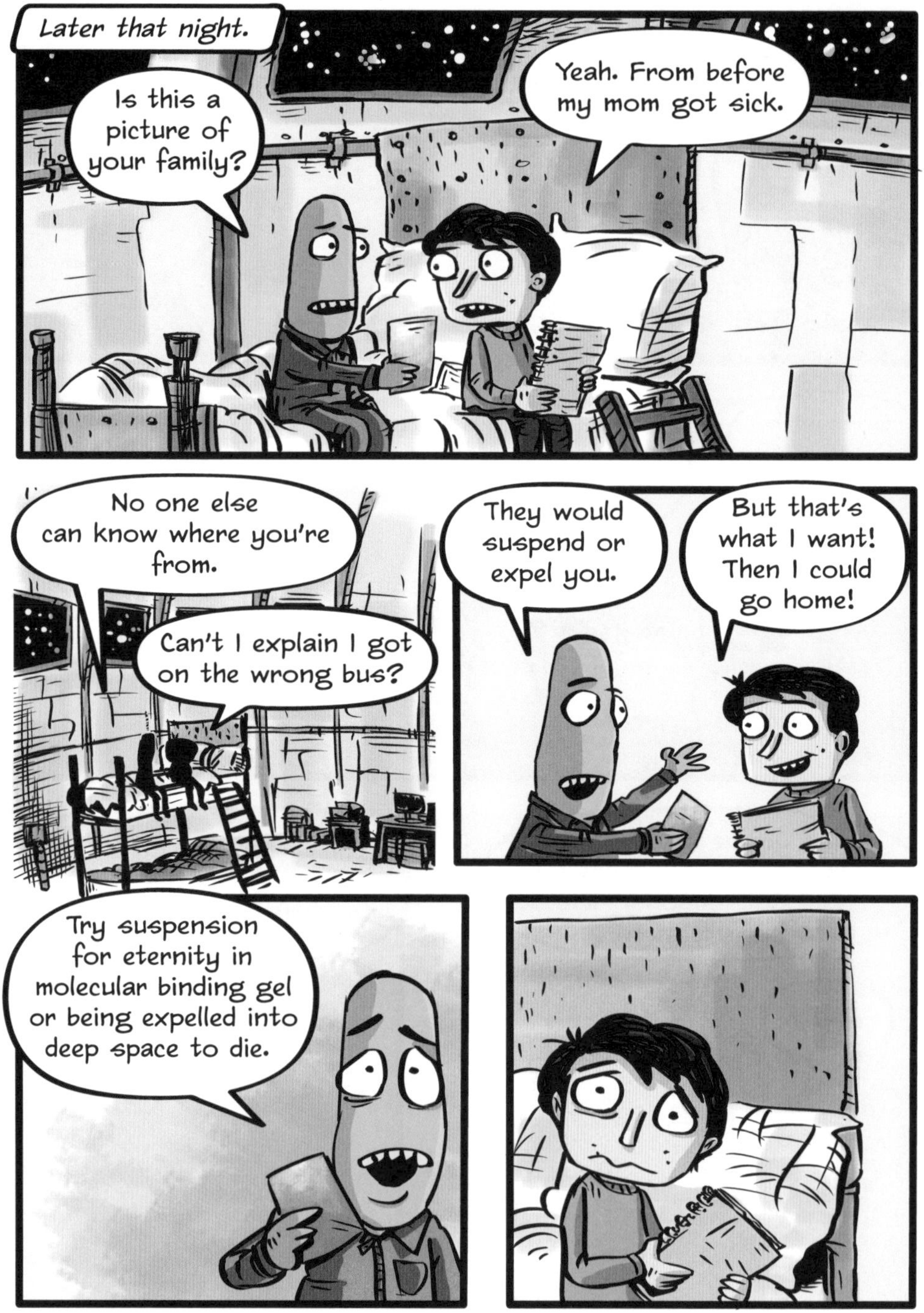
Later that night.
Is this a picture of your family?
Yeah. From before my mom got sick.
No one else can know where you're from.
Can't I explain I got on the wrong bus?
They would suspend or expel you.
But that's what I want! Then I could go home!
Try suspension for eternity in molecular binding gel or being expelled into deep space to die.

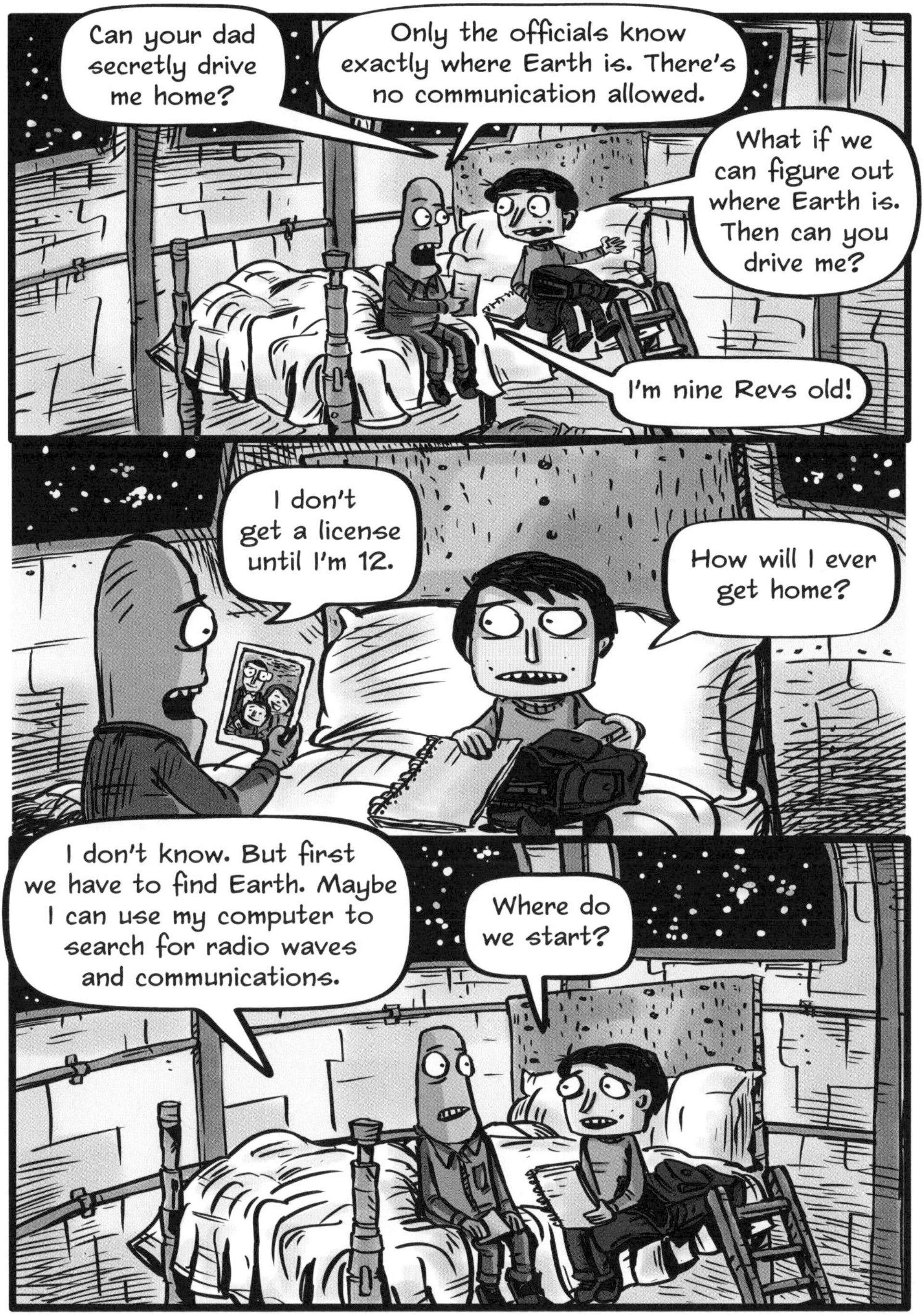
Can your dad secretly drive me home?
Only the officials know exactly where Earth is. There's no communication allowed.
What if we can figure out where Earth is. Then can you drive me?
I'm nine Revs old!
I don't get a license until I'm 12.
How will I ever get home?
I don't know. But first we have to find Earth. Maybe I can use my computer to search for radio waves and communications.
Where do we start?

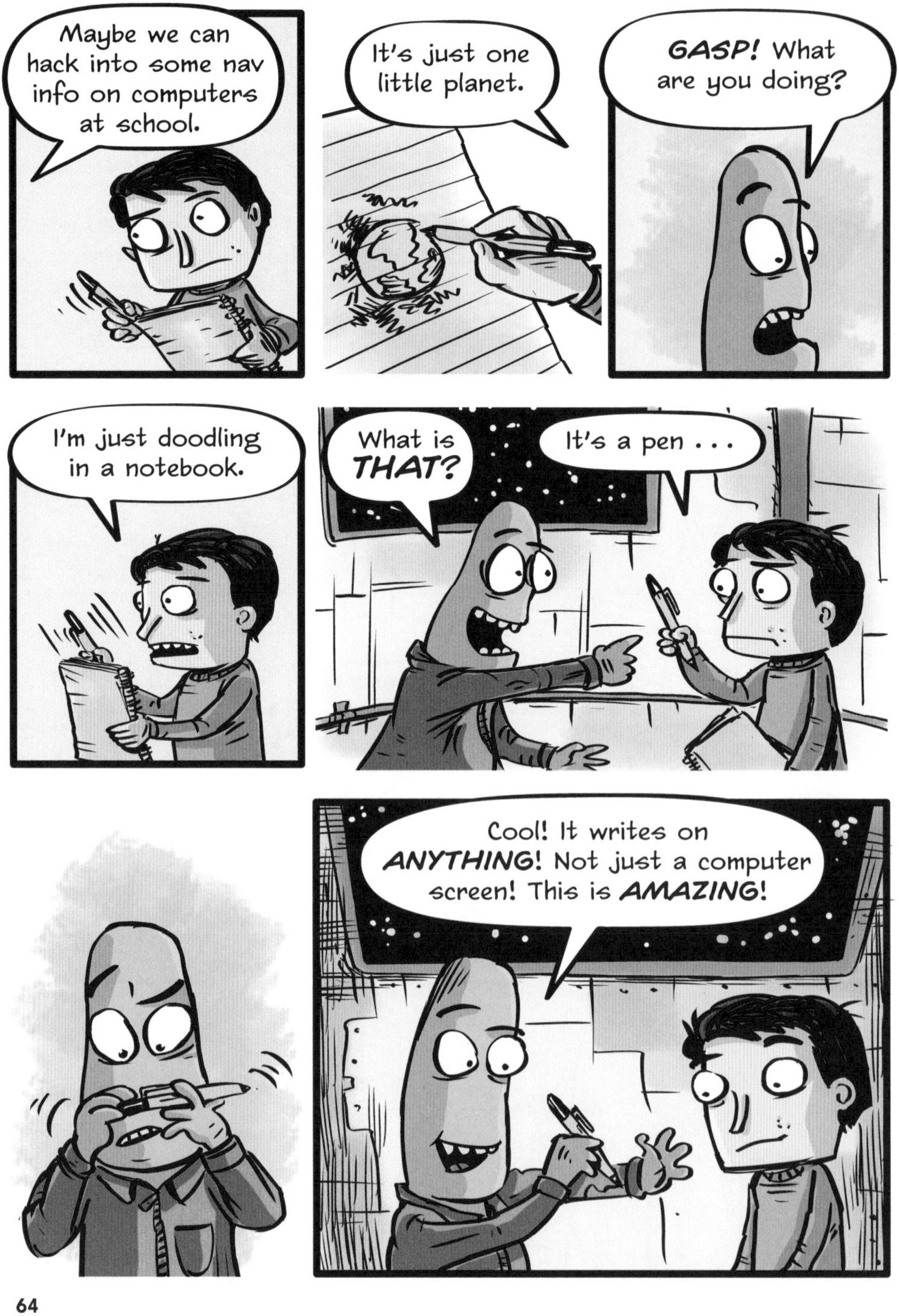
Maybe we can hack into some nav info on computers at school.
It's just one little planet.
GASP! What are you doing?
I'm just doodling in a notebook.
What is THAT?
It's a pen . . .
Cool! It writes on ANYTHING! Not just a computer screen! This is AMAZING!

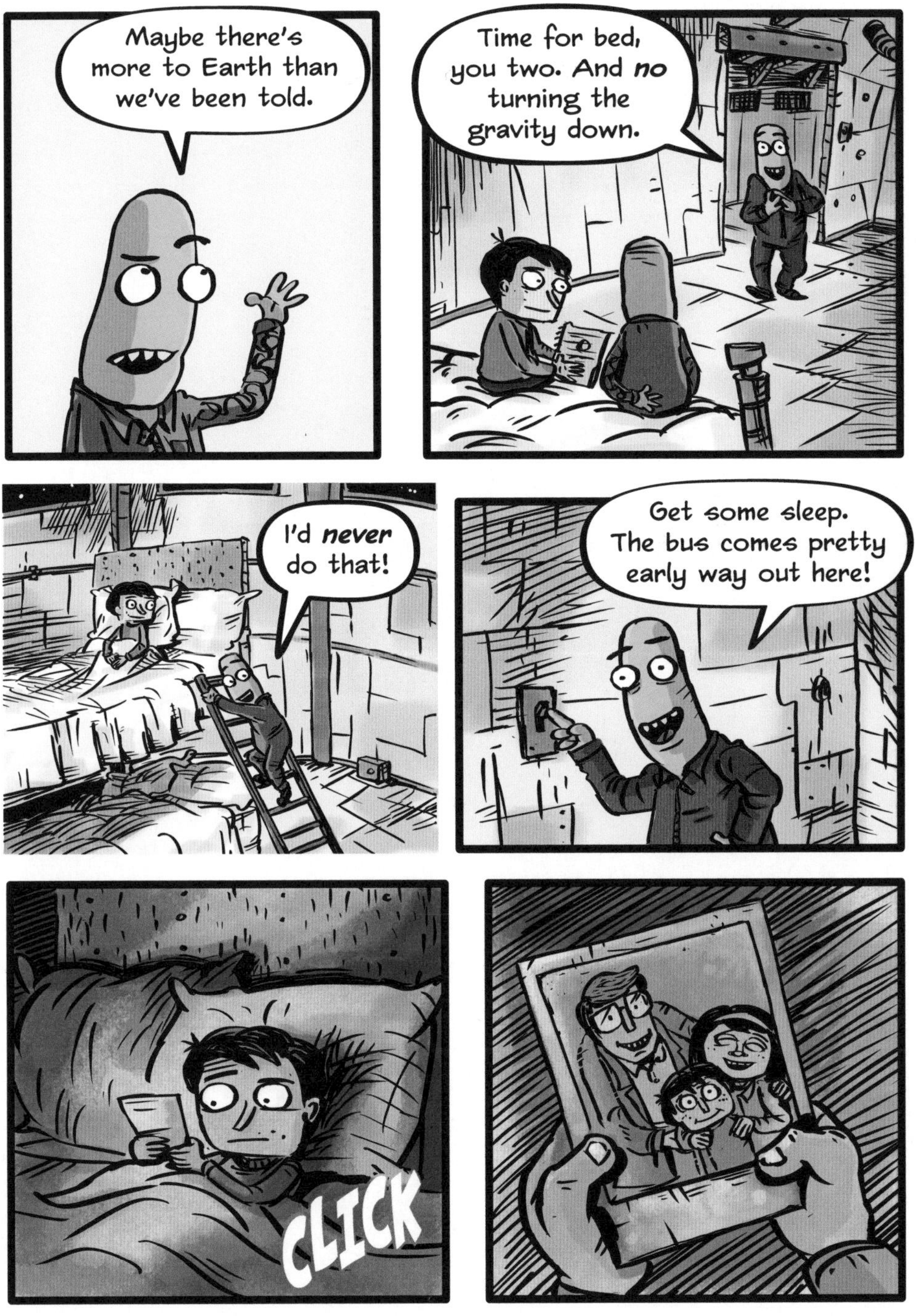
Maybe there's more to Earth than we've been told.
Time for bed, you two. And *no* turning the gravity down.
I'd *never* do that!
Get some sleep. The bus comes pretty early way out here!
CLICK

CHAPTER 3

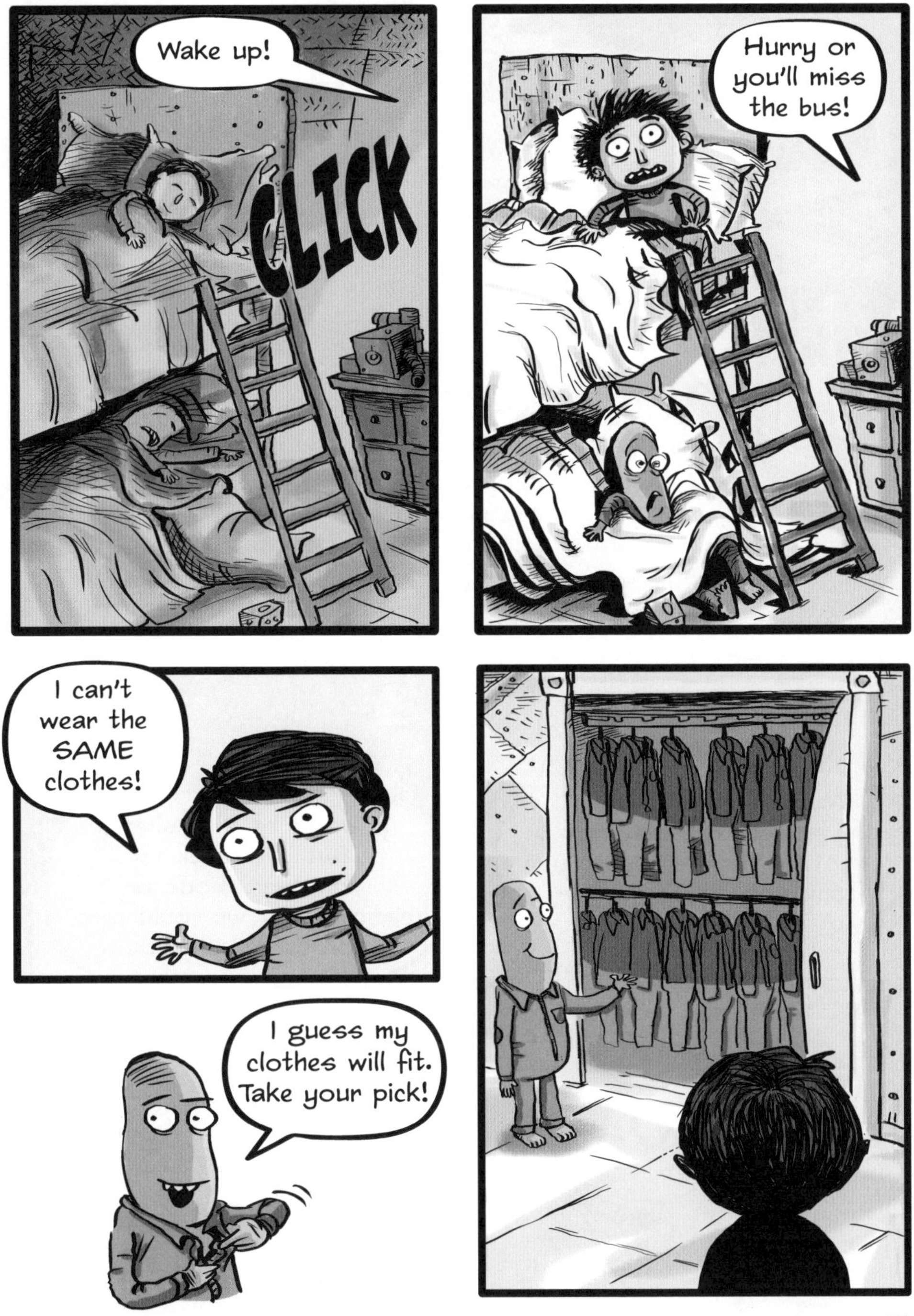
Wake up!
CLICK
Hurry or you'll miss the bus!
I can't wear the SAME clothes!
I guess my clothes will fit. Take your pick!

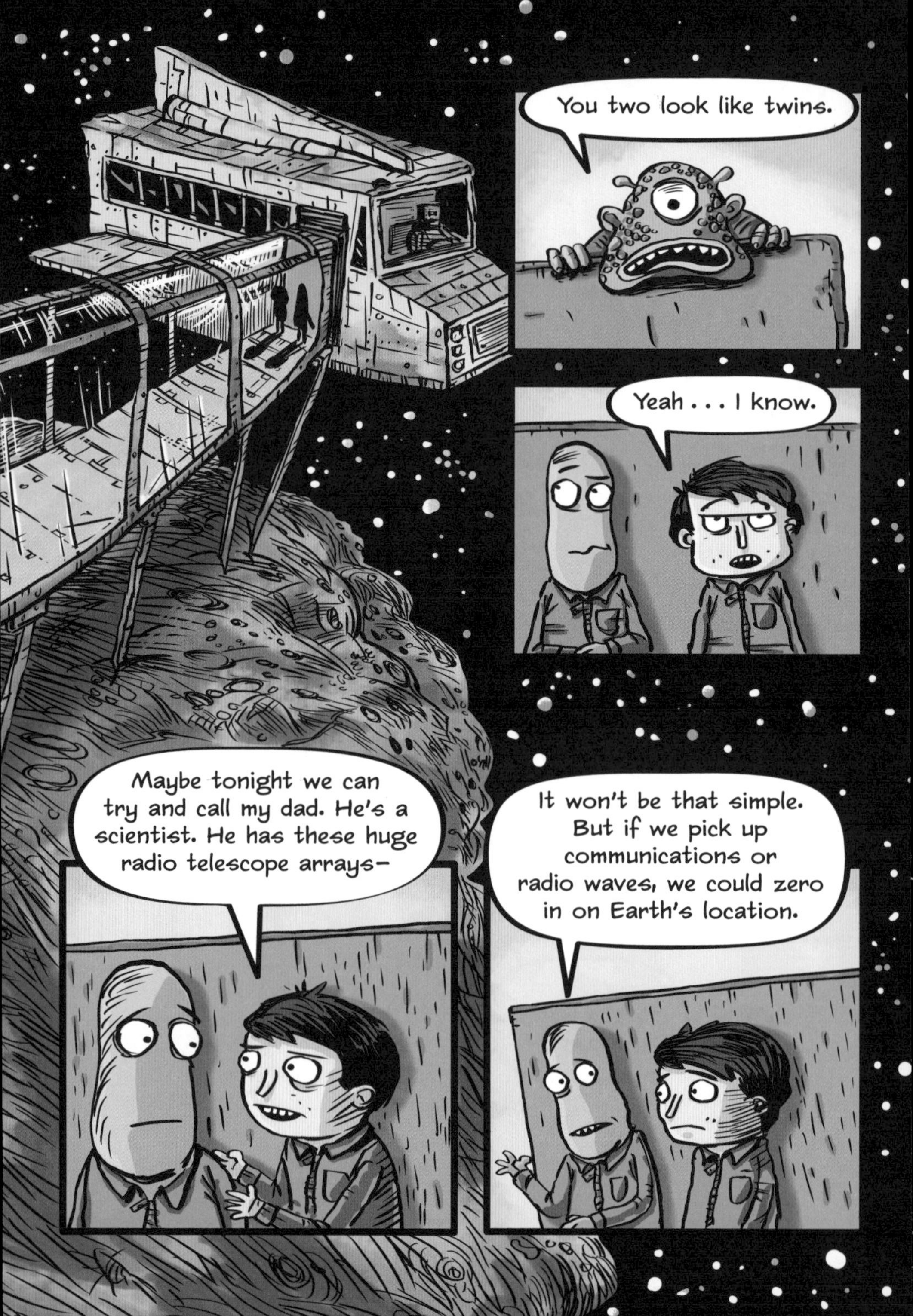
You two look like twins.
Yeah . . . I know.
Maybe tonight we can try and call my dad. He's a scientist. He has these huge radio telescope arrays-
It won't be that simple. But if we pick up communications or radio waves, we could zero in on Earth's location.

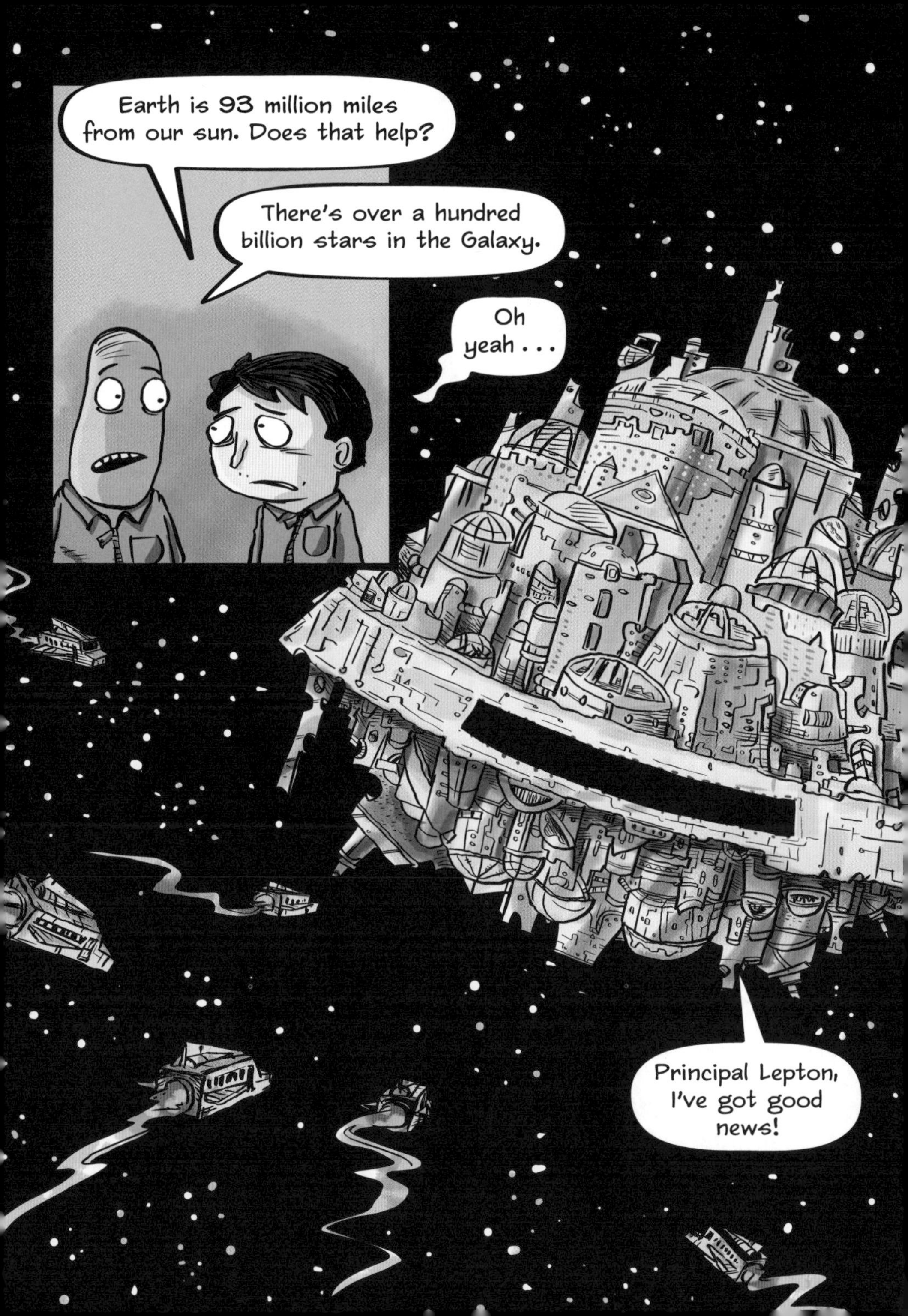
Earth is 93 million miles from our sun. Does that help?
There's over a hundred billion stars in the Galaxy.
Oh yeah . . .
Principal Lepton, I've got good news!

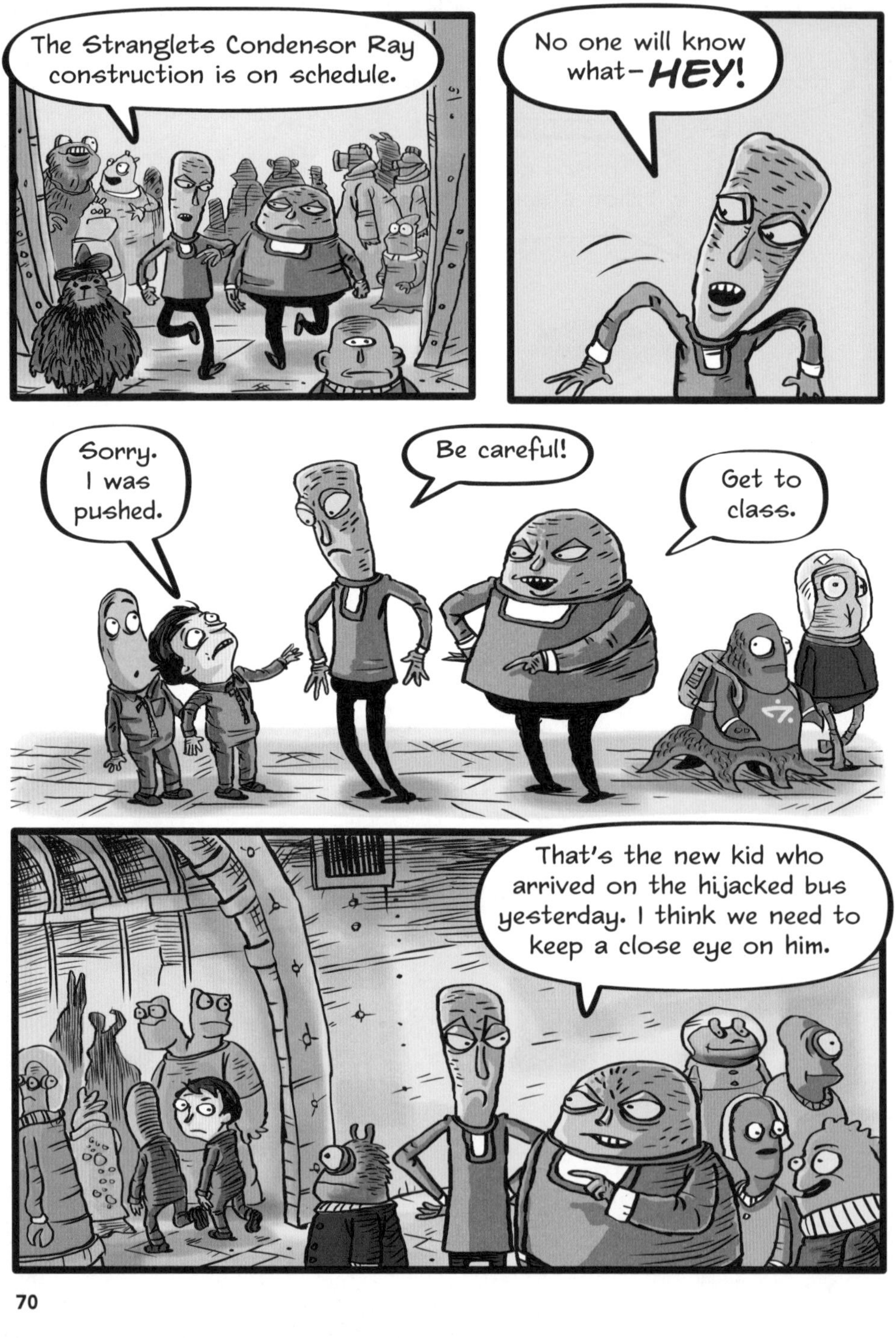
The Stranglets Condensor Ray construction is on schedule.
No one will know what–HEY!
Sorry. I was pushed.
Be careful!
Get to class.
That's the new kid who arrived on the hijacked bus yesterday. I think we need to keep a close eye on him.

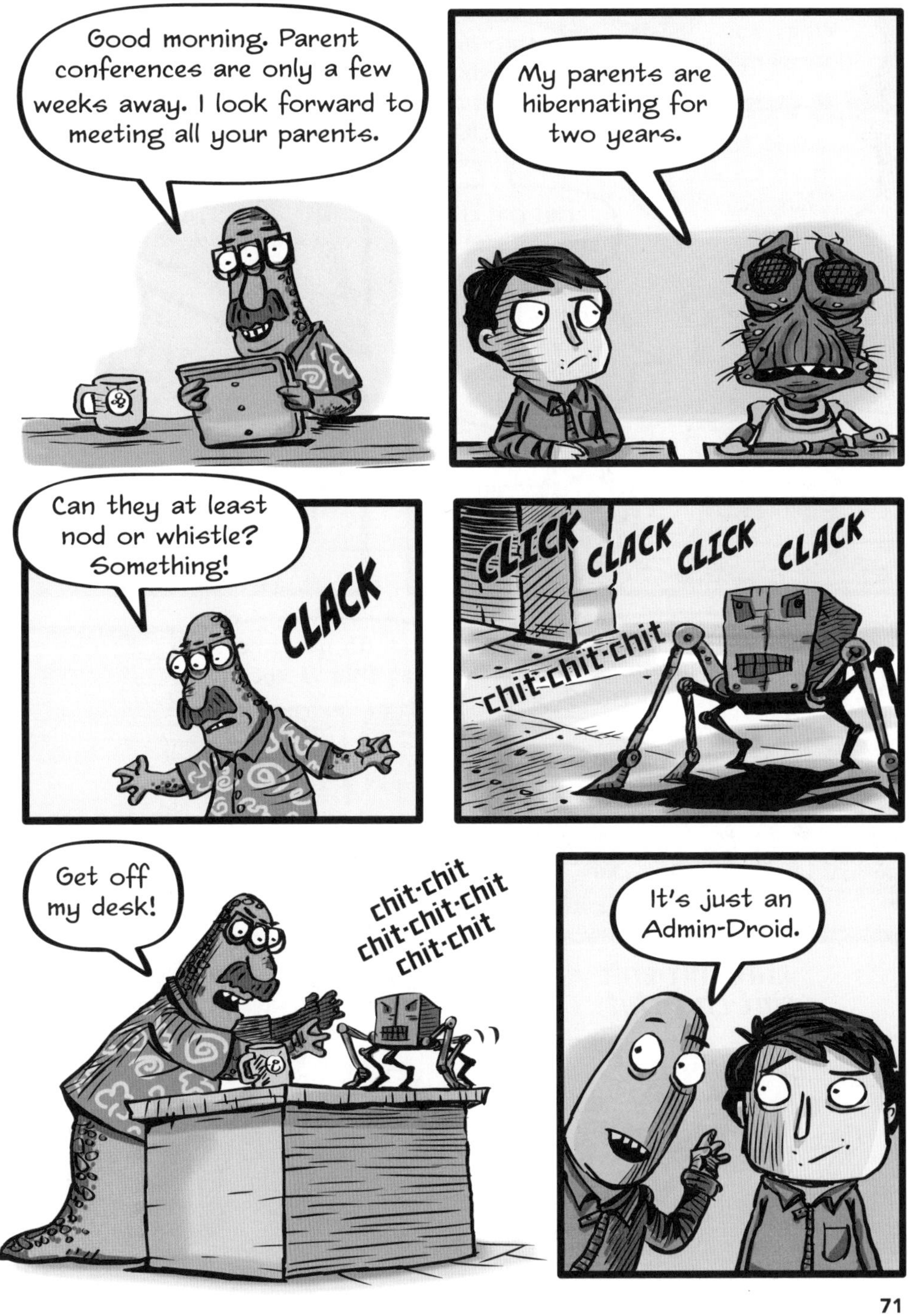
Good morning. Parent conferences are only a few weeks away. I look forward to meeting all your parents.
My parents are hibernating for two years.
Can they at least nod or whistle? Something!
CLACK
CLICK
CLACK
CLICK
CLACK
chit-chit-chit
Get off my desk!
chit-chit
chit-chit-chit
chit-chit
It's just an Admin-Droid.

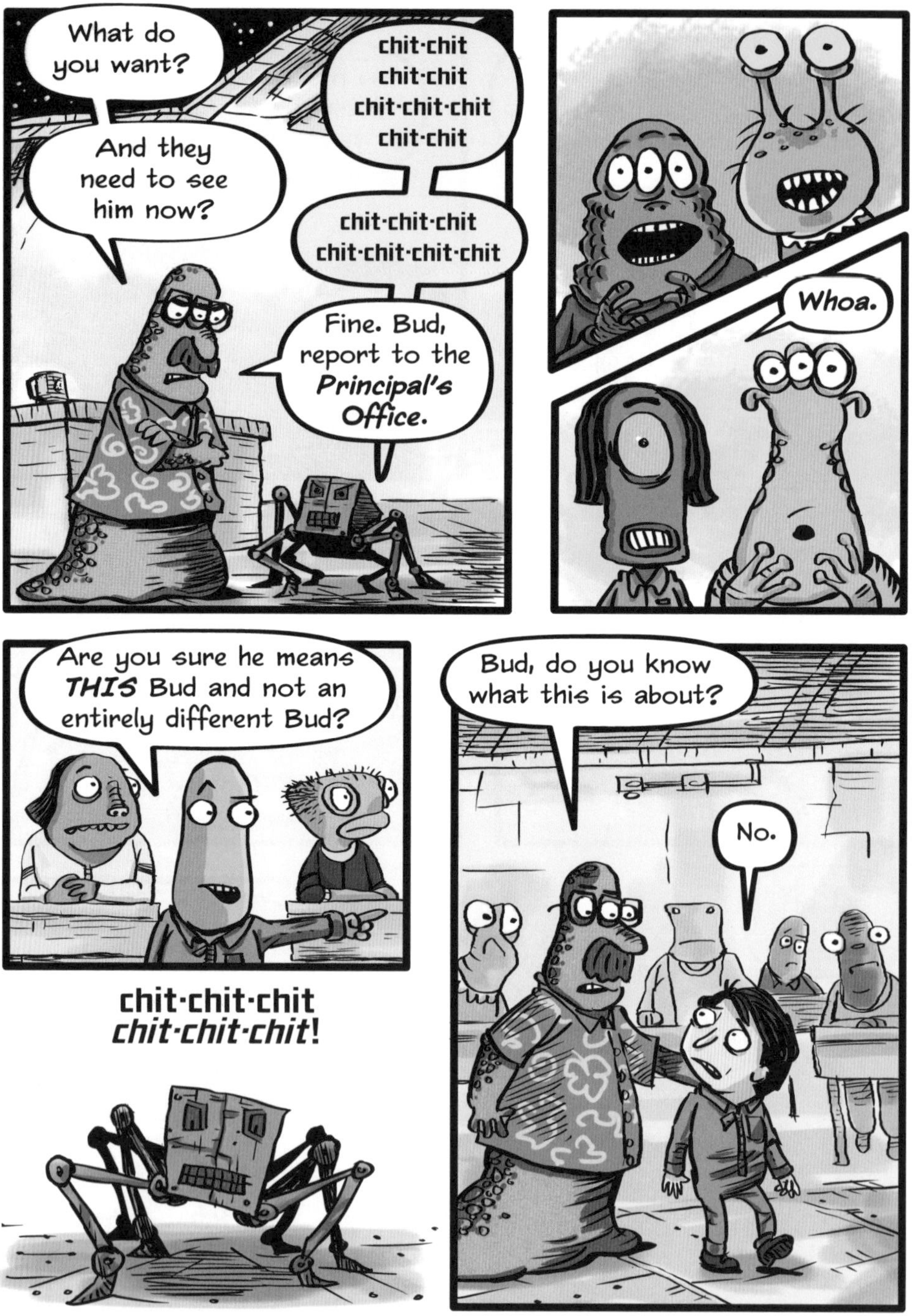
What do you want?
chit·chit chit·chit chit·chit·chit chit·chit
And they need to see him now?
chit·chit·chit chit·chit·chit·chit
Fine. Bud, report to the *Principal's* Office.
Whoa.
Are you sure he means *THIS* Bud and not an entirely different Bud?
Bud, do you know what this is about?
No.
chit·chit·chit *chit·chit·chit*!

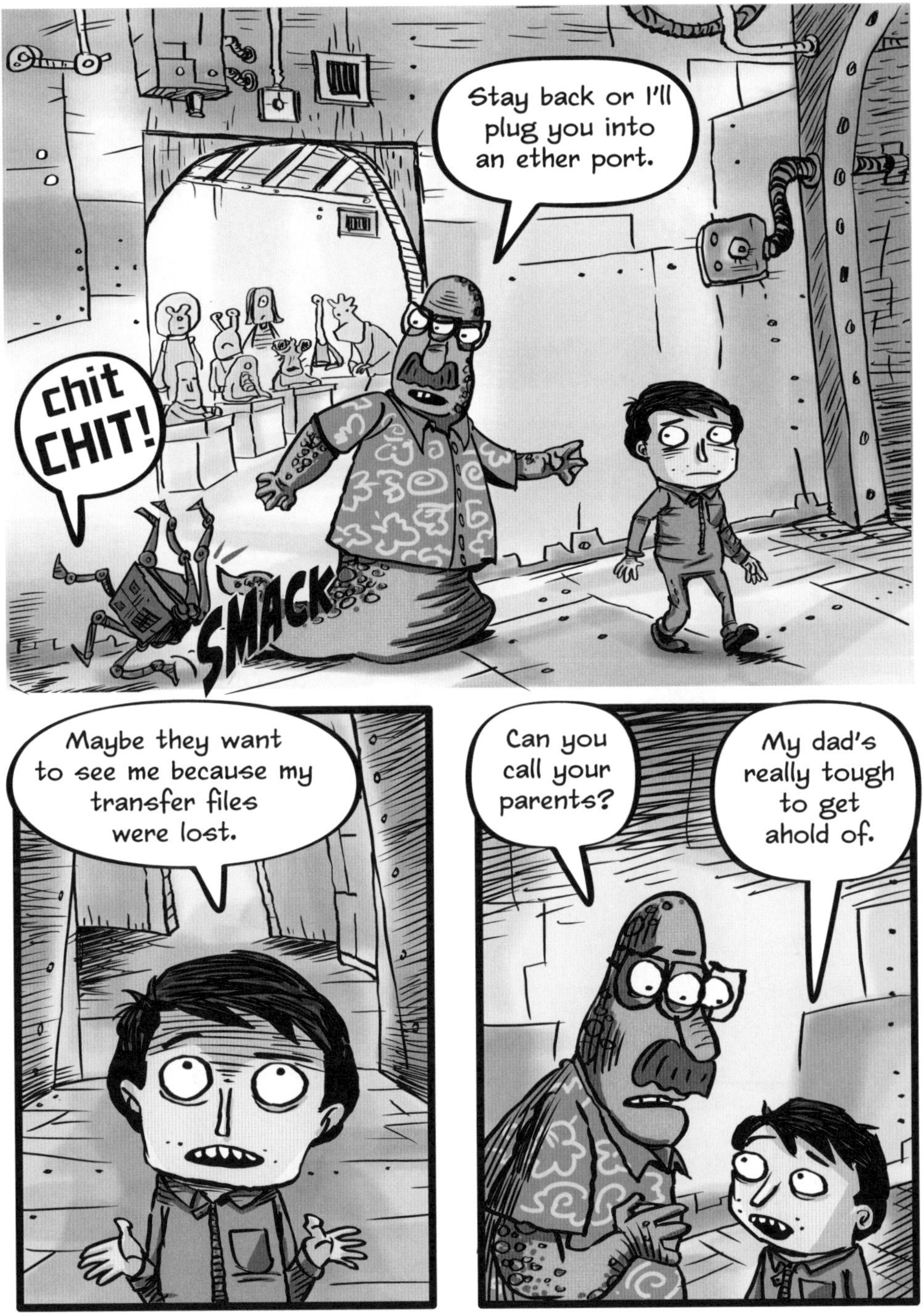
Stay back or I'll plug you into an ether port.
chit CHIT!
SMACK
Maybe they want to see me because my transfer files were lost.
Can you call your parents?
My dad's really tough to get ahold of.

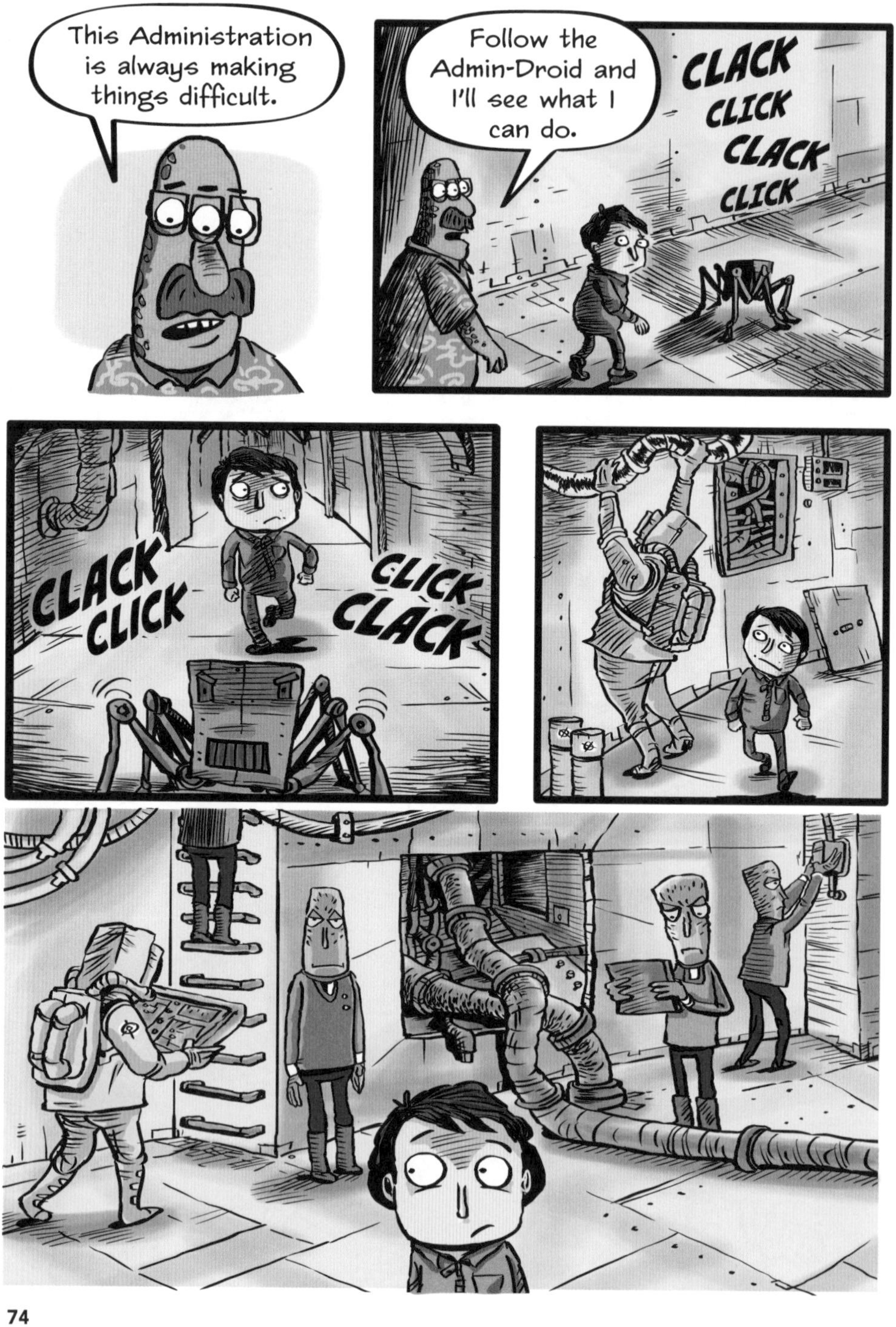
This Administration is always making things difficult.
Follow the Admin-Droid and I'll see what I can do.
CLACK
CLICK
CLACK
CLICK
CLACK
CLICK
CLICK
CLACK

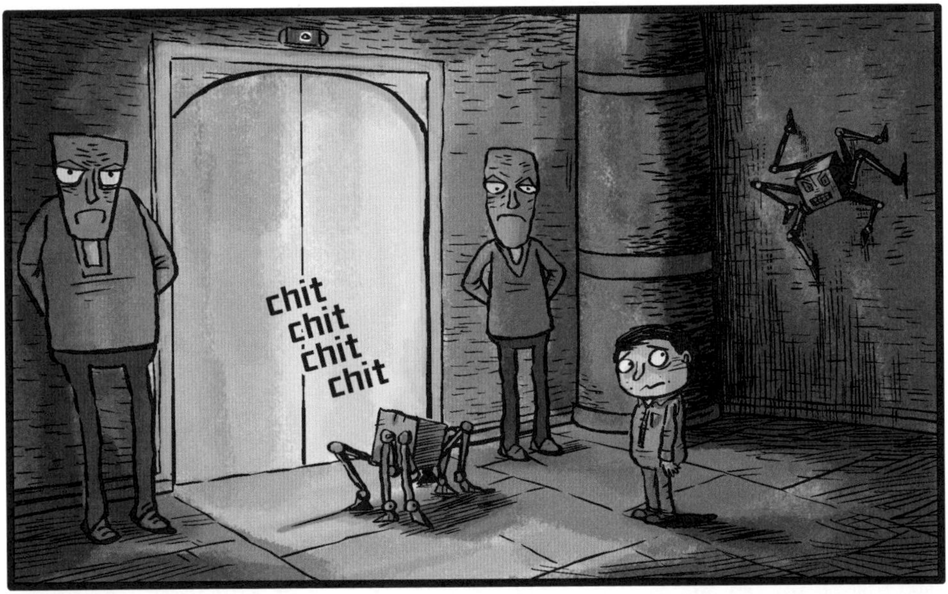
chit
chit
chit
chit

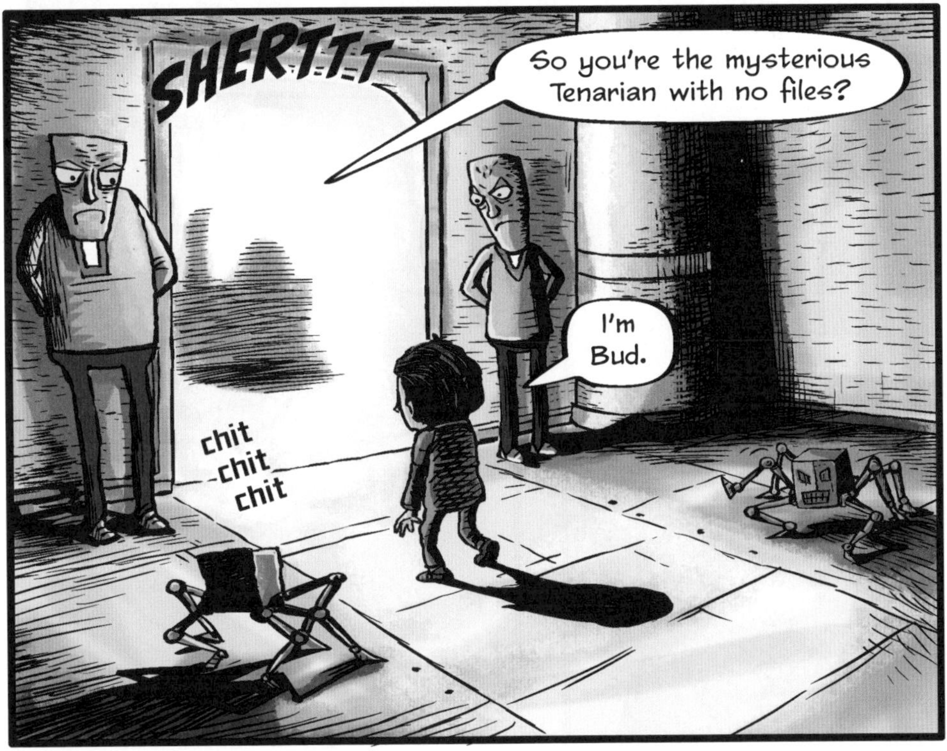
SHERTTT
So you're the mysterious Tenarian with no files?
I'm Bud.
chit
chit
chit

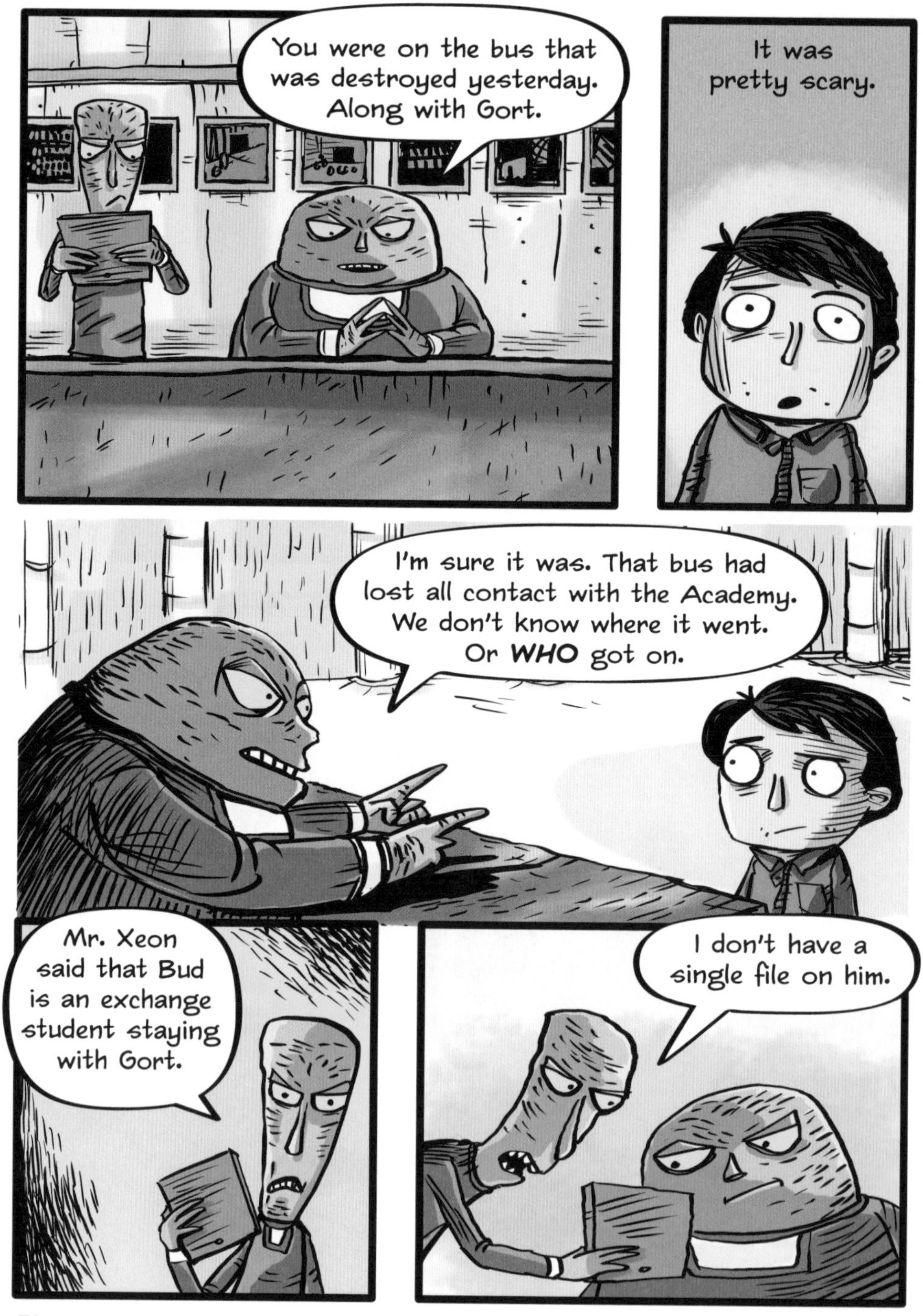
You were on the bus that was destroyed yesterday. Along with Gort.
It was pretty scary.
I'm sure it was. That bus had lost all contact with the Academy. We don't know where it went. Or **WHO** got on.
Mr. Xeon said that Bud is an exchange student staying with Gort.
I don't have a single file on him.

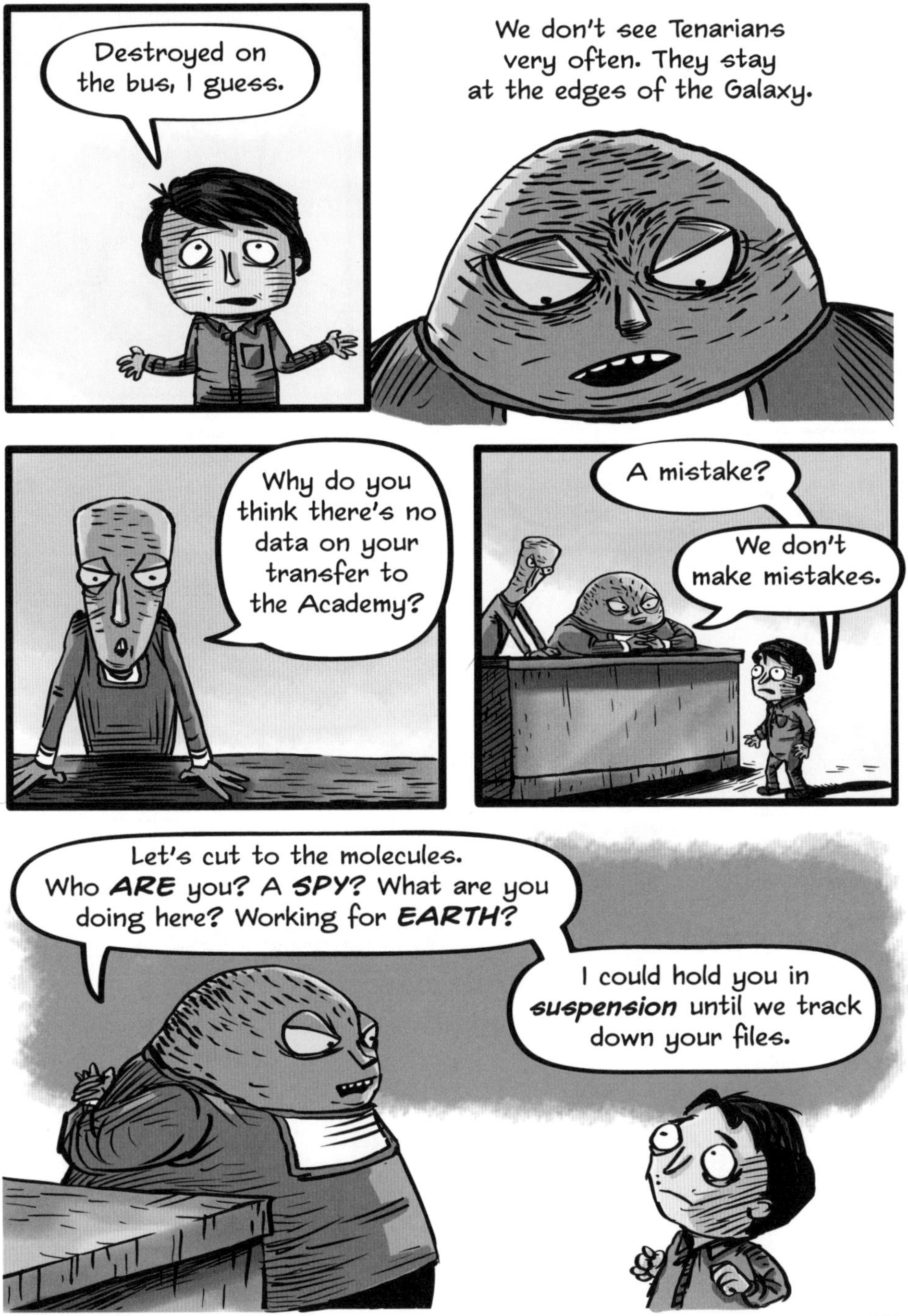
Destroyed on the bus, I guess.
We don't see Tenarians very often. They stay at the edges of the Galaxy.
Why do you think there's no data on your transfer to the Academy?
A mistake?
We don't make mistakes.
Let's cut to the molecules. Who **ARE** you? A **SPY**? What are you doing here? Working for **EARTH**?
I could hold you in **suspension** until we track down your files.

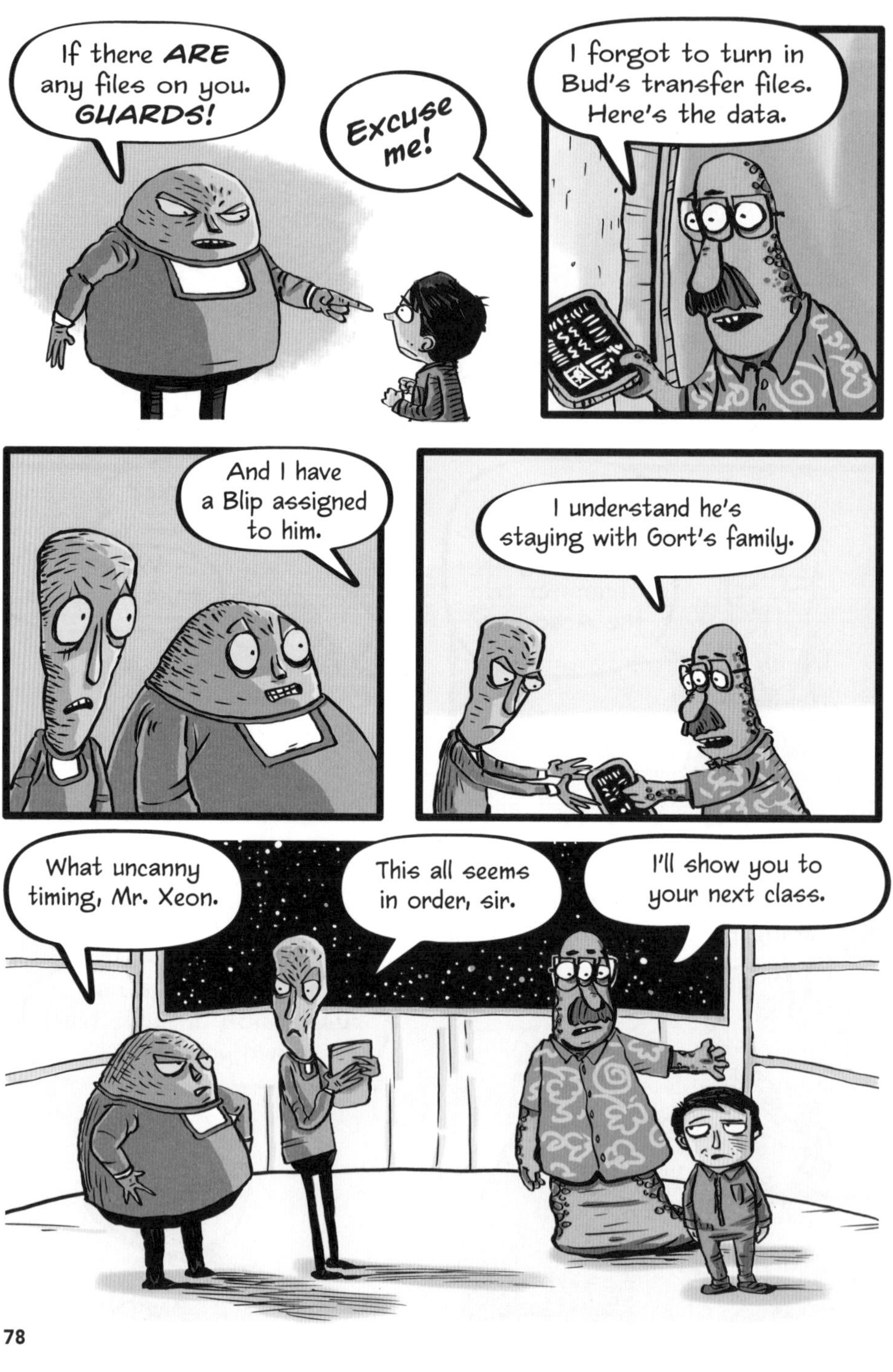
If there ARE any files on you. GUARDS!
Excuse me!
I forgot to turn in Bud's transfer files. Here's the data.
And I have a Blip assigned to him.
I understand he's staying with Gort's family.
What uncanny timing, Mr. Xeon.
This all seems in order, sir.
I'll show you to your next class.

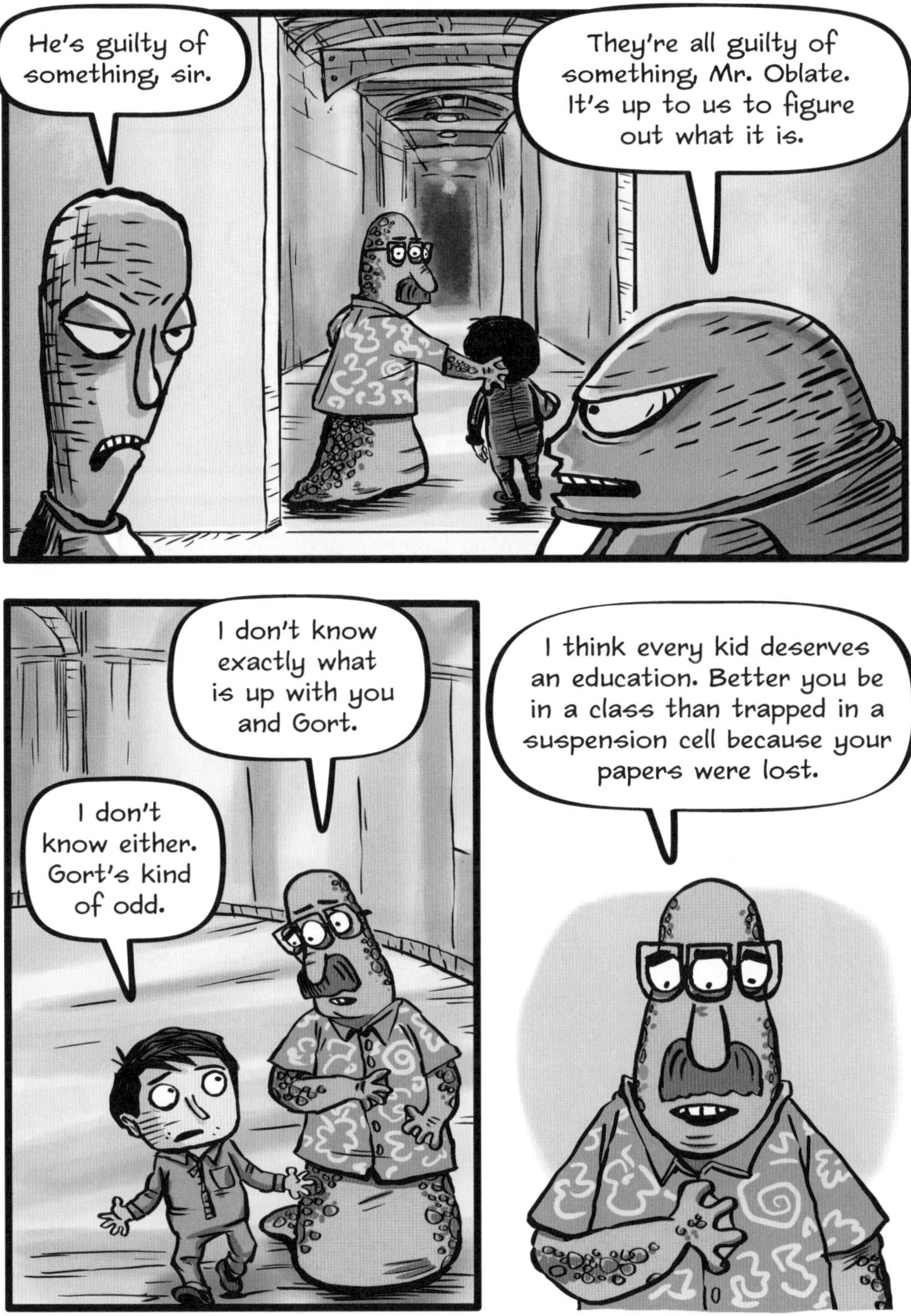
He's guilty of something, sir.
They're all guilty of something, Mr. Oblate. It's up to us to figure out what it is.
I don't know exactly what is up with you and Gort.
I don't know either. Gort's kind of odd.
I think every kid deserves an education. Better you be in a class than trapped in a suspension cell because your papers were lost.

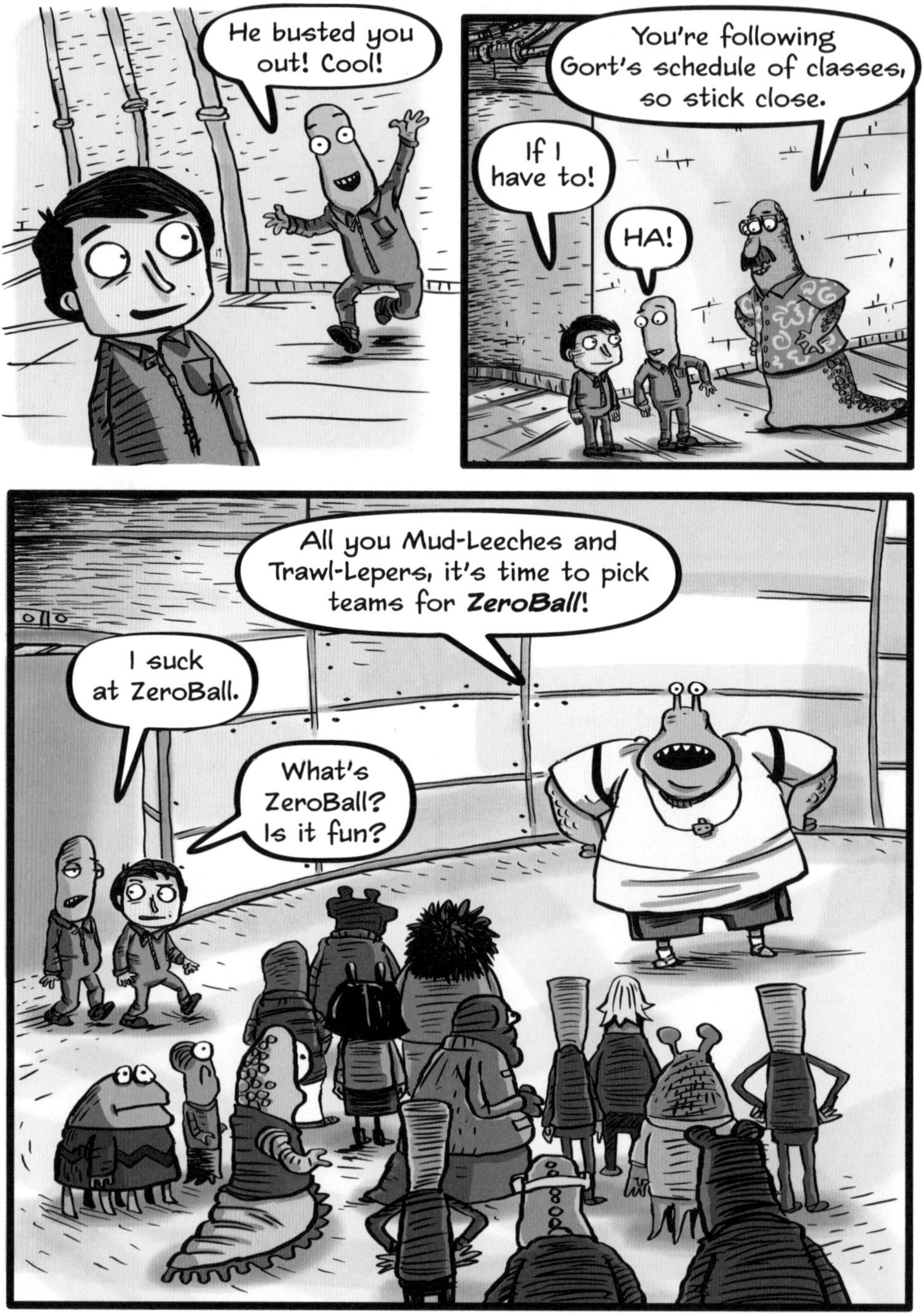

He busted you out! Cool!
You're following Gort's schedule of classes, so stick close.
If I have to!
HA!
All you Mud-Leeches and Trawl-Lepers, it's time to pick teams for ZeroBall!
I suck at ZeroBall.
What's ZeroBall? Is it fun?

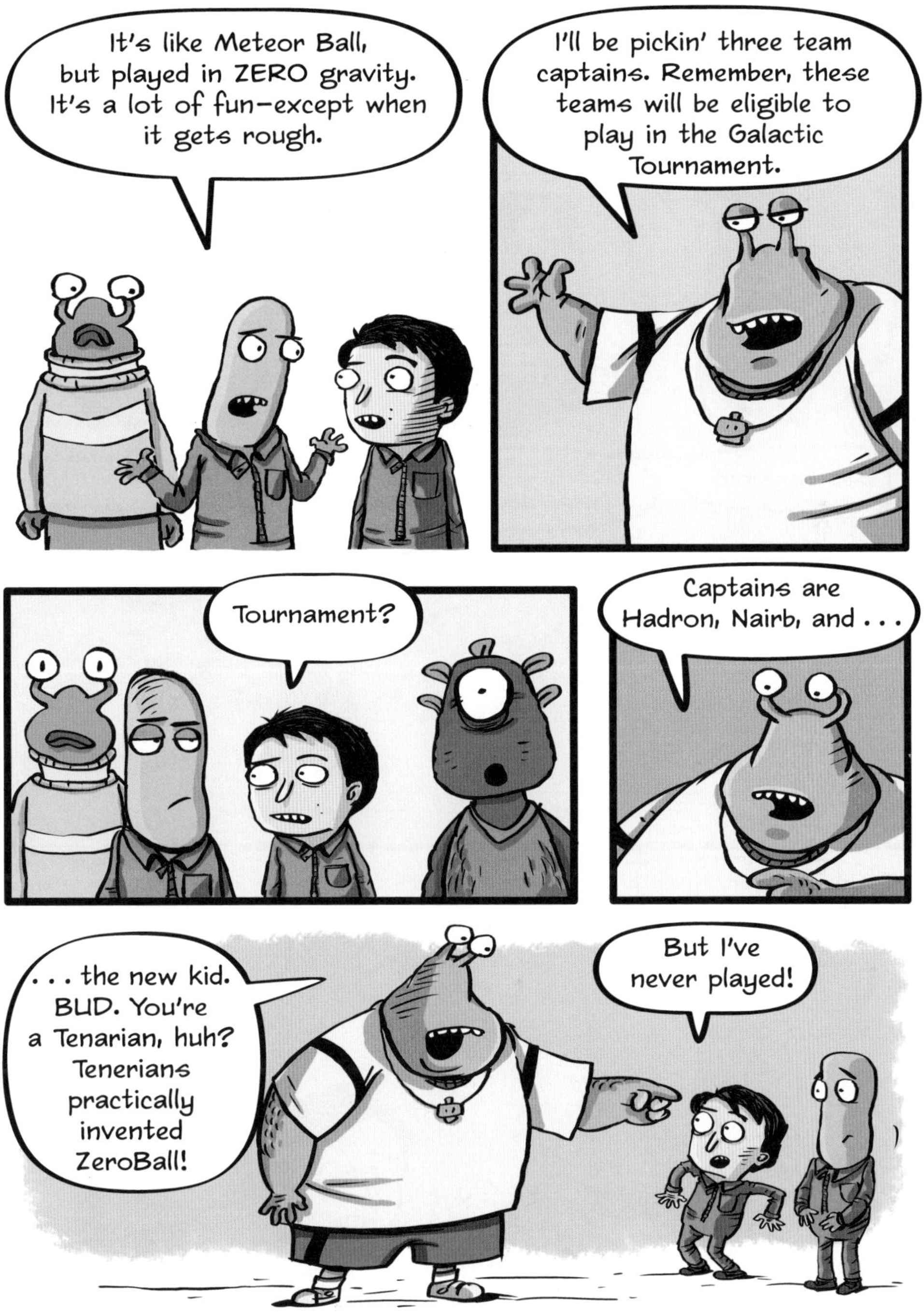
It's like Meteor Ball, but played in ZERO gravity. It's a lot of fun—except when it gets rough.
I'll be pickin' three team captains. Remember, these teams will be eligible to play in the Galactic Tournament.
Tournament?
Captains are Hadron, Nairb, and . . .
. . . the new kid. BUD. You're a Tenarian, huh? Tenerians practically invented ZeroBall!
But I've never played!

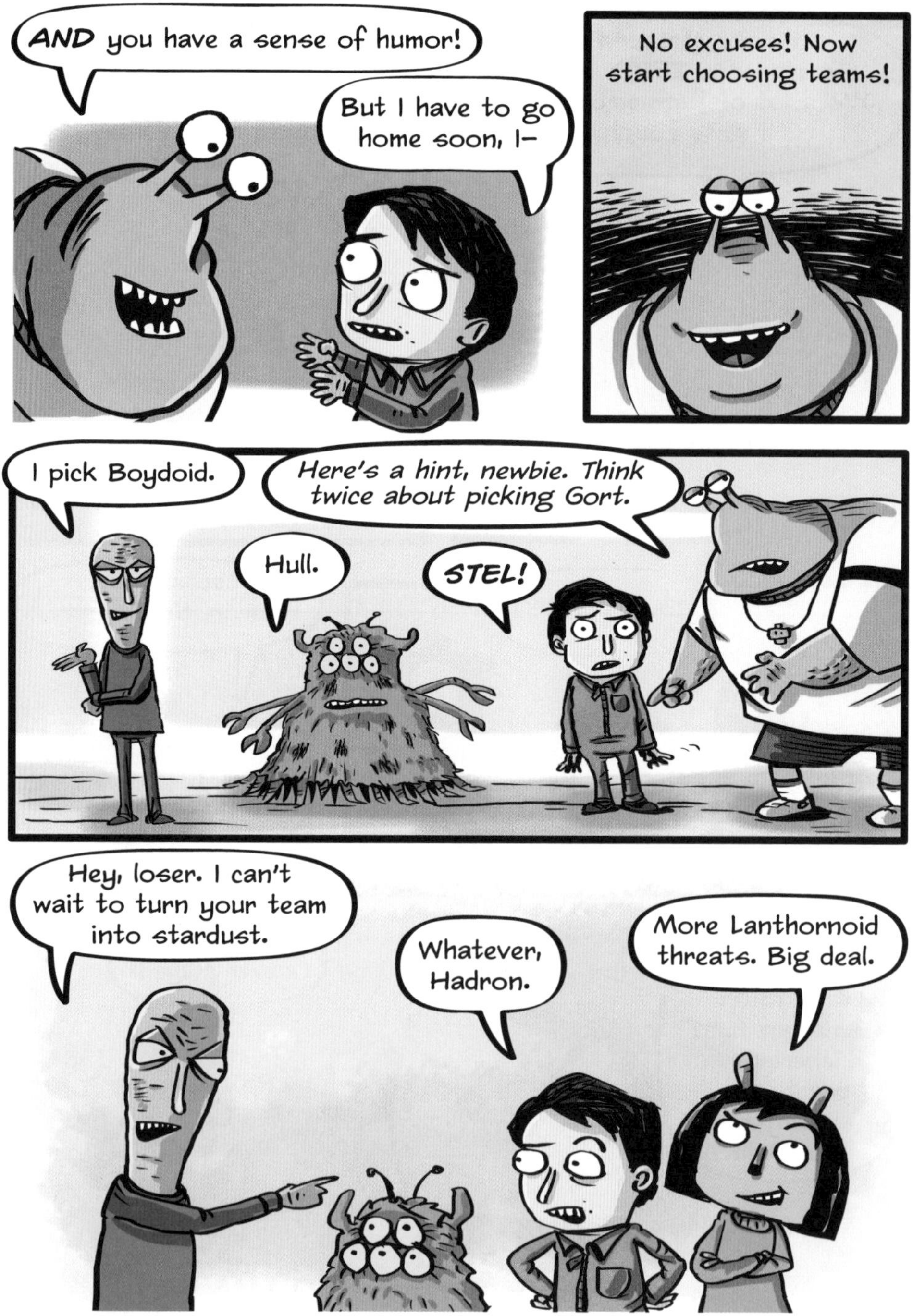
AND you have a sense of humor!
But I have to go home soon, I–
No excuses! Now start choosing teams!
I pick Boydoid.
Here's a hint, newbie. Think twice about picking Gort.
Hull.
STEL!
Hey, loser. I can't wait to turn your team into stardust.
Whatever, Hadron.
More Lanthornoid threats. Big deal.

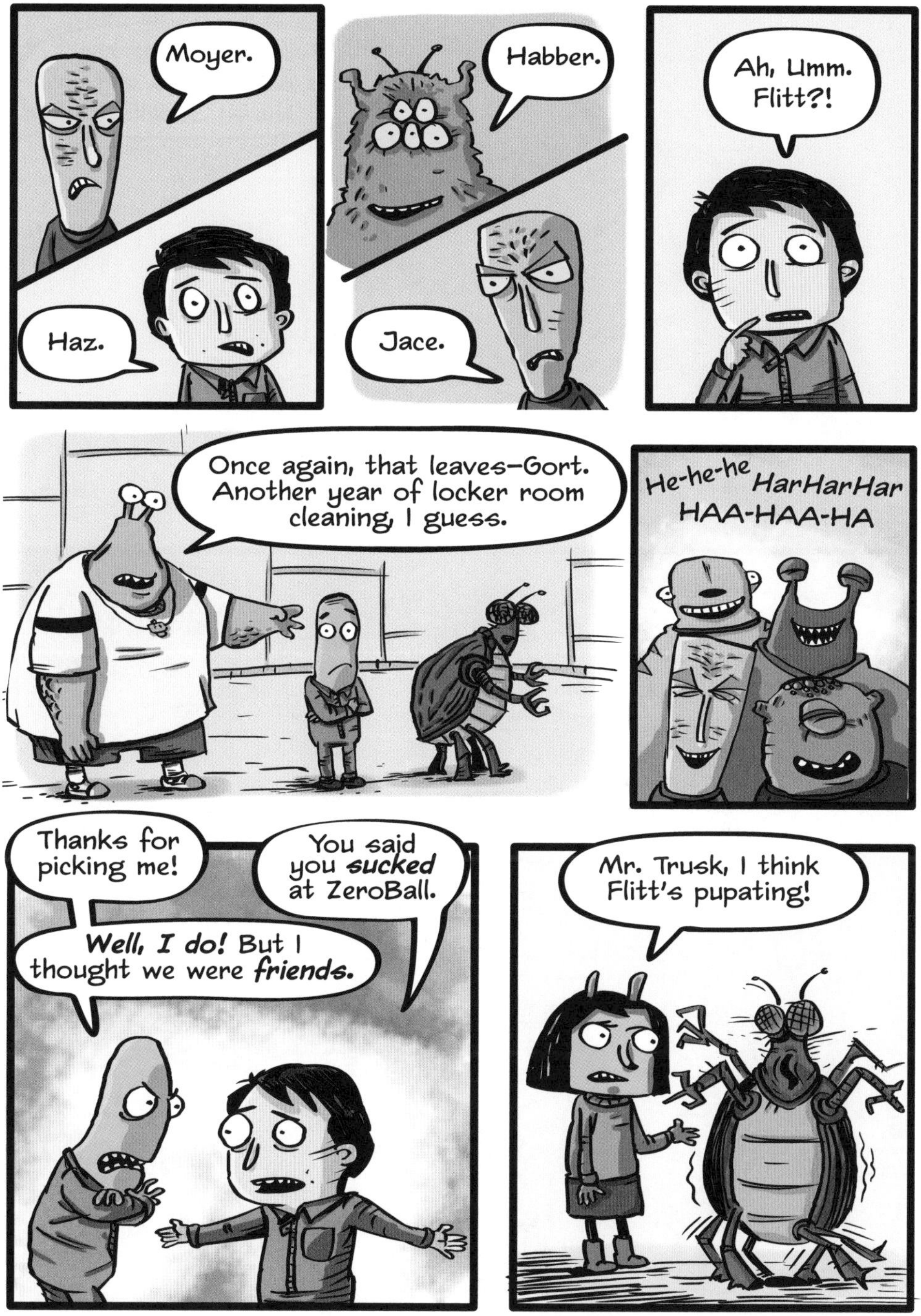
Moyer.
Haz.
Habber.
Jace.
Ah, Umm. Flitt?!
Once again, that leaves—Gort. Another year of locker room cleaning, I guess.
He-he-he HarHarHar HAA-HAA-HA
Thanks for picking me!
You said you *sucked* at ZeroBall.
Well, I do! But I thought we were ***friends.***
Mr. Trusk, I think Flitt's pupating!

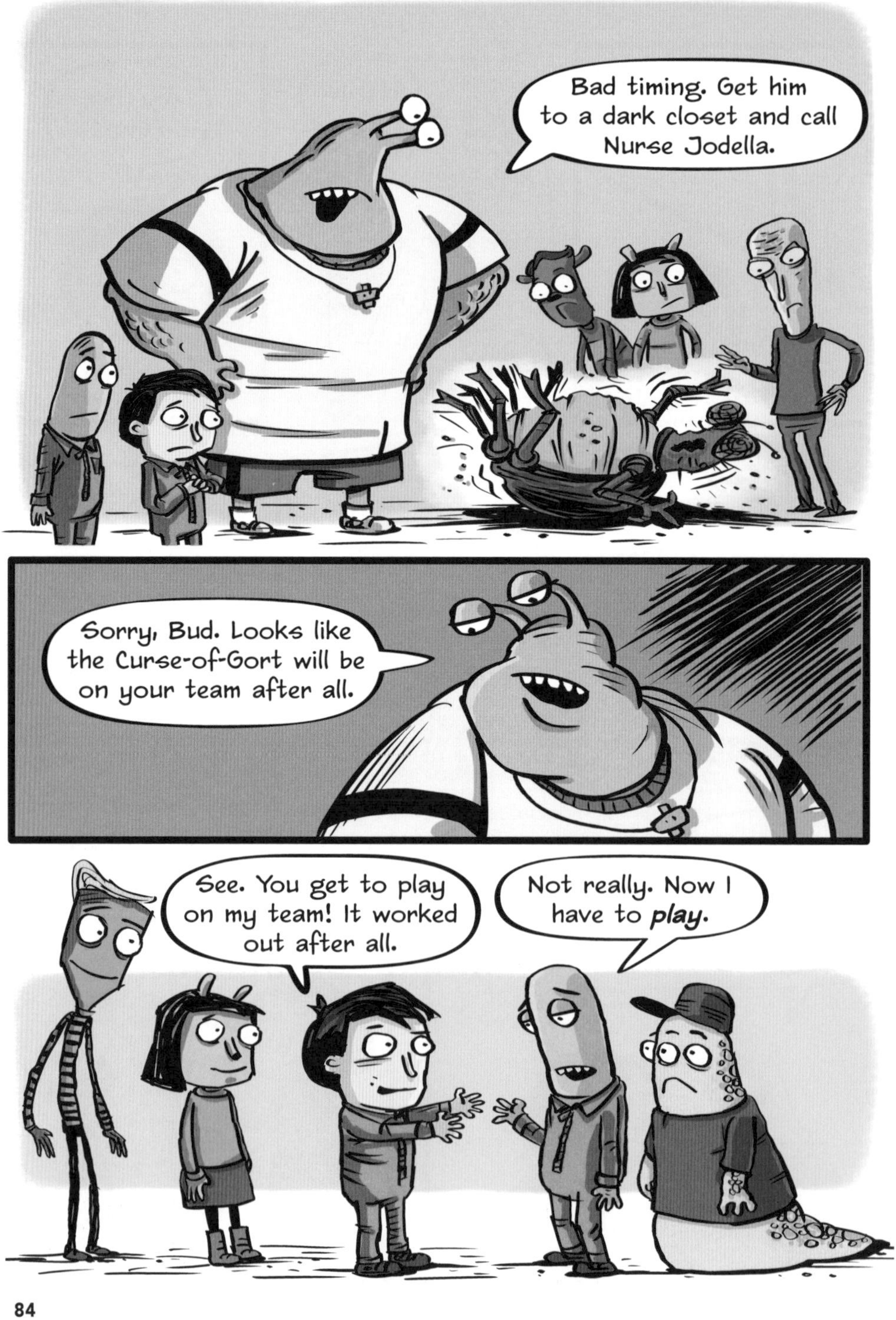
Bad timing. Get him to a dark closet and call Nurse Jodella.
Sorry, Bud. Looks like the Curse-of-Gort will be on your team after all.
See. You get to play on my team! It worked out after all.
Not really. Now I have to *play*.

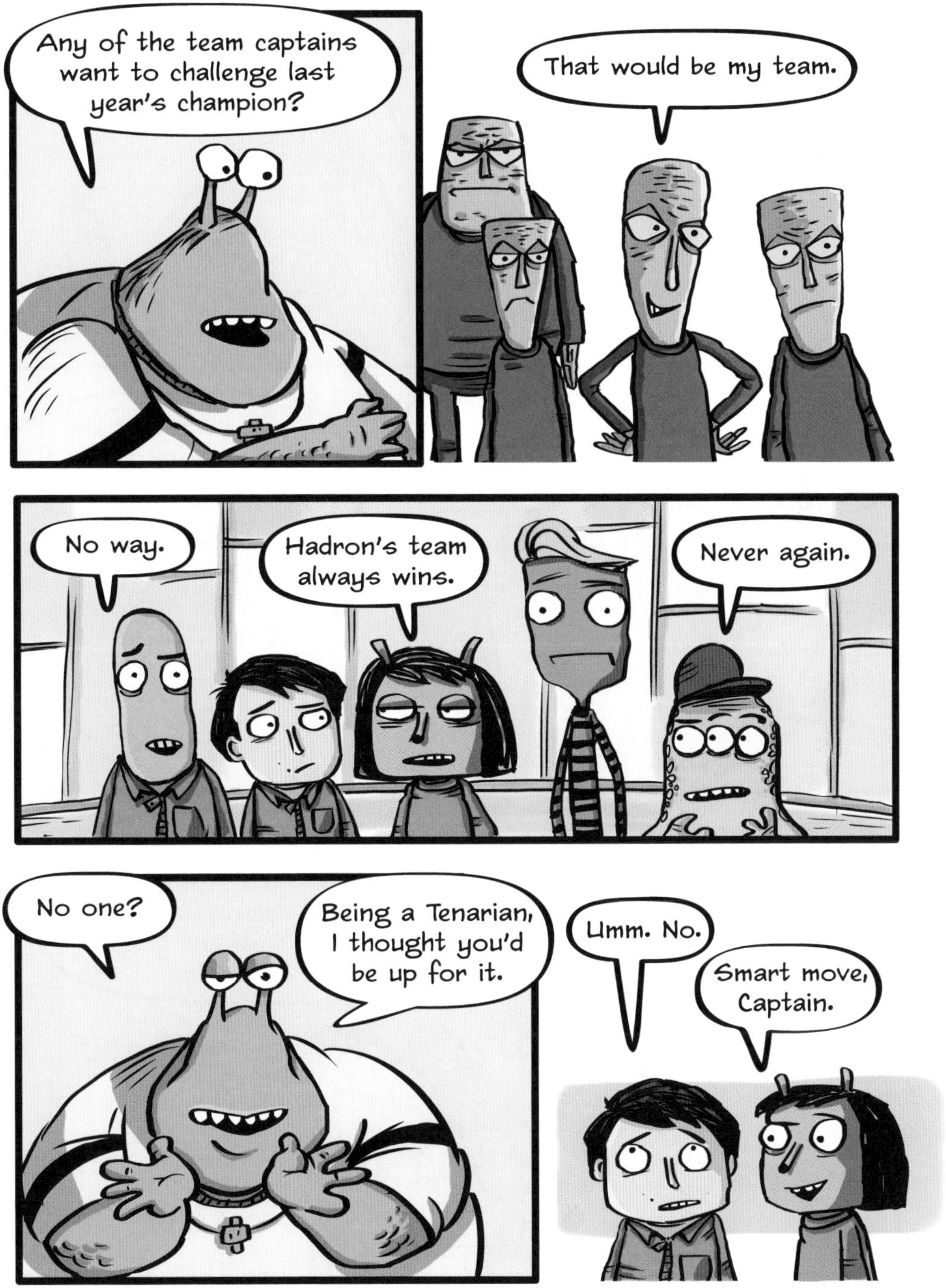
Any of the team captains want to challenge last year's champion?
That would be my team.
No way.
Hadron's team always wins.
Never again.
No one?
Being a Tenarian, I thought you'd be up for it.
Umm. No.
Smart move, Captain.

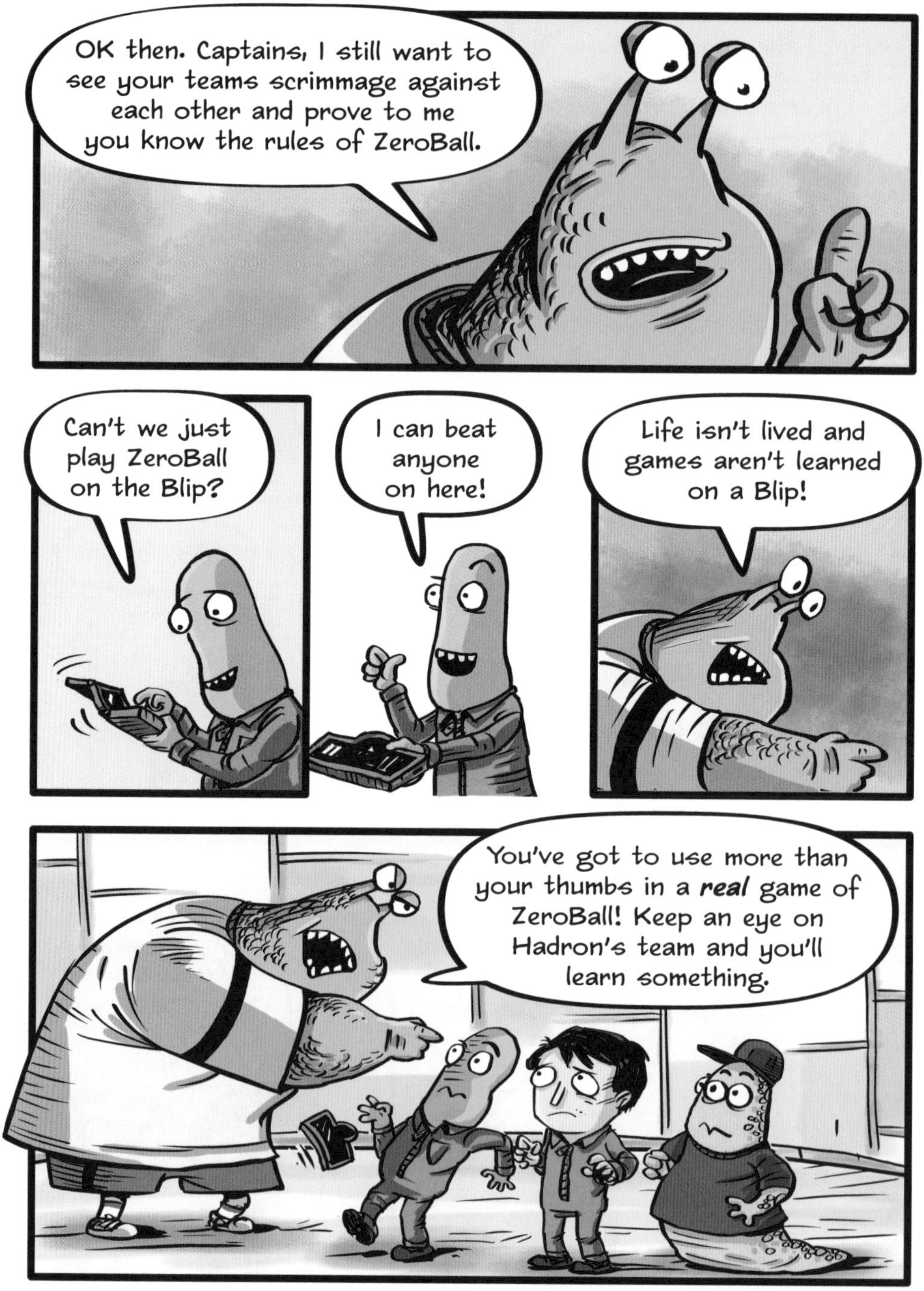
OK then. Captains, I still want to see your teams scrimmage against each other and prove to me you know the rules of ZeroBall.
Can't we just play ZeroBall on the Blip?
I can beat anyone on here!
Life isn't lived and games aren't learned on a Blip!
You've got to use more than your thumbs in a *real* game of ZeroBall! Keep an eye on Hadron's team and you'll learn something.

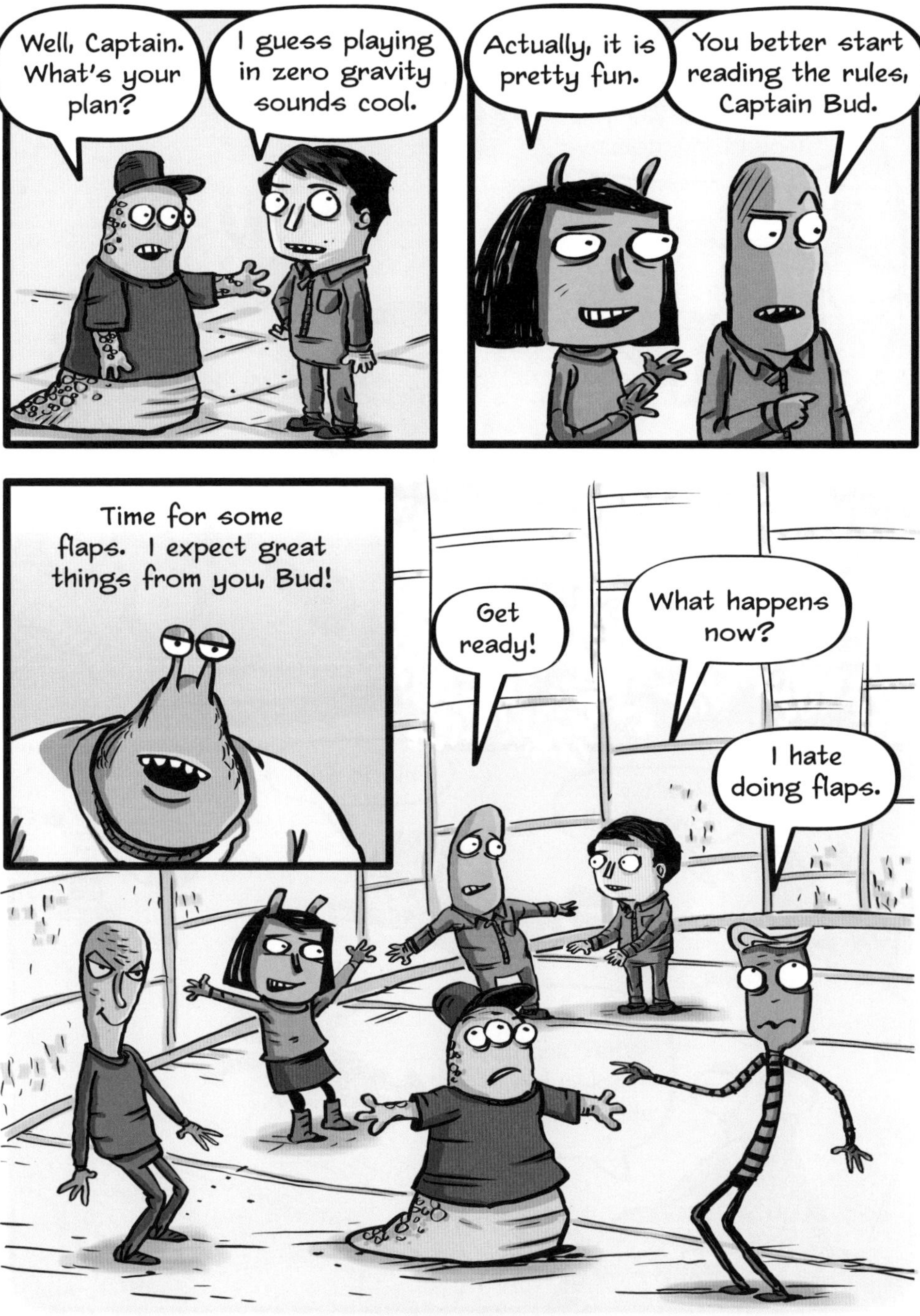
Well, Captain. What's your plan?
I guess playing in zero gravity sounds cool.
Actually, it is pretty fun.
You better start reading the rules, Captain Bud.
Time for some flaps. I expect great things from you, Bud!
Get ready!
What happens now?
I hate doing flaps.

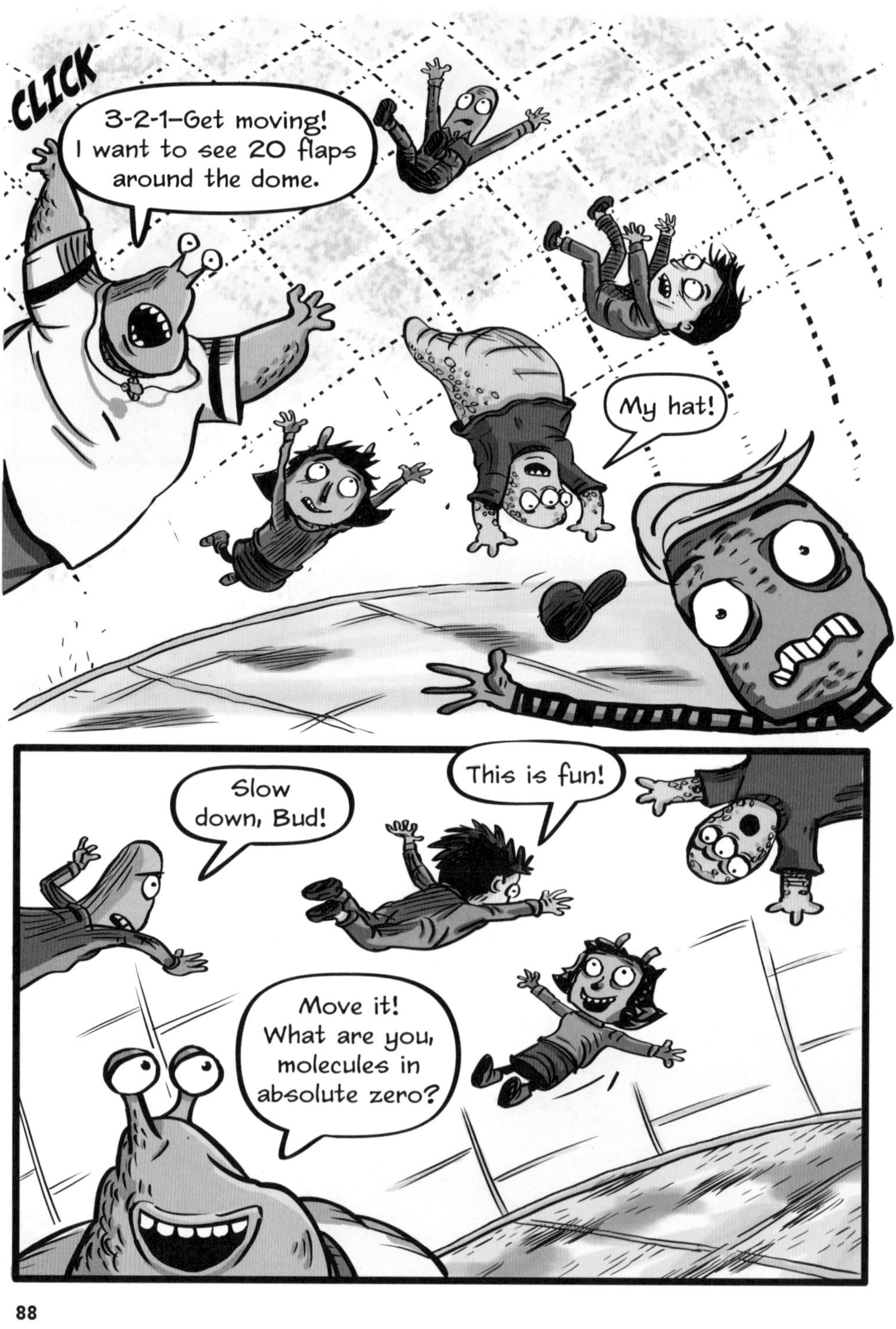
CLICK
3-2-1—Get moving! I want to see 20 flaps around the dome.
My hat!
Slow down, Bud!
This is fun!
Move it! What are you, molecules in absolute zero?

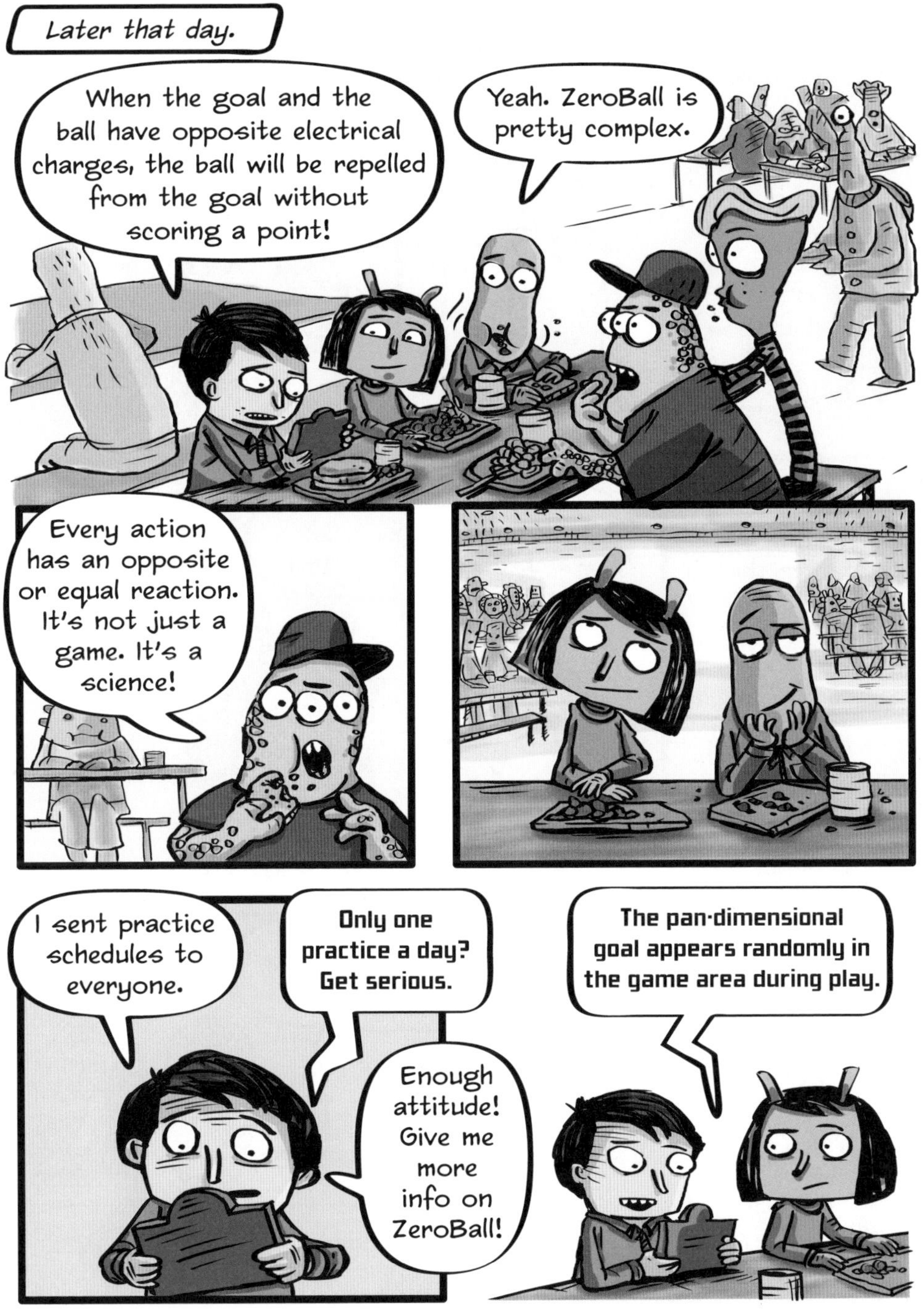
Later that day.
When the goal and the ball have opposite electrical charges, the ball will be repelled from the goal without scoring a point!
Yeah. ZeroBall is pretty complex.
Every action has an opposite or equal reaction. It's not just a game. It's a science!
I sent practice schedules to everyone.
Only one practice a day? Get serious.
Enough attitude! Give me more info on ZeroBall!
The pan-dimensional goal appears randomly in the game area during play.

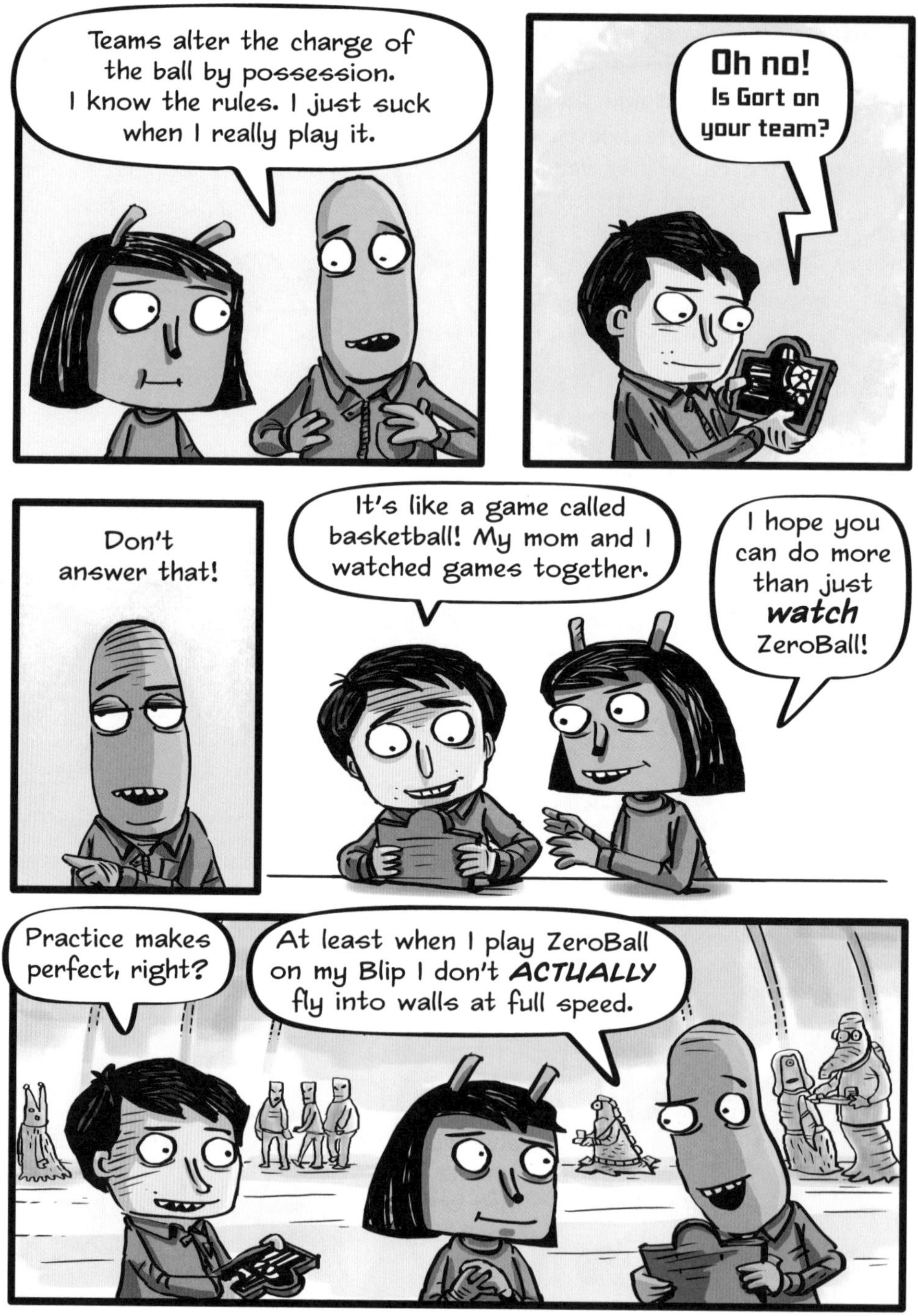
Teams alter the charge of the ball by possession. I know the rules. I just suck when I really play it.
Oh no! Is Gort on your team?
Don't answer that!
It's like a game called basketball! My mom and I watched games together.
I hope you can do more than just ***watch*** ZeroBall!
Practice makes perfect, right?
At least when I play ZeroBall on my Blip I don't ***ACTUALLY*** fly into walls at full speed.

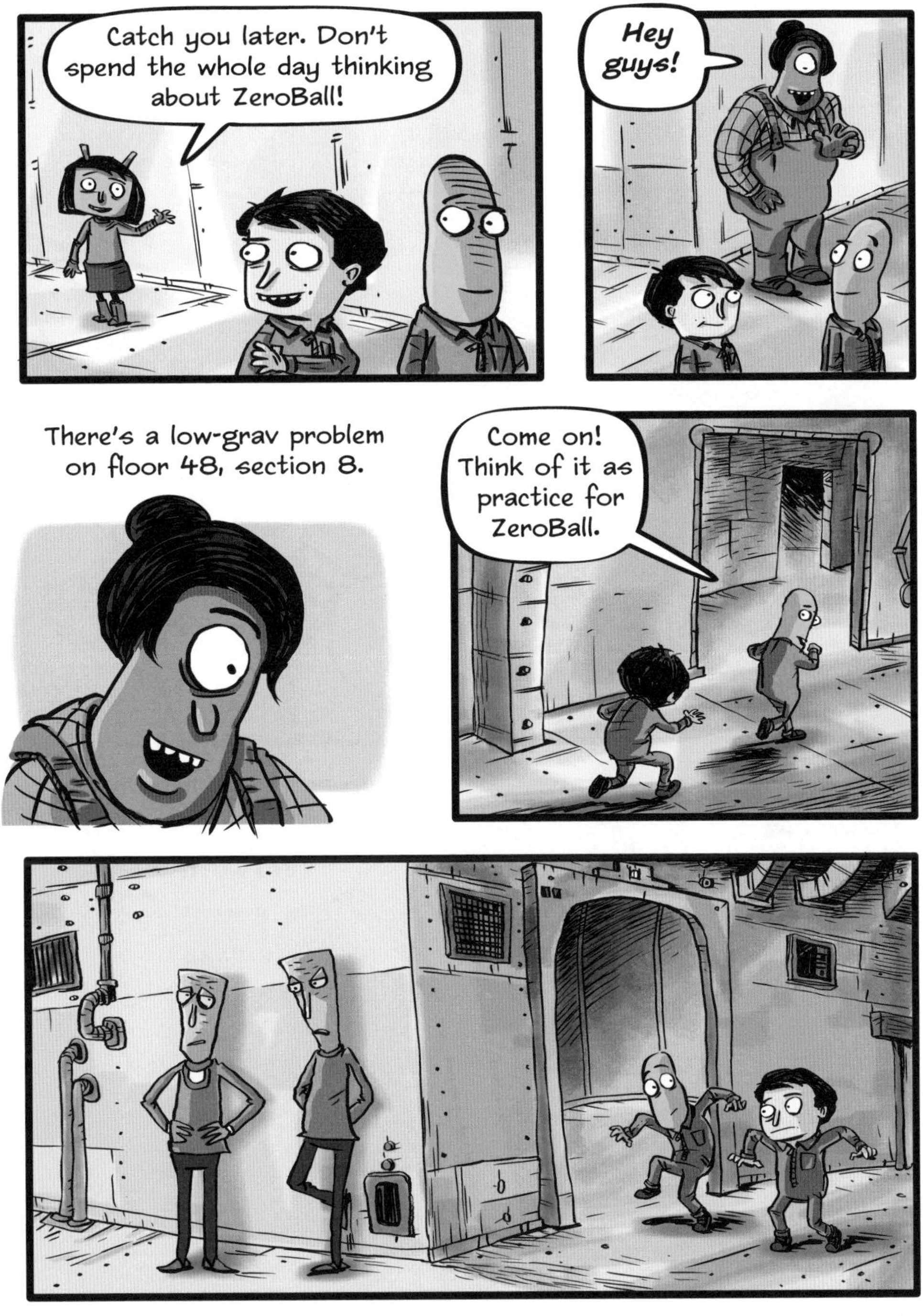

Catch you later. Don't spend the whole day thinking about ZeroBall!
Hey guys!
There's a low-grav problem on floor 48, section 8.
Come on! Think of it as practice for ZeroBall.

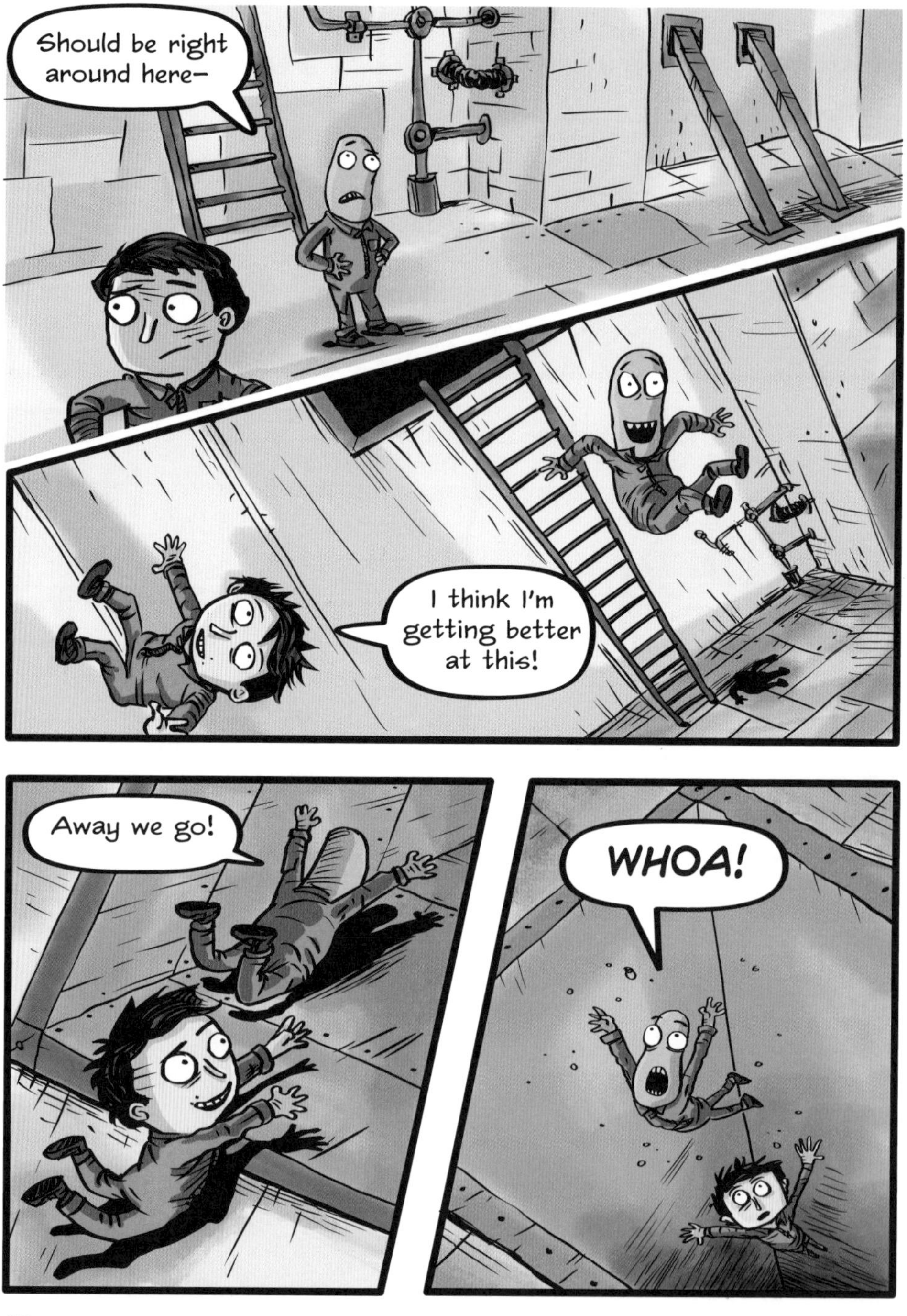
Should be right around here–
I think I'm getting better at this!
Away we go!
WHOA!

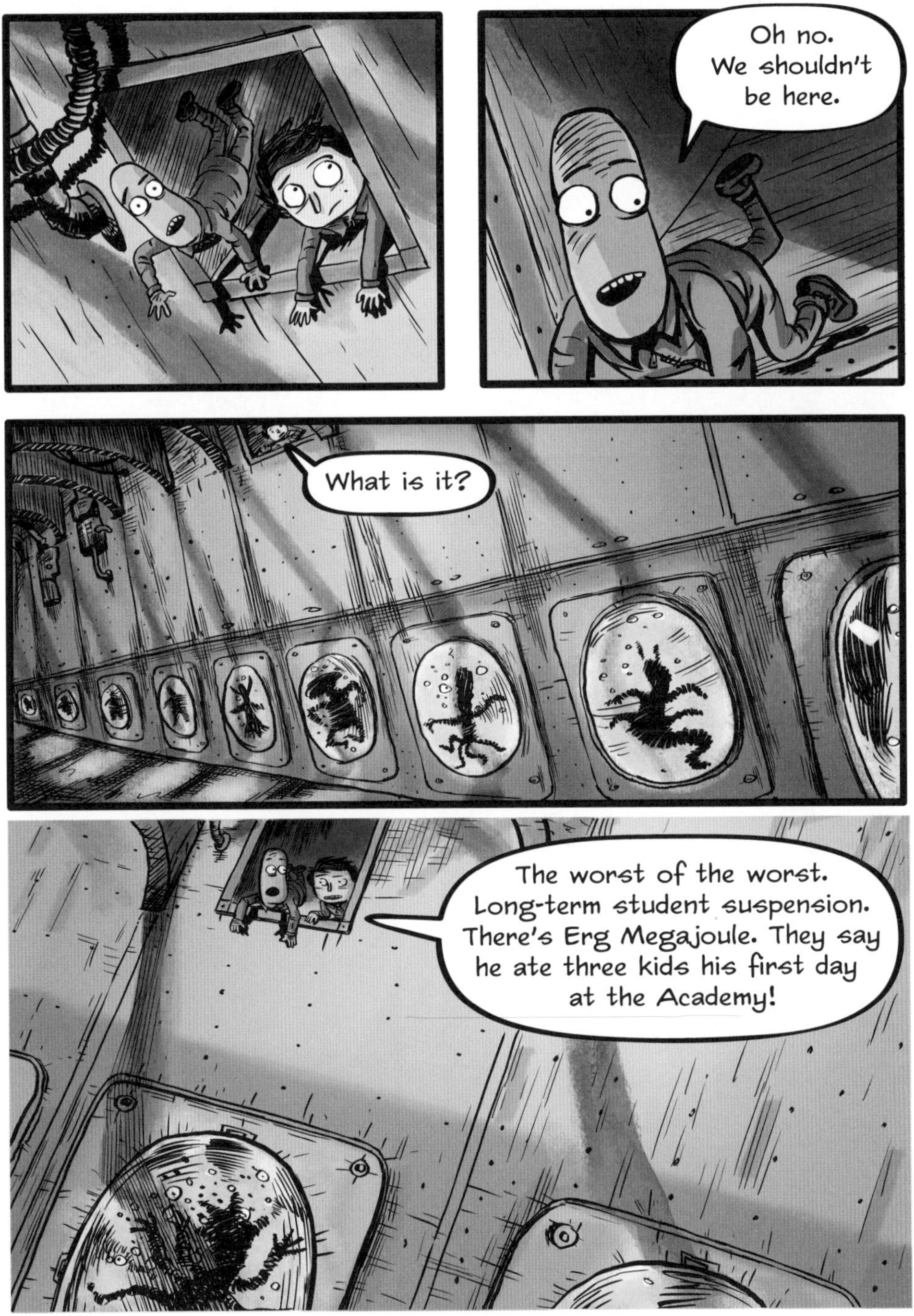
Oh no. We shouldn't be here.
What is it?
The worst of the worst. Long-term student suspension. There's Erg Megajoule. They say he ate three kids his first day at the Academy!

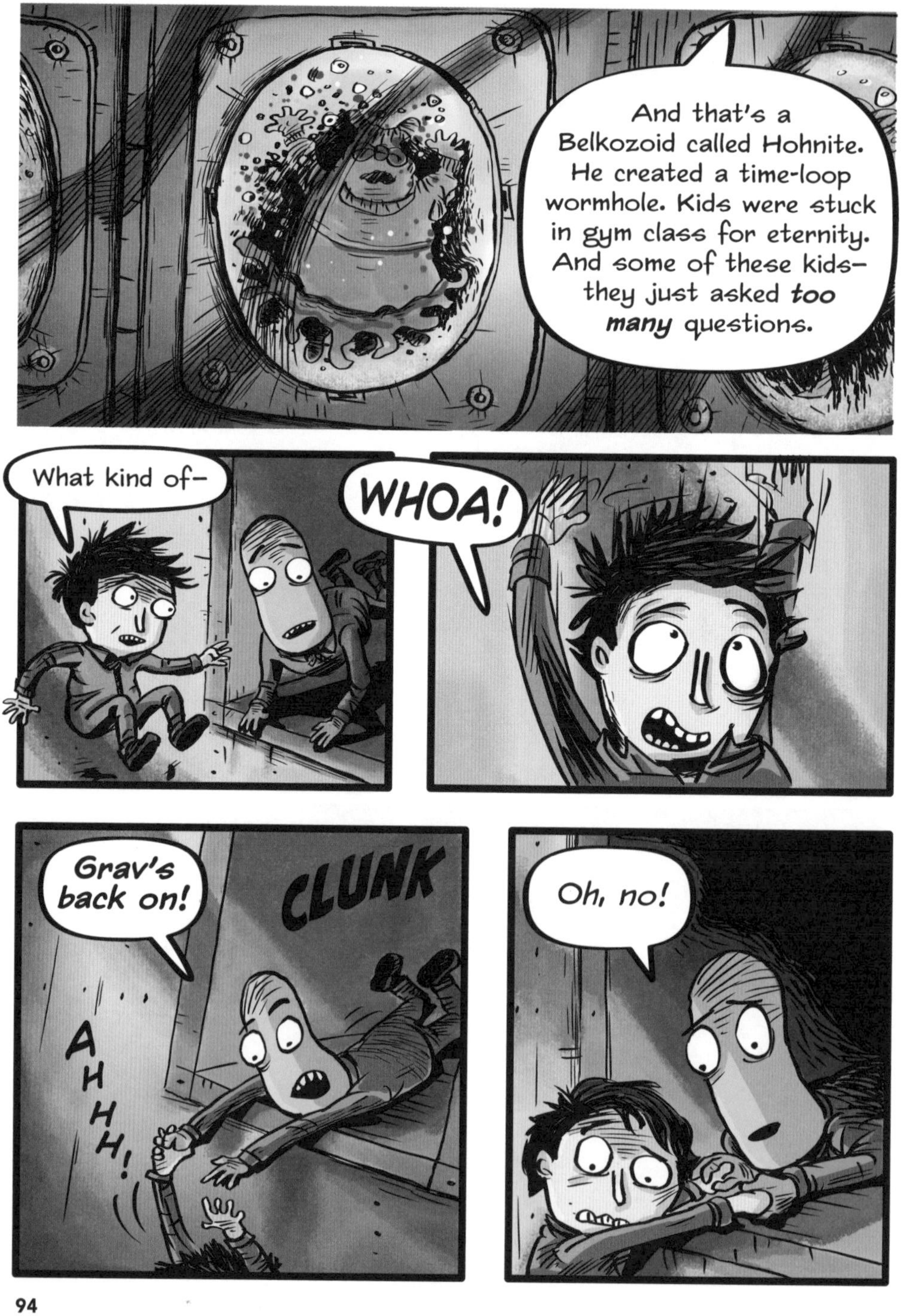
And that's a Belkozoid called Hohnite. He created a time-loop wormhole. Kids were stuck in gym class for eternity. And some of these kids–they just asked *too many* questions.
What kind of–
WHOA!
Grav's back on!
CLUNK
AHHH!
Oh, no!

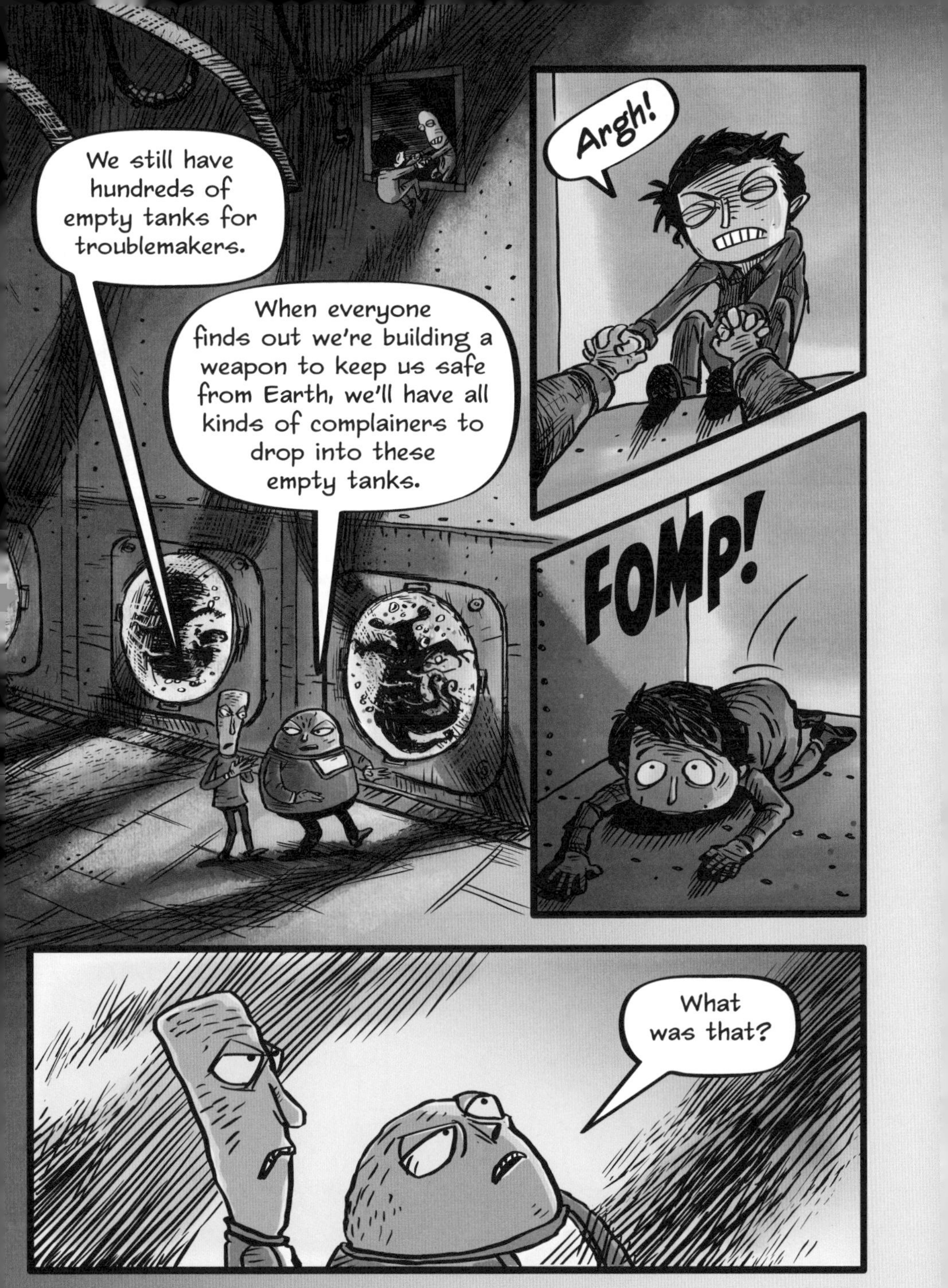
We still have hundreds of empty tanks for troublemakers.
When everyone finds out we're building a weapon to keep us safe from Earth, we'll have all kinds of complainers to drop into these empty tanks.
Argh!
FOMP!
What was that?

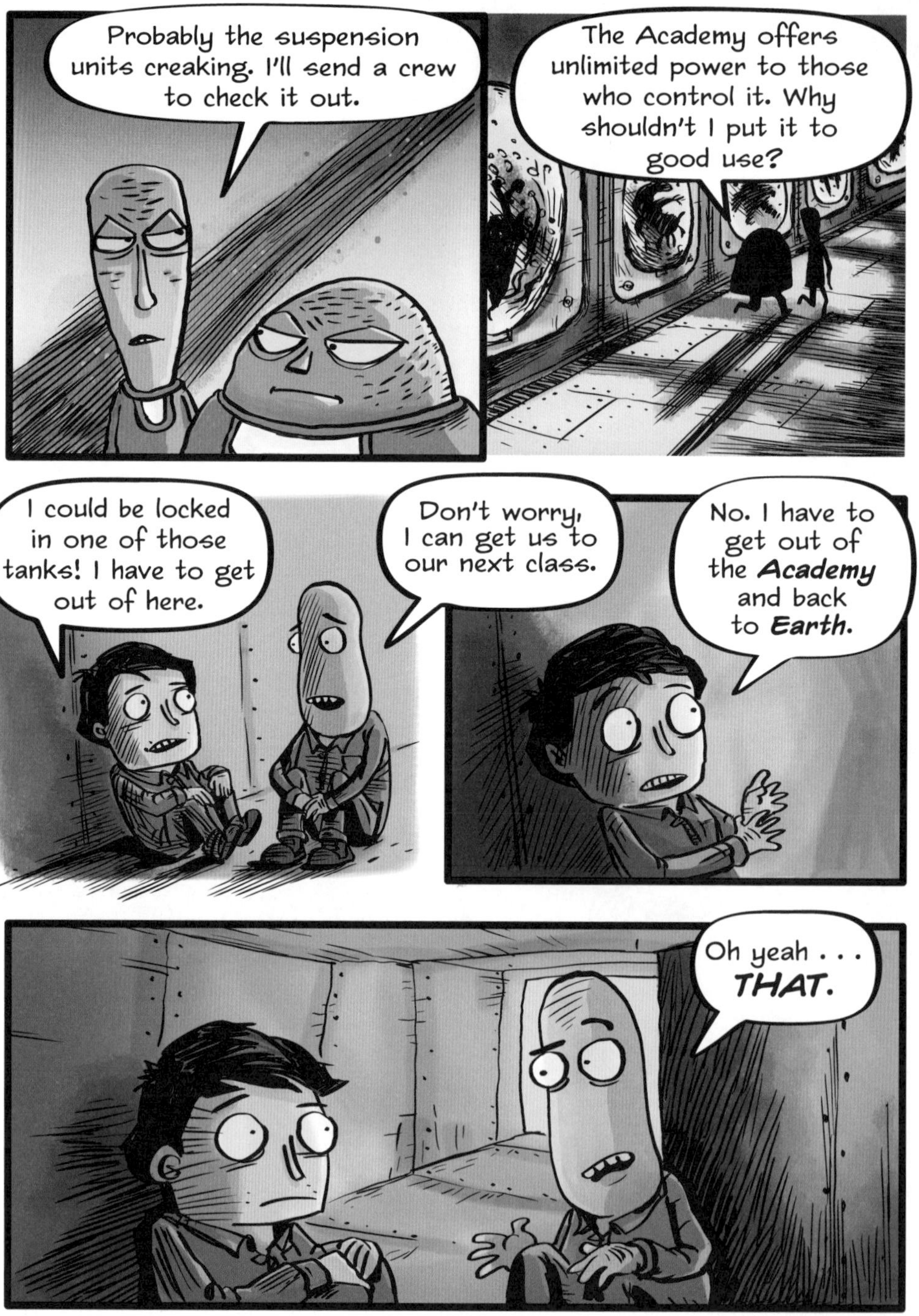
Probably the suspension units creaking. I'll send a crew to check it out.
The Academy offers unlimited power to those who control it. Why shouldn't I put it to good use?
I could be locked in one of those tanks! I have to get out of here.
Don't worry, I can get us to our next class.
No. I have to get out of the ***Academy*** and back to ***Earth***.
Oh yeah . . . ***THAT***.

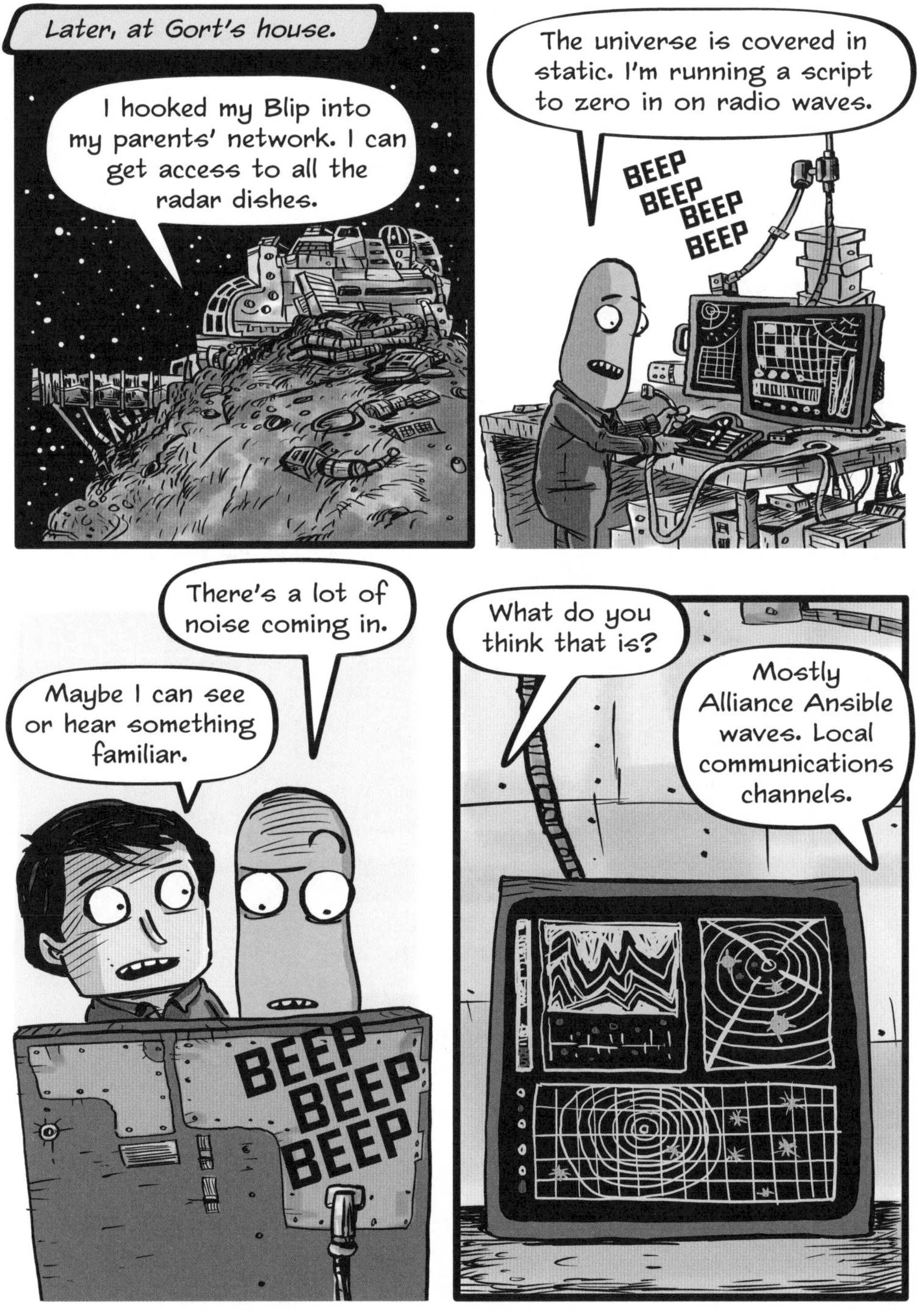
Later, at Gort's house.
I hooked my Blip into my parents' network. I can get access to all the radar dishes.
The universe is covered in static. I'm running a script to zero in on radio waves.
BEEP BEEP BEEP BEEP
There's a lot of noise coming in.
Maybe I can see or hear something familiar.
BEEP BEEP BEEP
What do you think that is?
Mostly Alliance Ansible waves. Local communications channels.

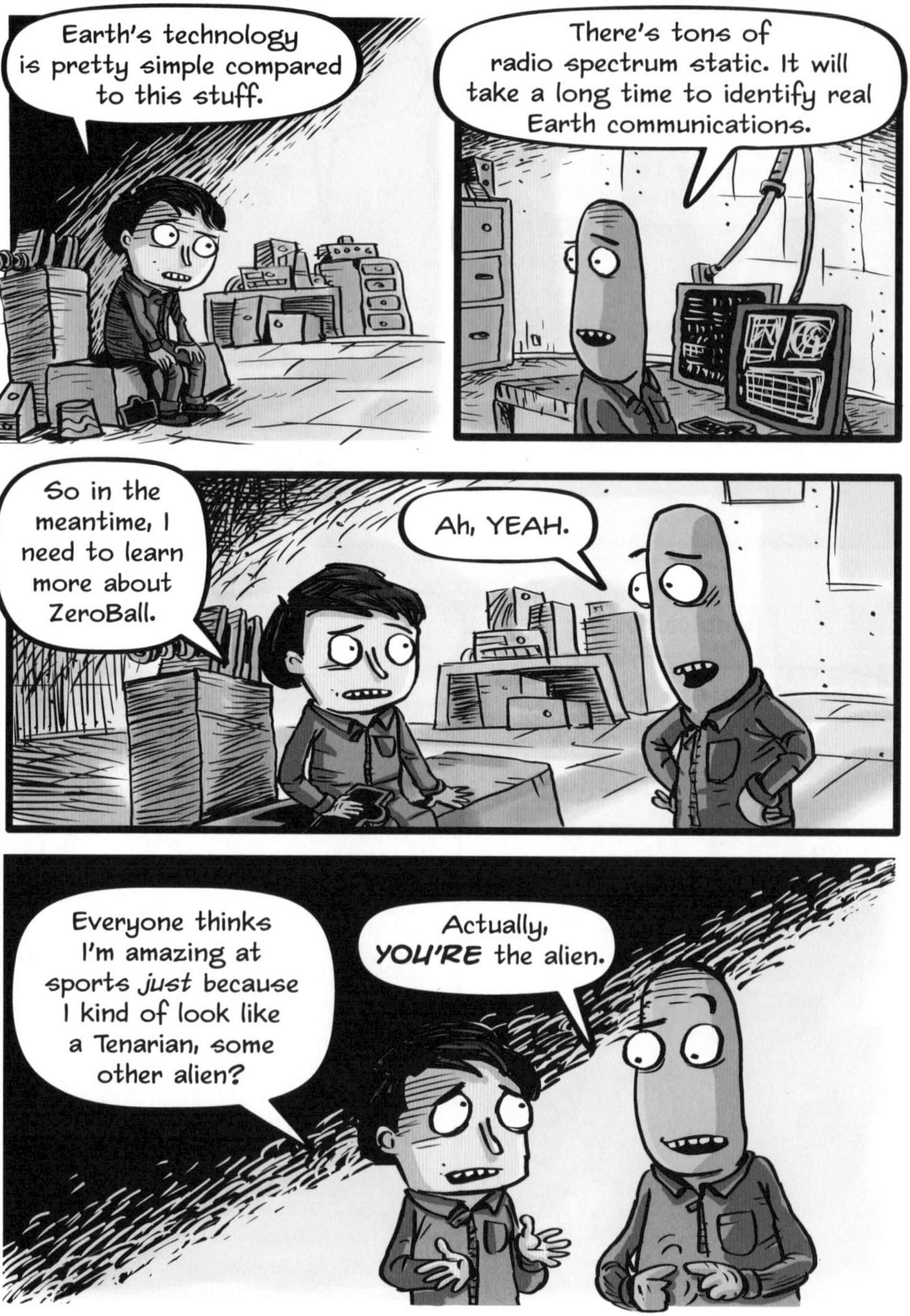

Earth's technology is pretty simple compared to this stuff.
There's tons of radio spectrum static. It will take a long time to identify real Earth communications.
So in the meantime, I need to learn more about ZeroBall.
Ah, YEAH.
Everyone thinks I'm amazing at sports *just* because I kind of look like a Tenarian, some other alien?
Actually, ***YOU'RE*** the alien.

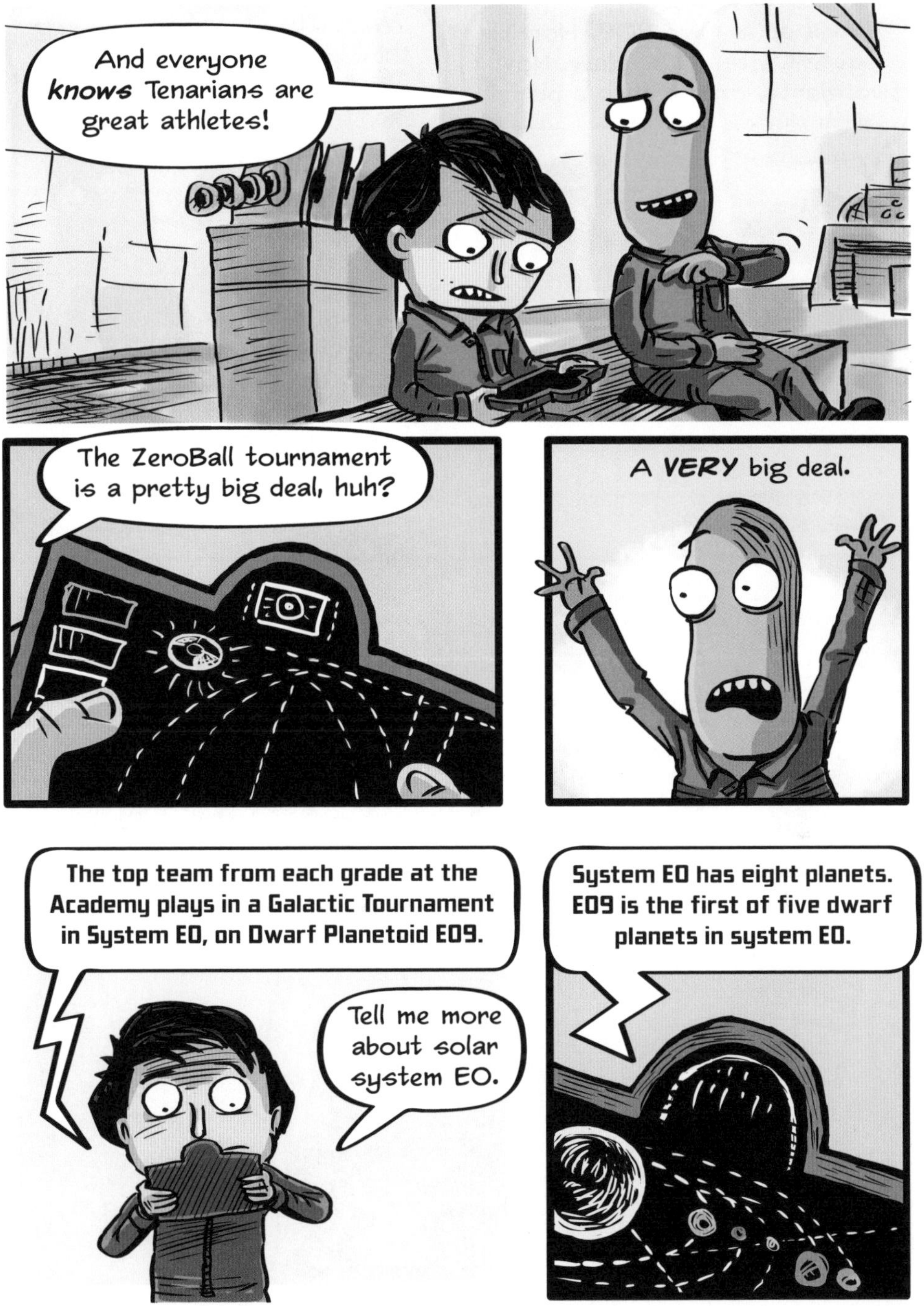
And everyone **knows** Tenarians are great athletes!
The ZeroBall tournament is a pretty big deal, huh?
A **VERY** big deal.
The top team from each grade at the Academy plays in a Galactic Tournament in System E0, on Dwarf Planetoid E09.
Tell me more about solar system E0.
System E0 has eight planets. E09 is the first of five dwarf planets in system E0.

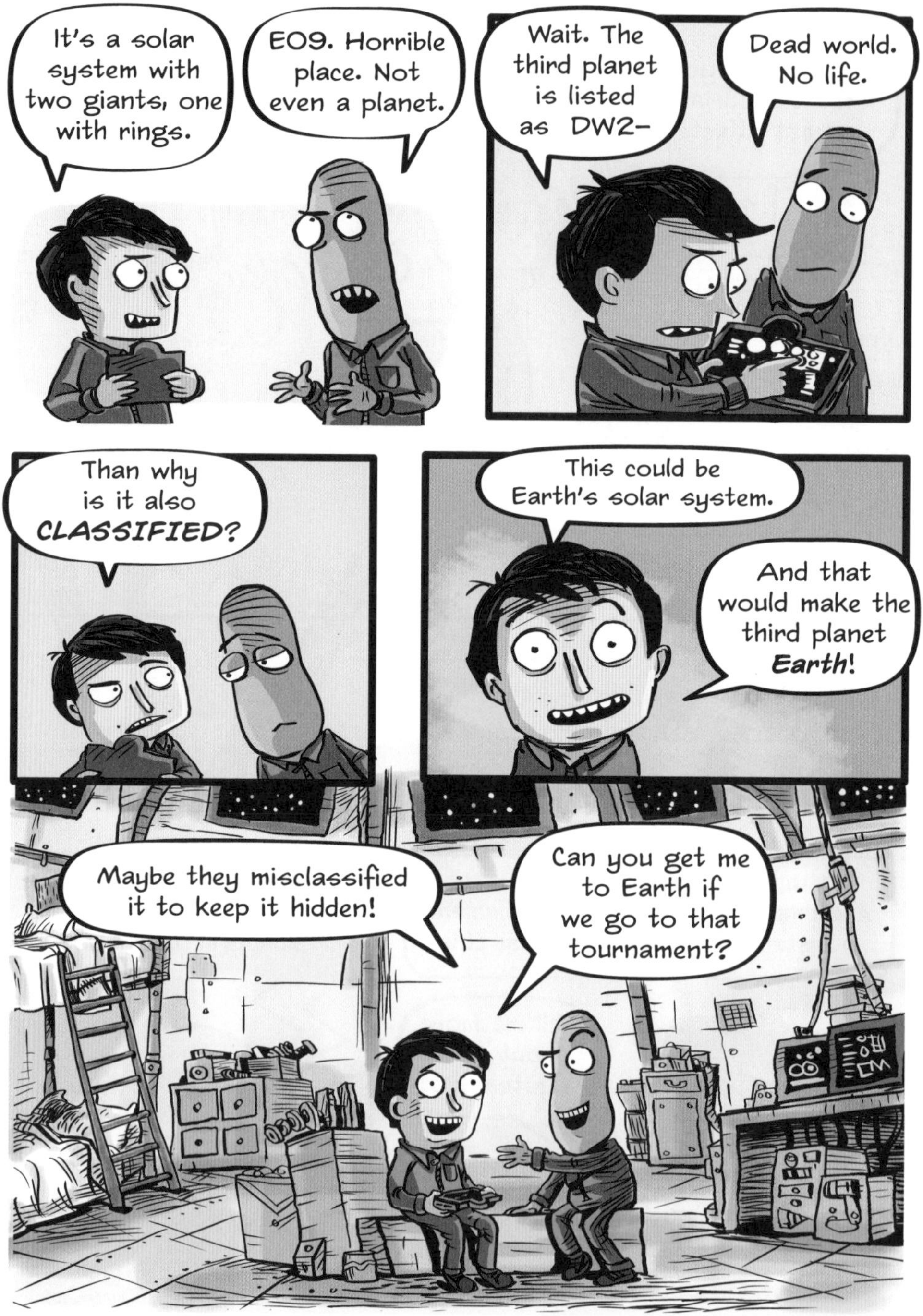
It's a solar system with two giants, one with rings.
E09. Horrible place. Not even a planet.
Wait. The third planet is listed as DW2–
Dead world. No life.
Than why is it also *CLASSIFIED*?
This could be Earth's solar system.
And that would make the third planet *Earth*!
Maybe they misclassified it to keep it hidden!
Can you get me to Earth if we go to that tournament?

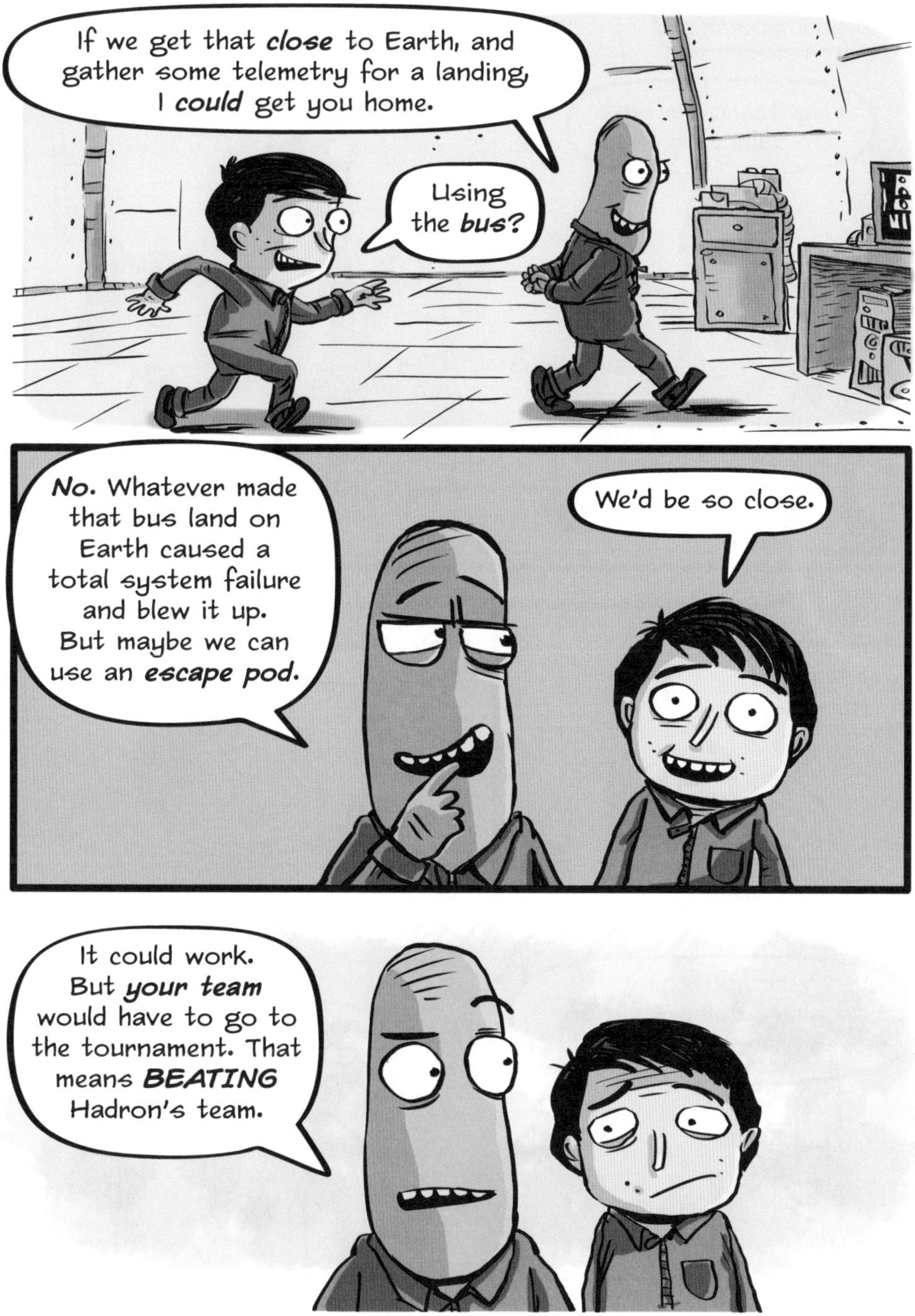
If we get that *close* to Earth, and gather some telemetry for a landing, I *could* get you home.
Using the *bus?*
No. Whatever made that bus land on Earth caused a total system failure and blew it up. But maybe we can use an *escape pod.*
We'd be so close.
It could work. But *your team* would have to go to the tournament. That means *BEATING* Hadron's team.

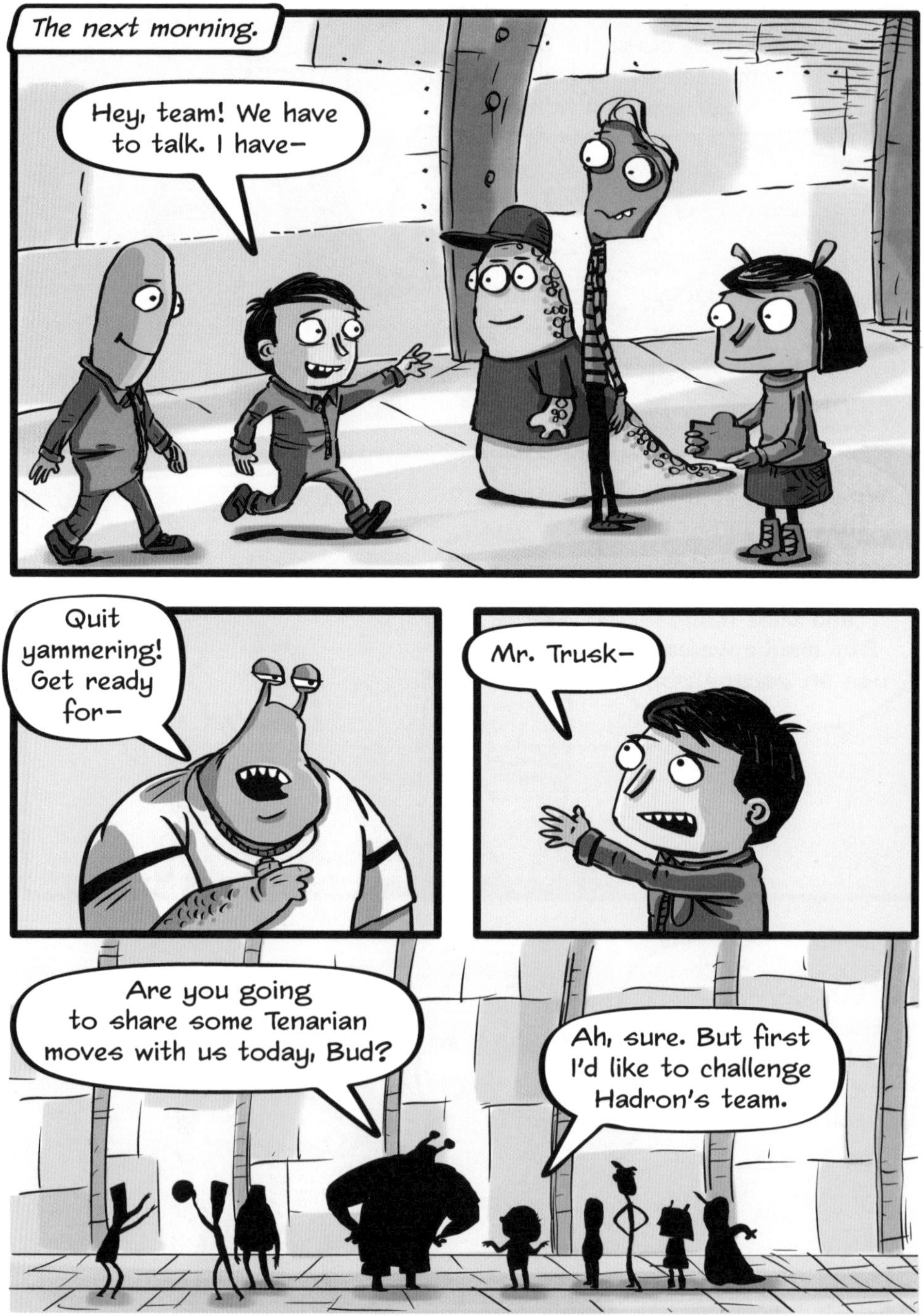
The next morning.
Hey, team! We have to talk. I have–
Quit yammering! Get ready for–
Mr. Trusk–
Are you going to share some Tenarian moves with us today, Bud?
Ah, sure. But first I'd like to challenge Hadron's team.

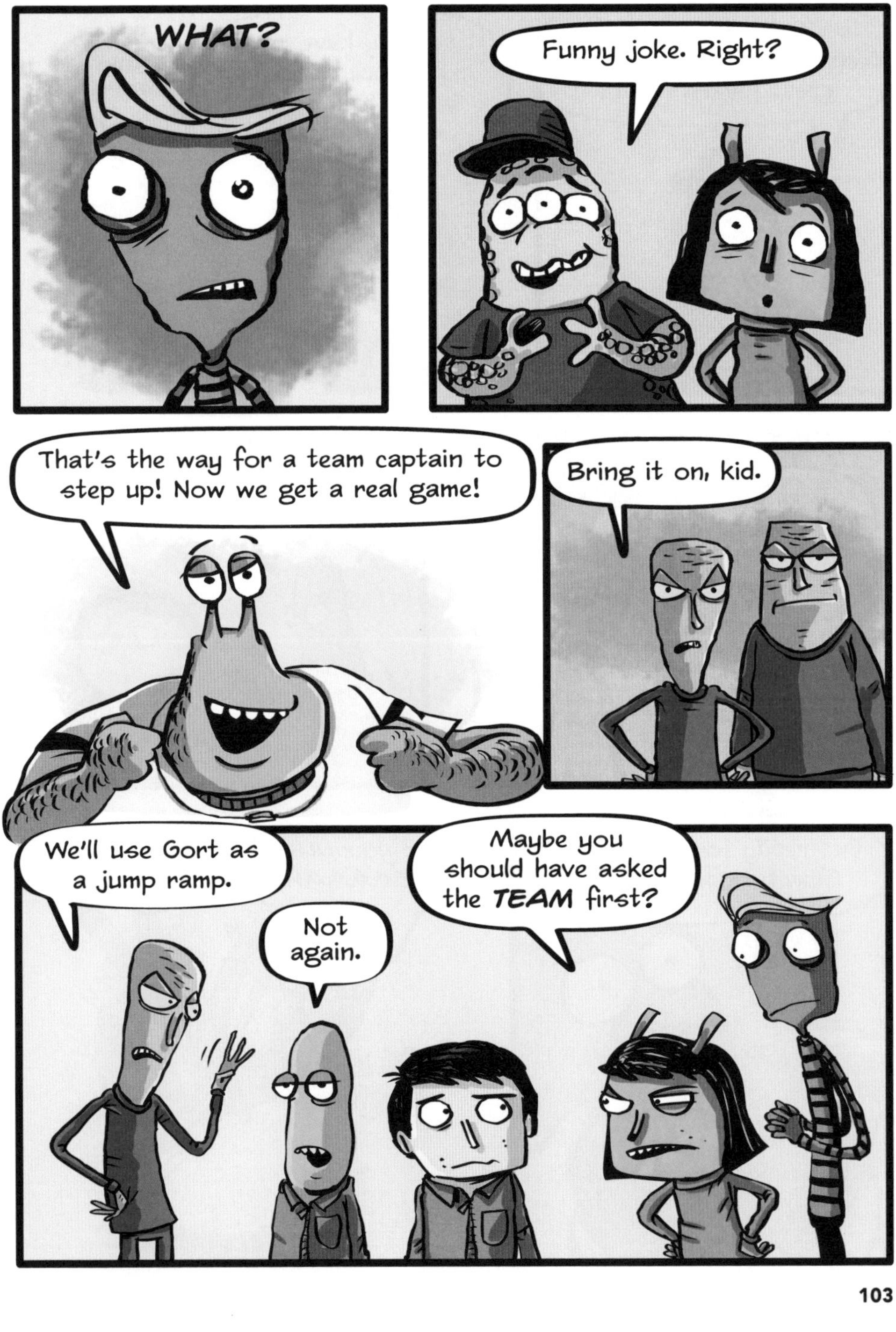

WHAT?
Funny joke. Right?
That's the way for a team captain to step up! Now we get a real game!
Bring it on, kid.
We'll use Gort as a jump ramp.
Not again.
Maybe you should have asked the TEAM first?

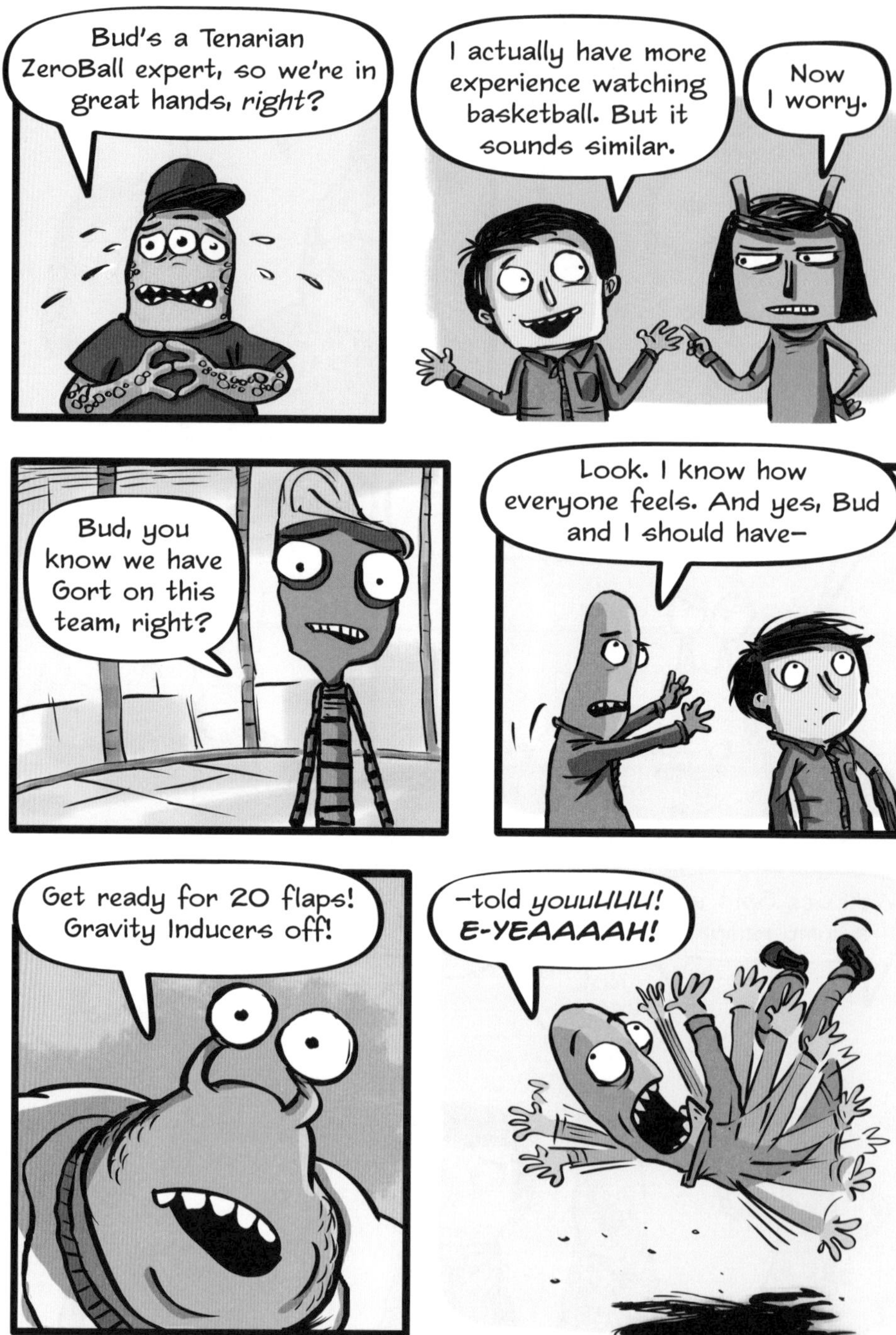
Bud's a Tenarian ZeroBall expert, so we're in great hands, *right*?
I actually have more experience watching basketball. But it sounds similar.
Now I worry.
Bud, you know we have Gort on this team, right?
Look. I know how everyone feels. And yes, Bud and I should have–
Get ready for 20 flaps! Gravity Inducers off!
–told *youuUUU*!
E-YEAAAAH!

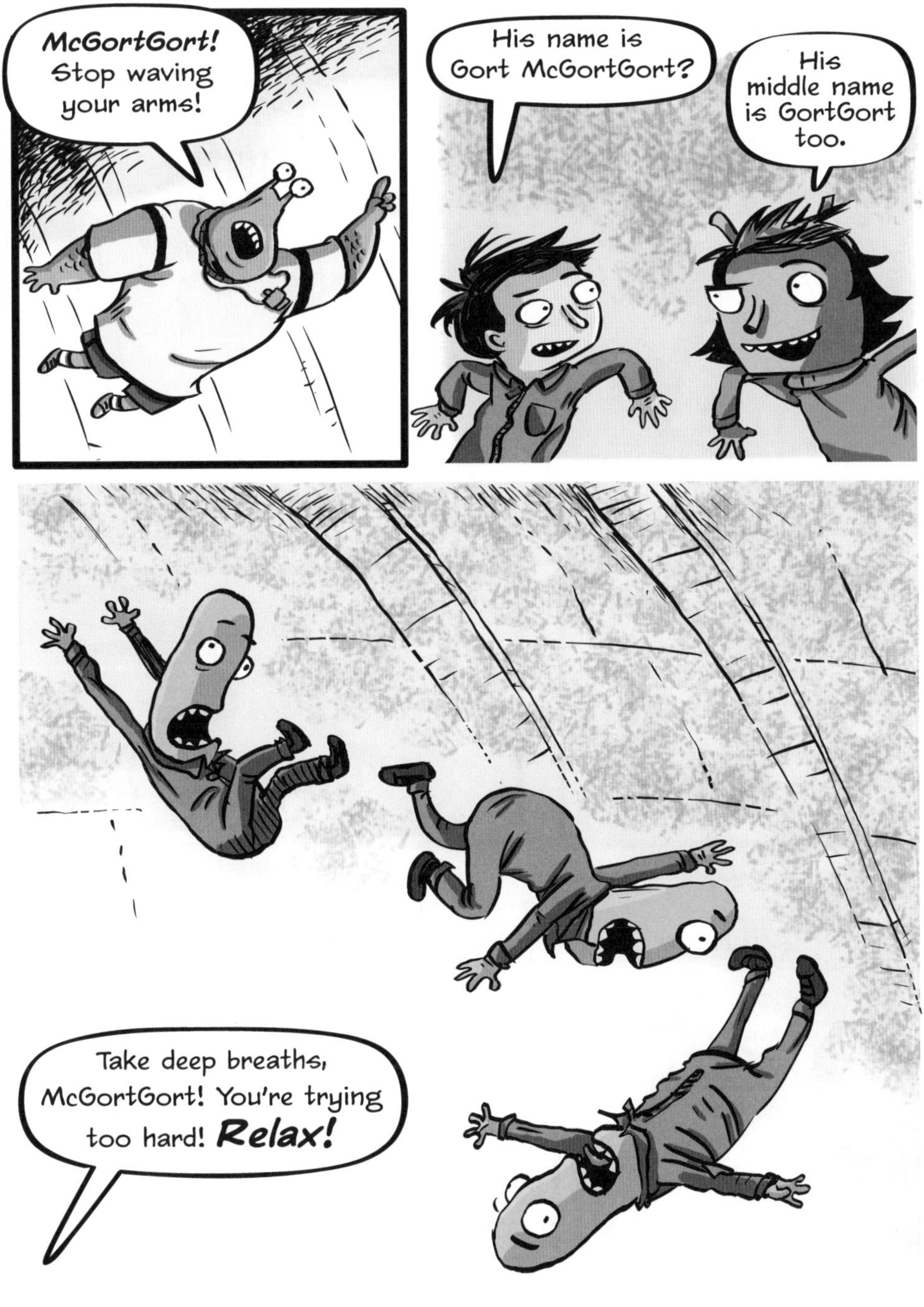

McGortGort! Stop waving your arms!
His name is Gort McGortGort?
His middle name is GortGort too.
Take deep breaths, McGortGort! You're trying too hard! Relax!

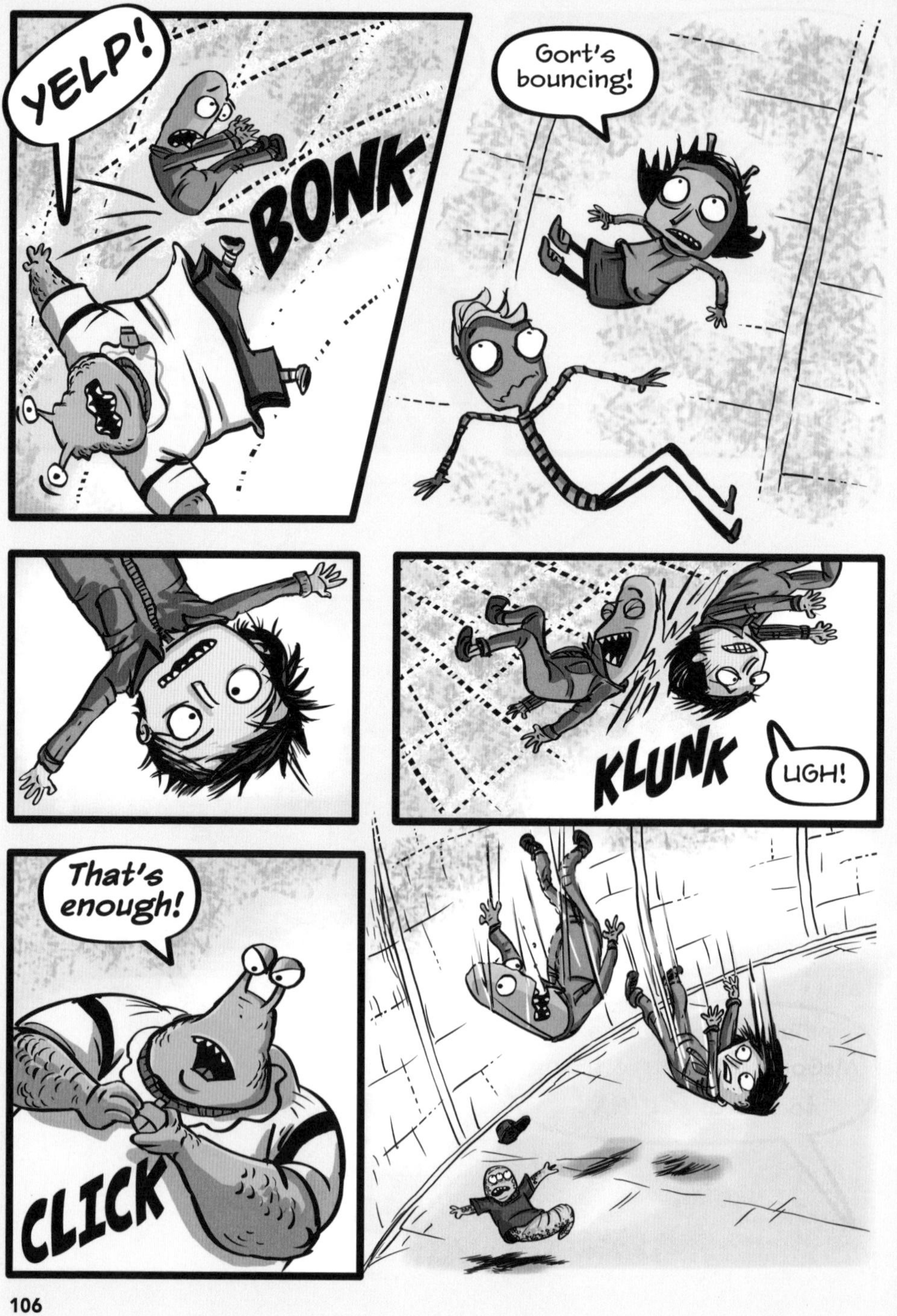
YELP!
BONK
Gort's bouncing!
KLUNK
UGH!
That's enough!
CLICK

PLOP

That wasn't so bad!

Why don't you just take the written test?

He's better off taking a molecular knitting class!

HAHAHAHA! HAR-HAR-HAR HEEHEE!

Go ahead and laugh! It won't be so funny—when you stop laughing.

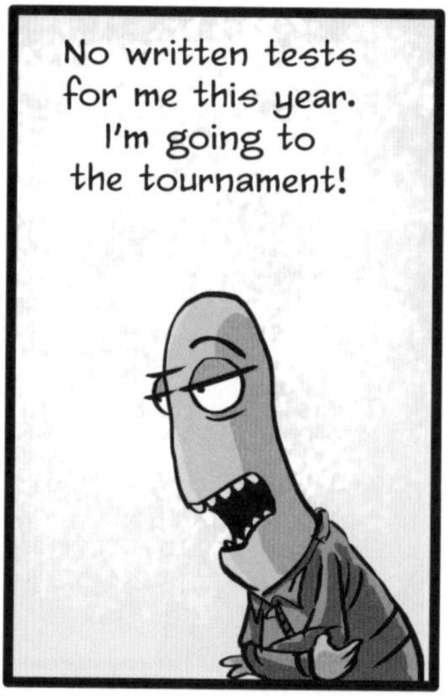
No written tests for me this year. I'm going to the tournament!

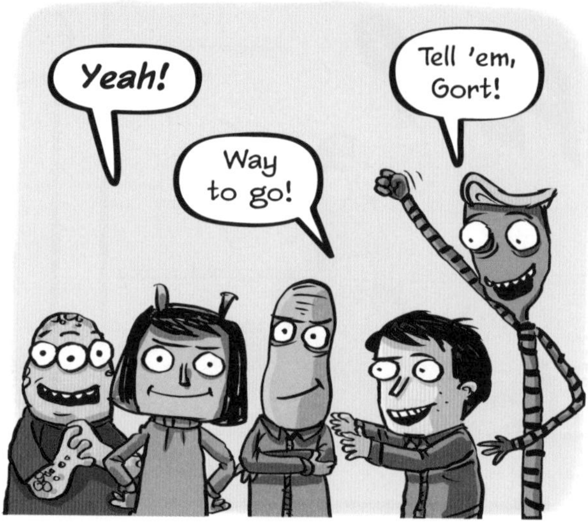
Yeah!
Way to go!
Tell 'em, Gort!

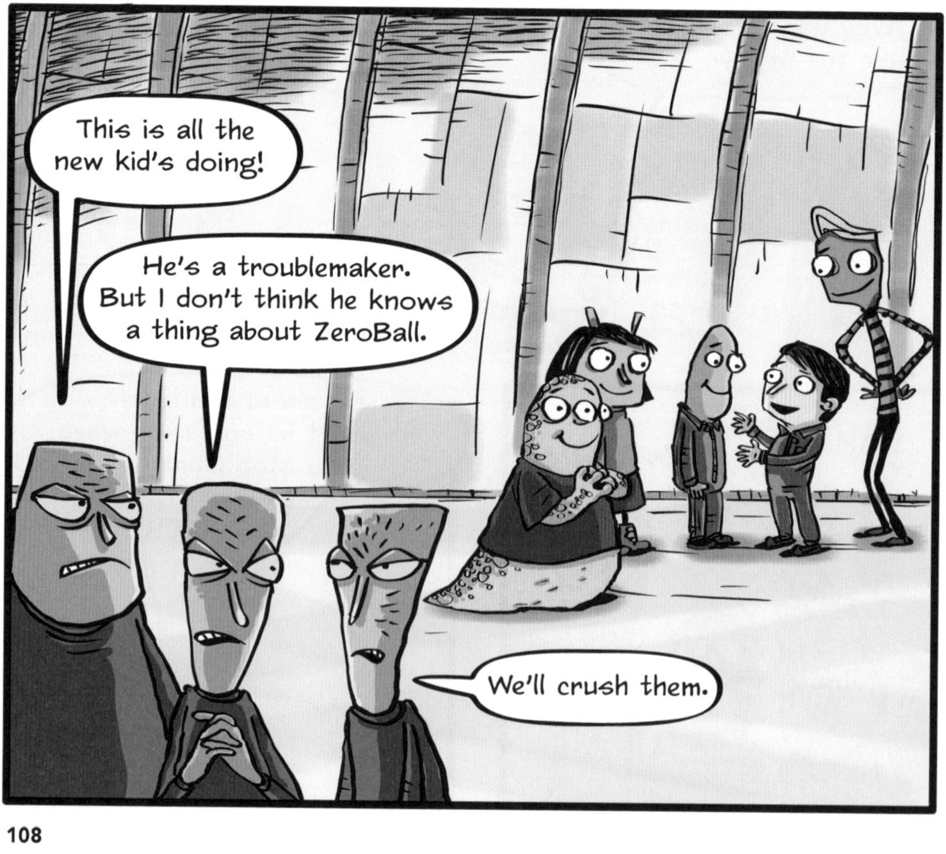
This is all the new kid's doing!
He's a troublemaker. But I don't think he knows a thing about ZeroBall.
We'll crush them.

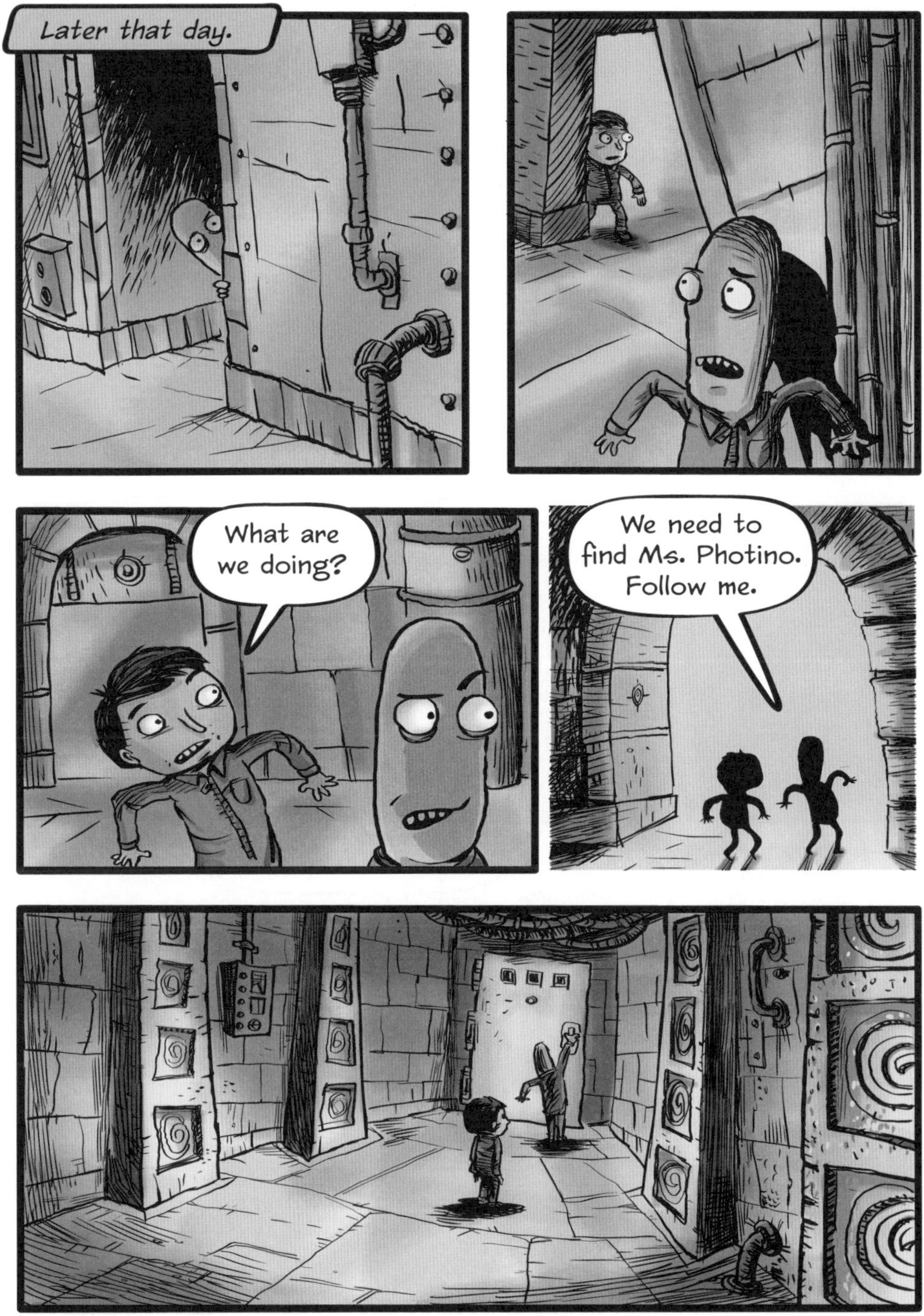
Later that day.
What are we doing?
We need to find Ms. Photino. Follow me.

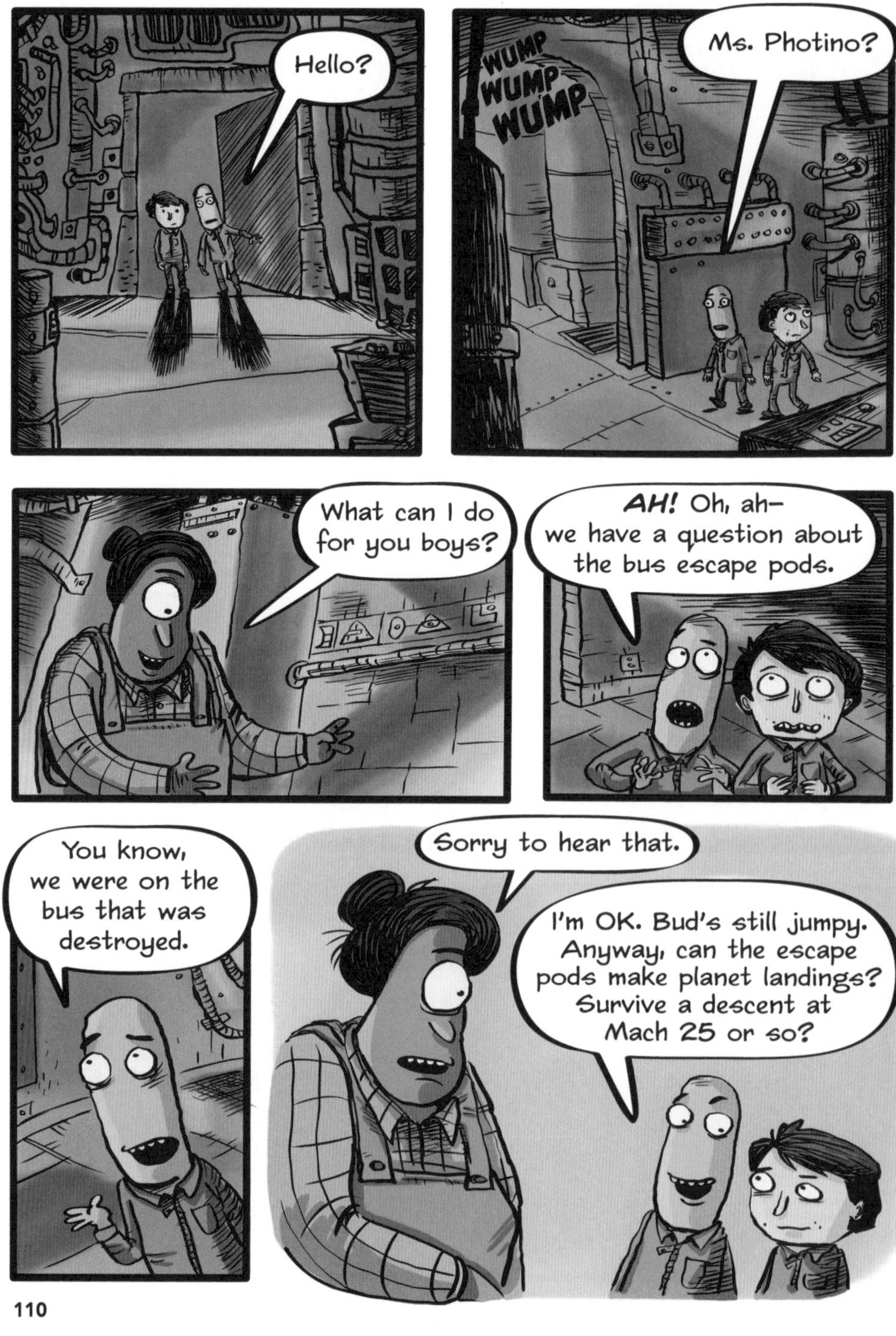
Hello?
WUMP
WUMP
WUMP
Ms. Photino?
What can I do for you boys?
AH! Oh, ah— we have a question about the bus escape pods.
You know, we were on the bus that was destroyed.
Sorry to hear that.
I'm OK. Bud's still jumpy. Anyway, can the escape pods make planet landings? Survive a descent at Mach 25 or so?

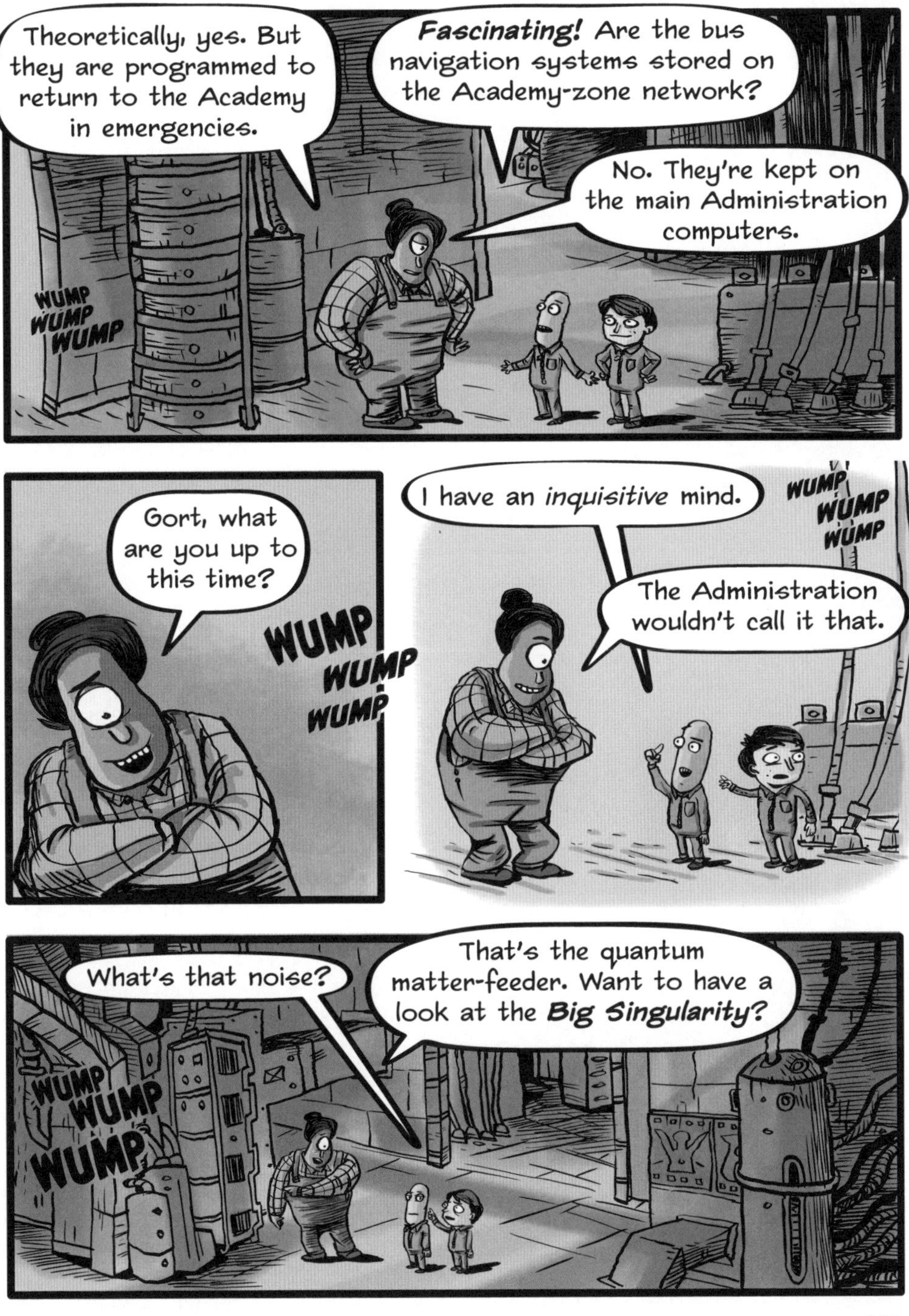
Theoretically, yes. But they are programmed to return to the Academy in emergencies.
Fascinating! Are the bus navigation systems stored on the Academy-zone network?
No. They're kept on the main Administration computers.
WUMP WUMP WUMP
Gort, what are you up to this time?
WUMP WUMP WUMP
I have an *inquisitive* mind.
WUMP WUMP WUMP
The Administration wouldn't call it that.
What's that noise?
That's the quantum matter-feeder. Want to have a look at the ***Big Singularity***?
WUMP WUMP WUMP

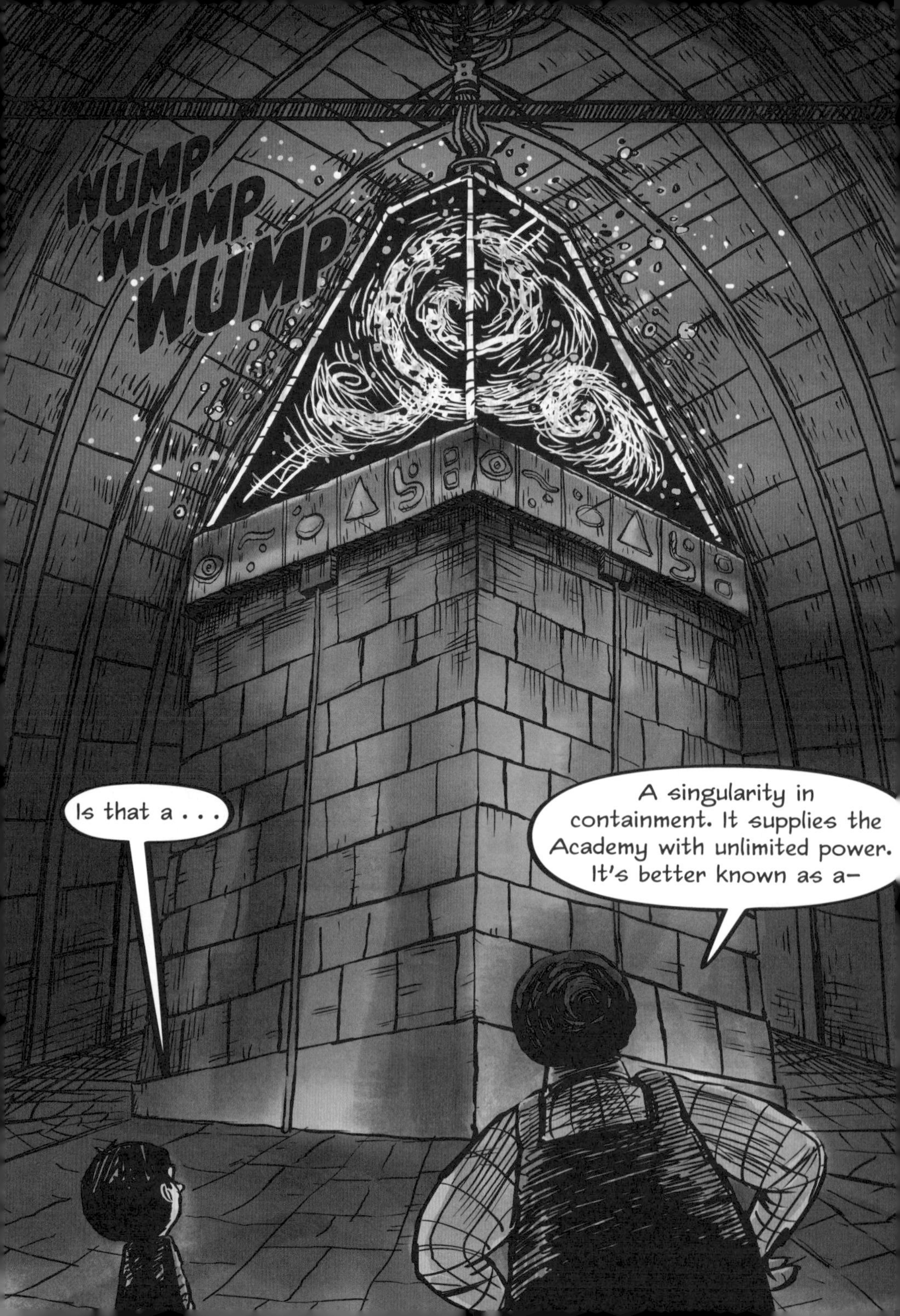
WUMP WUMP WUMP
Is that a . . .
A singularity in containment. It supplies the Academy with unlimited power. It's better known as a–

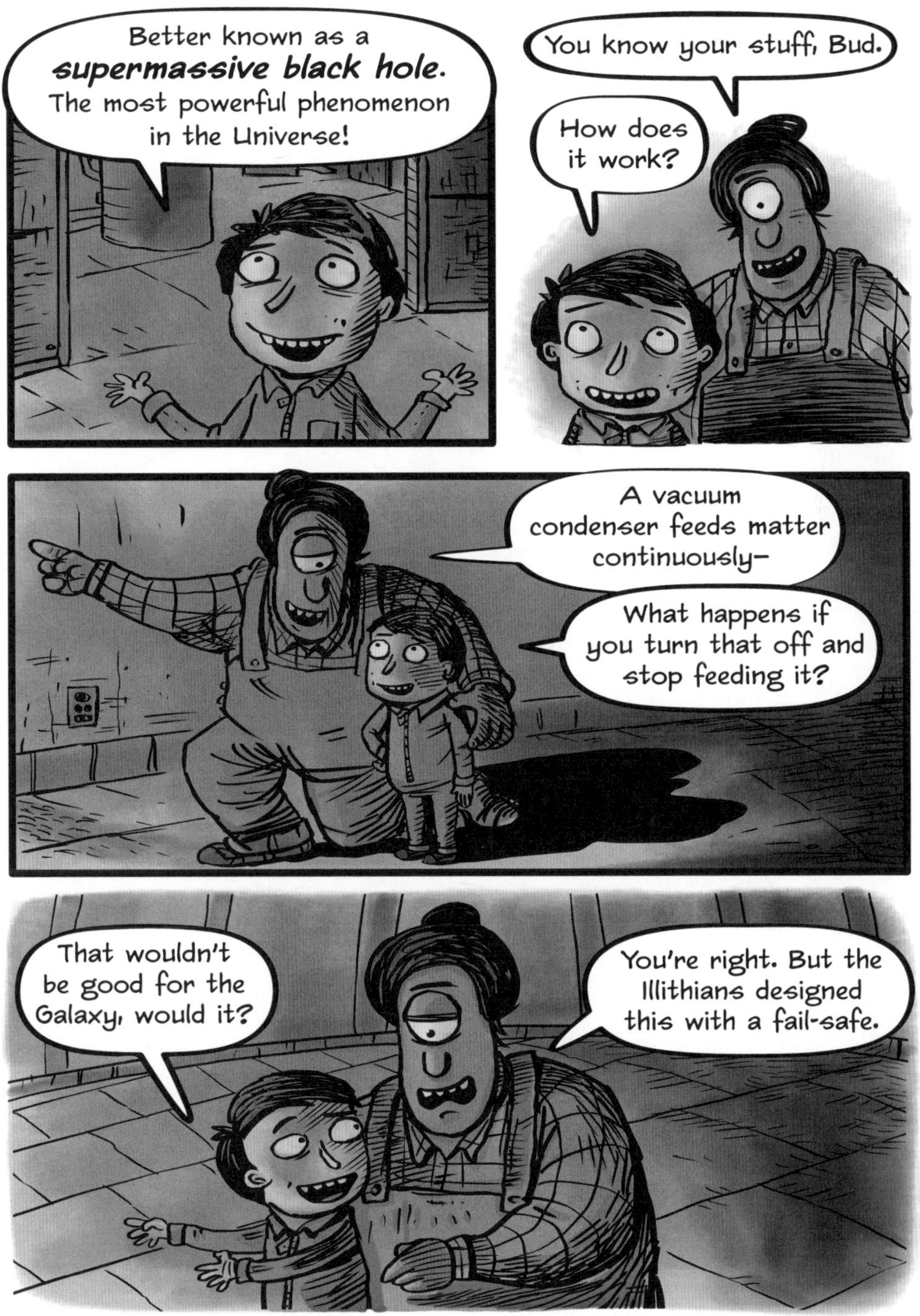
Better known as a *supermassive black hole.* The most powerful phenomenon in the Universe!
You know your stuff, Bud.
How does it work?
A vacuum condenser feeds matter continuously–
What happens if you turn that off and stop feeding it?
That wouldn't be good for the Galaxy, would it?
You're right. But the Illithians designed this with a fail-safe.

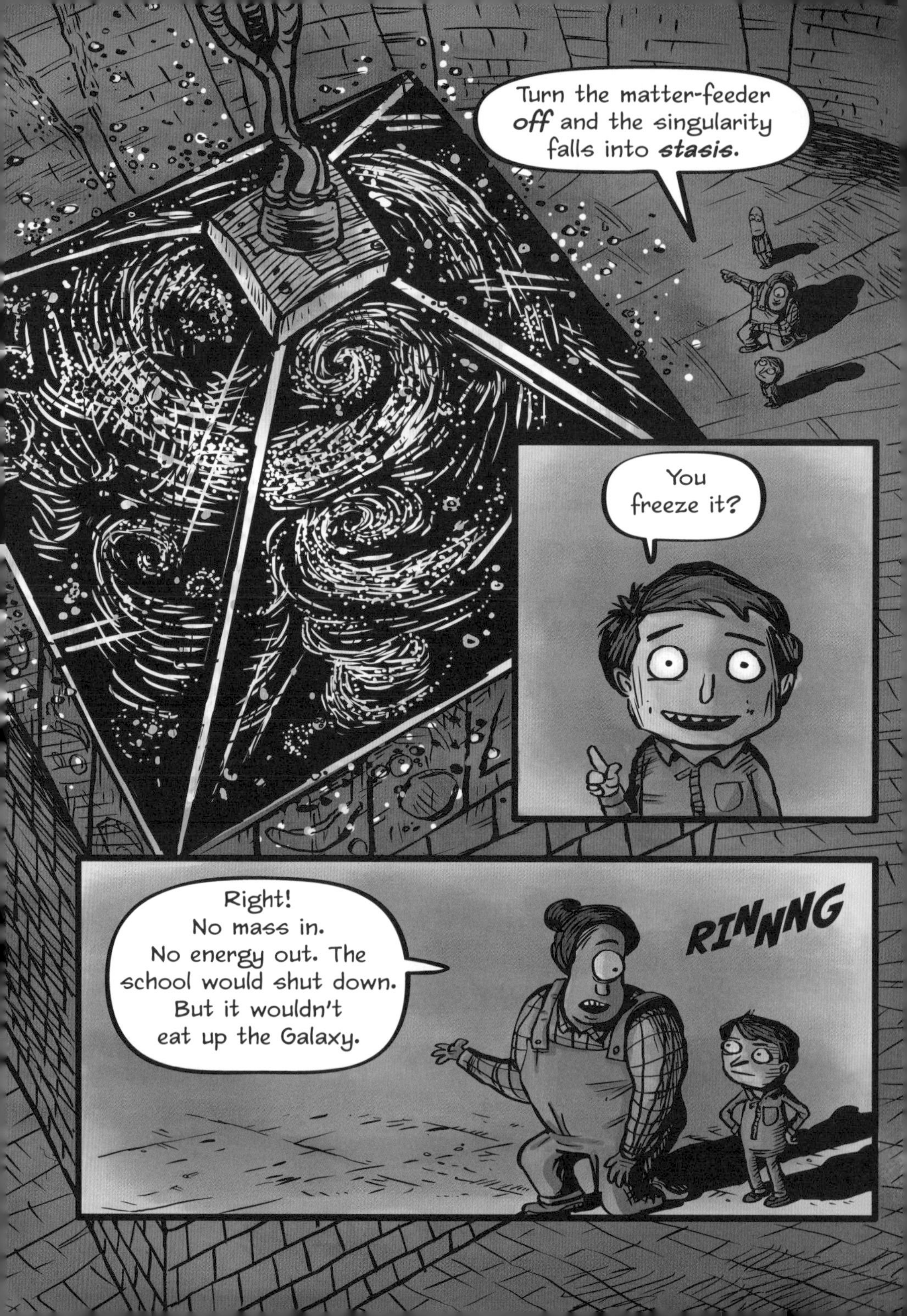
Turn the matter-feeder *off* and the singularity falls into *stasis.*
You freeze it?
Right! No mass in. No energy out. The school would shut down. But it wouldn't eat up the Galaxy.
RINNNG

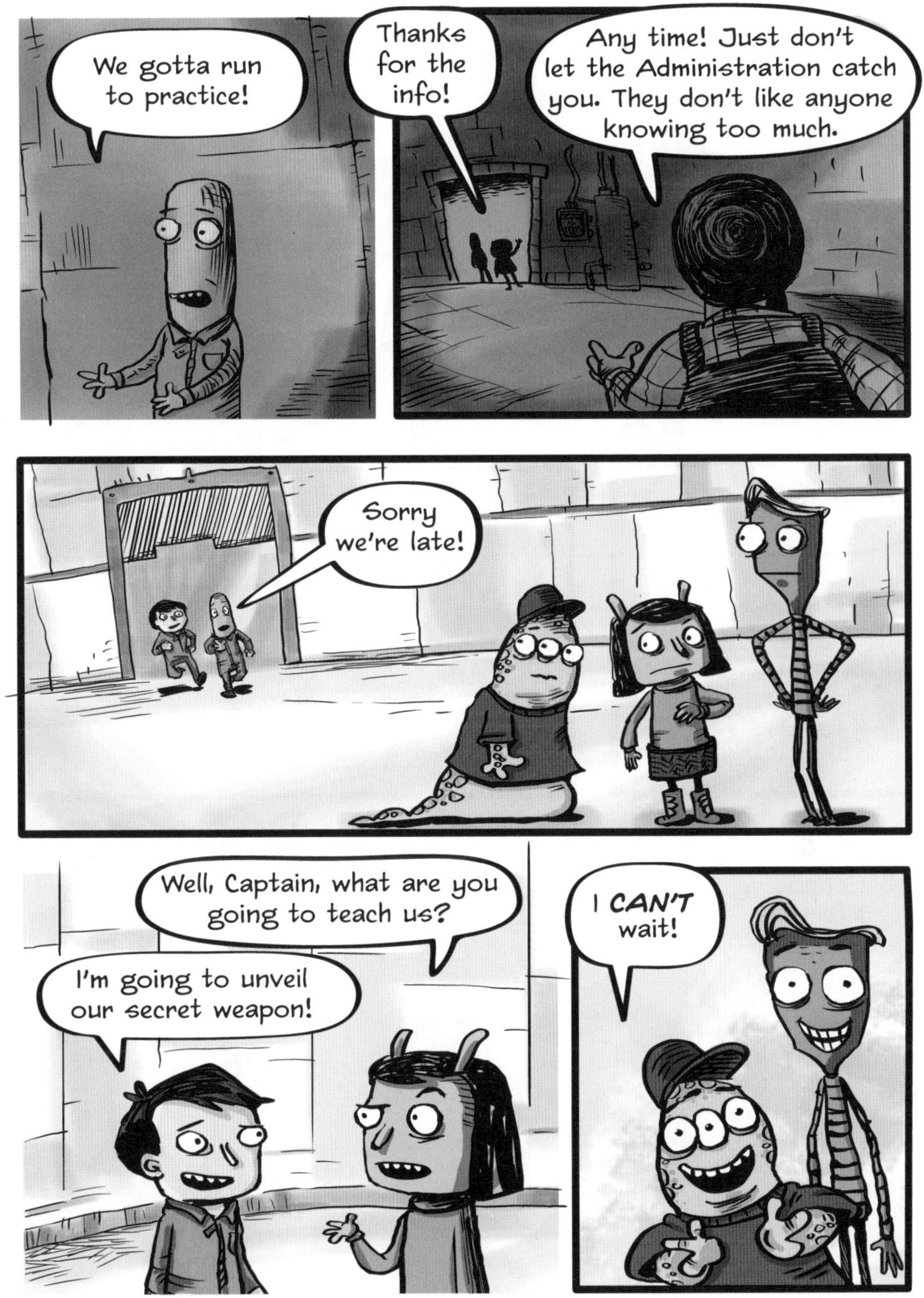
We gotta run to practice!
Thanks for the info!
Any time! Just don't let the Administration catch you. They don't like anyone knowing too much.
Sorry we're late!
Well, Captain, what are you going to teach us?
I'm going to unveil our secret weapon!
I **CAN'T** wait!

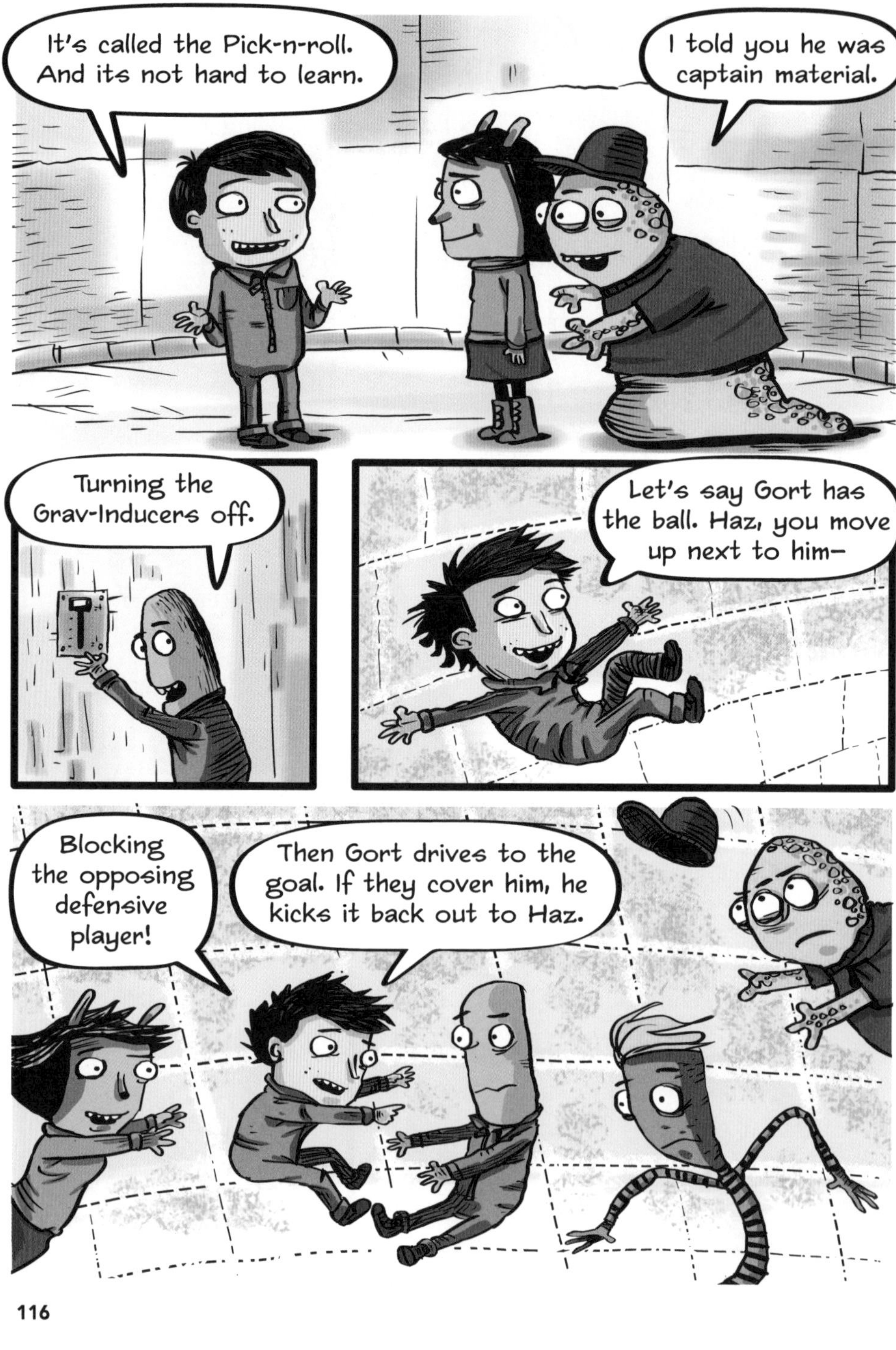
It's called the Pick-n-roll. And its not hard to learn.
I told you he was captain material.
Turning the Grav-Inducers off.
Let's say Gort has the ball. Haz, you move up next to him—
Blocking the opposing defensive player!
Then Gort drives to the goal. If they cover him, he kicks it back out to Haz.

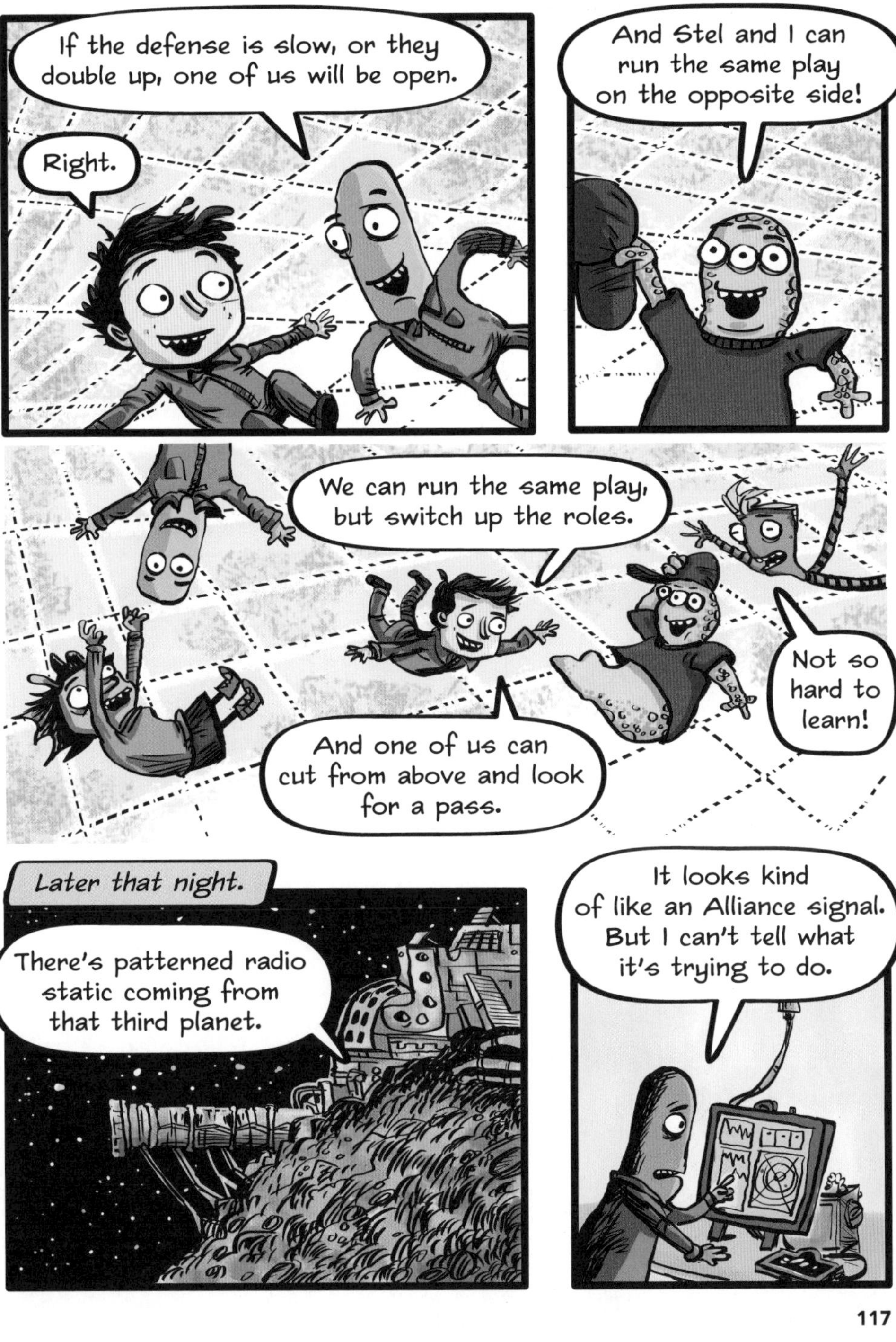

If the defense is slow, or they double up, one of us will be open.
Right.
And Stel and I can run the same play on the opposite side!
We can run the same play, but switch up the roles.
And one of us can cut from above and look for a pass.
Not so hard to learn!
Later that night.
There's patterned radio static coming from that third planet.
It looks kind of like an Alliance signal. But I can't tell what it's trying to do.

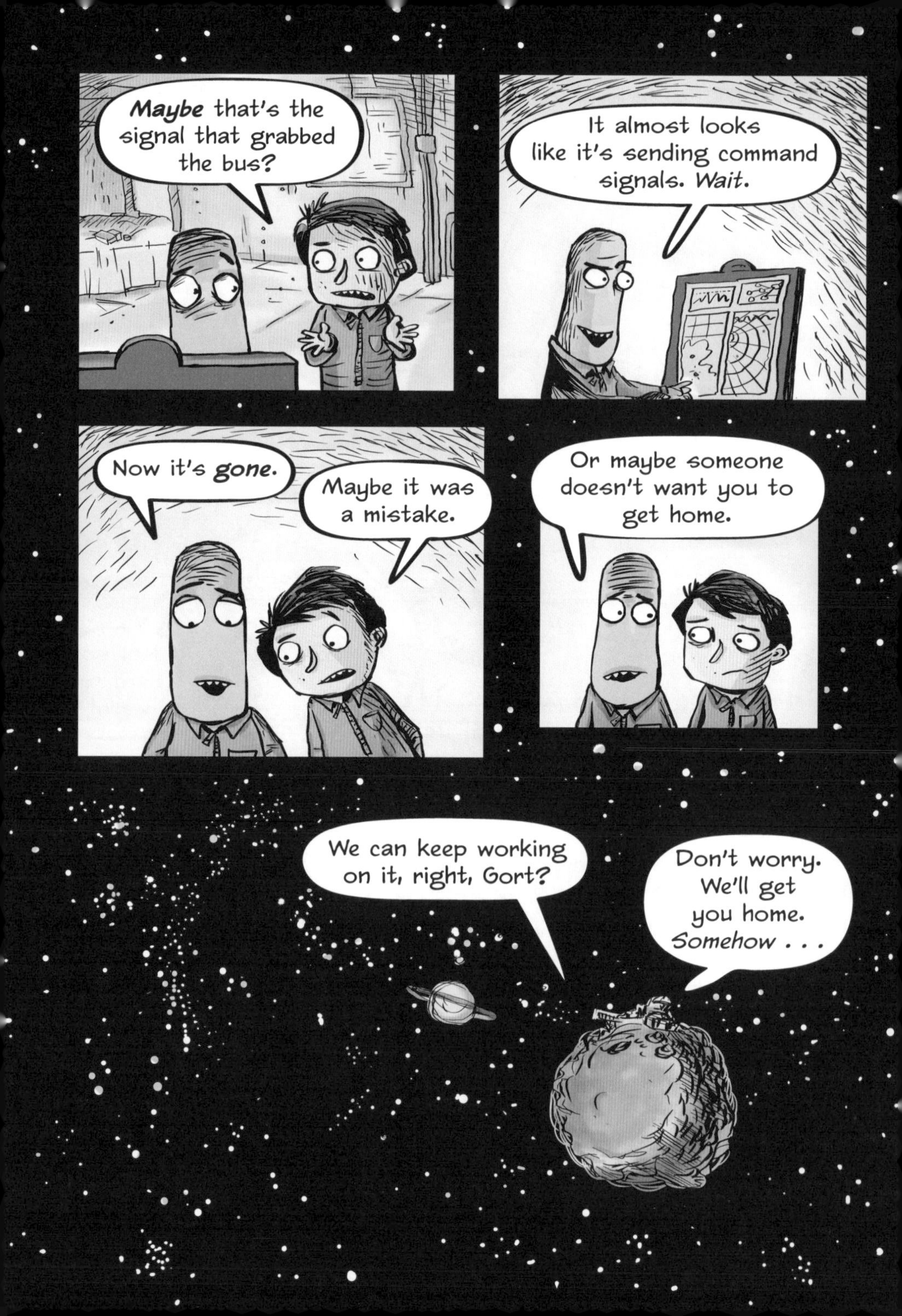
Maybe that's the signal that grabbed the bus?
It almost looks like it's sending command signals. *Wait*.
Now it's *gone*.
Maybe it was a mistake.
Or maybe someone doesn't want you to get home.
We can keep working on it, right, Gort?
Don't worry. We'll get you home. *Somehow . . .*

CHAPTER 4

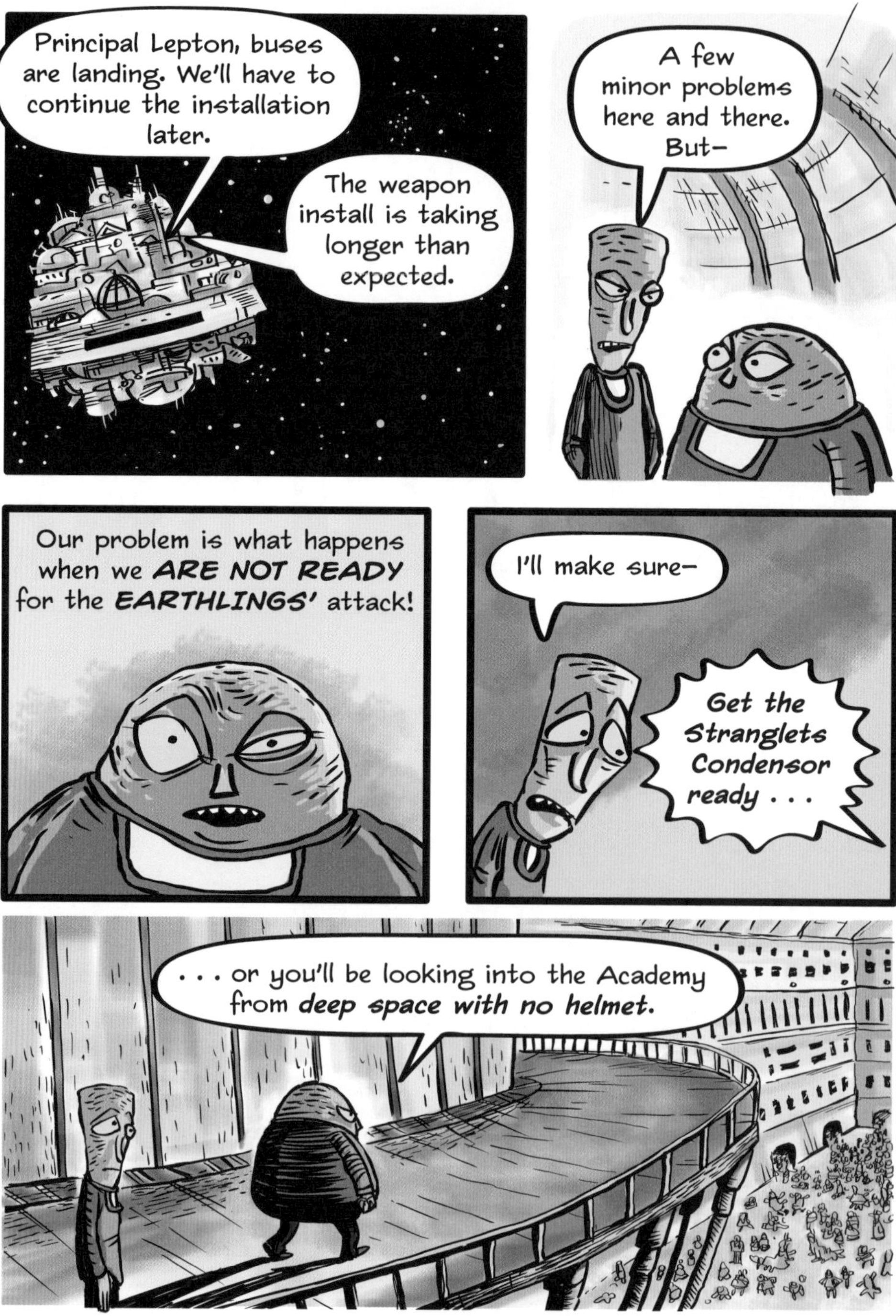
Principal Lepton, buses are landing. We'll have to continue the installation later.
The weapon install is taking longer than expected.
A few minor problems here and there. But—
Our problem is what happens when we ARE NOT READY for the EARTHLINGS' attack!
I'll make sure—
Get the Stranglets Condensor ready . . .
. . . or you'll be looking into the Academy from deep space with no helmet.

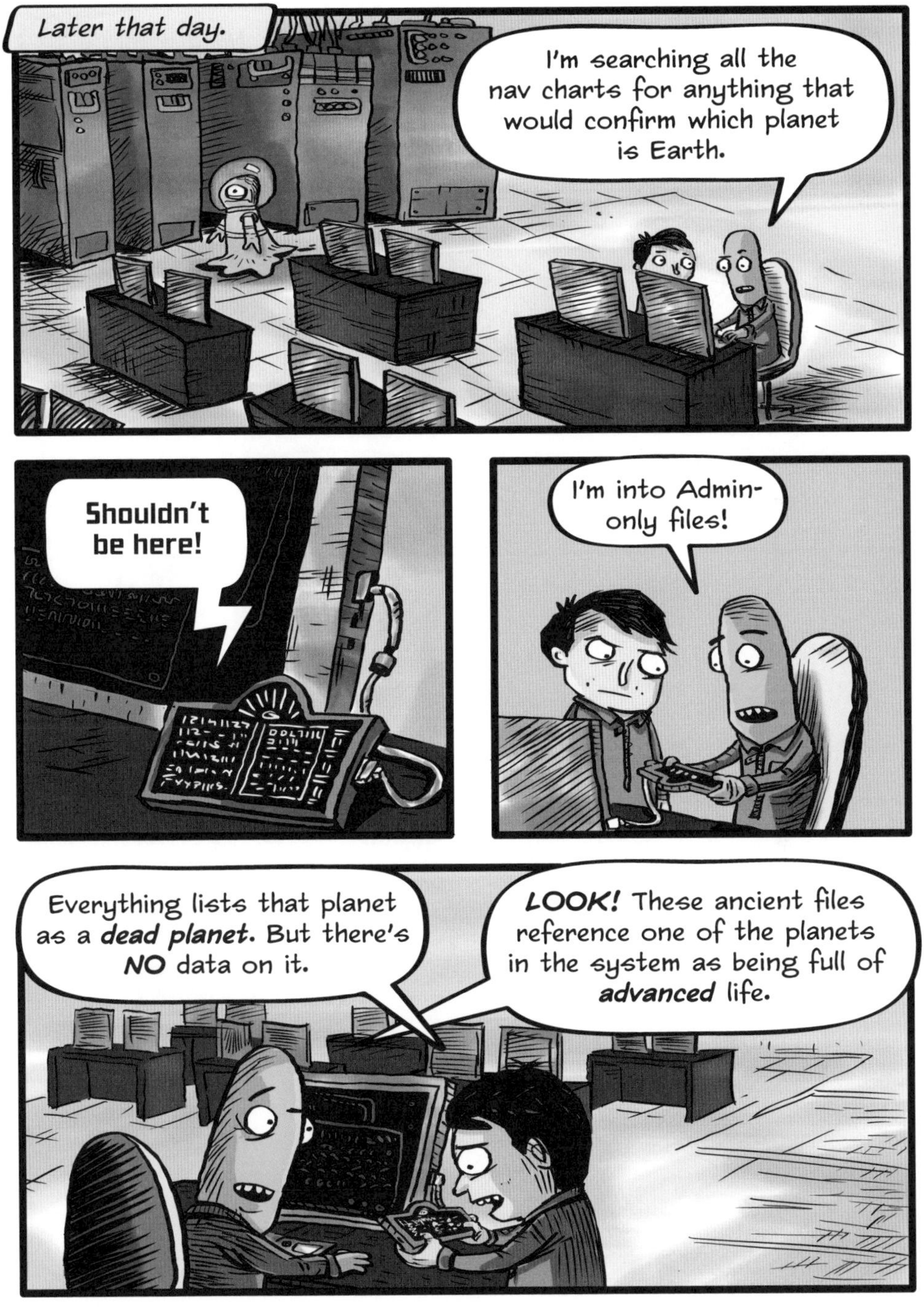
Later that day.
I'm searching all the nav charts for anything that would confirm which planet is Earth.
Shouldn't be here!
I'm into Admin-only files!
Everything lists that planet as a ***dead planet***. But there's ***NO*** data on it.
LOOK! These ancient files reference one of the planets in the system as being full of ***advanced*** life.

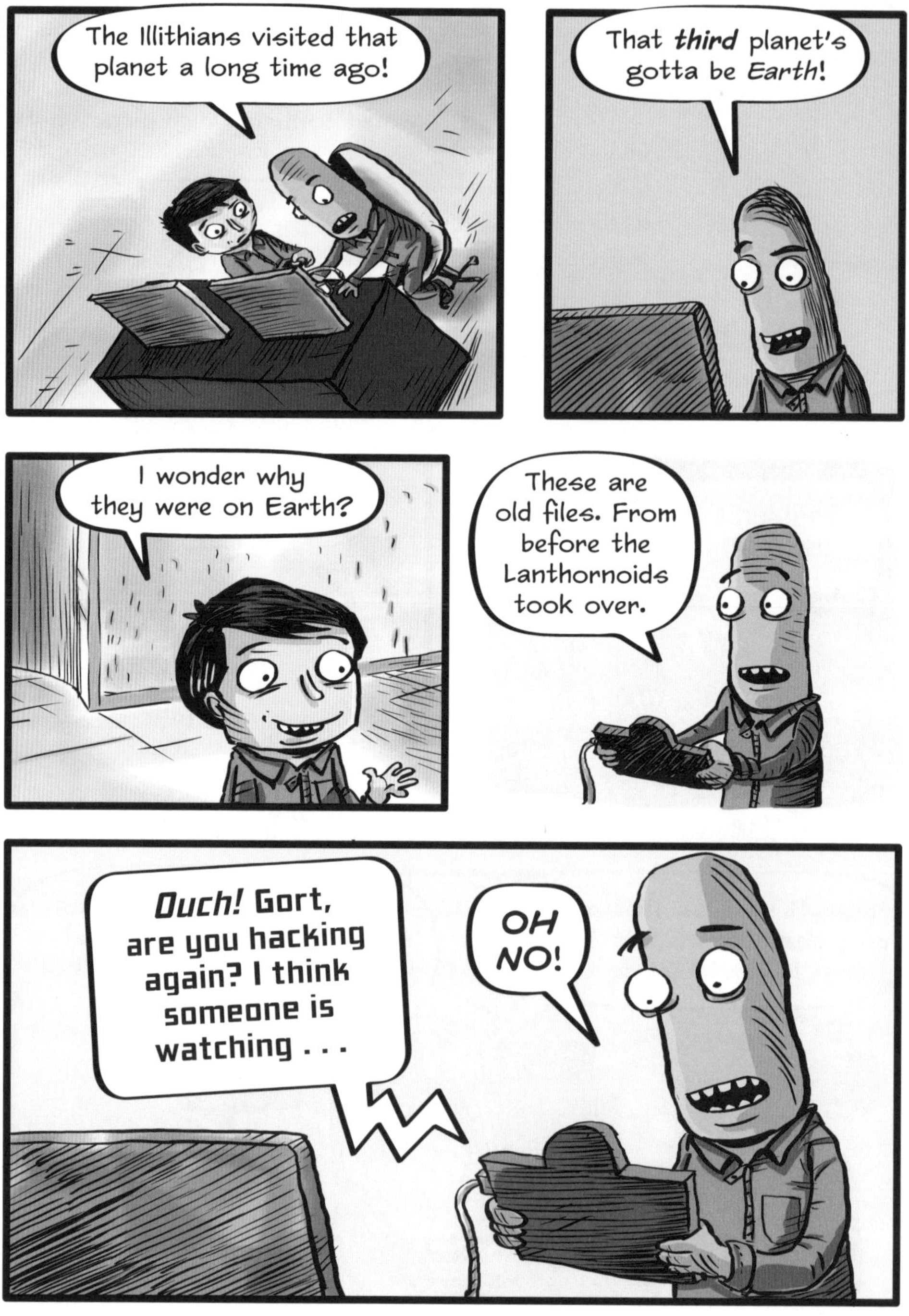
The Illithians visited that planet a long time ago!
That *third* planet's gotta be *Earth*!
I wonder why they were on Earth?
These are old files. From before the Lanthornoids took over.
Ouch! Gort, are you hacking again? I think someone is watching . . .
OH NO!

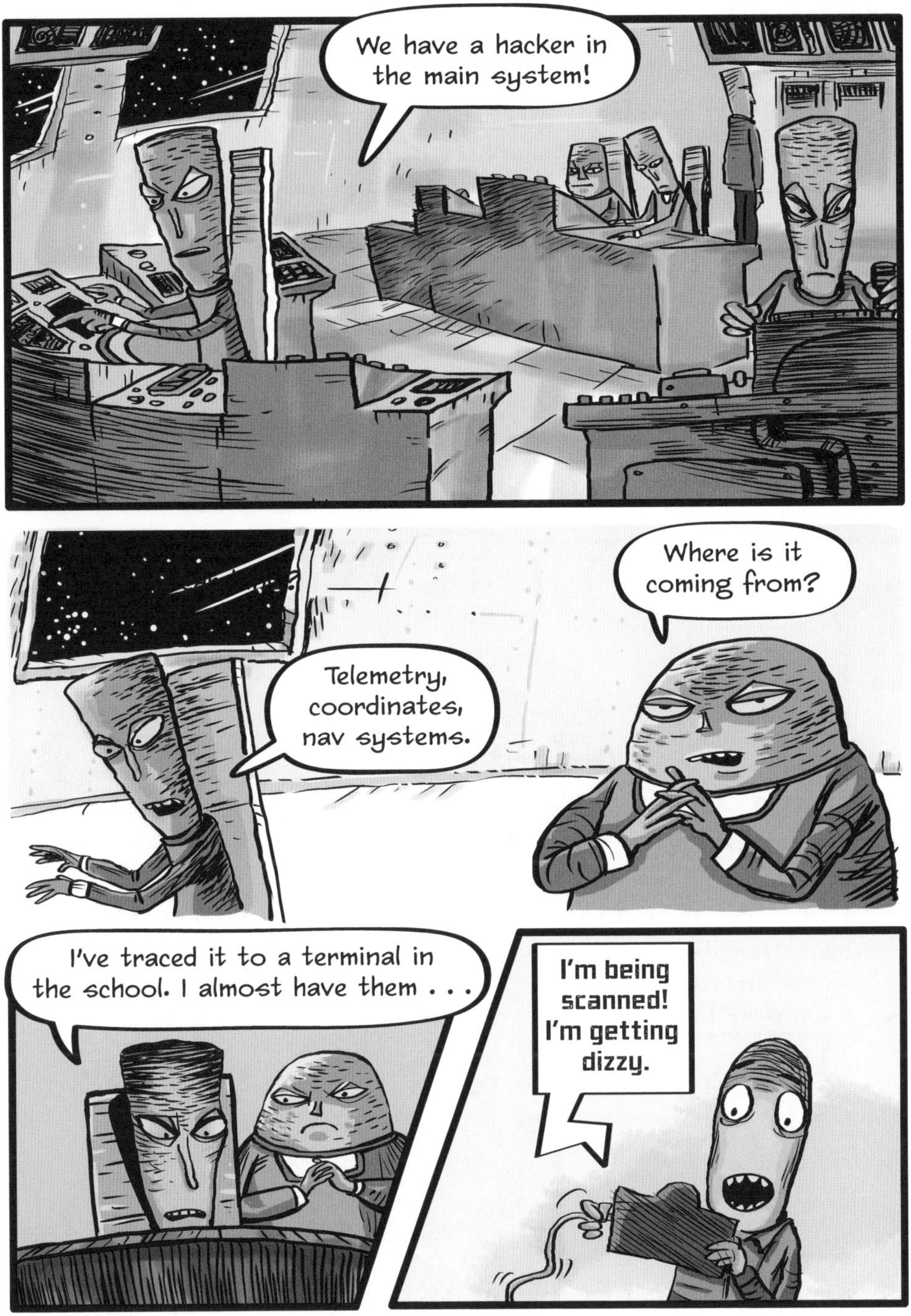
We have a hacker in the main system!
Where is it coming from?
Telemetry, coordinates, nav systems.
I've traced it to a terminal in the school. I almost have them . . .
I'm being scanned! I'm getting dizzy.

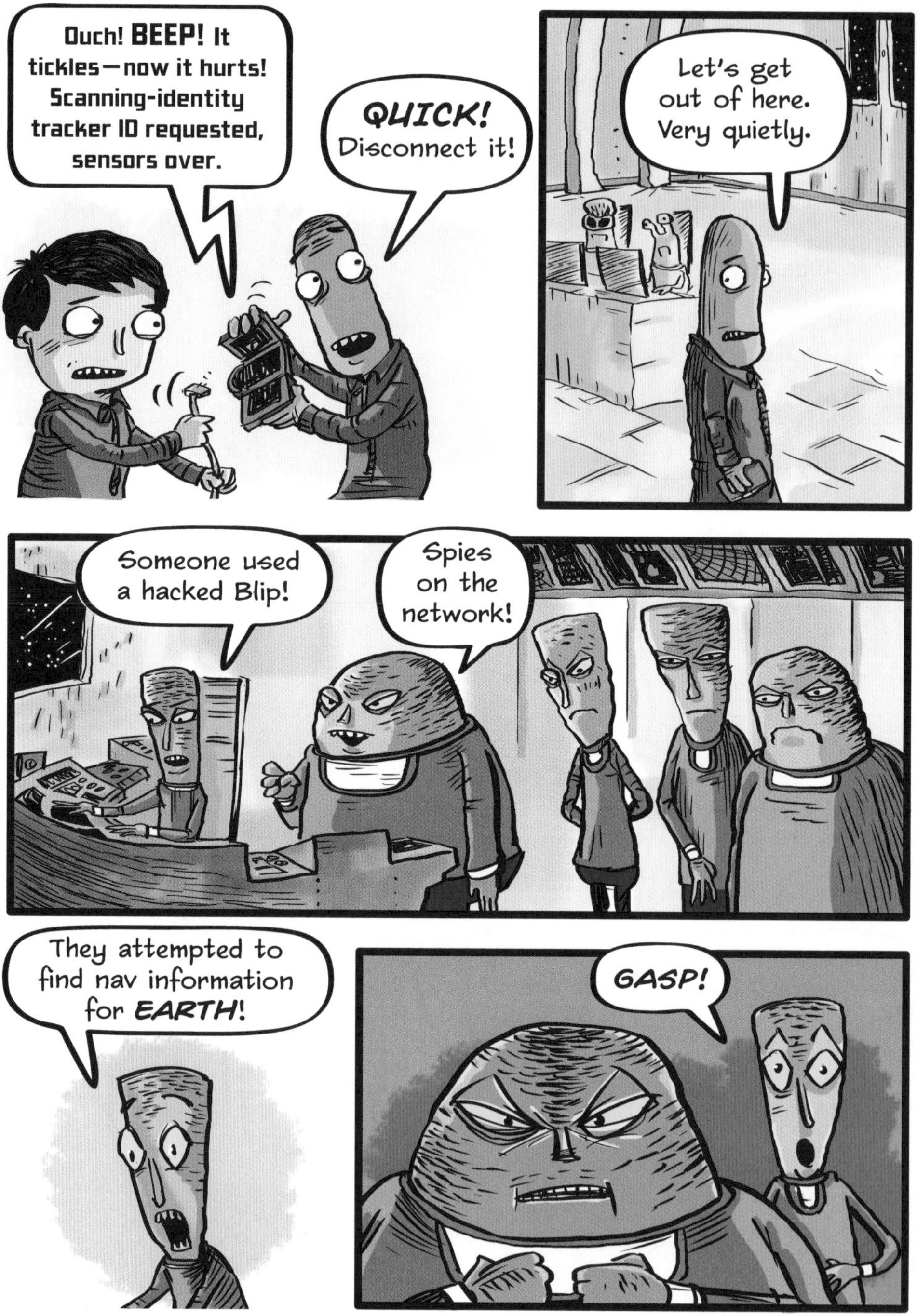
Ouch! BEEP! It tickles—now it hurts! Scanning-identity tracker ID requested, sensors over.
QUICK! Disconnect it!
Let's get out of here. Very quietly.
Someone used a hacked Blip!
Spies on the network!
They attempted to find nav information for EARTH!
GASP!

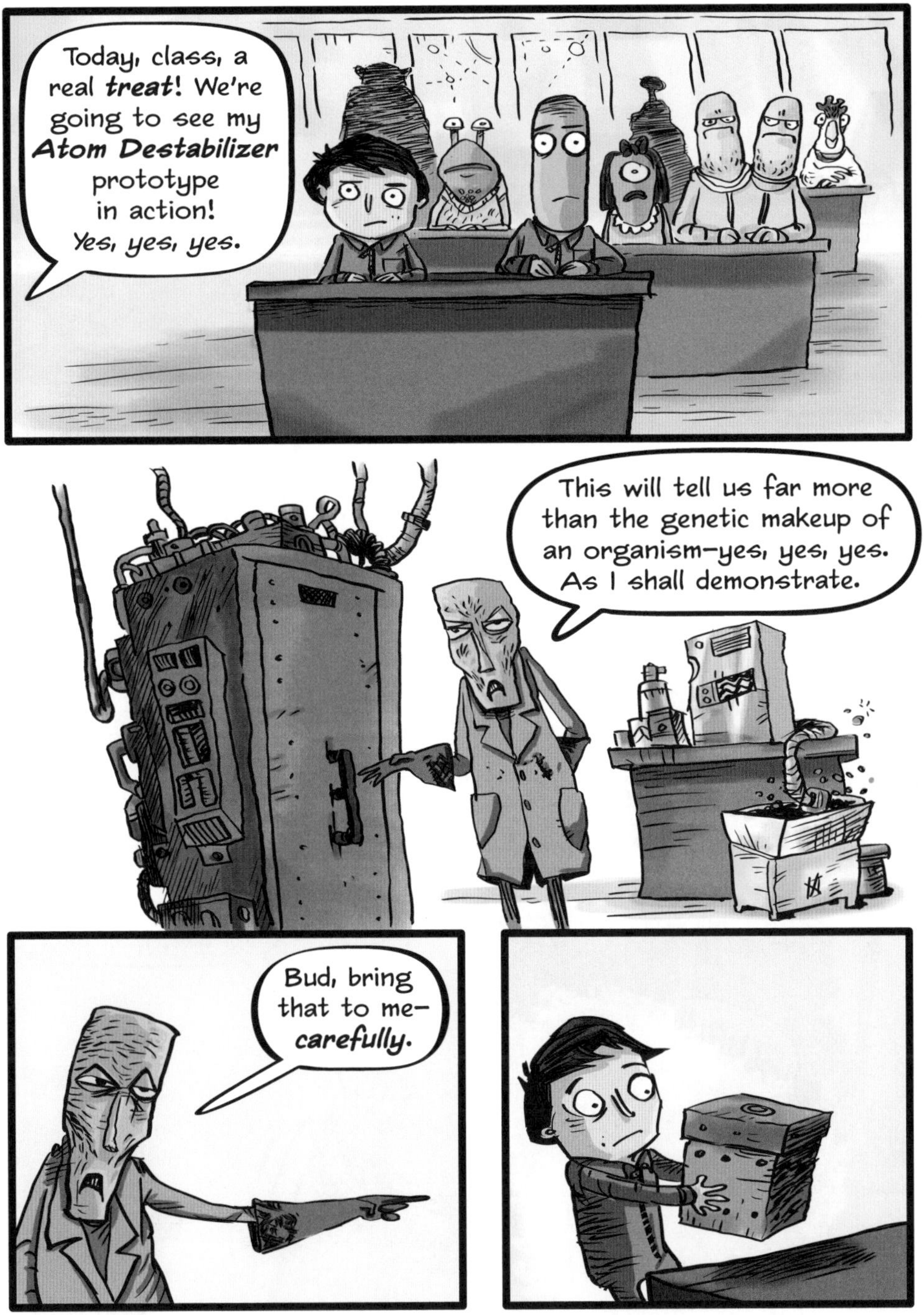
Today, class, a real **treat**! We're going to see my ***Atom Destabilizer*** prototype in action! *Yes, yes, yes.*
This will tell us far more than the genetic makeup of an organism—yes, yes, yes. As I shall demonstrate.
Bud, bring that to me— ***carefully.***

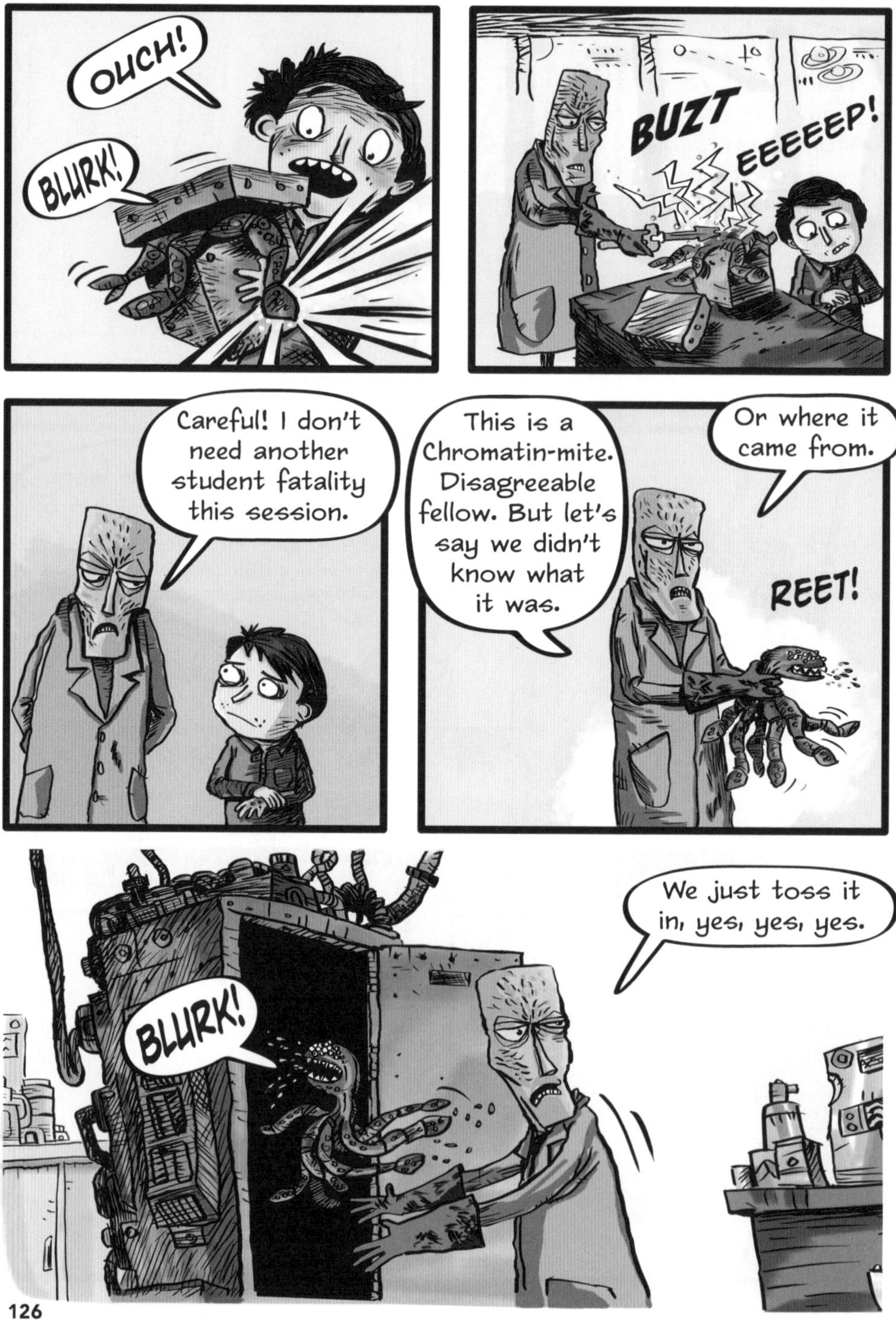
OUCH!
BLURK!
BUZT
EEEEEEP!
Careful! I don't need another student fatality this session.
This is a Chromatin-mite. Disagreeable fellow. But let's say we didn't know what it was.
Or where it came from.
REET!
We just toss it in, yes, yes, yes.
BLURK!

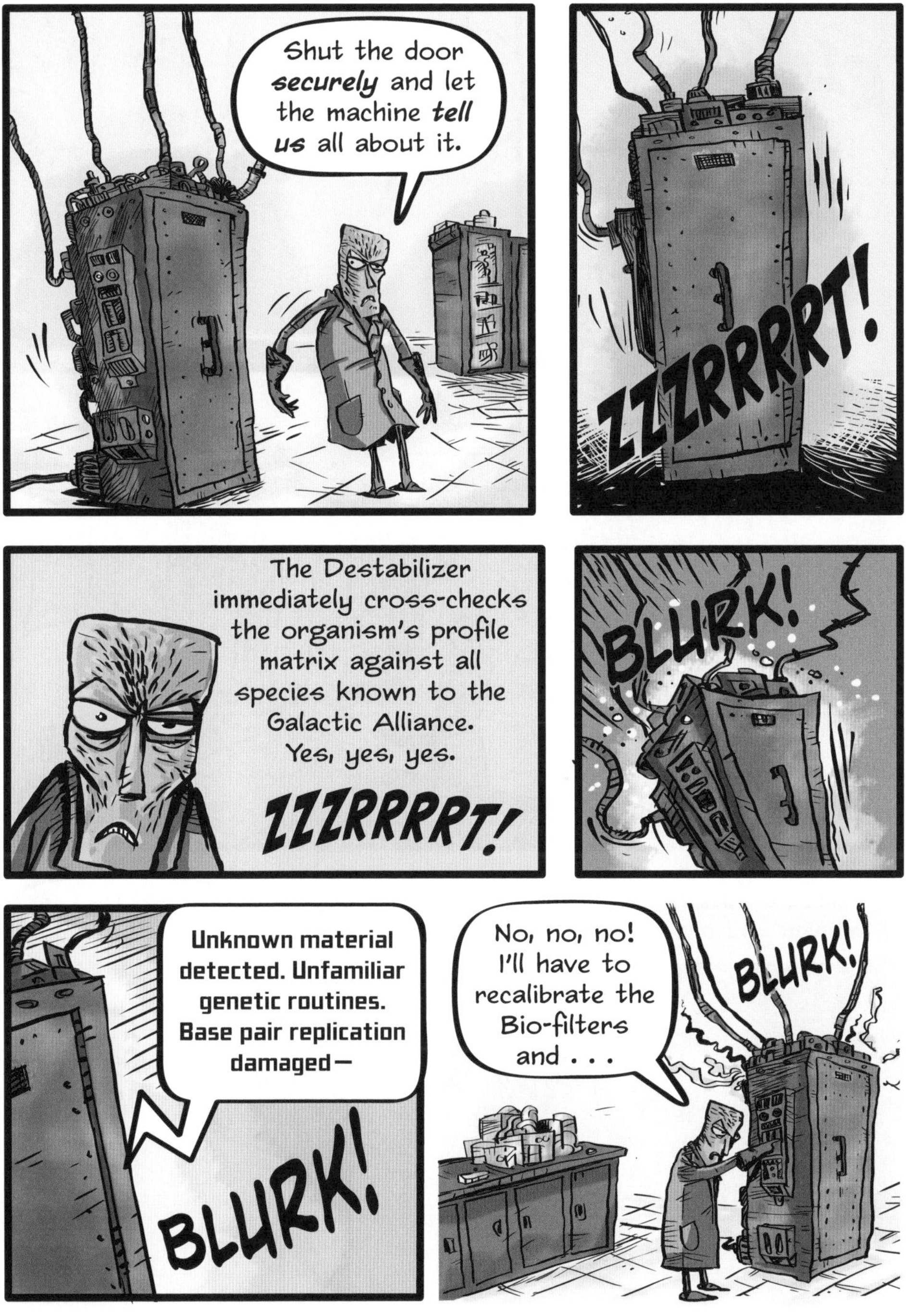
Shut the door *securely* and let the machine *tell us* all about it.
ZZZRRRRT!
The Destabilizer immediately cross-checks the organism's profile matrix against all species known to the Galactic Alliance. Yes, yes, yes.
ZZZRRRRT!
BLURK!
Unknown material detected. Unfamiliar genetic routines. Base pair replication damaged—
BLURK!
No, no, no! I'll have to recalibrate the Bio-filters and . . .
BLURK!

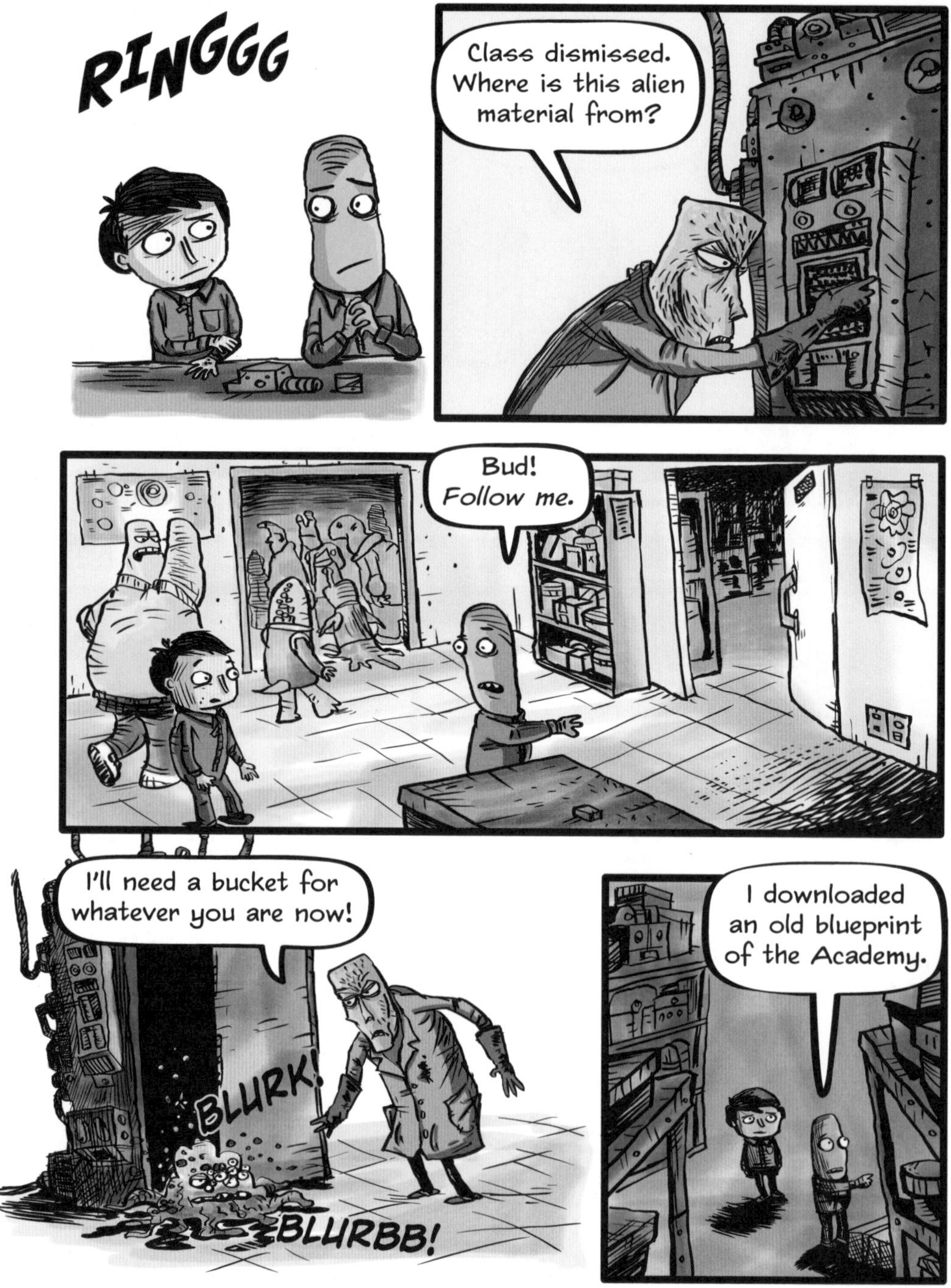
RINGGG
Class dismissed. Where is this alien material from?
Bud! Follow me.
I'll need a bucket for whatever you are now!
BLURK!
BLURBB!
I downloaded an old blueprint of the Academy.

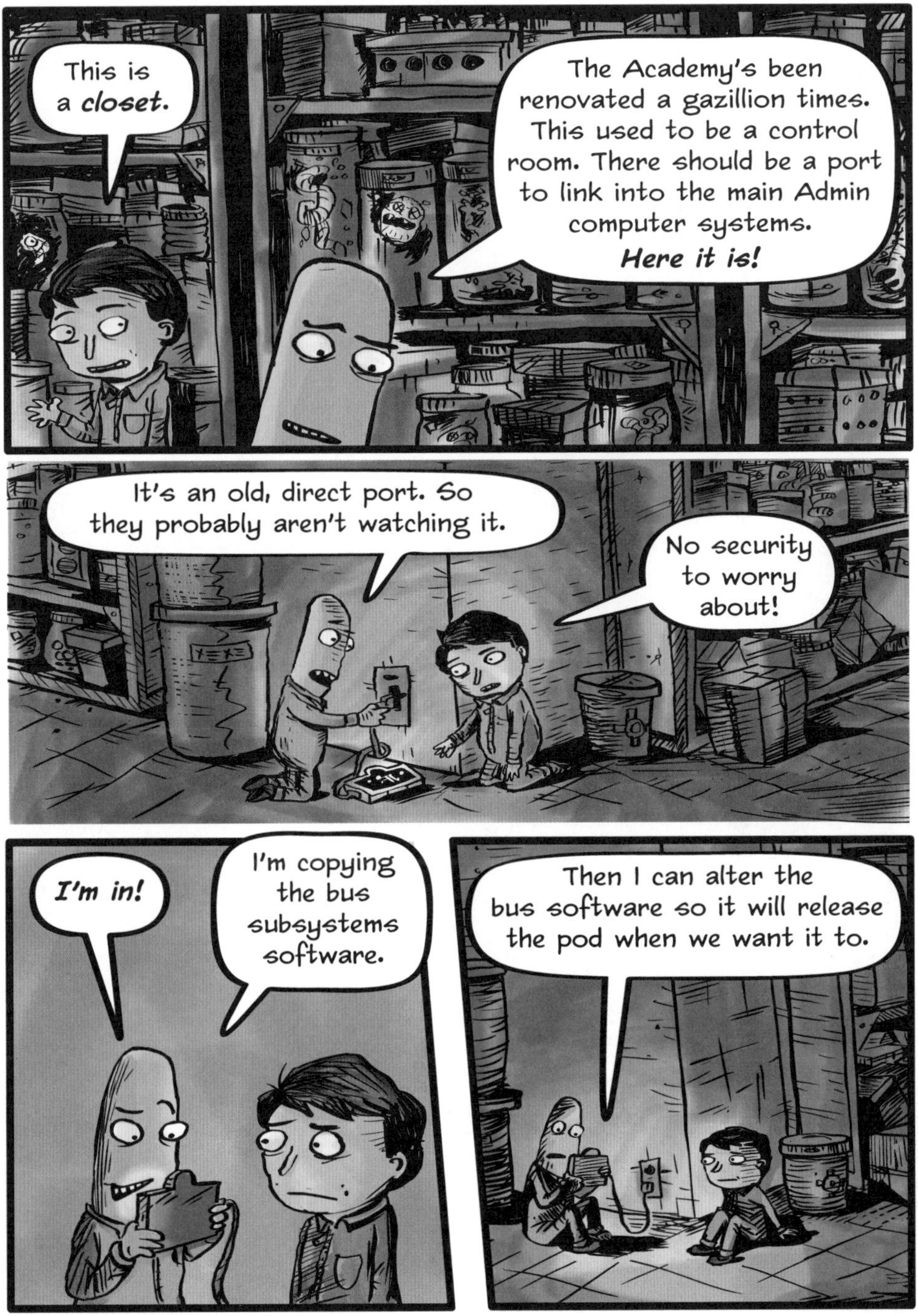
This is a *closet.*
The Academy's been renovated a gazillion times. This used to be a control room. There should be a port to link into the main Admin computer systems. ***Here it is!***
It's an old, direct port. So they probably aren't watching it.
No security to worry about!
I'm in!
I'm copying the bus subsystems software.
Then I can alter the bus software so it will release the pod when we want it to.

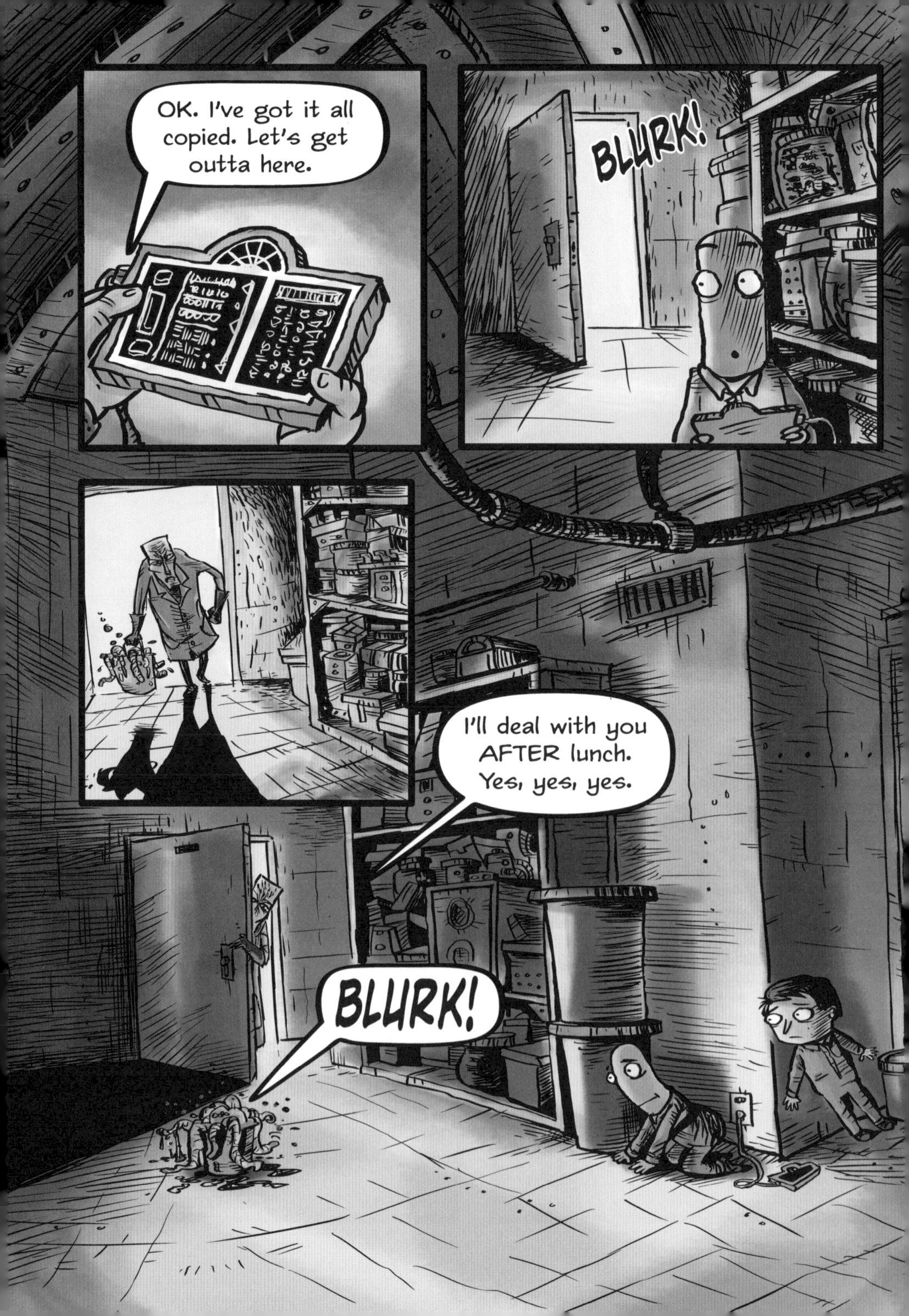
OK. I've got it all copied. Let's get outta here.
BLURK!
I'll deal with you AFTER lunch. Yes, yes, yes.
BLURK!

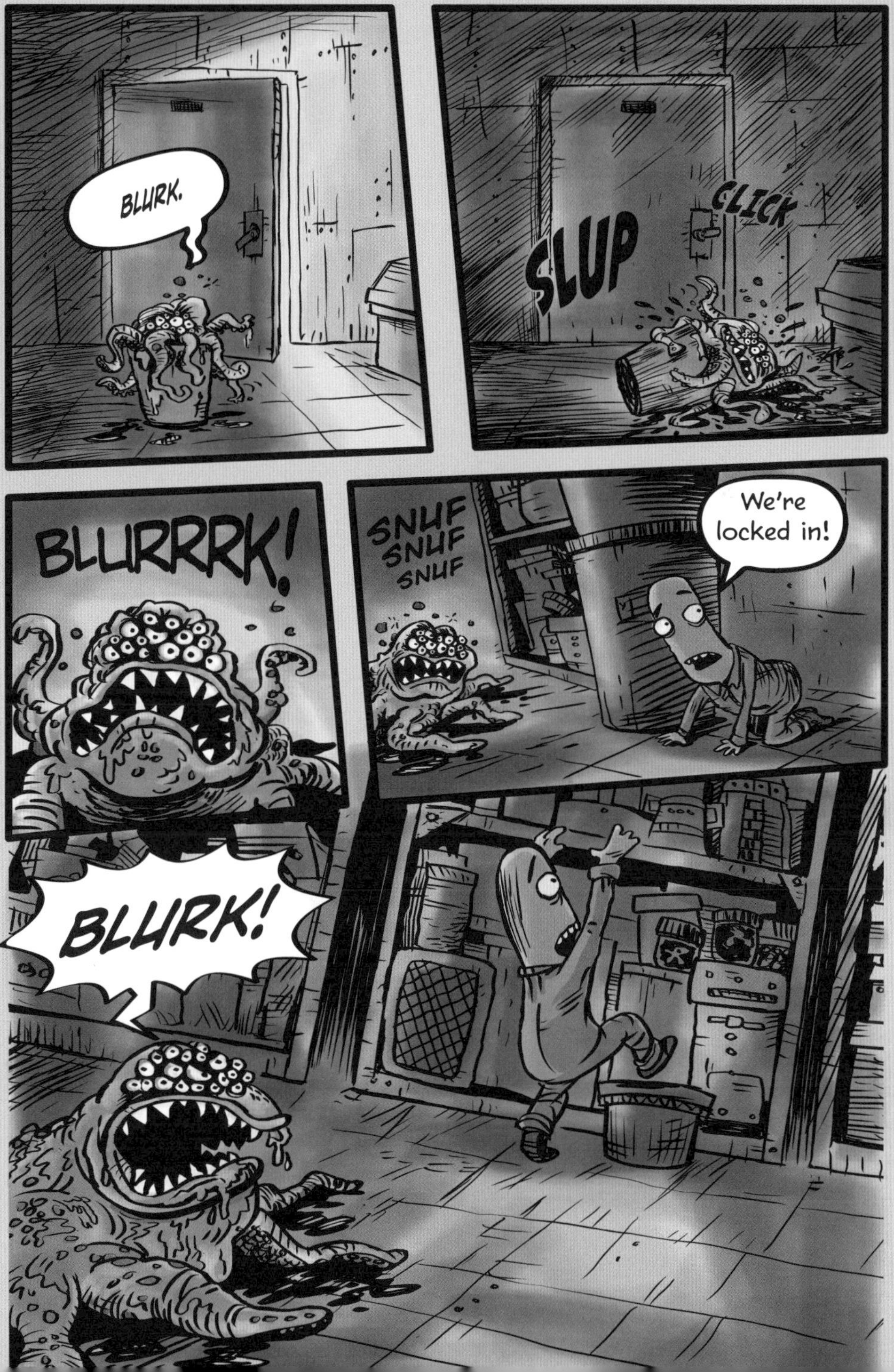
BLURK.
SLUP
CLICK
BLURRRK!
SNUF
SNUF
SNUF
We're locked in!
BLURK!

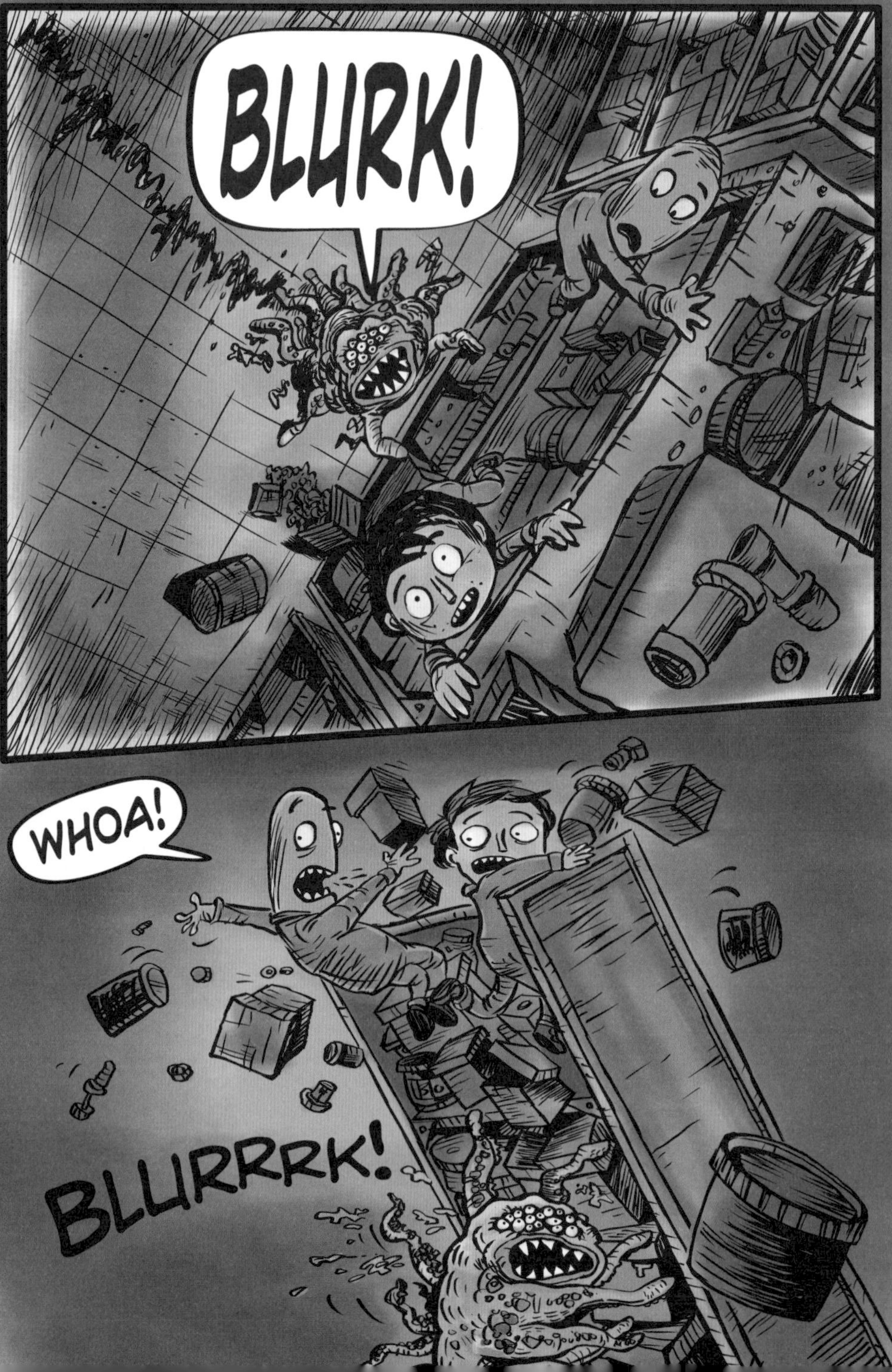
BLURK!
WHOA!
BLURRRK!

SLAM
AHHH!
CRASH
WHOOOSH
SCHRRRIT

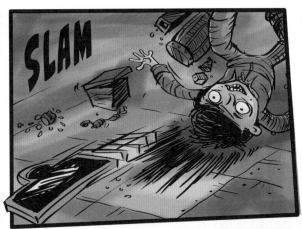

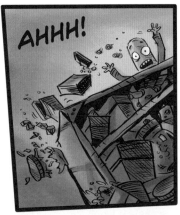

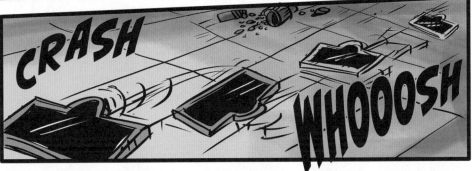

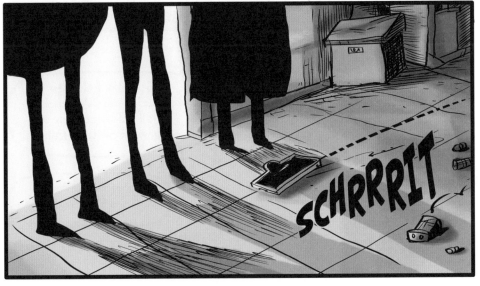

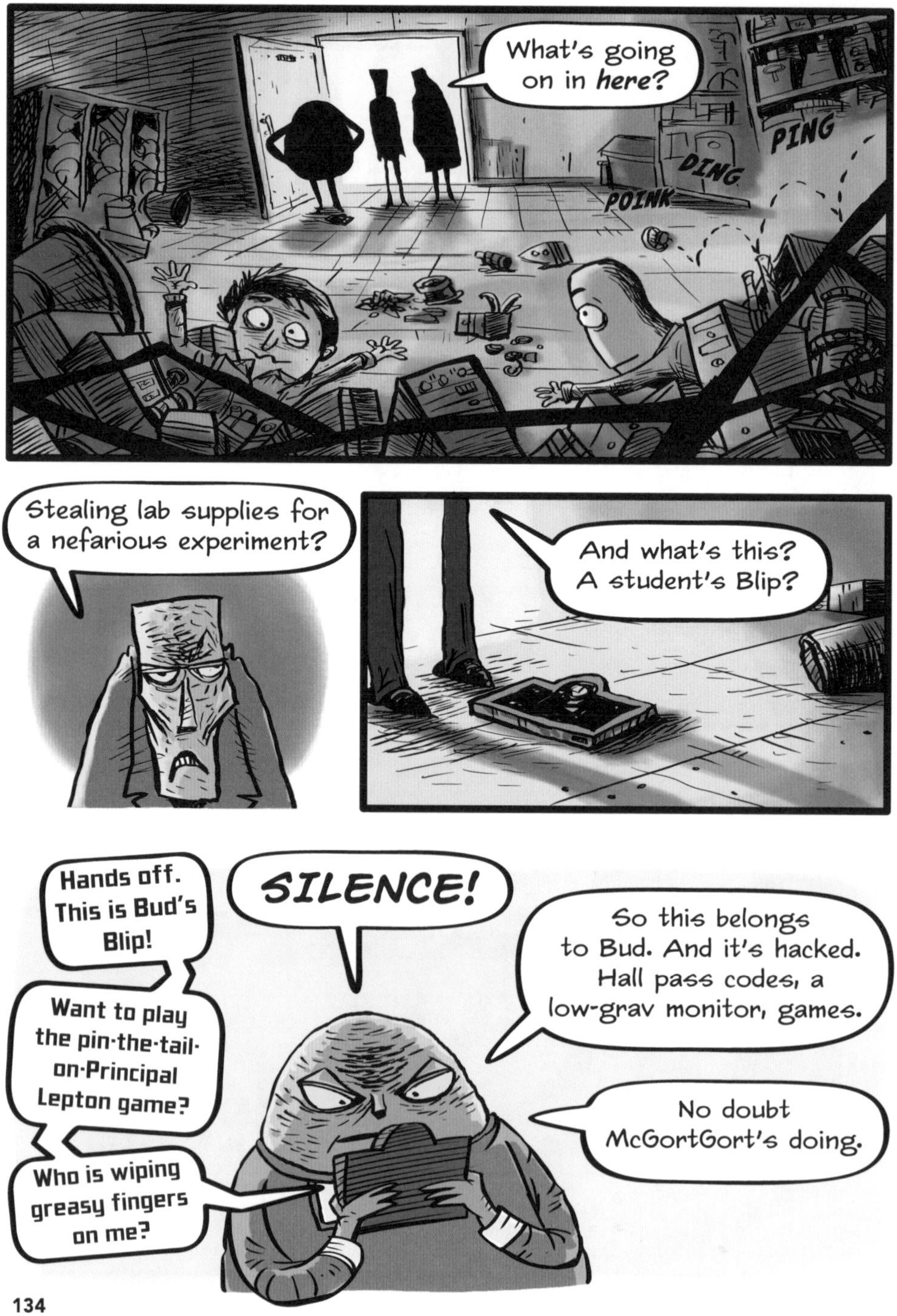
What's going on in *here?*
PING
DING
POINK
Stealing lab supplies for a nefarious experiment?
And what's this? A student's Blip?
Hands off. This is Bud's Blip!
Want to play the pin-the-tail-on-Principal Lepton game?
Who is wiping greasy fingers on me?
SILENCE!
So this belongs to Bud. And it's hacked. Hall pass codes, a low-grav monitor, games.
No doubt McGortGort's doing.

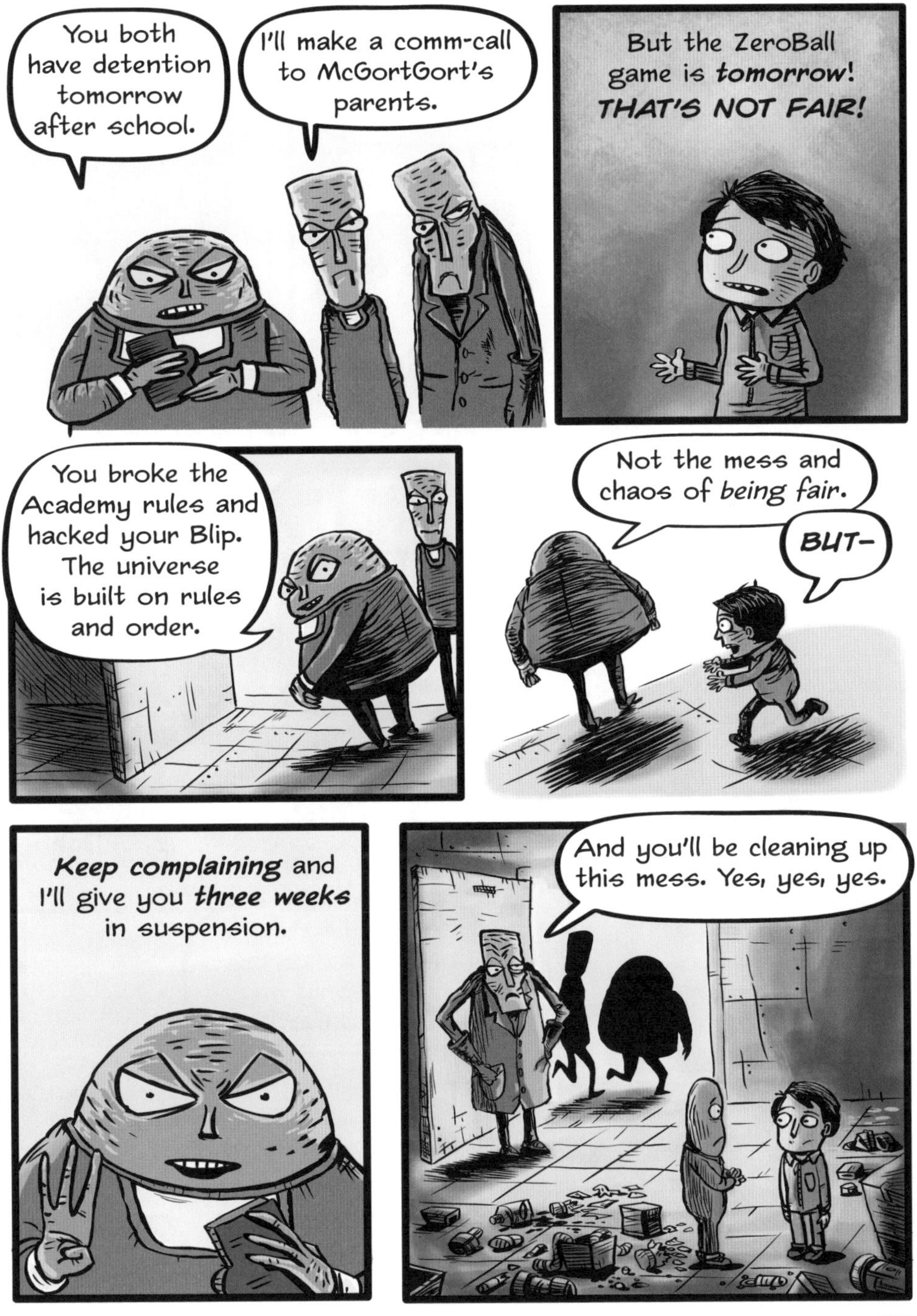

You both have detention tomorrow after school.
I'll make a comm-call to McGortGort's parents.
But the ZeroBall game is *tomorrow*! *THAT'S NOT FAIR!*
You broke the Academy rules and hacked your Blip. The universe is built on rules and order.
Not the mess and chaos of *being fair*.
BUT-
Keep complaining and I'll give you *three weeks* in suspension.
And you'll be cleaning up this mess. Yes, yes, yes.

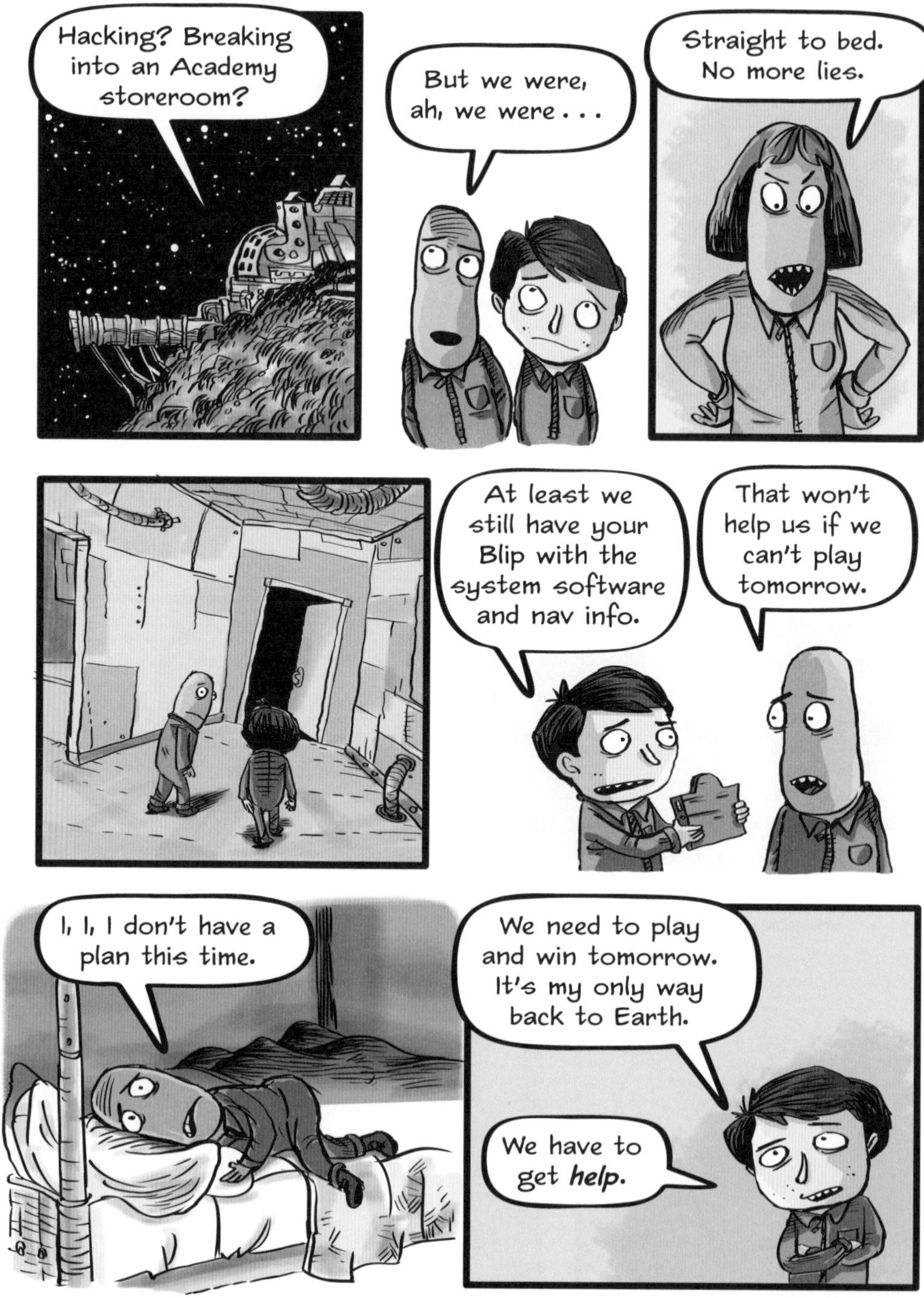
Hacking? Breaking into an Academy storeroom?
But we were, ah, we were . . .
Straight to bed. No more lies.
At least we still have your Blip with the system software and nav info.
That won't help us if we can't play tomorrow.
I, I, I don't have a plan this time.
We need to play and win tomorrow. It's my only way back to Earth.
We have to get ***help***.

CHAPTER 5

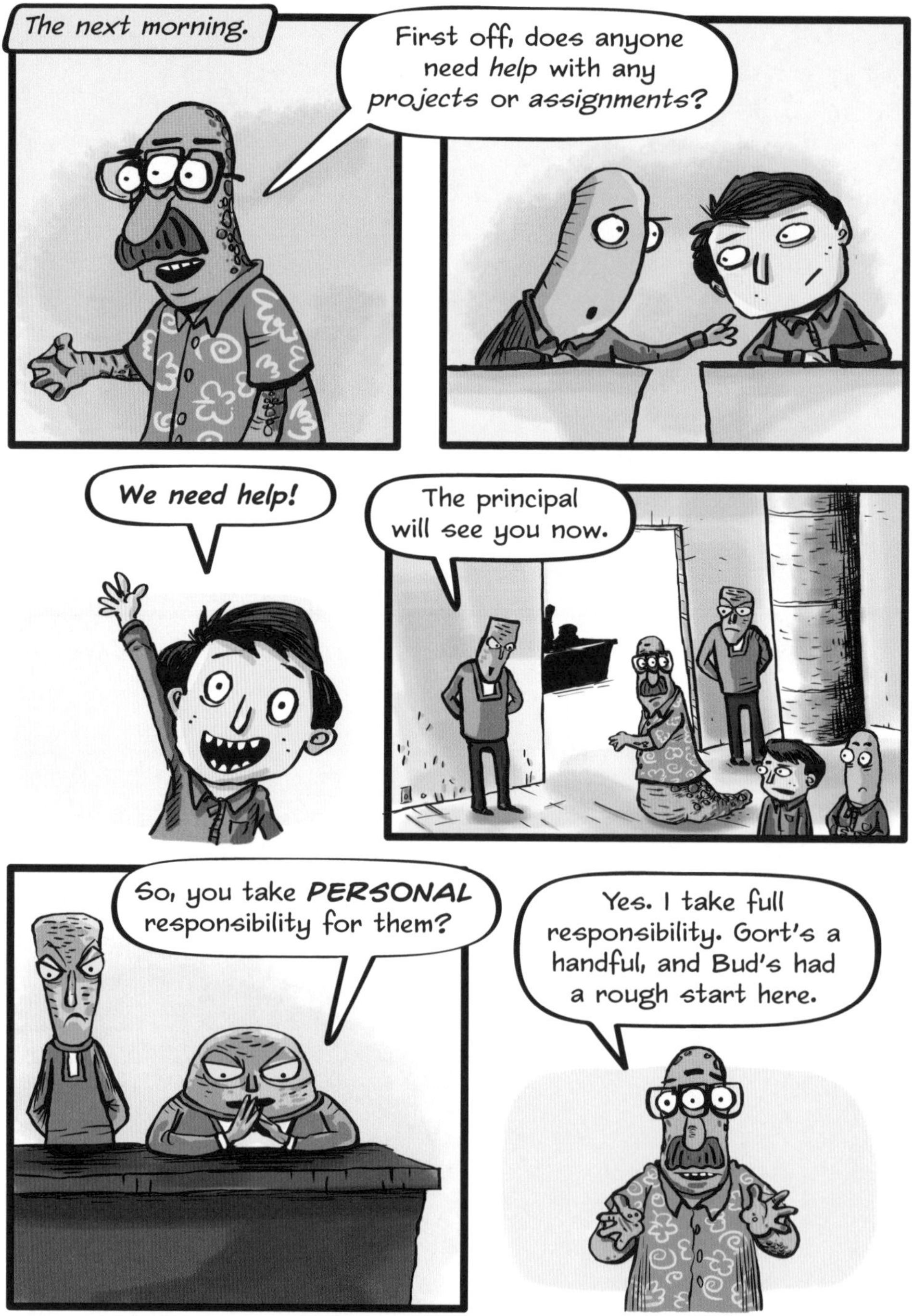
The next morning.
First off, does anyone need *help* with any *projects* or *assignments*?
We need help!
The principal will see you now.
So, you take **PERSONAL** responsibility for them?
Yes. I take full responsibility. Gort's a handful, and Bud's had a rough start here.

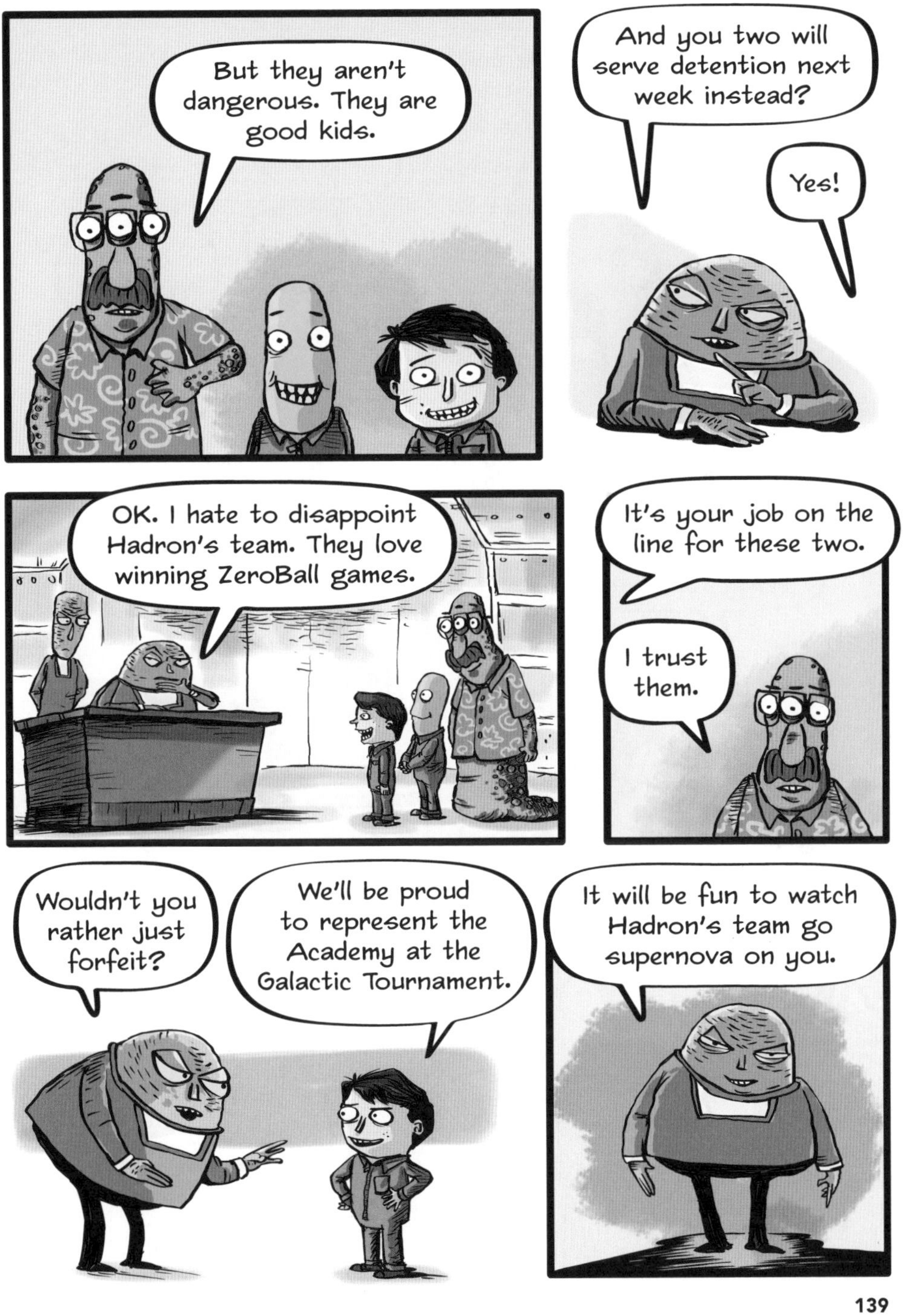
But they aren't dangerous. They are good kids.
And you two will serve detention next week instead?
Yes!
OK. I hate to disappoint Hadron's team. They love winning ZeroBall games.
It's your job on the line for these two.
I trust them.
Wouldn't you rather just forfeit?
We'll be proud to represent the Academy at the Galactic Tournament.
It will be fun to watch Hadron's team go supernova on you.

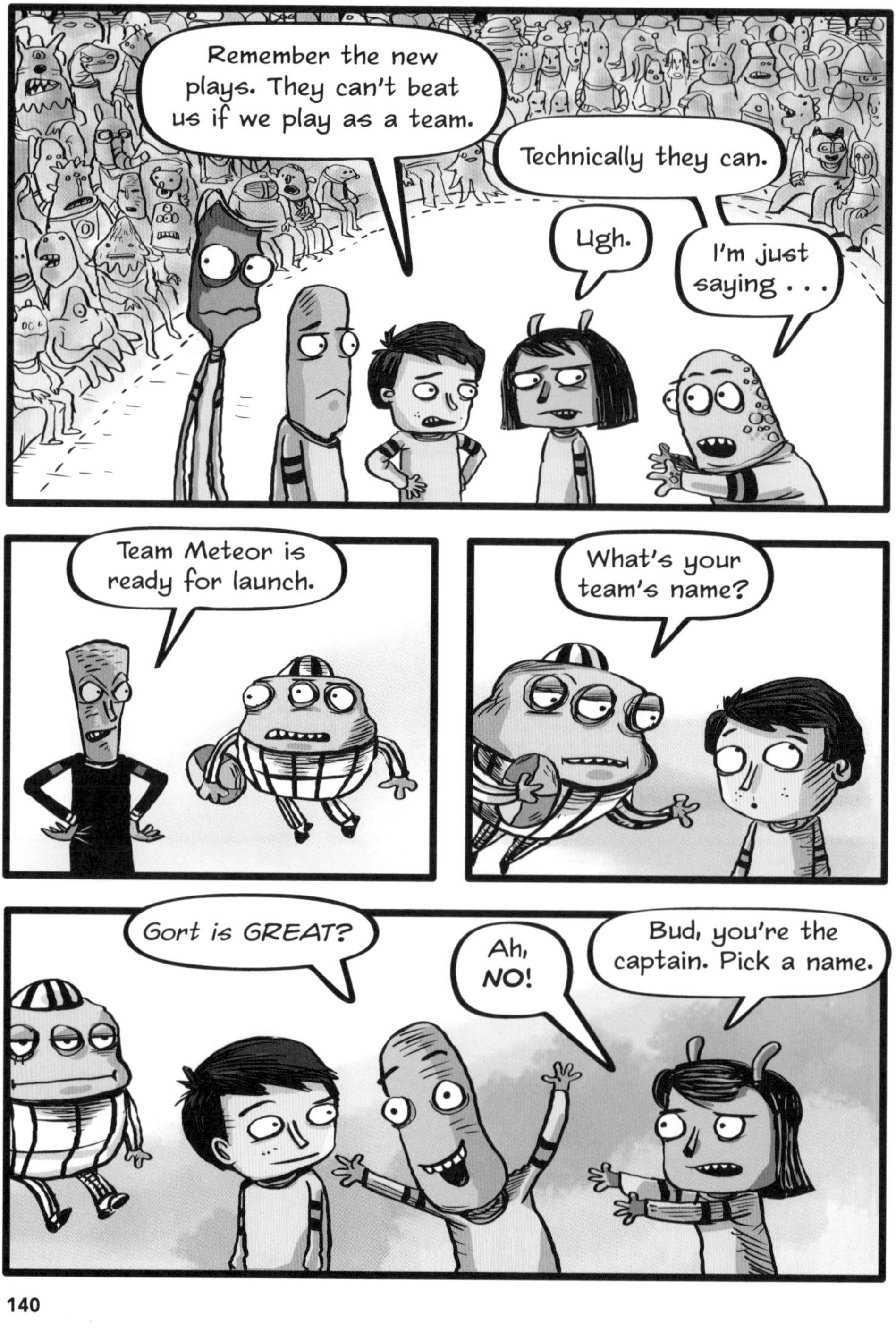
Remember the new plays. They can't beat us if we play as a team.
Technically they can.
Ugh.
I'm just saying . . .
Team Meteor is ready for launch.
What's your team's name?
Gort is GREAT?
Ah, NO!
Bud, you're the captain. Pick a name.

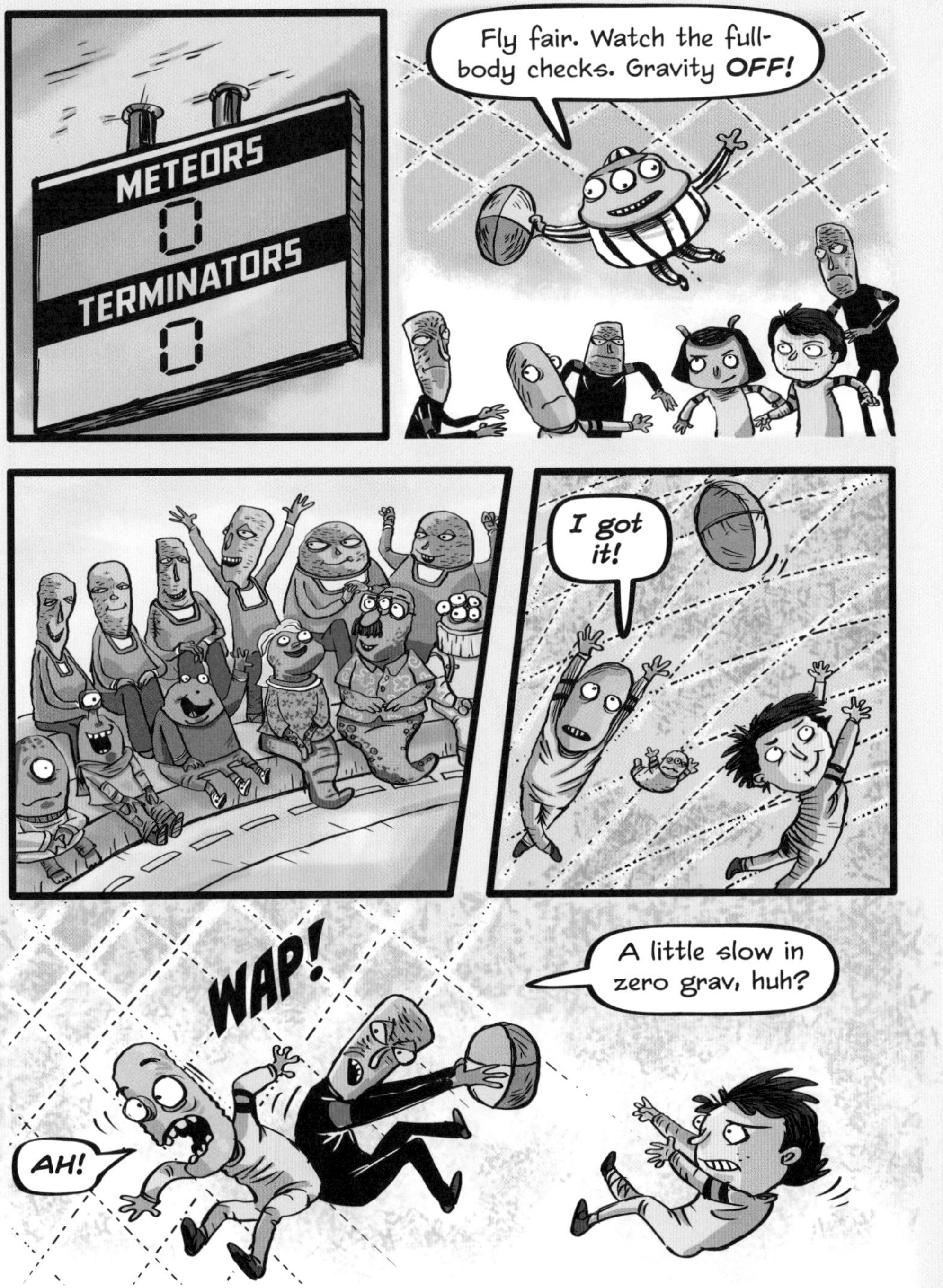
METEORS
0
TERMINATORS
0
Fly fair. Watch the full-body checks. Gravity **OFF!**
I got it!
WAP!
A little slow in zero grav, huh?
AH!

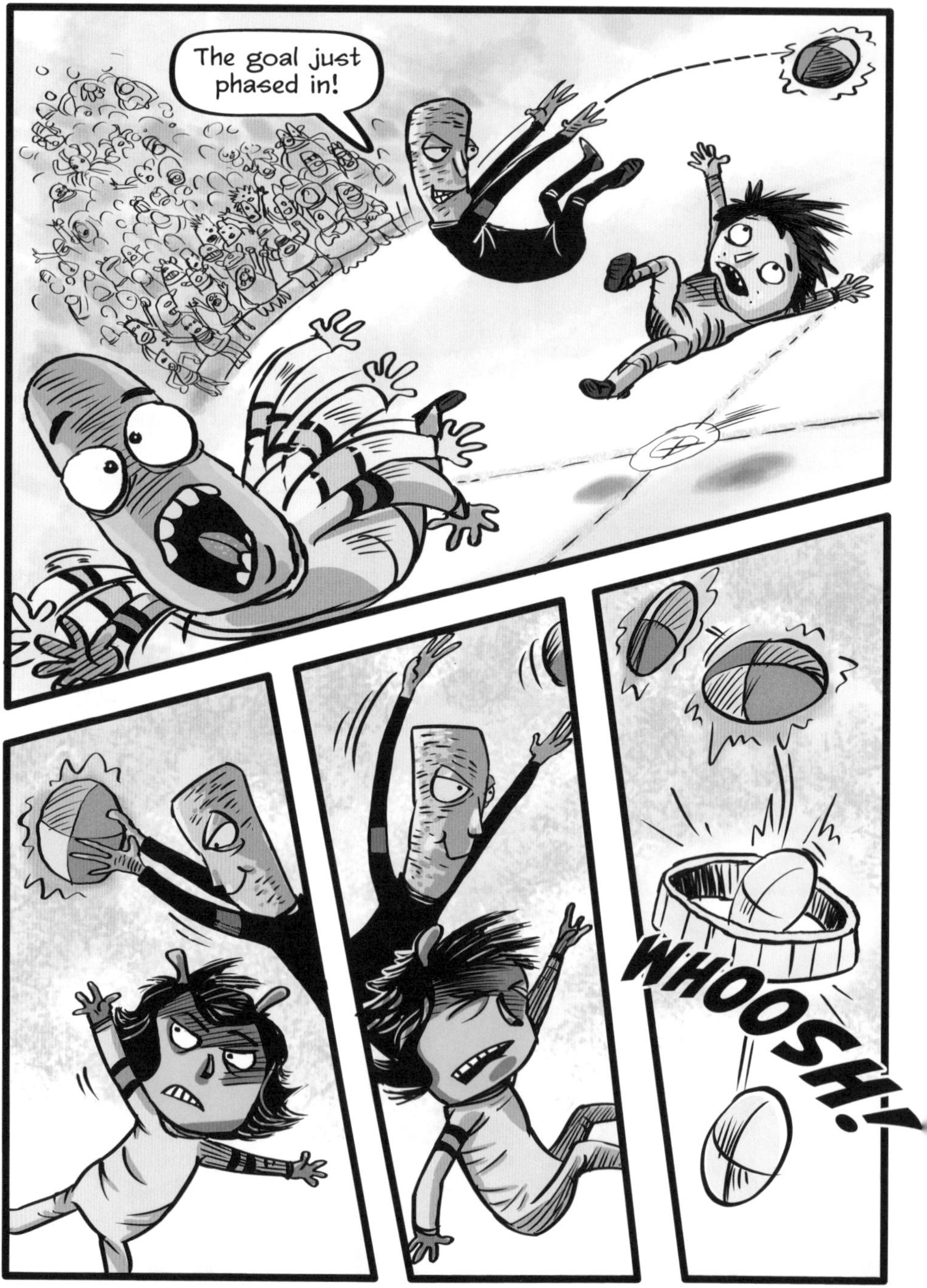
The goal just phased in!
WHOOSH!!

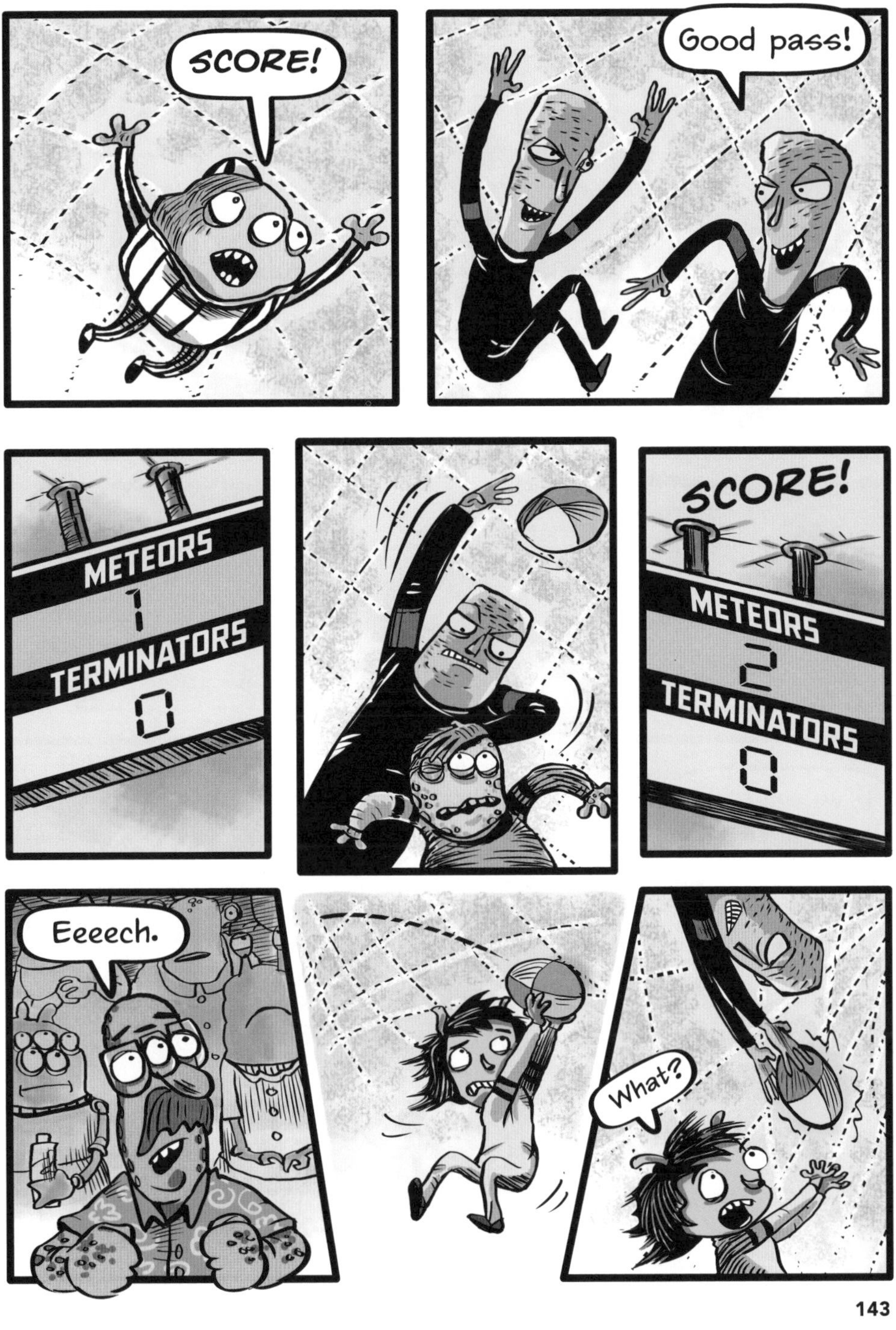
SCORE!
Good pass!
METEORS
1
TERMINATORS
0
SCORE!
METEORS
2
TERMINATORS
0
Eeeech.
What?

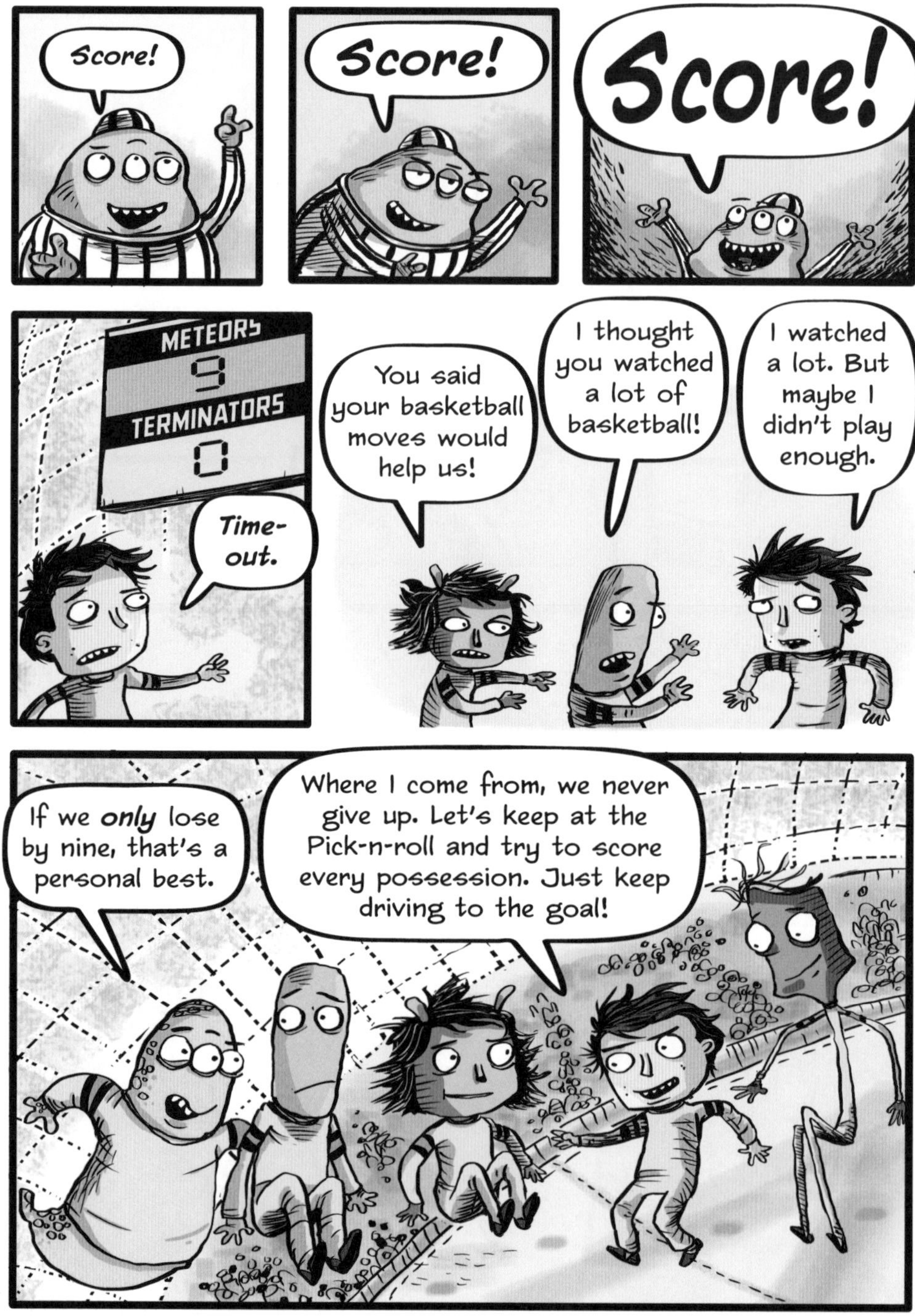
Score!
Score!
Score!
METEORS
9
TERMINATORS
0
Time-out.
You said your basketball moves would help us!
I thought you watched a lot of basketball!
I watched a lot. But maybe I didn't play enough.
If we *only* lose by nine, that's a personal best.
Where I come from, we never give up. Let's keep at the Pick-n-roll and try to score every possession. Just keep driving to the goal!

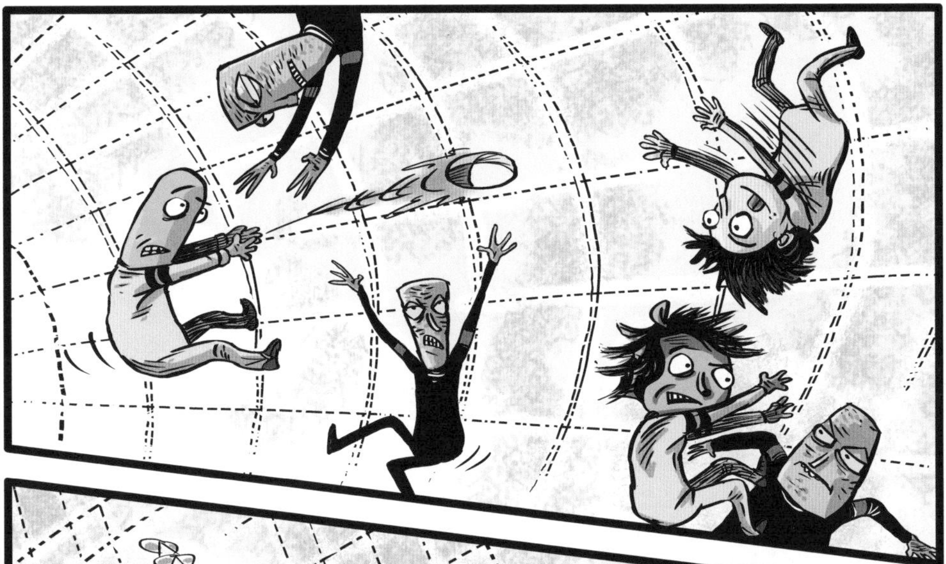

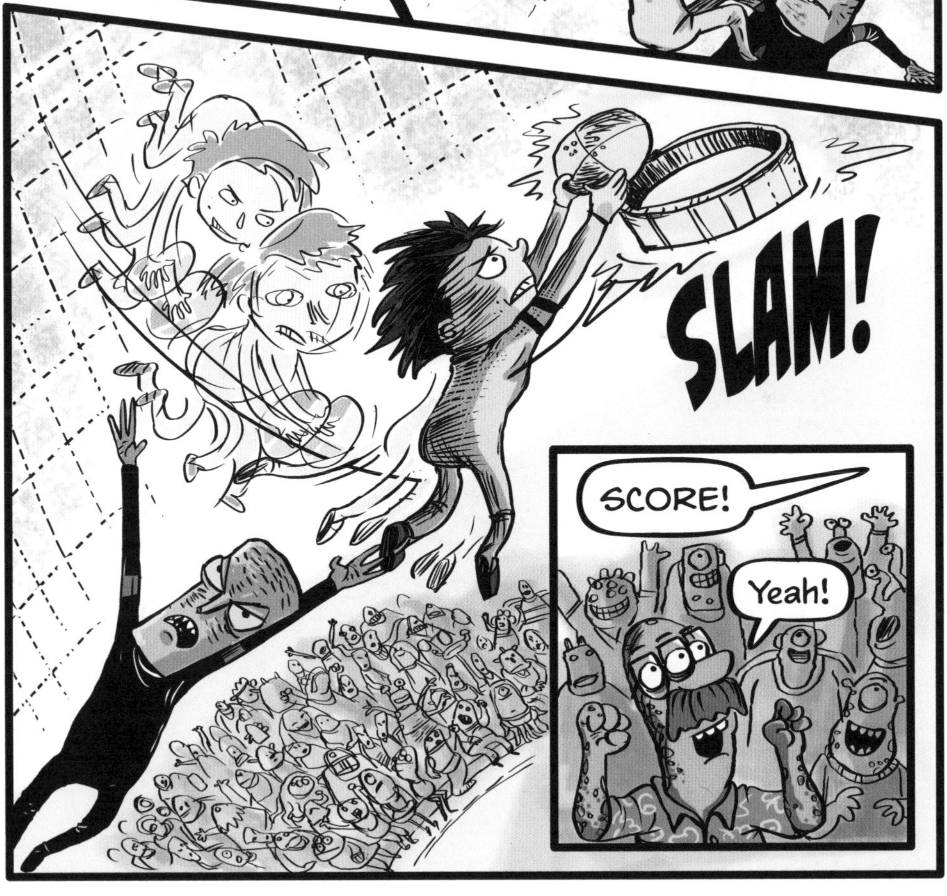
SLAM!
SCORE!
Yeah!

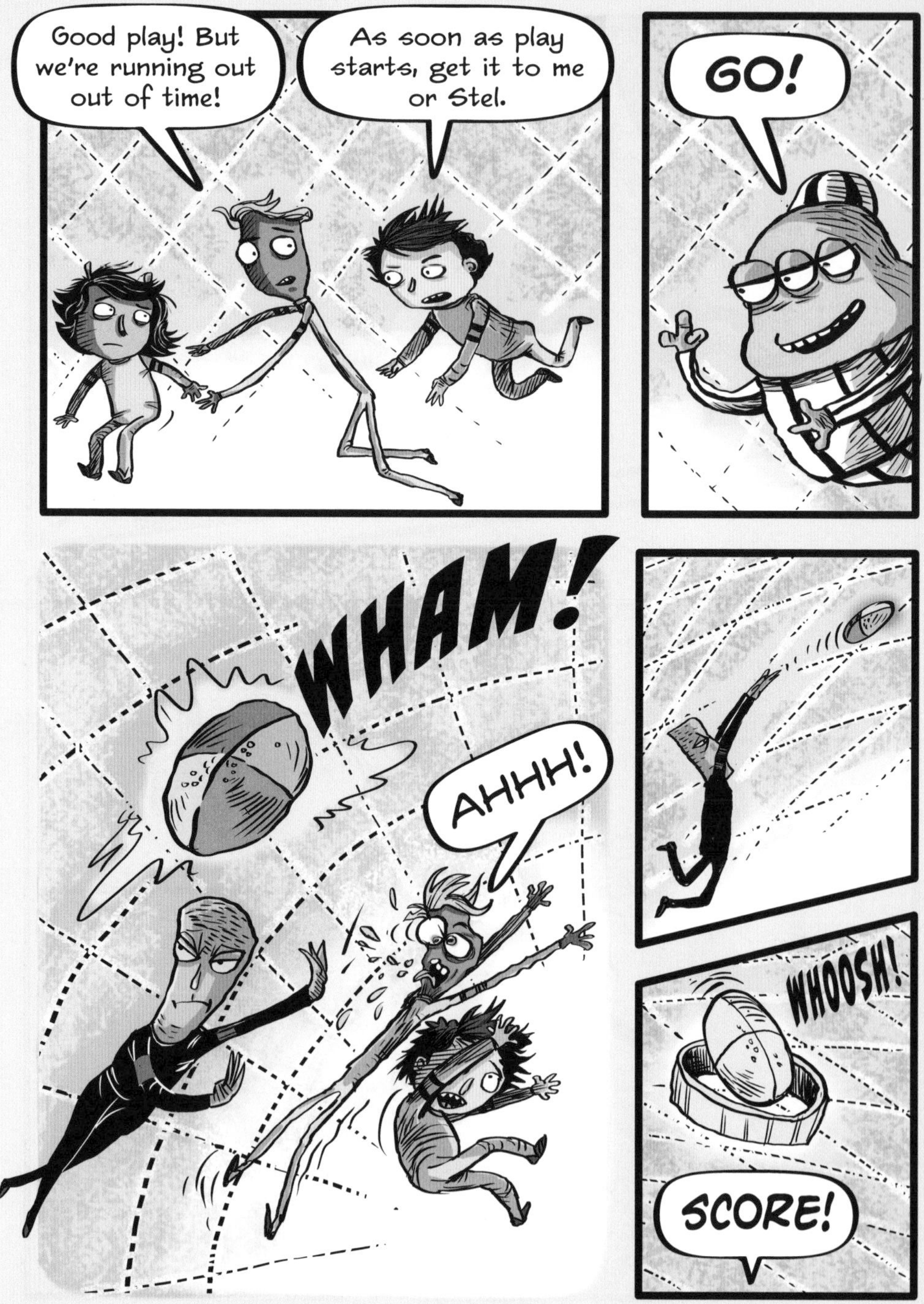
Good play! But we're running out out of time!
As soon as play starts, get it to me or Stel.
GO!
WHAM!
AHHH!
WHOOSH!
SCORE!

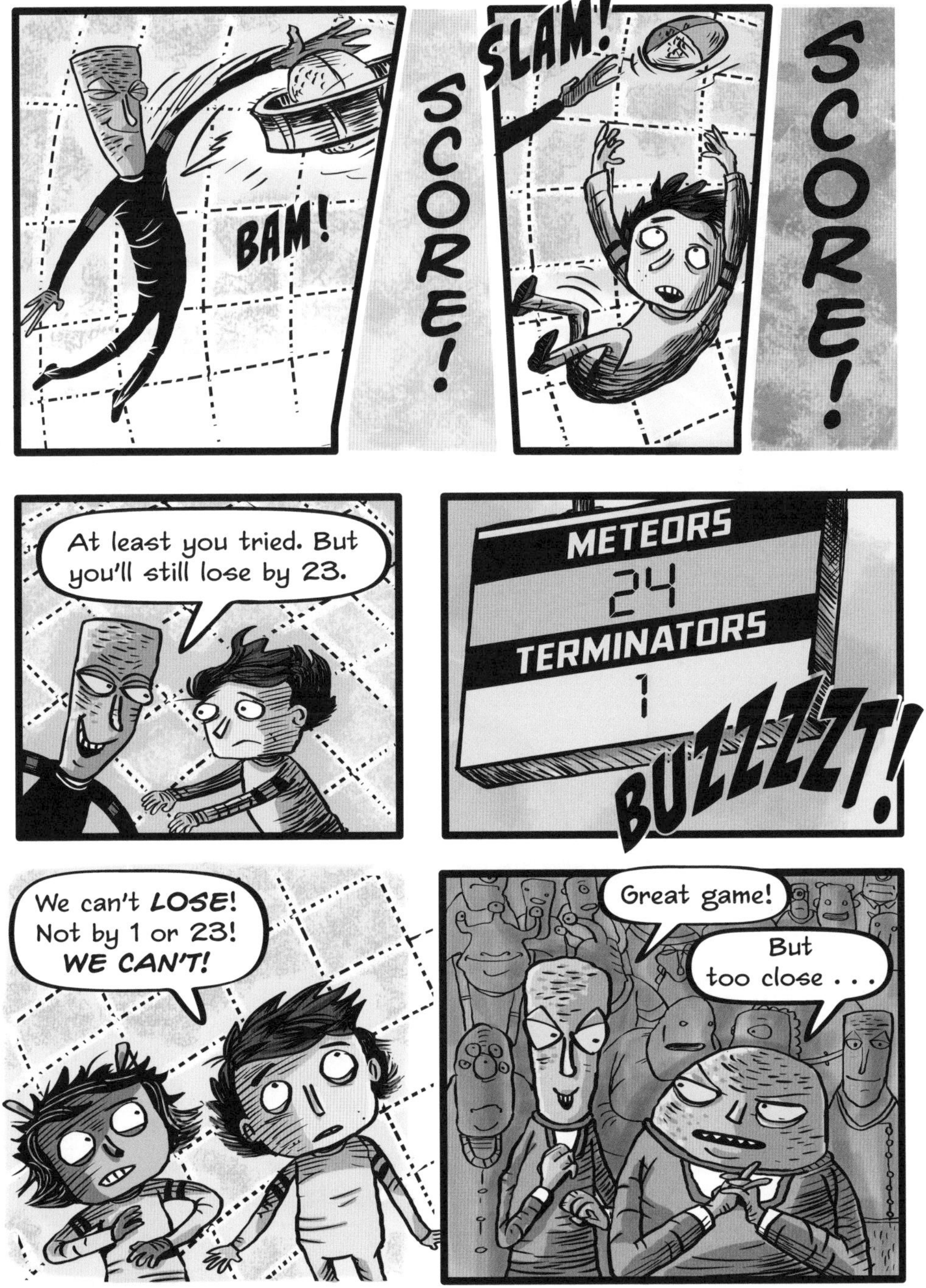
BAM!
SCORE!
SLAM!
SCORE!
At least you tried. But you'll still lose by 23.
METEORS
24
TERMINATORS
1
BUZZZZT!
We can't **LOSE**! Not by 1 or 23! ***WE CAN'T!***
Great game!
But too close . . .

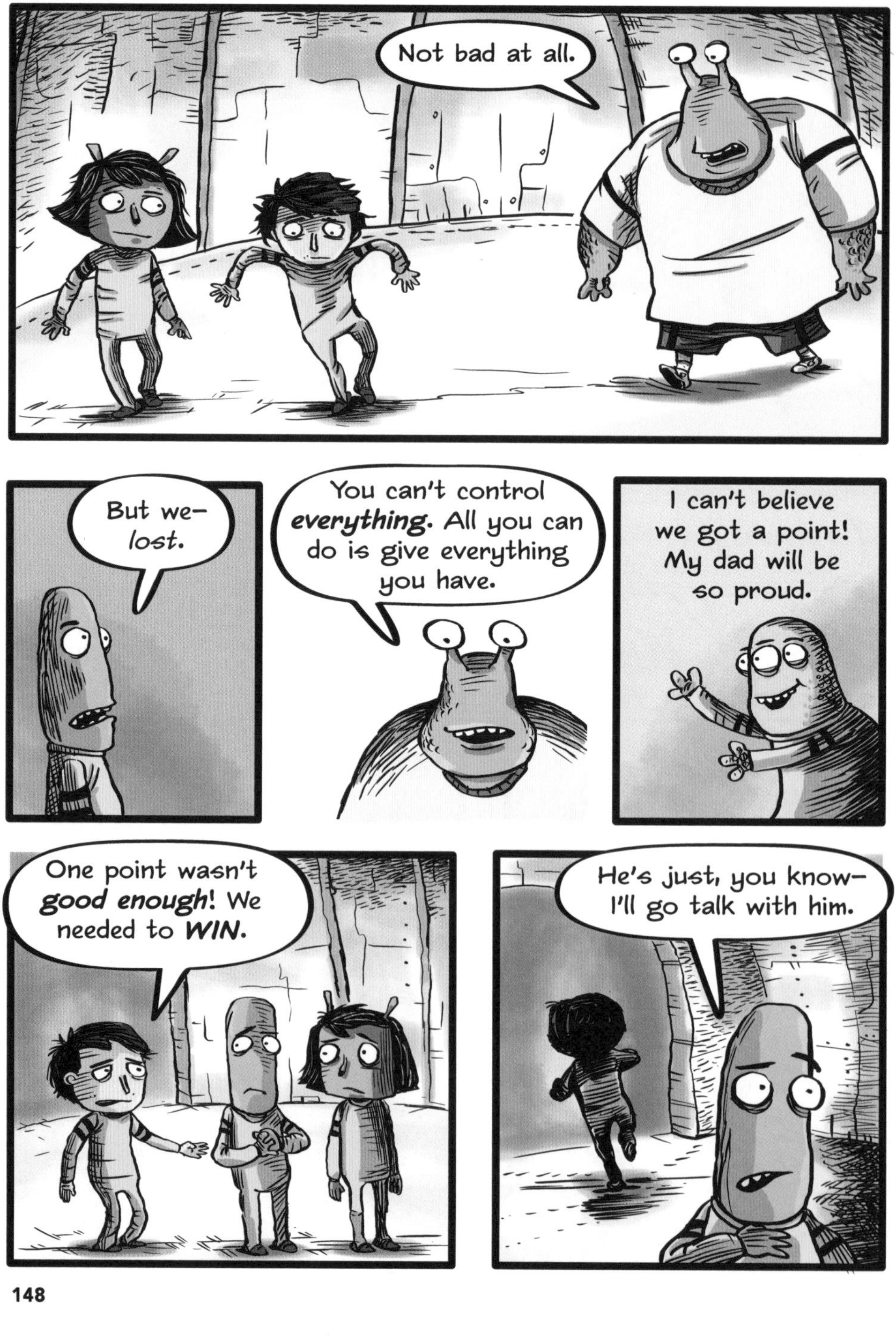
Not bad at all.
But we-
lost.
You can't control everything. All you can do is give everything you have.
I can't believe we got a point! My dad will be so proud.
One point wasn't good enough! We needed to WIN.
He's just, you know-
I'll go talk with him.

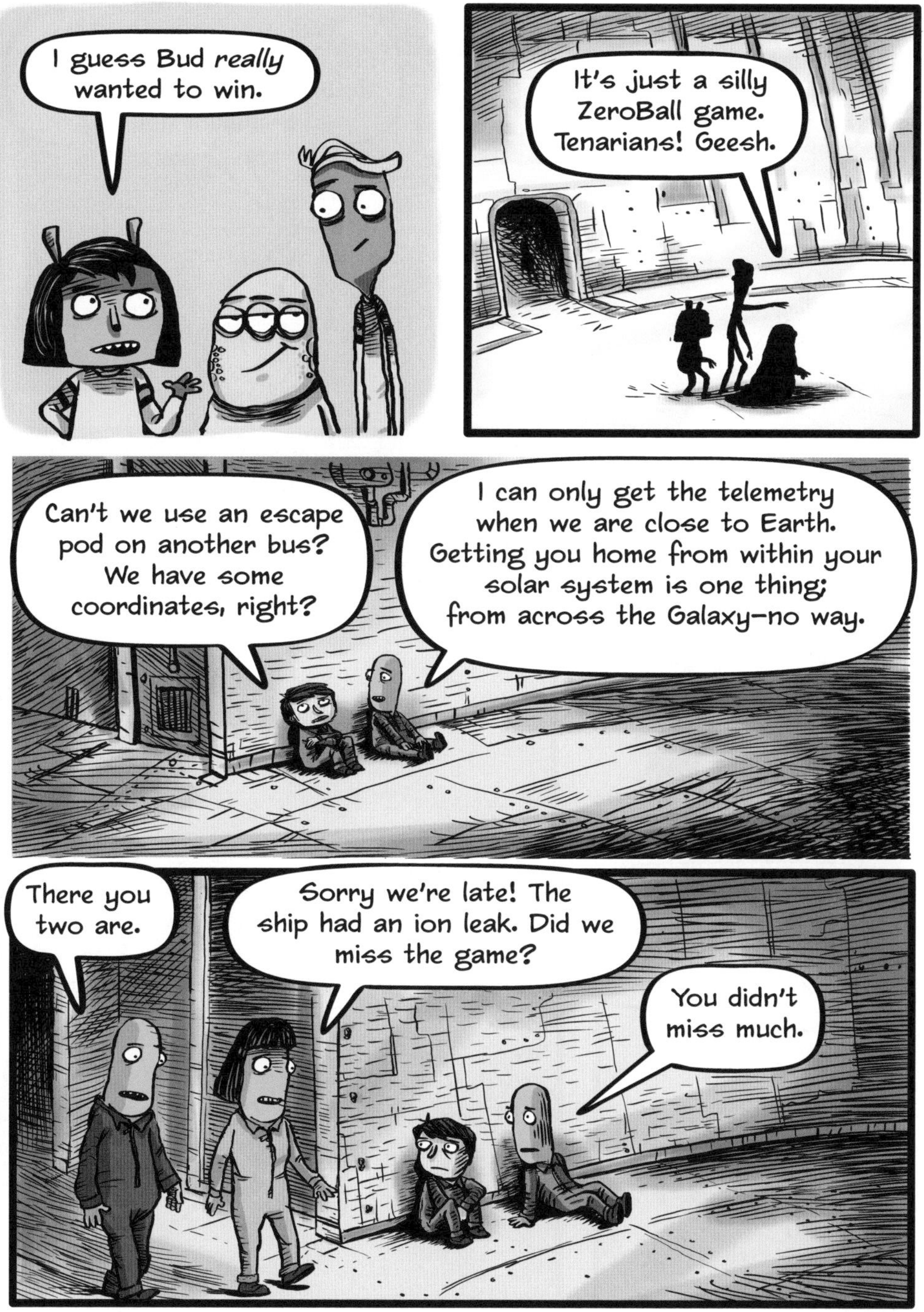
I guess Bud *really* wanted to win.
It's just a silly ZeroBall game. Tenarians! Geesh.
Can't we use an escape pod on another bus? We have some coordinates, right?
I can only get the telemetry when we are close to Earth. Getting you home from within your solar system is one thing; from across the Galaxy—no way.
There you two are.
Sorry we're late! The ship had an ion leak. Did we miss the game?
You didn't miss much.

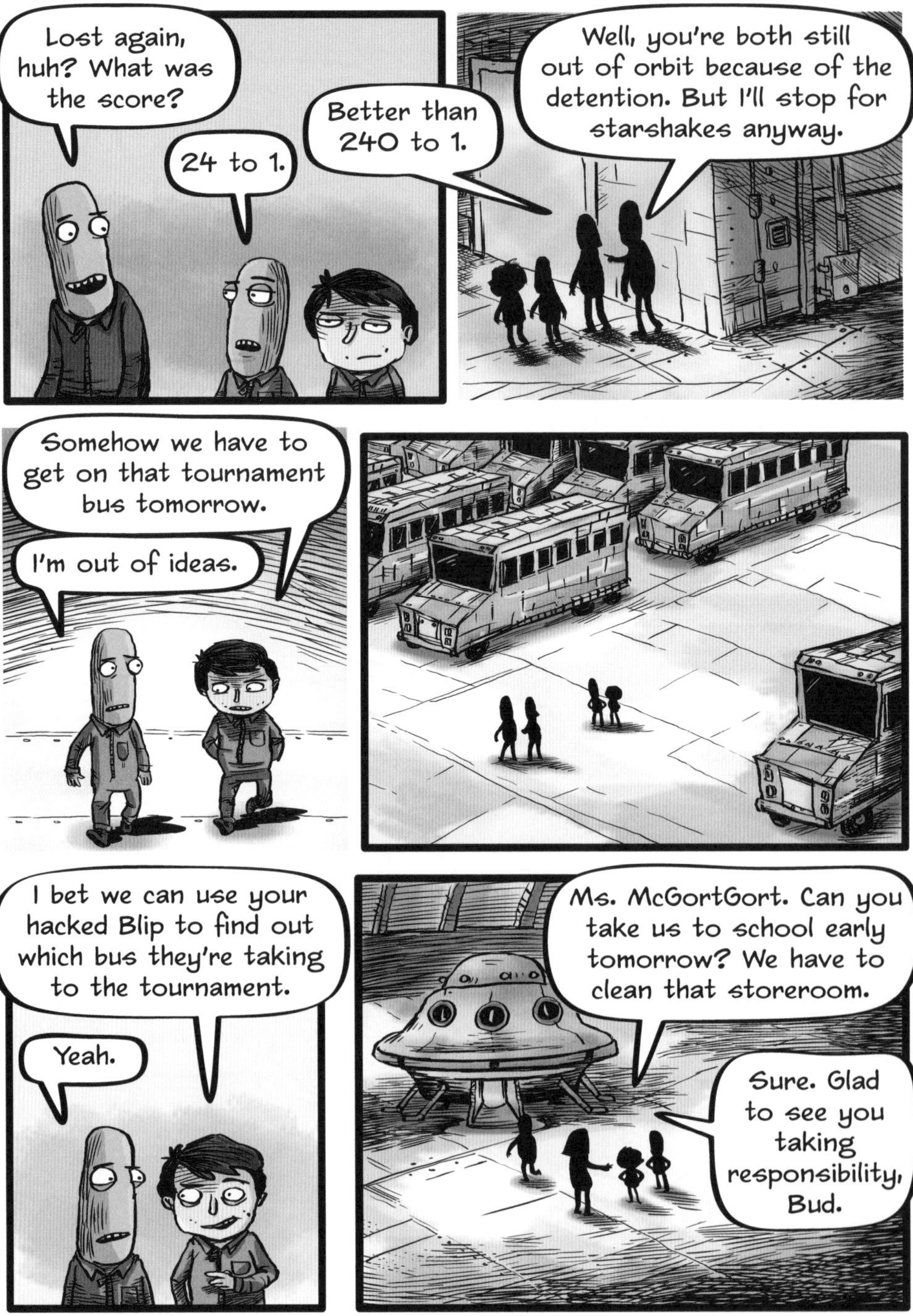
Lost again, huh? What was the score?
24 to 1.
Better than 240 to 1.
Well, you're both still out of orbit because of the detention. But I'll stop for starshakes anyway.
Somehow we have to get on that tournament bus tomorrow.
I'm out of ideas.
I bet we can use your hacked Blip to find out which bus they're taking to the tournament.
Yeah.
Ms. McGortGort. Can you take us to school early tomorrow? We have to clean that storeroom.
Sure. Glad to see you taking responsibility, Bud.

CHAPTER 6

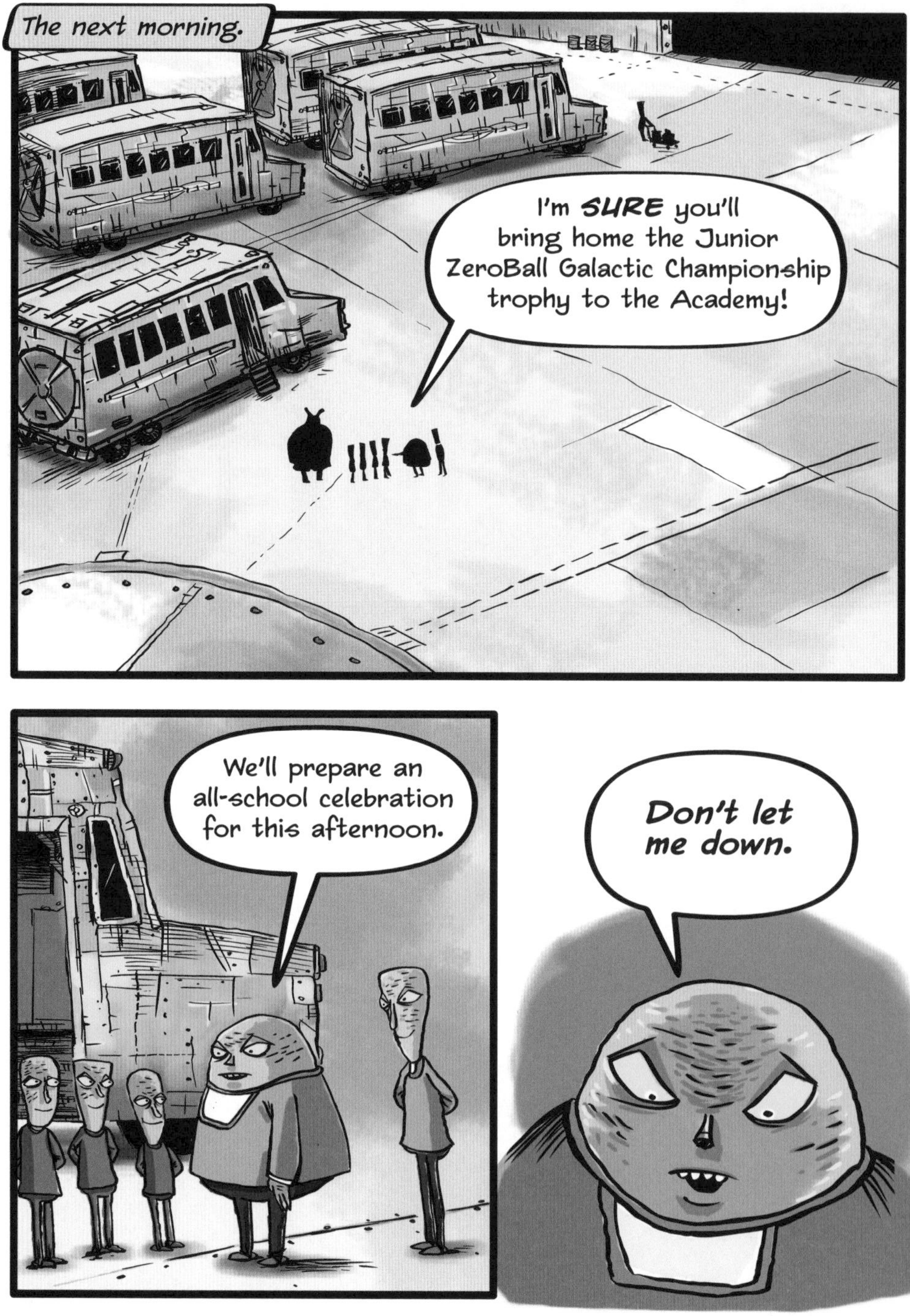
The next morning.
I'm **SURE** you'll bring home the Junior ZeroBall Galactic Championship trophy to the Academy!
We'll prepare an all-school celebration for this afternoon.
Don't let me down.

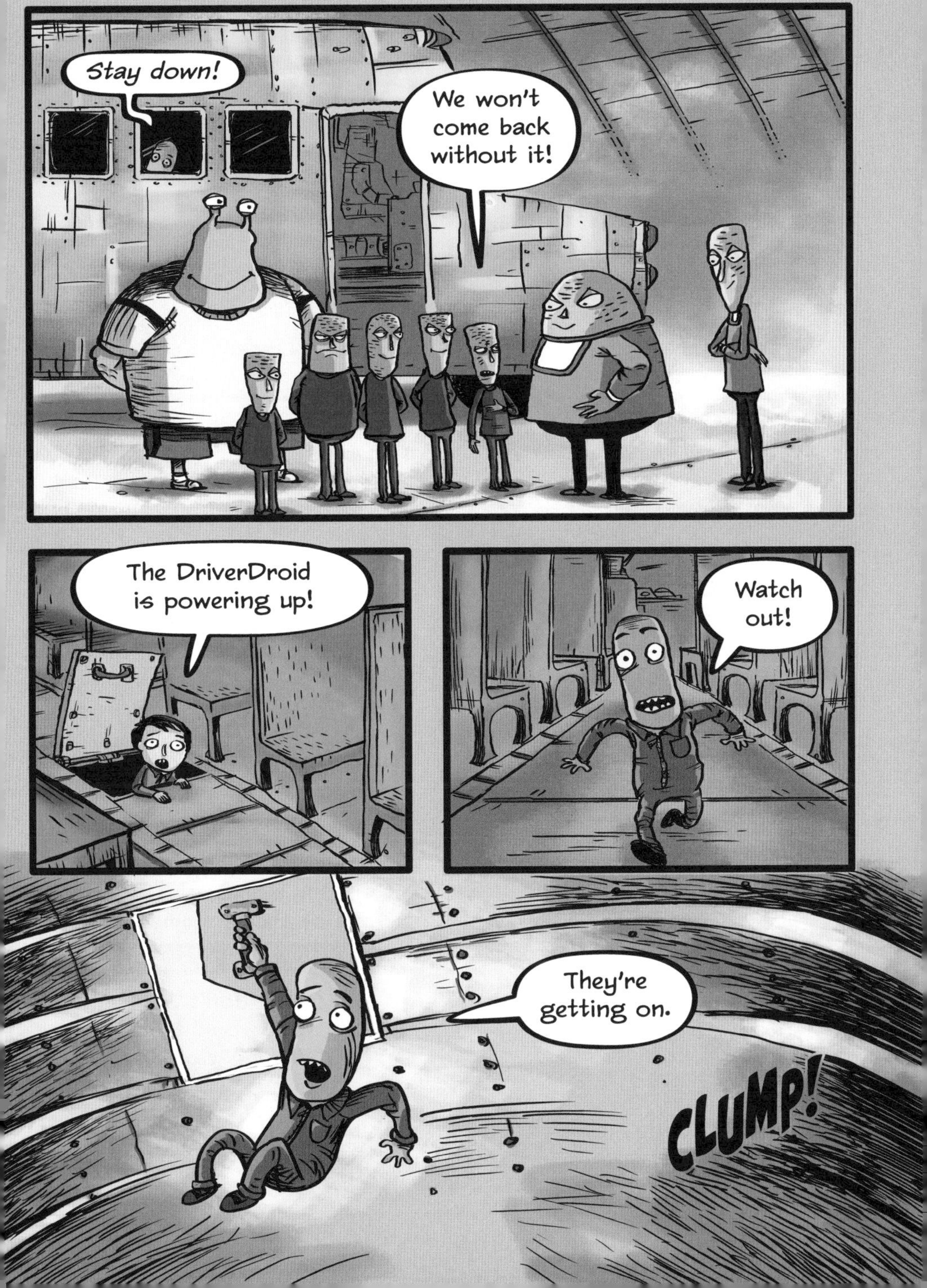
Stay down!
We won't come back without it!
The DriverDroid is powering up!
Watch out!
They're getting on.
CLUMP!

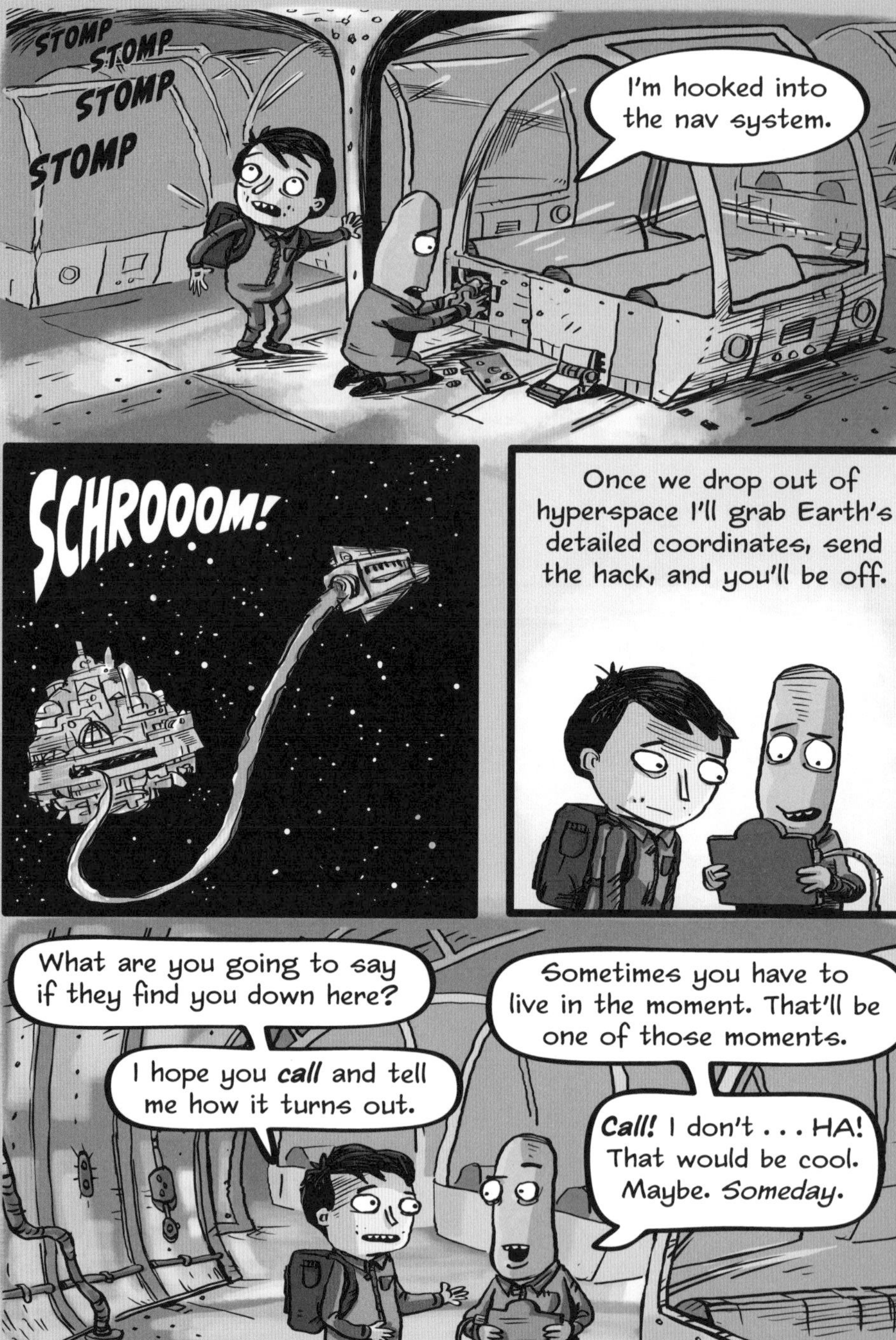
STOMP
STOMP
STOMP
STOMP
I'm hooked into the nav system.
SCHROOOM!
Once we drop out of hyperspace I'll grab Earth's detailed coordinates, send the hack, and you'll be off.
What are you going to say if they find you down here?
Sometimes you have to live in the moment. That'll be one of those moments.
I hope you *call* and tell me how it turns out.
Call! I don't . . . HA! That would be cool. Maybe. *Someday.*

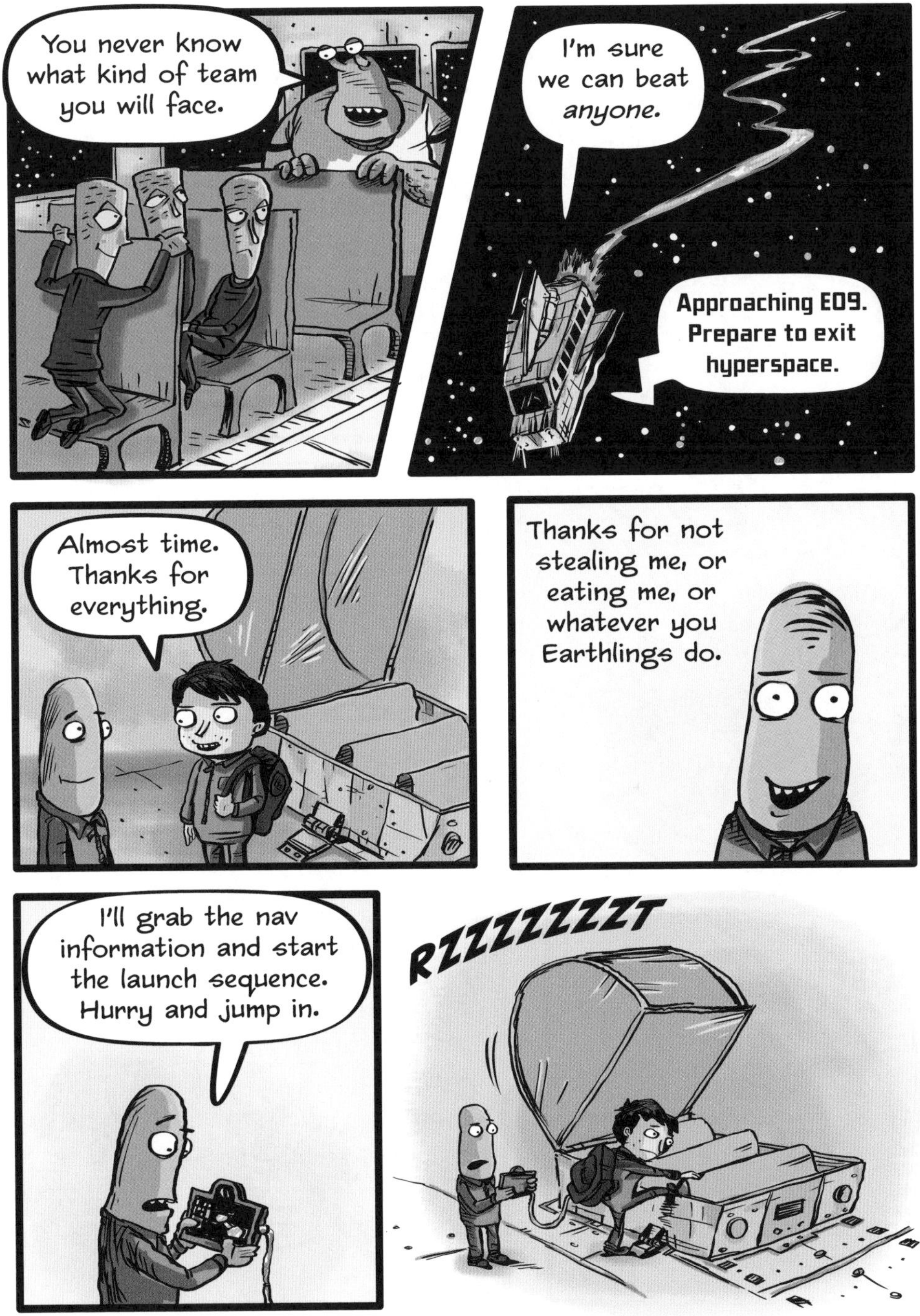
You never know what kind of team you will face.
I'm sure we can beat *anyone*.
Approaching E09. Prepare to exit hyperspace.
Almost time. Thanks for everything.
Thanks for not stealing me, or eating me, or whatever you Earthlings do.
I'll grab the nav information and start the launch sequence. Hurry and jump in.
RZZZZZZZT

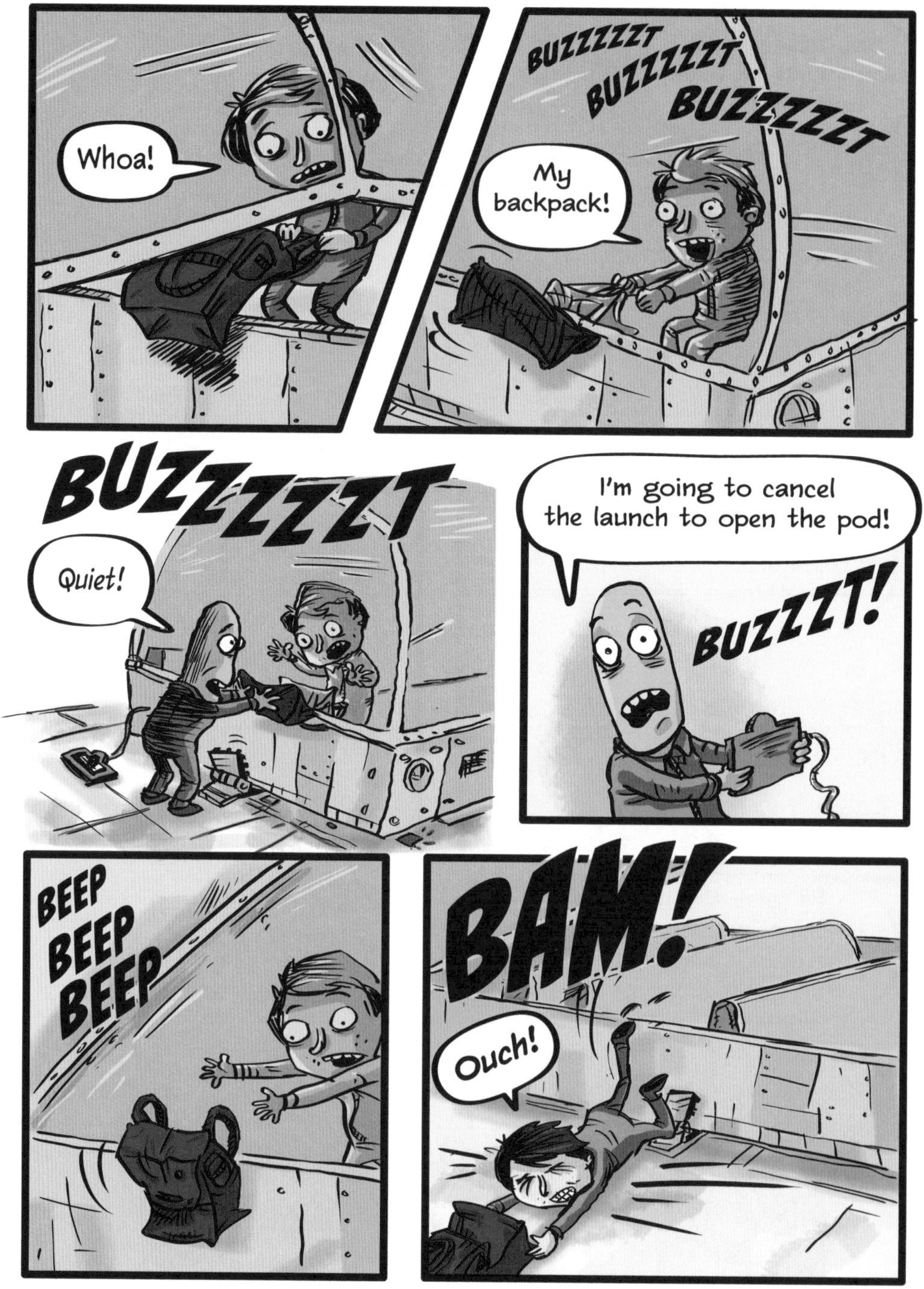
Whoa!
BUZZZZZT
BUZZZZZT
BUZZZZZZT
My backpack!
BUZZZZZT
Quiet!
I'm going to cancel the launch to open the pod!
BUZZZT!
BEEP
BEEP
BEEP
BAM!
Ouch!

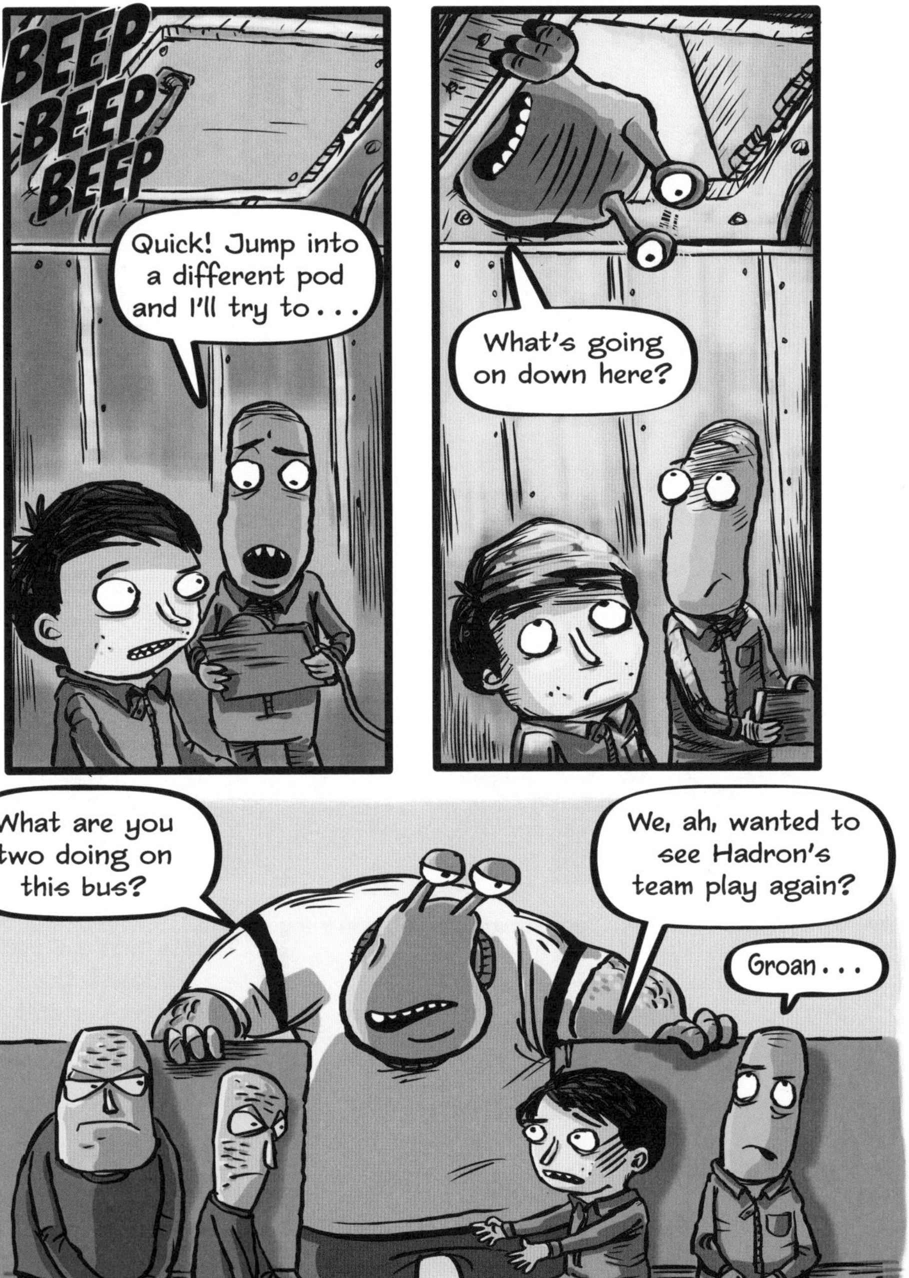
BEEP BEEP BEEP
Quick! Jump into a different pod and I'll try to . . .
What's going on down here?
What are you two doing on this bus?
We, ah, wanted to see Hadron's team play again?
Groan . . .

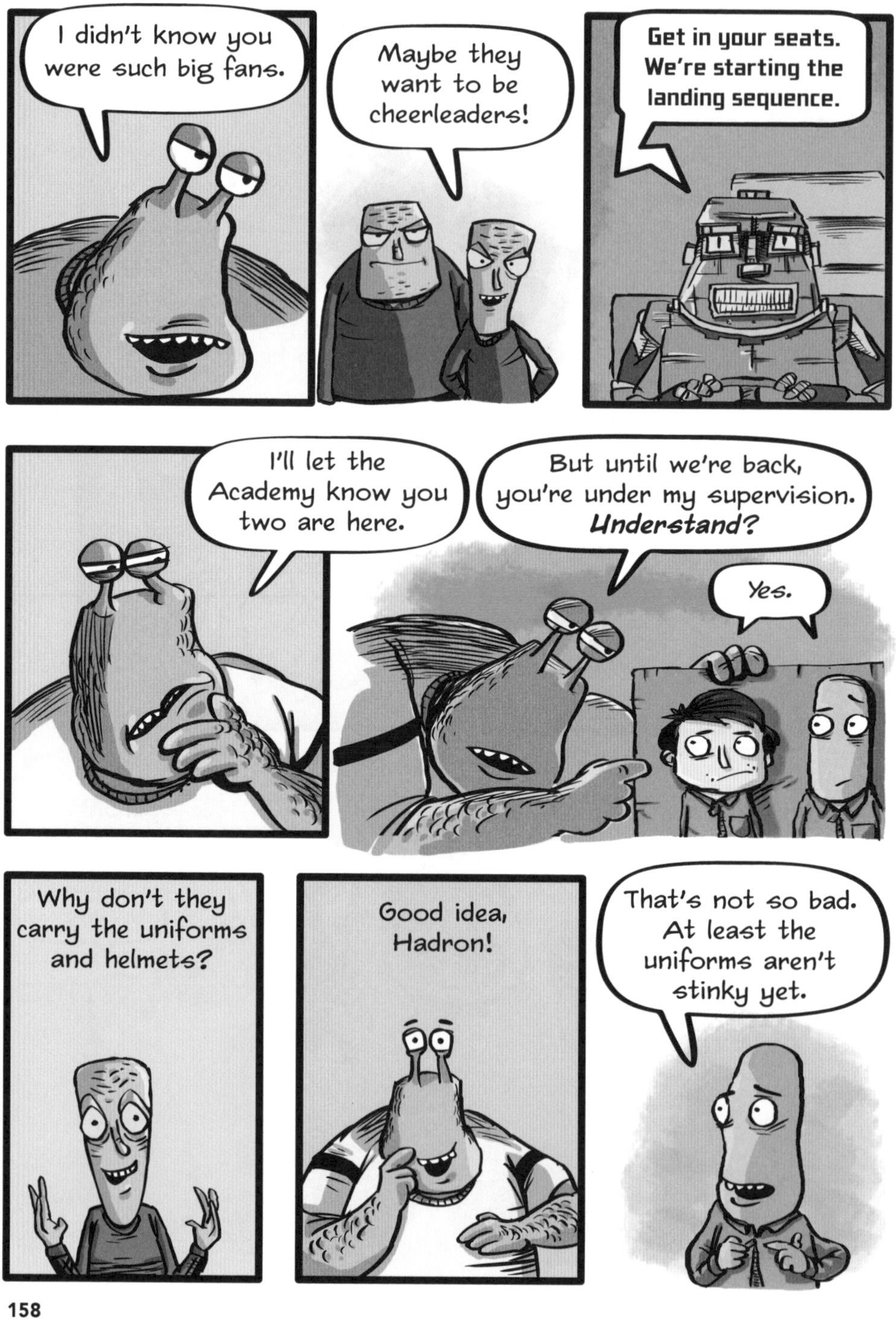
I didn't know you were such big fans.
Maybe they want to be cheerleaders!
Get in your seats. We're starting the landing sequence.
I'll let the Academy know you two are here.
But until we're back, you're under my supervision. *Understand?*
Yes.
Why don't they carry the uniforms and helmets?
Good idea, Hadron!
That's not so bad. At least the uniforms aren't stinky yet.

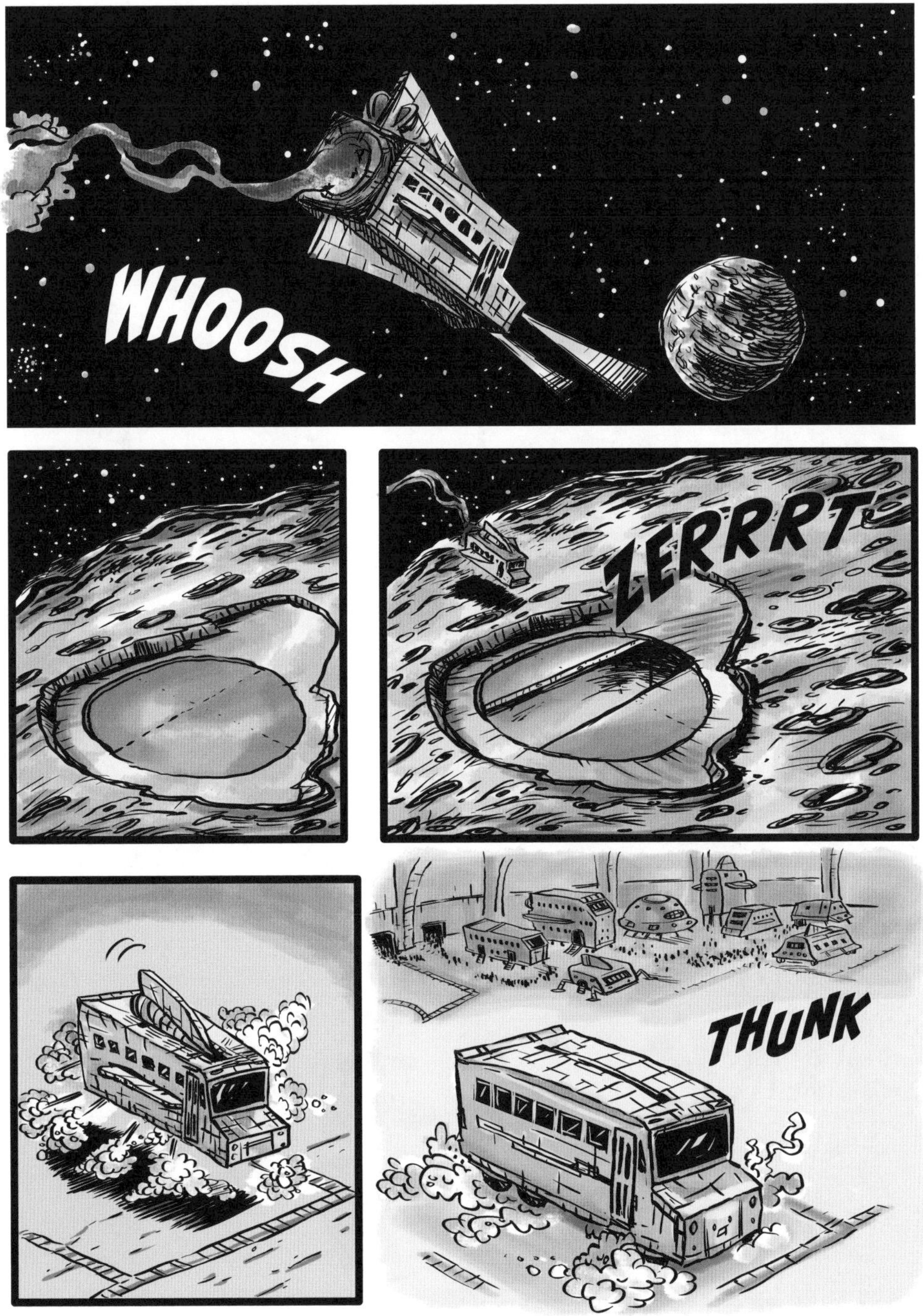
WHOOSH
ZERRRT
THUNK

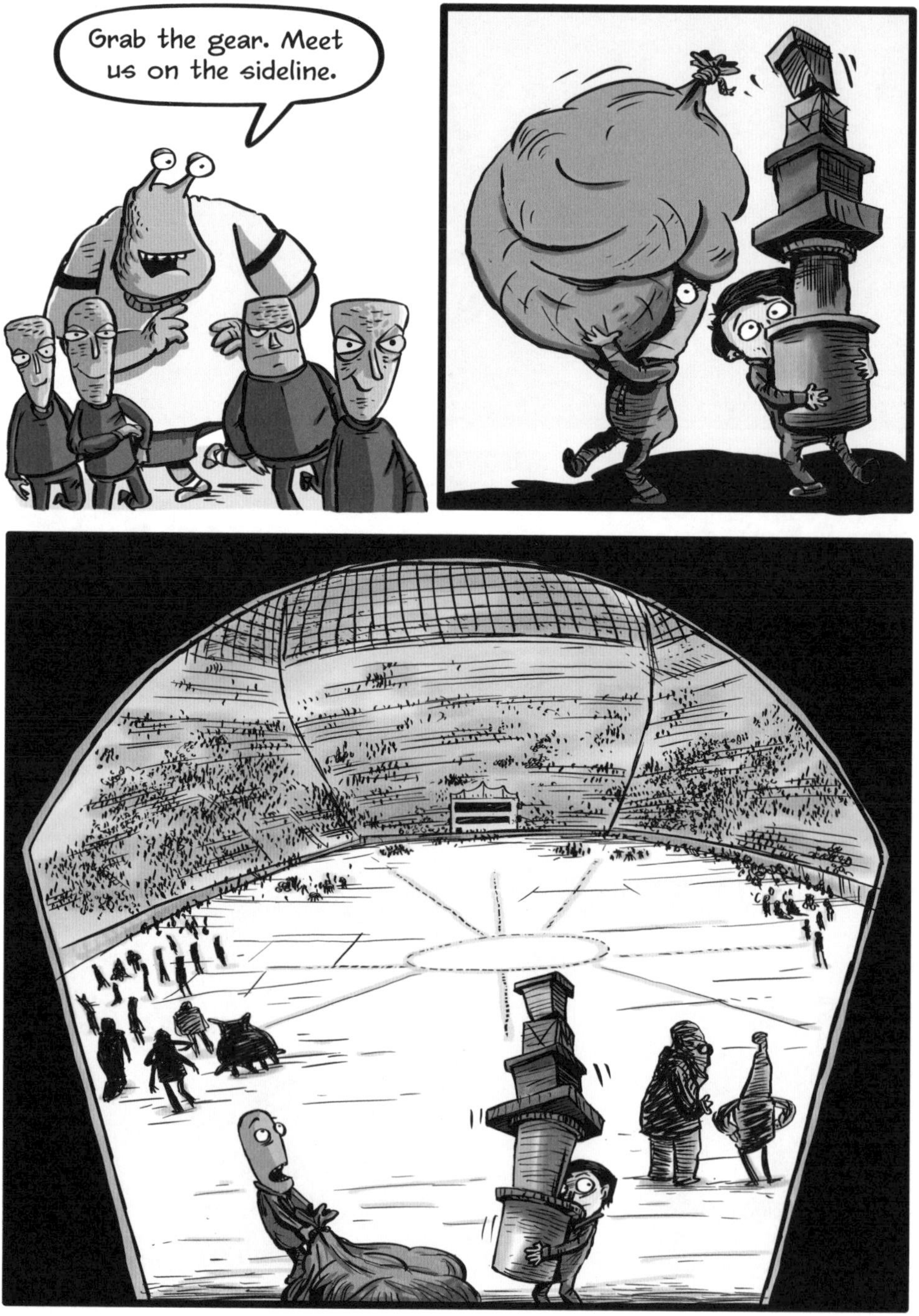
Grab the gear. Meet us on the sideline.

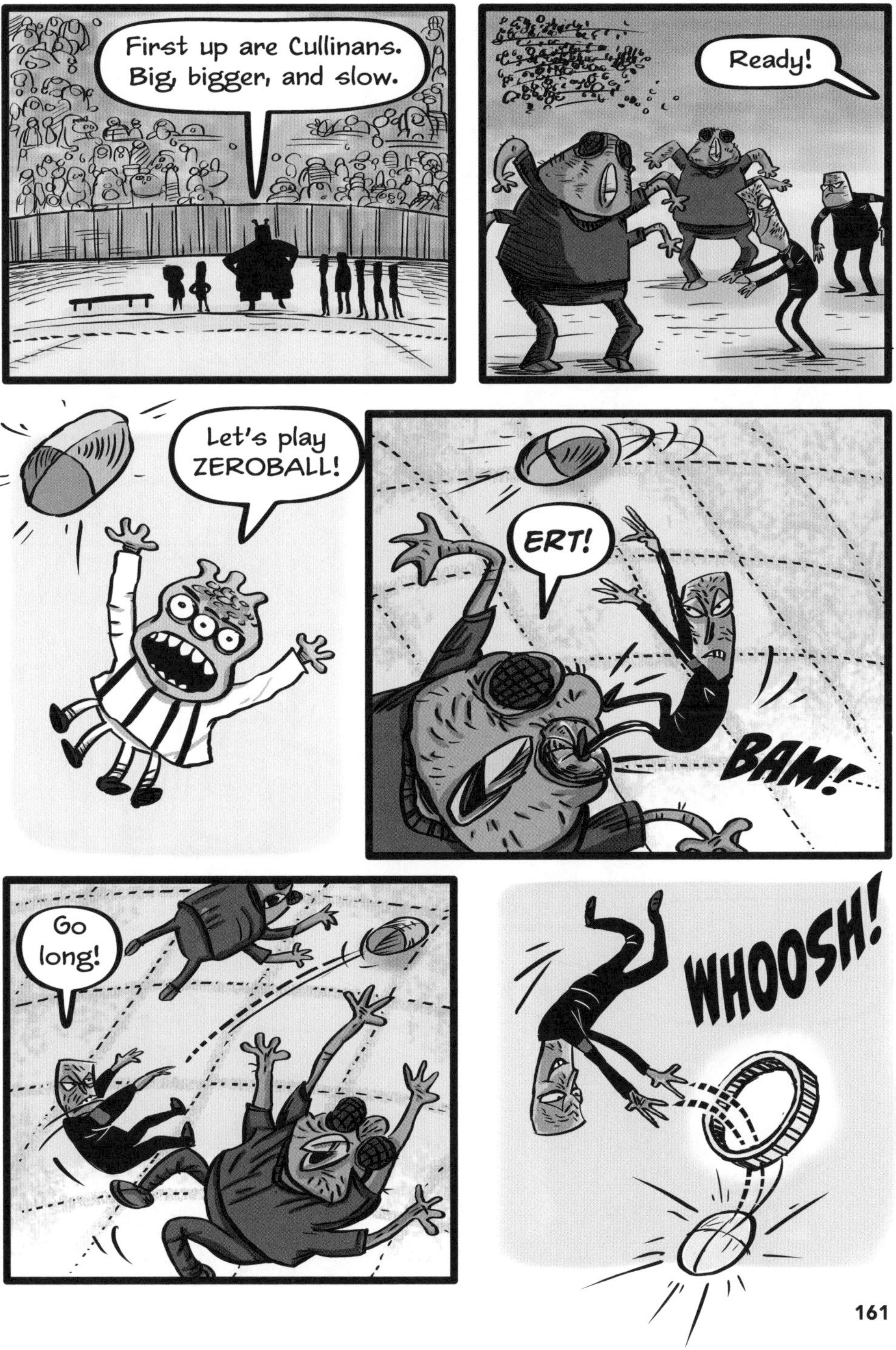
First up are Cullinans. Big, bigger, and slow.
Ready!
Let's play ZEROBALL!
ERT!
BAM!
Go long!
WHOOSH!

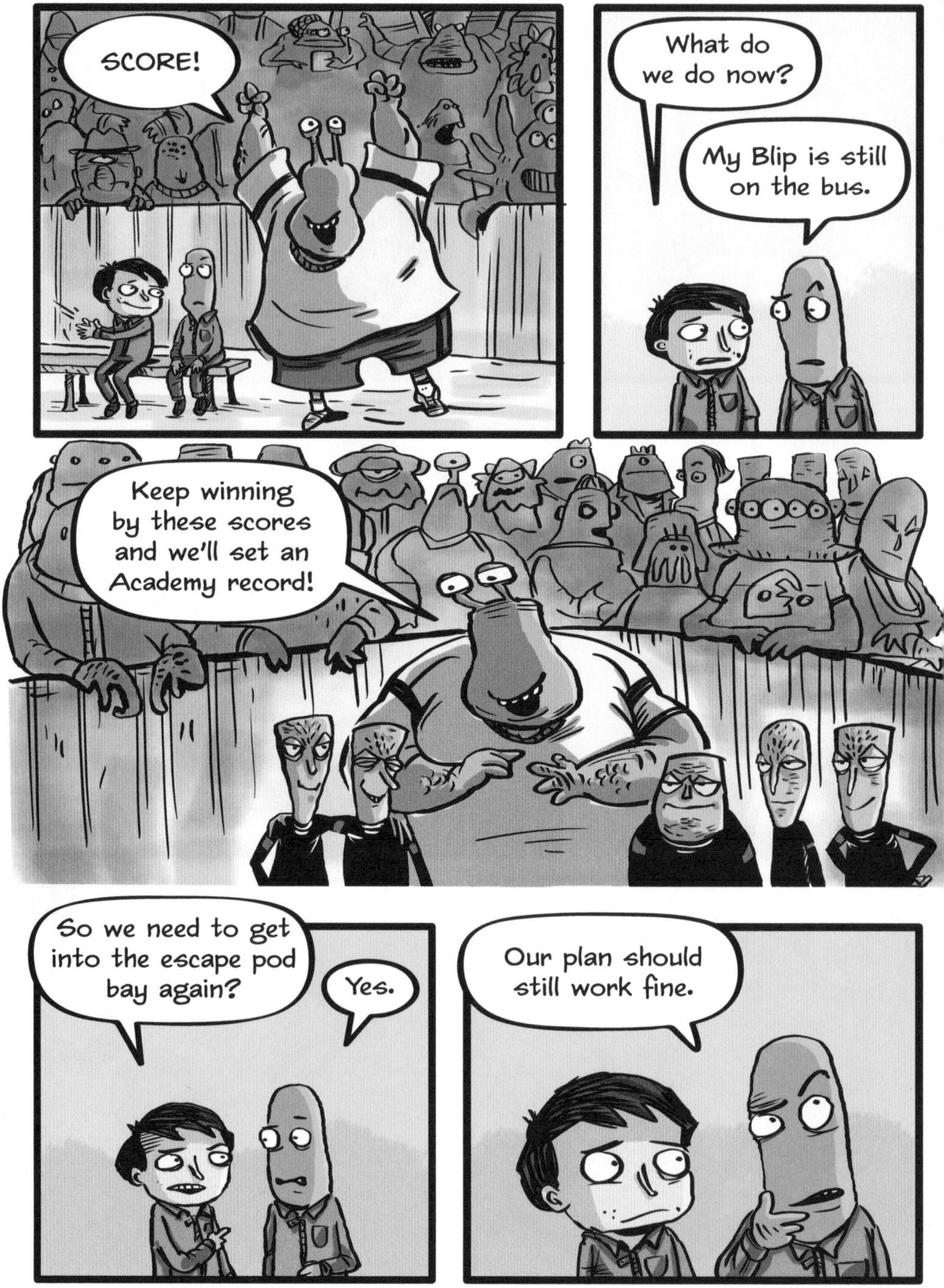
SCORE!
What do we do now?
My Blip is still on the bus.
Keep winning by these scores and we'll set an Academy record!
So we need to get into the escape pod bay again?
Yes.
Our plan should still work fine.

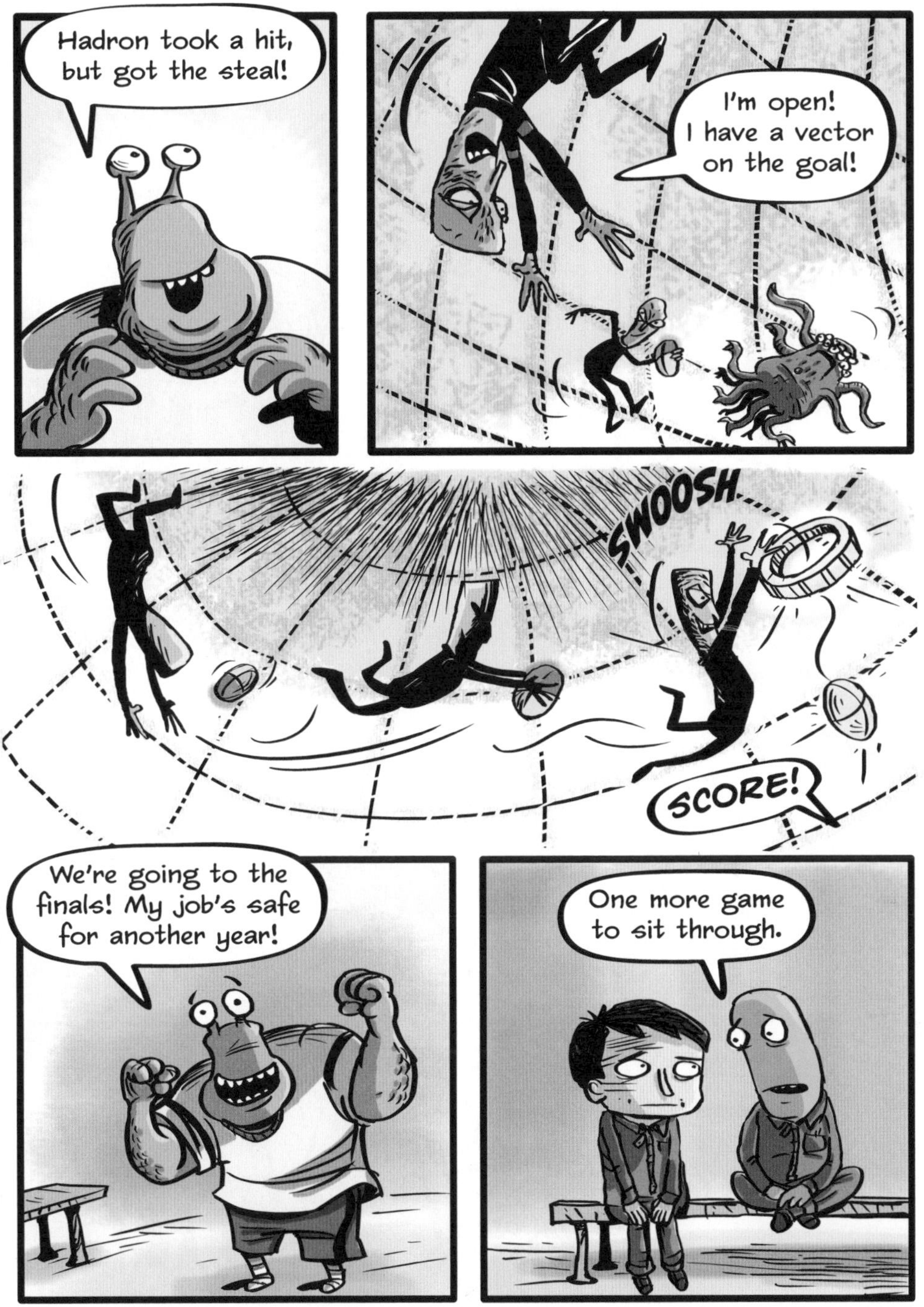

Hadron took a hit, but got the steal!
I'm open! I have a vector on the goal!
SWOOSH
SCORE!
We're going to the finals! My job's safe for another year!
One more game to sit through.

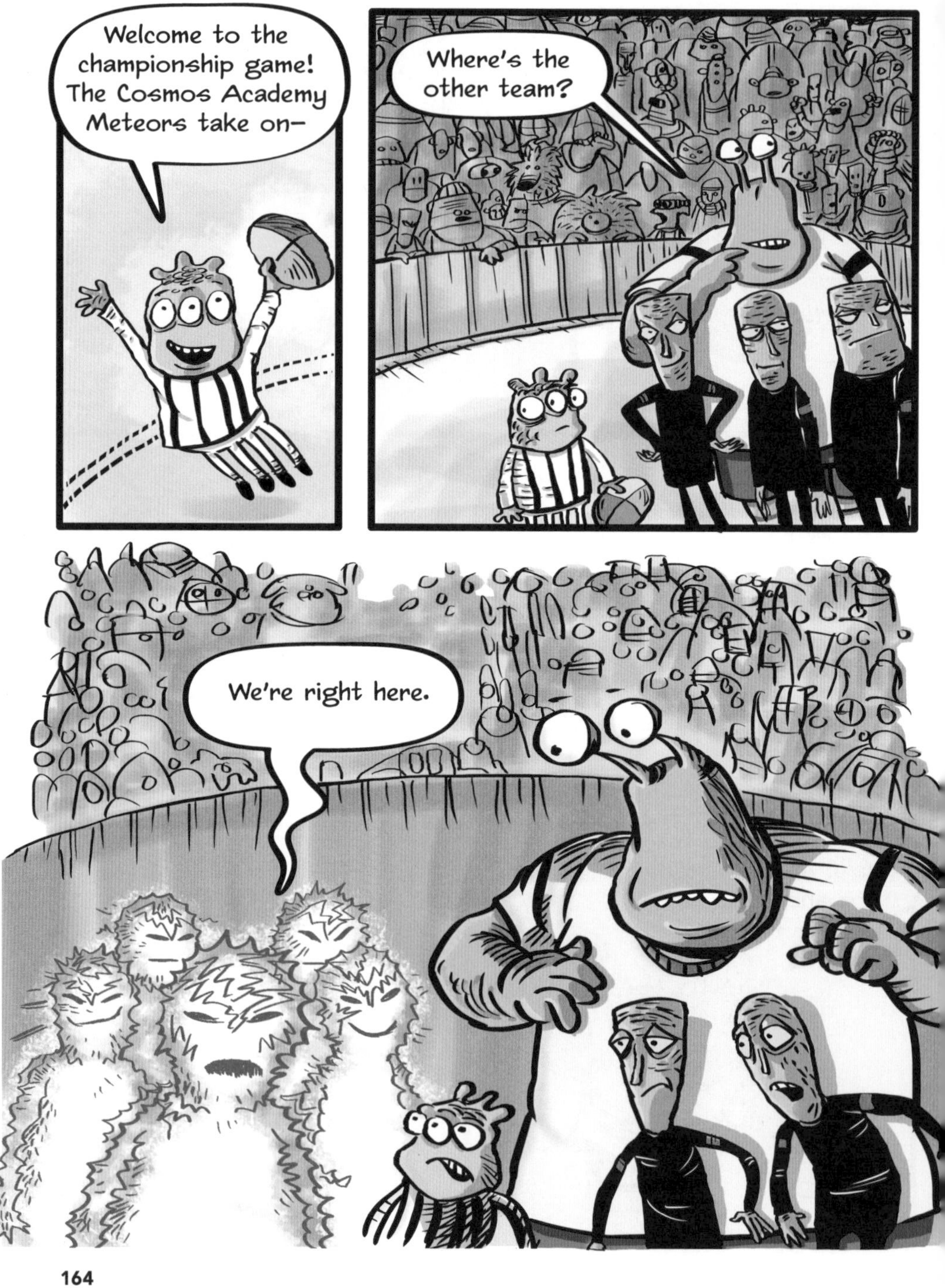
Welcome to the championship game! The Cosmos Academy Meteors take on–
Where's the other team?
We're right here.

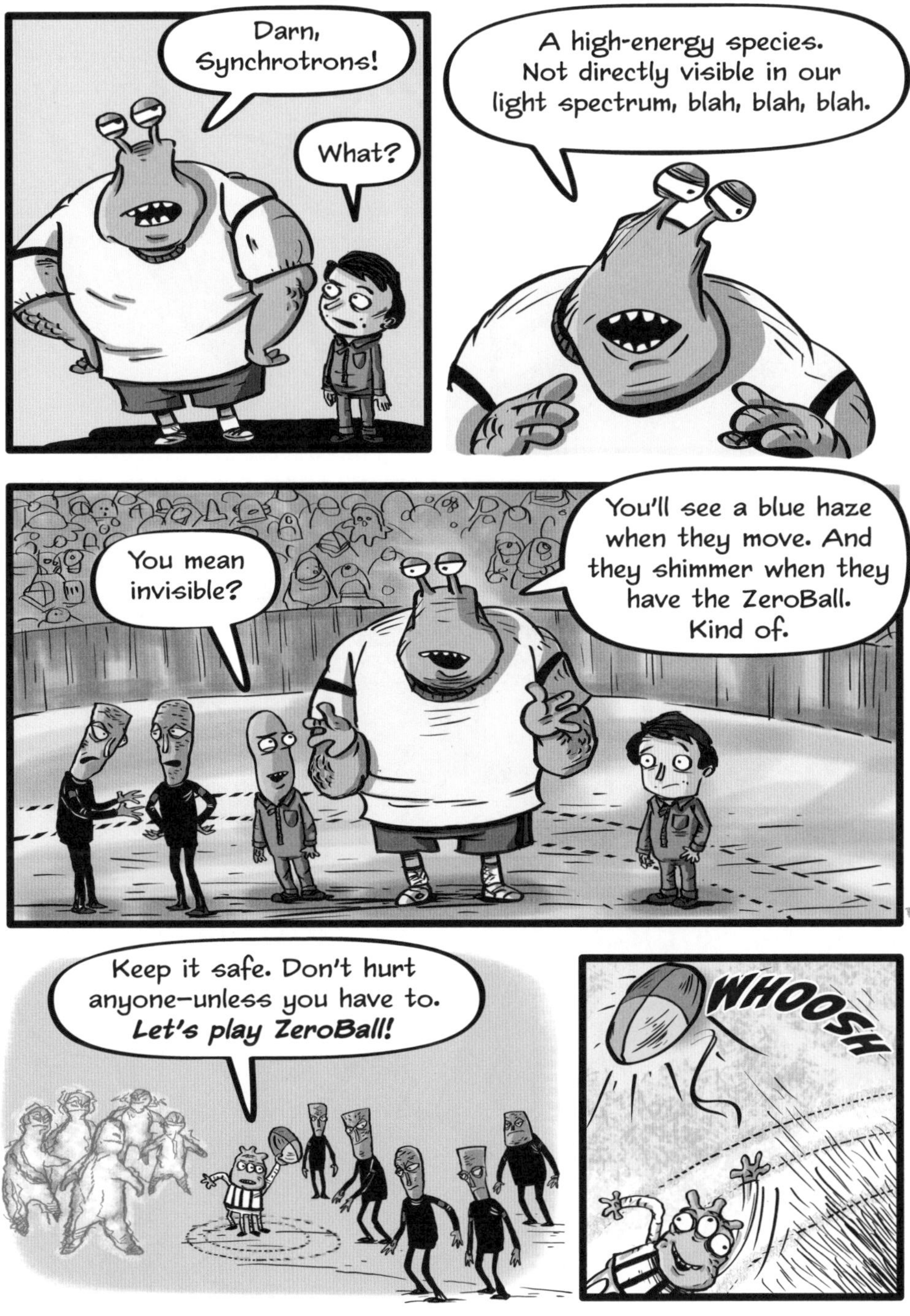
Darn, Synchrotrons!
What?
A high-energy species. Not directly visible in our light spectrum, blah, blah, blah.
You mean invisible?
You'll see a blue haze when they move. And they shimmer when they have the ZeroBall. Kind of.
Keep it safe. Don't hurt anyone—unless you have to. *Let's play ZeroBall!*
WHOOSH

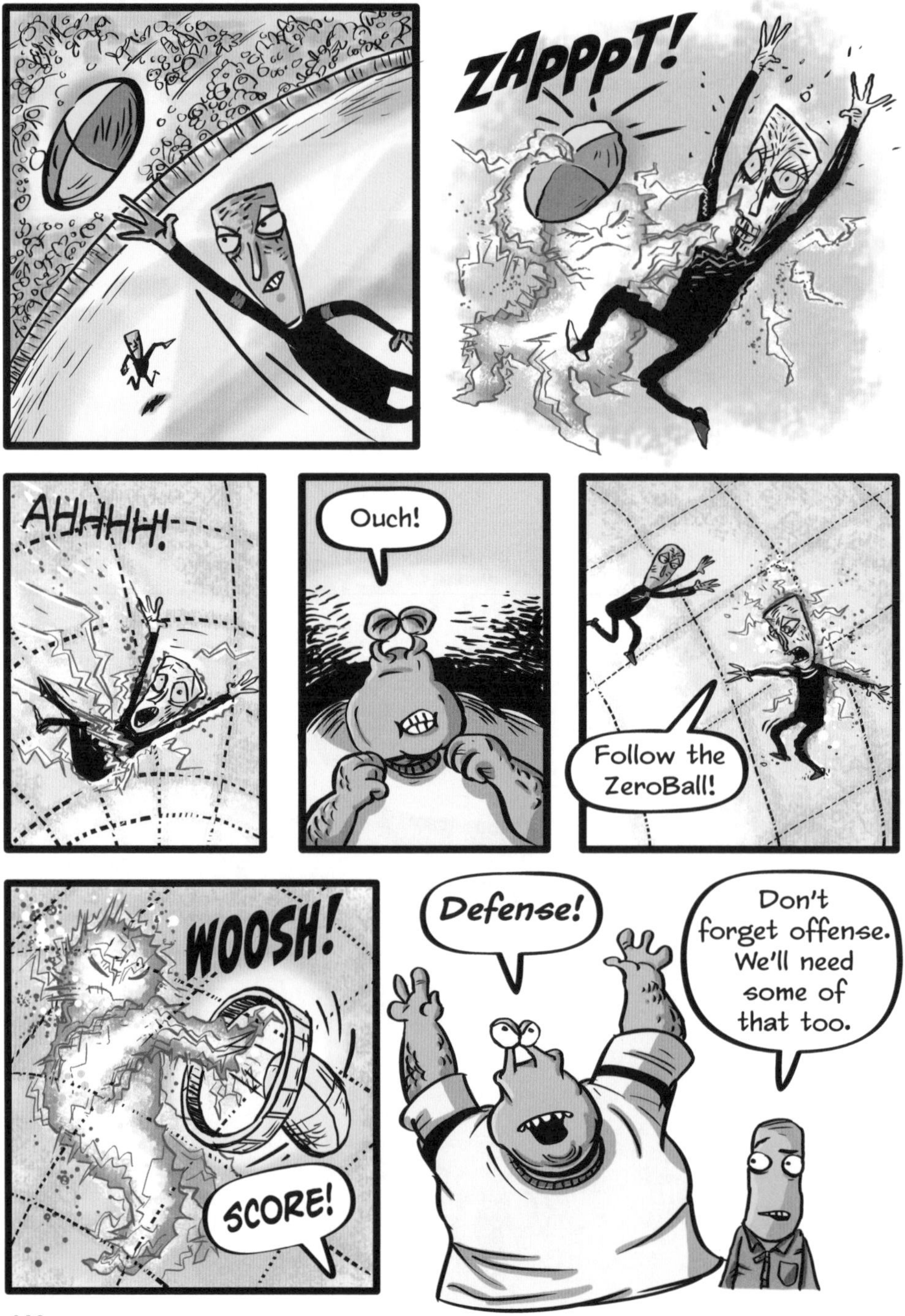
ZAPPPT!
AHHHH!
Ouch!
Follow the ZeroBall!
WOOSH!
SCORE!
Defense!
Don't forget offense. We'll need some of that too.

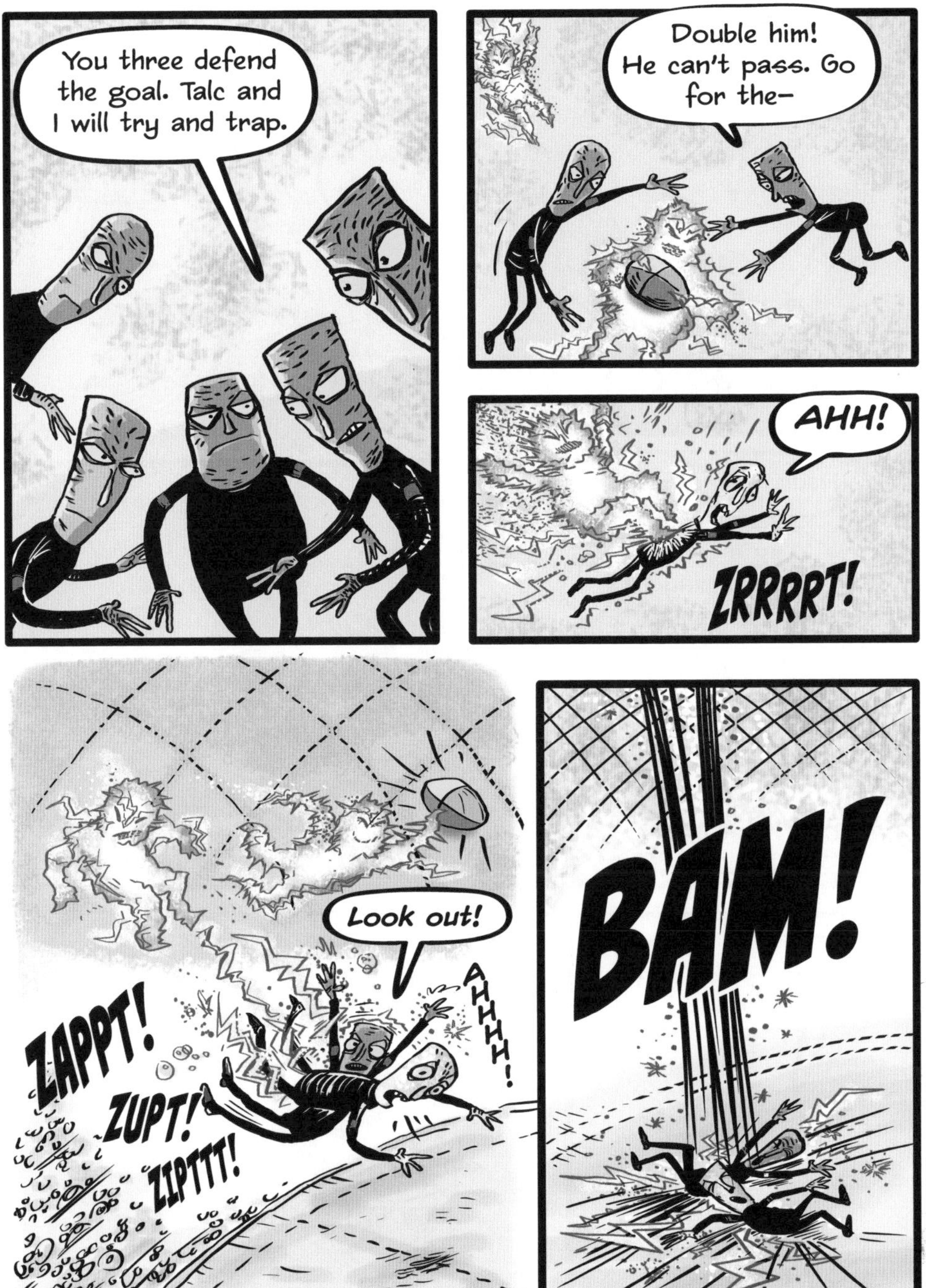
You three defend the goal. Talc and I will try and trap.
Double him! He can't pass. Go for the–
AHH!
ZRRRRT!
Look out!
AHHHH!
ZAPPT!
ZUPT!
ZIPTTT!
BAM!

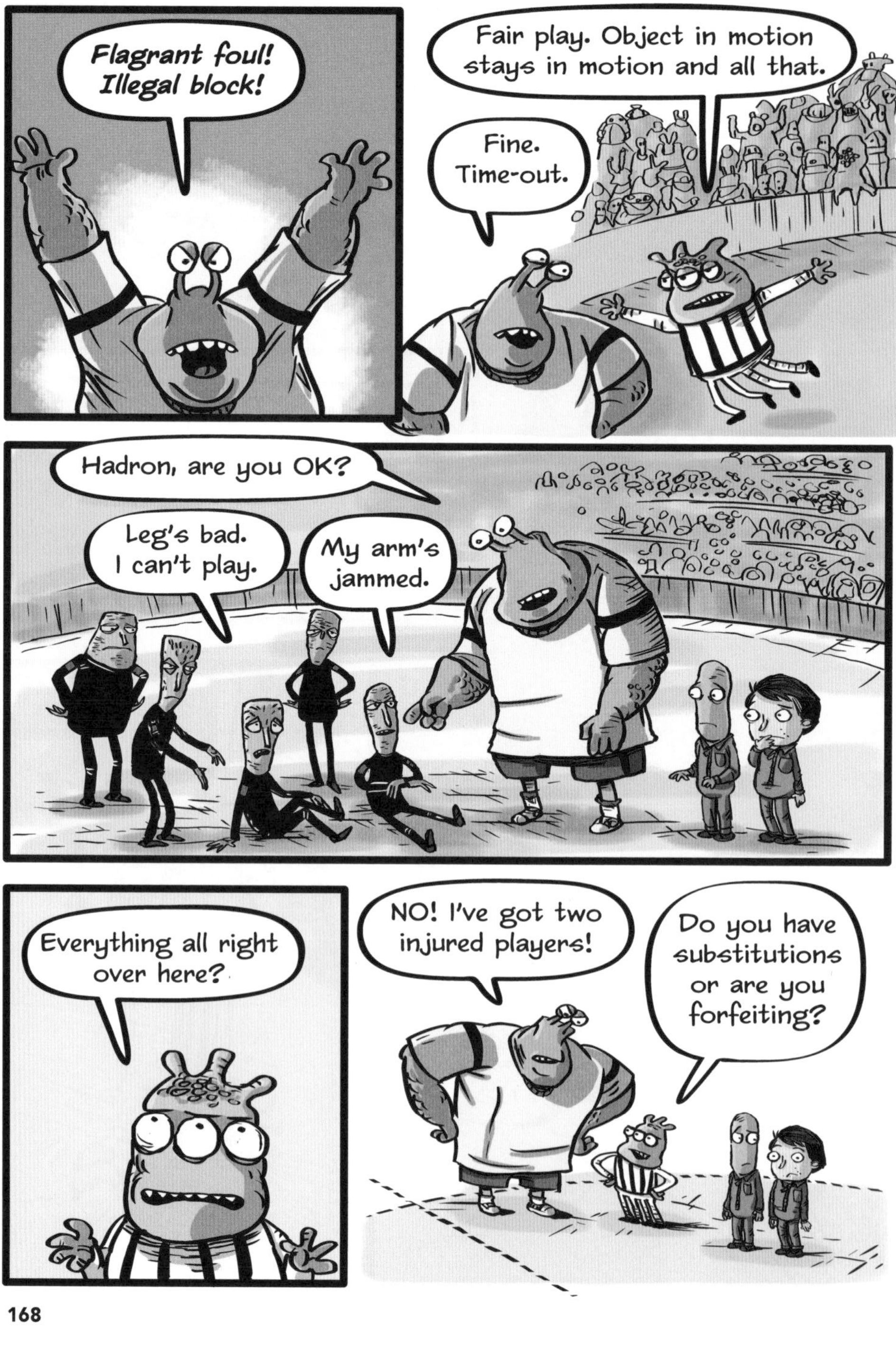
Flagrant foul! Illegal block!
Fair play. Object in motion stays in motion and all that.
Fine. Time-out.
Hadron, are you OK?
Leg's bad. I can't play.
My arm's jammed.
Everything all right over here?
NO! I've got two injured players!
Do you have substitutions or are you forfeiting?

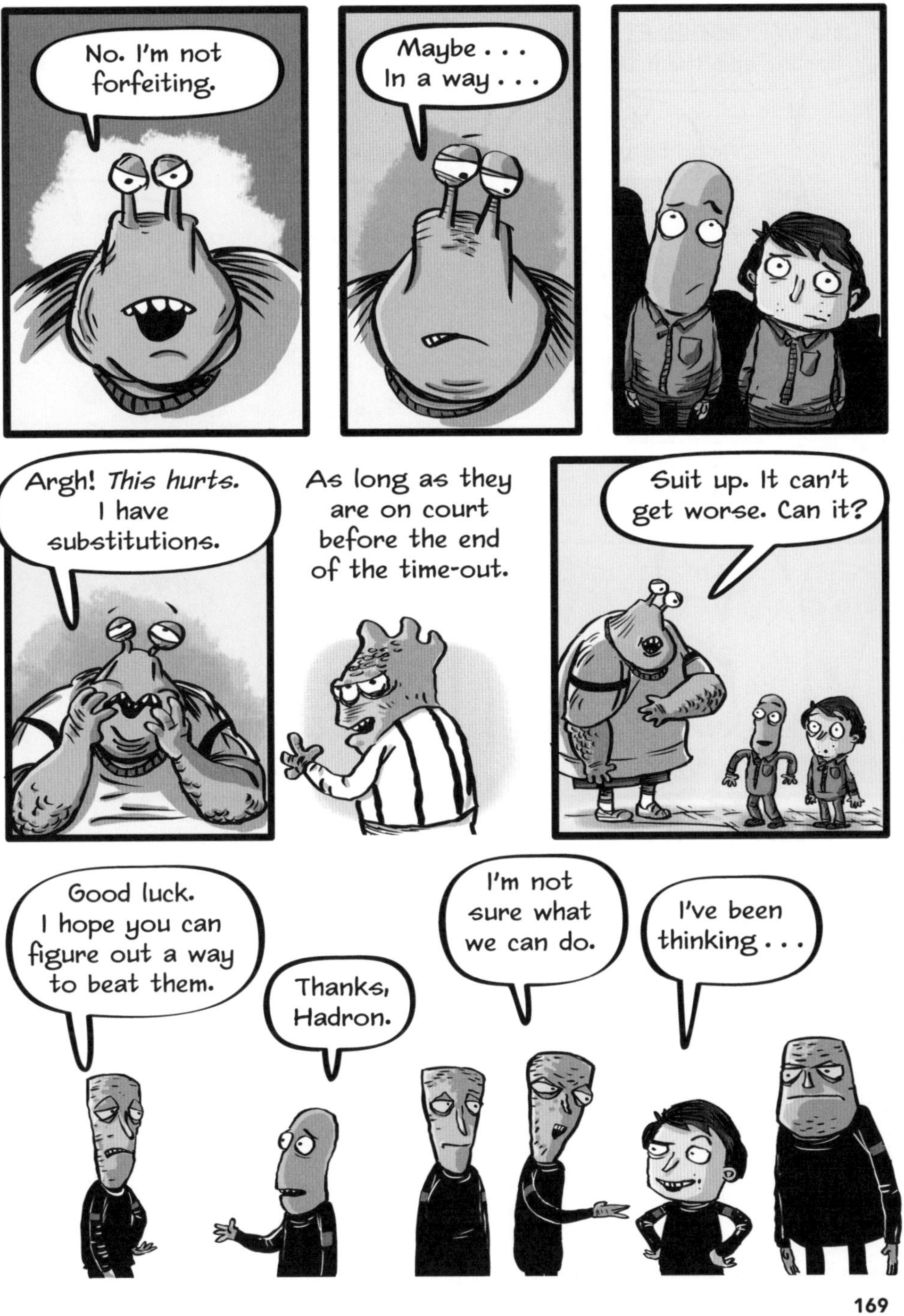
No. I'm not forfeiting.
Maybe . . . In a way . . .
Argh! *This hurts.* I have substitutions.
As long as they are on court before the end of the time-out.
Suit up. It can't get worse. Can it?
Good luck. I hope you can figure out a way to beat them.
Thanks, Hadron.
I'm not sure what we can do.
I've been thinking . . .

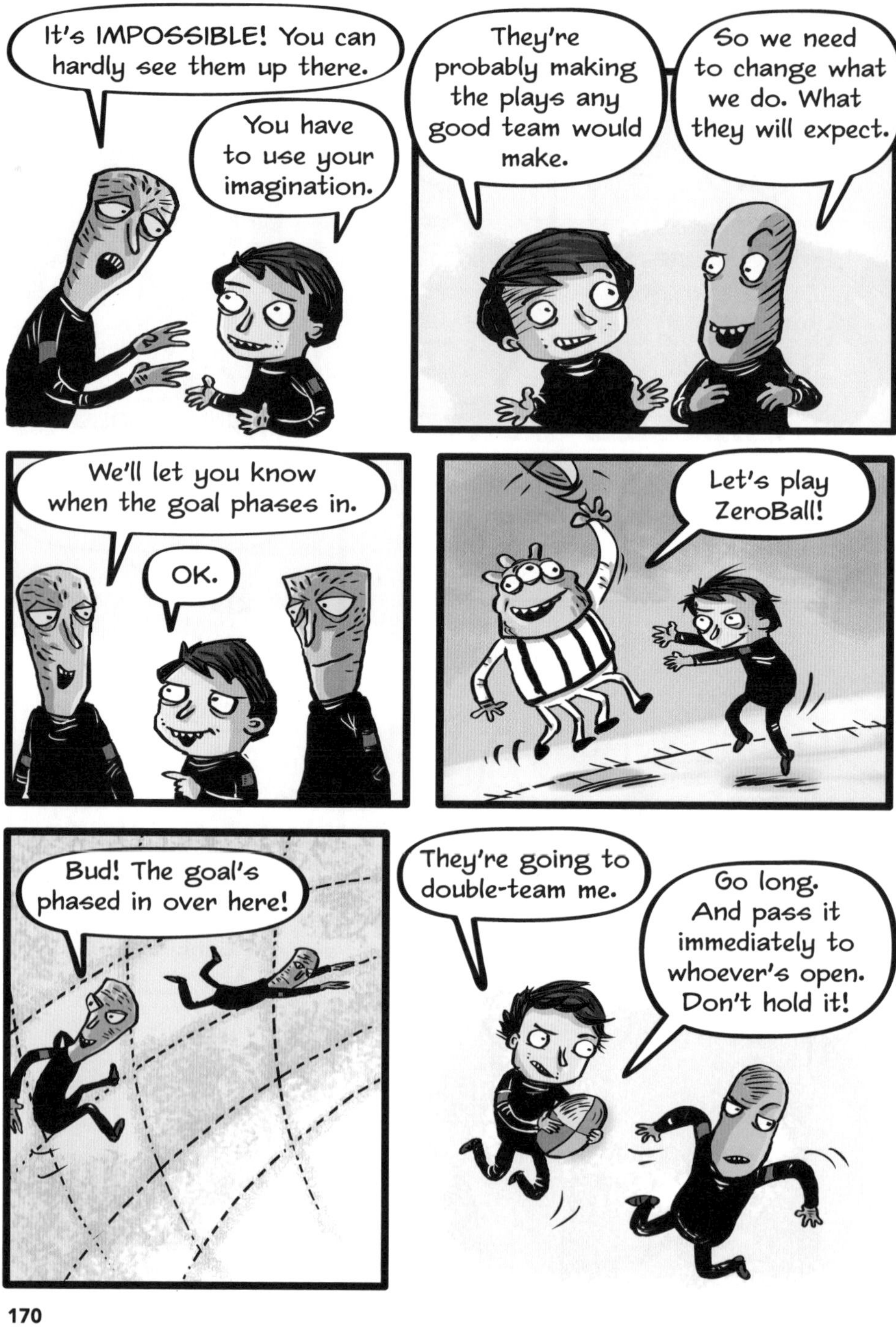
It's IMPOSSIBLE! You can hardly see them up there.
You have to use your imagination.
They're probably making the plays any good team would make.
So we need to change what we do. What they will expect.
We'll let you know when the goal phases in.
OK.
Let's play ZeroBall!
Bud! The goal's phased in over here!
They're going to double-team me.
Go long. And pass it immediately to whoever's open. Don't hold it!

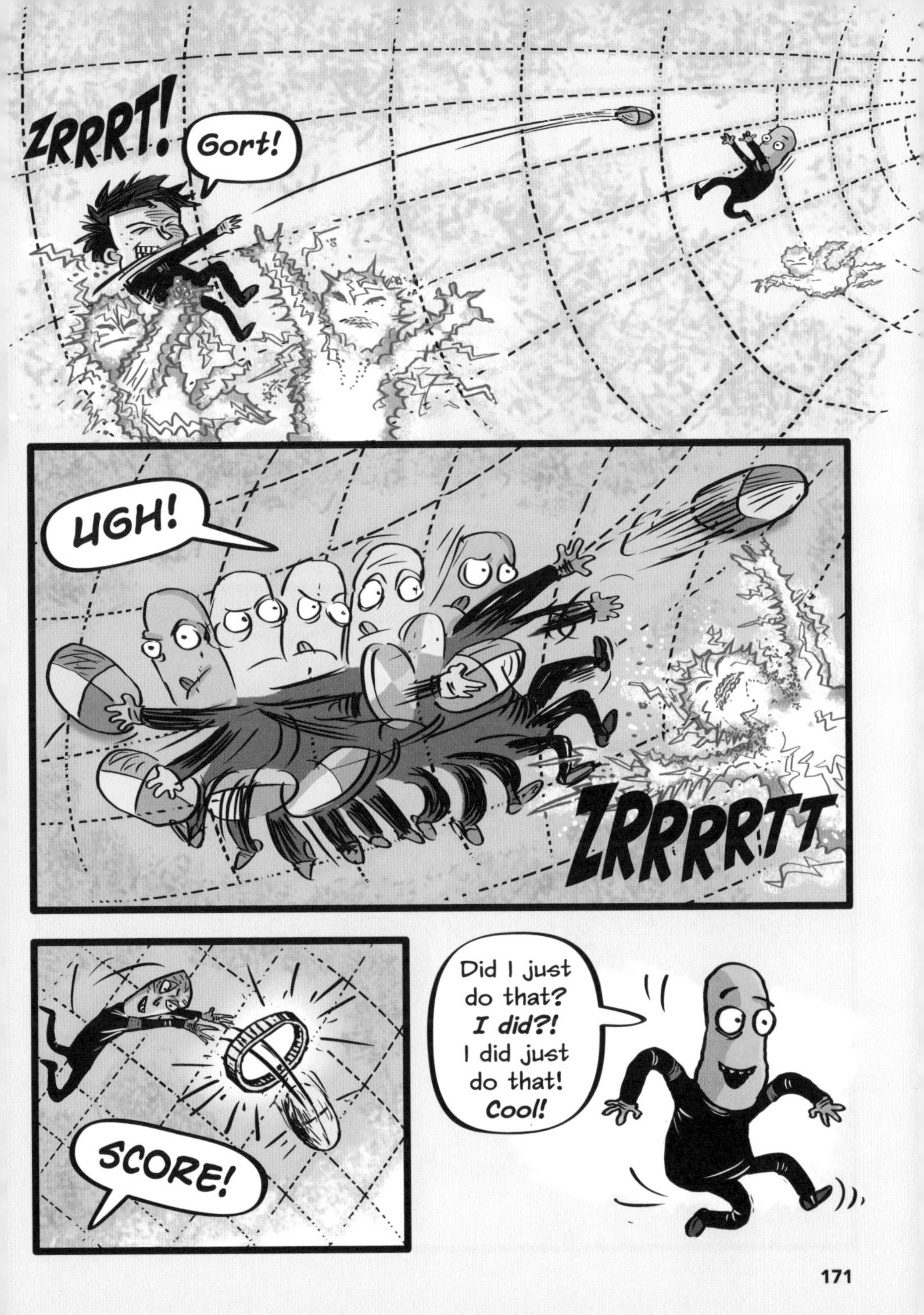
ZRRRT!
Gort!
UGH!
ZRRRRTT
SCORE!
Did I just do that? *I did?!* I did just do that! **Cool!**

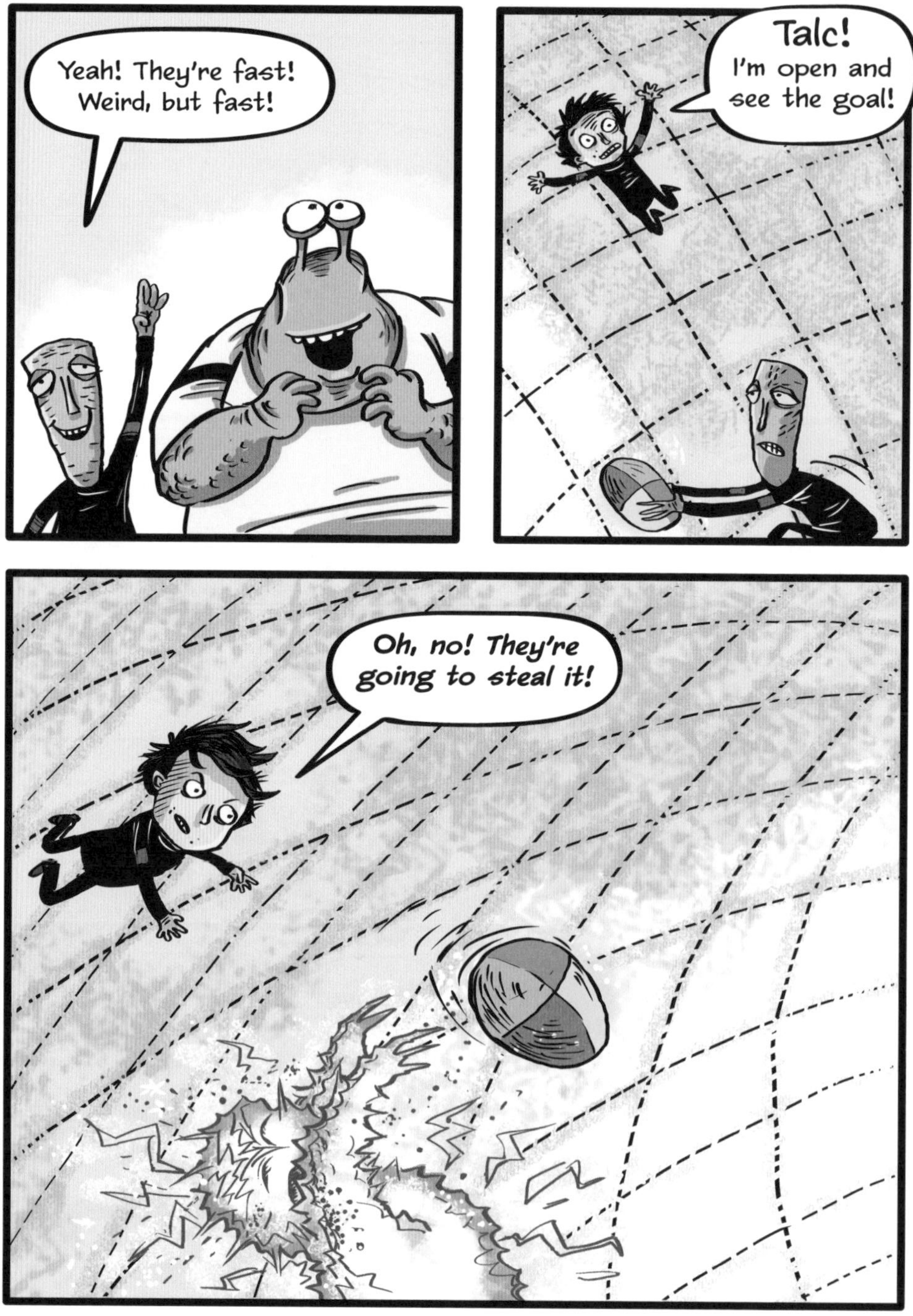
Yeah! They're fast! Weird, but fast!
Talc! I'm open and see the goal!
Oh, no! They're going to steal it!

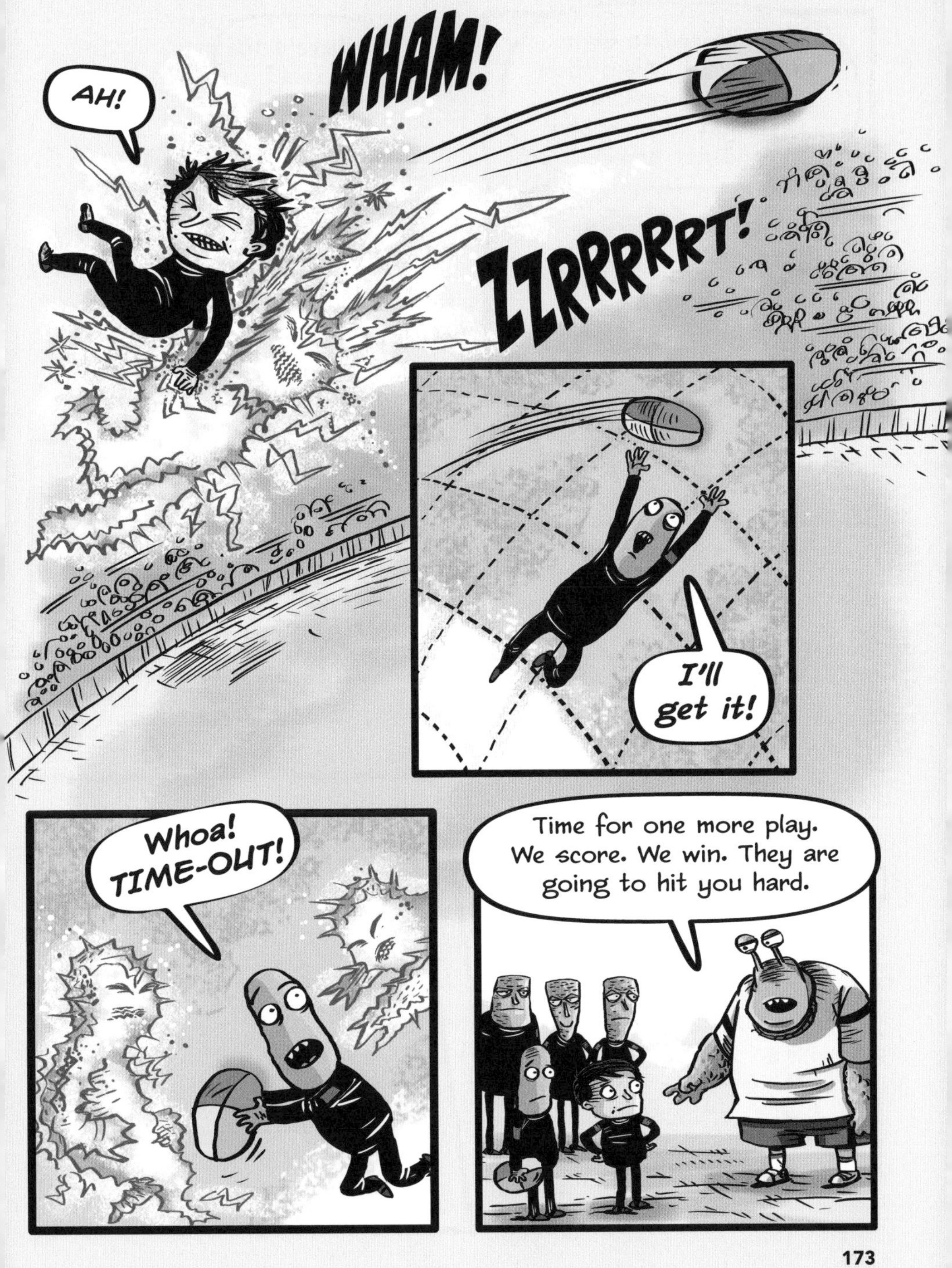
AH!
WHAM!
ZZRRRRRT!
I'll get it!
Whoa! TIME-OUT!
Time for one more play. We score. We win. They are going to hit you hard.

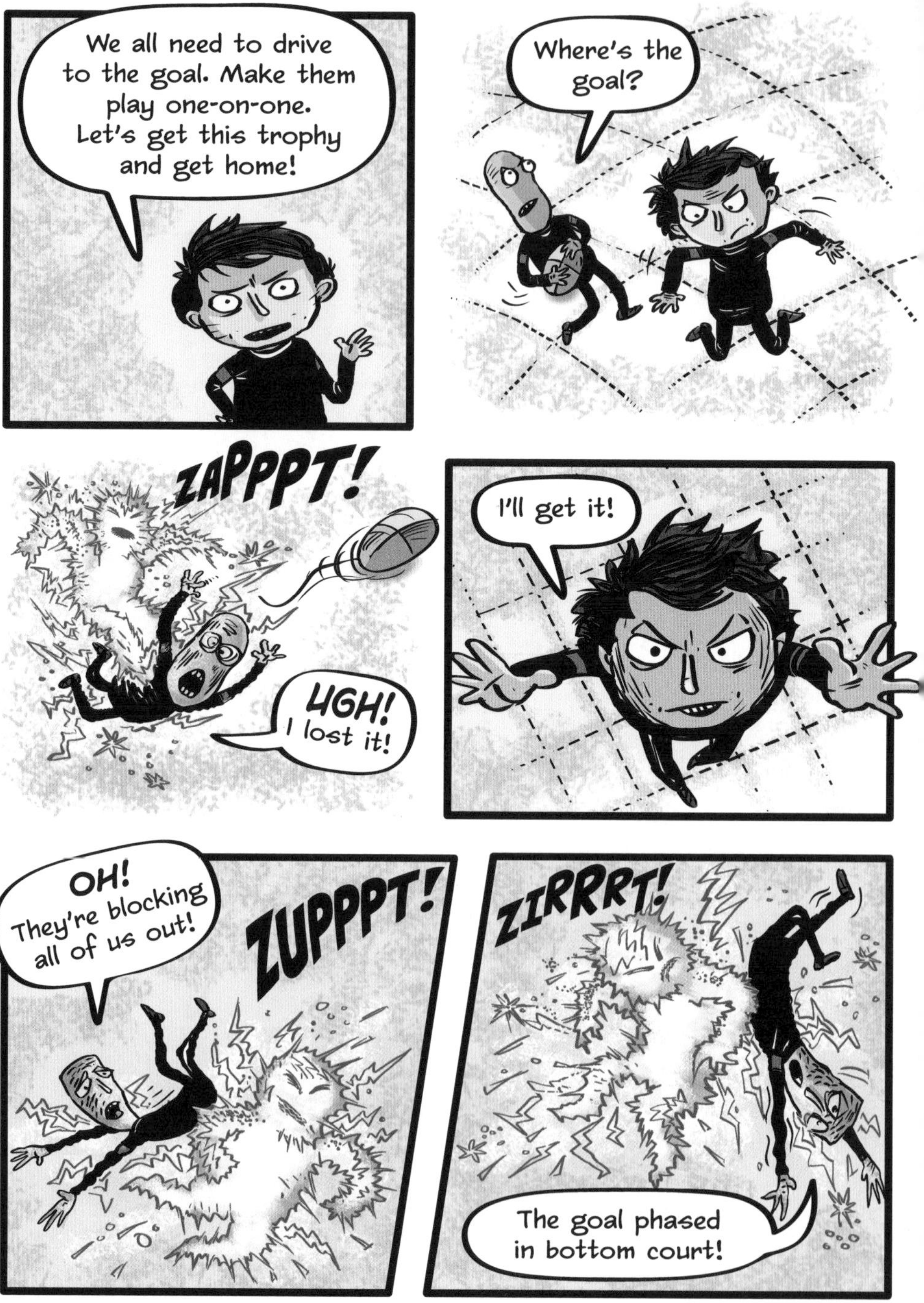

We all need to drive to the goal. Make them play one-on-one. Let's get this trophy and get home!
Where's the goal?
ZAPPPT!
UGH! I lost it!
I'll get it!
OH! They're blocking all of us out!
ZUPPPT!
ZIRRRT!
The goal phased in bottom court!

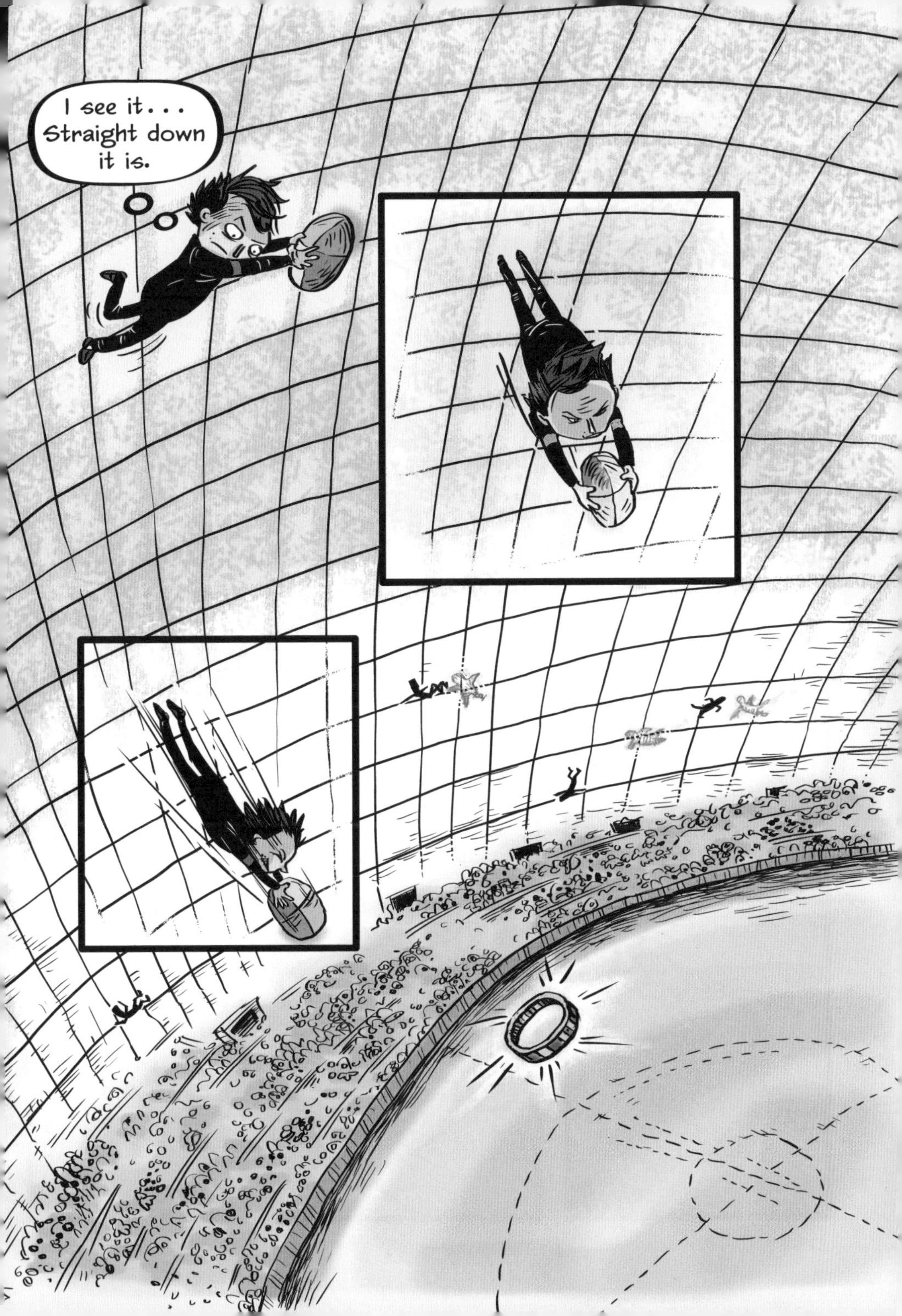
I see it . . . Straight down it is.

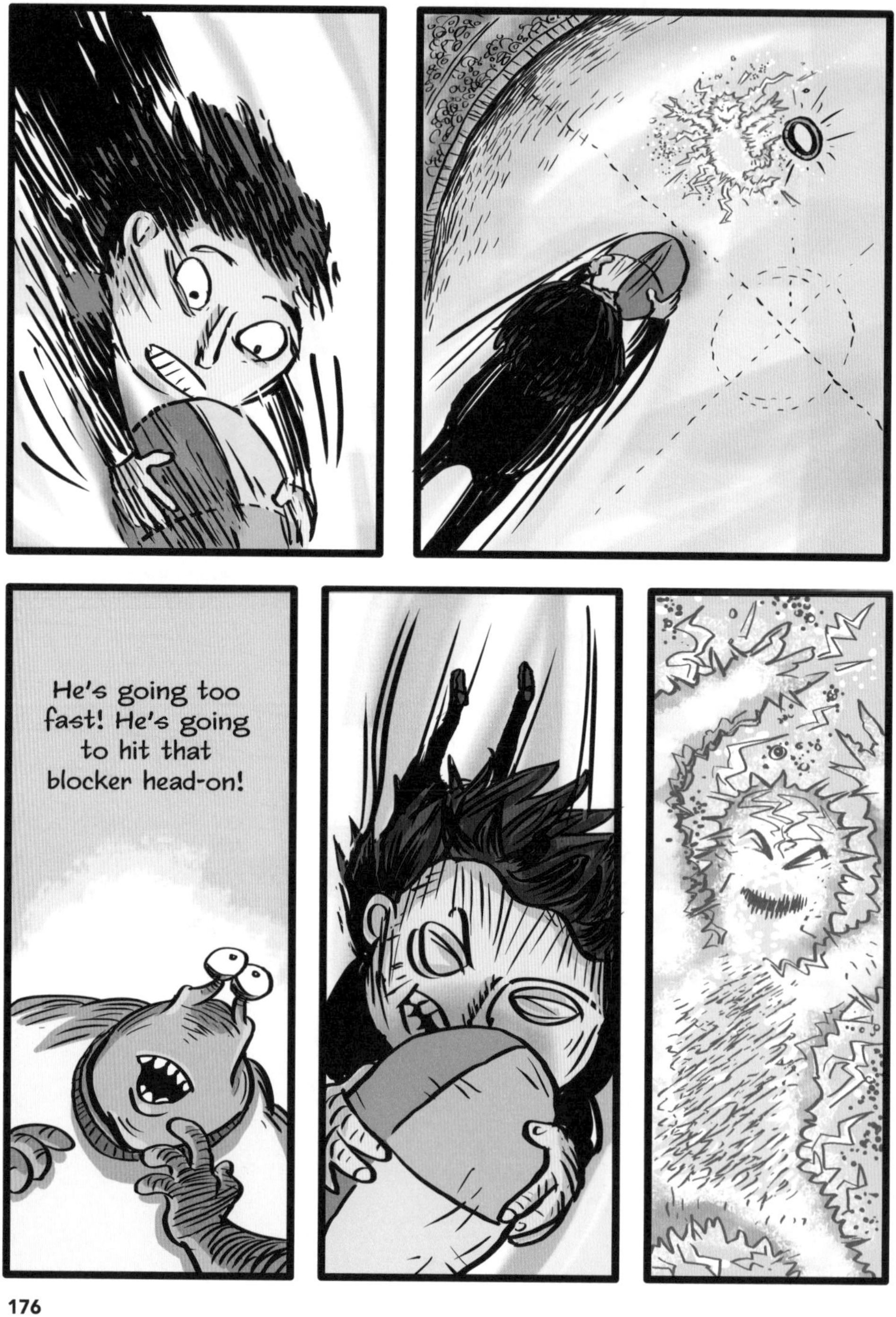
He's going too fast! He's going to hit that blocker head-on!

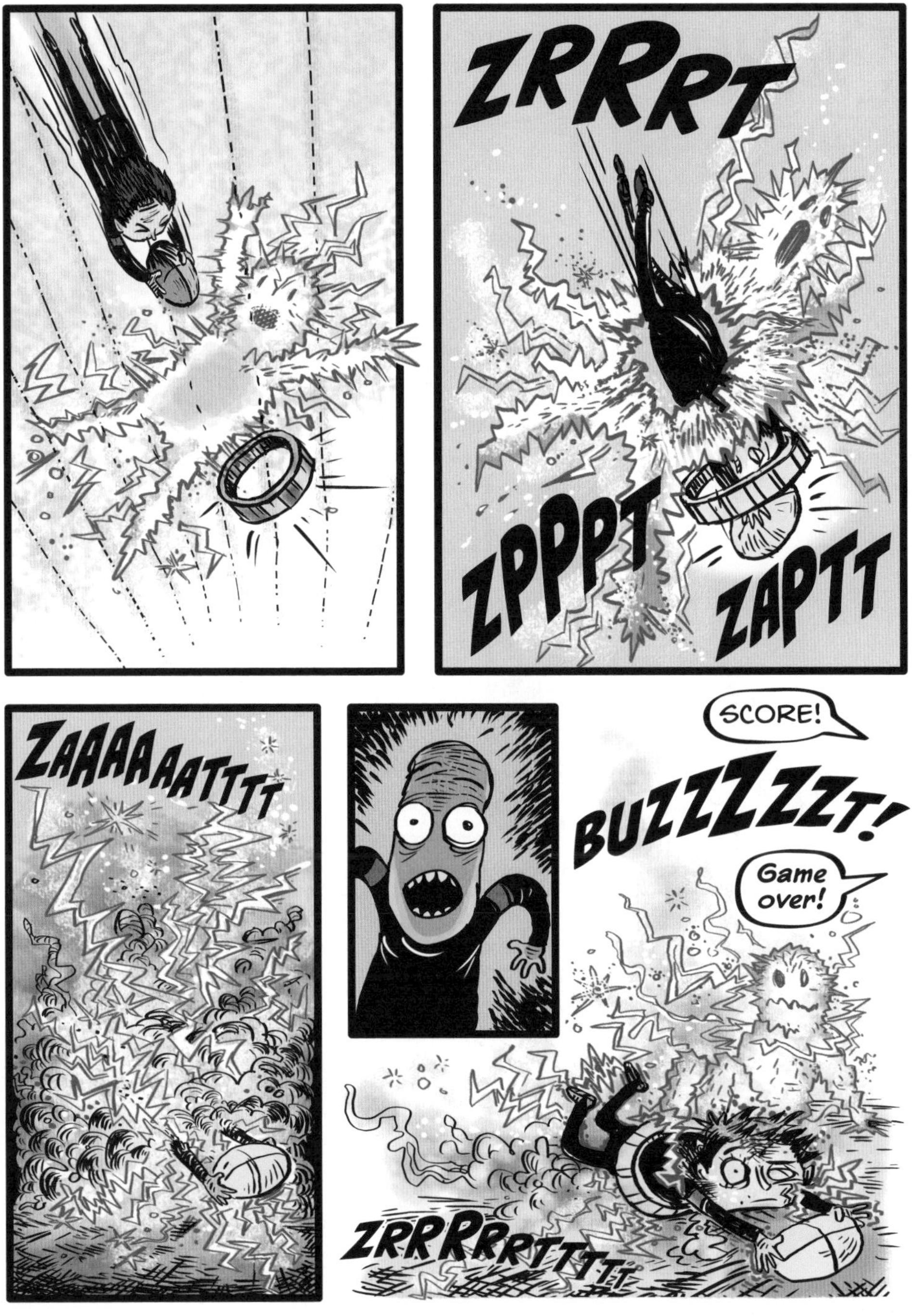
ZRRRT
ZPPPT
ZAPTT
ZAAAAATTTTT
SCORE!
BUZZZZZT!
Game over!
ZRRRRRTTTTT

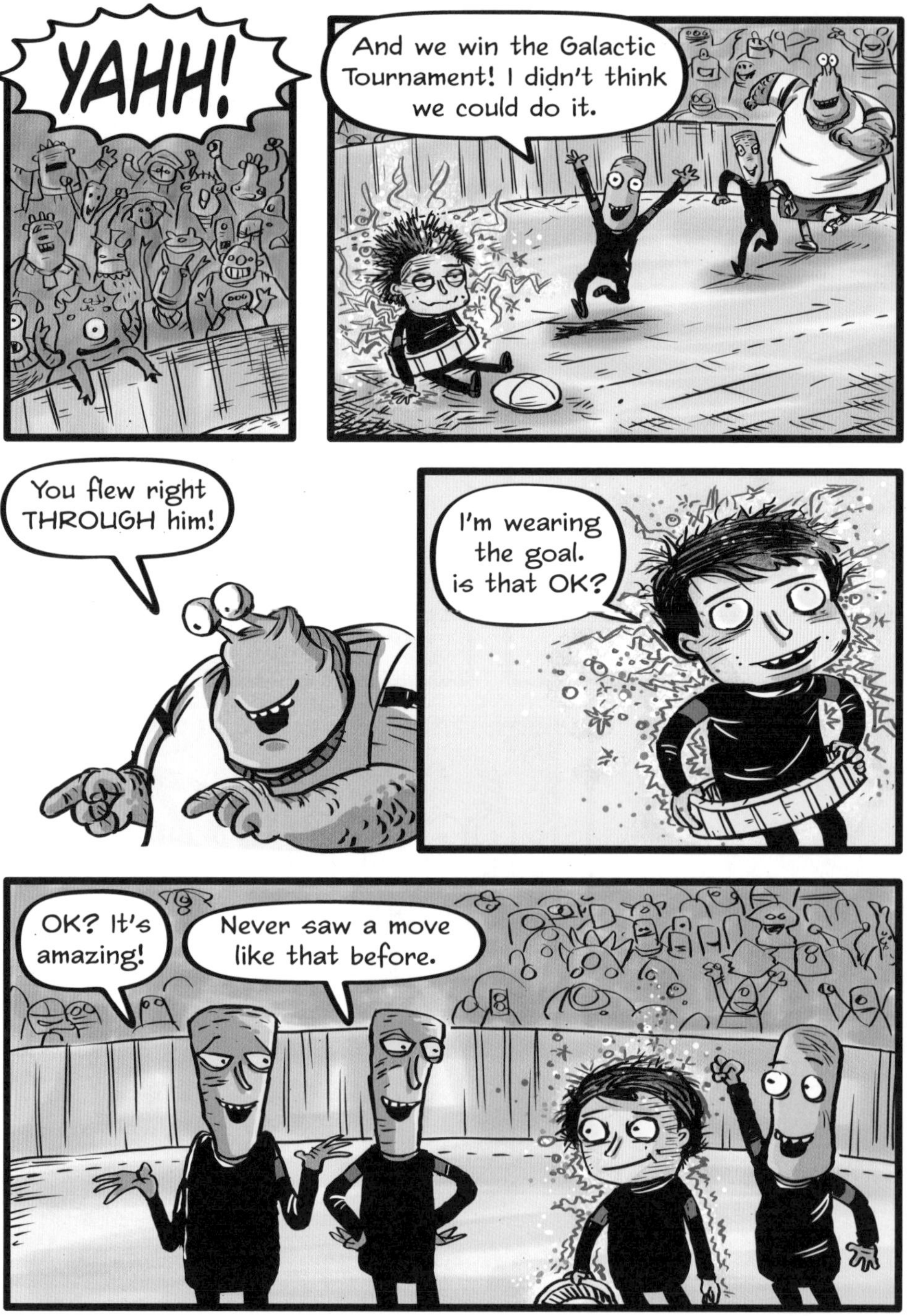
YAHH!
And we win the Galactic Tournament! I didn't think we could do it.
You flew right THROUGH him!
I'm wearing the goal. is that OK?
OK? It's amazing!
Never saw a move like that before.

CHAPTER 7

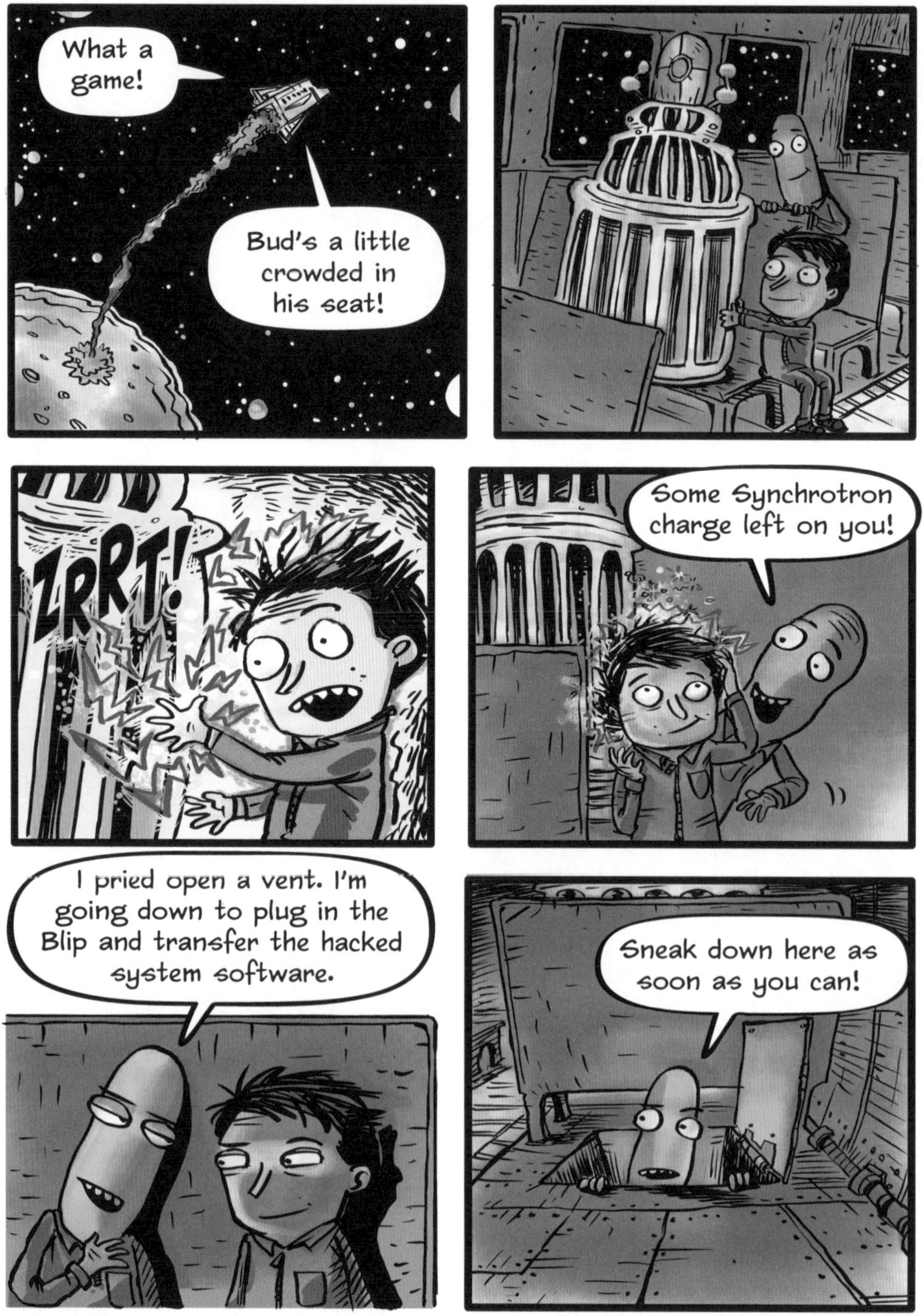
What a game!
Bud's a little crowded in his seat!
ZRRT!
Some Synchrotron charge left on you!
I pried open a vent. I'm going down to plug in the Blip and transfer the hacked system software.
Sneak down here as soon as you can!

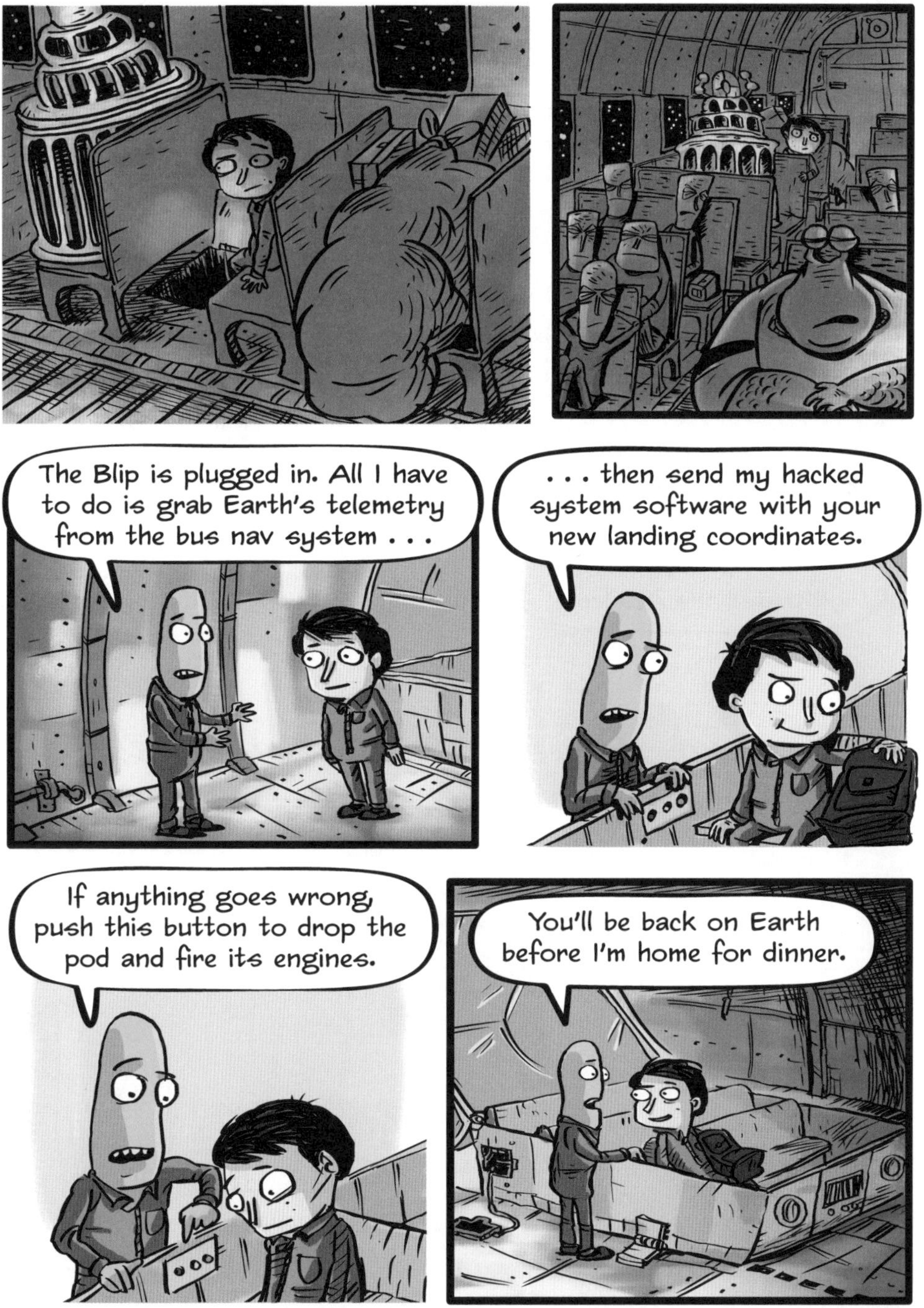
The Blip is plugged in. All I have to do is grab Earth's telemetry from the bus nav system . . .
. . . then send my hacked system software with your new landing coordinates.
If anything goes wrong, push this button to drop the pod and fire its engines.
You'll be back on Earth before I'm home for dinner.

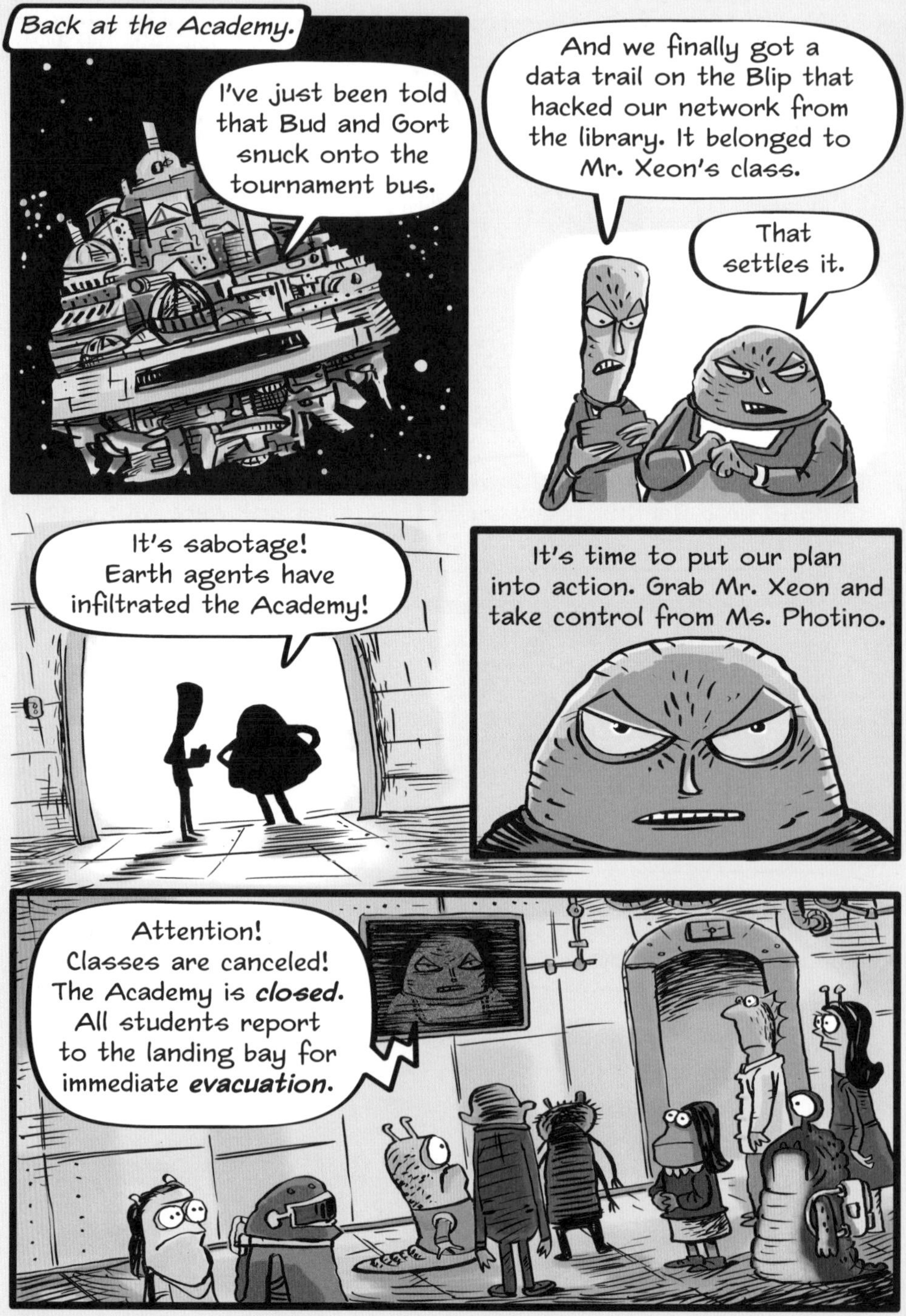

Back at the Academy.
I've just been told that Bud and Gort snuck onto the tournament bus.
And we finally got a data trail on the Blip that hacked our network from the library. It belonged to Mr. Xeon's class.
That settles it.
It's sabotage! Earth agents have infiltrated the Academy!
It's time to put our plan into action. Grab Mr. Xeon and take control from Ms. Photino.
Attention! Classes are canceled! The Academy is *closed.* All students report to the landing bay for immediate *evacuation.*

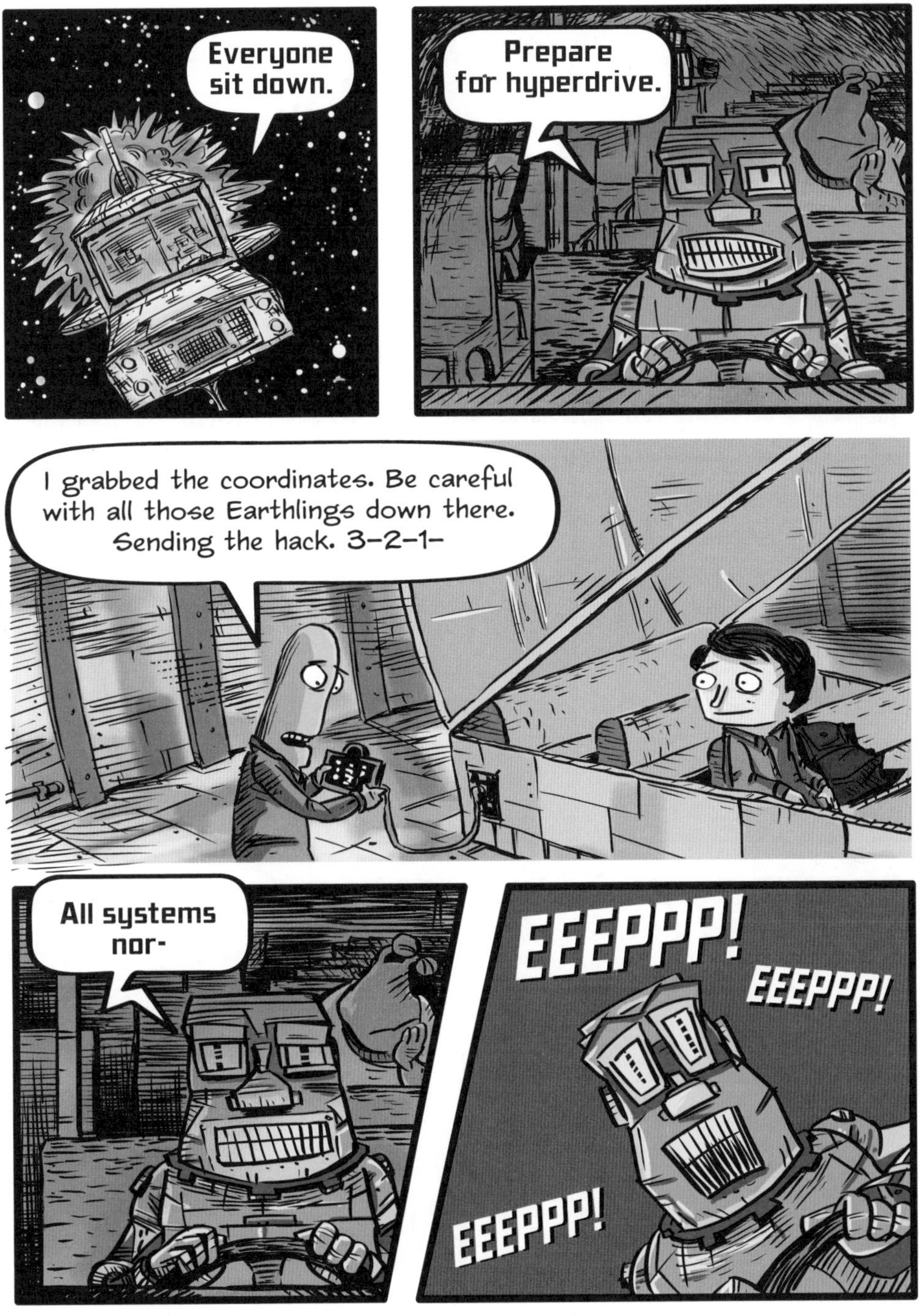
Everyone sit down.
Prepare for hyperdrive.
I grabbed the coordinates. Be careful with all those Earthlings down there. Sending the hack. 3-2-1-
All systems nor-
EEEPPP!
EEEPPP!
EEEPPP!

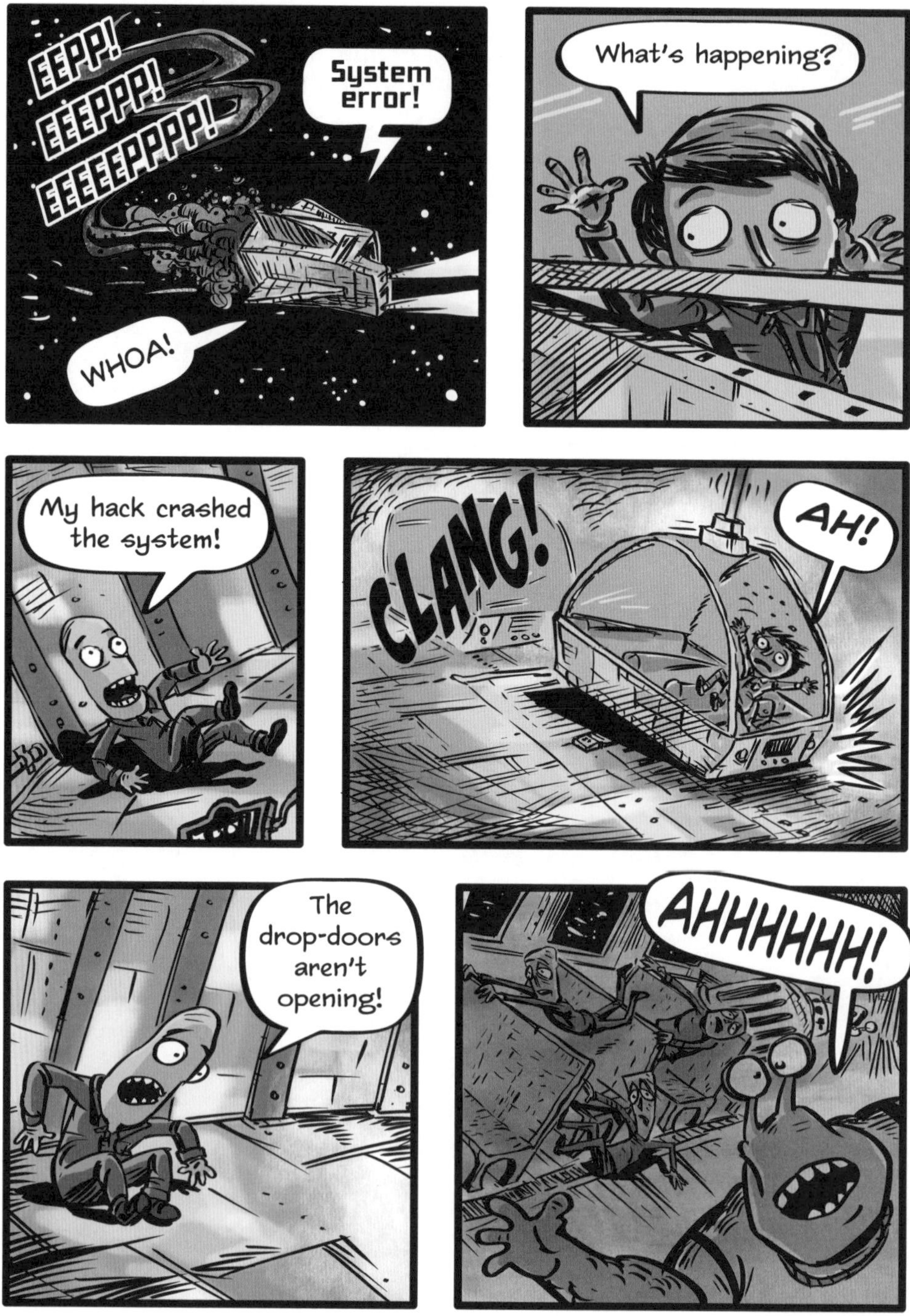
EEPP!
EEEPPP!
EEEEEPPPP!
System error!
WHOA!
What's happening?
My hack crashed the system!
CLANG!
AH!
The drop-doors aren't opening!
AHHHHHH!

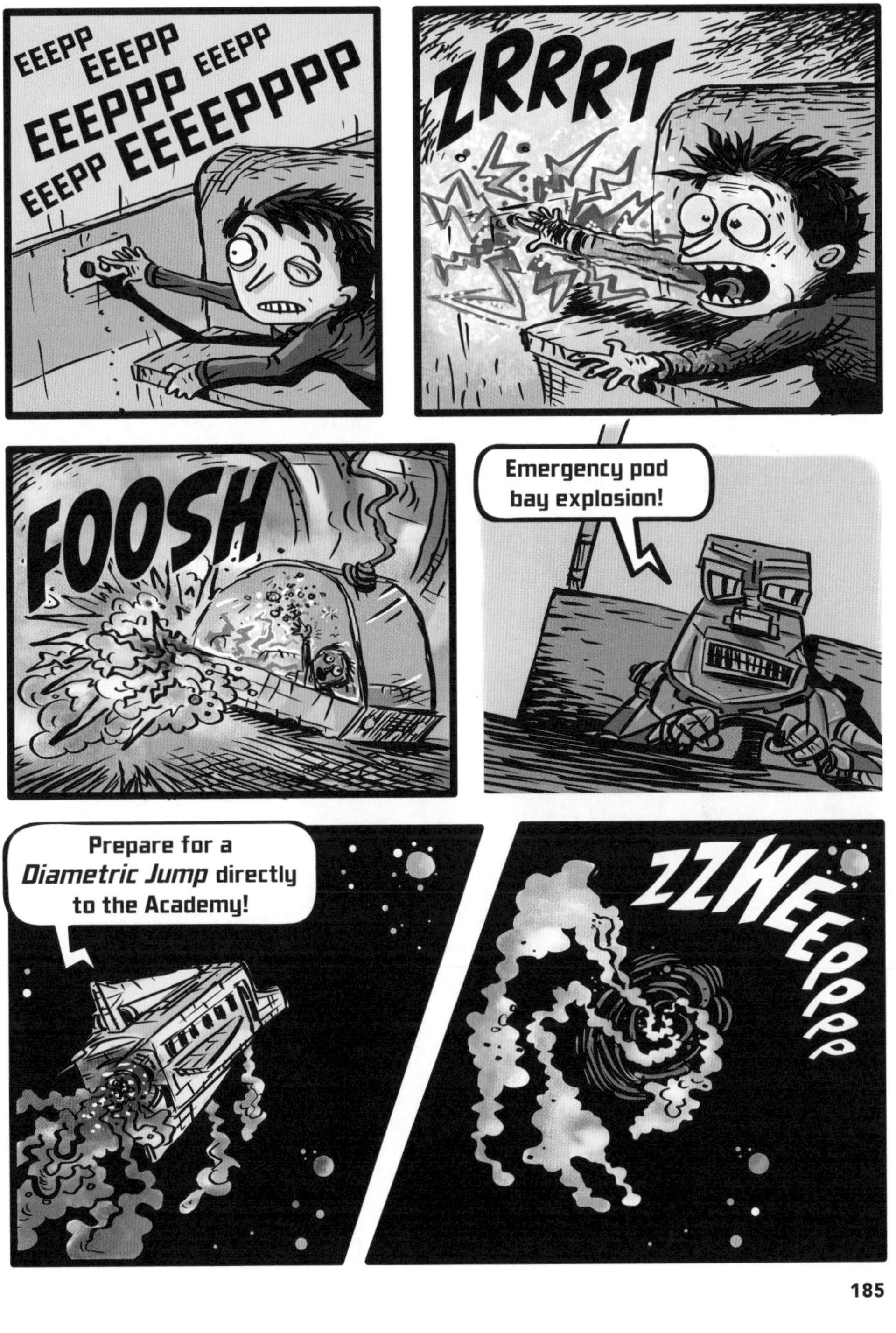
EEEPP EEEPP EEEPPP EEEPP EEEPP EEEEPPPP
ZRRRT
FOOSH
Emergency pod bay explosion!
Prepare for a *Diametric Jump* directly to the Academy!
ZZWEEPPP

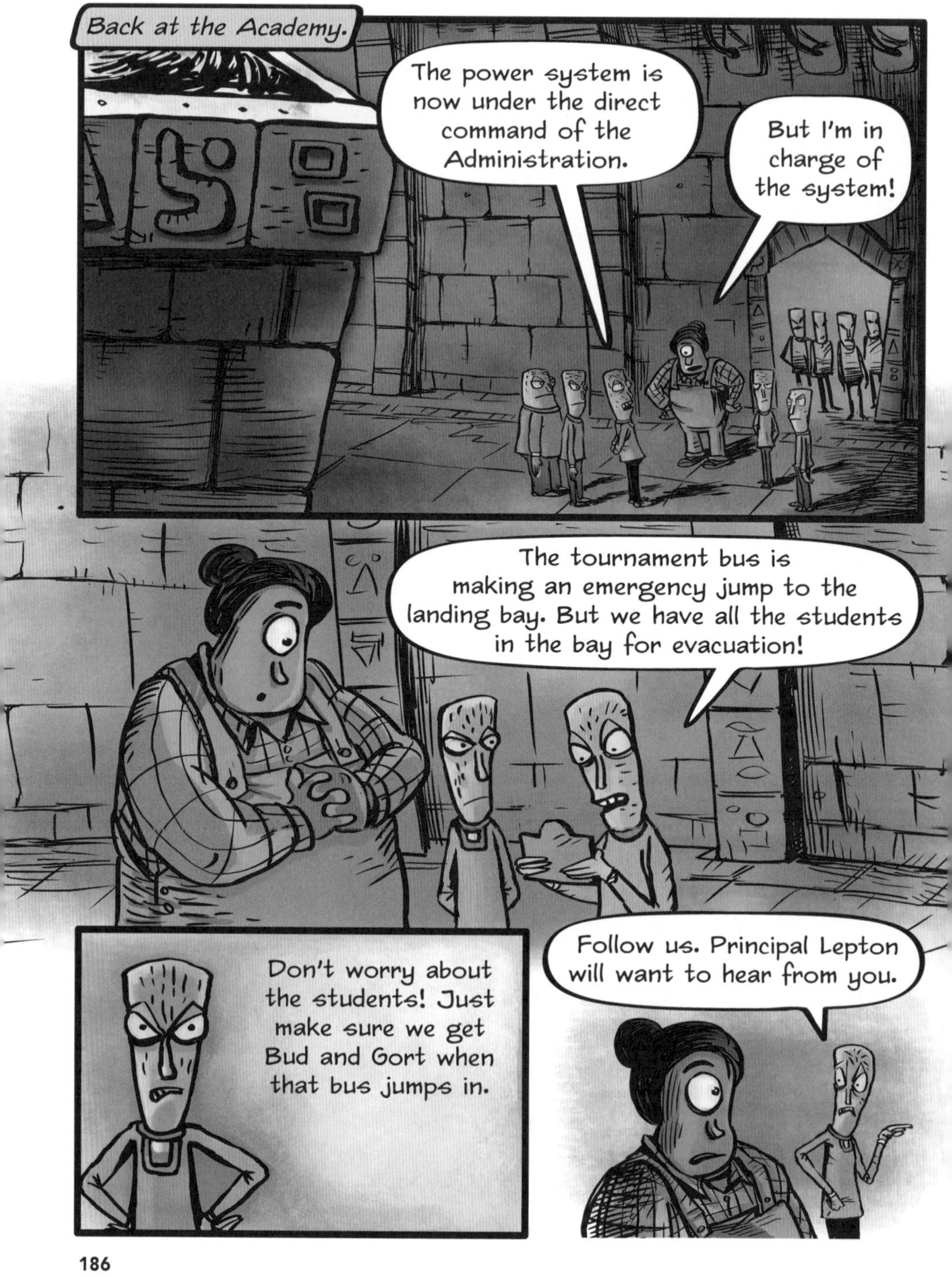
Back at the Academy.
The power system is now under the direct command of the Administration.
But I'm in charge of the system!
The tournament bus is making an emergency jump to the landing bay. But we have all the students in the bay for evacuation!
Don't worry about the students! Just make sure we get Bud and Gort when that bus jumps in.
Follow us. Principal Lepton will want to hear from you.

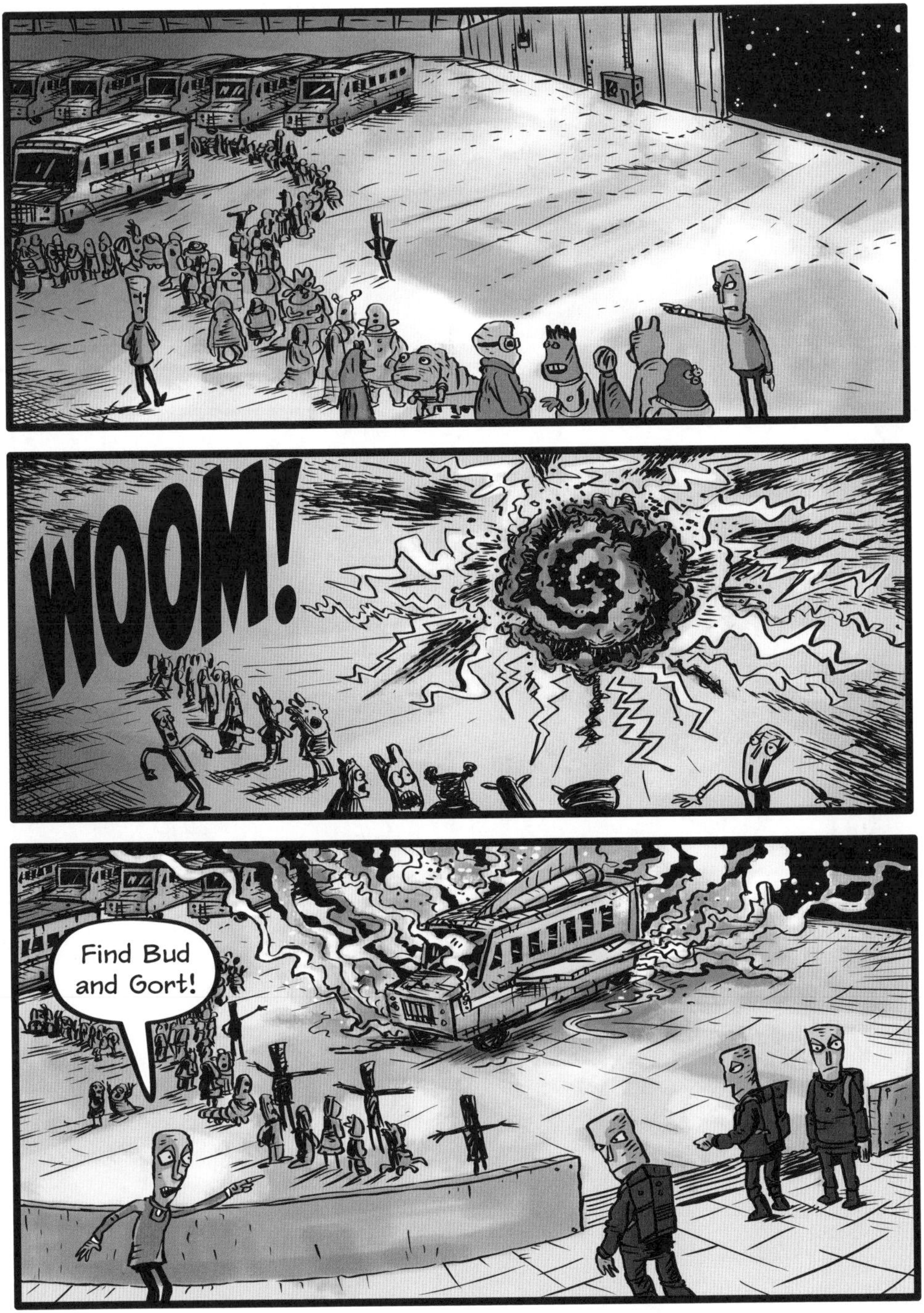
WOOM!
Find Bud and Gort!

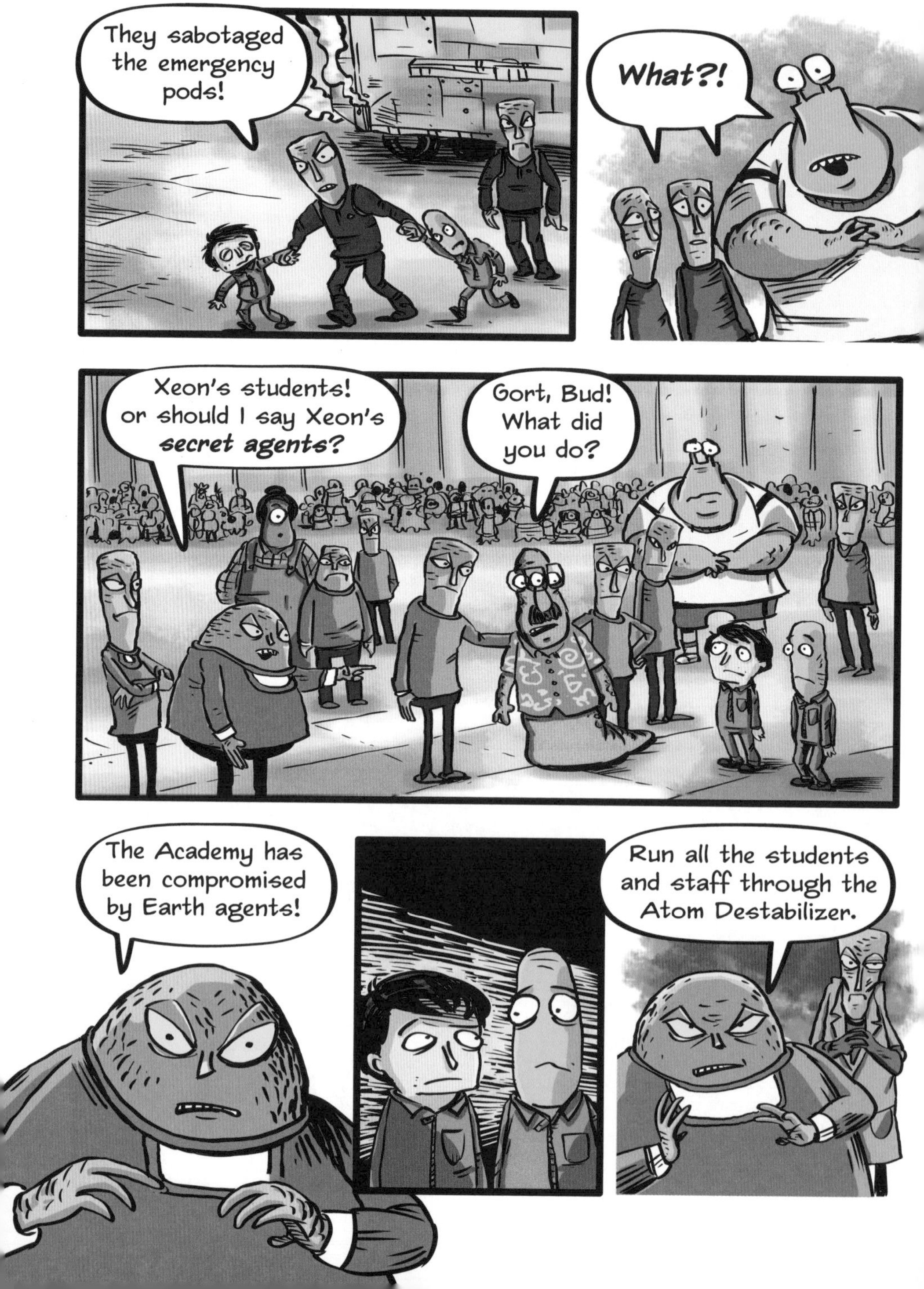
They sabotaged the emergency pods!
What?!
Xeon's students! or should I say Xeon's *secret agents?*
Gort, Bud! What did you do?
The Academy has been compromised by Earth agents!
Run all the students and staff through the Atom Destabilizer.

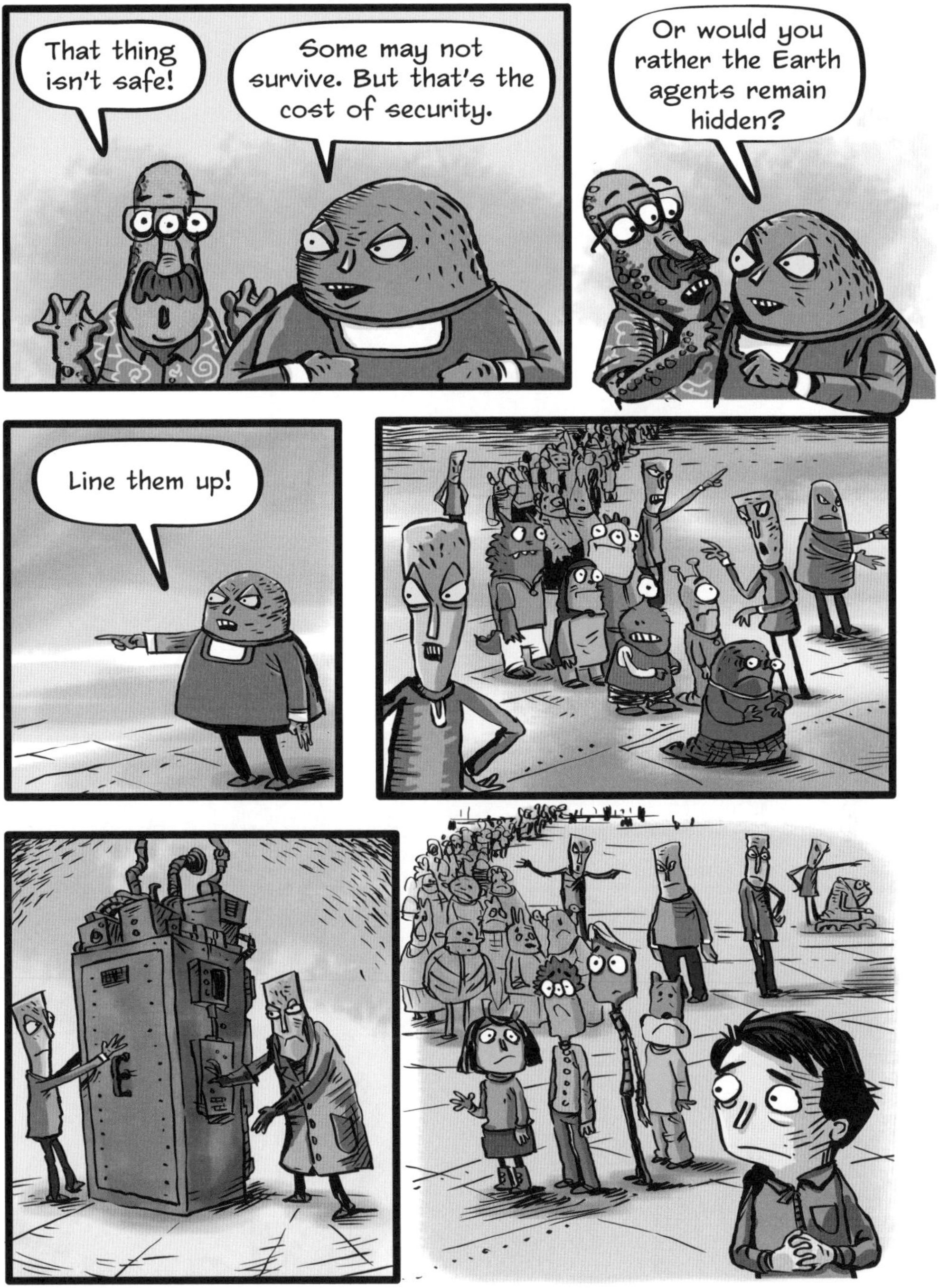
That thing isn't safe!
Some may not survive. But that's the cost of security.
Or would you rather the Earth agents remain hidden?
Line them up!

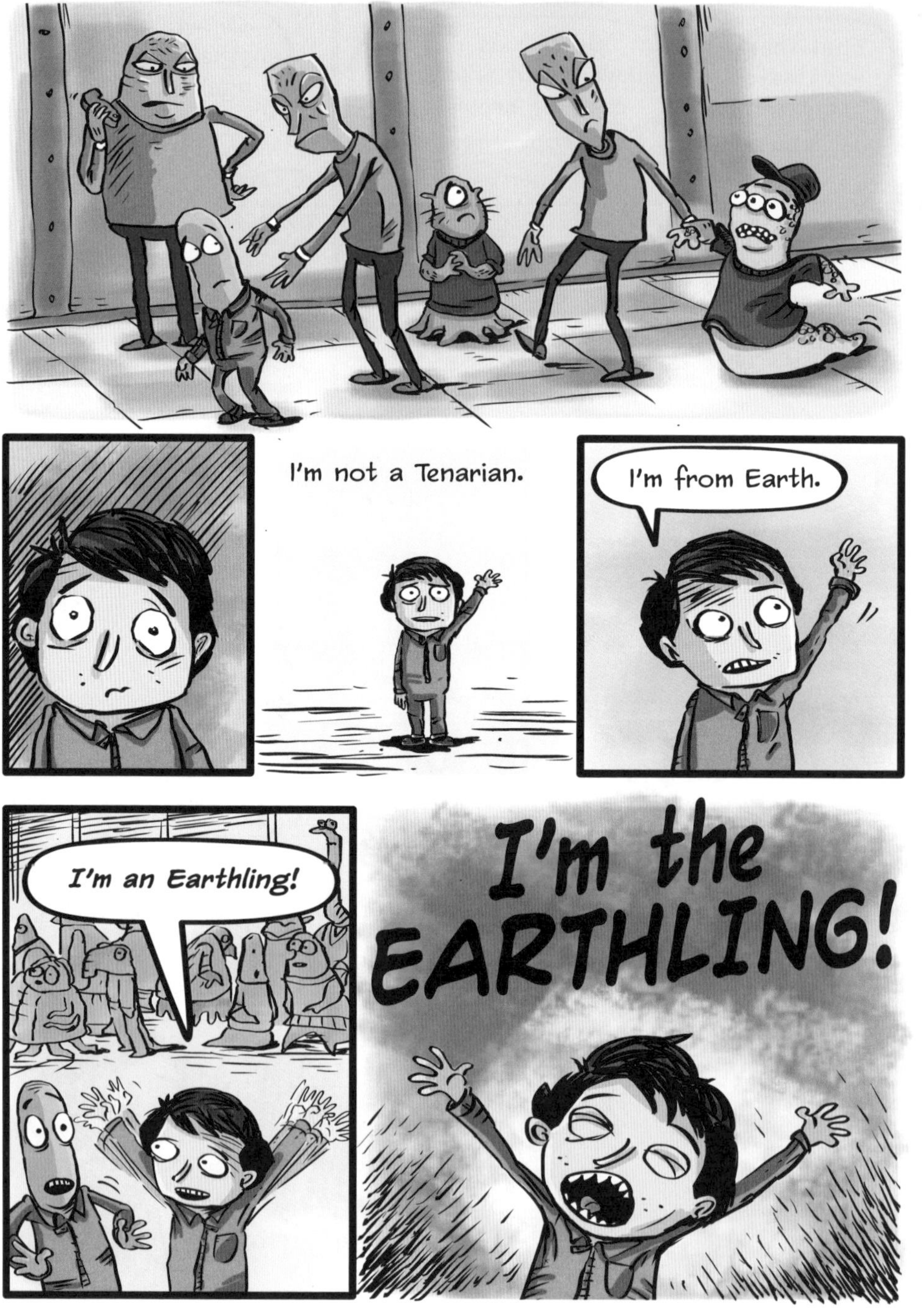
I'm not a Tenarian.
I'm from Earth.
I'm an Earthling!
I'm the EARTHLING!

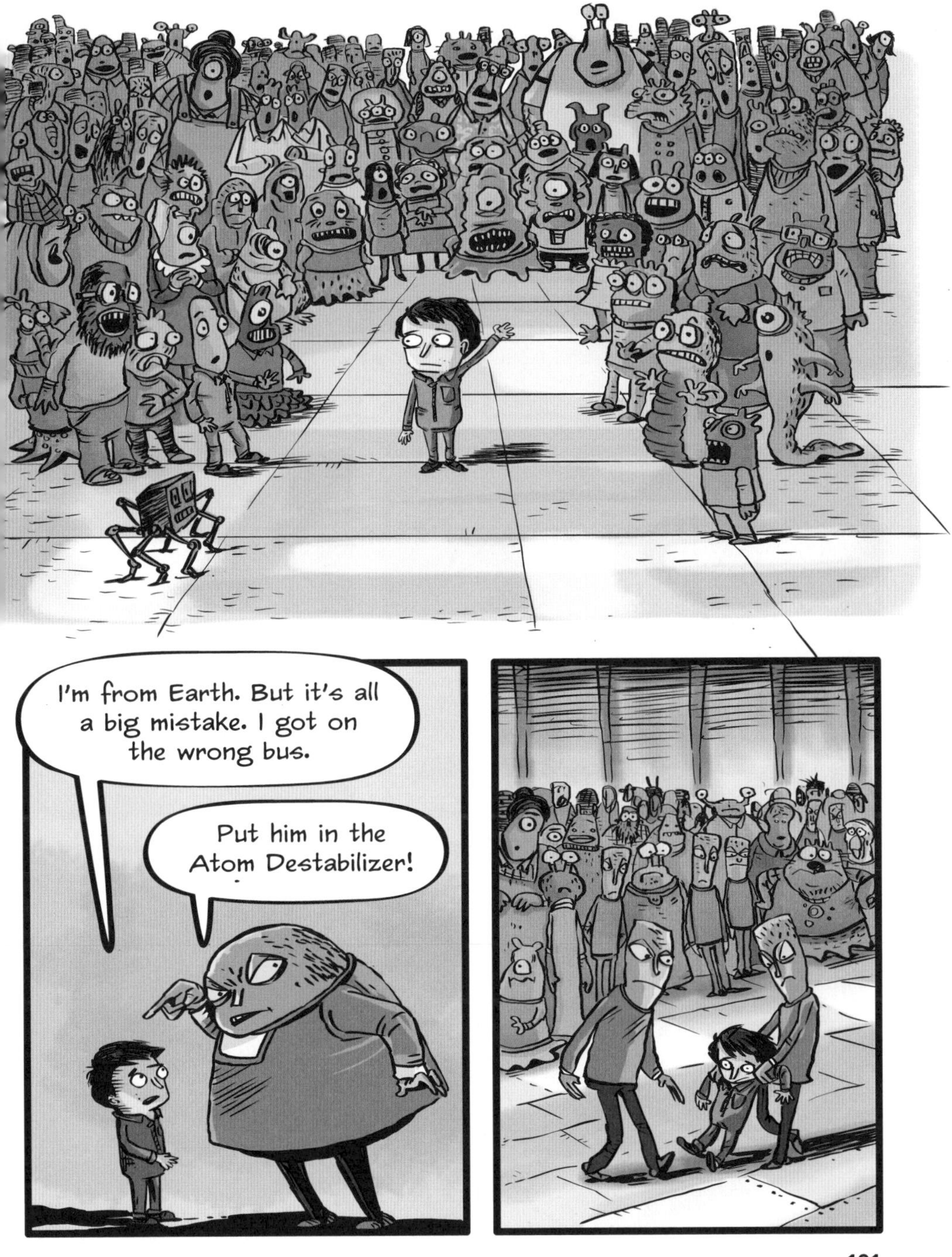
I'm from Earth. But it's all a big mistake. I got on the wrong bus.
Put him in the Atom Destabilizer!

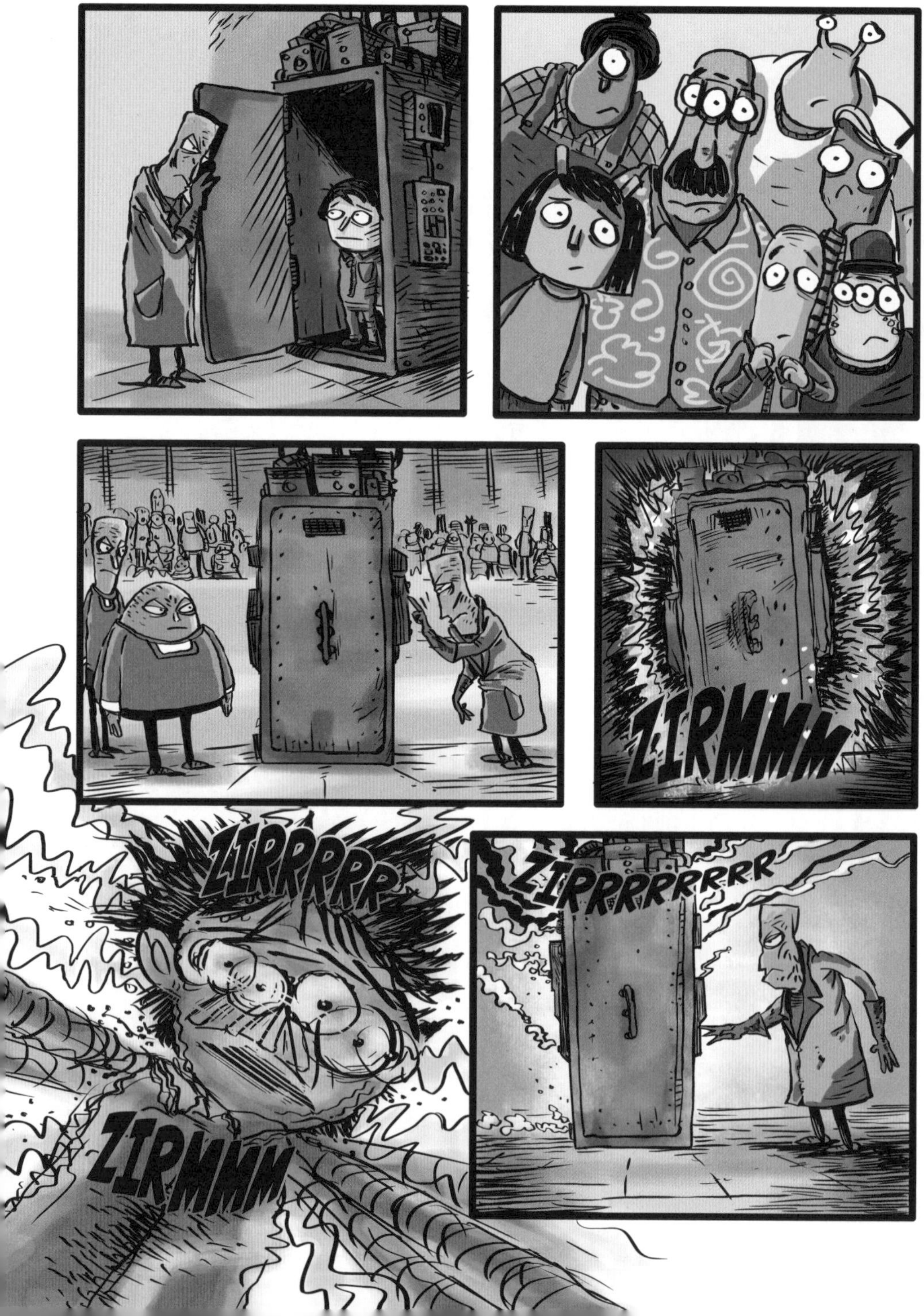
ZIRMMM
ZIRRRRRR
ZIRMMM
ZIRRRRRRRRR

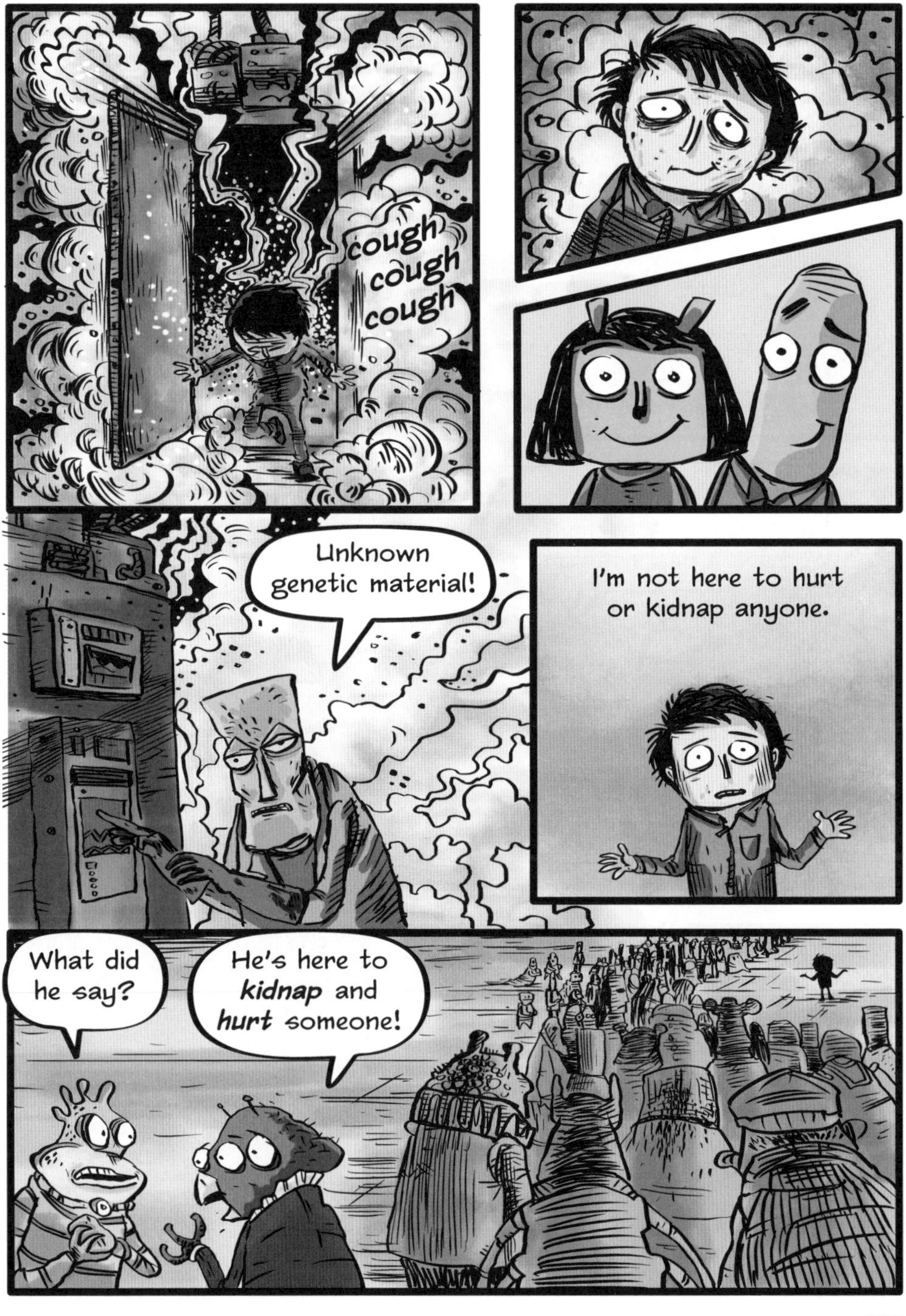
cough
cough
cough
Unknown genetic material!
I'm not here to hurt or kidnap anyone.
What did he say?
He's here to *kidnap* and *hurt* someone!

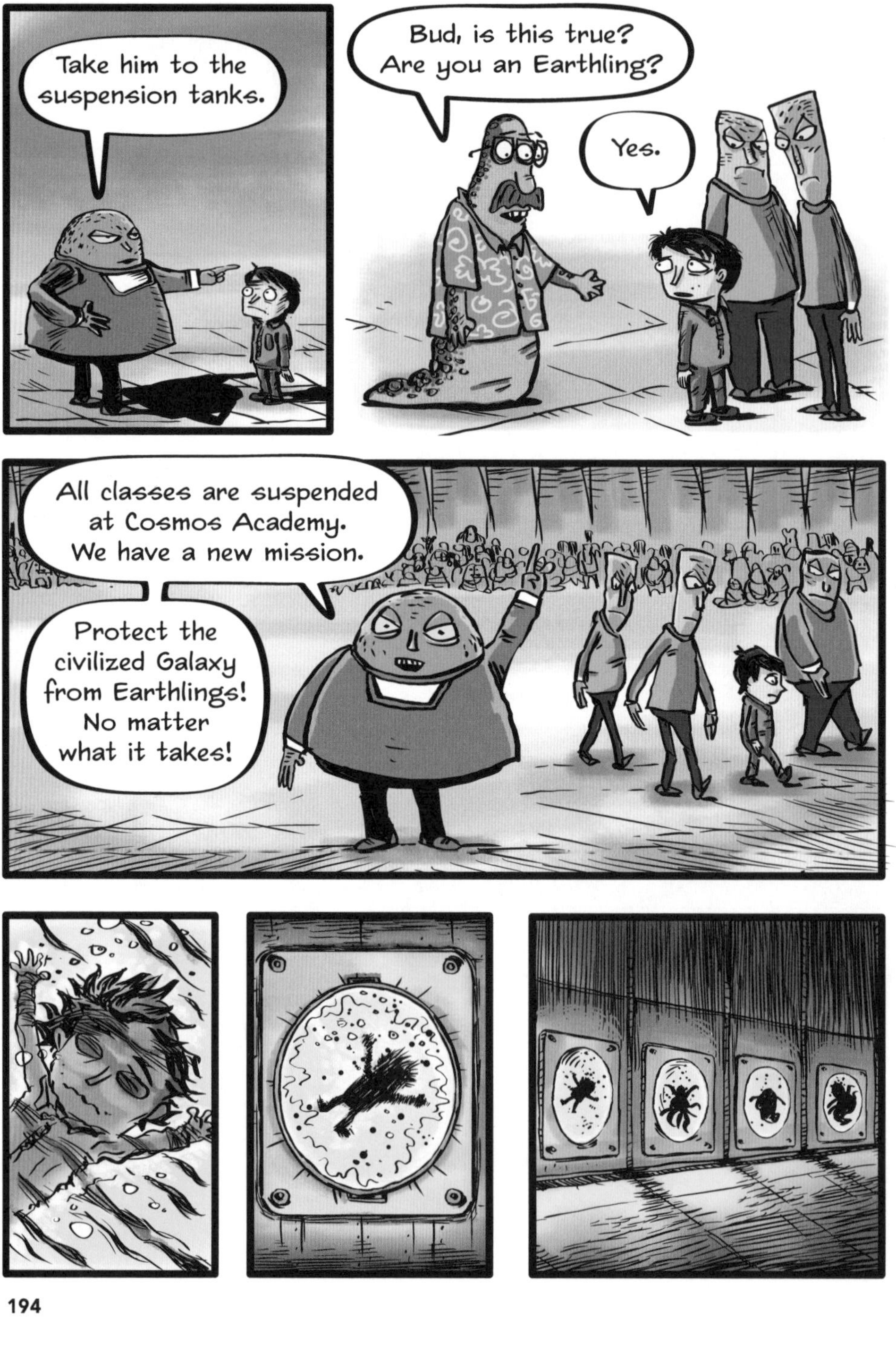
Take him to the suspension tanks.
Bud, is this true? Are you an Earthling?
Yes.
All classes are suspended at Cosmos Academy. We have a new mission.
Protect the civilized Galaxy from Earthlings! No matter what it takes!

CHAPTER 8

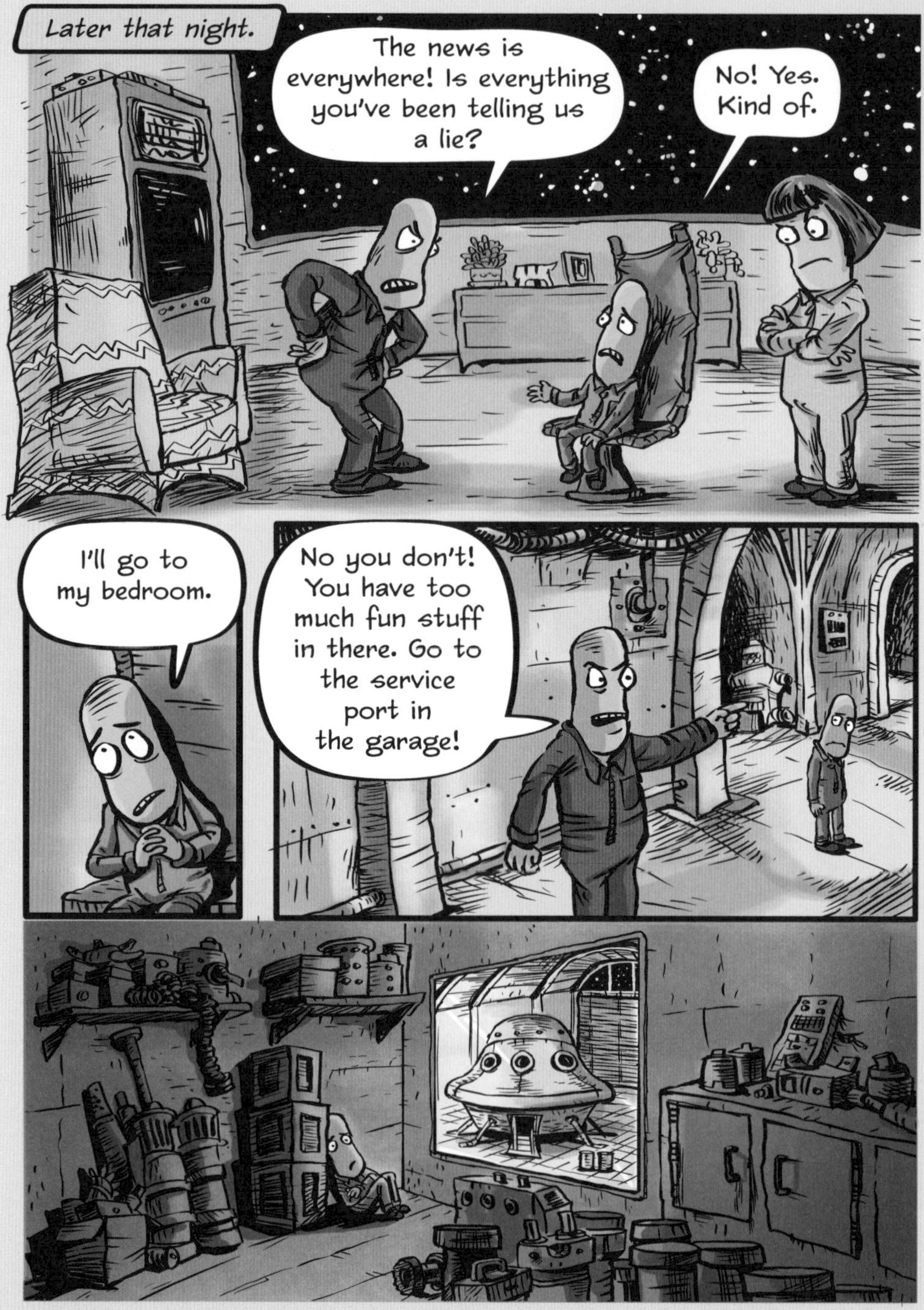
Later that night.
The news is everywhere! Is everything you've been telling us a lie?
No! Yes. Kind of.
I'll go to my bedroom.
No you don't! You have too much fun stuff in there. Go to the service port in the garage!

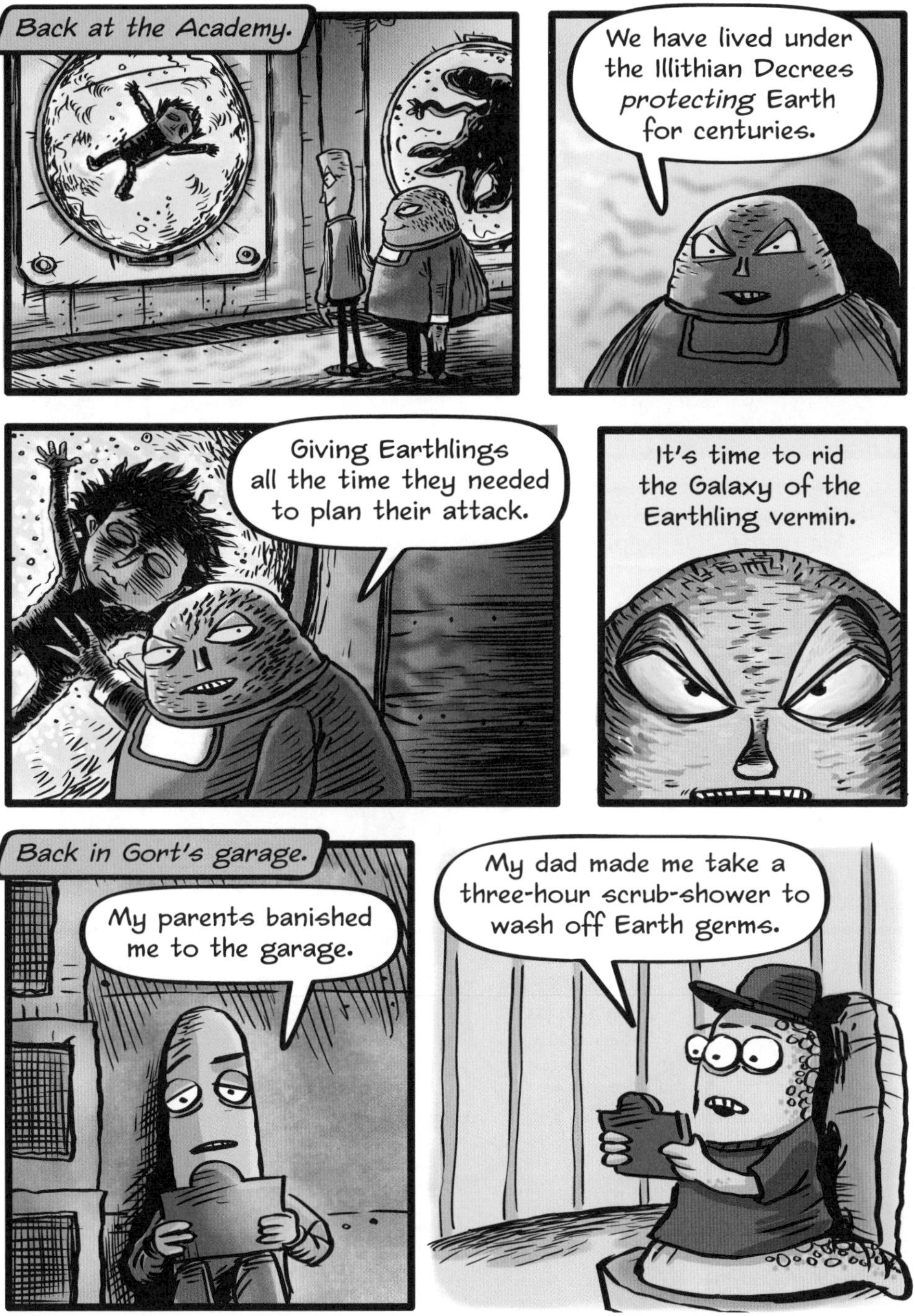
Back at the Academy.
We have lived under the Illithian Decrees *protecting* Earth for centuries.
Giving Earthlings all the time they needed to plan their attack.
It's time to rid the Galaxy of the Earthling vermin.
Back in Gort's garage.
My parents banished me to the garage.
My dad made me take a three-hour scrub-shower to wash off Earth germs.

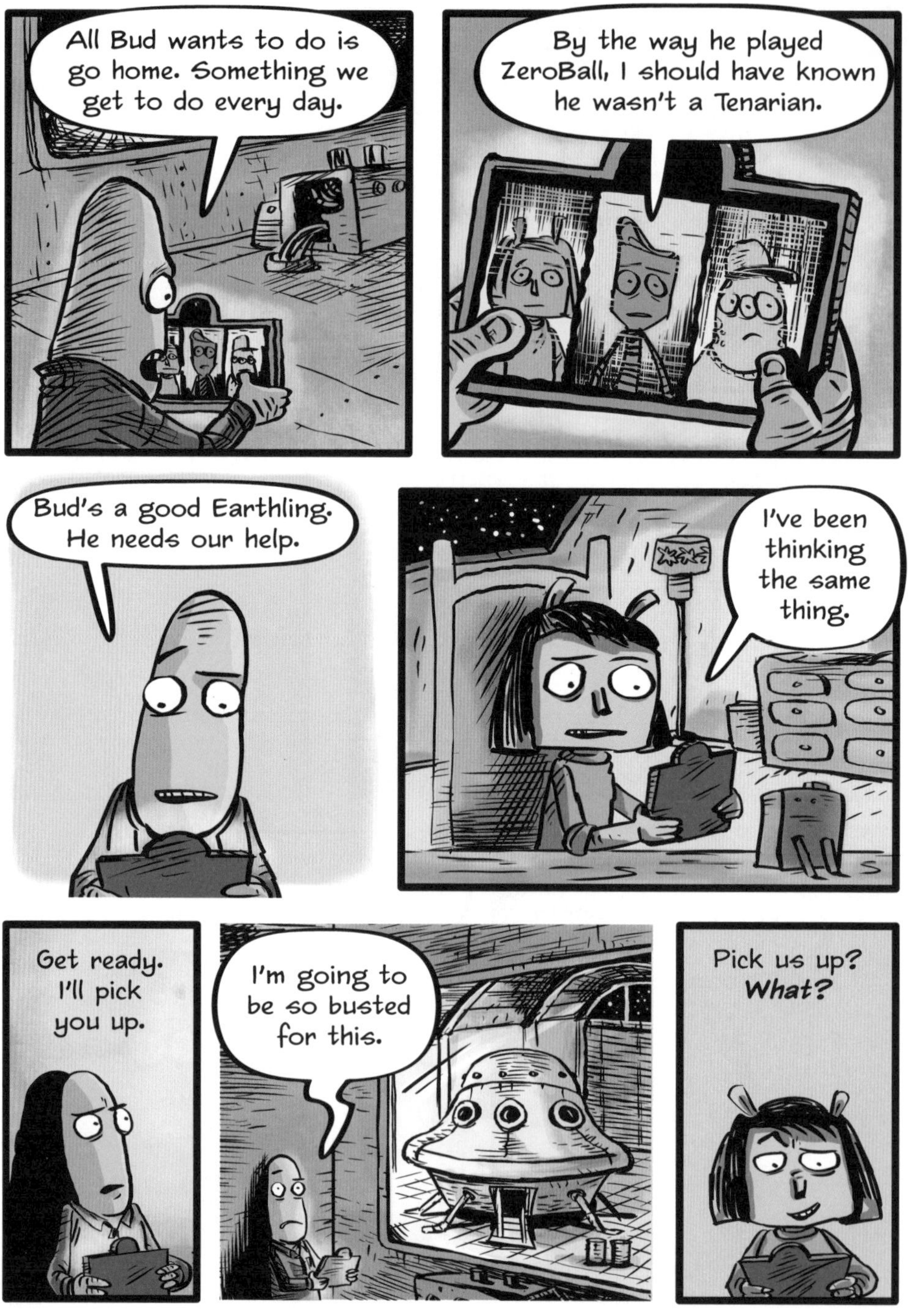
All Bud wants to do is go home. Something we get to do every day.
By the way he played ZeroBall, I should have known he wasn't a Tenarian.
Bud's a good Earthling. He needs our help.
I've been thinking the same thing.
Get ready. I'll pick you up.
I'm going to be so busted for this.
Pick us up? *What?*

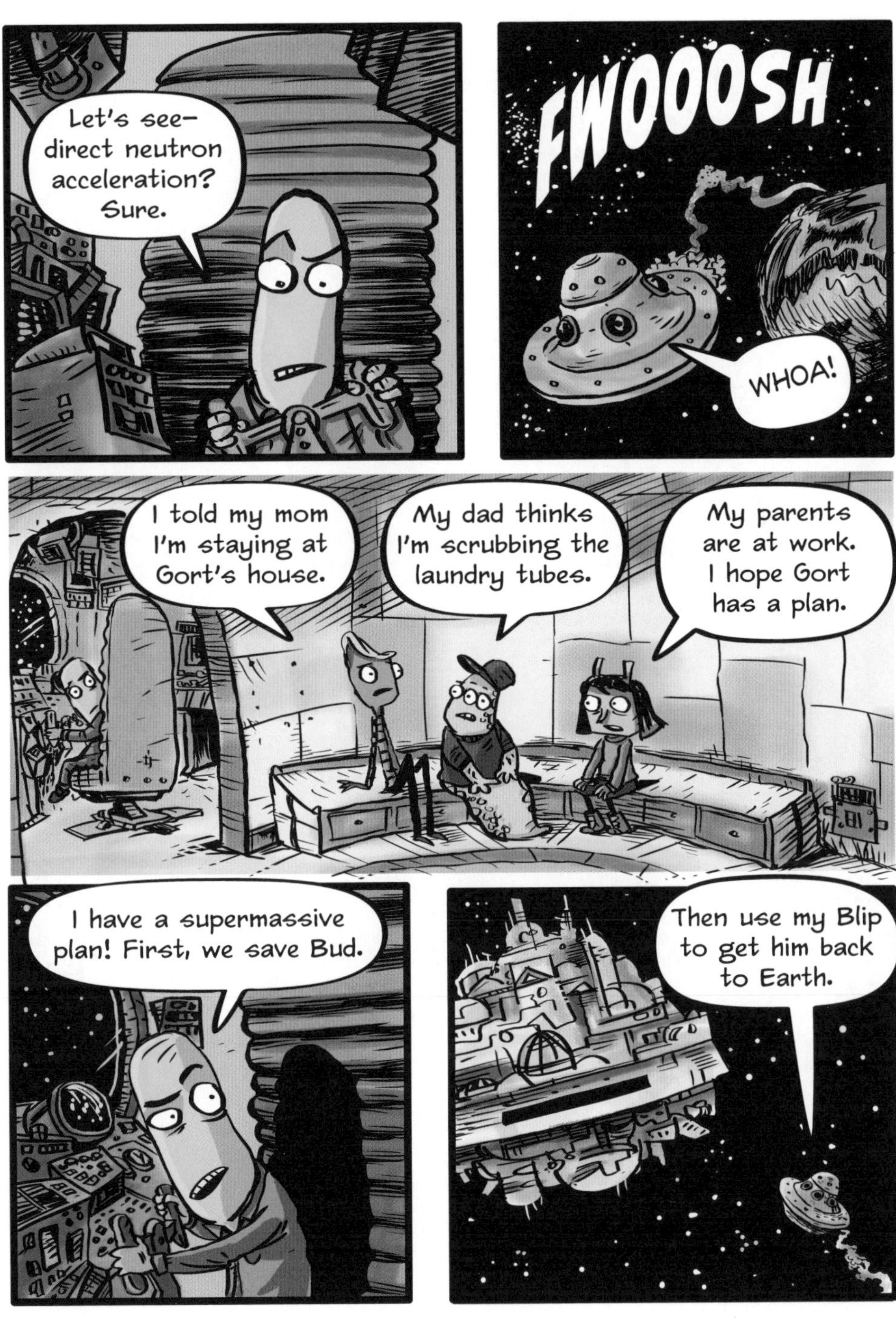

Let's see—direct neutron acceleration? Sure.
FWOOOSH
WHOA!
I told my mom I'm staying at Gort's house.
My dad thinks I'm scrubbing the laundry tubes.
My parents are at work. I hope Gort has a plan.
I have a supermassive plan! First, we save Bud.
Then use my Blip to get him back to Earth.

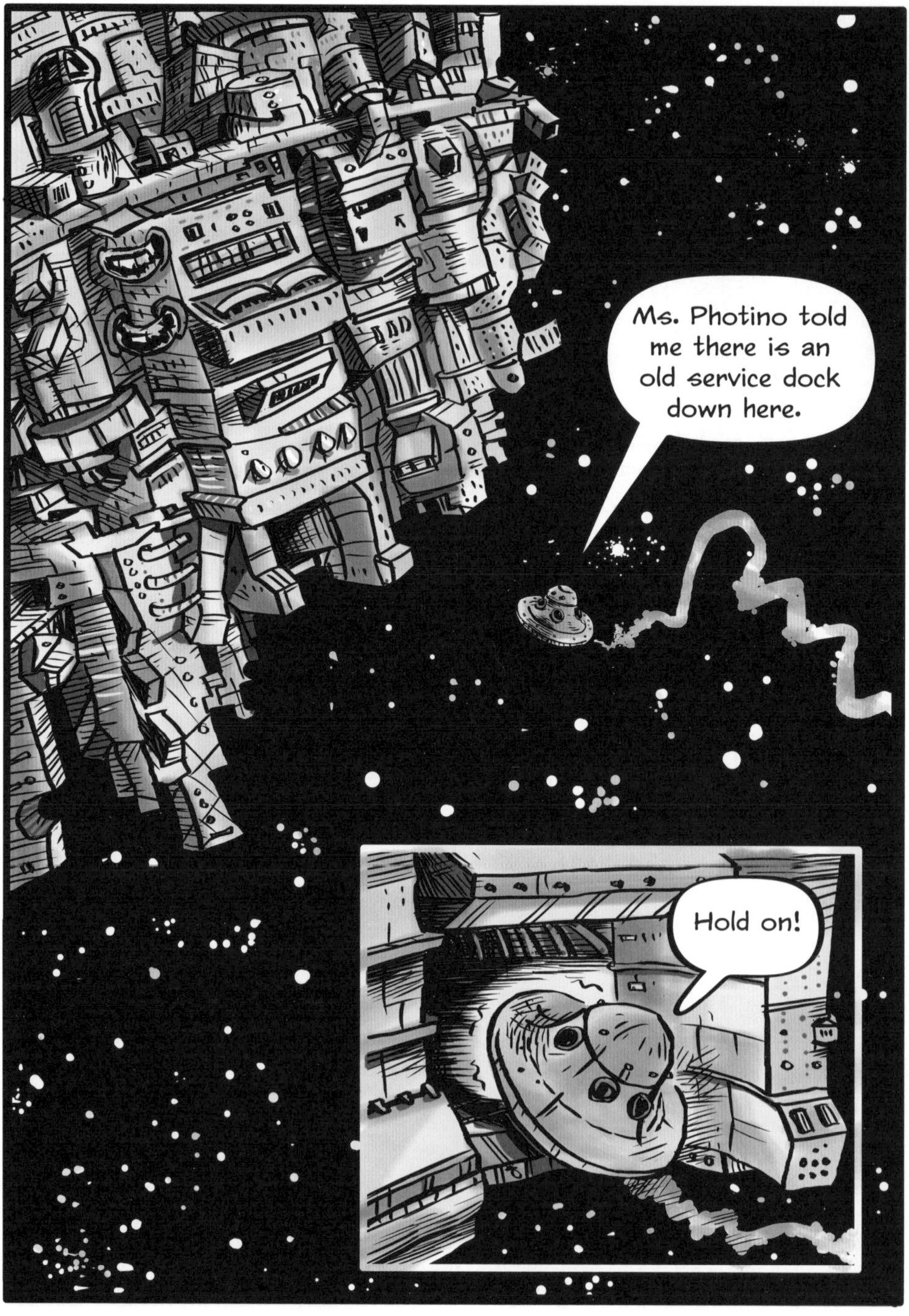
Ms. Photino told me there is an old service dock down here.
Hold on!

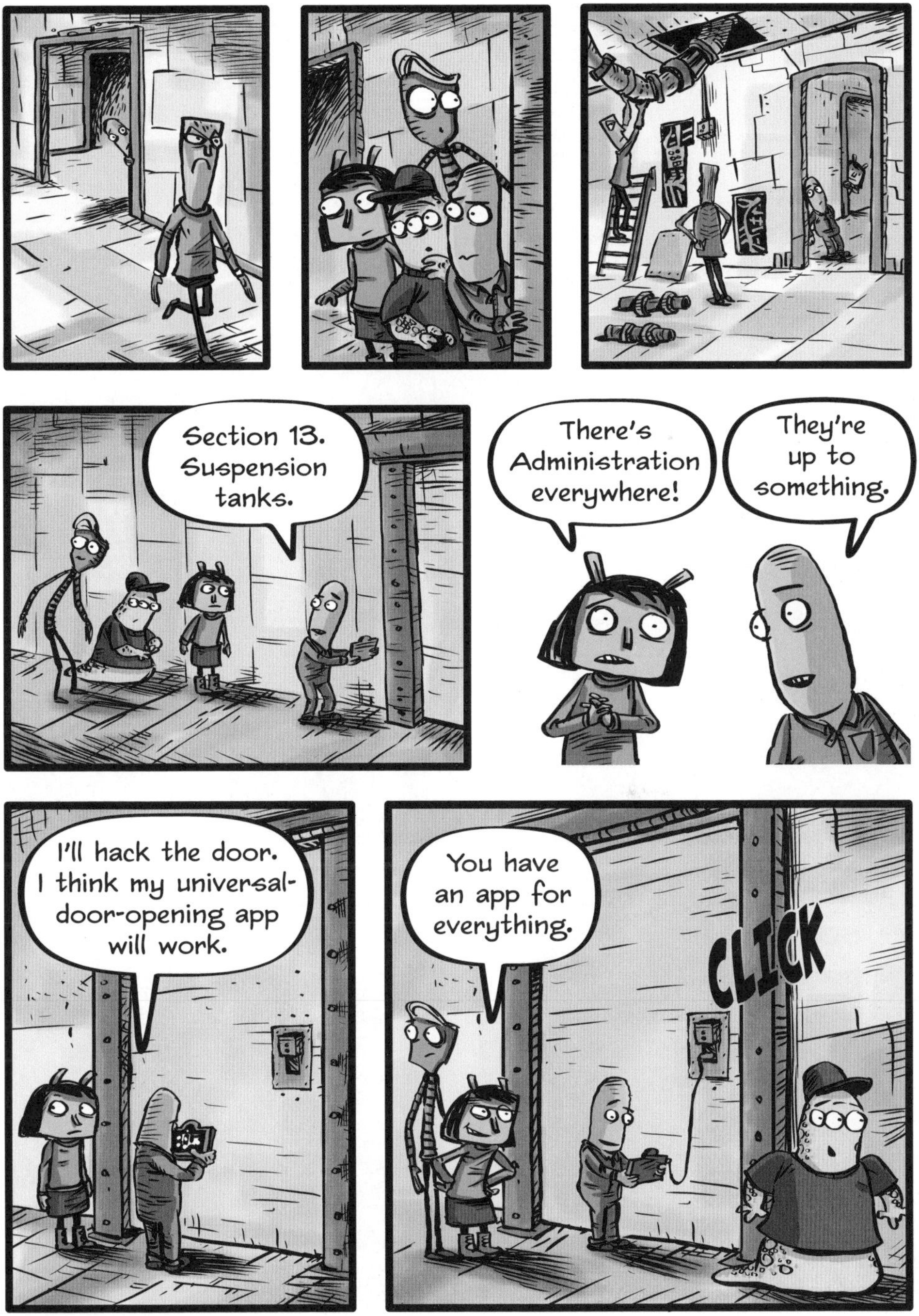
Section 13. Suspension tanks.
There's Administration everywhere!
They're up to something.
I'll hack the door. I think my universal-door-opening app will work.
You have an app for everything.
CLICK

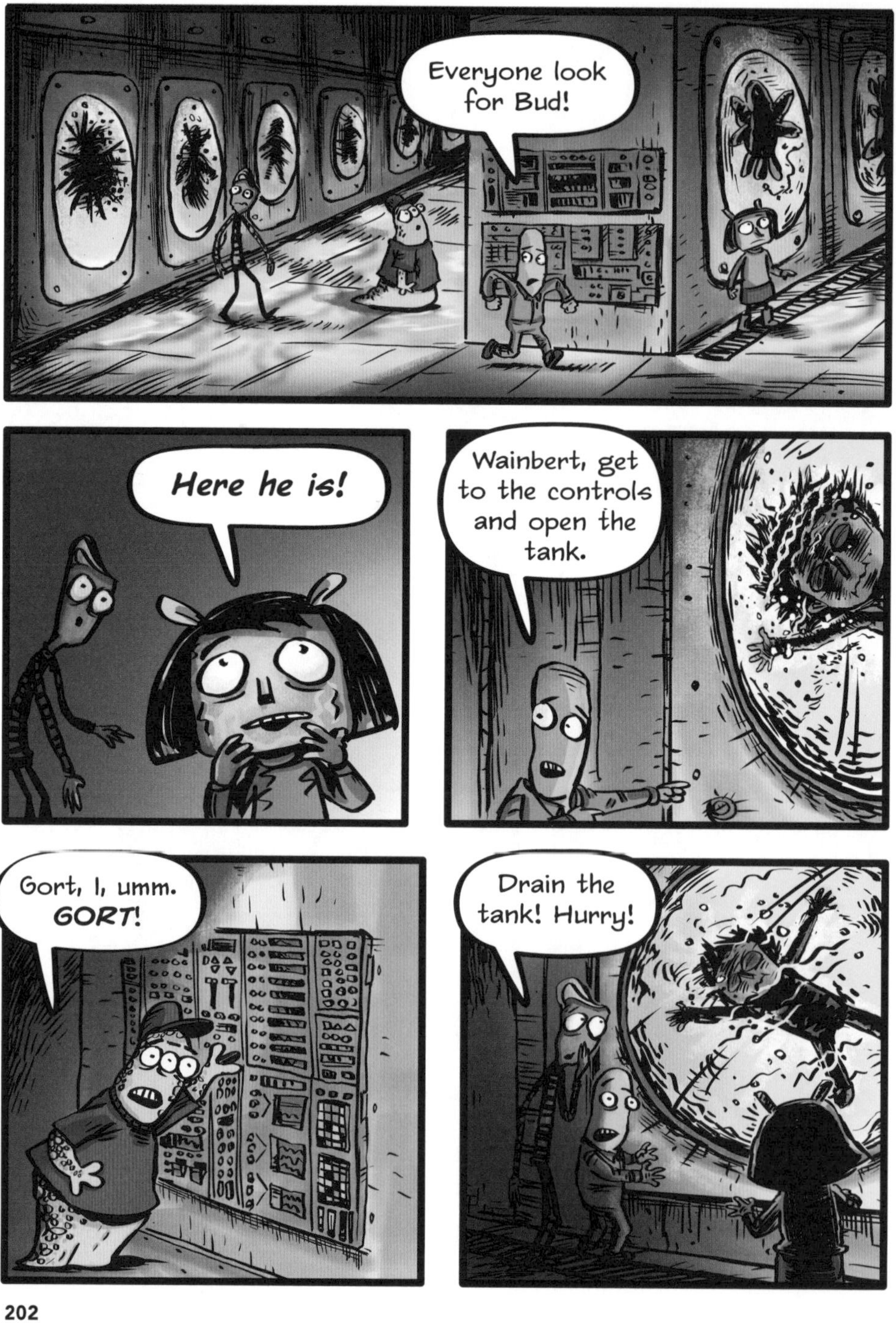
Everyone look for Bud!
Here he is!
Wainbert, get to the controls and open the tank.
Gort, I, umm. GORT!
Drain the tank! Hurry!

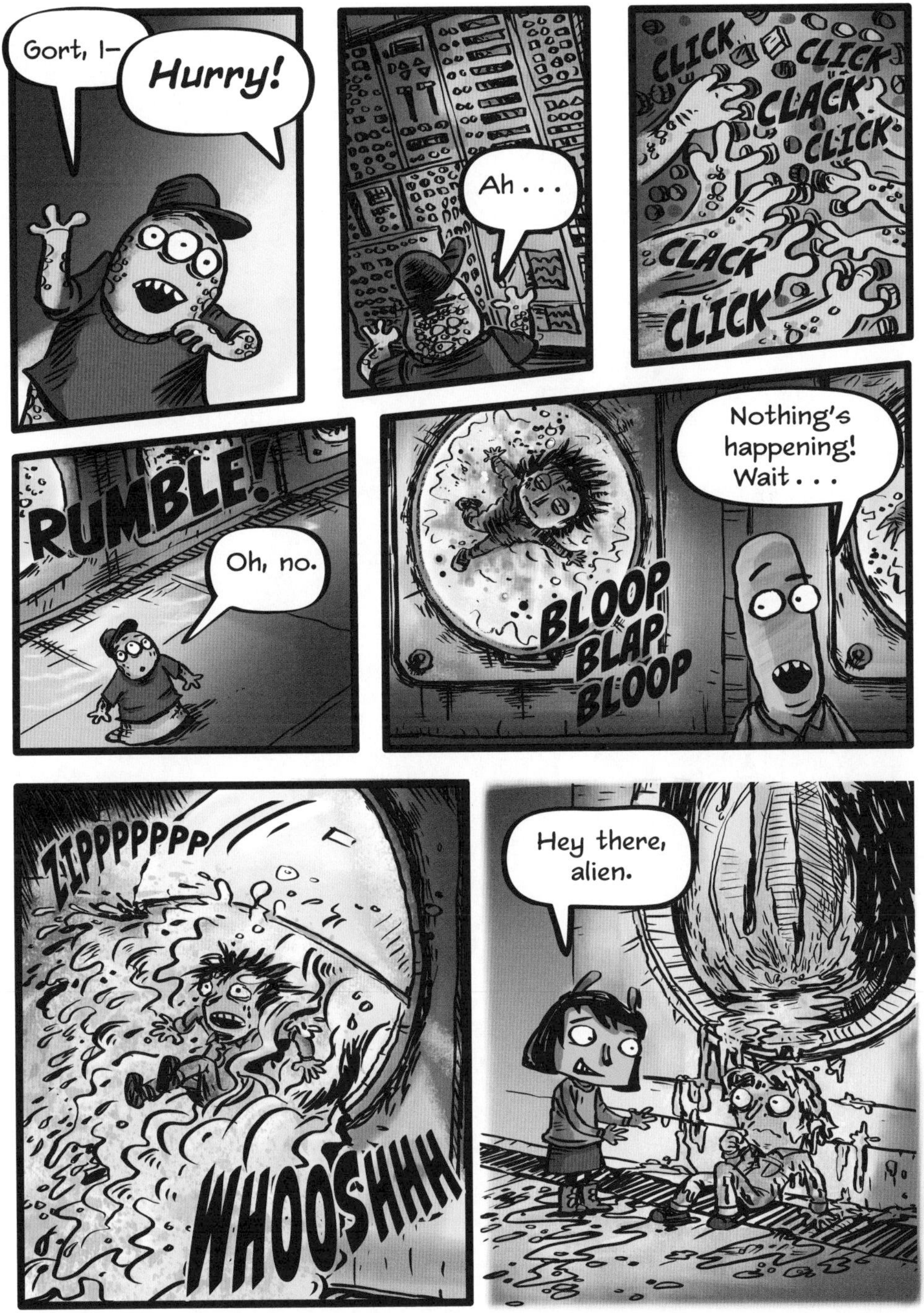

Gort, I—
Hurry!
Ah . . .
CLICK CLICK
CLACK
CLICK
CLACK
CLICK
RUMBLE!
Oh, no.
Nothing's happening! Wait . . .
BLOOP
BLAP
BLOOP
ZIPPPPPPP
WHOOSHHH
Hey there, alien.

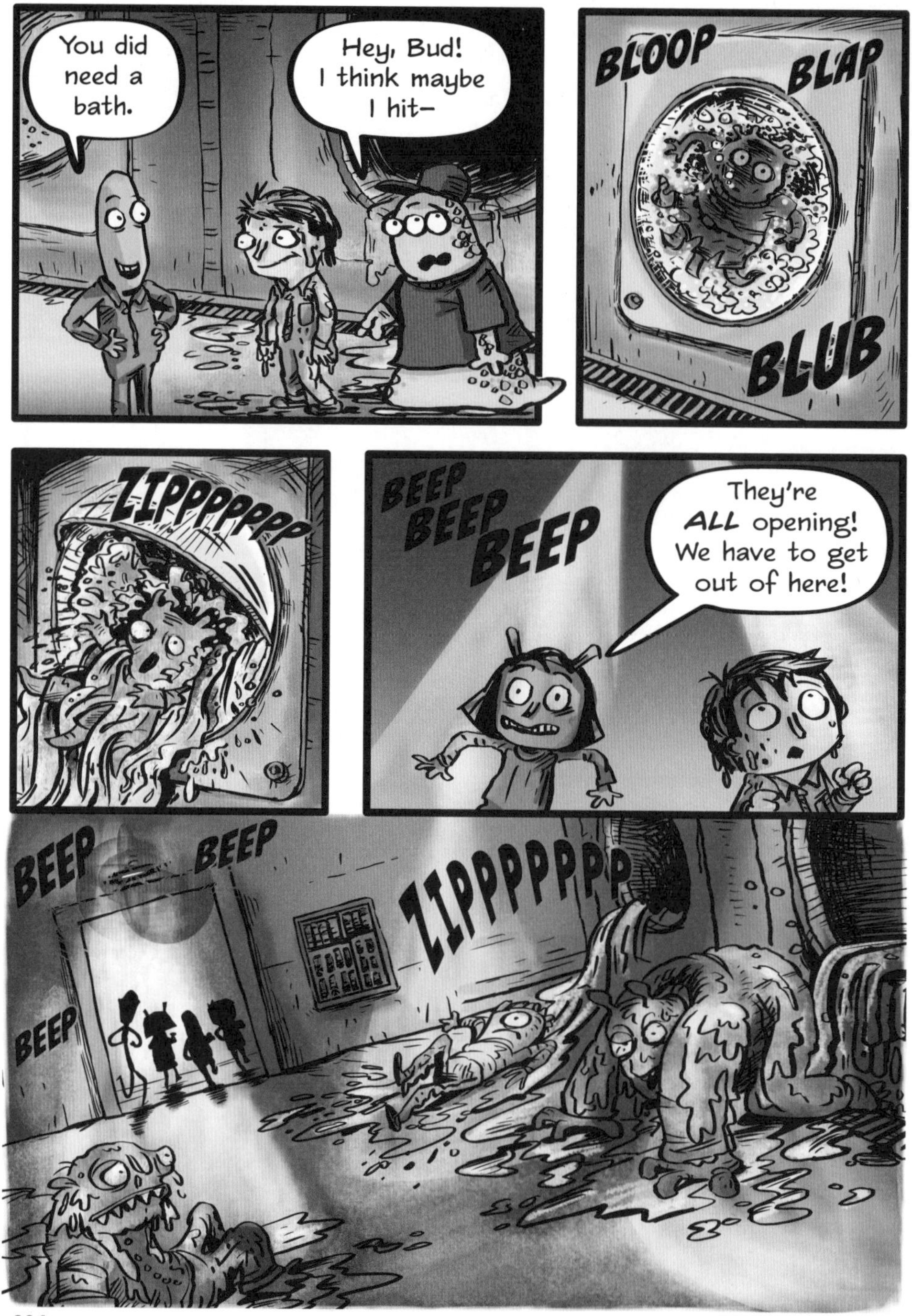
You did need a bath.
Hey, Bud! I think maybe I hit–
BLOOP
BLAP
BLUB
ZIPPPPPPP
BEEP
BEEP
BEEP
They're ALL opening! We have to get out of here!
BEEP
BEEP
ZIPPPPPPP
BEEP

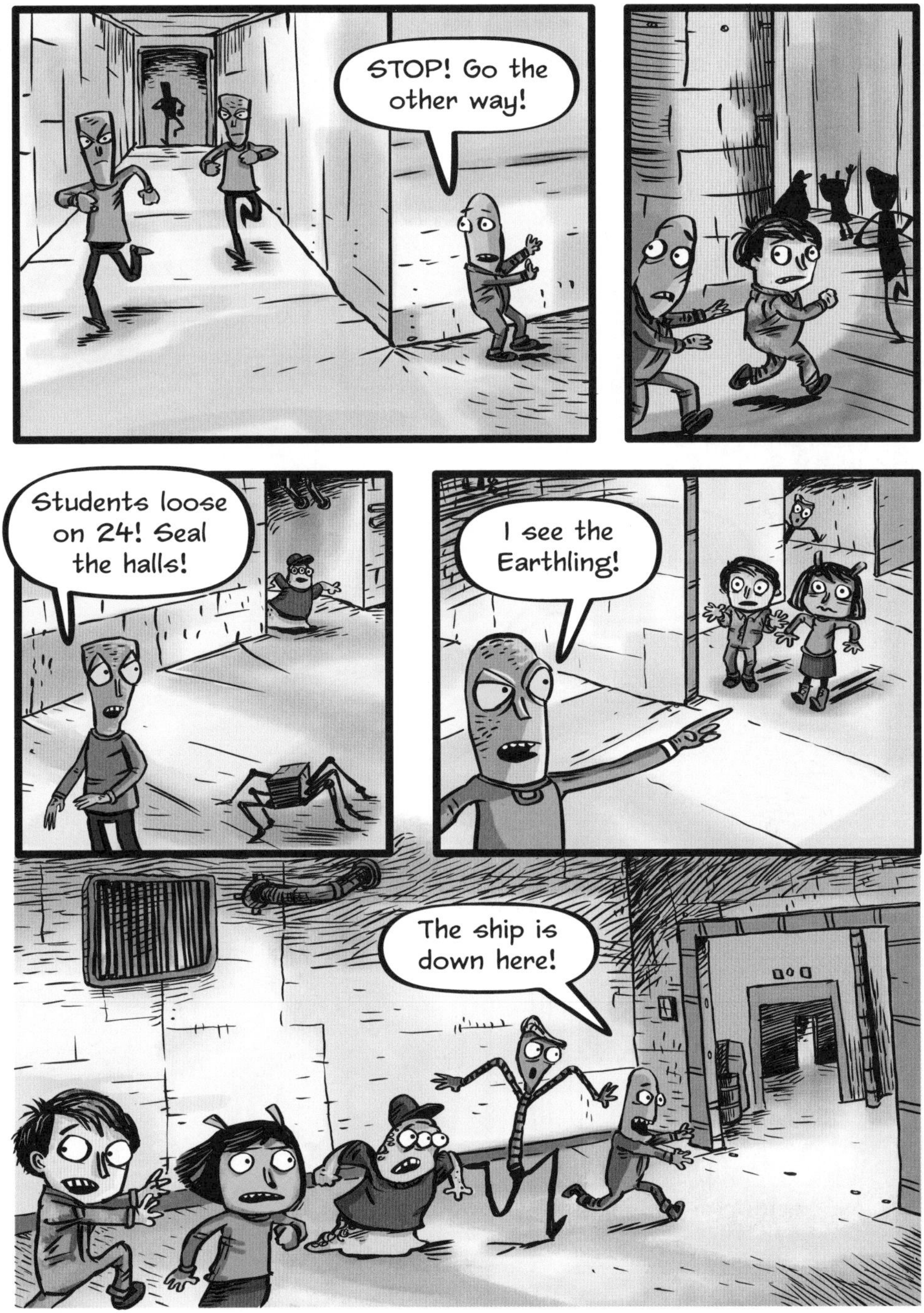
STOP! Go the other way!
Students loose on 24! Seal the halls!
I see the Earthling!
The ship is down here!

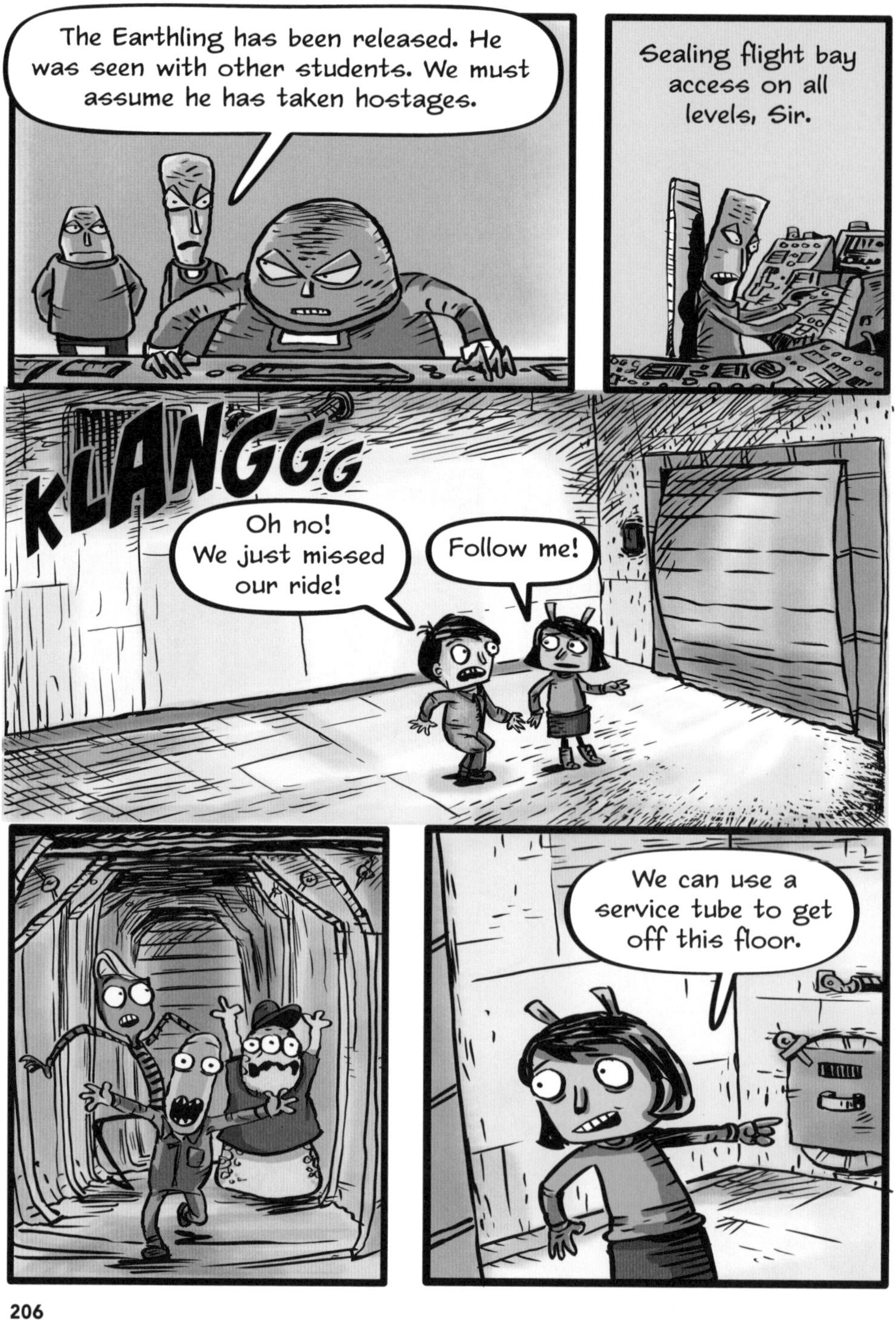
The Earthling has been released. He was seen with other students. We must assume he has taken hostages.
Sealing flight bay access on all levels, Sir.
KLANGGG
Oh no! We just missed our ride!
Follow me!
We can use a service tube to get off this floor.

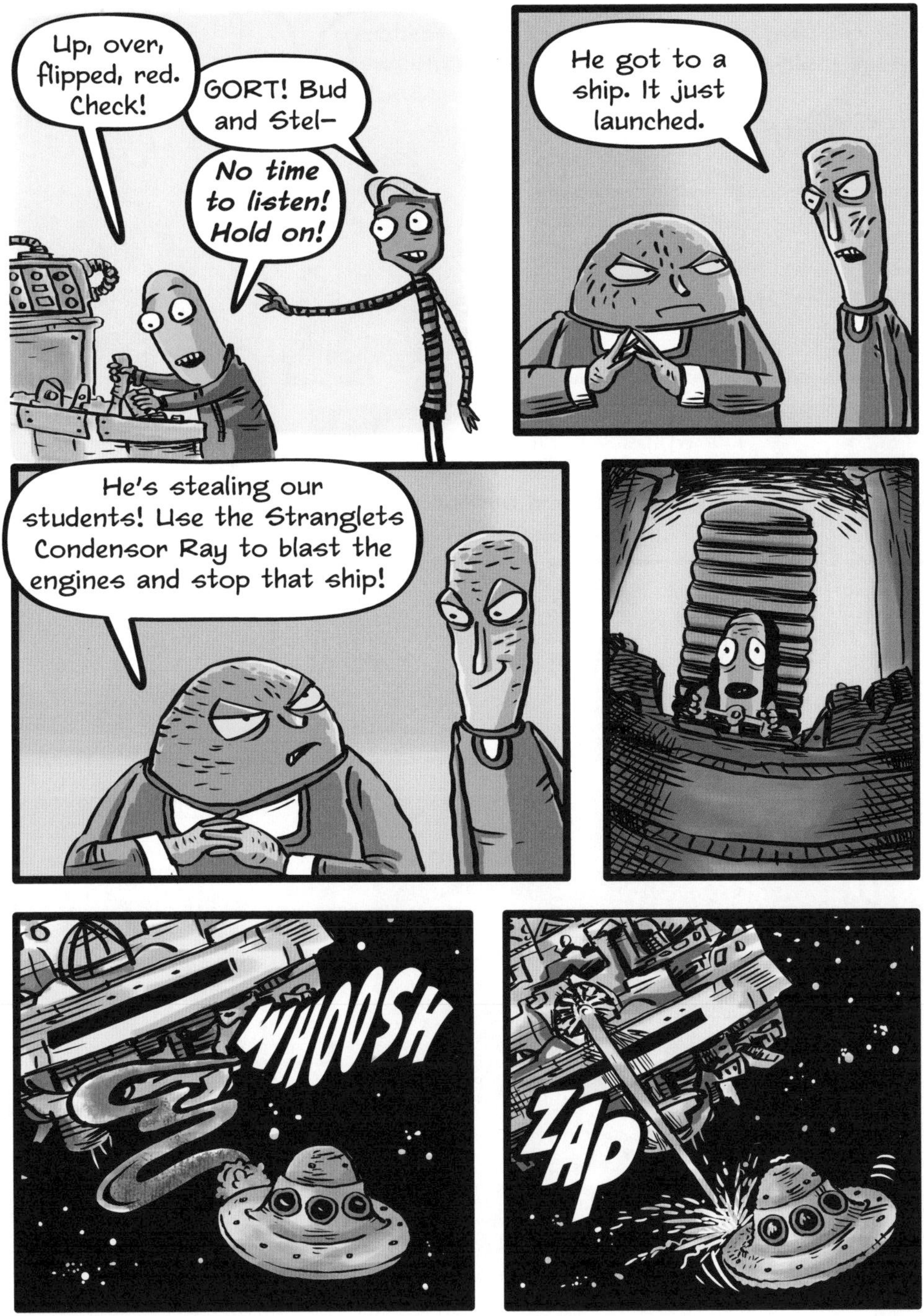
Up, over, flipped, red. Check!
GORT! Bud and Stel–
No time to listen! Hold on!
He got to a ship. It just launched.
He's stealing our students! Use the Stranglets Condensor Ray to blast the engines and stop that ship!
WHOOSH
ZAP

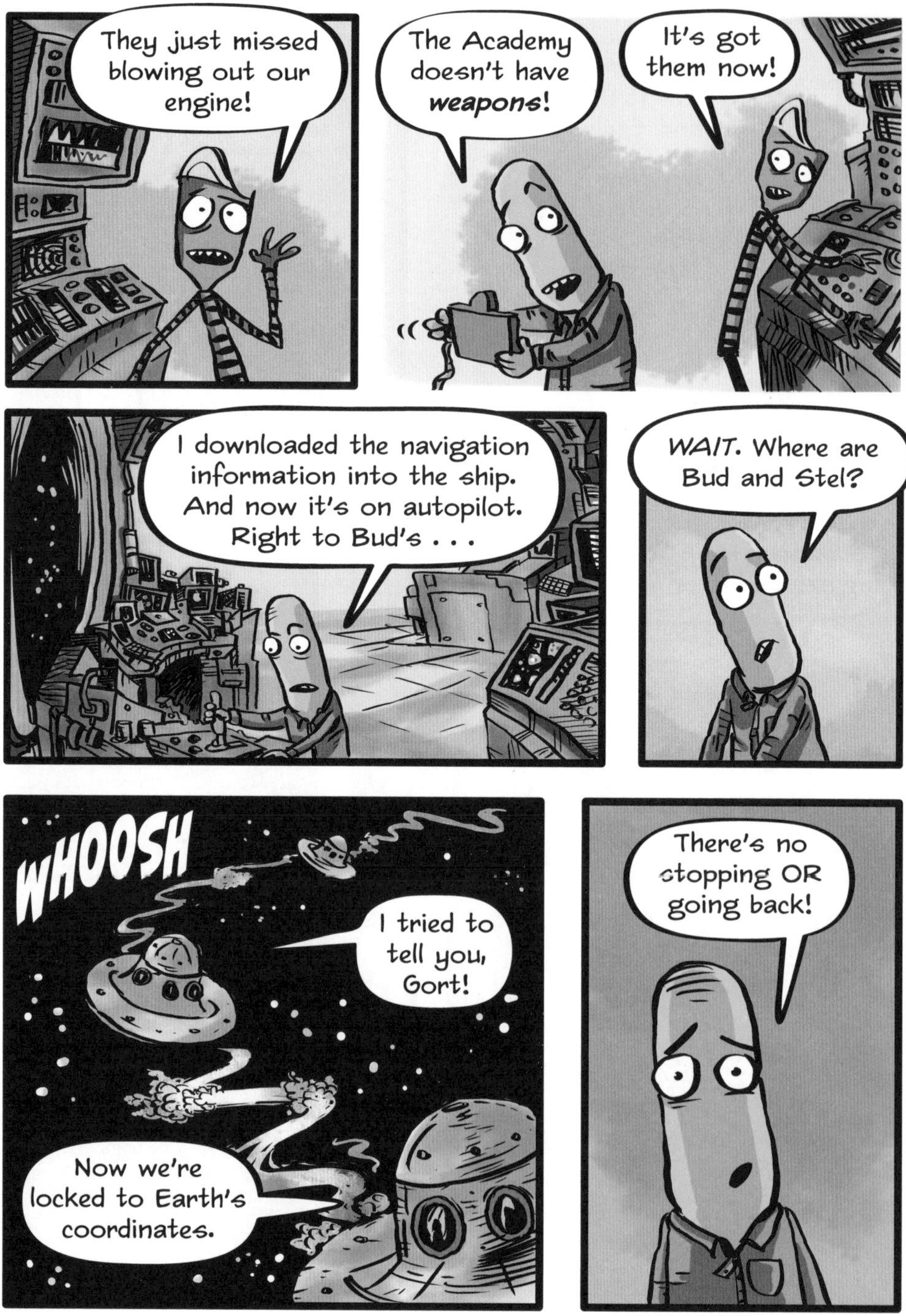
They just missed blowing out our engine!
The Academy doesn't have ***weapons***!
It's got them now!
I downloaded the navigation information into the ship. And now it's on autopilot. Right to Bud's . . .
WAIT. Where are Bud and Stel?
WHOOSH
I tried to tell you, Gort!
Now we're locked to Earth's coordinates.
There's no stopping OR going back!

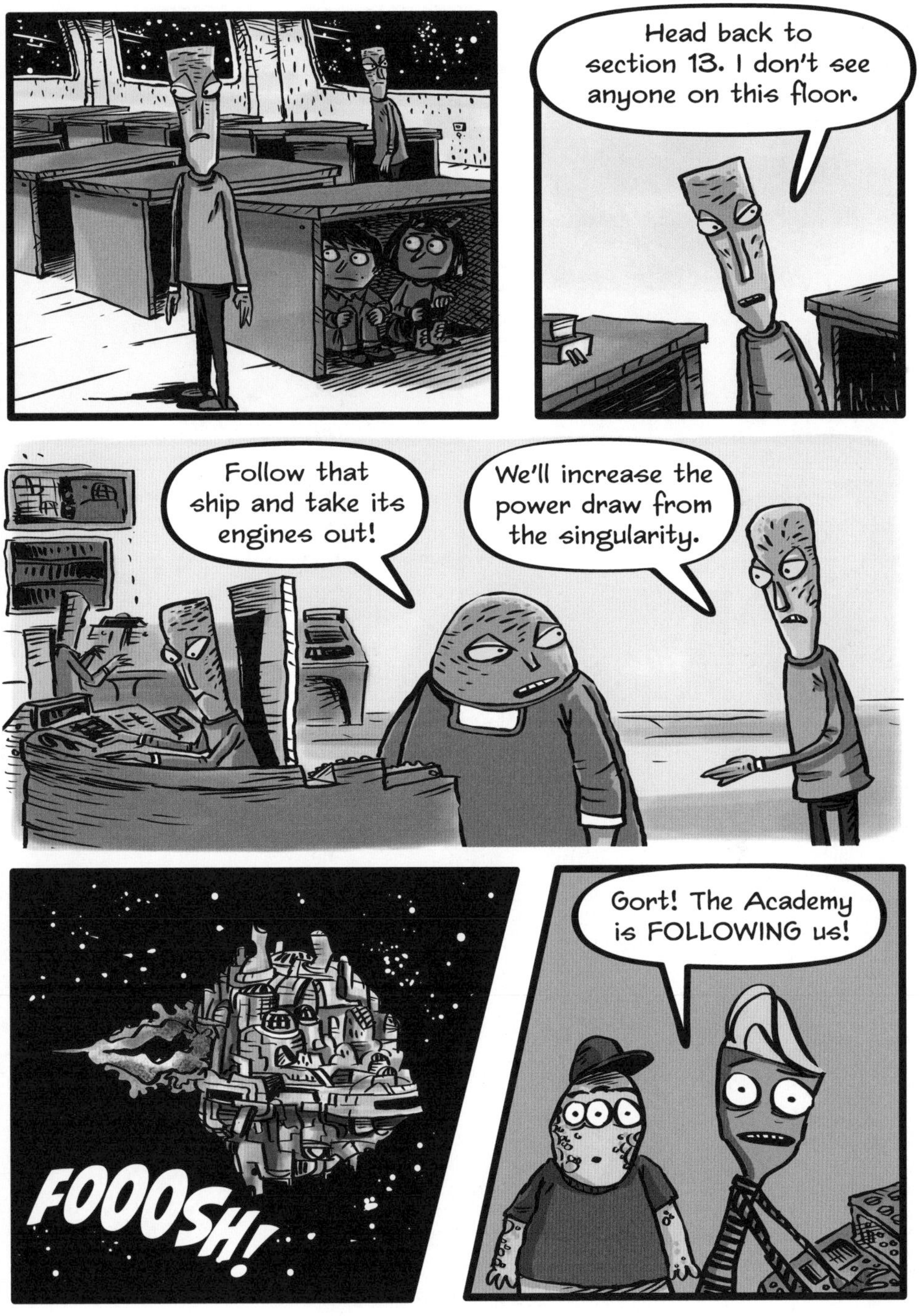
Head back to section 13. I don't see anyone on this floor.
Follow that ship and take its engines out!
We'll increase the power draw from the singularity.
FOOOSH!
Gort! The Academy is FOLLOWING us!

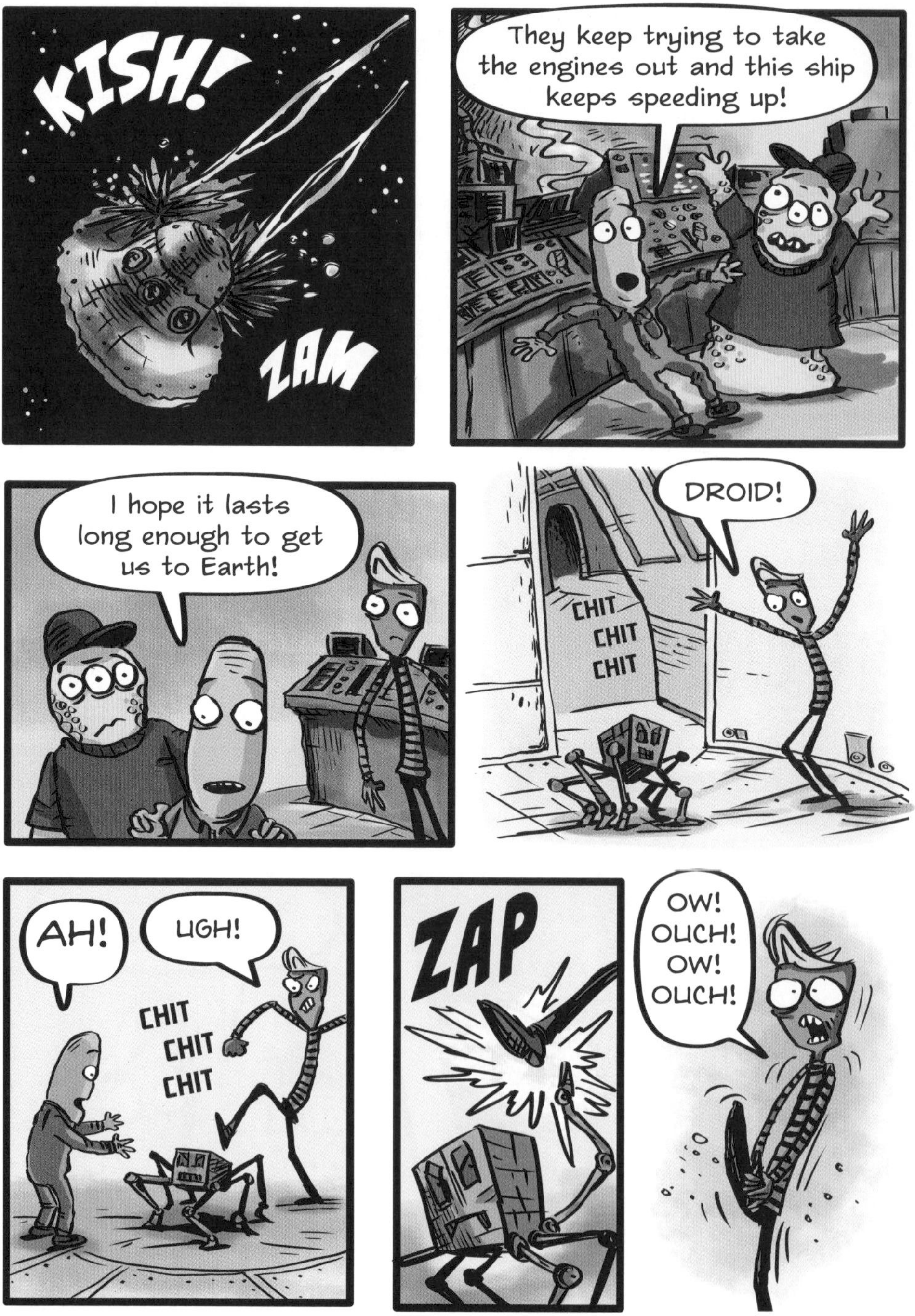
KISH!
ZAM
They keep trying to take the engines out and this ship keeps speeding up!
I hope it lasts long enough to get us to Earth!
DROID!
CHIT CHIT CHIT
AH!
UGH!
CHIT CHIT CHIT
ZAP
OW! OUCH! OW! OUCH!

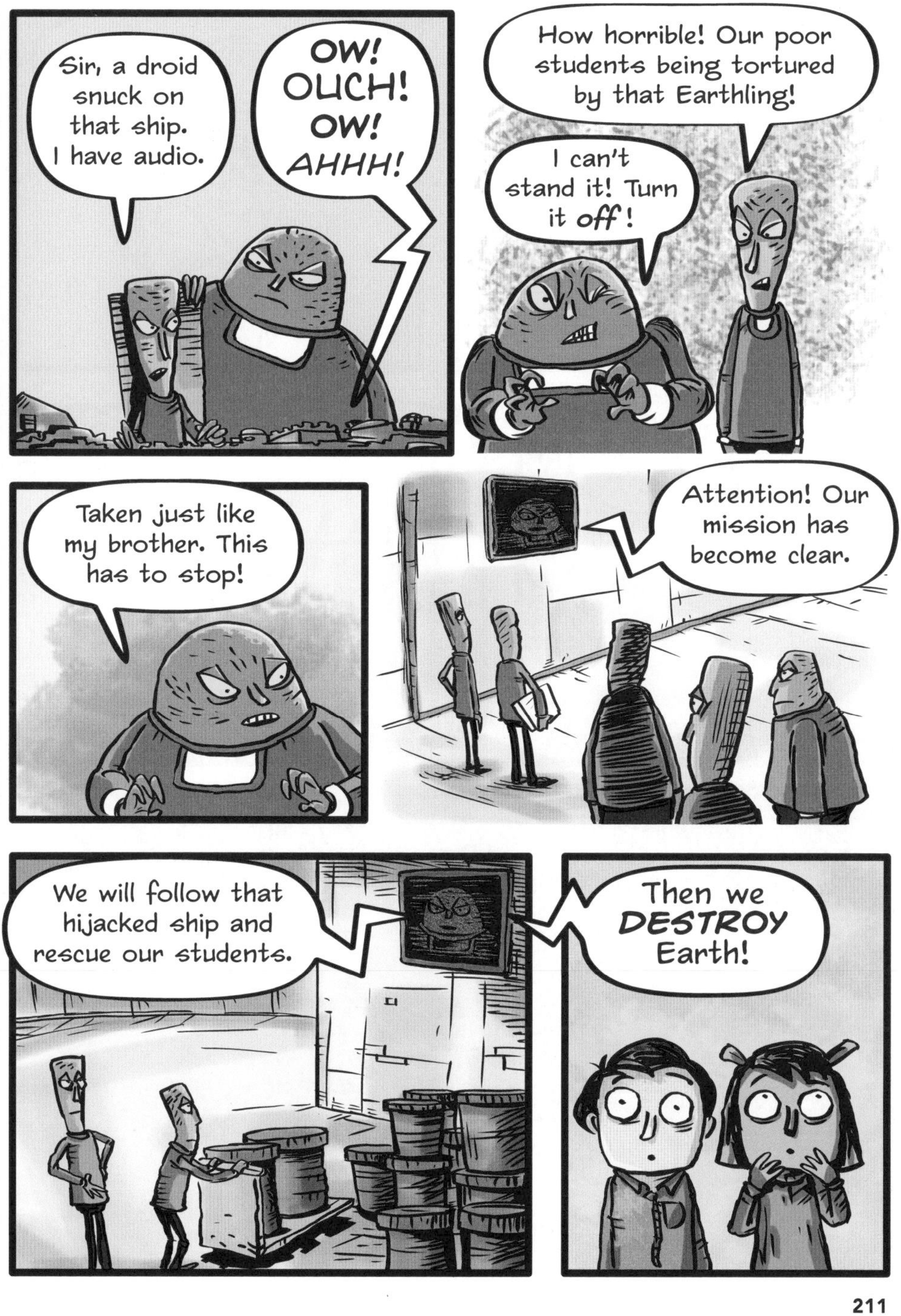
Sir, a droid snuck on that ship. I have audio.
OW! OUCH! OW! AHHH!
How horrible! Our poor students being tortured by that Earthling!
I can't stand it! Turn it *off*!
Taken just like my brother. This has to stop!
Attention! Our mission has become clear.
We will follow that hijacked ship and rescue our students.
Then we ***DESTROY*** Earth!

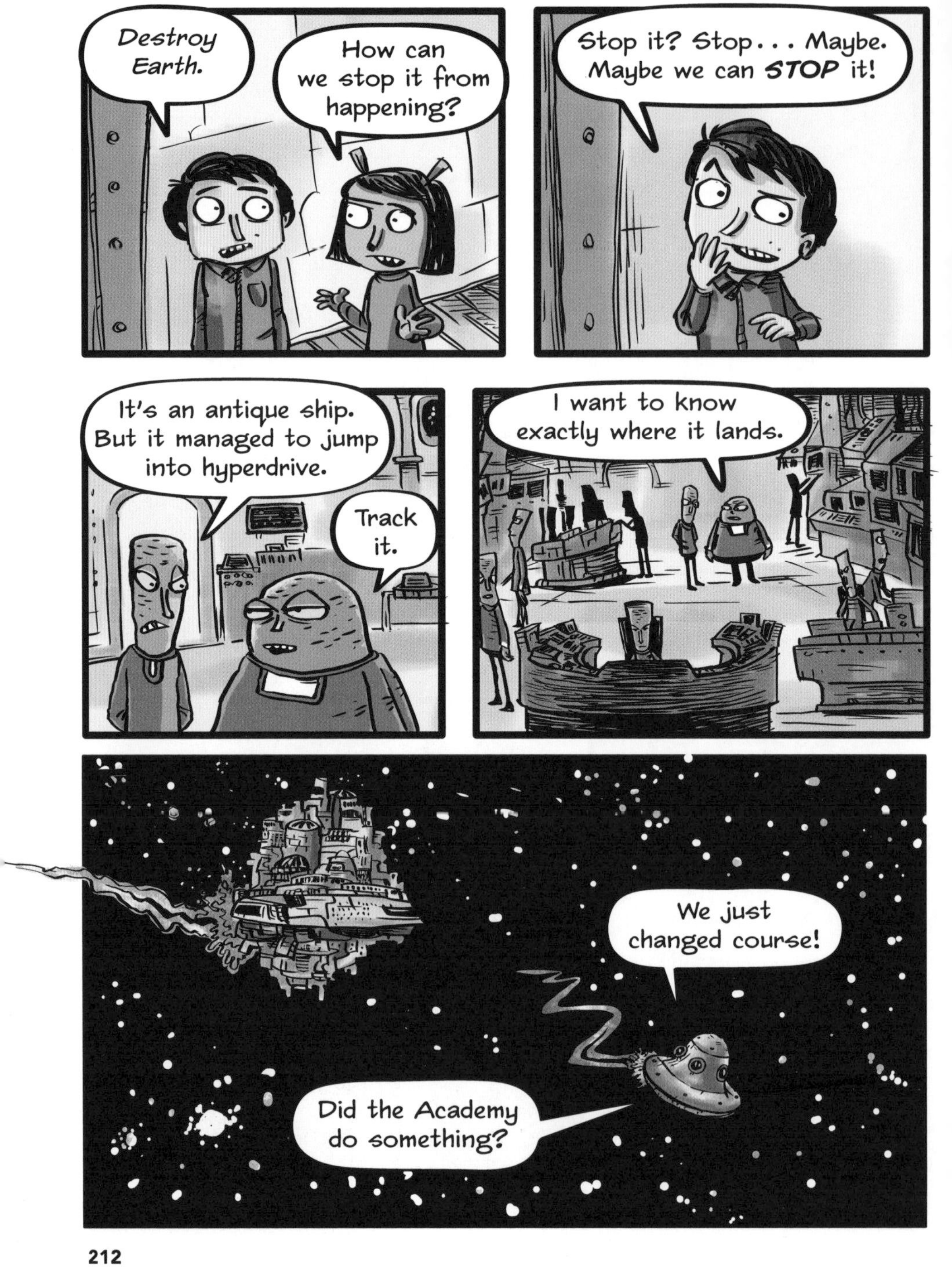
Destroy Earth.
How can we stop it from happening?
Stop it? Stop... Maybe. Maybe we can **STOP** it!
It's an antique ship. But it managed to jump into hyperdrive.
Track it.
I want to know exactly where it lands.
We just changed course!
Did the Academy do something?

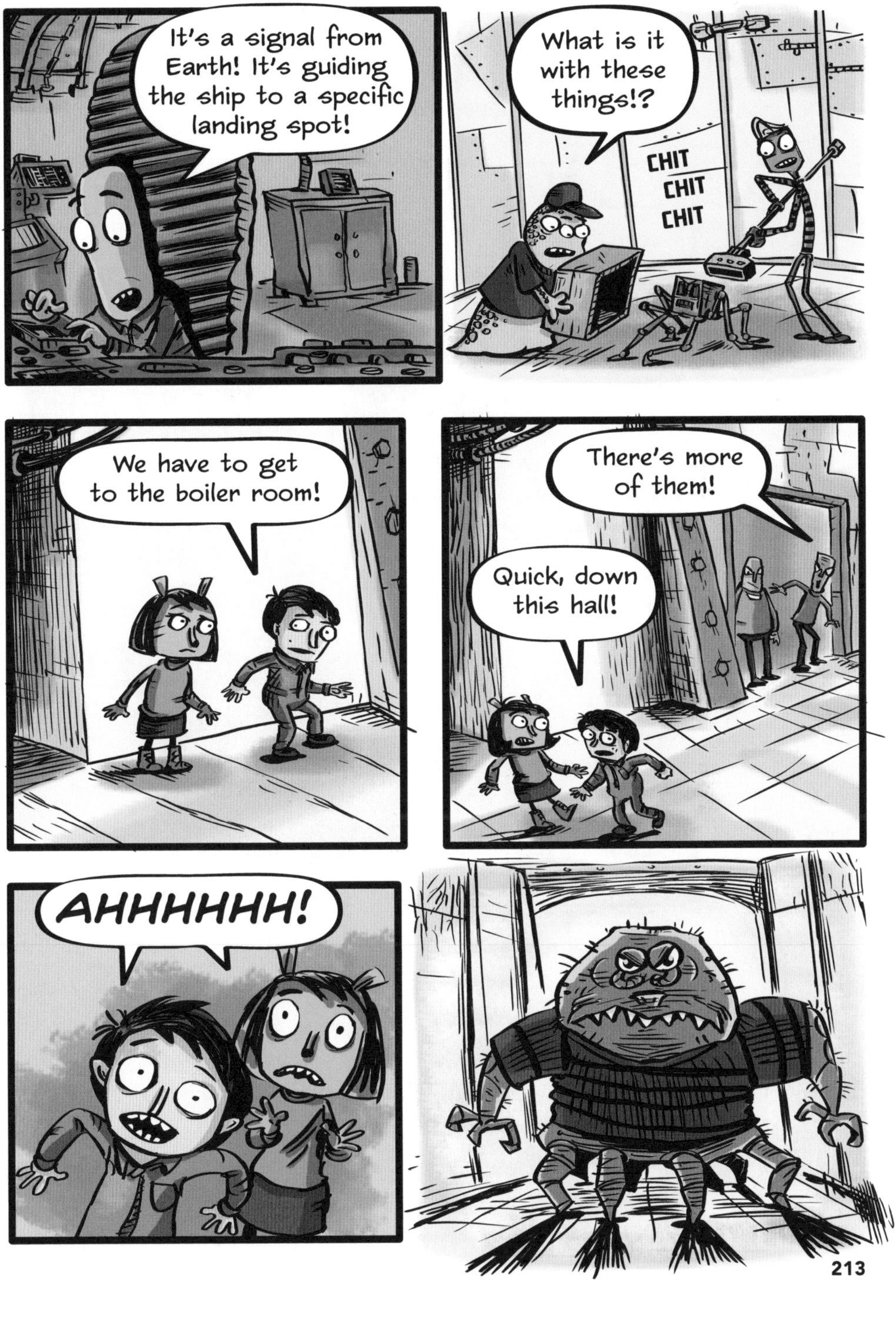
It's a signal from Earth! It's guiding the ship to a specific landing spot!
What is it with these things!?
CHIT
CHIT
CHIT
We have to get to the boiler room!
There's more of them!
Quick, down this hall!
AHHHHHH!

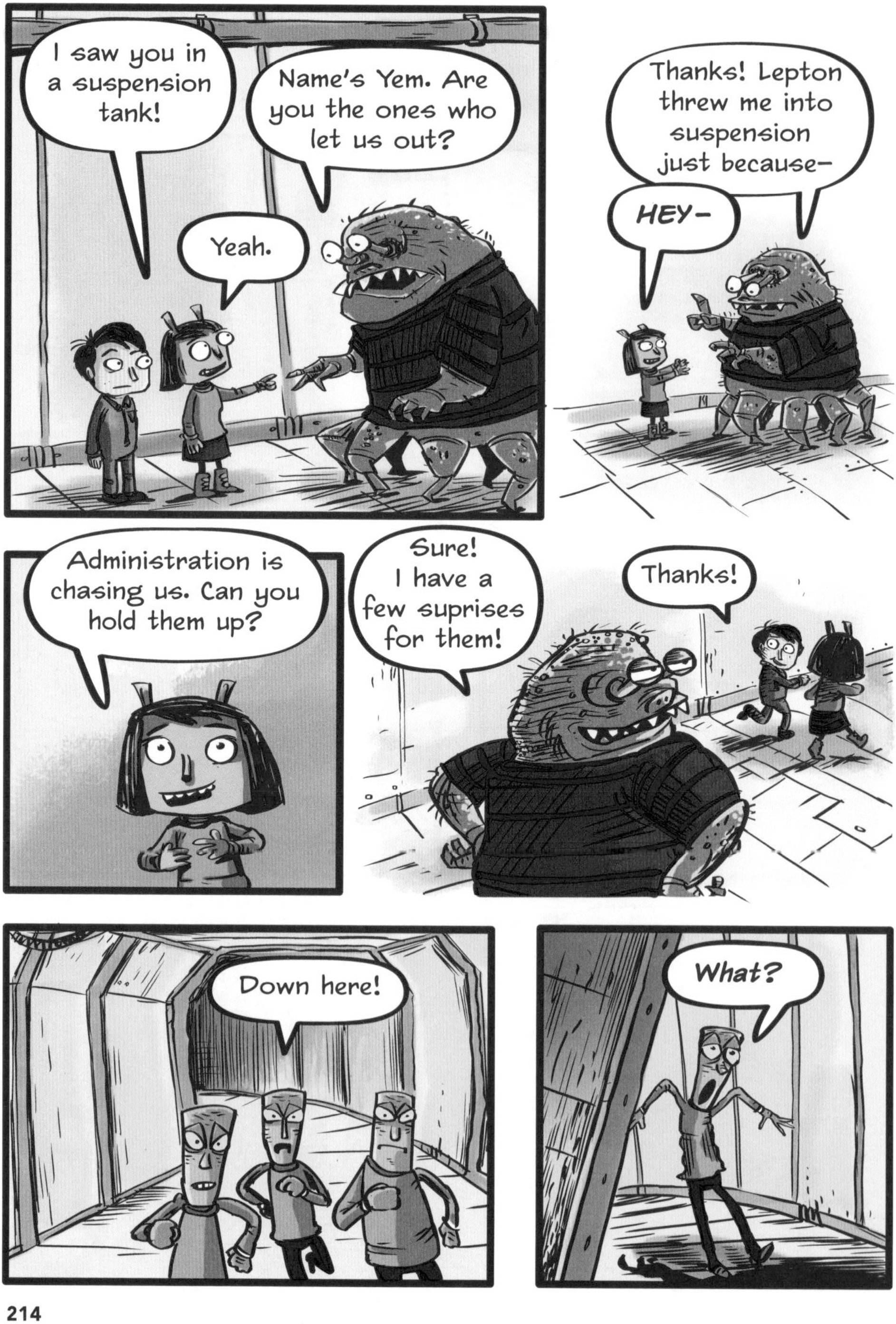
I saw you in a suspension tank!
Name's Yem. Are you the ones who let us out?
Yeah.
Thanks! Lepton threw me into suspension just because-
HEY-
Administration is chasing us. Can you hold them up?
Sure! I have a few suprises for them!
Thanks!
Down here!
What?

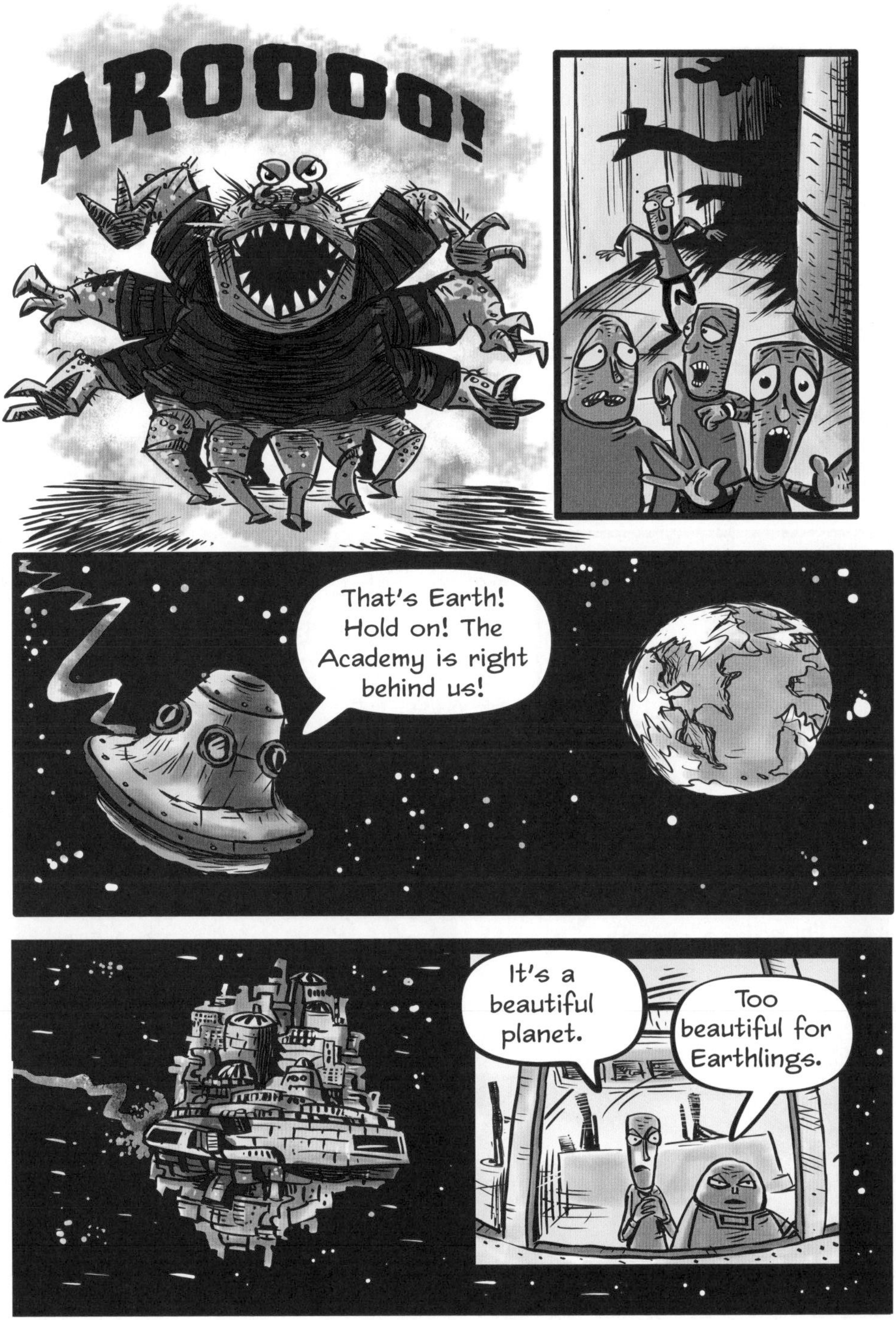
AROOOOO!
That's Earth! Hold on! The Academy is right behind us!
It's a beautiful planet.
Too beautiful for Earthlings.

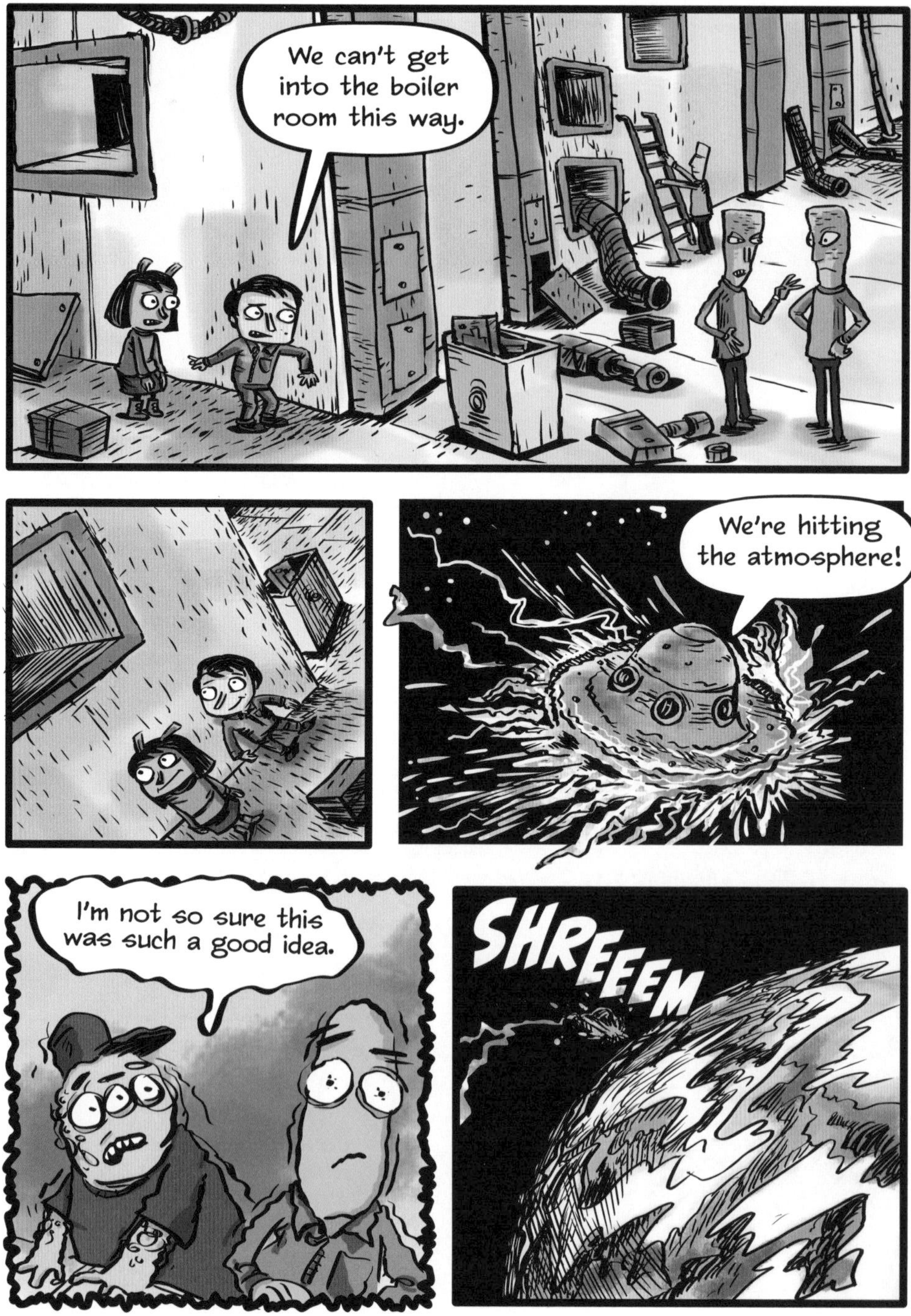
We can't get into the boiler room this way.
We're hitting the atmosphere!
I'm not so sure this was such a good idea.
SHREEEM

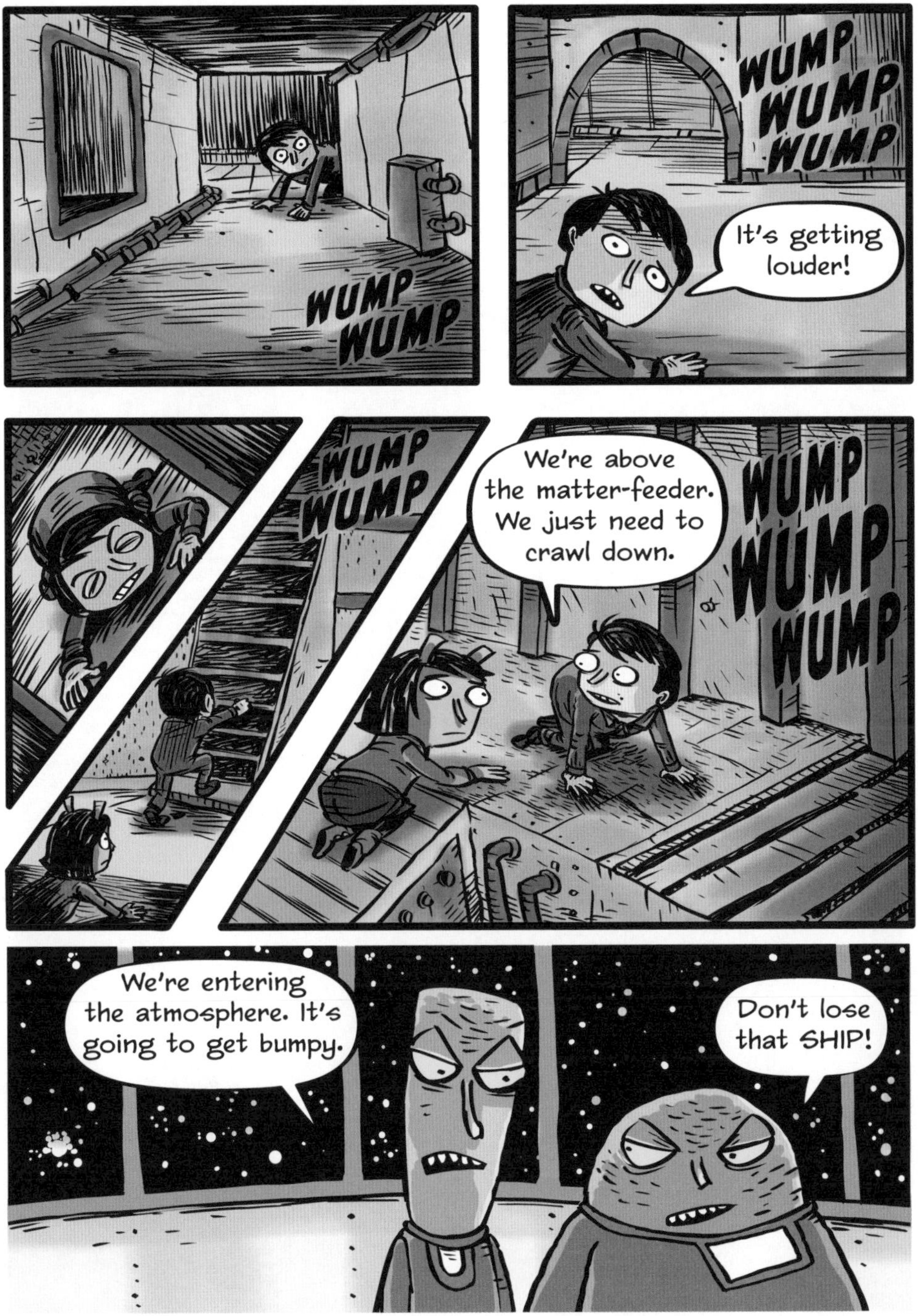
WUMP WUMP
WUMP WUMP WUMP
It's getting louder!
WUMP WUMP
We're above the matter-feeder. We just need to crawl down.
WUMP WUMP WUMP
We're entering the atmosphere. It's going to get bumpy.
Don't lose that SHIP!

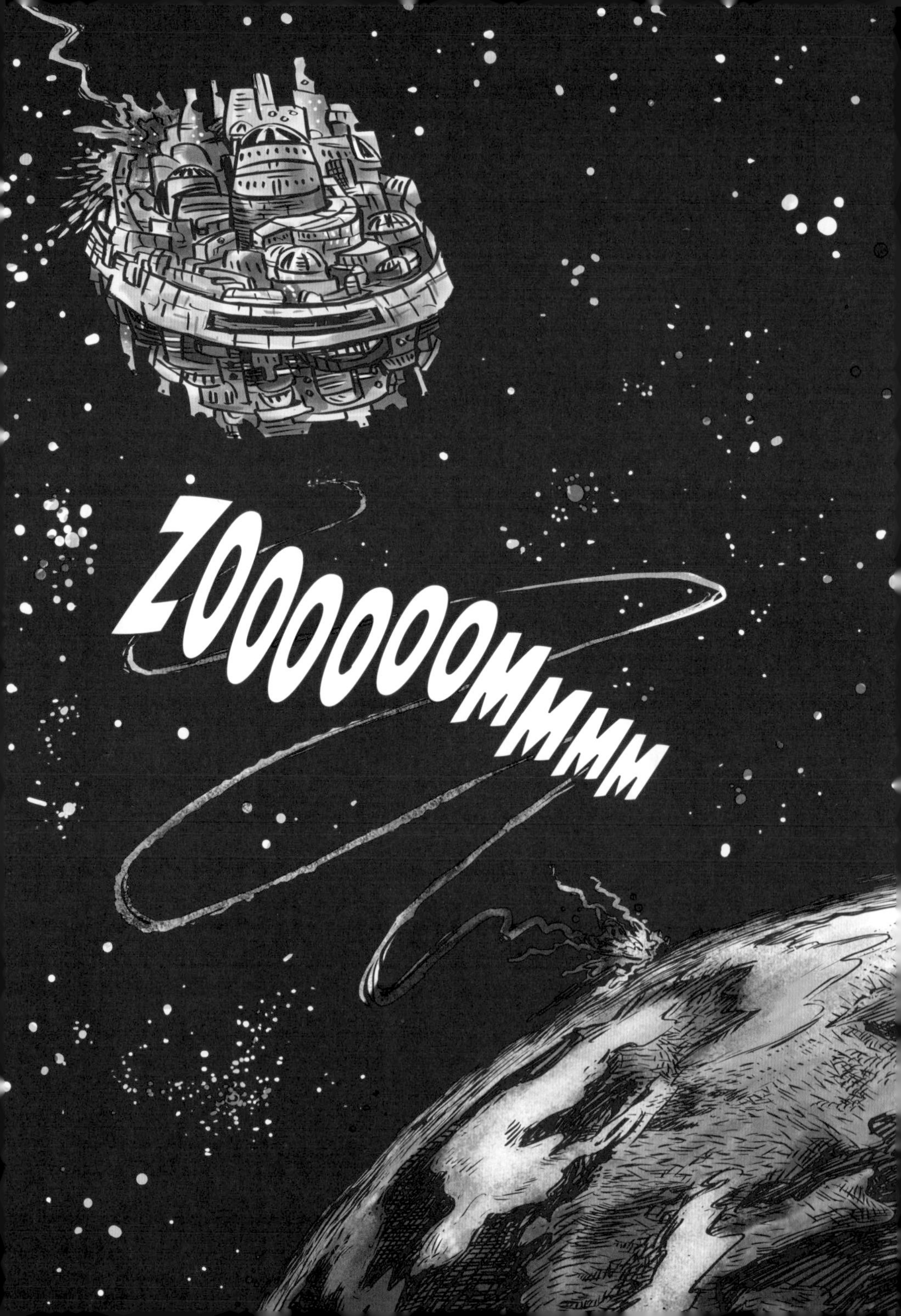
ZOOOOOOMMMMM

CHAPTER 9

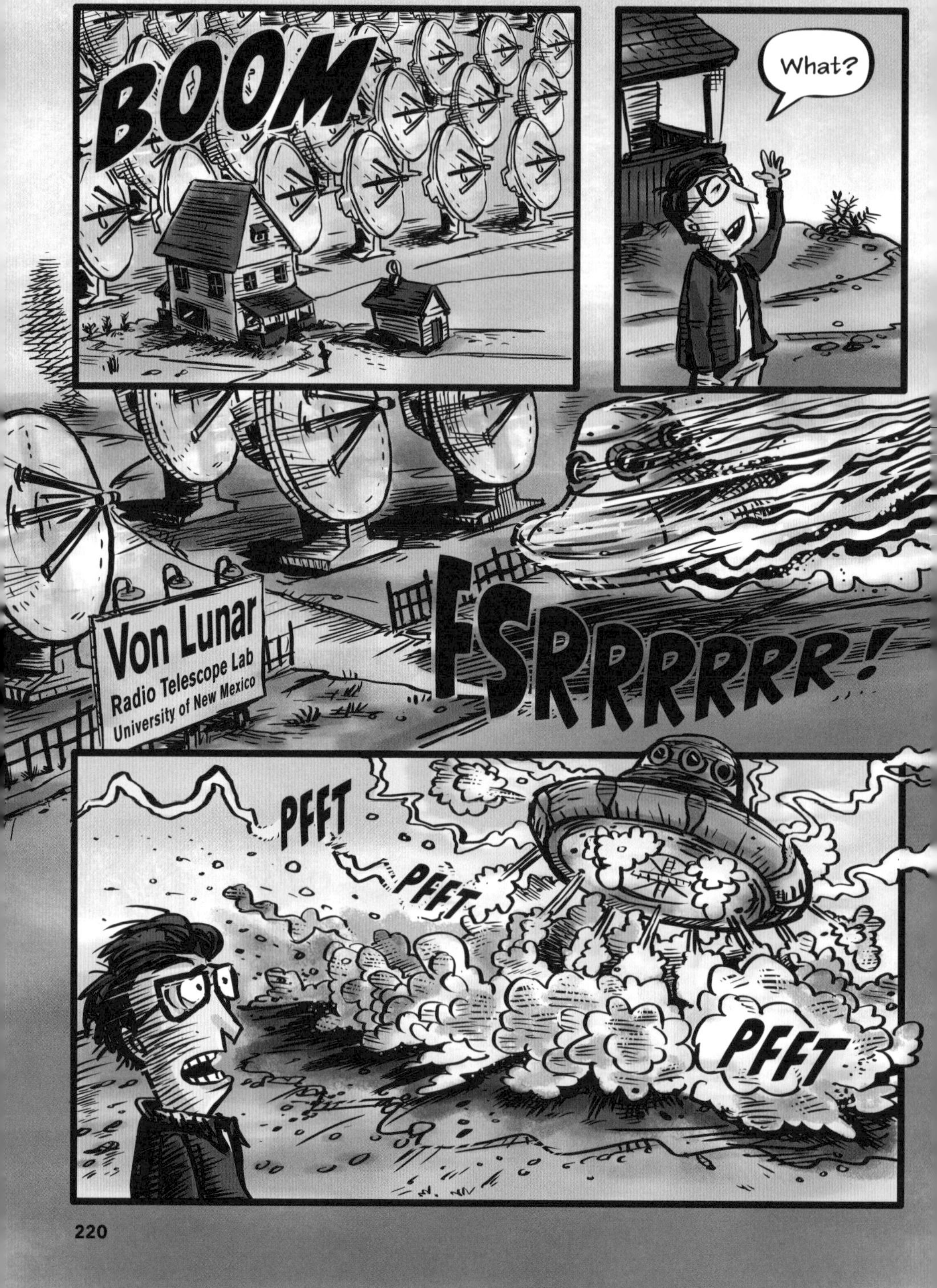
BOOM
What?
Von Lunar
Radio Telescope Lab
University of New Mexico
FSRRRRRR!
PFFT
PFFT
PFFT

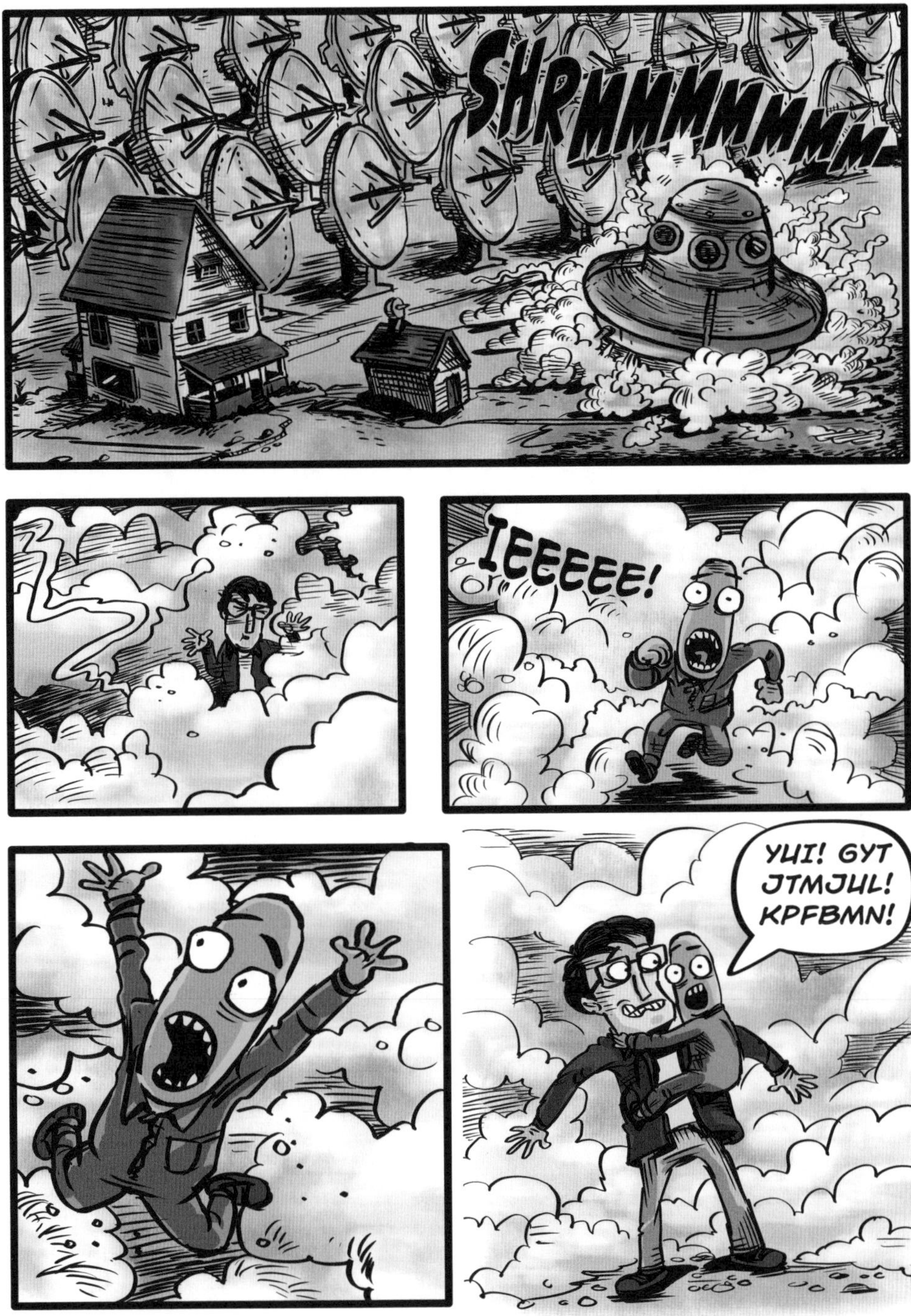
SHRMMMMMMMM-
IEEEEEE!
YUI! GYT JTMJUL! KPFBMN!

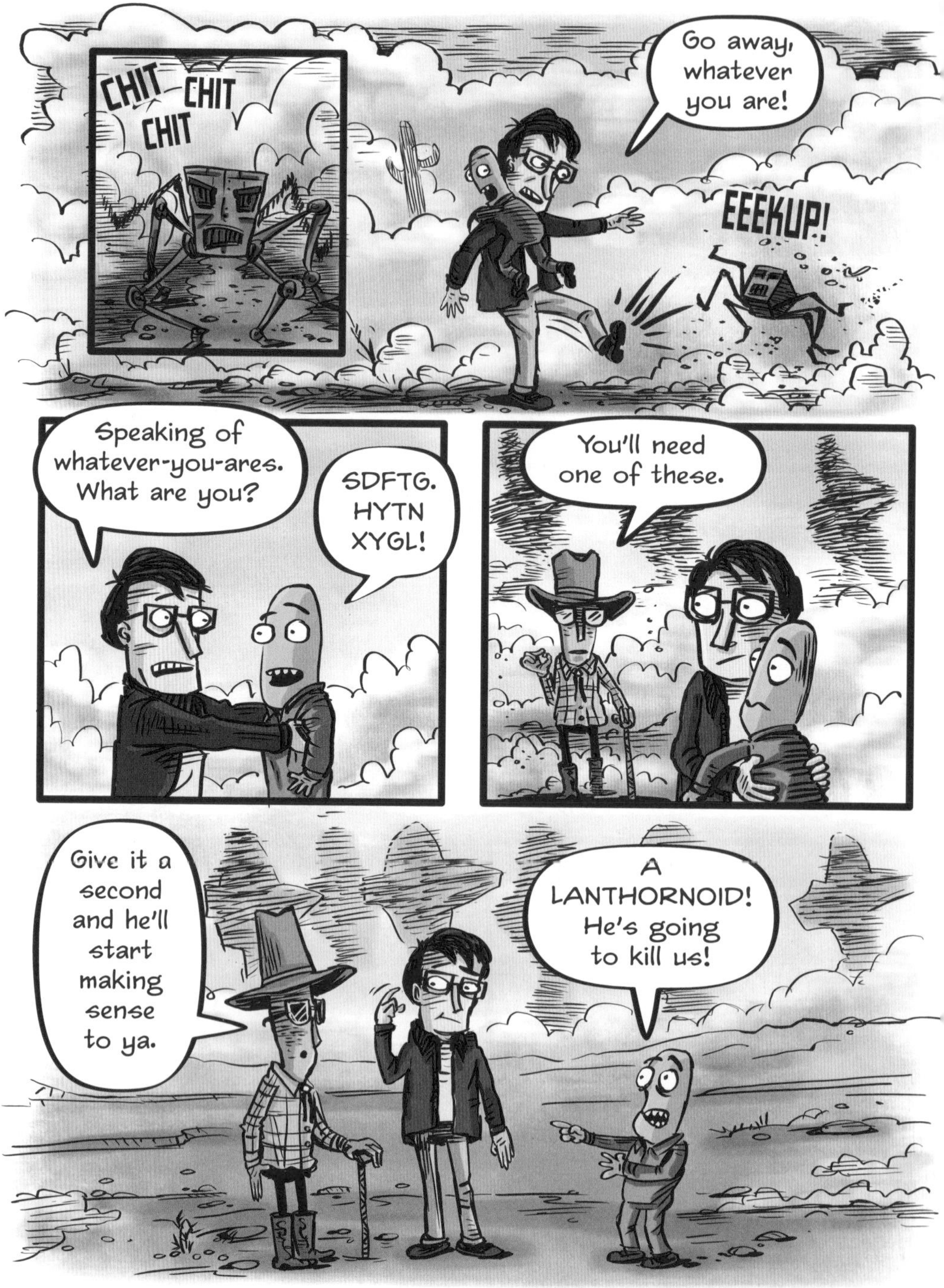
CHIT CHIT CHIT
Go away, whatever you are!
EEEKUP!
Speaking of whatever-you-ares. What are you?
SDFTG. HYTN XYGL!
You'll need one of these.
Give it a second and he'll start making sense to ya.
A LANTHORNOID! He's going to kill us!

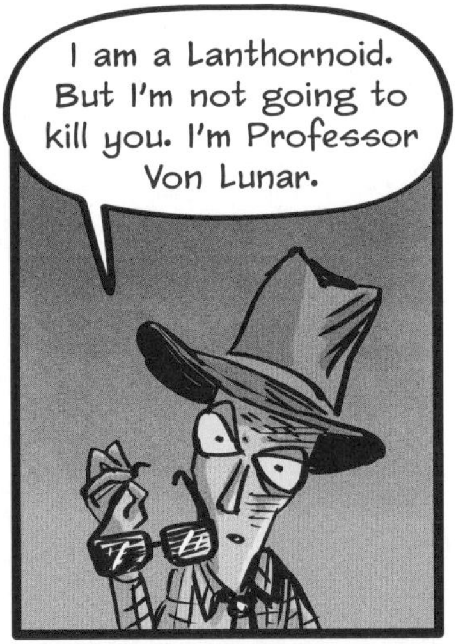
I am a Lanthornoid. But I'm not going to kill you. I'm Professor Von Lunar.

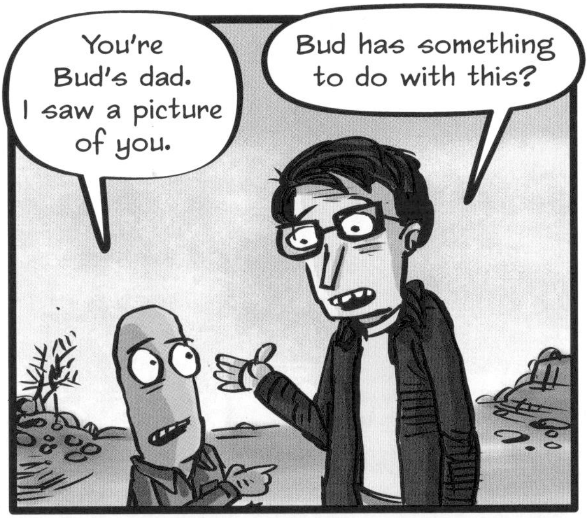
You're Bud's dad. I saw a picture of you.
Bud has something to do with this?

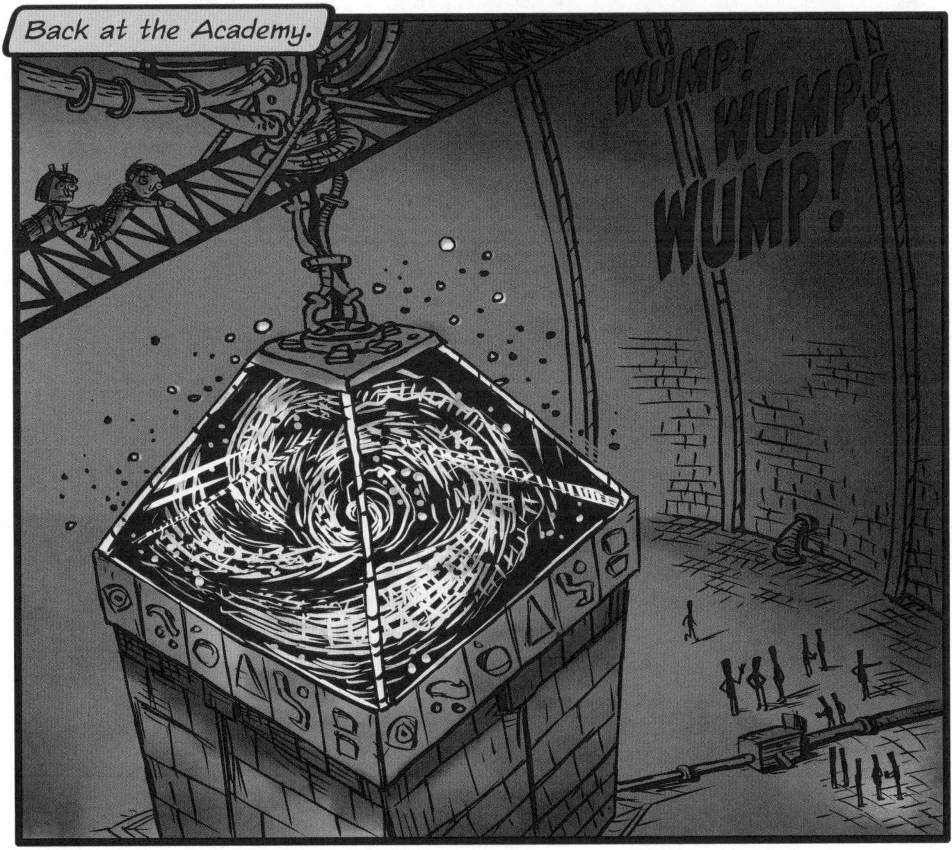
Back at the Academy.
WUMP! WUMP! WUMP!

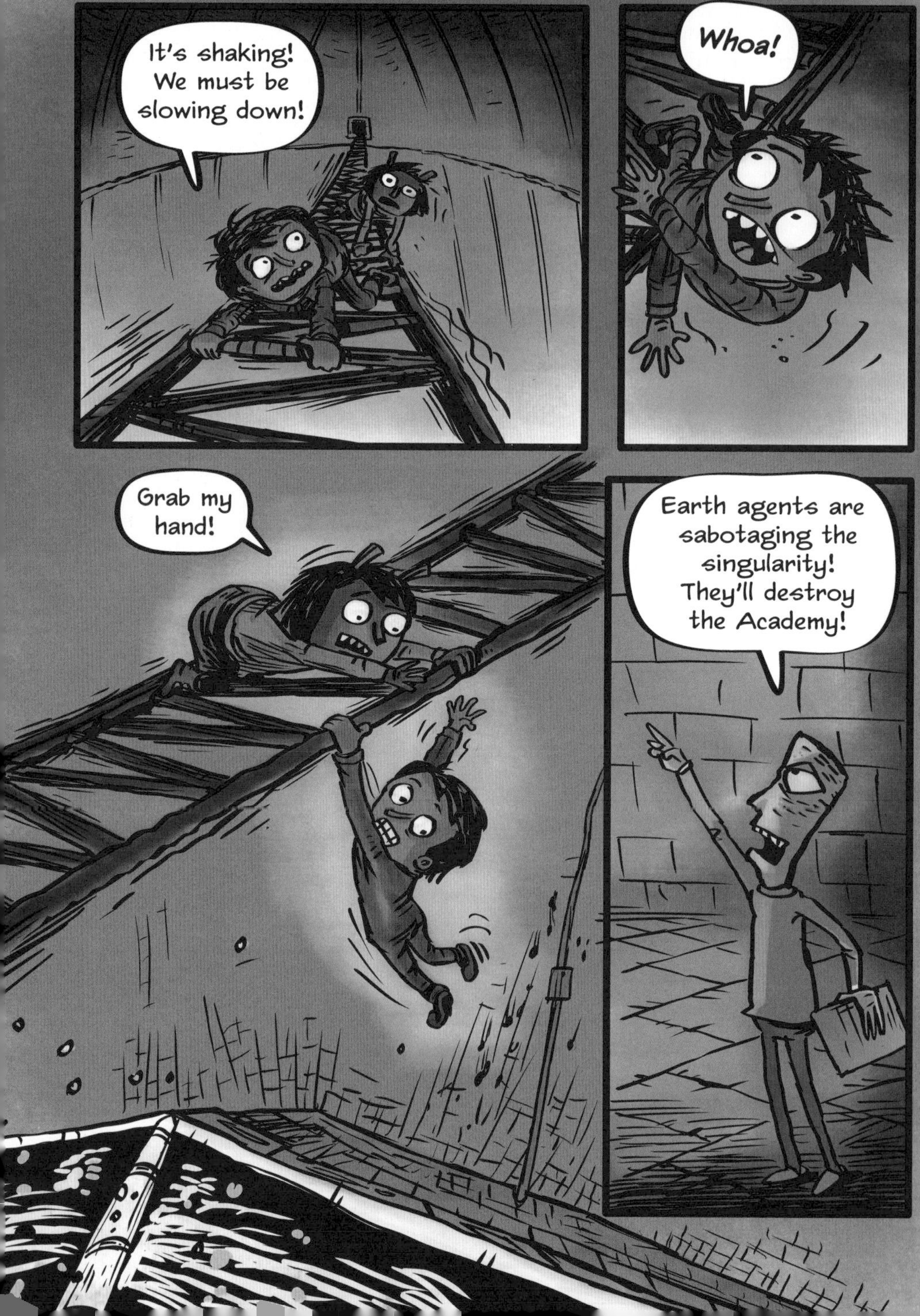
It's shaking! We must be slowing down!
Whoa!
Grab my hand!
Earth agents are sabotaging the singularity! They'll destroy the Academy!

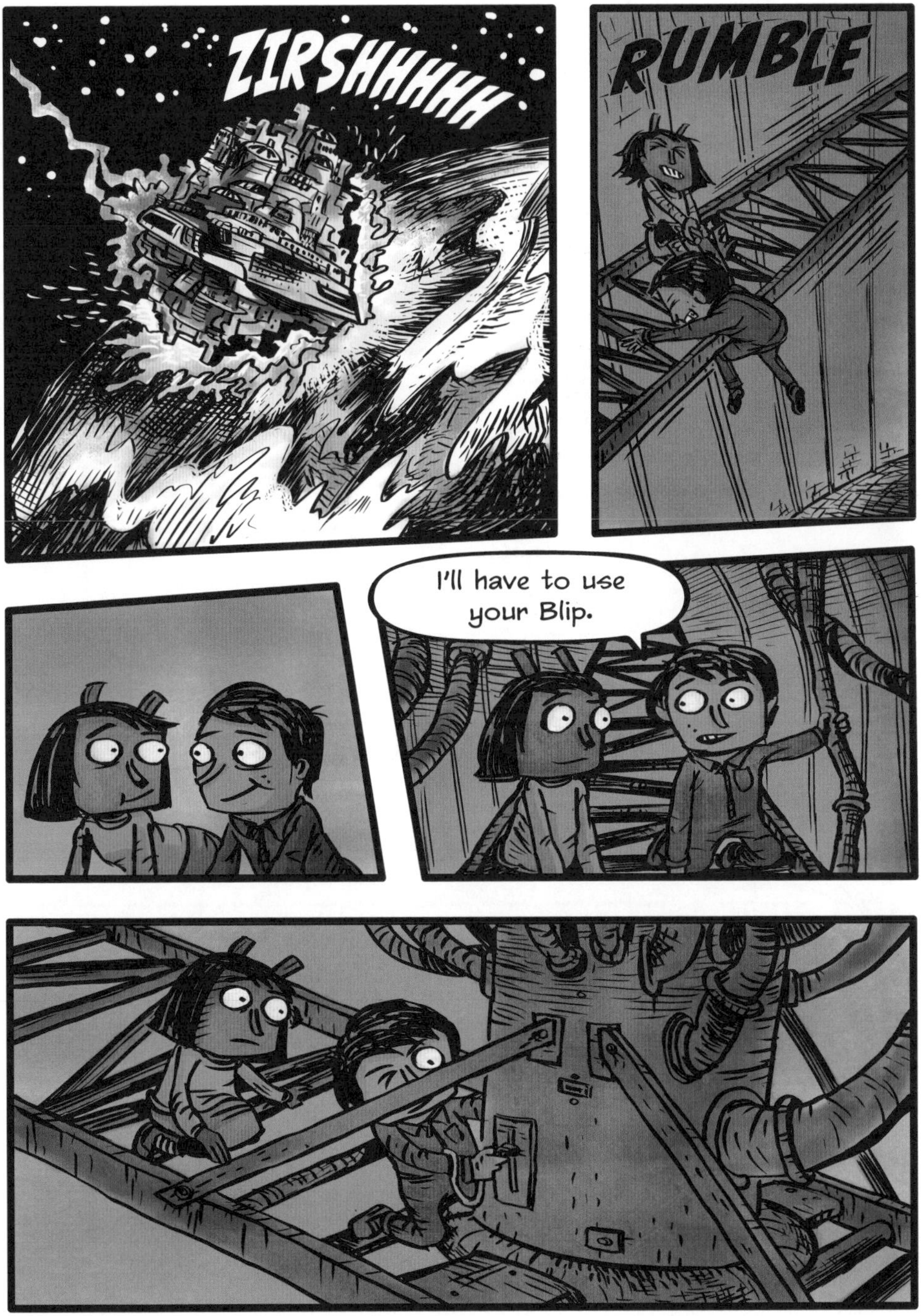
ZIRSHHHHH
RUMBLE
I'll have to use your Blip.

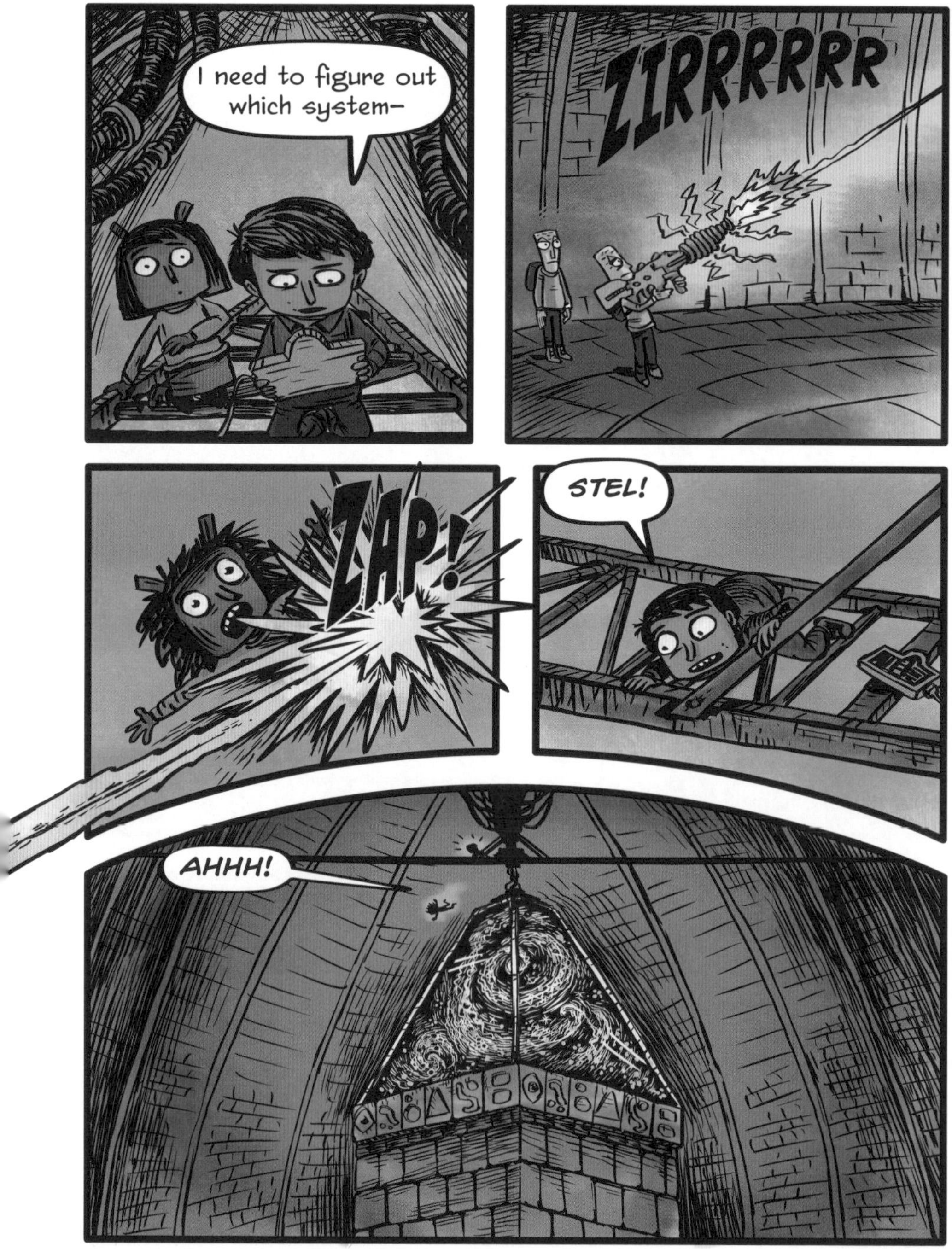
I need to figure out which system—
ZIRRRRRR
ZAP!
STEL!
AHHH!

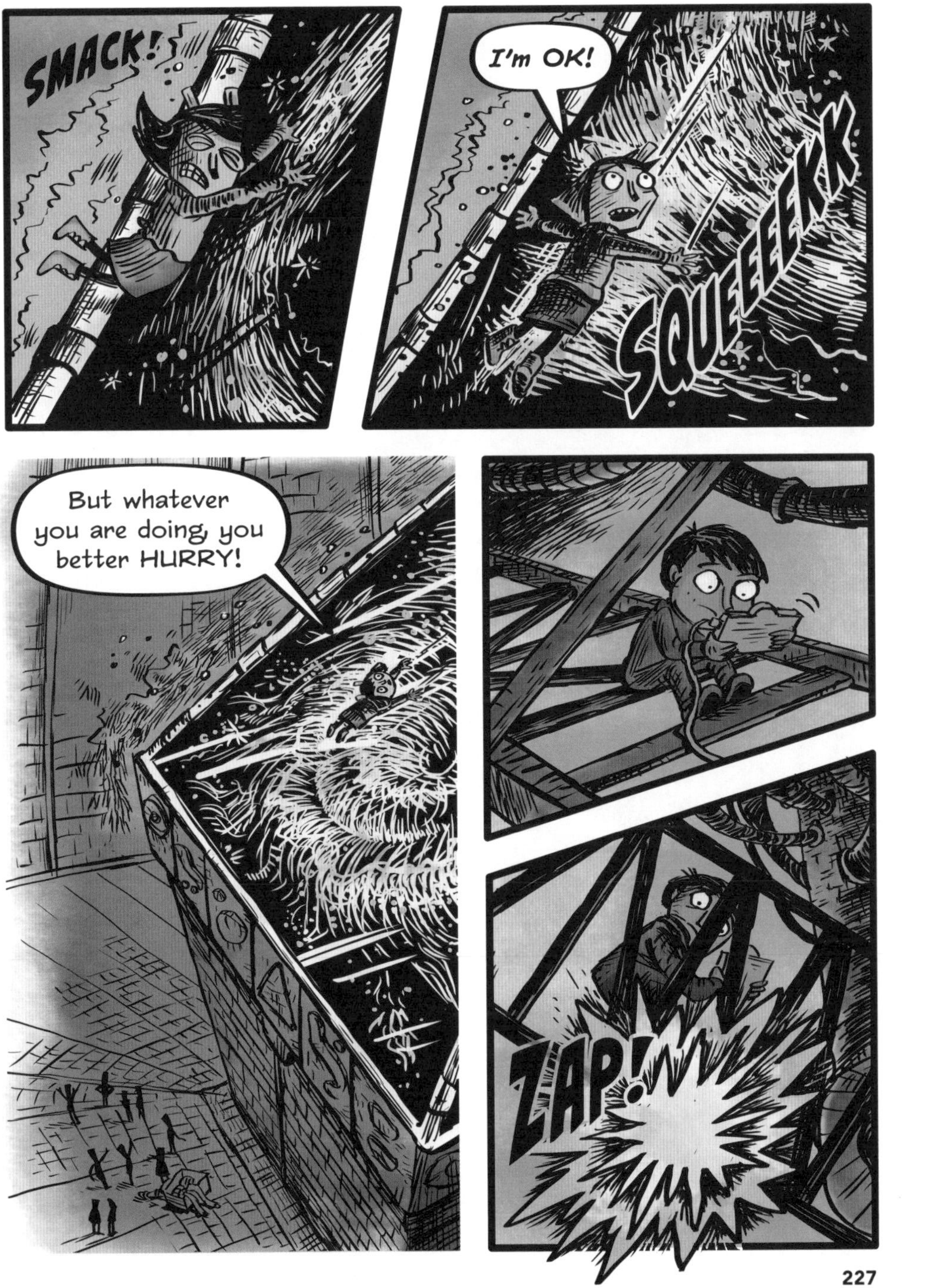
SMACK!
I'm OK!
SQUEEEEKK
But whatever you are doing, you better HURRY!
ZAP!

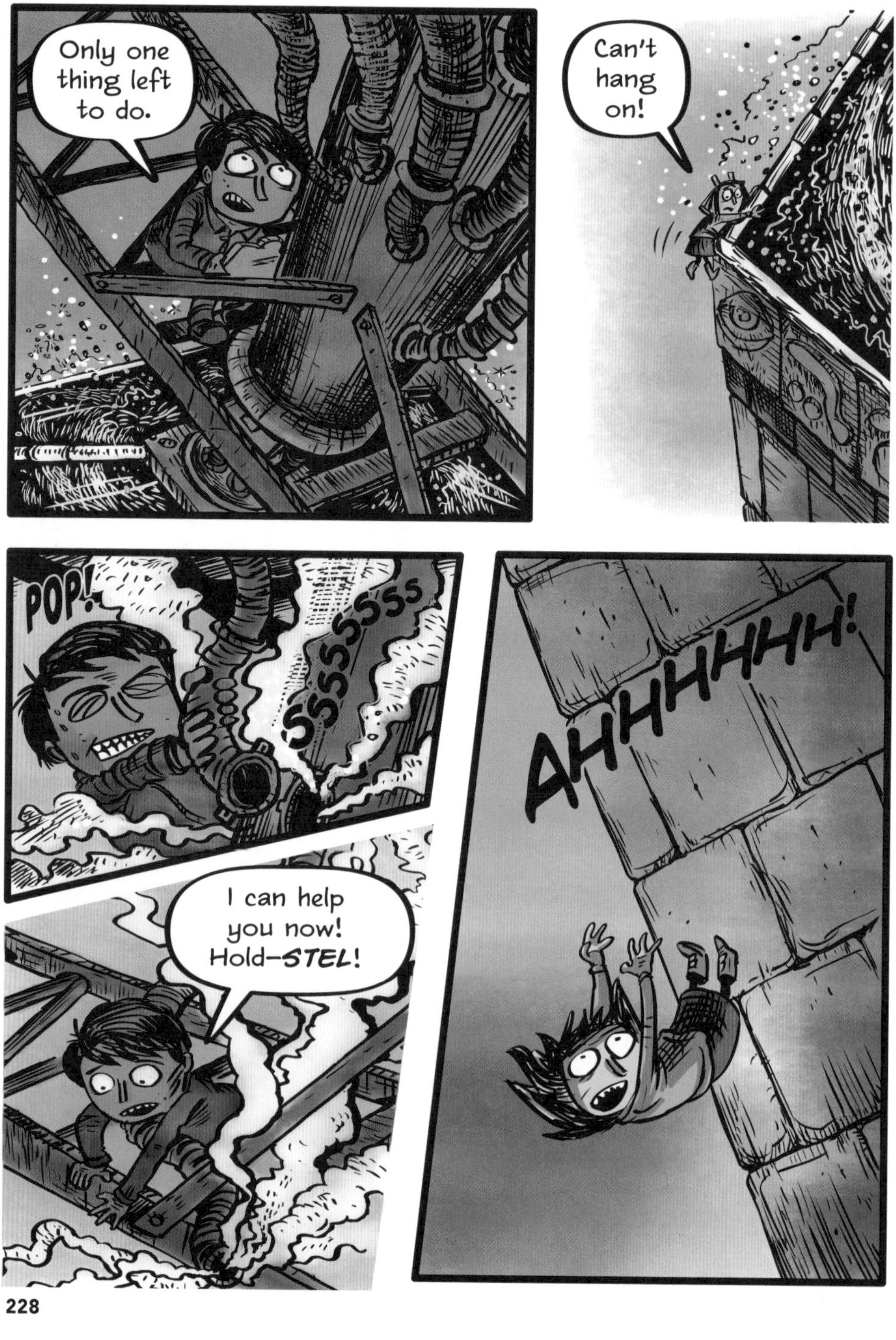
Only one thing left to do.
Can't hang on!
POP!
SSSSSSSSS
I can help you now! Hold-STEL!
AHHHHHHH!

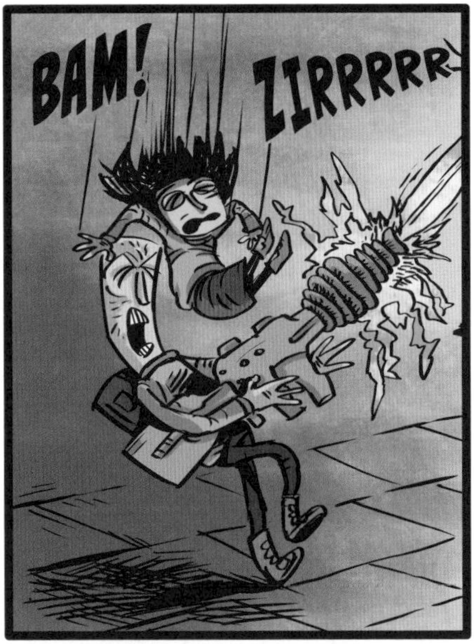
BAM!
ZIRRRRR

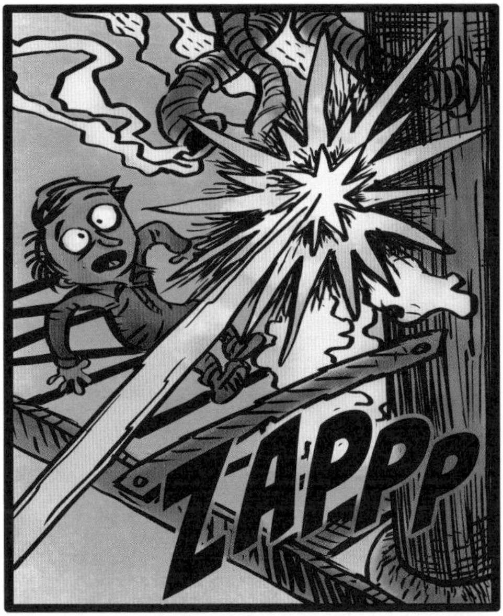
ZAPPP

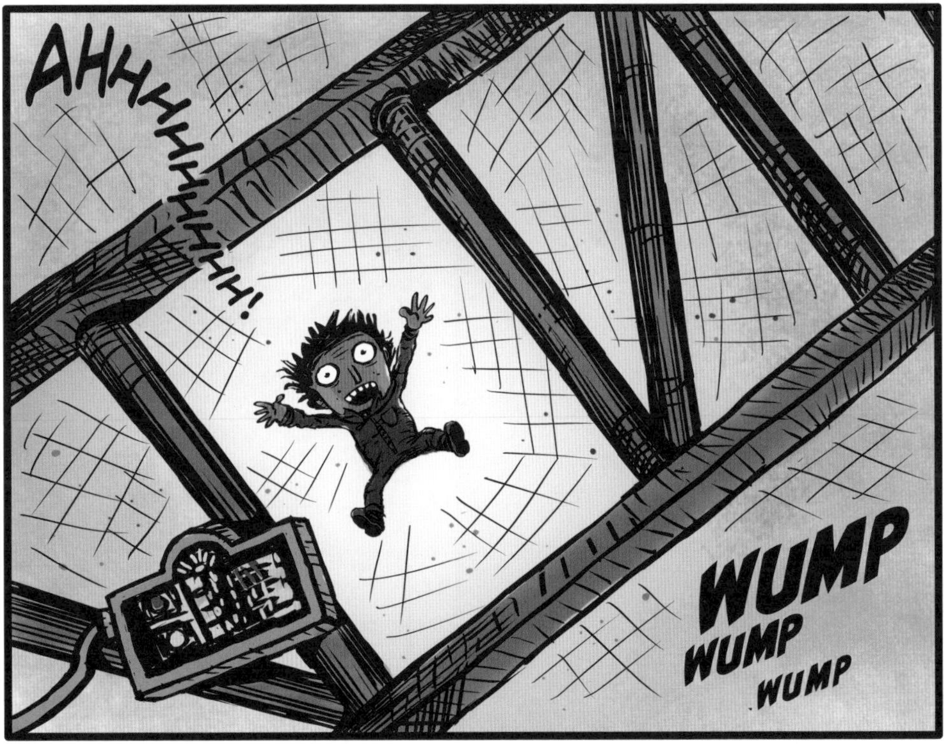
AHHHHHHHHHHH!
WUMP
WUMP
WUMP

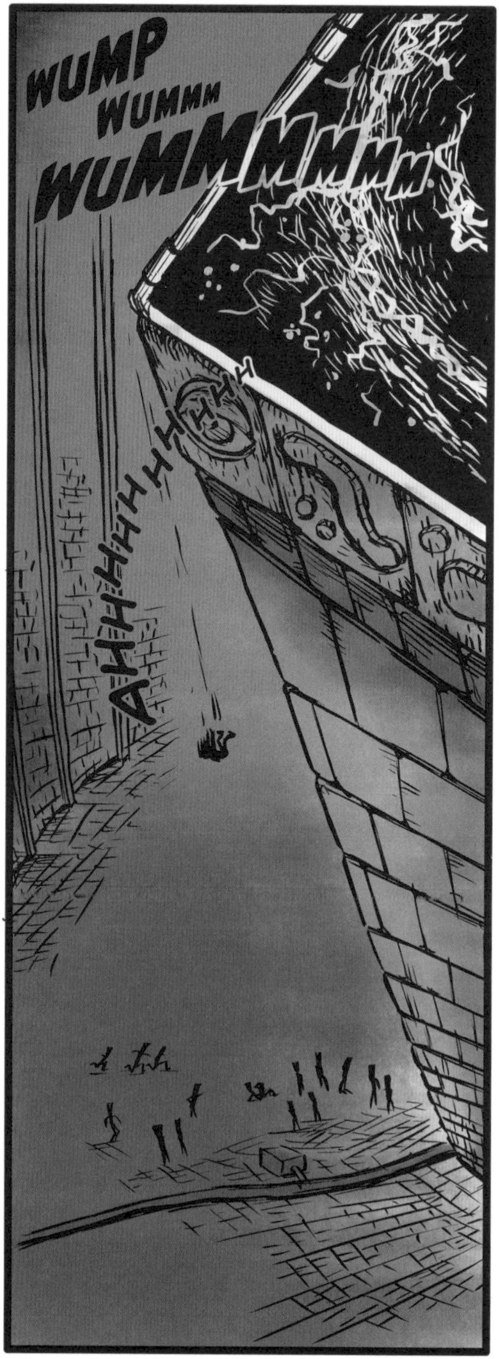
WUMP
WUMMM
WUMMMMMMM
AHHHHHHHH

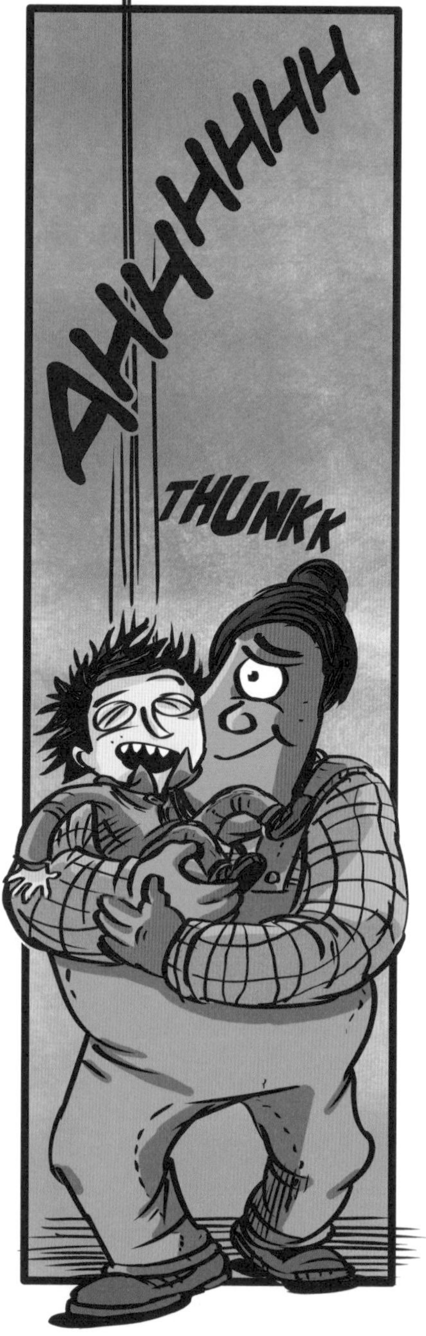
AHHHHHHH
THUNKK

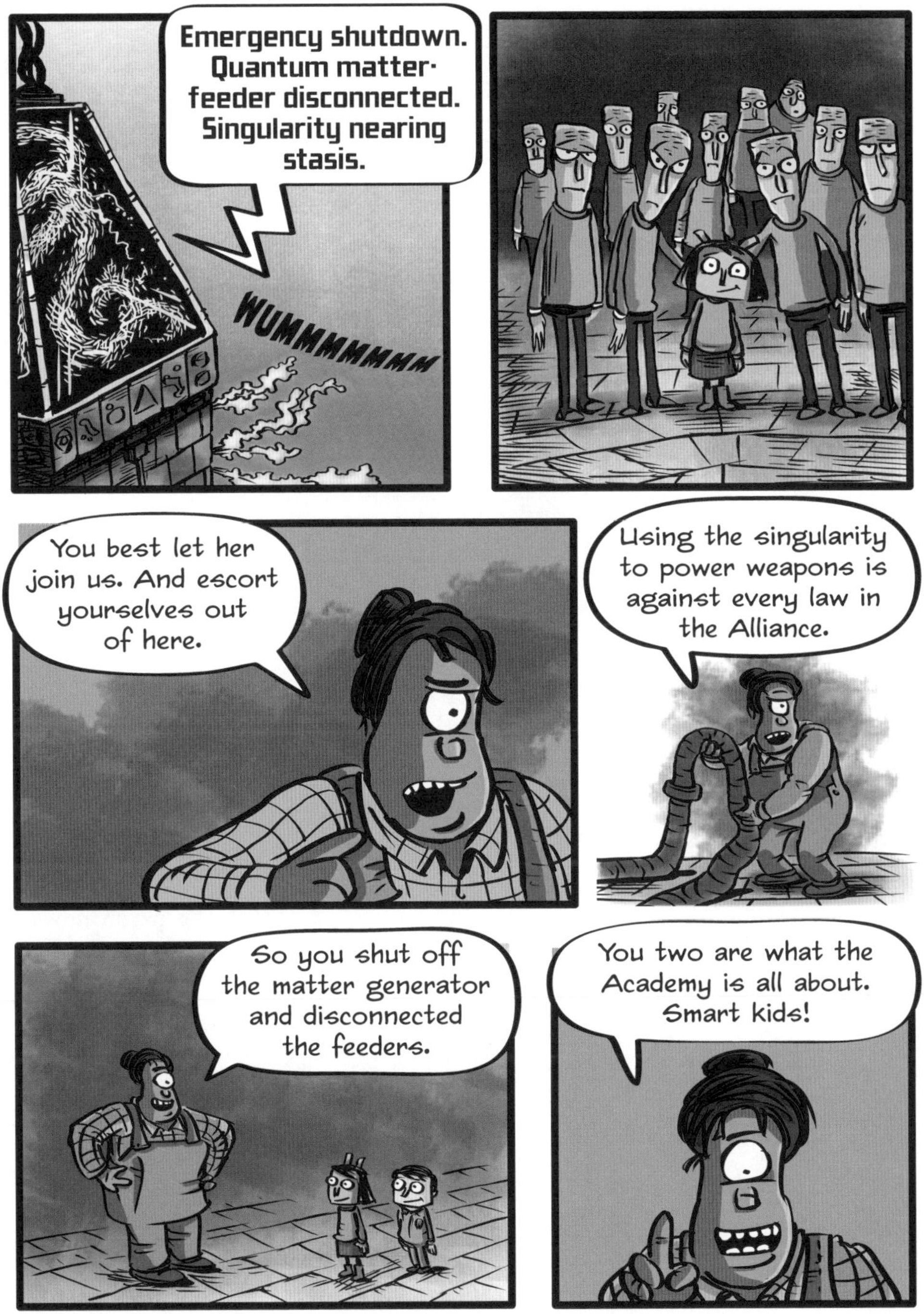
Emergency shutdown. Quantum matter-feeder disconnected. Singularity nearing stasis.
WUMMMMMMMM
You best let her join us. And escort yourselves out of here.
Using the singularity to power weapons is against every law in the Alliance.
So you shut off the matter generator and disconnected the feeders.
You two are what the Academy is all about. Smart kids!

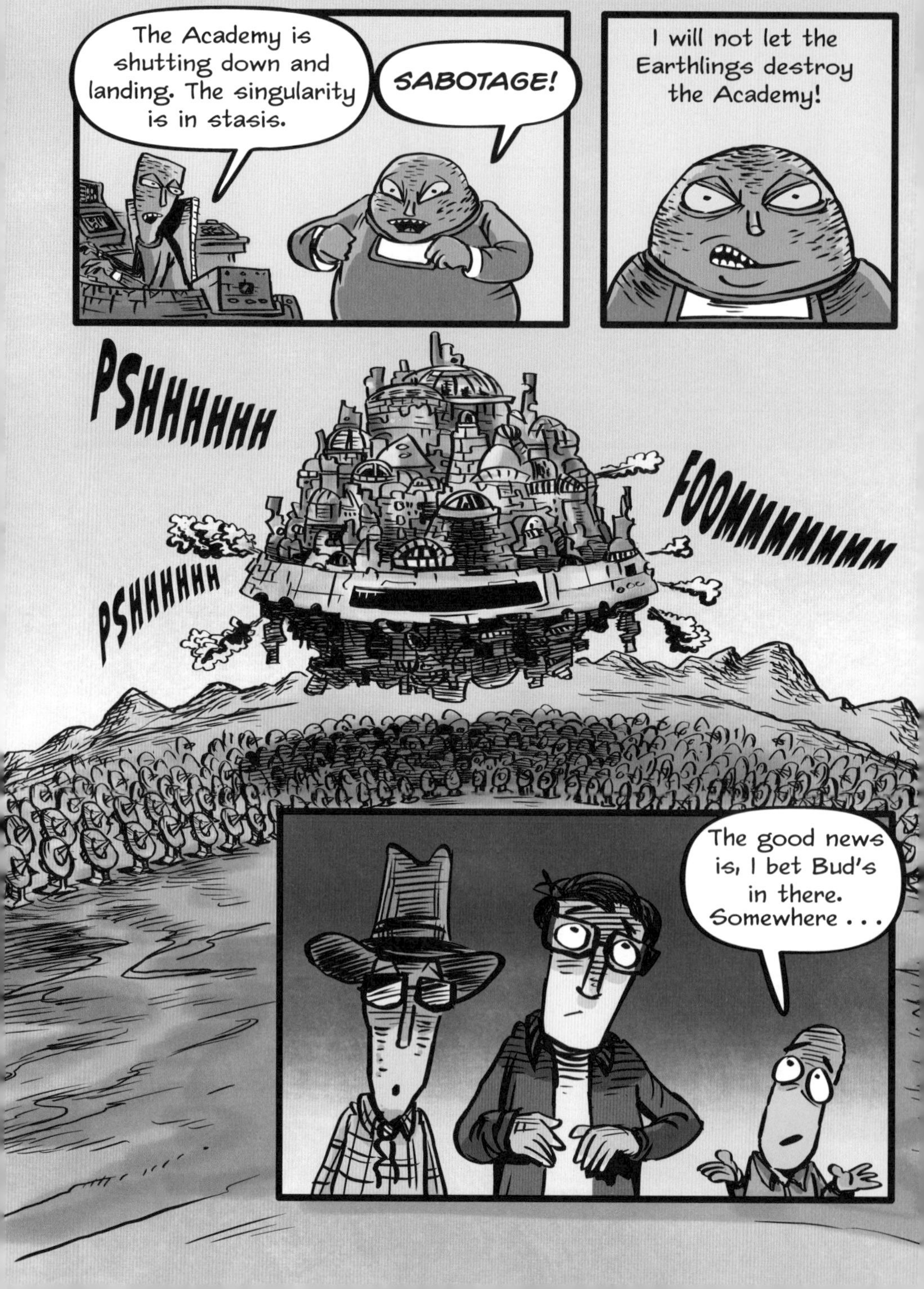

The Academy is shutting down and landing. The singularity is in stasis.
SABOTAGE!
I will not let the Earthlings destroy the Academy!
PSHHHHHH
PSHHHHHH
FOOMMMMMMM
The good news is, I bet Bud's in there. Somewhere . . .

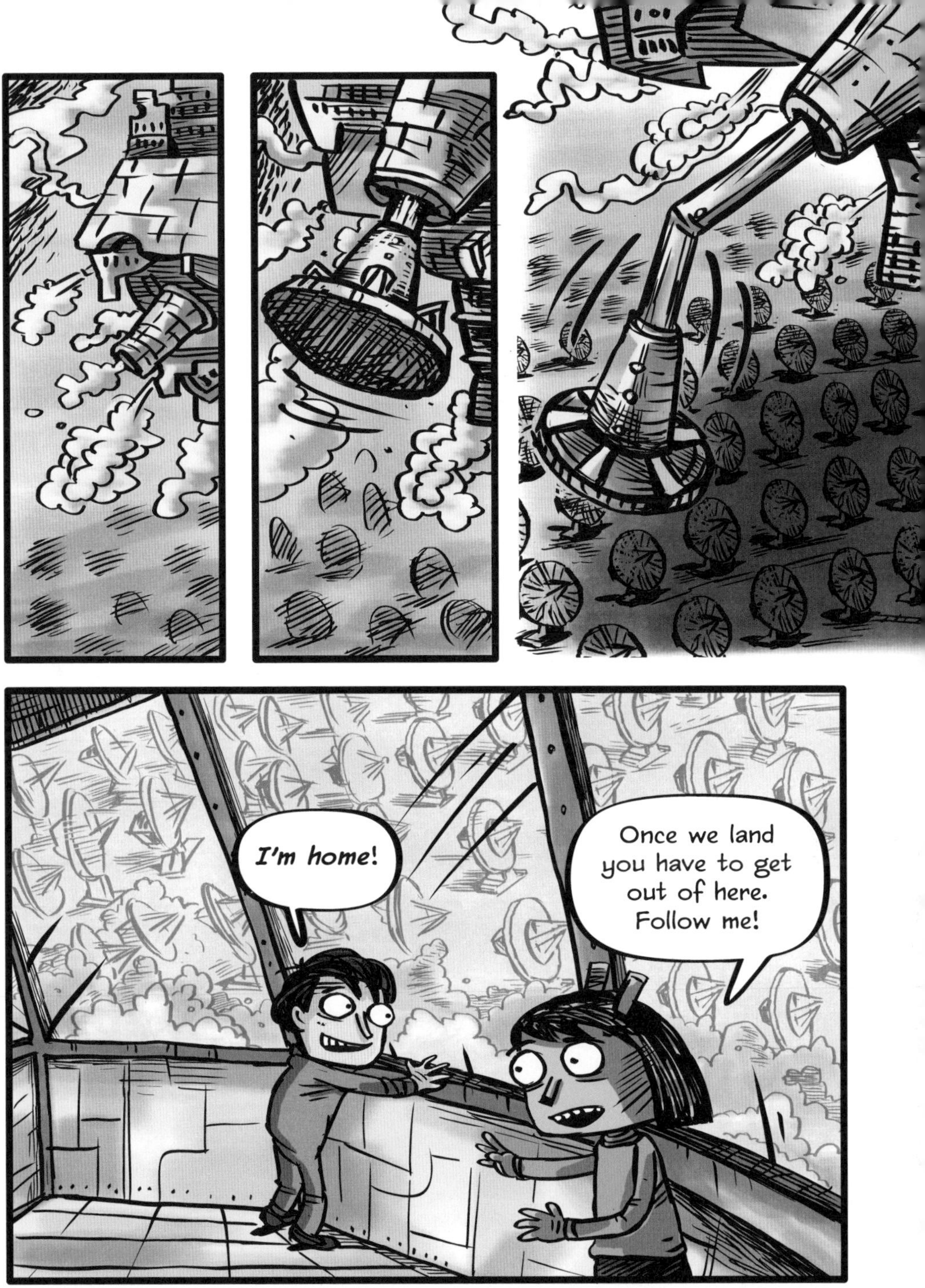
I'm home!
Once we land you have to get out of here. Follow me!

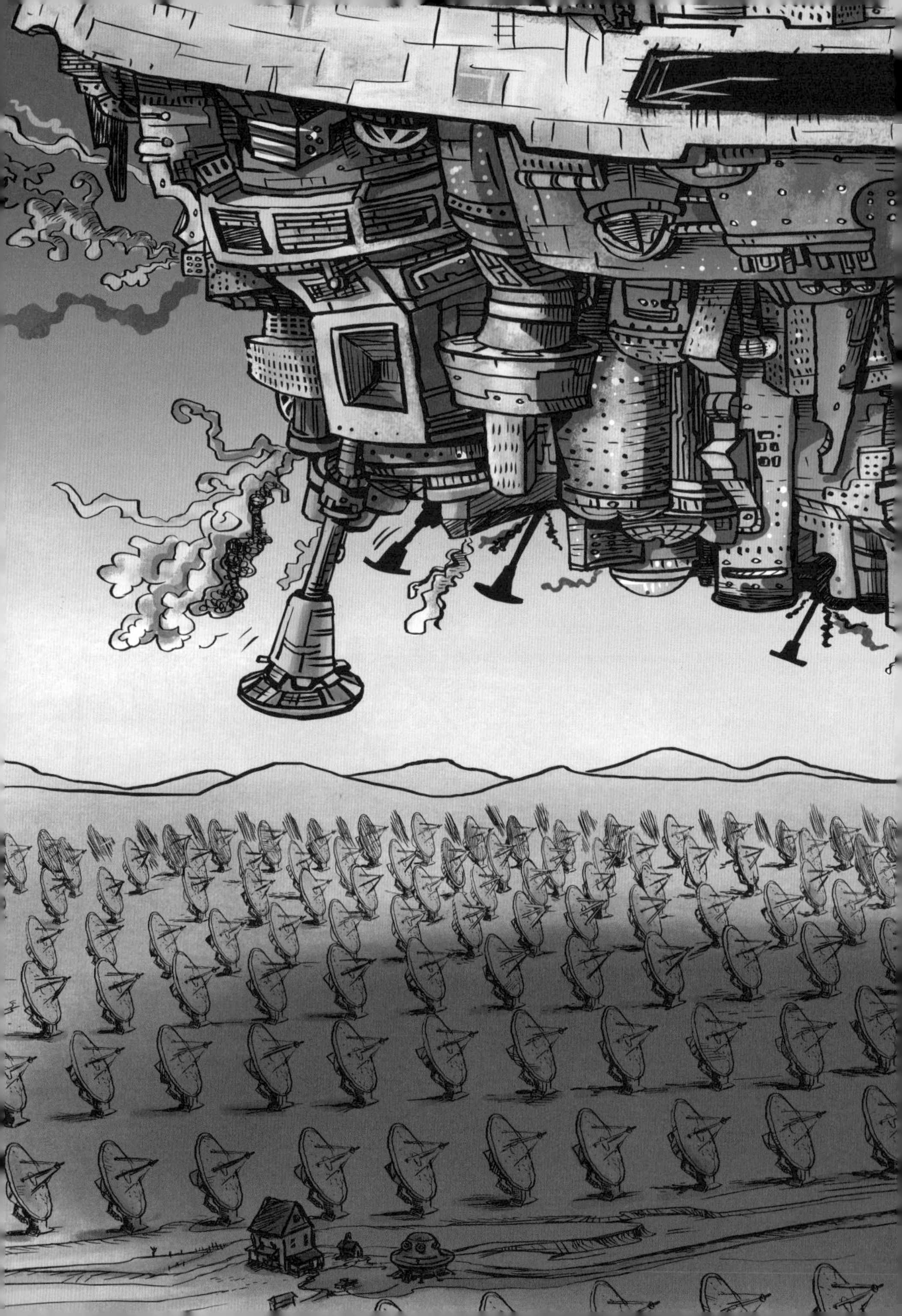

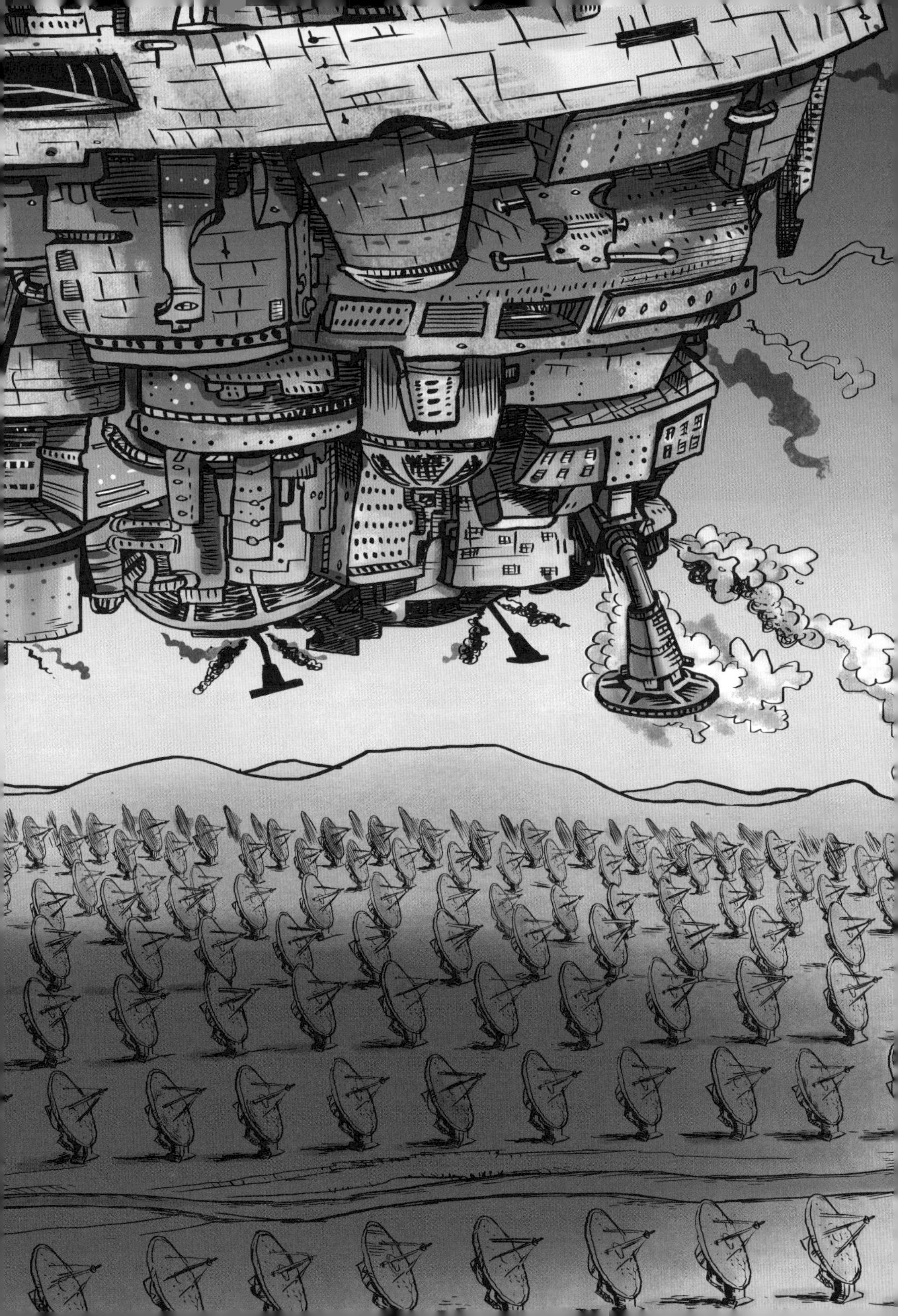

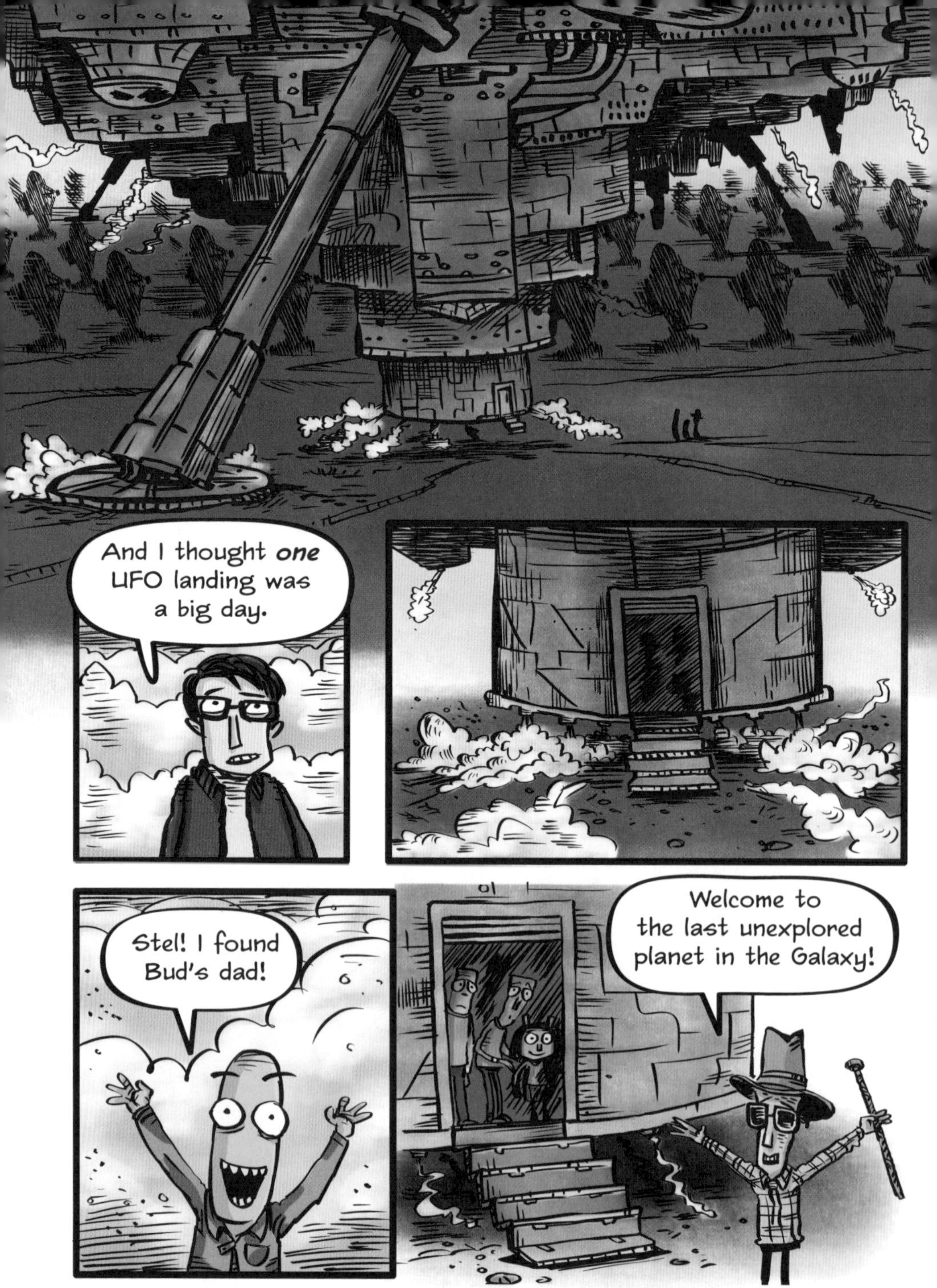
And I thought *one* UFO landing was a big day.
Stel! I found Bud's dad!
Welcome to the last unexplored planet in the Galaxy!

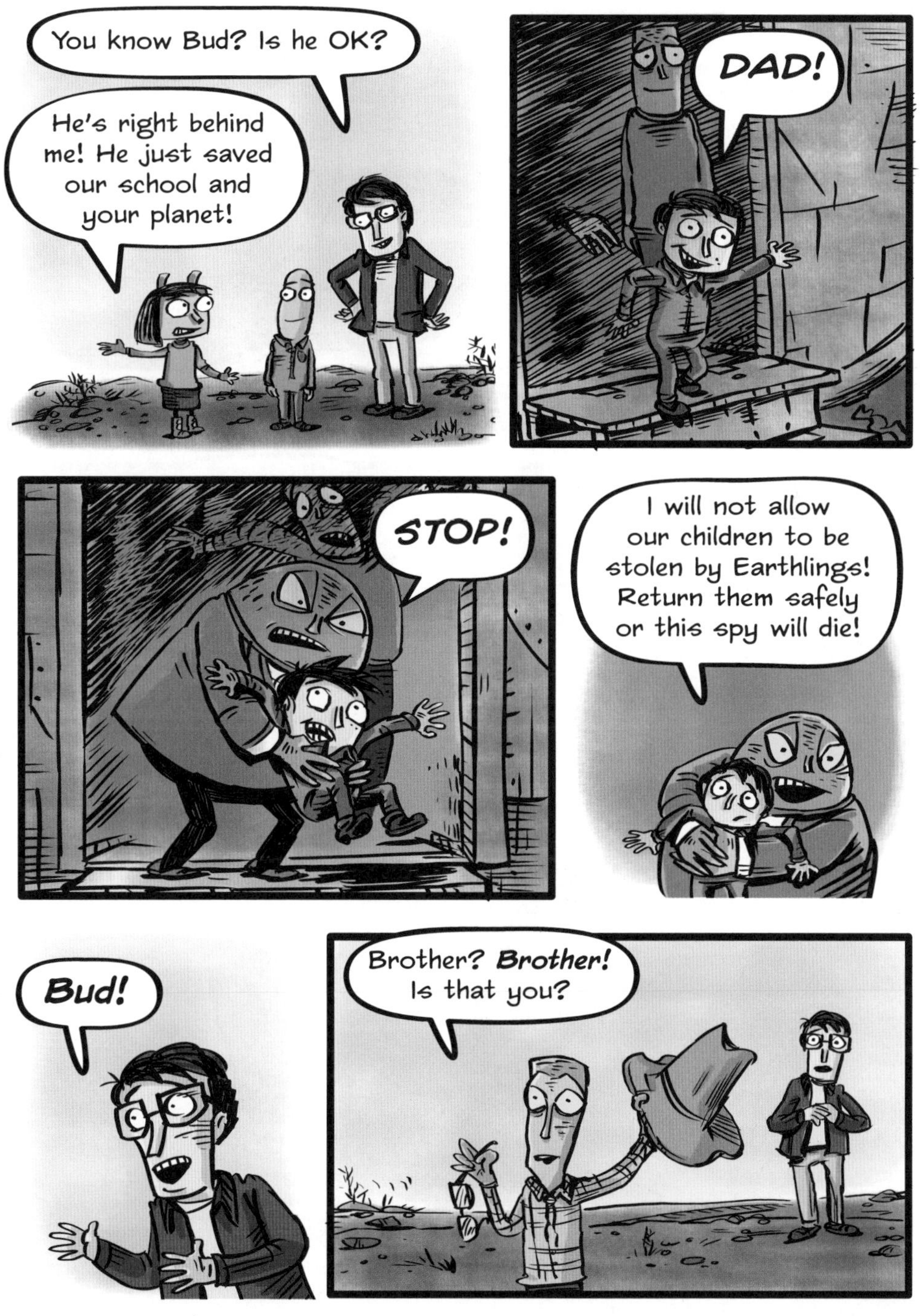
You know Bud? Is he OK?
He's right behind me! He just saved our school and your planet!
DAD!
STOP!
I will not allow our children to be stolen by Earthlings! Return them safely or this spy will die!
Bud!
Brother? **Brother!** Is that you?

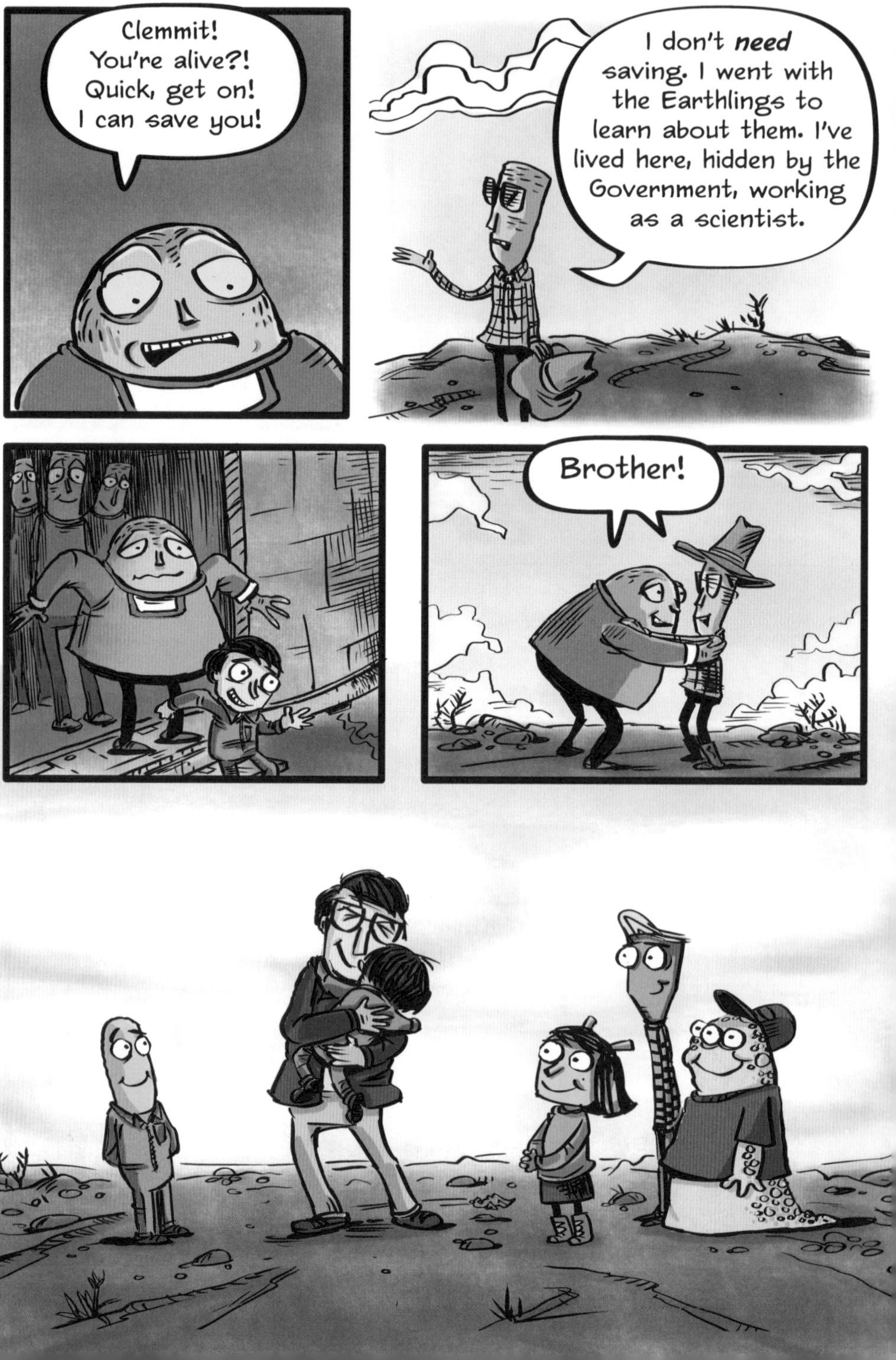
Clemmit! You're alive?! Quick, get on! I can save you!
I don't *need* saving. I went with the Earthlings to learn about them. I've lived here, hidden by the Government, working as a scientist.
Brother!

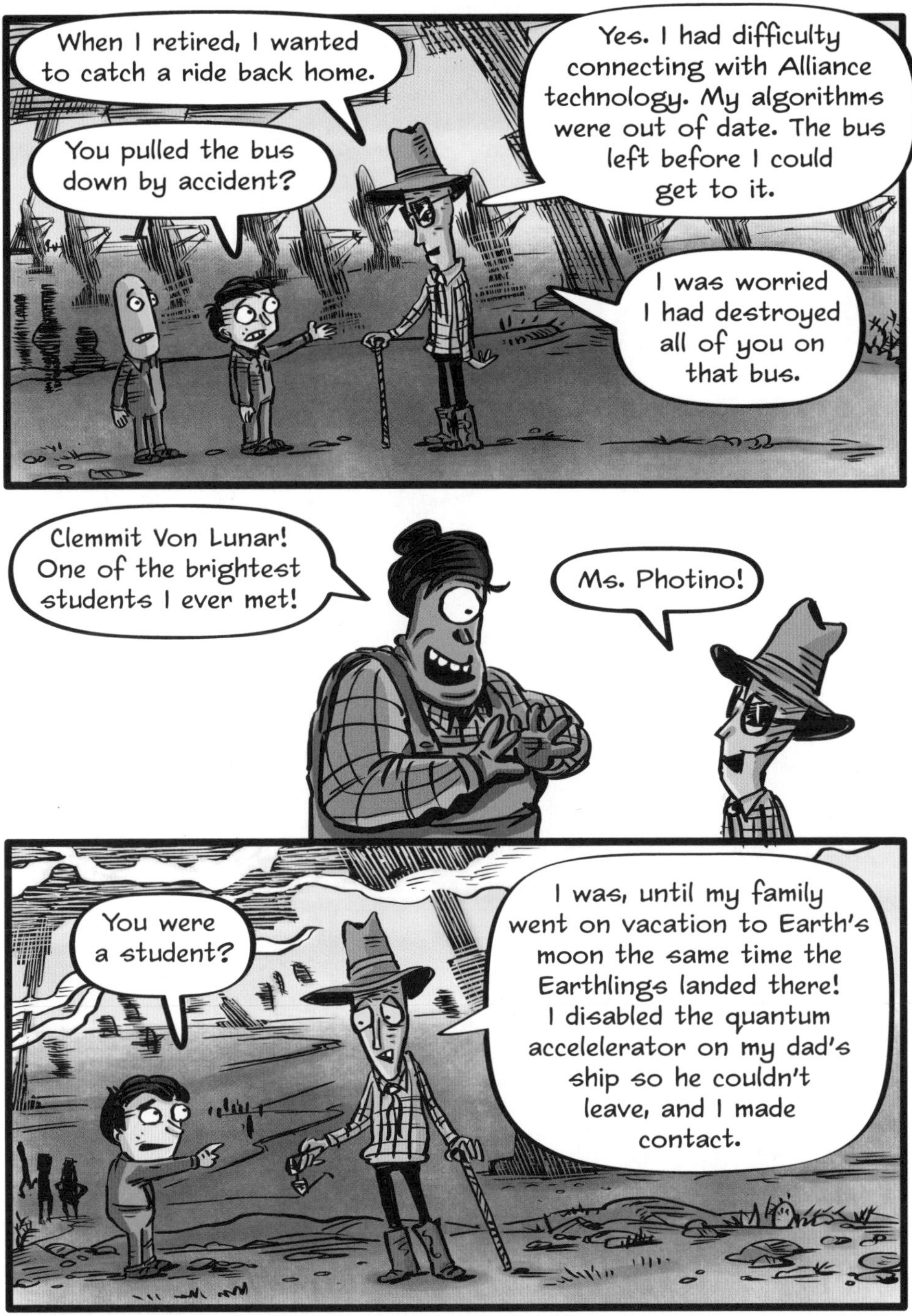
When I retired, I wanted to catch a ride back home.
You pulled the bus down by accident?
Yes. I had difficulty connecting with Alliance technology. My algorithms were out of date. The bus left before I could get to it.
I was worried I had destroyed all of you on that bus.
Clemmit Von Lunar! One of the brightest students I ever met!
Ms. Photino!
You were a student?
I was, until my family went on vacation to Earth's moon the same time the Earthlings landed there! I disabled the quantum accelelerator on my dad's ship so he couldn't leave, and I made contact.

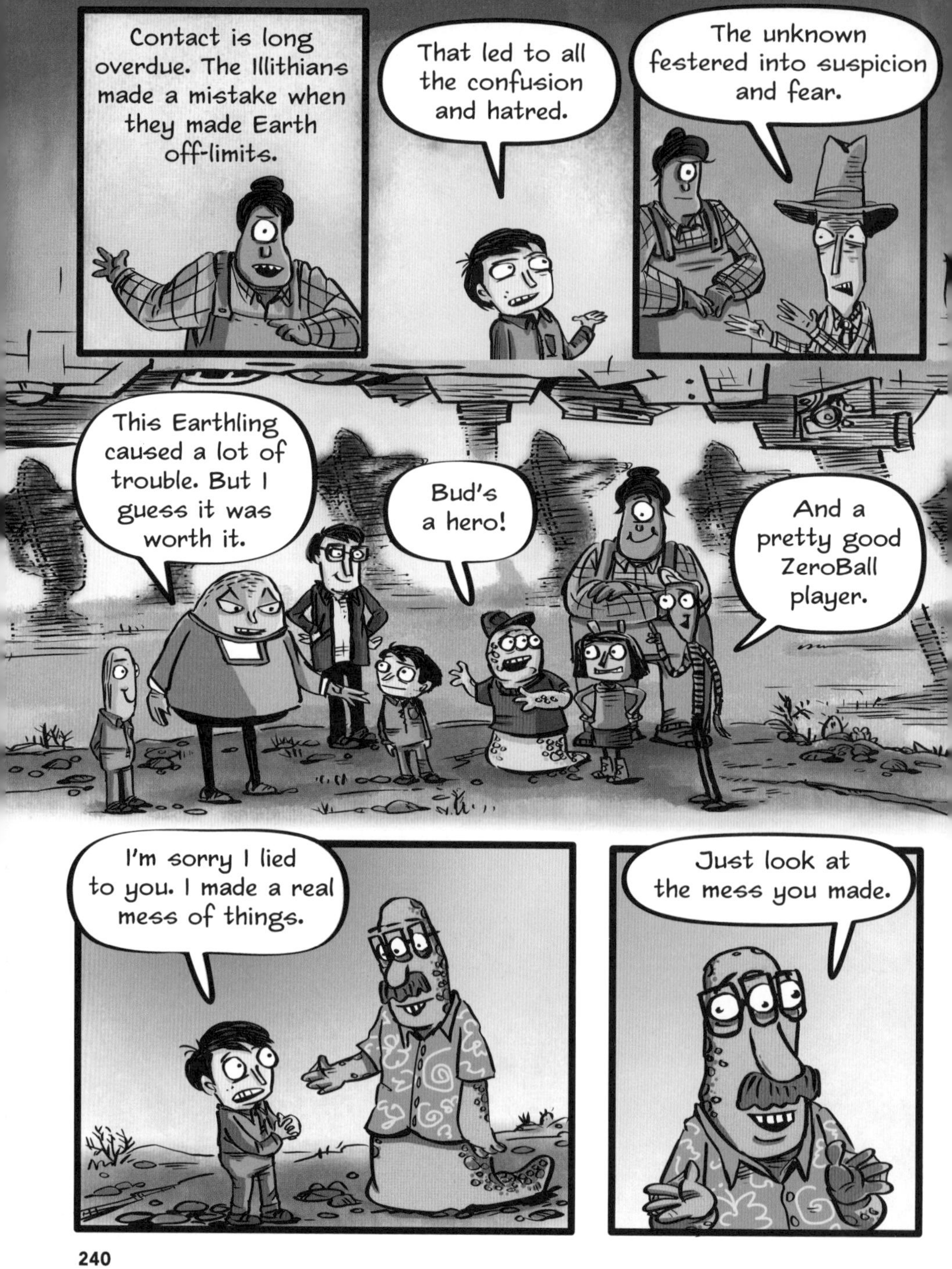
Contact is long overdue. The Illithians made a mistake when they made Earth off-limits.
That led to all the confusion and hatred.
The unknown festered into suspicion and fear.
This Earthling caused a lot of trouble. But I guess it was worth it.
Bud's a hero!
And a pretty good ZeroBall player.
I'm sorry I lied to you. I made a real mess of things.
Just look at the mess you made.

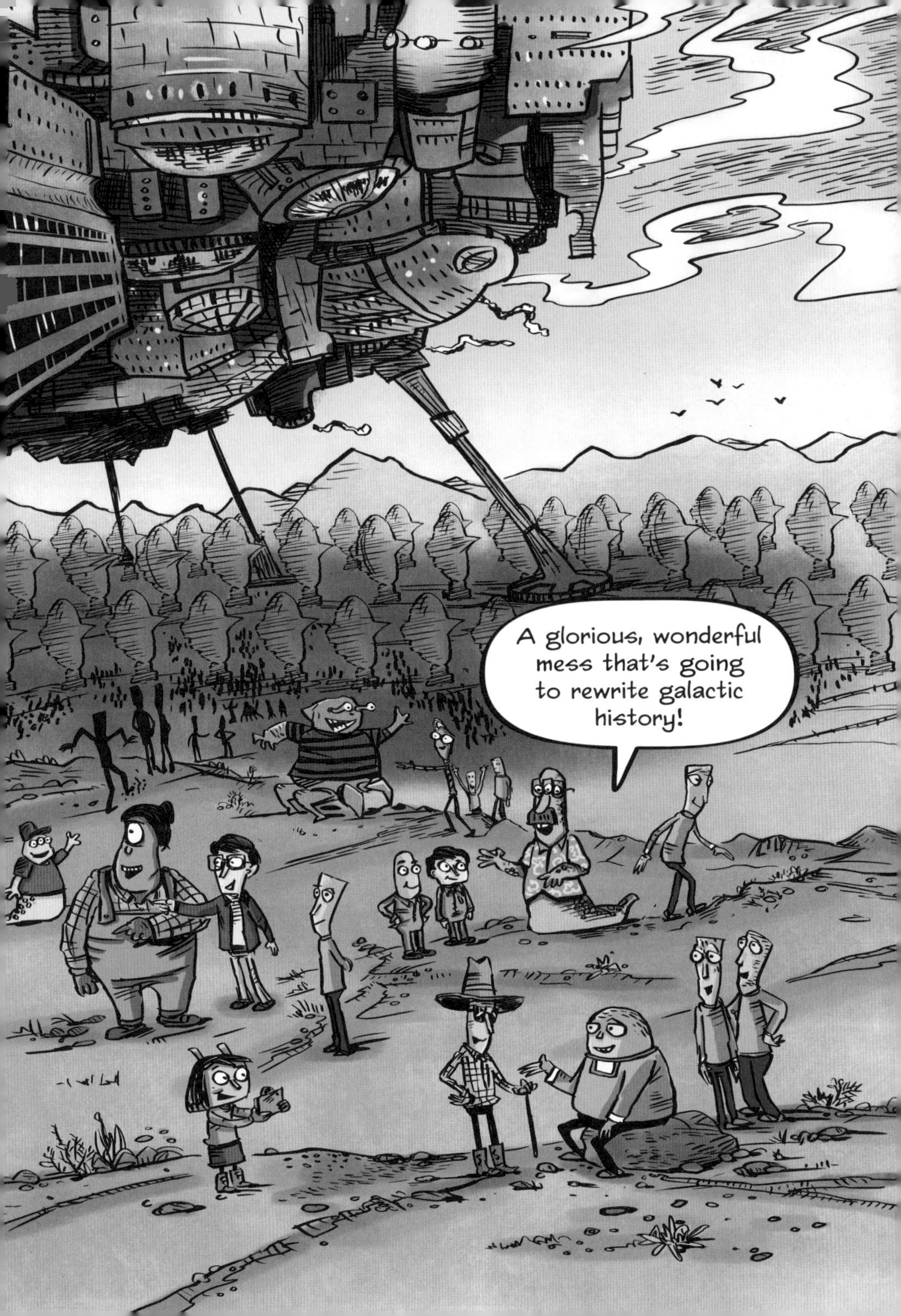
A glorious, wonderful mess that's going to rewrite galactic history!

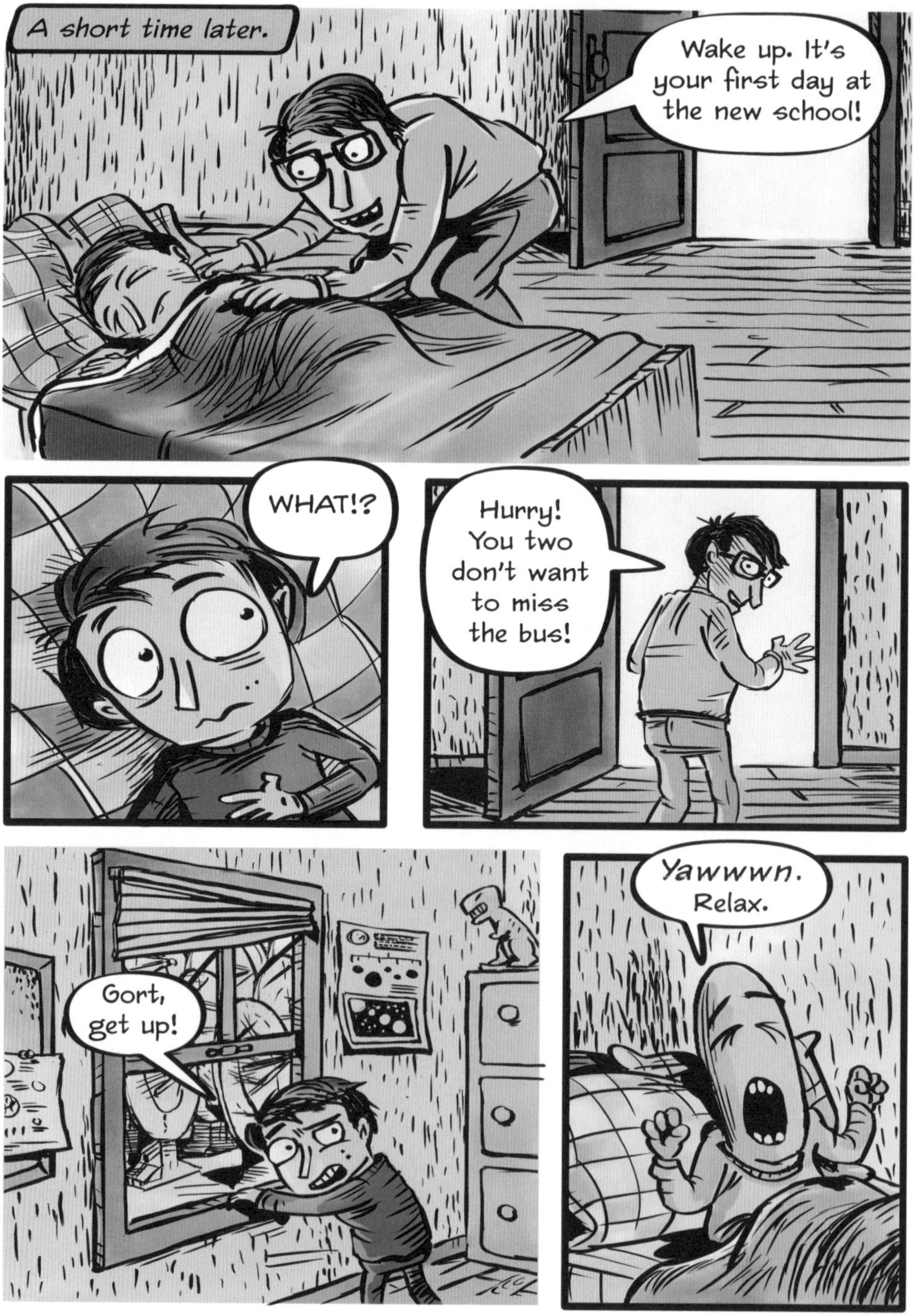
A short time later.
Wake up. It's your first day at the new school!
WHAT!?
Hurry! You two don't want to miss the bus!
Gort, get up!
Yawwwn. Relax.

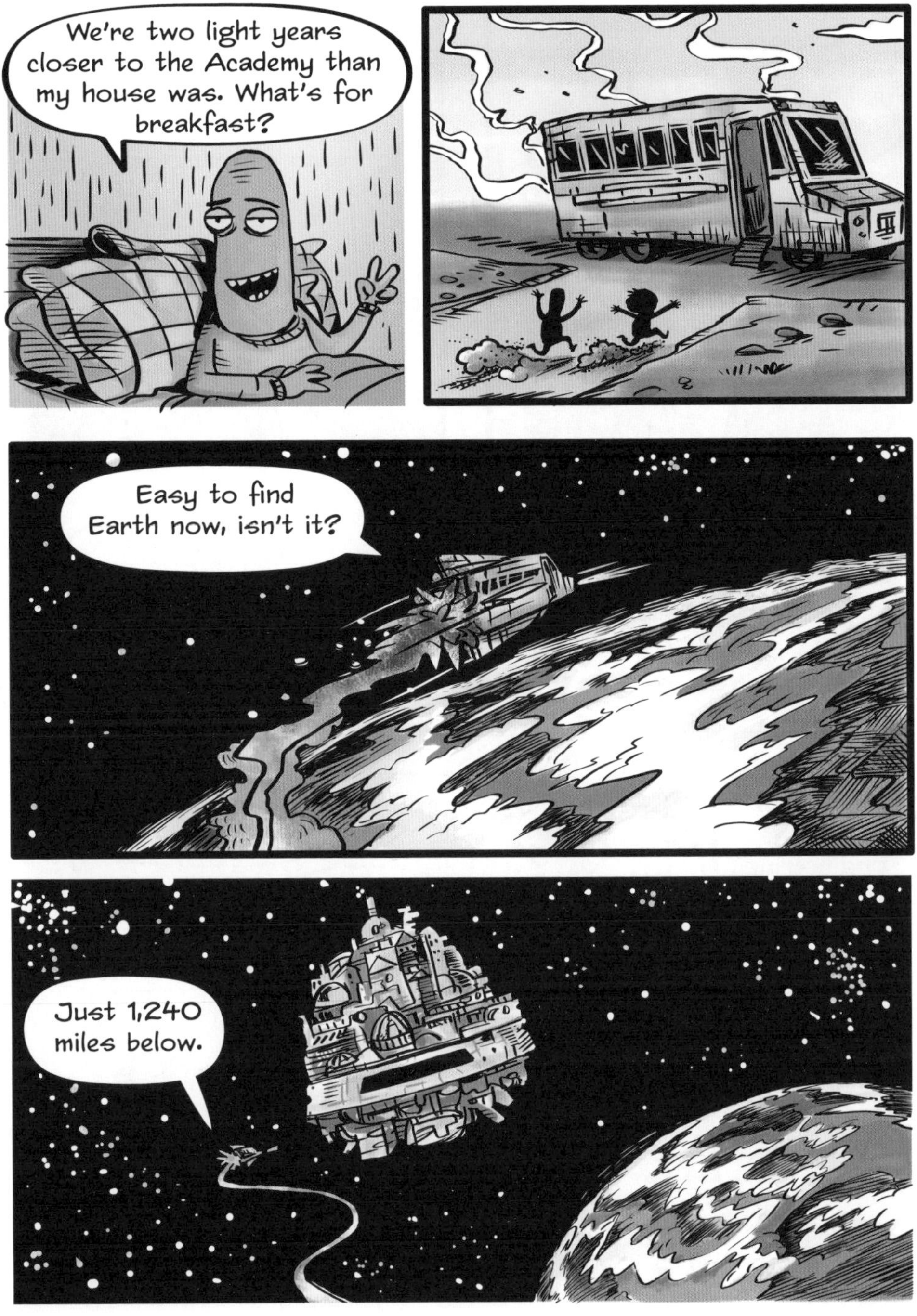
We're two light years closer to the Academy than my house was. What's for breakfast?
Easy to find Earth now, isn't it?
Just 1,240 miles below.

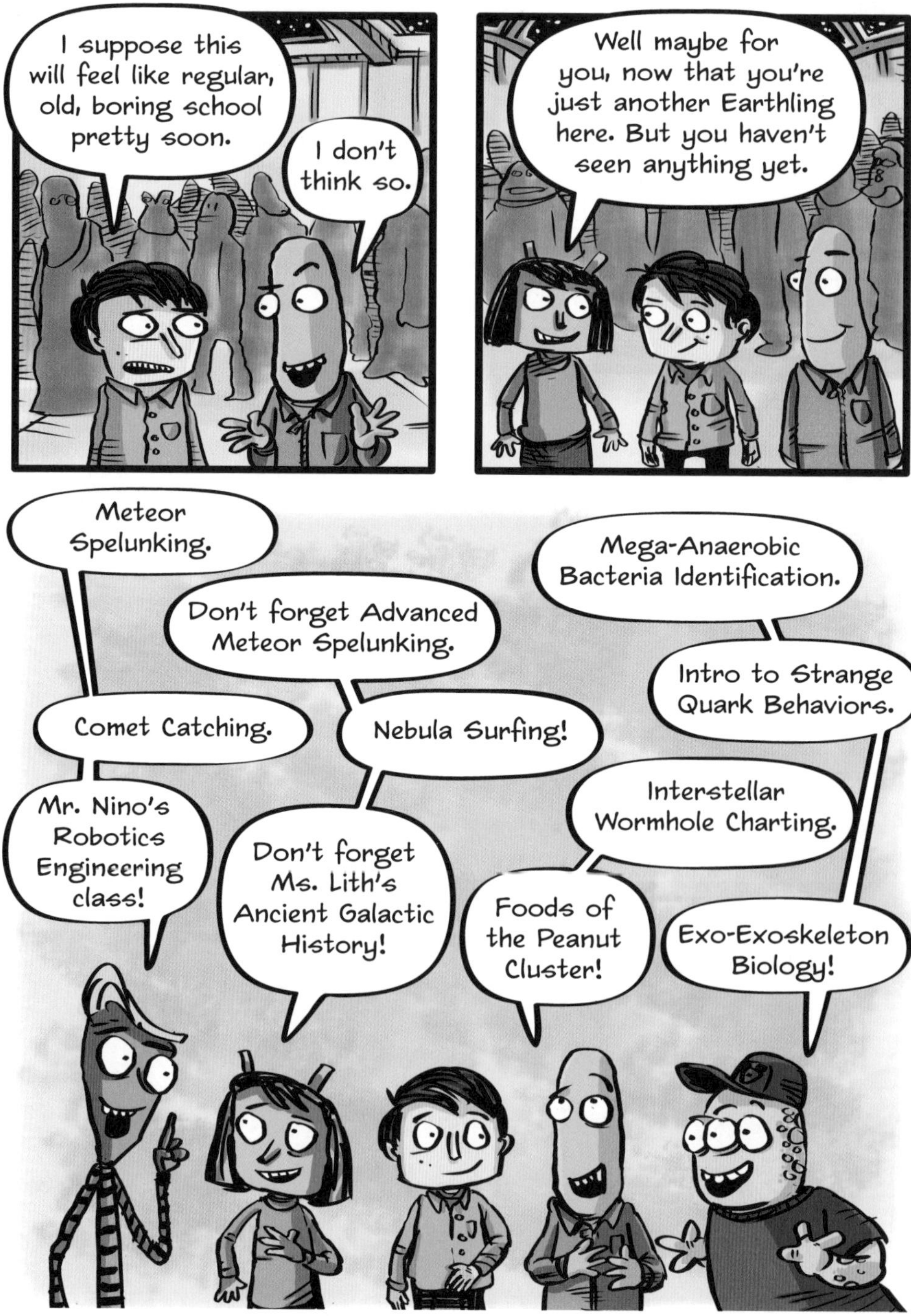
I suppose this will feel like regular, old, boring school pretty soon.
I don't think so.
Well maybe for you, now that you're just another Earthling here. But you haven't seen anything yet.
Meteor Spelunking.
Comet Catching.
Mr. Nino's Robotics Engineering class!
Don't forget Advanced Meteor Spelunking.
Nebula Surfing!
Don't forget Ms. Lith's Ancient Galactic History!
Mega-Anaerobic Bacteria Identification.
Intro to Strange Quark Behaviors.
Interstellar Wormhole Charting.
Foods of the Peanut Cluster!
Exo-Exoskeleton Biology!

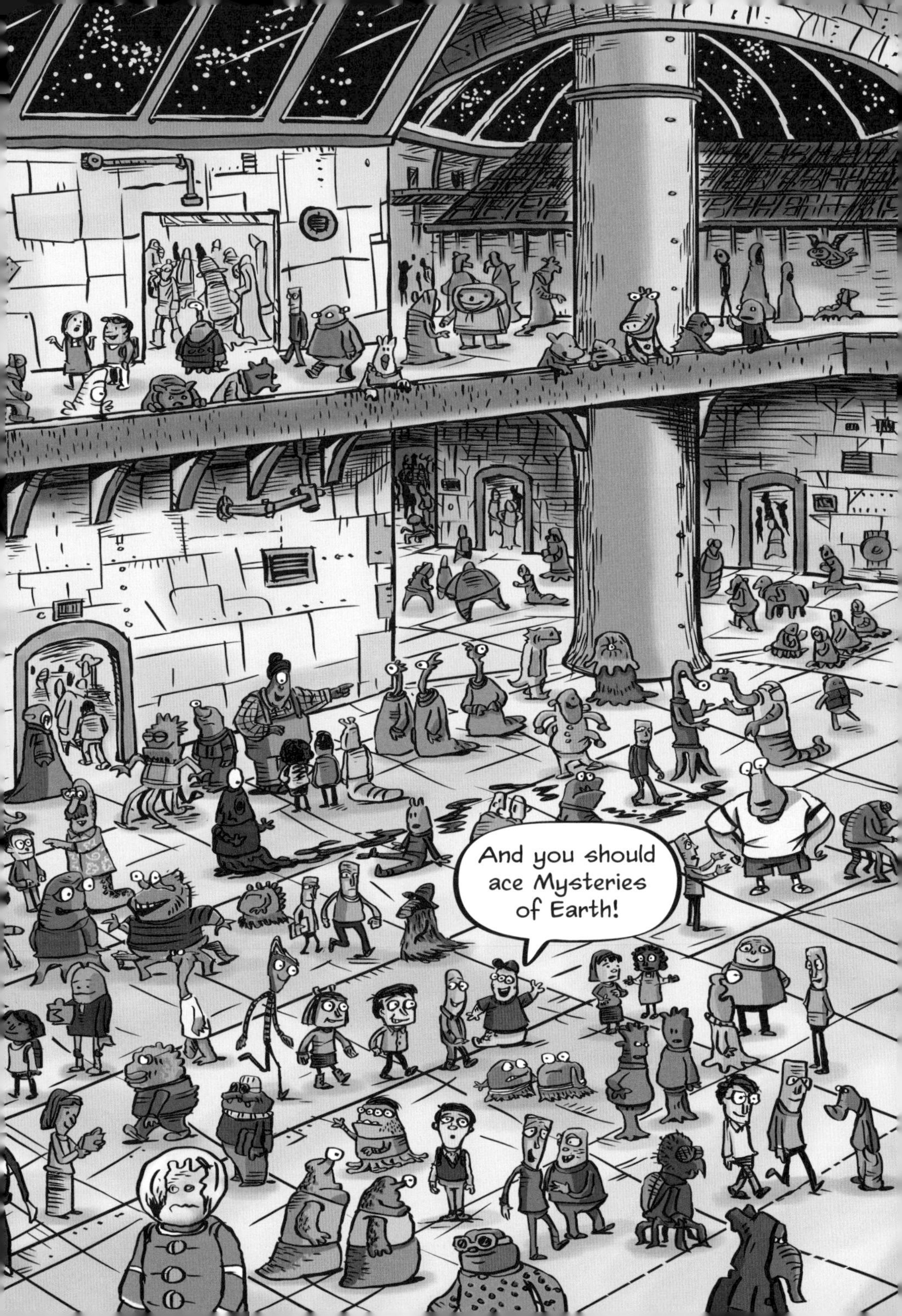
And you should ace Mysteries of Earth!

For Dad and the story-filled
hikes across northern Minnesota
and the arctic tundra.
—Mark

ACKNOWLEDGMENTS:

Tim Rummel who many years ago convinced me there was more to this story than just a ten-minute animated short.

My editor, Julie Romeis, who put up with my tantrums, made me concentrate on the characters, and was willing to let me take the long road to figure things out.

My agents, Denis Kitchen and John Lind, who believed in *Earthling!* from the start and acted generously and resolutely.

Brent Boyd for helping me cut the number of hugs in this story and telling me when characters were less than enthralling.

Ken Min who did far more than the marvelous painting in the book. He offered an additional set of visual notes that usually led to more work for me and for him.

Karen and Lily who for the last two years heard "I'm going to work on *Earthling!*" far too often.

And many other people who played a part in making *Earthling!* possible: Mary P., Ric H., Jon M., Jaime, Emmie, Justin, Erik J., John H., Bethany, Jenni, Omaha, Vicki A., Sean M., Martin, Fred M., and from what is now a long time ago, MooseyD.

Written and illustrated by Mark Fearing
Created by Mark Fearing and Tim Rummel
Color by Ken Min
Art direction and book design by John Lind

Library of Congress Cataloging-in-Publication Data available.

Hardcover ISBN 978-0-8118-7106-8
Paperback ISBN 978-1-4521-0906-0

Packaged for Chronicle Books by Kitchen, Lind & Associates LLC.
www.kitchenandlind.com

Typeset in **HEDGE BACKWARDS**, *BIFF BAM BOOM*, and **ELEPHANTMEN** from Comicraft,
and **AVINIR** from Linotype.

The illustrations in this book were rendered in pencil and inked and colored digitally using
Adobe Photoshop and Wacom tablets.

Manufactured in China.

10 9 8 7 6 5 4 3 2 1

Chronicle Books LLC
680 Second Street, San Francisco, California 94107

www.chroniclekids.com

THE CREATORS

MARK FEARING is an award-winning illustrator, cartoonist, and animator. He lives in Portland, Oregon, with his wife, daughter, two dogs, a cat, and a need to vacuum constantly. This is his first graphic novel. Visit Mark at: www.markfearing.

TIM RUMMEL is a television producer and creative executive. He lives with his wife in Los Angeles, California, Planet Earth.